ANARRES
11 LY from Terra

ATHSHE
also known as World 41
also known as New Tahiti
27 LY from Terra

CIME

ELEVEN-SORO

FOUR-TAURUS
also known as Iao

GANAM
also known as Tadkla
21 LY from Ollul

GETHEN
also known as Winter
72 LY from Hain

HUTHU

O
4 LY from Hain and from Ve

ORINT

ROKANAN
8 LY from New South Georgia

S

TERRA
140 LY from Hain

URRAS
11 LY from Terra

WEREL
80 LY from Hain and from Ve

Library of America, a nonprofit organization,
champions our nation's cultural heritage
by publishing America's greatest writing in
authoritative new editions and providing resources
for readers to explore this rich, living legacy.

URSULA K. LE GUIN
HAINISH NOVELS & STORIES

VOLUME TWO

URSULA K. LE GUIN

HAINISH NOVELS & STORIES

VOLUME TWO

The Word for World Is Forest
Stories
Five Ways to Forgiveness
The Telling

Brian Attebery, *editor*

THE LIBRARY OF AMERICA

Visit our website at www.loa.org.

Introduction copyright © 2017 by Ursula K. Le Guin.
The Word for World Is Forest copyright © 1972 by Ursula K. Le Guin.
Published by arrangement with Tom Doherty Associates.
The Telling copyright © 2000 by Ursula K. Le Guin. Published by
arrangement with Houghton Mifflin Harcourt Publishing Company.
All other texts published by arrangement with the author.

Endpaper by Donna G. Brown for Library of America.

This paper meets the requirements of
ANSI/NISO Z39.48–1992 (Permanence of Paper).

Distributed to the trade in the United States
by Penguin Random House Inc.
and in Canada by Penguin Random House Canada Ltd.

Library of Congress Control Number: 2016958894
ISBN 978–1–59853–539–6

First Printing
The Library of America—297

Contents

Introduction

The novels and stories of the Hainish Descent were written in two periods separated by at least a decade. Everything in the first volume of this collected edition dates from the 1960s and '70s, except one story from 1995; in the second volume, after one short novel from 1976, everything is from the 1990s. During the eighties I didn't revisit the Hainish Universe at all (nor, until 1989, did I go back to Earthsea). When I became aware of this discontinuity, I wondered what kept me away from these literary realms I had invented, explored, established, and what brought me back to them.

That's the sort of question interviewers and critics often ask and I usually dodge, uncomfortable with their assumption of rational choice guided by conscious decision. I may have intentions, as a writer, but they're seldom that clear. Sometimes I find there is a certain tendency to my readings and thoughts, a general direction in which I am drawn—evidenced in a wish to learn more about certain subjects or fields (sleep and dream studies, satyagraha, medieval mining, DNA research, slavery, gender frequency, the *Aeneid*, the Inca). If this impulsion continues and gains energy, the subject matter of a story or novel may emerge from it. But it is an impulsion, not a decision. The decisions will be called for when the planning and writing begin.

It is as if I were the skipper of a ship and find my ship sailing always, irresistibly, to the south. To sail safely southward, I must plot my course and trim my sails and look out for reefs. But what is the current that impels me? Am I going to Kerguelen, Cape Horn, Tierra del Fuego, Antarctica? Often there isn't much use asking until I'm halfway there and able to see the drift of my journey; sometimes only after I've come to the end of it can I look back on the way I took.

A line in one of Theodore Roethke's poems is a cornerstone of thought for me: "I learn by going where I have to go." The poet is saying that he didn't know where he had to go until he found himself going there, and also that by going where he must go he'd learn the way to it. Like Lao Tzu's "knowing by not knowing, doing by not doing," this is a willingness to re-linquish control, an act of trust. It both describes my own ex-perience as a writer and gives me guidance.

In retrospect, it seems that by 1980 I was ready to trust my luck. Written within the general conventions of science fiction and fantasy, my books had sold well enough and received enough favorable notice that my agent, Virginia Kidd, could find publishers who would take a chance on something unex-pected or unconventional from me. It must be hard for young writers to believe these days, but even some of the big, com-mercial, corporation-owned publishers used to allow their edi-tors to take chances.

I certainly gave those editors the opportunity to do so, and am grateful to them for taking it. I sailed right off the fantasy and science fiction maps, first with the ungenrifiable *Always Coming Home*, then by setting realistic stories on the Oregon coast and a fantasy in the Oregon desert, by publishing several books for children, two of poetry, and two of literary and po-litical essays. This might appear more like wandering fecklessly about than finding a way forward, but looking back on what I wrote and didn't write in that decade, I do see some pattern and direction to it. I was learning how to think what I thought and say it, how to write from and with my own body and mind, not a borrowed one. I was coming home to myself as a woman and as a woman of the American West. I learned by going where I had to go.

At the end of that ten-year exploration of my own inner territories, I was able to see my old Earthsea with new eyes, and to return to the worlds of the Hainish descent ready to play very freely with the imaginative opportunities they offered.

My 1977 introductory note for *The Word for World Is Forest* (in the Appendix of this volume) explains how and where the book came to be written, and expresses my fear that it might end up, like many passionate testimonies of political opinion, a victim of its own relevance. However, since my country learned nothing from its defeat in Vietnam and has held ever since to the policy of making war by invasion and attack, the story's argument against aggression continued and continues to apply. I wish it didn't.

In the introduction I wrote in 1977 for this novel, I tell the tale of how, after it was published, I came to believe—or to hope to believe—that counterparts of my Athsheans existed on our Earth in a Philippine people called the Senoi. But the seductively convincing study by Kilton Stewart of Senoi "dream culture," presented and published as anthropology, was presently shown to be largely wishful thinking.[1] There was no wonderful convergence of my fantasy with reality; my earthly models for Athshean dreaming must remain fragmentary. It was an excellent demonstration of the difference between science and science fictions, which it behoves both scientist and novelist to respect. On the other hand, the lack of a real-life model doesn't affect the fictional reality of my Athsheans; it reduces the scientific while increasing the speculative element of the novel. The powers of Athshean dreaming, its existence as the life-technique of a whole people, can be categorized only as fantasy. But the powers of the unconscious mind, the uses of dream, are central elements of twentieth-century psychology, and there the novel was and is on solid speculative ground.

A final note on *Word for World*: a high-budget, highly successful film resembled the novel in so many ways that people have often assumed I had some part in making it. Since the film completely reverses the book's moral premise, presenting the central and unsolved problem of the book, mass violence, as a solution, I'm glad I had nothing at all to do with it.

———————

Several of the short stories in this volume are connected. "The Shobies' Story" shares several characters with "Dancing to Ganam," and both of them share the idea of transilience with "Another Story."

Long ago I made up the ansible, a device that would permit people light-years apart to talk to one another without interval. Most science-fictional spaceships go much faster than light (FTL), but mine stolidly obey Einstein, going only nearly as

[1] "Dream Theory in Malaya," *Complex* (1951).

fast as light (NAFAL). Travel through the Hainish galaxy involves the Einsteinian paradoxes of time dilation. The traveler in a NAFAL ship traversing the distance of a hundred light-years experiences the interval between departure and arrival as very brief, perhaps an hour or two, while on the home world and the destination more than a century is passing. Such gaps in relative time would forbid any continuous interchange of information between worlds. This is why FTL is so popular: you really can't have a Galactic War without it. I didn't want a war, but I did want my worlds to be able to talk with one another, so in 1966 I introduced the ansible. Later on, I met its inventor, Shevek, the temporal physicist in *The Dispossessed*, who could explain the principles on which it functions much better than I can. I'm pleased that several other science fiction writers have found the ansible useful—stealing ideas is plagiarism, but both art and science function by sharing them.

Around 1990 I was allured by the notion of transilience, the transfer of a physical body from one point in space-time to another without interval. The Cetian word for it is churten. From time to time it has, as it were, been done. Madeleine L'Engle called it a wrinkle in time. Sometimes I think my cat churtens downstairs, but I do not know how he does it. My stories about churtening indicate that, even after doing it, nobody is certain how they did it or that it can be done more than once in the same way. In this it much resembles life.

In the introduction to the 1994 collection containing these stories, *A Fisherman of the Inland Sea*, I wrote: "All three of the churten stories are also metafictions, stories about story. In 'The Shobies' Story,' transilience acts as a metaphor for narration, and narration as the chancy and unreliable but most effective means of constructing a shared reality. 'Dancing to Ganam' continues with the theme of unreliable narration or differing witness, with a hi-tech hubristic hero at its eccentric center, and adds the lovely theory of entrainment to the churten stew. And finally, 'Another Story'—one of my very few experiments with time travel—explores the possibility of two stories about the same person in the same time being completely different and completely true."

The full title, "Another Story, or A Fisherman of the Inland

Sea," is both a self-referential in-joke about the story itself and a direct reference to the Japanese folktale I read as a child in Lafcadio Hearn's beautiful retelling. The tale went down deep in me and lived there until, as such stories will do, it came up and flowered again.

As a love story, it connects with two others, "Unchosen Love" and "Mountain Ways." All three take place on the world called O, a fairly near neighbor of Hain. Human beings have lived on both these worlds for hundreds of thousands of years, and their civilizations have reached a kind of steady state, like a climax forest, expressed in durable yet various, vigorous, and adaptable cultures. An element of the social structure on O is an unusual form of marriage, the sedoretu, which institutionalizes both homosexual and heterosexual relationships in an intricate four-part arrangement laden with infinite emotional possibilities—a seductive prospect to a storyteller. I explored a few such possibilities in the ghost story "Unchosen Love" and the semi-comedy "Mountain Ways," in which cross-gender role playing further convolutes the complicated.

In the mid-nineties I wrote at least six "gender-bending" stories (among them "Coming of Age in Karhide," in the first Hainish volume). I was solidifying and celebrating gains. The hard study I had put into rethinking my understanding of sexuality and gender was working itself out, paying off imaginatively. To escape from the misplaced expectations and demands of a male-centered literature, I'd had to learn how to write as a woman. Now I was ready—and had an audience ready—to learn what a woman might write about. We'd kicked the fence down—where to gallop?

I invented the sedoretu in a playful spirit, both enjoying my take-off on the elaborate descriptions required by anthropological kinship studies and trying to imagine how individuals would adapt (as we do adapt) to such complex sexual arrangements and consider them perfectly natural. My knowledge of anthropology is slight, but it is a familiar acquaintance, and it gave me some insight into the inexhaustible strangeness of human social customs and the all but universal human refusal to see anything strange about them if they're our own customs, and anything good about them if they're not.

"The Matter of Seggri," written in the same period as the

stories of O, was not written playfully. Still, I don't think I realised while I was working on the various sketches that compose it how bleak a picture I was drawing. It arose, as a good many science fiction stories do, from a question to which science has not yet found a generally accepted answer. There are a lot of such questions in gender studies, but this one is quite basic: Why are there as many men as there are women? It takes very few males (of any species) to impregnate a whole lot of females, ensuring the next generation. What's the need for all those extra males? Answers to this seemingly simple-minded question are complicated, involving the gene pool, probability theory, and more mathematics than I can follow, and no one of them is yet accepted as completely sufficient. There is no reason, after all, to expect a complex phenomenon to have a single cause. The uncertainty still surrounding the question gave some plausibility to the basic assumption, or gimmick, of my story: a human society consisting mostly of women. The idea has been explored many times from a somewhat excited male point of view—"hive worlds," Amazons, etc.—and, more recently, by feminists.

The women of Seggri, sixteen times more numerous than the men, have worked out a stable and generally harmonious society. They value their men highly, protect and segregate them as both endangered and dangerous, encourage their hormonal display via competitive feats and aggressive games, but keep them from any pursuit or knowledge that by empowering them as human beings might interfere with their function as sexual objects and breeding stock. The resulting misery, injustice, and waste of human potential, though differently gendered, is only too familiar.

In one section of "Seggri" the reversal of sexual stereotypes is particularly obvious, the sub-story called "Love Out of Place." It is a deliberate imitation of works I read in my youth by Maupassant, Flaubert, and others, which distressed and angered me deeply, though I had to wait for feminist thinkers to tell me why. The unquestioned assumption of the story is that men are what women perceive them to be. A man has no existence and can do nothing of any significance apart from his relationships to women. He accepts this extreme impoverishment of his being because his whole society—including the author—accepts it. I have seldom disliked a story so much as I wrote it. It was a relief to go on to the next section, unhappy as much of it is, written from the point of view of a man suffocating in such a life and struggling to escape—to be a person, to have a point of view.

The final story, "Solitude," takes an even more radical view of personhood. Having been an introvert all my life in a society that adores extraversion, I felt it was time to speak up for myself and my people, to imagine for us a society where loners are the norm and the gregarious and self-advertising are the oddballs, the misfits. I invented a peculiar social arrangement involving an extreme kind of gender segregation, only tenuously connected to the extra/introversion theme. My fear of the ongoing human catastrophe of unlimited growth, imagery of the ruinous aftermath of overpopulation and mindless exploitation, which has haunted much of my science fiction for forty years or more, is very clear in the story. All the same, I ended up feeling quite at home on poor, impoverished Soro, a world without crowds, teams, or armies, where *everybody* is an oddball and a misfit.

———

Joining protest movements and nonviolent demonstrations against nuclear bomb tests and wars and for abortion, women's, and lesbian-gay rights, I took a small active part in some of the immense social revolutions of my time. Racism I confronted only through my writing. In the late sixties, embarrassed by the traditional vanilla universe of science fiction and fantasy and wanting to subvert it, I took the simple course of basing my novels and stories on the (perfectly rational) assumption that "colored" is the human norm.

I made no fuss about this, and for a long time nobody said anything about it. The assumption that heroes are white men was so deeply ingrained that it blinded many readers to what the books state perfectly clearly. Almost all the books' publishers, despite my protests, permitted cover illustrations showing white faces only. Still, even if I could do it only in imaginary worlds, and nobody in this one seemed to notice, it was a satisfaction to me to dump the mechanical, vicious stereotypes of racial supremacy and do away with the sign on the doors of genre fiction that said to readers—silently but unmistakably—Whites Only.

In most of my invented societies skin color has no social implications at all. But when I came to write stories about slavery, as an American I could not in conscience escape the fatal connection of color and supremacy. To subvert it, I again reversed expectation, showing a dark-skinned people as masters of light-skinned slaves. But to reverse a wrong is not to escape from it. Writing of these worlds, I had to work my way through the terrible story that my own country is still telling.

The first of these slavery pieces, "Betrayals," takes place on the "plantation world" Yeowe after a successful slave revolution; the others are set at different times during the revolution, some on Yeowe and some on the home planet, Werel. As I wrote them, connections among them through both events and characters kept strengthening. The result was not a novel, but what I call a story suite.

As a set of stories thus connected has no generally accepted name, I took one from music. The several movements of a Bach cello suite don't assume a unified form like a sonata, and yet each of the six suites is undoubtedly an entity, unified by more than a common key. The parts of a suite discuss, as it were, the same subject in different ways. In fiction, at least two major nineteenth-century works are suites, Jewett's *The Country of the Pointed Firs* and Gaskell's *Cranford*, and the form continues to turn up—it could be argued that some of David Mitchell's novels are actually story suites.

Thinking that "A Woman's Liberation" was the final story of the suite, I published *Four Ways to Forgiveness*. But the character called Old Music began to tell me a fifth tale about the latter days of the civil war, and haunting memories of a tourist visit to a plantation in South Carolina gave me its setting. I'm glad to see it joined to the others at last. But it makes a very bitter ending to the suite, and in fact I didn't intend it to stop there. I wanted to follow the character Metoy back to the place where he was born a slave and made a eunuch; but that story would not come clear, and I have not been able to write the sixth and last way to forgiveness.

Like *The Word for World Is Forest*, *The Telling* had its origin in a moral and political issue or concern, and in a personal sense of shame.

Never having been forced to participate in or to escape from organized religion, I have been able to regard it peaceably, open to its great achievements in art and thought and to the life-giving winds of the spirit that blow through it. The wind of the spirit that blew earliest and sweetest on me was Lao Tzu's voice, speaking of the Way, the Tao. I knew it only in his book and Chuang Tzu's, and in Western philosophical commentaries on them. Of religious Taoism, I knew vaguely that it was highly institutionalized, with divinities, priests, rituals, and a great paraphernalia of practises and beliefs, and traced its origin back over the millennia somehow to Lao Tzu's spare, subversive, godless meditations. I did not know that during my adult lifetime this immense, ancient structure had been almost completely destroyed by an aggressive secular fundamentalism, a politics of belief demanding blind obedience to a nearly deified leader. When I did finally realize this, I was both shocked by the fact and ashamed of my ignorance. Moved both to understand and to make amends, I set out to learn, through imagining it in a story, how such destruction might take place so quickly.

In my story the secular persecution of an ancient, pacific, non-theistic religion on another world is instigated by a violent monotheistic sect on Earth. *The Telling* comes a lot ·closer home than China. Only recently have I ever feared institutionalized religion, as I see divisive, exclusive, aggressive fundamentalisms absorb and pervert the energy of every major creed, and Americans abandoning the secular vision of freedom on which our republic stands.

On a happier note, writing the book gave me the pleasure of exploring the old Akan way of life and thought, a peaceful journey up a river and a terrific one into the mountains, and a glimpse of a love so star-crossed, repressed, subliminal, and impossible that the lovers never know it's there.

Ursula K. Le Guin
Portland, Oregon
December 2016

THE WORD FOR WORLD
IS FOREST

I

TWO PIECES of yesterday were in Captain Davidson's mind when he woke, and he lay looking at them in the darkness for a while. One up: the new shipload of women had arrived. Believe it or not. They were here, in Centralville, twenty-seven lightyears from Earth by NAFAL and four hours from Smith Camp by hopper, the second batch of breeding females for the New Tahiti Colony, all sound and clean, 212 head of prime human stock. Or prime enough, anyhow. One down: the report from Dump Island of crop failures, massive erosion, a wipe-out. The line of 212 buxom beddable breasty little figures faded from Davidson's mind as he saw rain pouring down onto ploughed dirt, churning it to mud, thinning the mud to a red broth that ran down rocks into the rainbeaten sea. The erosion had begun before he left Dump Island to run Smith Camp, and being gifted with an exceptional visual memory, the kind they called eidetic, he could recall it now all too clearly. It looked like that bigdome Kees was right and you had to leave a lot of trees standing where you planned to put farms. But he still couldn't see why a soybean farm needed to waste a lot of space on trees if the land was managed really scientifically. It wasn't like that in Ohio; if you wanted corn you grew corn, and no space wasted on trees and stuff. But then Earth was a tamed planet and New Tahiti wasn't. That's what he was here for: to tame it. If Dump Island was just rocks and gullies now, then scratch it; start over on a new island and do better. Can't keep us down, we're Men. You'll learn what that means pretty soon, you godforsaken damn planet, Davidson thought, and he grinned a little in the darkness of the hut, for he liked challenges. Thinking Men, he thought Women, and again the line of little figures began to sway through his mind, smiling, jiggling.

"Ben!" he roared, sitting up and swinging his bare feet onto the bare floor. "Hot water get-ready, hurry-up-quick!" The roar woke him satisfyingly. He stretched and scratched his chest and pulled on his shorts and strode out of the hut into the sunlit clearing all in one easy series of motions. A big, hard-muscled man, he enjoyed using his well-trained body.

Ben, his creechie, had the water ready and steaming over the fire, as usual, and was squatting staring at nothing, as usual. Creechies never slept, they just sat and stared. "Breakfast. Hurry-up-quick!" Davidson said, picking up his razor from the rough board table where the creechie had laid it out ready with a towel and a propped-up mirror.

There was a lot to be done today, since he'd decided, that last minute before getting up, to fly down to Central and see the new women for himself. They wouldn't last long, 212 among over two thousand men, and like the first batch probably most of them were Colony Brides, and only twenty or thirty had come as Recreation Staff; but those babies were real good greedy girls and he intended to be first in line with at least one of them this time. He grinned on the left, the right cheek remaining stiff to the whining razor.

The old creechie was moseying round taking an hour to bring his breakfast from the cookhouse. "Hurry-up-quick!" Davidson yelled, and Ben pushed his boneless saunter into a walk. Ben was about a meter high and his back fur was more white than green; he was old, and dumb even for a creechie, but Davidson knew how to handle him. A lot of men couldn't handle creechies worth a damn, but Davidson had never had trouble with them; he could tame any of them, if it was worth the effort. It wasn't, though. Get enough humans here, build machines and robots, make farms and cities, and nobody would need the creechies any more. And a good thing too. For this world, New Tahiti, was literally made for men. Cleaned up and cleaned out, the dark forests cut down for open fields of grain, the primeval murk and savagery and ignorance wiped out, it would be a paradise, a real Eden. A better world than worn-out Earth. And it would be his world. For that's what Don Davidson was, way down deep inside him: a world-tamer. He wasn't a boastful man, but he knew his own size. It just happened to be the way he was made. He knew what he wanted, and how to get it. And he always got it.

Breakfast landed warm in his belly. His good mood wasn't spoiled even by the sight of Kees Van Sten coming towards him, fat, white, and worried, his eyes sticking out like blue golf-balls.

"Don," Kees said without greeting, "the loggers have been

hunting red deer in the Strips again. There are eighteen pair of antlers in the back room of the Lounge."

"Nobody ever stopped poachers from poaching, Kees."

"You can stop them. That's why we live under martial law, that's why the Army runs this colony. To keep the laws."

A frontal attack from Fatty Bigdome! It was almost funny. "All right," Davidson said reasonably, "I could stop 'em. But look, it's the men I'm looking after; that's my job, like you said. And it's the men that count. Not the animals. If a little extra-legal hunting helps the men get through this godforsaken life, then I intend to blink. They've got to have some recreation."

"They have games, sports, hobbies, films, teletapes of every major sporting event of the past century, liquor, marijuana, hallies, and a fresh batch of women at Central. For those unsatisfied by the Army's rather unimaginative arrangements for hygienic homosexuality. They are spoiled rotten, your frontier heroes, and they don't need to exterminate a rare native species 'for recreation.' If you don't act, I must record a major infraction of Ecological Protocols in my report to Captain Gosse."

"You can do that if you see fit, Kees," said Davidson, who never lost his temper. It was sort of pathetic the way a euro like Kees got all red in the face when he lost control of his emotions. "That's your job, after all. I won't hold it against you; they can do the arguing at Central and decide who's right. See, you want to keep this place just like it is, actually, Kees. Like one big National Forest. To look at, to study. Great, you're a spesh. But see we're just ordinary joes getting the work done. Earth needs wood, needs it bad. We find wood on New Tahiti. So—we're loggers. See, where we differ is that with you Earth doesn't come first, actually. With me it does."

Kees looked at him sideways out of those blue golf-ball eyes. "Does it? You want to make this world into Earth's image, eh? A desert of cement?"

"When I say Earth, Kees, I mean people. Men. You worry about deer and trees and fibreweed, fine, that's your thing. But I like to see things in perspective, from the top down, and the top, so far, is humans. We're here, now; and so this world's going to go our way. Like it or not, it's a fact you have to face; it happens to be the way things are. Listen, Kees, I'm going to hop down to Central and take a look at the new colonists. Want to come along?"

"No thanks, Captain Davidson," the spesh said, going on towards the Lab hut. He was really mad. All upset about those damn deer. They were great animals, all right. Davidson's vivid memory recalled the first one he had seen, here on Smith Land, a big red shadow, two meters at the shoulder, a crown of narrow golden antlers, a fleet, brave beast, the finest game-animal imaginable. Back on Earth they were using robodeer even in the High Rockies and Himalaya Parks now, the real ones were about gone. These things were a hunter's dream. So they'd be hunted. Hell, even the wild creechies hunted them, with their lousy little bows. The deer would be hunted because that's what they were there for. But poor old bleeding-heart Kees couldn't see it. He was actually a smart fellow, but not realistic, not tough-minded enough. He didn't see that you've got to play on the winning side or else you lose. And it's Man that wins, every time. The old Conquistador.

Davidson strode on through the settlement, morning sunlight in his eyes, the smell of sawn wood and woodsmoke sweet on the warm air. Things looked pretty neat, for a logging camp. The two hundred men here had tamed a fair patch of wilderness in just three E-months. Smith Camp: a couple of big corruplast geodesics, forty timber huts built by creechie-labor, the sawmill, the burner trailing a blue plume over acres of logs and cut lumber; uphill, the airfield and the big prefab hangar for helicopters and heavy machinery. That was all. But when they came here there had been nothing. Trees. A dark huddle and jumble and tangle of trees, endless, meaningless. A sluggish river overhung and choked by trees, a few creechie-warrens hidden among the trees, some red deer, hairy monkeys, birds. And trees. Roots, boles, branches, twigs, leaves, leaves overhead and underfoot and in your face and in your eyes, endless leaves on endless trees.

New Tahiti was mostly water, warm shallow seas broken here and there by reefs, islets, archipelagoes, and the five big Lands that lay in a 2500-kilo arc across the Northwest Quartersphere. And all those flecks and blobs of land were covered with trees. Ocean: forest. That was your choice on New Tahiti. Water and sunlight, or darkness and leaves.

But men were here now to end the darkness, and turn the tree-jumble into clean sawn planks, more prized on Earth than gold. Literally, because gold could be got from seawater and from under the Antarctic ice, but wood could not; wood came only from trees. And it was a really necessary luxury on Earth. So the alien forests became wood. Two hundred men with robosaws and haulers had already cut eight mile-wide Strips on Smith Land, in three months. The stumps of the Strip nearest camp were already white and punky; chemically treated, they would have fallen into fertile ash by the time the permanent colonists, the farmers, came to settle Smith Land. All the farmers would have to do was plant seeds and let 'em sprout.

It had been done once before. That was a queer thing, and the proof, actually, that New Tahiti was intended for humans to take over. All the stuff here had come from Earth, about a million years ago, and the evolution had followed so close a path that you recognised things at once: pine, oak, walnut, chestnut, fir, holly, apple, ash; deer, bird, mouse, cat, squirrel, monkey. The humanoids on Hain-Davenant of course claimed they'd done it at the same time as they colonised Earth, but if you listened to those ETs you'd find they claimed to have settled every planet in the Galaxy and invented everything from sex to thumbtacks. The theories about Atlantis were a lot more realistic, and this might well be a lost Atlantean colony. But the humans had died out. And the nearest thing that had developed from the monkey line to replace them was the creechie —a meter tall and covered with green fur. As ETs they were about standard, but as men they were a bust, they just hadn't made it. Give 'em another million years, maybe. But the Conquistadors had arrived first. Evolution moved now not at the pace of a random mutation once a millennium, but with the speed of the starships of the Terran Fleet.

"Hey Captain!"

Davidson turned, only a microsecond late in his reaction, but that was late enough to annoy him. There was something about this damn planet, its gold sunlight and hazy sky, its mild winds smelling of leafmould and pollen, something that made you daydream. You mooched along thinking about conquistadors and destiny and stuff, till you were acting as thick and slow as a creechie. "Morning, Ok!" he said crisply to the logging foreman.

Black and tough as wire rope, Oknanawi Nabo was Kees's physical opposite, but he had the same worried look. "You got half a minute?"

"Sure. What's eating you, Ok?"

"The little bastards."

They leaned their backsides on a split rail fence. Davidson lit his first reefer of the day. Sunlight, smoke-blued, slanted warm across the air. The forest behind camp, a quarter-mile-wide uncut strip, was full of the faint, ceaseless, cracking, chuckling, stirring, whirring, silvery noises that woods in the morning are full of. It might have been Idaho in 1950, this clearing. Or Kentucky in 1830. Or Gaul in 50 B.C. "Te-whet," said a distant bird.

"I'd like to get rid of 'em, Captain."

"The creechies? How d'you mean, Ok?"

"Just let 'em go. I can't get enough work out of 'em in the mill to make up for their keep. Or for their being such a damn headache. They just don't work."

"They do if you know how to make 'em. They built the camp."

Oknanawi's obsidian face was dour. "Well, you got the touch with 'em, I guess. I don't." He paused. "In that Applied History course I took in training for Far-out, it said that slavery never worked. It was uneconomical."

"Right, but this isn't slavery, Ok baby. Slaves are humans. When you raise cows, you call that slavery? No. And it works."

Impassive, the foreman nodded; but he said, "They're too little. I tried starving the sulky ones. They just sit and starve."

"They're little, all right, but don't let 'em fool you, Ok. They're tough; they've got terrific endurance; and they don't feel pain like humans. That's the part you forget, Ok. You think hitting one is like hitting a kid, sort of. Believe me, it's more like hitting a robot for all they feel it. Look, you've laid some of the females, you know how they don't seem to feel anything, no pleasure, no pain, they just lay there like mattresses no matter what you do. They're all like that. Probably they've got more primitive nerves than humans do. Like fish. I'll tell you a weird one about that. When I was in Central, before I came up here, one of the tame males jumped me once. I know they'll tell you they never fight, but this one went spla, right off his nut, and lucky he wasn't armed or he'd have killed me. I had to damn near kill him before he'd even let go. And he kept coming back. It was incredible the beating he took and never even felt it. Like some beetle you have to keep stepping on because it doesn't know it's been squashed already. Look at this." Davidson bent down his close-cropped head to show a gnarled lump behind one ear. "That was damn near a concussion. And he did it after I'd broken his arm and pounded his face into cranberry sauce. He just kept coming back and coming back. The thing is, Ok, the creechies are lazy, they're dumb, they're treacherous, and they don't feel pain. You've got to be tough with 'em, and stay tough with 'em."

"They aren't worth the trouble, Captain. Damn sulky little green bastards, they won't fight, won't work, won't nothing. Except give me the pip." There was a geniality in Oknanawi's grumbling which did not conceal the stubbornness beneath. He wouldn't beat up creechies because they were so much smaller; that was clear in his mind, and clear now to Davidson, who at once accepted it. He knew how to handle his men. "Look, Ok. Try this. Pick out the ringleaders and tell 'em you're going to give them a shot of hallucinogen. Mesc, lice, any one, they don't know one from the other. But they're scared of them. Don't overwork it, and it'll work. I can guarantee."

"Why are they scared of hallies?" the foreman asked curiously.

"How do I know? Why are women scared of rats? Don't look for good sense from women or creechies, Ok! Speaking of which I'm on the way to Central this morning, shall I put the finger on a Collie Girl for you?"

"Just keep the finger off a few till I get my leave," Ok said grinning. A group of creechies passed, carrying a long 12 × 12 beam for the Rec Room being built down by the river. Slow, shambling little figures, they worried the big beam along like a lot of ants with a dead caterpillar, sullen and inept. Oknanawi watched them and said, "Fact is, Captain, they give me the creeps."

That was queer, coming from a tough, quiet guy like Ok.

"Well, I agree with you, actually, Ok, that they're not worth the trouble, or the risk. If that fart Lyubov wasn't around and the Colonel wasn't so stuck on following the Code, I think we

might just clean out the areas we settle, instead of this Voluntary Labor routine. They're going to get rubbed out sooner or
later, and it might as well be sooner. It's just how things happen to be. Primitive races always have to give way to civilised
ones. Or be assimilated. But we sure as hell can't assimilate a
lot of green monkeys. And like you say, they're just bright
enough that they'll never be quite trustworthy. Like those big
monkeys used to live in Africa, what were they called."

"Gorillas?"

"Right. We'll get on better without creechies here, just like
we get on better without gorillas in Africa. They're in our
way. . . . But Daddy Ding-Dong he say use creechie-labor, so
we use creechie-labor. For a while. Right? See you tonight, Ok."

"Right, Captain."

Davidson checked out the hopper from Smith Camp HQ: a
pine-plank 4-meter cube, two desks, a watercooler, Lt. Birno
repairing a walkytalky. "Don't let the camp burn down, Birno."

"Bring me back a Collie, Cap. Blonde. 34-22-36."

"Christ, is that all?"

"I like 'em neat, not floppy, see." Birno expressively outlined
his preference in the air. Grinning, Davidson went on up to
the hangar. As he brought the helicopter back over camp he
looked down at it: kid's blocks, sketch-lines of paths, long
stump-stubbled clearings, all shrinking as the machine rose and
he saw the green of the uncut forests of the great island, and
beyond that dark green the pale green of the sea going on
and on. Now Smith Camp looked like a yellow spot, a fleck on a
vast green tapestry.

He crossed Smith Straits and the wooded, deep-folded
ranges of north Central Island, and came down by noon in
Centralville. It looked like a city, at least after three months in
the woods; there were real streets, real buildings, it had been
there since the Colony began four years ago. You didn't see
what a flimsy little frontier-town it really was, until you looked
south of it a halfmile and saw glittering above the stumplands
and the concrete pads a single golden tower, taller than anything in Centralville. The ship wasn't a big one but it looked so
big, here. And it was only a launch, a lander, a ship's boat; the
NAFAL ship of the line, *Shackleton*, was half a million kilos up,
in orbit. The launch was just a hint, just a fingertip of the

hugeness, the power, the golden precision and grandeur of the star-bridging technology of Earth.

That was why tears came to Davidson's eyes for a second at the sight of the ship from home. He wasn't ashamed of it. He was a patriotic man, it just happened to be the way he was made.

Soon enough, walking down those frontier-town streets with their wide vistas of nothing much at each end, he began to smile. For the women were there, all right, and you could tell they were fresh ones. They mostly had long tight skirts and big shoes like galoshes, red or purple or gold, and gold or silver frilly shirts. No more nipplepeeps. Fashions had changed; too bad. They all wore their hair piled up high, it must be sprayed with that glue stuff they used. Ugly as hell, but it was the sort of thing only women would do to their hair, and so it was provocative. Davidson grinned at a chesty little euraf with more hair than head; he got no smile, but a wag of the retreating hips that said plainly, Follow follow follow me. But he didn't. Not yet. He went to Central HQ: quickstone and plastiplate Standard Issue, 40 offices 10 watercoolers and a basement arsenal, and checked in with New Tahiti Central Colonial Administration Command. He met a couple of the launch-crew, put in a request for a new semirobo barkstripper at Forestry, and got his old pal Juju Sereng to meet him at the Luau Bar at fourteen hundred.

He got to the bar an hour early to stock up on a little food before the drinking began. Lyubov was there, sitting with a couple of guys in Fleet uniform, some kind of speshes that had come down on the *Shackleton*'s launch. Davidson didn't have a high regard for the Navy, a lot of fancy sunhoppers who left the dirty, muddy, dangerous on-planet work to the Army; but brass was brass, and anyhow it was funny to see Lyubov acting chummy with anybody in uniform. He was talking, waving his hands around the way he did. Just in passing Davidson tapped his shoulder and said, "Hi, Raj old pal, how's tricks?" He went on without waiting for the scowl, though he hated to miss it. It was really funny the way Lyubov hated him. Probably the guy was effeminate like a lot of intellectuals, and resented Davidson's virility. Anyhow Davidson wasn't going to waste any time hating Lyubov, he wasn't worth the trouble.

The Luau served a first-rate venison steak. What would they say on old Earth if they saw one man eating a kilogram of meat at one meal? Poor damn soybeansuckers! Then Juju arrived with—as Davidson had confidently expected—the pick of the new Collie Girls: two fruity beauties, not Brides, but Recreation Staff. Oh the old Colonial Administration sometimes came through! It was a long, hot afternoon.

Flying back to camp he crossed Smith Straits level with the sun that lay on top of a great gold bed of haze over the sea. He sang as he lolled in the pilot's seat. Smith Land came in sight hazy, and there was smoke over the camp, a dark smudge as if oil had got into the waste-burner. He couldn't even make out the buildings through it. It was only as he dropped down to the landing-field that he saw the charred jet, the wrecked hoppers, the burned-out hangar.

He pulled the hopper up again and flew back over the camp, so low that he might have hit the high cone of the burner, the only thing left sticking up. The rest was gone, mill, furnace, lumberyards, HQ, huts, barracks, creechie compound, everything. Black hulks and wrecks, still smoking. But it hadn't been a forest fire. The forest stood there, green, next to the ruins. Davidson swung back round to the field, set down and lit out looking for the motorbike, but it too was a black wreck along with the stinking, smouldering ruins of the hangar and the machinery. He loped down the path to camp. As he passed what had been the radio hut, his mind snapped back into gear. Without hesitating for even a stride he changed course, off the path, behind the gutted shack. There he stopped. He listened.

There was nobody. It was all silent. The fires had been out a long time; only the great lumber-piles still smouldered, showing a hot red under the ash and char. Worth more than gold, those oblong ash-heaps had been. But no smoke rose from the black skeletons of the barracks and huts; and there were bones among the ashes.

Davidson's brain was super-clear and active, now, as he crouched behind the radio shack. There were two possibilities. One: an attack from another camp. Some officer on King or New Java had gone spla and was trying a coup de planète. Two: an attack from off-planet. He saw the golden tower on the space-dock at Central. But if the *Shackleton* had gone privateer why would she start by rubbing out a small camp, instead of taking over Centralville? No, it must be invasion, aliens. Some unknown race, or maybe the Cetians or the Hainish had decided to move in on Earth's colonies. He'd never trusted those damned smart humanoids. This must have been done with a heatbomb. The invading force, with jets, aircars, nukes, could easily be hidden on an island or reef anywhere in the SW Quartersphere. He must get back to his hopper and send out the alarm, then try a look around, reconnoiter, so he could tell HQ his assessment of the actual situation. He was just straightening up when he heard the voices.

Not human voices. High, soft, gabble-gobble. Aliens.

Ducking on hands and knees behind the shack's plastic roof, which lay on the ground deformed by heat into a batwing shape, he held still and listened.

Four creechies walked by a few yards from him, on the path. They were wild creechies, naked except for loose leather belts on which knives and pouches hung. None wore the shorts and leather collar supplied to tame creechies. The Volunteers in the compound must have been incinerated along with the humans.

They stopped a little way past his hiding-place, talking their slow gabble-gobble, and Davidson held his breath. He didn't want them to spot him. What the devil were creechies doing here? They could only be serving as spies and scouts for the invaders.

One pointed south as it talked, and turned, so that Davidson saw its face. And he recognised it. Creechies all looked alike, but this one was different. He had written his own signature all over that face, less than a year ago. It was the one that had gone spla and attacked him down in Central, the homicidal one, Lyubov's pet. What in the blue hell was it doing here?

Davidson's mind raced, clicked; reactions fast as always, he stood up, sudden, tall, easy, gun in hand. "You creechies. Stop. Stay-put. No moving!"

His voice cracked out like a whiplash. The four little green creatures did not move. The one with the smashed-in face looked at him across the black rubble with huge, blank eyes that had no light in them.

"Answer now. This fire, who start it?"

No answer.

"Answer now: hurry-up-quick! No answer, then I burn-up first one, then one, then one, see? This fire, who start it?"

"We burned the camp, Captain Davidson," said the one from Central, in a queer soft voice that reminded Davidson of some human. "The humans are all dead."

"You burned it, what do you mean?"

He could not recall Scarface's name for some reason.

"There were two hundred humans here. Ninety slaves of my people. Nine hundred of my people came out of the forest. First we killed the humans in the place in the forest where they were cutting trees, then we killed those in this place, while the houses were burning. I had thought you were killed. I am glad to see you, Captain Davidson."

It was all crazy, and of course a lie. They couldn't have killed all of them, Ok, Birno, Van Sten, all the rest, two hundred men, some of them would have got out. All the creechies had was bows and arrows. Anyway the creechies couldn't have done this. Creechies didn't fight, didn't kill, didn't have wars. They were intraspecies non-aggressive, that meant sitting ducks. They didn't fight back. They sure as hell didn't massacre two hundred men at a swipe. It was crazy. The silence, the faint stink of burning in the long, warm evening light, the pale-green faces with unmoving eyes that watched him, it all added up to nothing, to a crazy bad dream, a nightmare.

"Who did this for you?"

"Nine hundred of my people," Scarface said in that damned fake-human voice.

"No, not that. Who else? Who were you acting for? Who told you what to do?"

"My wife did."

Davidson saw then the telltale tension of the creature's stance, yet it sprang at him so lithe and oblique that his shot missed, burning an arm or shoulder instead of smack between the eyes. And the creechie was on him, half his size and weight yet knocking him right off balance by its onslaught, for he had been relying on the gun and not expecting attack. The thing's arms were thin, tough, coarse-furred in his grip, and as he struggled with it, it sang.

He was down on his back, pinned down, disarmed. Four

green muzzles looked down at him. The scarfaced one was still singing, a breathless gabble, but with a tune to it. The other three listened, their white teeth showing in grins. He had never seen a creechie smile. He had never looked up into a creechie's face from below. Always down, from above. From on top. He tried not to struggle, for at the moment it was wasted effort. Little as they were, they outnumbered him, and Scarface had his gun. He must wait. But there was a sickness in him, a nausea that made his body twitch and strain against his will. The small hands held him down effortlessly, the small green faces bobbed over him grinning.

Scarface ended his song. He knelt on Davidson's chest, a knife in one hand, Davidson's gun in the other.

"You can't sing, Captain Davidson, is that right? Well, then, you may run to your hopper, and fly away, and tell the Colonel in Central that this place is burned and the humans are all killed."

Blood, the same startling red as human blood, clotted the fur of the creechie's right arm, and the knife shook in the green paw. The sharp, scarred face looked down into Davidson's from very close, and he could see now the queer light that burned way down in the charcoal-dark eyes. The voice was still soft and quiet.

They let him go.

He got up cautiously, still dizzy from the fall Scarface had given him. The creechies stood well away from him now, knowing his reach was twice theirs; but Scarface wasn't the only one armed, there was a second gun pointing at his guts. That was Ben holding the gun. His own creechie Ben, the little grey mangy bastard, looking stupid as always but holding a gun.

It's hard to turn your back on two pointing guns, but Davidson did it and started walking towards the field.

A voice behind him said some creechie word, shrill and loud. Another said, "Hurry-up-quick!" and there was a queer noise like birds twittering that must be creechie laughter. A shot clapped and whined on the road right by him. Christ, it wasn't fair, they had the guns and he wasn't armed. He began to run. He could outrun any creechie. They didn't know how to shoot a gun.

"Run," said the quiet voice far behind him. That was Scarface
—Selver, that was his name. Sam, they'd called him, till Lyubov
stopped Davidson from giving him what he deserved and
made a pet out of him, then they'd called him Selver. Christ, what
was all this, it was a nightmare. He ran. The blood thundered
in his ears. He ran through the golden, smoky evening. There
was a body by the path, he hadn't even noticed it coming. It
wasn't burned, it looked like a white balloon with the air gone
out. It had staring blue eyes. They didn't dare kill him, Davidson. They hadn't shot at him again. It was impossible. They
couldn't kill him. There was the hopper, safe and shining, and
he lunged into the seat and had her up before the creechies
could try anything. His hands shook, but not much, just
shock. They couldn't kill him. He circled the hill and then
came back fast and low, looking for the four creechies. But
nothing moved in the streaky rubble of the camp.

There had been a camp there this morning. Two hundred
men. There had been four creechies there just now. He hadn't
dreamed all this. They couldn't just disappear. They were
there, hiding. He opened up the machinegun in the hopper's
nose and raked the burned ground, shot holes in the green
leaves of the forest, strafed the burned bones and cold bodies
of his men and the wrecked machinery and the rotting white
stumps, returning again and again until the ammo was gone
and the gun's spasms stopped short.

Davidson's hands were steady now, his body felt appeased,
and he knew he wasn't caught in any dream. He headed back
over the Straits, to take the news to Centralville. As he flew he
could feel his face relax into its usual calm lines. They couldn't
blame the disaster on him, for he hadn't even been there.
Maybe they'd see that it was significant that the creechies had
struck while he was gone, knowing they'd fail if he was there to
organise the defense. And there was one good thing would
come out of this. They'd do like they should have done to start
with, and clean up the planet for human occupation. Not even
Lyubov could stop them from rubbing out the creechies now,
not when they heard it was Lyubov's pet creechie who'd led
the massacre! They'd go in for rat-extermination for a while,
now; and maybe, just maybe, they'd hand that little job over to

him. At that thought he could have smiled. But he kept his face calm.

The sea under him was greyish with twilight, and ahead of him lay the island hills, the deep-folded, many-streamed, many-leaved forests in the dusk.

2

All the colors of rust and sunset, brown-reds and pale greens, changed ceaselessly in the long leaves as the wind blew. The roots of the copper willows, thick and ridged, were moss-green down by the running water, which like the wind moved slowly with many soft eddies and seeming pauses, held back by rocks, roots, hanging and fallen leaves. No way was clear, no light un-broken, in the forest. Into wind, water, sunlight, starlight, there always entered leaf and branch, bole and root, the shadowy, the complex. Little paths ran under the branches, around the boles, over the roots; they did not go straight, but yielded to every obstacle, devious as nerves. The ground was not dry and solid but damp and rather springy, product of the collaboration of living things with the long, elaborate death of leaves and trees; and from that rich graveyard grew ninety-foot trees, and tiny mushrooms that sprouted in circles half an inch across. The smell of the air was subtle, various, and sweet. The view was never long, unless looking up through the branches you caught sight of the stars. Nothing was pure, dry, arid, plain. Revelation was lacking. There was no seeing everything at once: no cer-tainty. The colors of rust and sunset kept changing in the hang-ing leaves of the copper willows, and you could not say even whether the leaves of the willows were brownish-red, or reddish-green, or green.

Selver came up a path beside the water, going slowly and often stumbling on the willow roots. He saw an old man dreaming, and stopped. The old man looked at him through the long willow-leaves and saw him in his dreams.

"May I come to your Lodge, my Lord Dreamer? I've come a long way."

The old man sat still. Presently Selver squatted down on his heels just off the path, beside the stream. His head drooped down, for he was worn out and had to sleep. He had been walking five days.

"Are you of the dream-time or of the world-time?" the old man asked at last.

"Of the world-time."

"Come along with me then." The old man got up promptly and led Selver up the wandering path out of the willow grove into dryer, darker regions of oak and thorn. "I took you for a god," he said, going a pace ahead. "And it seemed to me I had seen you before, perhaps in dream."

"Not in the world-time. I come from Sornol, I have never been here before."

"This town is Cadast. I am Coro Mena. Of the Whitethorn."

"Selver is my name. Of the Ash."

"There are Ash people among us, both men and women. Also your marriage-clans, Birch and Holly; we have no women of the Apple. But you don't come looking for a wife, do you?"

"My wife is dead," Selver said.

They came to the Men's Lodge, on high ground in a stand of young oaks. They stooped and crawled through the tunnel-entrance. Inside, in the firelight, the old man stood up, but Selver stayed crouching on hands and knees, unable to rise. Now that help and comfort was at hand his body, which he had forced too far, would not go farther. It lay down and the eyes closed; and Selver slipped, with relief and gratitude, into the great darkness.

The men of the Lodge of Cadast looked after him, and their healer came to tend the wound in his right arm. In the night Coro Mena and the healer Torber sat by the fire. Most of the other men were with their wives that night; there were only a couple of young prentice-dreamers over on the benches, and they had both gone fast asleep. "I don't know what would give a man such scars as he has on his face," said the healer, "and much less, such a wound as that in his arm. A very queer wound."

"It's a queer engine he wore on his belt," said Coro Mena.

"I saw it and didn't see it."

"I put it under his bench. It looks like polished iron, but not like the handiwork of men."

"He comes from Sornol, he said to you."

They were both silent a while. Coro Mena felt unreasoning fear press upon him, and slipped into dream to find the reason for the fear; for he was an old man, and long adept. In the dream the giants walked, heavy and dire. Their dry scaly limbs were swathed in cloths; their eyes were little and light, like tin beads. Behind them crawled huge moving things made of polished iron. The trees fell down in front of them.

Out from among the falling trees a man ran, crying aloud, with blood on his mouth. The path he ran on was the door-path of the Lodge of Cadast.

"Well, there's little doubt of it," Coro Mena said, sliding out of the dream. "He came oversea straight from Sornol, or else came afoot from the coast of Kelme Deva on our own land. The giants are in both those places, travellers say."

"Will they follow him," said Torber; neither answered the question, which was no question but a statement of possibility.

"You saw the giants once, Coro?"

"Once," the old man said.

He dreamed; sometimes, being very old and not so strong as he had been, he slipped off to sleep for a while. Day broke, noon passed. Outside the Lodge a hunting-party went out, children chirped, women talked in voices like running water. A dryer voice called Coro Mena from the door. He crawled out into the evening sunlight. His sister stood outside, sniffing the aromatic wind with pleasure, but looking stern all the same. "Has the stranger waked up, Coro?"

"Not yet. Torber's looking after him."

"We must hear his story."

"No doubt he'll wake soon."

Ebor Dendep frowned. Headwoman of Cadast, she was anxious for her people; but she did not want to ask that a hurt man be disturbed, nor to offend the Dreamers by insisting on her right to enter their Lodge. "Can't you wake him, Coro?" she asked at last. "What if he is . . . being pursued?"

He could not run his sister's emotions on the same rein with his own, yet he felt them; her anxiety bit him. "If Torber permits, I will," he said.

"Try to learn his news, quickly. I wish he was a woman and would talk sense. . . ."

The stranger had roused himself, and lay feverish in the

halfdark of the Lodge. The unreined dreams of illness moved in his eyes. He sat up, however, and spoke with control. As he listened Coro Mena's bones seemed to shrink within him trying to hide from this terrible story, this new thing.

"I was Selver Thele, when I lived in Eshreth in Sornol. My city was destroyed by the yumens when they cut down the trees in that region. I was one of those made to serve them, with my wife Thele. She was raped by one of them and died. I attacked the yumen that killed her. He would have killed me then, but another of them saved me and set me free. I left Sornol, where no town is safe from the yumens now, and came here to the North Isle, and lived on the coast of Kelme Deva in the Red Groves. There presently the yumens came and began to cut down the world. They destroyed a city there, Penle. They caught a hundred of the men and women and made them serve them, and live in the pen. I was not caught. I lived with others who had escaped from Penle, in the bogland north of Kelme Deva. Sometimes at night I went among the people in the yumens' pens. They told me that that one was there. That one whom I had tried to kill. I thought at first to try again; or else to set the people in the pen free. But all the time I watched the trees fall and saw the world cut open and left to rot. The men might have escaped, but the women were locked in more safely and could not, and they were beginning to die. I talked with the people hiding there in the boglands. We were all very frightened and very angry, and had no way to let our fear and anger free. So at last after long talking, and long dreaming, and the making of a plan, we went in daylight, and killed the yumens of Kelme Deva with arrows and hunting-lances, and burned their city and their engines. We left nothing. But that one had gone away. He came back alone. I sang over him, and let him go."

Selver fell silent.

"Then," Coro Mena whispered.

"Then a flying ship came from Sornol, and hunted us in the forest, but found nobody. So they set fire to the forest; but it rained, and they did little harm. Most of the people freed from the pens and the others have gone farther north and east, towards the Holle Hills, for we were afraid many yumens might come hunting us. I went alone. The yumens know me, you see, they know my face; and this frightens me, and those I stay with."

"What is your wound?" Torber asked.

"That one, he shot me with their kind of weapon; but I sang him down and let him go."

"Alone you downed a giant?" said Torber with a fierce grin, wishing to believe.

"Not alone. With three hunters, and with his weapon in my hand—this."

Torber drew back from the thing.

None of them spoke for a while. At last Coro Mena said, "What you tell us is very black, and the road goes down. Are you a Dreamer of your Lodge?"

"I was. There's no Lodge of Eshreth any more."

"That's all one; we speak the Old Tongue together. Among the willows of Asta you first spoke to me calling me Lord Dreamer. So I am. Do you dream, Selver?"

"Seldom now," Selver answered, obedient to the catechism, his scarred, feverish face bowed.

"Awake?"

"Awake."

"Do you dream well, Selver?"

"Not well."

"Do you hold the dream in your hands?"

"Yes."

"Do you weave and shape, direct and follow, start and cease at will?"

"Sometimes, not always."

"Can you walk the road your dream goes?"

"Sometimes. Sometimes I am afraid to."

"Who is not? It is not altogether bad with you, Selver."

"No, it is altogether bad," Selver said, "there's nothing good left," and he began to shake.

Torber gave him the willow-draught to drink and made him lie down. Coro Mena still had the headwoman's question to ask; reluctantly he did so, kneeling by the sick man. "Will the giants, the yumens you call them, will they follow your trail, Selver?"

"I left no trail. No one has seen me between Kelme Deva and this place, six days. That's not the danger." He struggled to sit up again. "Listen, listen. You don't see the danger. How can you see it? You haven't done what I did, you have never dreamed of it, making two hundred people die. They will not follow me, but they may follow us all. Hunt us, as hunters drive coneys. That is the danger. They may try to kill us. To kill us all, all men."

"Lie down—"

"No, I'm not raving, this is true fact and dream. There were two hundred yumens at Kelme Deva and they are dead. We killed them. We killed them as if they were not men. So will they not turn and do the same? They have killed us by ones, now they will kill us as they kill the trees, by hundreds, and hundreds, and hundreds."

"Be still," Torber said. "Such things happen in the fever-dream, Selver. They do not happen in the world."

"The world is always new," said Coro Mena, "however old its roots. Selver, how is it with these creatures, then? They look like men and talk like men, are they not men?"

"I don't know. Do men kill men, except in madness? Does any beast kill its own kind? Only the insects. These yumens kill us as lightly as we kill snakes. The one who taught me said that they kill one another, in quarrels, and also in groups, like ants fighting. I haven't seen that. But I know they don't spare one who asks life. They will strike a bowed neck, I have seen it! There is a wish to kill in them, and therefore I saw fit to put them to death."

"And all men's dreams," said Coro Mena, cross-legged in shadow, "will be changed. They will never be the same again. I shall never walk again that path I came with you yesterday, the way up from the willow grove that I've walked on all my life. It is changed. You have walked on it and it is utterly changed. Before this day the thing we had to do was the right thing to do; the way we had to go was the right way and led us home. Where is our home now? For you've done what you had to do, and it was not right. You have killed men. I saw them, five years ago, in the Lemgan Valley, where they came in a flying ship; I hid and watched the giants, six of them, and saw them speak, and look at rocks and plants, and cook food. They are men. But you have lived among them, tell me, Selver: do they dream?"

"As children do, in sleep."

"They have no training?"

"No. Sometimes they talk of their dreams, the healers try to use them in healing, but none of them are trained, or have any skill in dreaming. Lyubov, who taught me, understood me when I showed him how to dream, and yet even so he called the world-time 'real' and the dream-time 'unreal,' as if that were the difference between them."

"You have done what you had to do," Coro Mena repeated after a silence. His eyes met Selver's, across shadows. The desperate tension lessened in Selver's face; his scarred mouth relaxed, and he lay back without saying more. In a little while he was asleep.

"He's a god," Coro Mena said.

Torber nodded, accepting the old man's judgment almost with relief.

"But not like the others. Not like the Pursuer, nor the Friend who has no face, nor the Aspen-leaf Woman who walks in the forest of dreams. He is not the Gatekeeper, nor the Snake. Nor the Lyre-player nor the Carver nor the Hunter, though he comes in the world-time like them. We may have dreamed of Selver these last few years, but we shall no longer; he has left the dream-time. In the forest, through the forest he comes, where leaves fall, where trees fall, a god that knows death, a god that kills and is not himself reborn."

The headwoman listened to Coro Mena's reports and prophecies, and acted. She put the town of Cadast on alert, making sure that each family was ready to move out, with some food packed, and litters ready for the old and ill. She sent young women scouting south and east for news of the yumens. She kept one armed hunting-group always around town, though the others went out as usual every night. And when Selver grew stronger she insisted that he come out of the Lodge and tell his story: how the yumens killed and enslaved people in Sornol, and cut down the forests; how the people of Kelme Deva had killed the yumens. She forced women and undreaming men who did not understand these things to listen again, until they understood, and were frightened. For Ebor Dendep was a practical woman. When a Great Dreamer, her brother, told her that Selver was a god, a changer, a bridge between realities, she believed and acted. It was the Dreamer's responsibility to be careful, to be certain that his judgment was true. Her responsibility was then to take that judgment and act upon it. He saw what must be done; she saw that it was done.

"All the cities of the forest must hear," Coro Mena said. So the headwoman sent out her young runners, and headwomen in other towns listened, and sent out their runners. The killing at Kelme Deva and the name of Selver went over North Island and oversea to the other lands, from voice to voice, or in writing; not very fast, for the Forest People had no quicker messengers than footrunners; yet fast enough.

They were not all one people on the Forty Lands of the world. There were more languages than lands, and each with a different dialect for every town that spoke it; there were infinite ramifications of manners, morals, customs, crafts; physical types differed on each of the five Great Lands. The people of Sornol were tall, and pale, and great traders; the people of Rieshwel were short, and many had black fur, and they ate monkeys; and so on and on. But the climate varied little, and the forest little, and the sea not at all. Curiosity, regular trade-routes, and the necessity of finding a husband or wife of the proper Tree, kept up an easy movement of people among the towns and between the lands, and so there were certain likenesses among all but the remotest extremes, the half-rumored barbarian isles of the Far East and South. In all the Forty Lands, women ran the cities and towns, and almost every town had a Men's Lodge. Within the Lodges the Dreamers spoke an old tongue, and this varied little from land to land. It was rarely learned by women or by men who remained hunters, fishers, weavers, builders, those who dreamed only small dreams outside the Lodge. As most writing was in this Lodge-tongue, when headwomen sent fleet girls carrying messages, the letters went from Lodge to Lodge, and so were interpreted by the Dreamers to the Old Women, as were other documents, rumors, problems, myths, and dreams. But it was always the Old Women's choice whether to believe or not.

Selver was in a small room at Eshsen. The door was not locked, but he knew if he opened it something bad would come in. So

long as he kept it shut everything would be all right. The
trouble was that there were young trees, a sapling orchard,
planted out in front of the house; not fruit or nut trees but
some other kind, he could not remember what kind. He went
out to see what kind of trees they were. They all lay broken
and uprooted. He picked up the silvery branch of one and a
little blood ran out of the broken end. No, not here, not again,
Thele, he said: O Thele, come to me before your death! But
she did not come. Only her death was there, the broken
birchtree, the opened door. Selver turned and went quickly
back into the house, discovering that it was all built above
ground like a yumen house, very tall and full of light. Outside
the other door, across the tall room, was the long street of the
yumen city Central. Selver had the gun in his belt. If Davidson
came, he could shoot him. He waited, just inside the open
door, looking out into the sunlight. Davidson came, huge,
running so fast that Selver could not keep him in the sights of
the gun as he doubled crazily back and forth across the wide
street, very fast, always closer. The gun was heavy. Selver fired
it but no fire came out of it, and in rage and terror he threw
the gun and the dream away.

Disgusted and depressed, he spat, and sighed.

"A bad dream?" Ebor Dendep inquired.

"They're all bad, and all the same," he said, but the deep
unease and misery lessened a little as he answered. Cool morning sunlight fell flecked and shafted through the fine leaves
and branches of the birch grove of Cadast. There the headwoman sat weaving a basket of blackstem fern, for she liked to
keep her fingers busy, while Selver lay beside her in half-dream
and dream. He had been fifteen days at Cadast, and his wound
was healing well. He still slept much, but for the first time in
many months he had begun to dream waking again, regularly,
not once or twice in a day and night but in the true pulse and
rhythm of dreaming which should rise and fall ten to fourteen
times in the diurnal cycle. Bad as his dreams were, all terror
and shame, yet he welcomed them. He had feared that he was
cut off from his roots, that he had gone too far into the dead
land of action ever to find his way back to the springs of reality.
Now, though the water was very bitter, he drank again.

Briefly he had Davidson down again among the ashes of the

burned camp, and instead of singing over him this time he hit him in the mouth with a rock. Davidson's teeth broke, and blood ran between the white splinters.

The dream was useful, a straight wish-fulfilment, but he stopped it there, having dreamed it many times, before he met Davidson in the ashes of Kelme Deva, and since. There was nothing to that dream but relief. A sip of bland water. It was the bitter he needed. He must go clear back, not to Kelme Deva but to the long dreadful street in the alien city called Central, where he had attacked Death, and had been defeated.

Ebor Dendep hummed as she worked. Her thin hands, their silky green down silvered with age, worked black fern-stems in and out, fast and neat. She sang a song about gathering ferns, a girl's song: I'm picking ferns, I wonder if he'll come back. . . . Her faint old voice trilled like a cricket's. Sun trembled in birch leaves. Selver put his head down on his arms.

The birch grove was more or less in the center of the town of Cadast. Eight paths led away from it, winding narrowly off among trees. There was a whiff of woodsmoke in the air; where the branches were thin at the south edge of the grove you could see smoke rise from a house-chimney, like a bit of blue yarn unravelling among the leaves. If you looked closely among the live-oaks and other trees you would find houseroofs sticking up a couple of feet above ground, between a hundred and two hundred of them, it was very hard to count. The timber houses were three-quarters sunk, fitted in among tree-roots like badgers' setts. The beam roofs were mounded over with a thatch of small branches, pinestraw, reeds, earthmould. They were insulating, waterproof, almost invisible. The forest and the community of eight hundred people went about their business all around the birch grove where Ebor Dendep sat making a basket of fern. A bird among the branches over her head said, "Te-whet," sweetly. There was more people-noise than usual, for fifty or sixty strangers, young men and women mostly, had come drifting in these last few days, drawn by Selver's presence. Some were from other cities of the North, some were those who had done the killing at Kelme Deva with him; they had followed rumor here to follow him. Yet the voices calling here and there and the babble of women bathing or children playing down by the stream, were not so loud as the morning birdsong and insect-drone and under-noise of the living forest of which the town was one element.

A girl came quickly, a young huntress the color of the pale birch leaves. "Word of mouth from the southern coast, mother," she said. "The runner's at the Women's Lodge."

"Send her here when she's eaten," the headwoman said softly. "Sh, Tolbar, can't you see he's asleep?"

The girl stooped to pick a large leaf of wild tobacco, and laid it lightly over Selver's eyes, on which a shaft of the steepening, bright sunlight had fallen. He lay with his hands half open and his scarred, damaged face turned upward, vulnerable and foolish, a Great Dreamer gone to sleep like a child. But it was the girl's face that Ebor Dendep watched. It shone, in that uneasy shade, with pity and terror, with adoration.

Tolbar darted away. Presently two of the Old Women came with the messenger, moving silent in single file along the sun-flecked path. Ebor Dendep raised her hand, enjoining silence. The messenger promptly lay down flat, and rested; her brown-dappled green fur was dusty and sweaty, she had run far and fast. The Old Women sat down in patches of sun, and became still. Like two old grey-green stones they sat there, with bright living eyes.

Selver, struggling with a sleep-dream beyond his control, cried out as if in great fear, and woke.

He went to drink from the stream; when he came back he was followed by six or seven of those who always followed him. The headwoman put down her half-finished work and said, "Now be welcome, runner, and speak."

The runner stood up, bowed her head to Ebor Dendep, and spoke her message: "I come from Trethat. My words come from Sorbron Deva, before that from sailors of the Strait, before that from Broter in Sornol. They are for the hearing of all Cadast but they are to be spoken to the man called Selver who was born of the Ash in Eshreth. Here are the words: There are new giants in the great city of the giants in Sornol, and many of these new ones are females. The yellow ship of fire goes up and down at the place that was called Peha. It is known in Sornol that Selver of Eshreth burned the city of the giants at Kelme

Deva. The Great Dreamers of the Exiles in Broter have dreamed giants more numerous than the trees of the Forty Lands. These are all the words of the message I bear."

After the singsong recitation they were all silent. The bird, a little farther off, said, "Whet-whet?" experimentally.

"This is a very bad world-time," said one of the Old Women, rubbing a rheumatic knee.

A grey bird flew from a huge oak that marked the north edge of town, and went up in circles, riding the morning updraft on lazy wings. There was always a roosting-tree of these grey kites near a town; they were the garbage service.

A small, fat boy ran through the birch grove, pursued by a slightly larger sister, both shrieking in tiny voices like bats. The boy fell down and cried, the girl stood him up and scrubbed his tears off with a large leaf. They scuttled off into the forest hand in hand.

"There was one called Lyubov," Selver said to the headwoman. "I have spoken of him to Coro Mena, but not to you. When that one was killing me, it was Lyubov who saved me. It was Lyubov who healed me, and set me free. He wanted to know about us; so I would tell him what he asked, and he too would tell me what I asked. Once I asked how his race could survive, having so few women. He said that in the place where they come from, half the race is women; but the men would not bring women to the Forty Lands until they had made a place ready for them."

"Until the men made a fit place for the women? Well! they may have quite a wait," said Ebor Dendep. "They're like the people in the Elm Dream who come at you rump-first, with their heads put on front to back. They make the forest into a dry beach"—her language had no word for "desert"—"and call that making things ready for the women? They should have sent the women first. Maybe with them the women do the Great Dreaming, who knows? They are backwards, Selver. They are insane."

"A people can't be insane."

"But they only dream in sleep, you said; if they want to dream waking they take poisons so that the dreams go out of control, you said! How can people be any madder? They don't know the dream-time from the world-time, any more than a baby does. Maybe when they kill a tree they think it will come alive again!"

Selver shook his head. He still spoke to the headwoman as if he and she were alone in the birch grove, in a quiet hesitant voice, almost drowsily. "No, they understand death very well. . . . Certainly they don't see as we do, but they know more and understand more about certain things than we do. Lyubov mostly understood what I told him. Much of what he told me, I couldn't understand. It wasn't the language that kept me from understanding; I know his tongue, and he learned ours; we made a writing of the two languages together. Yet there were things he said I could never understand. He said the yumens are from outside the forest. That's quite clear. He said they want the forest: the trees for wood, the land to plant grass on." Selver's voice, though still soft, had taken on resonance; the people among the silver trees listened. "That too is clear, to those of us who've seen them cutting down the world. He said the yumens are men like us, that we're indeed related, as close kin maybe as the Red Deer to the Greybuck. He said that they come from another place which is not the forest; the trees there are all cut down; it has a sun, not our sun, which is a star. All this, as you see, wasn't clear to me. I say his words but don't know what they mean. It does not matter much. It is clear that they want our forest for themselves. They are twice our stature, they have weapons that outshoot ours by far, and fire-throwers, and flying ships. Now they have brought more women, and will have children. There are maybe two thousand, maybe three thousand of them here now, mostly in Sornol. But if we wait a lifetime or two they will breed; their numbers will double and redouble. They kill men and women; they do not spare those who ask life. They cannot sing in contest. They have left their roots behind them, perhaps, in this other forest from which they came, this forest with no trees. So they take poison to let loose the dreams in them, but it only makes them drunk or sick. No one can say certainly whether they're men or not men, whether they're sane or insane, but that does not matter. They must be made to leave the forest, because they are dangerous. If they will not go they must be burned out of the Lands, as nests of stinging-ants must be burned out of the groves of cities. If we wait, it is we that will be smoked out and burned. They can step on us as we step on stinging-ants. Once I saw a woman, it was when they burned my city Eshreth, she lay down in the path before a yumen to ask him for life, and he stepped on her back and broke the spine, and then kicked her aside as if she was a dead snake. I saw that. If the yumens are men they are men unfit or untaught to dream and to act as men. Therefore they go about in torment killing and destroying, driven by the gods within, whom they will not set free but try to uproot and deny. If they are men they are evil men, having denied their own gods, afraid to see their own faces in the dark. Headwoman of Cadast, hear me." Selver stood up, tall and abrupt among the seated women. "It's time, I think, that I go back to my own land, to Sornol, to those that are in exile and those that are enslaved. Tell any people who dream of a city burning to come after me to Broter." He bowed to Ebor Dendep and left the birch grove, still walking lame, his arm bandaged; yet there was a quickness to his walk, a poise to his head, that made him seem more whole than other men. The young people followed quietly after him.

"Who is he?" asked the runner from Trethat, her eyes following him.

"The man to whom your message came, Selver of Eshreth, a god among us. Have you ever seen a god before, daughter?"

"When I was ten the Lyre-Player came to our town."

"Old Ertel, yes. He was of my Tree, and from the North Vales like me. Well, now you've seen a second god, and a greater. Tell your people in Trethat of him."

"Which god is he, mother?"

"A new one," Ebor Dendep said in her dry old voice. "The son of forest-fire, the brother of the murdered. He is the one who is not reborn. Now go on, all of you, go on to the Lodge. See who'll be going with Selver, see about food for them to carry. Let me be a while. I'm as full of forebodings as a stupid old man, I must dream. . . ."

Coro Mena went with Selver that night as far as the place where they first met, under the copper willows by the stream. Many people were following Selver south, some sixty in all, as great a troop as most people had ever seen on the move at once. They would cause great stir and thus gather many more to them, on their way to the sea-crossing to Sornol. Selver had claimed his Dreamer's privilege of solitude for this one night. He was setting off alone. His followers would catch him up in the morning; and thenceforth, implicated in crowd and act, he would have little time for the slow and deep running of the great dreams.

"Here we met," the old man said, stopping among the bowing branches, the veils of dropping leaves, "and here part. This will be called Selver's Grove, no doubt, by the people who walk our paths hereafter."

Selver said nothing for a while, standing still as a tree, the restless leaves about him darkening from silver as clouds thickened over the stars. "You are surer of me than I am," he said at last, a voice in darkness.

"Yes, I'm sure, Selver. . . . I was well taught in dreaming, and then I'm old. I dream very little for myself any more. Why should I? Little is new to me. And what I wanted from my life, I have had, and more. I have had my whole life. Days like the leaves of the forest. I'm an old hollow tree, only the roots live. And so I dream only what all men dream. I have no visions and no wishes. I see what is. I see the fruit ripening on the branch. Four years it has been ripening, that fruit of the deep-planted tree. We have all been afraid for four years, even we who live far from the yumens' cities, and have only glimpsed them from hiding, or seen their ships fly over, or looked at the dead places where they cut down the world, or heard mere tales of these things. We are all afraid. Children wake from sleep crying of giants; women will not go far on their trading-journeys; men in the Lodges cannot sing. The fruit of fear is ripening. And I see you gather it. You are the harvester. All that we fear to know, you have seen, you have known: exile, shame, pain, the roof and walls of the world fallen, the mother dead in misery, the children untaught, uncherished. . . . This is a new time for the world: a bad time. And you have suffered it all. You have gone farthest. And at the farthest, at the end of the black path, there grows the Tree; there the fruit ripens; now you reach up, Selver, now you gather it. And the world changes wholly, when a man holds in his hand the fruit of that tree, whose roots are deeper than the forest. Men will know it. They will know you, as we did. It doesn't take an old man or a Great Dreamer to recognise a god! Where you go, fire burns; only the blind cannot see it. But listen, Selver, this is what I see that perhaps others do not, this is why I have loved you: I dreamed of you before we met here. You were walking on a path, and behind you the young trees grew up, oak and birch, willow and holly, fir and pine, alder, elm, white-flowering ash, all the roof and walls of the world, forever renewed. Now farewell, dear god and son, go safely."

The night darkened as Selver went, until even his night-seeing eyes saw nothing but masses and planes of black. It began to rain. He had gone only a few miles from Cadast when he must either light a torch, or halt. He chose to halt, and groping found a place among the roots of a great chestnut tree. There he sat, his back against the broad, twisting bole that seemed to hold a little sun-warmth in it still. The fine rain, falling unseen in darkness, pattered on the leaves overhead, on his arms and neck and head protected by their thick silk-fine hair, on the earth and ferns and undergrowth nearby, on all the leaves of the forest, near and far. Selver sat as quiet as the grey owl on a branch above him, unsleeping, his eyes wide open in the rainy dark.

3

Captain Raj Lyubov had a headache. It began softly in the muscles of his right shoulder, and mounted crescendo to a smashing drumbeat over his right ear. The speech centers are in the left cerebral cortex, he thought, but he couldn't have said it; couldn't speak, or read, or sleep, or think. Cortex, vortex. Migraine headache, margarine breadache, ow, ow, ow. Of course he had been cured of migraine once at college and again during his obligatory Army Prophylactic Psychotherapy Sessions, but he had brought along some ergotamine pills when he left Earth, just in case. He had taken two, and a superhyperduper-analgesic, and a tranquillizer, and a digestive pill to counteract the caffeine which counteracted the ergotamine, but the awl still bored out from within, just over his right ear, to the beat of the big bass drum. Awl, drill, ill, pill, oh God. Lord deliver us. Liver sausage. What would the Athsheans do for a migraine? They wouldn't have one, they would have daydreamed the tensions away a week before they got them. Try it, try daydreaming. Begin as Selver taught you. Although knowing nothing of electricity he could not really grasp the principle of the EEG, as soon as he heard about alpha waves and when they appear he had said, "Oh yes, you mean this," and there appeared the unmistakable alpha-squiggles on the graph recording what went on inside his small green head; and he had taught Lyubov how to turn on and off the alpha-rhythms in one half-hour lesson. There really was nothing to it. But not now, the world is too much with us, ow, ow, ow above the right ear I always hear Time's winged chariot hurrying near, for the Athsheans had burned Smith Camp day before yesterday and killed two hundred men. Two hundred and seven to be precise. Every man alive except the Captain. No wonder pills couldn't get at the center of his migraine, for it was on an island two hundred miles away two days ago. Over the hills and far away. Ashes, ashes, all fall down. And amongst the ashes, all his knowledge of the High Intelligence Life Forms of World 41. Dust, rubbish, a mess of false data and fake hypotheses. Nearly five E-years here, and he had believed the Athsheans to be incapable of killing men, his kind or their kind. He had written long papers to explain how and why they couldn't kill men. All wrong. Dead wrong.

What had he failed to see?

It was nearly time to be going over to the meeting at HQ. Cautiously Lyubov stood up, moving all in one piece so that the right side of his head would not fall off; he approached his desk with the gait of a man underwater, poured out a shot of General Issue vodka, and drank it. It turned him inside out: it extraverted him: it normalized him. He felt better. He went out, and unable to stand the jouncing of his motorbike, started to walk down the long, dusty main street of Centralville to HQ. Passing the Luau he thought with greed of another vodka; but Captain Davidson was just going in the door, and Lyubov went on.

The people from the *Shackleton* were already in the conference room. Commander Yung, whom he had met before, had brought some new faces down from orbit this time. They were not in Navy uniform; after a moment Lyubov recognised them, with a slight shock, as non-Terran humans. He sought an introduction at once. One, Mr Or, was a Hairy Cetian, dark grey, stocky, and dour; the other, Mr Lepennon, was tall, white, and comely: a Hainishman. They greeted Lyubov with interest, and Lepennon said, "I've just been reading your report on the conscious control of paradoxical sleep among the Athsheans, Dr Lyubov," which was pleasant, and it was pleasant also to be called by his own, earned title of doctor. Their conversation indicated that they had spent some years on Earth, and that they might be hilfers, or something like it; but the Commander, introducing them, had not mentioned their status or position.

The room was filling up. Gosse, the colony ecologist, came in; so did all the high brass; so did Captain Susun, head of Planet Development—logging operations—whose captaincy like Lyubov's was an invention necessary to the peace of the military mind. Captain Davidson came in alone, straight-backed and handsome, his lean, rugged face calm and rather stern. Guards stood at all the doors. The Army necks were all stiff as crowbars. The conference was plainly an Investigation. *Whose fault?* My fault, Lyubov thought despairingly; but out of his despair he looked across the table at Captain Don Davidson with detestation and contempt.

Commander Yung had a very quiet voice. "As you know, gentlemen, my ship stopped here at World 41 to drop you off a new load of colonists, and nothing more; *Shackleton*'s mission is to World 88, Prestno, one of the Hainish Group. However, this attack on your outpost camp, since it chanced to occur during our week here, can't be simply ignored; particularly in the light of certain developments which you would have been informed of a little later, in the normal course of events. The fact is that the status of World 41 as an Earth Colony is now subject to revision, and the massacre at your camp may precipitate the Administration's decisions on it. Certainly the decisions *we* can make must be made quickly, for I can't keep my ship here long. Now first, we wish to make sure that the relevant facts are all in the possession of those present. Captain Davidson's report on the events at Smith Camp was taped and heard by all of us on ship; by all of you here also? Good. Now if there are questions any of you wish to ask Captain Davidson, go ahead. I have one myself. You returned to the site of the camp the following day, Captain Davidson, in a large hopper with eight soldiers; had you the permission of a senior officer here at Central for that flight?"

Davidson stood up. "I did, sir."

"Were you authorised to land and to set fires in the forest near the campsite?"

"No, sir."

"You did, however, set fires?"

"I did, sir. I was trying to smoke out the creechies that killed my men."

"Very well. Mr Lepennon?"

The tall Hainishman cleared his throat. "Captain Davidson," he said, "do you think that the people under your command at Smith Camp were mostly content?"

"Yes, I do."

Davidson's manner was firm and forthright; he seemed indifferent to the fact that he was in trouble. Of course these Navy officers and foreigners had no authority over him; it was to his own Colonel that he must answer for losing two hundred men and making unauthorized reprisals. But his Colonel was right there, listening.

"They were well fed, well housed, not overworked, then, as well as can be managed in a frontier camp?"

"Yes."

"Was the discipline maintained very harsh?"

"No, it was not."

"What, then, do you think motivated the revolt?"

"I don't understand."

"If none of them were discontented, why did some of them massacre the rest and destroy the camp?"

There was a worried silence.

"May I put in a word," Lyubov said. "It was the native hilfs, the Athsheans employed in the camp, who joined with an attack by the forest people against the Terran humans. In his report Captain Davidson referred to the Athsheans as 'creechies.'"

Lepennon looked embarrassed and anxious. "Thank you, Dr Lyubov. I misunderstood entirely. Actually I took the word 'creechie' to stand for a Terran caste that did rather menial work in the logging camps. Believing, as we all did, that the Athsheans were intraspecies non-aggressive, I never thought they might be the group meant. In fact I didn't realise that they cooperated with you in your camps. —However, I am more at a loss than ever to understand what provoked the attack and mutiny."

"I don't know, sir."

"When he said the people under his command were content, did the Captain include native people?" said the Cetian, Or, in a dry mumble. The Hainishman picked it up at once, and asked Davidson, in his concerned, courteous voice, "Were the Athsheans living at the camp content, do you think?"

"So far as I know."

"There was nothing unusual in their position there, or the work they had to do?"

Lyubov felt the heightening of tension, one turn of the screw, in Colonel Dongh and his staff, and also in the starship commander. Davidson remained calm and easy. "Nothing unusual."

Lyubov knew now that only his scientific studies had been sent up to the *Shackleton*; his protests, even his annual assessments of 'Native Adjustment to Colonial Presence' required by the Administration, had been kept in some desk drawer deep in HQ. These two N.-T.H.'s knew nothing about the exploitation of the Athsheans. Commander Yung did, of course; he had been down before today and had probably seen the creechie-pens. In any case a Navy commander on Colony runs wouldn't have much to learn about Terran-hilf relations. Whether or not he approved of how the Colonial Administration ran its business, not much would come as a shock to him. But a Cetian and a Hainishman, how much would they know about Terran colonies, unless chance brought them to one on the way to somewhere else? Lepennon and Or had not intended to come on-planet here at all. Or possibly they had not been intended to come on-planet, but, hearing of trouble, had insisted. Why had the commander brought them down: his will, or theirs? Whoever they were they had about them a hint of authority, a whiff of the dry, intoxicating odor of power. Lyubov's headache had gone, he felt alert and excited, his face was rather hot. "Captain Davidson," he said, "I have a couple

of questions, concerning your confrontation with the four natives, day before yesterday. You're certain that one of them was
Sam, or Selver Thele?"

"I believe so."

"You're aware that he has a personal grudge against you."

"I don't know."

"You don't? Since his wife died in your quarters immediately
subsequent to sexual intercourse with you, he holds you responsible for her death; you didn't know that? He attacked you
once before, here in Centralville; you had forgotten that? Well,
the point is, that Selver's personal hatred for Captain Davidson
may serve as a partial explanation or motivation for this un-
precedented assault. The Athsheans aren't incapable of personal
violence, that's never been asserted in any of my studies of them.
Adolescents who haven't mastered controlled dreaming or
competitive singing do a lot of wrestling and fist-fighting, not
all of it good-tempered. But Selver is an adult and an adept;
and his first, personal attack on Captain Davidson, which I
happened to witness part of, was pretty certainly an attempt to
kill. As was the Captain's retaliation, incidentally. At the time, I
thought that attack an isolated psychotic incident, resulting
from grief and stress, not likely to be repeated. I was wrong.
—Captain, when the four Athsheans jumped you from am-
bush, as you describe in your report, did you end up prone on
the ground?"

"Yes."

"In what position?"

Davidson's calm face tensed and stiffened, and Lyubov felt a
pang of compunction. He wanted to corner Davidson in his
lies, to force him into speaking truth once, but not to humiliate him before others. Accusations of rape and murder supported Davidson's image of himself as the totally virile man, but
now that image was endangered: Lyubov had called up a picture of him, the soldier, the fighter, the cool tough man, being
knocked down by enemies the size of six-year-olds. . . . What
did it cost Davidson, then, to recall that moment when he had
lain looking up at the little green men, for once, not down at
them?

"I was on my back."

"Was your head thrown back, or turned aside?"

"I don't know."

"I'm trying to establish a fact here, Captain, one that might help explain why Selver didn't kill you, although he had a grudge against you and had helped kill two hundred men a few hours earlier. I wondered if you might by chance have been in one of the positions which, when assumed by an Athshean, prevent his opponent from further physical aggression."

"I don't know."

Lyubov glanced round the conference table; all the faces showed curiosity and some tension. "These aggression-halting gestures and positions may have some innate basis, may rise from a surviving trigger-response, but they are socially developed and expanded, and of course learned. The strongest and completest of them is a prone position, on the back, eyes shut, head turned so the throat is fully exposed. I think an Athshean of the local cultures might find it impossible to hurt an enemy who took that position. He would have to do something else to release his anger or aggressive drive. —When they had all got you down, Captain, did Selver by any chance sing?"

"Did he what?"

"Sing."

"I don't know."

Block. No go. Lyubov was about to shrug and give it up when the Cetian said, "Why, Mr Lyubov?" The most winning characteristic of the rather harsh Cetian temperament was curiosity, inopportune and inexhaustible curiosity; Cetians died eagerly, curious as to what came next.

"You see," Lyubov said, "the Athsheans use a kind of ritualised singing to replace physical combat. Again it's a universal social phenomenon that might have a physiological foundation, though it's very hard to establish anything as 'innate' in human beings. However the higher primates here all go in for vocal competing between two males, a lot of howling and whistling; the dominant male may finally give the other a cuff, but usually they just spend an hour or so trying to outbellow each other. The Athsheans themselves see the similarity to their singing-matches, which are also only between males; but as they observe, theirs are not only aggression-releases, but an art-form. The better artist wins. I wondered if Selver sang over Captain Davidson, and if so, whether he did because he could not kill, or because he preferred the bloodless victory. These questions have suddenly become rather urgent."

"Dr Lyubov," said Lepennon, "how effective are these aggression-channelling devices? Are they universal?"

"Among adults, yes. So my informants state, and all my observation supported them, until day before yesterday. Rape, violent assault, and murder virtually don't exist among them. There are accidents, of course. And there are psychotics. Not many of the latter."

"What do they do with dangerous psychotics?"

"Isolate them. Literally. On small islands."

"The Athsheans are carnivorous, they hunt animals?"

"Yes, meat is a staple."

"Wonderful," Lepennon said, and his white skin paled further with pure excitement. "A human society with an effective war-barrier! What's the cost, Dr Lyubov?"

"I'm not sure, Mr Lepennon. Perhaps change. They're a static, stable, uniform society. They have no history. Perfectly integrated, and wholly unprogressive. You might say that like the forest they live in, they've attained a climax state. But I don't mean to imply that they're incapable of adaptation."

"Gentlemen, this is very interesting but in a somewhat specialist frame of reference, and it may be somewhat out of the context which we're attempting to clarify here—"

"No, excuse me, Colonel Dongh, this may be the point. Yes, Dr Lyubov?"

"Well, I wonder if they're not proving their adaptability, now. By adapting their behavior to us. To the Earth Colony. For four years they've behaved to us as they do to one another. Despite the physical differences, they recognised us as members of their species, as men. However, we have not responded as members of their species should respond. We have ignored the responses, the rights and obligations of non-violence. We have killed, raped, dispersed, and enslaved the native humans, destroyed their communities, and cut down their forests. It wouldn't be surprising if they'd decided that we are not human."

"And therefore can be killed, like animals, yes yes," said the Cetian, enjoying logic; but Lepennon's face now was stiff as white stone. "Enslaved?" he said.

"Captain Lyubov is expressing his personal opinions and

theories," said Colonel Dongh, "which I should state I consider possibly to be erroneous, and he and I have discussed this type of thing previously, although the present context is unsuitable. We do not employ slaves, sir. Some of the natives serve a useful role in our community. The Voluntary Autochthonous Labor Corps is a part of all but the temporary camps here. We have very limited personnel to accomplish our tasks here and we need workers and use all we can get, but on any kind of basis that could be called a slavery basis, certainly not."

Lepennon was about to speak, but deferred to the Cetian, who said only, "How many of each race?"

Gosse replied: "2641 Terrans, now. Lyubov and I estimate the native hilf population very roughly at 3 million."

"You should have considered these statistics, gentlemen, before you altered the native traditions!" said Or, with a disagreeable but perfectly genuine laugh.

"We are adequately armed and equipped to resist any type of aggression these natives could offer," said the Colonel. "However there was a general consensus by both the first Exploratory Missions and our own research staff of specialists here headed by Captain Lyubov, giving us to understand that the New Tahitians are a primitive, harmless, peace-loving species. Now this information was obviously erroneous—"

Or interrupted the Colonel. "Obviously! You consider the human species to be primitive, harmless, and peace-loving, Colonel? No. But you knew that the hilfs of this planet are human? As human as you or I or Lepennon—since we all came from the same, original, Hainish stock?"

"That is the scientific theory, I am aware—"

"Colonel, it is the historic fact."

"I am not forced to accept it as a fact," the old Colonel said, getting hot, "and I don't like opinions stuffed into my own mouth. The fact is that these creechies are a meter tall, they're covered with green fur, they don't sleep, and they're not human beings in my frame of reference!"

"Captain Davidson," said the Cetian, "do you consider the native hilfs human, or not?"

"I don't know."

"But you had sexual intercourse with one—this Selver's wife. Would you have sexual intercourse with a female animal? What about the rest of you?" He looked about at the purple colonel, the glowering majors, the livid captains, the cringing specialists. Contempt came into his face. "You have not thought things through," he said. By his standards it was a brutal insult.

The Commander of the *Shackleton* at last salvaged words from the gulf of embarrassed silence. "Well, gentlemen, the tragedy at Smith Camp clearly is involved with the entire colony-native relationship, and is not by any means an insignificant or isolated episode. That's what we had to establish. And this being the case, we can make a certain contribution towards easing your problem here. The main purpose of our journey was not to drop off a couple of hundred girls here, though I know you've been waiting for 'em, but to get to Prestno, which has been having some difficulties, and give the government there an ansible. That is, an ICD transmitter."

"What?" said Sereng, an engineer. Stares became fixed, all round the table.

"The one we have aboard is an early model, and it cost a planetary annual revenue, roughly. That, of course, was 27 years ago planetary time, when we left Earth. Nowadays they're making them relatively cheaply; they're SI on Navy ships; and in the normal course of things a robo or manned ship would be coming out here to give your colony one. As a matter of fact it's a manned Administration ship, and is on the way, due here in 9.4 E-years if I recall the figure."

"How do you know that?" somebody said, setting it up for Commander Yung, who replied smiling, "By the ansible: the one we have aboard. Mr Or, your people invented the device, perhaps you'd explain it to those here who are unfamiliar with the terms?"

The Cetian did not unbend. "I shall not attempt to explain the principles of ansible operation to those present," he said. "Its effect can be stated simply: the instantaneous transmission of a message over any distance. One element must be on a large-mass body, the other can be anywhere in the cosmos. Since arrival in orbit the *Shackleton* has been in daily communication with Terra, now 27 lightyears distant. The message does not take 54 years for delivery and response, as it does on an electromagnetic device. It takes no time. There is no more time-gap between worlds."

"As soon as we came out of NAFAL time-dilatation into planetary space-time, here, we rang up home, as you might say," the soft-voiced Commander went on. "And were told what had happened during the 27 years we were travelling. The time-gap for bodies remains, but the information lag does not. As you can see, this is as important to us as an interstellar species, as speech itself was to us earlier in our evolution. It'll have the same effect: to make a society possible."

"Mr Or and I left Earth, 27 years ago, as Legates for our respective governments, Tau II and Hain," said Lepennon. His voice was still gentle and civil, but the warmth had gone out of it. "When we left, people were talking about the possibility of forming some kind of league among the civilised worlds, now that communication was possible. The League of Worlds now exists. It has existed for 18 years. Mr Or and I are now Emissaries of the Council of the League, and so have certain powers and responsibilities we did not have when we left Earth."

The three of them from the ship kept saying these things: an instantaneous communicator exists, an interstellar supergovernment exists. . . . Believe it or not. They were in league, and lying. This thought went through Lyubov's mind; he considered it, decided it was a reasonable but unwarranted suspicion, a defense-mechanism, and discarded it. Some of the military staff, however, trained to compartmentalize their thinking, specialists in self-defense, would accept it as unhesitatingly as he discarded it. They must believe that anyone claiming a sudden new authority was a liar or conspirator. They were no more constrained than Lyubov, who had been trained to keep his mind open whether he wanted to or not.

"Are we to take all—all this simply on your word, sir?" said Colonel Dongh, with dignity and some pathos; for he, too muddleheaded to compartmentalize neatly, knew that he shouldn't believe Lepennon and Or and Yung, but did believe them, and was frightened.

"No," said the Cetian. "That's done with. A colony like this had to believe what passing ships and outdated radio-messages told them. Now you don't. You can verify. We are going to give you the ansible destined for Prestno. We have League authority to do so. Received, of course, by ansible. Your colony here is in a bad way. Worse than I thought from your reports. Your reports are very incomplete; censorship or stupidity have been at work. Now, however, you'll have the ansible, and can talk with your Terran Administration; you can ask for orders, so you'll know how to proceed. Given the profound changes that have been occurring in the organisation of the Terran Government since we left there, I should recommend that you do so at once. There is no longer any excuse for acting on outdated orders; for ignorance; for irresponsible autonomy."

Sour a Cetian and, like milk, he stayed sour. Mr Or was being overbearing, and Commander Yung should shut him up. But could he? How did an "Emissary of the Council of the League of Worlds" rank? Who's in charge here, thought Lyubov, and he too felt a qualm of fear. His headache had returned as a sense of constriction, a sort of tight headband over the temples.

He looked across the table at Lepennon's white, long-fingered hands, lying left over right, quiet, on the bare polished wood of the table. The white skin was a defect to Lyubov's Earth-formed aesthetic taste, but the serenity and strength of those hands pleased him very much. To the Hainish, he thought, civilisation came naturally. They had been at it so long. They lived the social-intellectual life with the grace of a cat hunting in a garden, the certainty of a swallow following summer over the sea. They were experts. They never had to pose, to fake. They were what they were. Nobody seemed to fit the human skin so well. Except, perhaps, the little green men? the deviant, dwarfed, over-adapted, stagnated creechies, who were as absolutely, as honestly, as serenely what they were. . . .

An officer, Benton, was asking Lepennon if he and Or were on this planet as observers for the (he hesitated) League of Worlds, or if they claimed any authority to . . . Lepennon took him up politely: "We are observers here, not empowered to command, only to report. You are still answerable only to your own government on Earth."

Colonel Dongh said with relief, "Then nothing has essentially changed—"

"You forget the ansible," Or interrupted. "I'll instruct you in its operation, Colonel, as soon as this discussion is over. You can then consult with your Colonial Administration."

"Since your problem here is rather urgent, and since Earth is now a League member and may have changed the Colonial Code somewhat during recent years, Mr Or's advice is both proper and timely. We should be very grateful to Mr Or and Mr Lepennon for their decision to give this Terran colony the ansible destined for Prestno. It was their decision; I can only applaud it. Now, one more decision remains to be made, and this one I have to make, using your judgment as my guide. If you feel the colony is in imminent peril of further and more massive attacks from the natives, I can keep my ship here for a week or two as a defense arsenal; I can also evacuate the women. No children yet, right?"

"No, sir," said Gosse. "482 women, now."

"Well, I have space for 380 passengers; we might crowd a hundred more in; the extra mass would add a year or so to the trip home, but it could be done. Unfortunately that's all I can do. We must proceed to Prestno; your nearest neighbor, as you know, 1.8 lightyears distant. We'll stop here on the way home to Terra, but that's going to be three and a half more E-years at least. Can you stick it out?"

"Yes," said the Colonel, and others echoed him. "We've had warning now and we won't be caught napping again."

"Equally," said the Cetian, "can the native inhabitants stick it out for three and a half Earth-years more?"

"Yes," said the Colonel. "No," said Lyubov. He had been watching Davidson's face, and a kind of panic had taken hold of him.

"Colonel?" said Lepennon, politely.

"We've been here four years now and the natives are flourishing. There's room enough and to spare for all of us, as you can see the planet's heavily underpopulated and the Administration wouldn't have cleared it for colonisation purposes if that hadn't been as it is. As for if this entered anyone's head, they won't catch us off guard again, we were erroneously briefed concerning the nature of these natives, but we're fully armed and able to defend ourselves, but we aren't planning any reprisals. That is expressly forbidden in the Colonial Code, though I don't know what new rules this new government may have added on, but we'll just stick to our own as we have been doing and they definitely negative mass reprisals or genocide. We won't be sending any messages for help out, after all a colony 27 lightyears from home has come out expecting to be on its own and to in fact be completely self-sufficient, and I don't see that the ICD really changes that, due to ship and men and material still have to travel at near lightspeed. We'll just keep on shipping the lumber home, and look out for ourselves. The women are in no danger."

"Mr Lyubov?" said Lepennon.

"We've been here four years. I don't know if the native human culture will survive four more. As for the total land ecology, I think Gosse will back me if I say that we've irrecoverably wrecked the native life-systems on one large island, have done great damage on this subcontinent Sornol, and if we go on logging at the present rate, may reduce the major habitable lands to desert within ten years. This isn't the fault of the colony's HQ or Forestry Bureau; they've simply been following a Development Plan drawn up on Earth without sufficient knowledge of the planet to be exploited, its life-systems, or its native human inhabitants."

"Mr Gosse?" said the polite voice.

"Well, Raj, you're stretching things a bit. There's no denying that Dump Island, which was overlogged in direct contravention to my recommendations, is a dead loss. If more than a certain percentage of the forest is cut over a certain area, then the fibreweed doesn't reseed, you see, gentlemen, and the fibreweed root-system is the main soil-binder on clear land; without it the soil goes dusty and drifts off very fast under wind-erosion and the heavy rainfall. But I can't agree that our basic directives are at fault, so long as they're scrupulously followed. They were based on careful study of the planet. We've succeeded, here on Central, by following the Plan: erosion is minimal, and the cleared soil is highly arable. To log off a forest doesn't, after all, mean to make a desert—except perhaps from the point of view of a squirrel. We can't forecast precisely how the native forest life-systems will adapt to the new woodland-prairie-plowland ambiance foreseen in the Development Plan, but we know the chances are good for a large percentage of adaptation and survival."

"That's what the Bureau of Land Management said about Alaska during the First Famine," said Lyubov. His throat had tightened so that his voice came out high and husky. He had counted on Gosse for support. "How many Sitka spruce have you seen in your lifetime, Gosse? Or snowy owl? or wolf? or Eskimo? The survival percentage of native Alaskan species in habitat, after 15 years of the Development Program, was .3%. It's now zero. —A forest ecology is a delicate one. If the forest perishes, its fauna may go with it. The Athshean word for *world* is also the word for *forest*. I submit, Commander Yung, that though the colony may not be in imminent danger, the planet is—"

"Captain Lyubov," said the old Colonel, "such submissions are not properly submitted by staff specialist officers to officers of other branches of the service but should rest on the judgment of the senior officers of the Colony, and I cannot tolerate any further such attempts as this to give advice without previous clearance."

Caught off guard by his own outburst, Lyubov apologised and tried to look calm. If only he didn't lose his temper, if his voice didn't go weak and husky, if he had poise. . . .

The Colonel went on. "It appears to us that you made some serious erroneous judgments concerning the peacefulness and non-aggressiveness of the natives here, and because we counted on this specialist description of them as non-aggressive is why we left ourselves open to this terrible tragedy at Smith Camp, Captain Lyubov. So I think we have to wait until some other specialists in hilfs have had time to study them, because evidently your theories were basically erroneous to some extent."

Lyubov sat and took it. Let the men from the ship see them all passing the blame around like a hot brick: all the better. The more dissension they showed, the likelier were these Emissaries to have them checked and watched over. And he was to blame; he had been wrong. To hell with my self-respect so long as the forest people get a chance, Lyubov thought, and so strong a sense of his own humiliation and self-sacrifice came over him that tears rose to his eyes.

He was aware that Davidson was watching him.

He sat up stiff, the blood hot in his face, his temples drumming. He would not be sneered at by that bastard Davidson. Couldn't Or and Lepennon see what kind of man Davidson was, and how much power he had here, while Lyubov's powers, called "advisory," were simply derisory? If the colonists were left to go on with no check on them but a super-radio, the Smith Camp massacre would almost certainly become the excuse for systematic aggression against the natives. Bacteriological extermination, most likely. The *Shackleton* would come back in three and a half or four years to "New Tahiti," and find a thriving Terran colony, and no more Creechie Problem. None at all. Pity about the plague, we took all precautions required by the Code, but it must have been some kind of mutation, they had no natural resistance, but we did manage to save a group of them by transporting them to the New Falkland Isles in the southern hemisphere and they're doing fine there, all sixty-two of them. . . .

The conference did not last much longer. When it ended he stood up and leaned across the table to Lepennon. "You must tell the League to do something to save the forests, the forest people," he said almost inaudibly, his throat constricted, "you must, please, you must."

The Hainishman met his eyes; his gaze was reserved, kindly, and deep as a well. He said nothing.

4

It was unbelievable. They'd all gone insane. This damned alien world had sent them all right round the bend, into byebye dreamland, along with the creechies. He still wouldn't believe what he'd seen at that "conference" and the briefing after it, if he saw it all over again on film. A Starfleet ship's commander bootlicking two humanoids. Engineers and techs cooing and ooing over a fancy radio presented to them by a Hairy Cetian with a lot of sneering and boasting, as if ICD's hadn't been predicted by Terran science years ago! The humanoids had stolen the idea, implemented it, and called it an "ansible" so nobody would realise it was just an ICD. But the worst part of it had been the conference, with that psycho Lyubov raving and crying, and Colonel Dongh letting him do it, letting him insult Davidson and HQ staff and the whole Colony; and all the time the two aliens sitting and grinning, the little grey ape and the big white fairy, sneering at humans.

It had been pretty bad. It hadn't got any better since the

Shackleton left. He didn't mind being sent down to New Java Camp under Major Muhamed. The Colonel had to discipline him; old Ding Dong might actually be very happy about that fire-raid he'd pulled in reprisal on Smith Island, but the raid had been a breach of discipline and he had to reprimand Davidson. All right, rules of the game. But what wasn't in the rules was this stuff coming over that overgrown TV set they called the ansible—their new little tin god at HQ.

Orders from the Bureau of Colonial Administration in Karachi: *Restrict Terran-Athshean contact to occasions arranged by Athsheans.* In other words you couldn't go into a creechie warren and round up a workforce any more. *Employment of volunteer labor is not advised; employment of forced labor is forbidden.* More of same. How the hell were they supposed to get the work done? Did Earth want this wood or didn't it? They were still sending the robot cargo ships to New Tahiti, weren't they, four a year, each carrying about 30 million new-dollars worth of prime lumber back to Mother Earth. Sure the Development people wanted those millions. They were businessmen. These messages weren't coming from them, any fool could see that.

The colonial status of World 41—why didn't they call it New Tahiti any more?—*is under consideration. Until decision is reached colonists should observe extreme caution in all dealings with native inhabitants. . . . The use of weapons of any kind except small side-arms carried in self-defense is absolutely forbidden*—just as on Earth, except that there a man couldn't even carry side-arms any more. But what the hell was the use coming 27 lightyears to a frontier world and then get told No guns, no firejelly, no bugbombs, no no, just sit like nice little boys and let the creechies come spit in your faces and sing songs at you and then stick a knife in your guts and burn down your camp, but don't you hurt the cute little green fellers, no sir!

A policy of avoidance is strongly advised; a policy of aggression or retaliation is strictly forbidden.

That was the gist of all the messages actually, and any fool could tell that that wasn't the Colonial Administration talking. They couldn't have changed that much in thirty years. They were practical, realistic men who knew what life was like on frontier planets. It was clear, to anybody who hadn't gone spla from geoshock, that the "ansible" messages were phoneys. They might be planted right in the machine, a whole set of answers to high-probability questions, computer run. The engineers said they could have spotted that; maybe so. In that case the thing did communicate instantaneously with another world. But that world wasn't Earth. Not by a long long shot! There weren't any men typing the answers onto the other end of that little trick: they were aliens, humanoids. Probably Cetians, for the machine was Cetian-made, and they were a smart bunch of devils. They were the kind that might make a real bid for interstellar supremacy. The Hainish would be in the conspiracy with them, of course; all that bleeding-heart stuff in the so-called directives had a Hainish sound to it. What the long-term objective of the aliens was, was hard to guess from here; it probably involved weakening the Terran Government by tying it up in this "league of worlds" business, until the aliens were strong enough to make an armed takeover. But their plan for New Tahiti was easy to see. They'd let the creechies wipe out the humans for them. Just tie the humans' hands with a lot of fake "ansible" directives and let the slaughter begin. Humanoids help humanoids: rats help rats.

And Colonel Dongh had swallowed it. He intended to obey orders. He had actually said that to Davidson. "I intend to obey my orders from Terra-HQ, and by God, Don, you'll obey my orders the same way, and in New Java you'll obey Major Muhamed's orders there." He was stupid, old Ding Dong, but he liked Davidson, and Davidson liked him. If it meant betraying the human race to an alien conspiracy then he couldn't obey his orders, but he still felt sorry for the old soldier. A fool, but a loyal and brave one. Not a born traitor like that whining, tattling prig Lyubov. If there was one man he hoped the creechies did get, it was bigdome Raj Lyubov, the alien-lover.

Some men, especially the asiatiforms and hindi types, are actually born traitors. Not all, but some. Certain other men are born saviors. It just happened to be the way they were made, like being of euraf descent, or like having a good physique; it wasn't anything he claimed credit for. If he could save the men and women of New Tahiti, he would; if he couldn't, he'd make a damn good try; and that was all there was to it, actually.

The women, now, that rankled. They'd pulled out the 10 Collies who'd been in New Java and none of the new ones were being sent out from Centralville. "Not safe yet," HQ bleated. Pretty rough on the three outpost camps. What did they expect the outposters to do when it was hands off the she-creechies, and all the she-humans were for the lucky bastards at Central? It was going to cause terrific resentment. But it couldn't last long, the whole situation was too crazy to be stable. If they didn't start easing back to normal now the *Shackleton* was gone, then Captain D. Davidson would just have to do a little extra work to get things headed back towards normalcy.

The morning of the day he left Central, they had let loose the whole creechie work-force. Made a big noble speech in pidgin, opened the compound gates, and let out every single tame creechie, carriers, diggers, cooks, dustmen, houseboys, maids, the lot. Not one had stayed. Some of them had been with their masters ever since the start of the colony, four E-years ago. But they had no loyalty. A dog, a chimp would have hung around. These things weren't even that highly developed, they were just about like snakes or rats, just smart enough to turn around and bite you as soon as you let 'em out of the cage. Ding Dong was spla, letting all those creechies loose right in the vicinity. Dumping them on Dump Island and letting them starve would have been actually the best final solution. But Dongh was still panicked by that pair of humanoids and their talky-box. So if the wild creechies on Central were planning to imitate the Smith Camp atrocity, they now had lots of real handy new recruits, who knew the layout of the whole town, the routines, where the arsenal was, where guards were posted, and the rest. If Centralville got burned down, HQ could thank themselves. It would be what they deserved, actually. For letting traitors dupe them, for listening to humanoids and ignoring the advice of men who really knew what the creechies were like.

None of those guys at HQ had come back to camp and found ashes and wreckage and burned bodies, like he had. And Ok's body, out where they'd slaughtered the logging crew, it had had an arrow sticking out of each eye like some sort of weird insect with antennae sticking out feeling the air, Christ, he kept seeing that.

One thing anyhow, whatever the phoney "directives" said, the boys at Central wouldn't be stuck with trying to use "small side-arms" for self-defense. They had fire throwers and machine guns; the 16 little hoppers had machine guns and were useful for dropping firejelly cans from; the five big hoppers had full armament. But they wouldn't need the big stuff. Just take up a hopper over one of the deforested areas and catch a mess of creechies there, with their damned bows and arrows, and start dropping firejelly cans and watch them run around and burn. It would be all right. It made his belly churn a little to imagine it, just like when he thought about making a woman, or whenever he remembered about when that Sam creechie had attacked him and he had smashed in his whole face with four blows one right after the other. It was eidetic memory plus a more vivid imagination than most men had, no credit due, just happened to be the way he was made.

The fact is, the only time a man is really and entirely a man is when he's just had a woman or just killed another man. That wasn't original, he'd read it in some old books; but it was true. That was why he liked to imagine scenes like that. Even if the creechies weren't actually men.

New Java was the southernmost of the five big lands, just north of the equator, and so was hotter than Central or Smith which were just about perfect climate-wise. Hotter and a lot wetter. It rained all the time in the wet seasons anywhere on New Tahiti, but in the northern lands it was a kind of quiet fine rain that went on and on and never really got you wet or cold. Down here it came in buckets, and there was a monsoon-type storm that you couldn't even walk in, let alone work in. Only a solid roof kept that rain off you, or else the forest. The damn forest was so thick it kept out the storms. You'd get wet from all the dripping off the leaves, of course, but if you were really inside the forest during one of those monsoons you'd hardly notice the wind was blowing; then you came out in the open and wham! got knocked off your feet by the wind and slobbered all over with the red liquid mud that the rain turned the cleared ground into, and you couldn't duck back into the forest quick enough; and inside the forest it was dark, and hot, and easy to get lost.

Then the C.O., Major Muhamed, was a sticky bastard. Everything at N. J. was done by the book: the logging all in kilo-strips, the fibreweed crap planted in the logged strips, leave to Central granted in strict non-preferential rotation, hallucinogens rationed and their use on duty punished, and so on and so on. However, one good thing about Muhamed was he wasn't always radioing Central. New Java was his camp, and he ran it his way. He didn't like orders from HQ. He obeyed them all right, he'd let the creechies go, and locked up all the guns except little popgun pistols, as soon as the orders came. But he didn't go looking for orders, or for advice. Not from Central or anybody else. He was a self-righteous type: knew he was right. That was his big fault.

When he was on Dongh's staff at HQ Davidson had had occasion sometimes to see the officers' records. His unusual memory held on to such things, and he could recall for instance that Muhamed's IQ was 107. Whereas his own happened to be 118. There was a difference of 11 points; but of course he couldn't say that to old Moo, and Moo couldn't see it, and so there was no way to get him to listen. He thought he knew better than Davidson, and that was that.

They were all a bit sticky at first, actually. None of these men at N. J. knew anything about the Smith Camp atrocity, except that the camp C.O. had left for Central an hour before it happened, and so was the only human that escaped alive. Put like that, it did sound bad. You could see why at first they looked at him like a kind of Jonah, or worse, a kind of Judas even. But when they got to know him they'd know better. They'd begin to see that, far from being a deserter or traitor, he was dedicated to preventing the colony of New Tahiti from betrayal. And they'd realise that getting rid of the creechies was going to be the only way to make this world safe for the Terran way of life.

It wasn't too hard to start getting that message across to the loggers. They'd never liked the little green rats, having to drive them to work all day and guard them all night; but now they began to understand that the creechies were not only repulsive but dangerous. When Davidson told them what he'd found at Smith; when he explained how the two humanoids on the Fleet ship had brainwashed HQ; when he showed them that wiping out the Terrans on New Tahiti was just a small part of the whole alien conspiracy against Earth; when he reminded them of the cold hard figures, twenty-five *hundred* humans to three *million* creechies—then they began to really get behind him.

Even the Ecological Control Officer here was with him. Not like poor old Kees, mad because men shot red deer and then getting shot in the guts himself by the sneaking creechies. This fellow, Atranda, was a creechie-hater. Actually he was kind of spla about them, he had geoshock or something; he was so afraid the creechies were going to attack the camp that he acted like some woman afraid of getting raped. But it was useful to have the local spesh on his side anyhow.

No use trying to line up the C.O.; a good judge of men, Davidson had seen it was no use almost at once. Muhamed was rigid-minded. Also he had a prejudice against Davidson which he wouldn't drop; it had something to do with the Smith Camp affair. He as much as told Davidson he didn't consider him a trustworthy officer.

He was a self-righteous bastard, but his running N. J. camp on such rigid lines was an advantage. A tight organization, used to obeying orders, was easier to take over than a loose one full of independent characters, and easier to keep together as a unit for defensive and offensive military operations, once he was in command. He would have to take command. Moo was a good logging-camp boss, but no soldier.

Davidson kept busy getting some of the best loggers and junior officers really firmly with him. He didn't hurry. When he had enough of them he could really trust, a squad of ten lifted a few items from old Moo's locked-up room in the Rec House basement full of war toys, and then went off one Sunday into the woods to play.

Davidson had located the creechie town some weeks ago, and had saved up the treat for his men. He could have done it singlehanded, but it was better this way. You got the sense of comradeship, of a real bond among men. They just walked into the place in broad open daylight, and coated all the creechies caught above-ground with firejelly and burned them, then poured kerosene over the warren-roofs and roasted the rest. Those that tried to get out got jellied; that was the artistic part, waiting at the rat-holes for the little rats to come out, letting them think they'd made it, and then just frying them from the feet up so they made torches. That green fur sizzled like crazy.

It actually wasn't much more exciting than hunting real rats, which were about the only wild animals left on Mother Earth, but there was more thrill to it; the creechies were a lot bigger than rats, and you knew they could fight back, though this time they didn't. In fact some of them even lay down instead of running away, just lay there on their backs with their eyes shut. It was sickening. The other fellows thought so too, and one of them actually got sick and vomited after he'd burned up one of the lying-down ones.

Hard up as the men were, they didn't leave even one of the females alive to rape. They had all agreed with Davidson beforehand that it was too damn near perversity. Homosexuality was with other humans, it was normal. These things might be built like human women but they weren't human, and it was better to get your kicks from killing them, and stay *clean*. That had made good sense to all of them, and they stuck to it.

Every one of them kept his trap shut back at camp, no boasting even to their buddies. They were sound men. Not a word of the expedition got to Muhamed's ears. So far as old Moo knew, all his men were good little boys just sawing up logs and keeping away from creechies, yes sir; and he could go on believing that until D-Day came.

For the creechies would attack. Somewhere. Here, or one of the camps on King Island, or Central. Davidson knew that. He was the only officer in the entire colony that did know it. No credit due, he just happened to know he was right. Nobody else had believed him, except these men here whom he'd had time to convince. But the others would all see, sooner or later, that he was right.

And he was right.

5

It had been a shock, meeting Selver face to face. As he flew back to Central from the foothill village, Lyubov tried to decide why it had been a shock, to analyse out the nerve that had jumped. For after all one isn't usually terrified by a chance meeting with a good friend.

It hadn't been easy to get the headwoman to invite him. Tuntar had been his main locus of study all summer; he had several excellent informants there and was on good terms with the Lodge and with the headwoman, who had let him observe and participate in the community freely. Wangling an actual invitation out of her, via some of the ex-serfs still in the area, had taken a long time, but at last she had complied, giving him, according to the new directives, a genuine "occasion arranged by the Athsheans." His own conscience, rather than the Colonel, had insisted on this. Dongh wanted him to go. He was worried about the Creechie Threat. He told Lyubov to size them up, to "see how they're reacting now that we're leaving them strictly alone." He hoped for reassurance. Lyubov couldn't decide whether the report he'd be turning in would reassure Colonel Dongh, or not.

For ten miles out of Central, the plain had been logged and the stumps had all rotted away; it was now a great dull flat of fibreweed, hairy grey in the rain. Under those hirsute leaves the seedling shrubs got their first growth, the sumacs, dwarf aspens, and salviforms which, grown, would in turn protect the seedling trees. Left alone, in this even, rainy climate, this area might reforest itself within thirty years and reattain the full climax forest within a hundred. Left alone.

Suddenly the forest began again, in space not time: under the helicopter the infinitely various green of leaves covered the slow swells and foldings of the hills of North Sornol.

Like most Terrans on Terra, Lyubov had never walked among wild trees at all, never seen a wood larger than a city block. At first on Athshe he had felt oppressed and uneasy in the forest, stifled by its endless crowd and incoherence of trunks, branches, leaves in the perpetual greenish or brownish twilight. The mass and jumble of various competitive lives all pushing and swelling outwards and upwards towards light, the silence made up of many little meaningless noises, the total vegetable indifference to the presence of mind, all this had troubled him, and like the others he had kept to clearings and to the beach. But little by little he had begun to like it. Gosse teased him, calling him Mr Gibbon; in fact Lyubov looked rather like a gibbon, with a round, dark face, long arms, and hair greying early; but gibbons were extinct. Like it or not, as a hilfer he had to go into the forests to find the hilfs; and now after four years of it he was completely at home under the trees, more so perhaps than anywhere else.

He had also come to like the Athsheans' names for their own lands and places, sonorous two-syllabled words: Sornol, Tuntar, Eshreth, Eshsen—that was now Centralville—Endtor, Abtan, and above all Athshe, which meant the Forest, and the World. So earth, terra, tellus mean both the soil and the planet, two meanings and one. But to the Athsheans soil, ground, earth was not that to which the dead return and by which the living live: the substance of their world was not earth, but forest. Terran man was clay, red dust. Athshean man was branch and root. They did not carve figures of themselves in stone, only in wood.

He brought the hopper down in a small glade north of the town, and walked in past the Women's Lodge. The smell of an Athshean settlement hung pungent in the air, woodsmoke, dead fish, aromatic herbs, alien sweat. The atmosphere of an underground house, if a Terran could fit himself in at all, was a rare compound of CO_2 and stinks. Lyubov had spent many intellectually stimulating hours doubled up and suffocating in the reeking gloom of the Men's Lodge in Tuntar. But it didn't look as if he would be invited in this time.

Of course the townsfolk knew of the Smith Camp massacre, now six weeks ago. They would have known of it soon, for word got around fast among the islands, though not so fast as to constitute a "mysterious power of telepathy" as the loggers liked to believe. The townsfolk also knew that the 1200 slaves at Centralville had been freed soon after the Smith Camp massacre, and Lyubov agreed with the Colonel that the natives might take the second event to be a result of the first. That gave what Colonel Dongh would call "an erroneous impression," but it probably wasn't important. What was important was that the slaves had been freed. Wrongs done could not be righted, but at least they were not still being done. They could start over: the natives without that painful, unanswerable wonder as to why the "yumens" treated men like animals; and he without the burden of explanation and the gnawing of irremediable guilt.

Knowing how they valued candor and direct speech concerning frightening or troublous matters, he expected that people in Tuntar would talk about these things with him, in triumph, or apology, or rejoicing, or puzzlement. No one did. No one said much of anything to him.

He had come in late afternoon, which was like arriving in a Terran city just after dawn. Athsheans did sleep—the colonists' opinion, as often, ignored observable fact—but their physiological low was between noon and four P.M., whereas with Terrans it is usually between two and five A.M.; and they had a double-peak cycle of high temperature and high activity, coming in the two twilights, dawn and evening. Most adults slept five or six hours in 24, in several catnaps; and adept men slept as little as two hours in 24; so, if one discounted both their naps and their dreaming-states as "laziness," one might say they never slept. It was much easier to say that than to understand what they actually did do. —At this point, in Tuntar, things were just beginning to stir again after the late-day slump.

Lyubov noticed a good many strangers. They looked at him, but none approached; they were mere presences passing on other paths in the dusk of the great oaks. At last someone he knew came along his path, the headwoman's cousin Sherrar, an old woman of small importance and small understanding. She greeted him civilly, but did not or would not respond to his inquiries about the headwoman and his two best informants, Egath the orchard-keeper and Tubab the Dreamer. Oh, the headwoman was very busy, and who was Egath, did he mean Geban, and Tubab might be here or perhaps he was there, or not. She stuck to Lyubov, and nobody else spoke to him. He worked his way, accompanied by the hobbling, complaining, tiny, green crone, across the groves and glades of Tuntar to the Men's Lodge. "They're busy in there," said Sherrar.

"Dreaming?"

"However should I know? Come along now, Lyubov, come see . . ." She knew he always wanted to see things, but she couldn't think what to show him to draw him away. "Come see the fishing-nets," she said feebly.

A girl passing by, one of the Young Hunters, looked up at

him: a black look, a stare of animosity such as he had never received from any Athshean, unless perhaps from a little child frightened into scowling by his height and his hairless face. But this girl was not frightened.

"All right," he said to Sherrar, feeling that his only course was docility. If the Athsheans had indeed developed—at last, and abruptly—the sense of group enmity, then he must accept this, and simply try to show them that he remained a reliable, unchanging friend.

But how could their way of feeling and thinking have changed so fast, after so long? And why? At Smith Camp, provocation had been immediate and intolerable: Davidson's cruelty would drive even Athsheans to violence. But this town, Tuntar, had never been attacked by the Terrans, had suffered no slave-raids, had not seen the local forest logged or burned. He, Lyubov himself, had been there—the anthropologist cannot always leave his own shadow out of the picture he draws—but not for over two months now. They had got the news from Smith, and there were among them now refugees, ex-slaves, who had suffered at the Terrans' hands and would talk about it. But would news and hearsay change the hearers, change them radically?—when their unaggressiveness ran so deep in them, right through their culture and society and on down into their subconscious, their "dream time," and perhaps into their very physiology? That an Athshean could be provoked, by atrocious cruelty, to attempt murder, he knew: he had seen it happen—once. That a disrupted community might be similarly provoked by similarly intolerable injuries, he had to believe: it had happened at Smith Camp. But that talk and hearsay, no matter how frightening and outrageous, could enrage a settled community of these people to the point where they acted against their customs and reason, broke entirely out of their whole style of living, this he couldn't believe. It was psychologically improbable. Some element was missing.

Old Tubab came out of the Lodge, just as Lyubov passed in front of it. Behind the old man came Selver.

Selver crawled out of the tunnel-door, stood upright, blinked at the rain-greyed, foliage-dimmed brightness of daylight. His dark eyes met Lyubov's, looking up. Neither spoke. Lyubov was badly frightened.

Flying home in the hopper, analysing out the shocked nerve, he thought, why fear? Why was I afraid of Selver? Unprovable intuition or mere false analogy? Irrational in any case.

Nothing between Selver and Lyubov had changed. What Selver had done at Smith Camp could be justified; even if it couldn't be justified, it made no difference. The friendship between them was too deep to be touched by moral doubt. They had worked very hard together; they had taught each other, in rather more than the literal sense, their languages. They had spoken without reserve. And Lyubov's love for his friend was deepened by that gratitude the savior feels toward the one whose life he has been privileged to save.

Indeed he had scarcely realised until that moment how deep his liking and loyalty to Selver were. Had his fear in fact been the personal fear that Selver might, having learned racial hatred, reject him, despise his loyalty, and treat him not as "you," but as "one of them"?

After that long first gaze Selver came forward slowly and greeted Lyubov, holding out his hands.

Touch was a main channel of communication among the forest people. Among Terrans touch is always likely to imply threat, aggression, and so for them there is often nothing between the formal handshake and the sexual caress. All that blank was filled by the Athsheans with varied customs of touch. Caress as signal and reassurance was as essential to them as it is to mother and child or to lover and lover; but its significance was social, not only maternal and sexual. It was part of their language. It was therefore patterned, codified, yet infinitely modifiable. "They're always pawing each other," some of the colonists sneered, unable to see in these touch-exchanges anything but their own eroticism which, forced to concentrate itself exclusively on sex and then repressed and frustrated, invades and poisons every sensual pleasure, every humane response: the victory of a blinded, furtive Cupid over the great brooding mother of all the seas and stars, all the leaves of trees, all the gestures of men, Venus Genetrix. . . .

So Selver came forward with his hands held out, shook Lyubov's hand Terran fashion, and then took both his arms with a stroking motion just above the elbow. He was not much more than half Lyubov's height, which made all gestures difficult and ungainly for both of them, but there was nothing uncertain or childlike in the touch of his small, thin-boned, green-furred hand on Lyubov's arms. It was a reassurance. Lyubov was very glad to get it.

"Selver, what luck to meet you here. I want very much to talk with you—"

"I can't, now, Lyubov."

He spoke gently, but when he spoke Lyubov's hope of an unaltered friendship vanished. Selver had changed. He was changed, radically: from the root.

"Can I come back," Lyubov said urgently, "another day, and talk with you, Selver? It is important to me—"

"I leave here today," Selver said even more gently, but letting go Lyubov's arms, and also looking away. He thus put himself literally out of touch. Civility required that Lyubov do the same, and let the conversation end. But then there would be no one to talk to. Old Tubab had not even looked at him; the town had turned its back on him. And this was Selver, who had been his friend.

"Selver, this killing at Kelme Deva, maybe you think that lies between us. But it does not. Maybe it brings us closer together. And your people in the slave-pens, they've all been set free, so that wrong no longer lies between us. And even if it does—it always did—all the same I . . . I am the same man I was, Selver."

At first the Athshean made no response. His strange face, the large deep-set eyes, the strong features misshapen by scars and blurred by the short silken fur that followed and yet obscured all contours, this face turned from Lyubov, shut, obstinate. Then suddenly he looked round as if against his own intent. "Lyubov, you shouldn't have come here. You should leave Central two nights from now. I don't know what you are. It would be better if I had never known you."

And with that he was off, a light walk like a long-legged cat, a green flicker among the dark oaks of Tuntar, gone. Tubab followed slowly after him, still without a glance at Lyubov. A fine rain fell without sound on the oak-leaves and on the narrow pathways to the Lodge and the river. Only if you listened intently could you hear the rain, too multitudinous a music for one mind to grasp, a single endless chord played on the entire forest.

"Selver is a god," said old Sherrar. "Come and see the fishing-nets now."

Lyubov declined. It would be impolite and impolitic to stay; anyway he had no heart to.

He tried to tell himself that Selver had not been rejecting him, Lyubov, but him as a Terran. It made no difference. It never does.

He was always disagreeably surprised to find how vulnerable his feelings were, how much it hurt him to be hurt. This sort of adolescent sensitivity was shameful, he should have a tougher hide by now.

The little crone, her green fur all dusted and besilvered with raindrops, sighed with relief when he said goodbye. As he started the hopper he had to grin at the sight of her, hop-hobbling off into the trees as fast as she could go, like a little toad that has escaped a snake.

Quality is an important matter, but so is quantity: relative size. The normal adult reaction to a very much smaller person may be arrogant, or protective, or patronising, or affectionate, or bullying, but whatever it is it's liable to be better fitted to a child than to an adult. Then, when the child-sized person was furry, a further response got called upon, which Lyubov had labelled the Teddybear Reaction. Since the Athsheans used caress so much, its manifestation was not inappropriate, but its motivation remained suspect. And finally there was the inevitable Freak Reaction, the flinching away from what is human but does not quite look so.

But quite outside of all that was the fact that the Athsheans, like Terrans, were simply funny-looking at times. Some of them did look like little toads, owls, caterpillars. Sherrar was not the first little old lady who had struck Lyubov as looking funny from behind. . . .

And that's one trouble with the colony, he thought as he lifted the hopper and Tuntar vanished beneath the oaks and the leafless orchards. We haven't got any old women. No old men either, except Dongh and he's only about sixty. But old women are different from everybody else, they say what they think. The Athsheans are governed, in so far as they have government, by old women. Intellect to the men, politics to the women, and ethics to the interaction of both: that's their arrangement. It has charm, and it works—for them. I wish the Administration had sent out a couple of grannies along with all those nubile fertile high-breasted young women. Now that girl I had over the other night, she's really very nice, and nice in bed, she has a kind heart, but my God it'll be forty years before she'll say anything to a man. . . .

But all the time, beneath his thoughts concerning old women and young ones, the shock persisted, the intuition or recognition that would not let itself be recognised.

He must think this out before he reported to HQ.

Selver: what about Selver, then?

Selver was certainly a key figure to Lyubov. Why? Because he knew him well, or because of some actual power in his personality, which Lyubov had never consciously appreciated?

But he had appreciated it; he had picked Selver out very soon as an extraordinary person. "Sam," he had been then, bodyservant for three officers sharing a prefab. Lyubov remembered Benson boasting what a good creechie they'd got, they'd broke him in right.

Many Athsheans, especially Dreamers from the Lodges, could not change their polycyclic sleep-pattern to fit the Terran one. If they caught up with their normal sleep at night, that prevented them from catching up with the REM or paradoxical sleep, whose 120-minute cycle ruled their life both day and night, and could not be fitted in to the Terran workday. Once you have learned to do your dreaming wide awake, to balance your sanity not on the razor's edge of reason but on the double support, the fine balance, of reason and dream, once you have learned that, you cannot unlearn it any more than you can unlearn to think. So many of the men became groggy, confused, withdrawn, even catatonic. Women, bewildered and abased, behaved with the sullen listlessness of the newly enslaved. Male non-adepts and some of the younger Dreamers did best; they adapted, working hard in the logging camps or becoming clever servants. Sam had been one of these, an efficient, characterless bodyservant, cook, laundry-boy, butler, backsoaper and scapegoat for his three masters. He had learned how to be invisible. Lyubov borrowed him as an ethnological informant, and had, by some affinity of mind and nature, won Sam's trust at once. He found Sam the ideal informant, trained in his people's customs, perceptive of their significances, and quick to translate them, to make them intelligible to Lyubov, bridging the gap between two languages, two cultures, two species of the genus Man.

For two years Lyubov had been travelling, studying, interviewing, observing, and had failed to get at the key that would let him into the Athshean mind. He didn't even know where the lock was. He had studied the Athsheans' sleeping-habits and found that they apparently had no sleeping-habits. He had wired countless electrodes onto countless furry green skulls, and failed to make any sense at all out of the familiar patterns, the spindles and jags, the alphas and deltas and thetas, that appeared on the graph. It was Selver who had made him understand, at last, the Athshean significance of the word "dream," which was also the word for "root," and so hand him the key of the kingdom of the forest people. It was with Selver as EEG subject that he had first seen with comprehension the extraordinary impulse-patterns of a brain entering a dreamstate neither sleeping nor awake: a condition which related to Terran dreaming-sleep as the Parthenon to a mud hut: the same thing basically, but with the addition of complexity, quality, and control.

What then, what more?

Selver might have escaped. He stayed, first as a valet, then (through one of Lyubov's few useful perquisites as a Spesh) as Scientific Aide, still locked up nightly with all other creechies in the pen (the Voluntary Autochthonous Labor Personnel Quarters). "I'll fly you up to Tuntar and work with you there," Lyubov had said, about the third time he talked with Selver, "for God's sake why stay here?"—"My wife Thele is in the pen," Selver had said. Lyubov had tried to get her released, but she was in the HQ kitchen, and the sergeants who managed the kitchen-gang resented any interference from "brass" and "speshes." Lyubov had to be very careful, lest they take out their resentment on the woman. She and Selver had both seemed willing to wait patiently until both could escape or be freed. Male and female creechies were strictly segregated in the pens—why, no one seemed to know—and husband and wife rarely saw each other. Lyubov managed to arrange meetings for them in his hut, which he had to himself at the north end of town. It was when Thele was returning to HQ from one such meeting that Davidson had seen her and apparently been struck by her frail, frightened grace. He had had her brought to his quarters that night, and had raped her.

He had killed her in the act, perhaps; this had happened before, a result of the physical disparity; or else she had stopped living. Like some Terrans the Athsheans had the knack of the authentic death-wish, and could cease to live. In either case it was Davidson who had killed her. Such murders had occurred before. What had not occurred before was what Selver did, the second day after her death.

Lyubov had got there only at the end. He could recall the sounds; himself running down Main Street in hot sunlight; the dust, the knot of men. The whole thing could have lasted only five minutes, a long time for a homicidal fight. When Lyubov got there Selver was blinded with blood, a sort of toy for Davidson to play with, and yet he had picked himself up and was coming back, not with berserk rage but with intelligent despair. He kept coming back. It was Davidson who was scared into rage at last by that terrible persistence; knocking Selver down with a side-blow he had moved forward lifting his booted foot to stamp on the skull. Even as he moved, Lyubov had broken into the circle. He stopped the fight (for whatever blood-thirst the ten or twelve men watching had had, was more than appeased, and they backed Lyubov when he told Davidson hands off); and thenceforth he hated Davidson, and was hated by him, having come between the killer and his death.

For if it's all the rest of us who are killed by the suicide, it's himself whom the murderer kills; only he has to do it over, and over, and over.

Lyubov had picked up Selver, a light weight in his arms. The mutilated face had pressed against his shirt so that the blood soaked through against his own skin. He had taken Selver to his own bungalow, splinted his broken wrist, done what he could for his face, kept him in his own bed, night after night tried to talk to him, to reach him in the desolation of his grief and shame. It was, of course, against regulations.

Nobody mentioned the regulations to him. They did not have to. He knew he was forfeiting most of what favor he had ever had with the officers of the colony.

He had been careful to keep on the right side of HQ, objecting only to extreme cases of brutality against the natives, using persuasion not defiance, and conserving what shred of power and influence he had. He could not prevent the exploitation of the Athsheans. It was much worse than his training had led him to expect, but he could do little about it here and now. His reports to the Administration and to the Committee on Rights might—after the roundtrip of 54 years—have some effect; Terra might even decide that the Open Colony policy for Athshe was a bad mistake. Better 54 years late than never. If he lost the tolerance of his superiors here they would censor or invalidate his reports, and there would be no hope at all.

But he was too angry now to keep up his strategy. To hell with the others, if they insisted on seeing his care of a friend as an insult to Mother Earth and a betrayal of the colony. If they labelled him "creechie-lover" his usefulness to the Athsheans would be impaired; but he could not set a possible, general good above Selver's imperative need. You can't save a people by selling your friend. Davidson, curiously infuriated by the minor injuries Selver had done him and by Lyubov's interference, had gone around saying he intended to finish off that rebel creechie; he certainly would do so if he got the chance. Lyubov stayed with Selver night and day for two weeks, and then flew him out of Central and put him down in a west coast town, Broter, where he had relatives.

There was no penalty for aiding slaves to escape, since the Athsheans were not slaves at all except in fact: they were Voluntary Autochthonous Labor Personnel. Lyubov was not even reprimanded. But the regular officers distrusted him totally, instead of partially, from then on; and even his colleagues in the Special Services, the exobiologist, the ag and forestry coordinators, the ecologists, variously let him know that he had been irrational, quixotic, or stupid. "Did you think you were coming on a picnic?" Gosse had demanded.

"No. I didn't think it would be any bloody picnic," Lyubov answered, morose.

"I can't see why any hilfer voluntarily ties himself up to an Open Colony. You know the people you're studying are going to get plowed under, and probably wiped out. It's the way things are. It's human nature, and you must know you can't change that. Then why come and watch the process? Masochism?"

"I don't know what 'human nature' is. Maybe leaving descriptions of what we wipe out is part of human nature. —Is it much pleasanter for an ecologist, really?"

Gosse ignored this. "All right then, write up your descriptions. But keep out of the carnage. A biologist studying a rat colony doesn't start reaching in and rescuing pet rats of his that get attacked, you know."

At this Lyubov had blown loose. He had taken too much. "No, of course not," he said. "A rat can be a pet, but not a friend. Selver is my friend. In fact he's the only man on this world whom I consider to be a friend." That had hurt poor old Gosse, who wanted to be a father-figure to Lyubov, and it had done nobody any good. Yet it had been true. And the truth shall make you free. . . . I like Selver, respect him; saved him; suffered with him; fear him. Selver is my friend.

Selver is a god.

So the little green crone had said as if everybody knew it, as flatly as she might have said So-and-so is a hunter. "Selver sha'ab." What did *sha'ab* mean, though? Many words of the Women's Tongue, the everyday speech of the Athsheans, came from the Men's Tongue that was the same in all communities, and these words often were not only two-syllabled but two-sided. They were coins, obverse and reverse. *Sha'ab* meant god, or numinous entity, or powerful being; it also meant something quite different, but Lyubov could not remember what. By this stage in his thinking, he was home in his bungalow, and had only to look it up in the dictionary which he and Selver had compiled in four months of exhausting but harmonious work. Of course: *sha'ab*, translator.

It was almost too pat, too apposite.

Were the two meanings connected? Often they were, yet not so often as to constitute a rule. If a god was a translator, what did he translate? Selver was indeed a gifted interpreter, but that gift had found expression only through the fortuity of a truly foreign language having been brought into his world. Was a *sha'ab* one who translated the language of dream and philosophy, the Men's Tongue, into the everyday speech? But all

Dreamers could do that. Might he then be one who could translate into waking life the central experience of vision: one serving as a link between the two realities, considered by the Athsheans as equal, the dream-time and the world-time, whose connections, though vital, are obscure. A link: one who could speak aloud the perceptions of the subconscious. To "speak" that tongue is to act. To do a new thing. To change or to be changed, radically, from the root. For the root is the dream.

And the translator is the god. Selver had brought a new word into the language of his people. He had done a new deed. The word, the deed, murder. Only a god could lead so great a newcomer as Death across the bridge between the worlds.

But had he learned to kill his fellowmen among his own dreams of outrage and bereavement, or from the undreamed-of actions of the strangers? Was he speaking his own language, or was he speaking Captain Davidson's? That which seemed to rise from the root of his own suffering and express his own changed being, might in fact be an infection, a foreign plague, which would not make a new people of his race, but would destroy them.

It was not in Raj Lyubov's nature to think, "What can I do?" Character and training disposed him not to interfere in other men's business. His job was to find out what they did, and his inclination was to let them go on doing it. He preferred to be enlightened, rather than to enlighten; to seek facts rather than the Truth. But even the most unmissionary soul, unless he pretend he has no emotions, is sometimes faced with a choice between commission and omission. "What are they doing?" abruptly becomes, "What are we doing?" and then, "What must I do?"

That he had reached such a point of choice now, he knew, and yet did not know clearly why, nor what alternatives were offered him.

He could do no more to improve the Athsheans' chance of survival at the moment; Lepennon, Or, and the ansible had done more than he had hoped to see done in his lifetime. The Administration on Terra was explicit in every ansible communication, and Colonel Dongh, though under pressure from some of his staff and the logging bosses to ignore the directives, was carrying out orders. He was a loyal officer; and besides, the *Shackleton* would be coming back to observe and report on how orders were being carried out. Reports home meant something, now that this ansible, this *machina ex machina*, functioned to prevent all the comfortable old colonial autonomy, and make you answerable within your own lifetime for what you did. There was no more 54-year margin for error. Policy was no longer static. A decision by the League of Worlds might now lead overnight to the colony's being limited to one Land, or forbidden to cut trees, or encouraged to kill natives—no telling. How the League worked and what sort of policies it was developing could not yet be guessed from the flat directives of the Administration. Dongh was worried by these multiple-choice futures, but Lyubov enjoyed them. In diversity is life and where there's life there's hope, was the general sum of his creed, a modest one to be sure.

The colonists were letting the Athsheans alone and they were letting the colonists alone. A healthy situation, and one not to be disturbed unnecessarily. The only thing likely to disturb it was fear.

At the moment the Athsheans might be expected to be suspicious and still resentful, but not particularly afraid. As for the panic felt in Centralville at news of the Smith Camp massacre, nothing had happened to revive it. No Athshean anywhere had shown any violence since; and with the slaves gone, the creechies all vanished back into their forests, there was no more constant irritation of xenophobia. The colonists were at last beginning to relax.

If Lyubov reported that he had seen Selver at Tuntar, Dongh and the others would be alarmed. They might insist on trying to capture Selver and bring him in for trial. The Colonial Code forbade prosecution of a member of one planetary society under the laws of another, but the Court Martial over-rode such distinctions. They could try, convict, and shoot Selver. With Davidson brought back from New Java to give evidence. Oh no, Lyubov thought, shoving the dictionary onto an overcrowded shelf. Oh no, he thought, and thought no more about it. So he made his choice without even knowing he had made one.

He turned in a brief report next day. It said that Tuntar was going about its business as usual, and that he had not been turned away or threatened. It was a soothing report, and the most inaccurate one Lyubov ever wrote. It omitted everything of significance: the headwoman's non-appearance, Tubab's refusal to greet Lyubov, the large number of strangers in town, the young huntress' expression, Selver's presence. . . . Of course that last was an intentional omission, but otherwise the report was quite factual, he thought; he had merely omitted subjective impressions, as a scientist should. He had a severe migraine whilst writing the report, and a worse one after submitting it.

He dreamed a lot that night, but could not remember his dreams in the morning. Late in the second night after his visit to Tuntar he woke, and in the hysterical whooping of the alarm-siren and the thudding of explosions he faced, at last, what he had refused. He was the only man in Centralville not taken by surprise. In that moment he knew what he was: a traitor.

And yet even now it was not clear in his mind that this was an Athshean raid. It was the terror in the night.

His own hut had been ignored, standing in its yard away from other houses; perhaps the trees around it protected it, he thought as he hurried out. The center of town was all on fire. Even the stone cube of HQ burned from within like a broken kiln. The ansible was in there: the precious link. There were fires also in the direction of the helicopter port and the Field. Where had they got explosives? How had the fires got going all at once? All the buildings along both sides of Main Street, built of wood, were burning; the sound of the burning was terrible. Lyubov ran towards the fires. Water flooded the way; he thought at first it was from a fire-hose, then realised the main from the river Menend was flooding uselessly over the ground while the houses burned with that hideous sucking roar. How had they done this? There were guards, there were always guards in jeeps at the Field. . . . Shots: volleys, the yatter of a machine gun. All around Lyubov were small running figures, but he ran among them without giving them much thought. He was abreast of the Hostel now, and saw a girl standing in the doorway, fire flickering at her back and a clear escape before her. She did not move. He shouted at her, then ran across the yard to her and wrested her hands free of the doorjambs which she clung to in panic, pulling her away by force, saying gently, "Come on, honey, come on." She came then, but not quite soon enough. As they crossed the yard the front of the upper storey, blazing from within, fell slowly forward, pushed by the timbers of the collapsing roof. Shingles and beams shot out like shell-fragments; a blazing beam-end struck Lyubov and knocked him sprawling. He lay face down in the firelit lake of mud. He did not see a little green-furred huntress leap at the girl, drag her down backwards, and cut her throat. He did not see anything.

6

No songs were sung that night. There was only shouting and silence. When the flying ships burned Selver exulted, and tears came into his eyes, but no words into his mouth. He turned away in silence, the fire thrower heavy in his arms, to lead his group back into the city.

Each group of people from the West and North was led by an ex-slave like himself, one who had served the yumens in Central and knew the buildings and ways of the city.

Most of the people who came to the attack that night had never seen the yumen city; many of them had never seen a yumen. They had come because they followed Selver, because they were driven by the evil dream and only Selver could teach them how to master it. There were hundreds and hundreds of them, men and women; they had waited in utter silence in the rainy darkness all around the edges of the city, while the ex-slaves, two or three at a time, did those things which they judged must be done first: break the water-pipe, cut the wires that carried light from Generator House, break into and rob the Arsenal. The first deaths, those of guards, had been silent, accomplished with hunting weapons, noose, knife, arrow, very quickly, in the dark. The dynamite, stolen earlier in the night from the logging camp ten miles south, was prepared in the Arsenal, the basement of HQ Building, while fires were set in other places; and then the alarm went off and the fires blazed and both night and silence fled. Most of the thunderclap and tree-fall crashing of gunfire came from the yumens defending themselves, for only ex-slaves had taken weapons from the Arsenal and used them; all the rest kept to their own lances, knives, and bows. But it was the dynamite, placed and ignited by Reswan and others who had worked in the loggers' slave-pen, that made the noise that conquered all other noises, and blew out the walls of the HQ Building and destroyed the hangars and the ships.

There were about seventeen hundred yumens in the city that night, about five hundred of them female; all the yumen females were said to be there now, that was why Selver and the others had decided to act, though not all the people who wished to come had yet gathered. Between four and five thousand men and women had come through the forests to the Meeting at Endtor, and from there to this place, to this night.

The fires burned huge, and the smell of burning and of butchering was foul.

Selver's mouth was dry and his throat sore, so that he could not speak, and longed for water to drink. As he led his group down the middle path of the city, a yumen came running towards him, looming huge in the black and dazzle of the smoky air. Selver lifted the fire thrower and pulled back on the tongue of it, even as the yumen slipped in mud and fell scrambling to its knees. No hissing jet of flame sprang from the machine, it had all been spent on burning the airships that had not been in the hangar. Selver dropped the heavy machine. The yumen was not armed, and was male. Selver tried to say, "Let him run away," but his voice was weak, and two men, hunters of the Abtam Glades, had leapt past him even as he spoke, holding their long knives up. The big, naked hands clutched at air, and dropped limp. The big corpse lay in a heap on the path. There were many others lying dead, there in what had been the center of the city. There was not much noise any more except the noise of the fires.

Selver parted his lips and hoarsely sent up the home-call that ends the hunt; those with him took it up more clearly and loudly, in carrying falsetto; other voices answered it, near and far off in the mist and reek and flame-shot darkness of the night. Instead of leading his group at once from the city, he signalled them to go on, and himself went aside, onto the muddy ground between the path and a building which had burned and fallen. He stepped across a dead female yumen and bent over one that lay pinned down under a great, charred beam of wood. He could not see the features obliterated by mud and shadow.

It was not just; it was not necessary; he need not have looked at that one among so many dead. He need not have known him in the dark. He started to go after his group. Then he turned back; straining, lifted the beam off Lyubov's back; knelt down, slipping one hand under the heavy head so that Lyubov seemed to lie easier, his face clear of the earth; and so knelt there, motionless.

He had not slept for four days and had not been still to dream for longer than that—he did not know how long. He had acted, spoken, travelled, planned, night and day, ever since he left Broter with his followers from Cadast. He had gone from city to city speaking to the people of the forest, telling them the new thing, waking them from the dream into the world, arranging the thing done this night, talking, always talking and hearing others talk, never in silence and never alone. They had listened, they had heard and had come to follow him, to follow the new path. They had taken up the fire they feared into their own hands: taken up the mastery over the evil dream: and loosed the death they feared upon their enemy. All had been done as he said it should be done. All had gone as he said it would go. The lodges and many dwellings of the yumens were burnt, their airships burnt or broken, their weapons stolen or destroyed: and their females were dead. The fires were burning out, the night growing very dark, fouled with smoke. Selver could scarcely see; he looked up to the east, wondering if it were nearing dawn. Kneeling there in the mud among the dead he thought, This is the dream now, the evil dream. I thought to drive it, but it drives me.

In the dream, Lyubov's lips moved a little against the palm of his own hand; Selver looked down and saw the dead man's eyes open. The glare of dying fires shone on the surface of them. After a while he spoke Selver's name.

"Lyubov, why did you stay here? I told you to be out of the city this night." So Selver spoke in dream, harshly, as if he were angry at Lyubov.

"Are you the prisoner?" Lyubov said, faintly and not lifting his head, but in so commonplace a voice that Selver knew for a moment that this was not the dream-time but the world-time, the forest's night. "Or am I?"

"Neither, both, how do I know? All the engines and machines are burned. All the women are dead. We let the men run away if they would. I told them not to set fire to your house, the books will be all right. Lyubov, why aren't you like the others?"

"I am like them. A man. Like them. Like you."

"No. You are different—"

"I am like them. And so are you. Listen, Selver. Don't go on. You must not go on killing other men. You must go back . . . to your own . . . to your roots."

"When your people are gone, then the evil dream will stop."

"*Now*," Lyubov said, trying to lift his head, but his back was broken. He looked up at Selver and opened his mouth to speak. His gaze dropped away and looked into the other time, and his lips remained parted, unspeaking. His breath whistled a little in his throat.

They were calling Selver's name, many voices far away, calling over and over. "I can't stay with you, Lyubov!" Selver said in tears, and when there was no answer stood up and tried to run away. But in the dream-darkness he could go only very slowly, like one wading through deep water. The Ash Spirit walked in front of him, taller than Lyubov or any yumen, tall as a tree, not turning its white mask to him. As Selver went he spoke to Lyubov: "We'll go back," he said. "I will go back. Now. We will go back, now, I promise you, Lyubov!"

But his friend, the gentle one, who had saved his life and betrayed his dream, Lyubov did not reply. He walked somewhere in the night near Selver, unseen, and quiet as death.

A group of the people of Tuntar came on Selver wandering in the dark, weeping and speaking, overmastered by dream; they took him with them in their swift return to Endtor.

In the makeshift Lodge there, a tent on the river-bank, he lay helpless and insane for two days and nights, while the Old Men tended him. All that time people kept coming in to Endtor and going out again, returning to the Place of Eshsen which had been called Central, burying their dead there and the alien dead: of theirs more than three hundred, of the others more than seven hundred. There were about five hundred yumens locked into the compound, the creechie-pens, which, standing empty and apart, had not been burnt. As many more had escaped, some of whom had got to the logging camps farther south, which had not been attacked; those who were still hiding and wandering in the forest or the Cut Lands were hunted down. Some were killed, for many of the younger hunters and huntresses still heard only Selver's voice saying *Kill them*. Others had left the night of killing behind them as if it had been a nightmare, the evil dream that must be understood lest it be repeated; and these, faced with a thirsty, exhausted yumen cowering in a thicket, could not kill him. So maybe he killed them. There were groups of ten and twenty yumens, armed with logger's axes and hand-guns, though few had ammunition left; these groups were tracked until sufficient numbers were hidden in the forest about them, then overpowered, bound, and led back to Eshsen. They were all captured within two or three days, for all that part of Sornol was swarming with the people of the forest, there had never in the knowledge of any man been half or a tenth so great a gathering of people in one place; some still coming in from distant towns and other Lands, others already going home again. The captured yumens were put in among the others in the compound, though it was overcrowded and the huts were too small for yumens. They were watered, fed twice daily, and guarded by a couple of hundred armed hunters at all times.

In the afternoon following the Night of Eshsen an airship came rattling out of the east and flew low as if to land, then shot upward like a bird of prey that misses its kill, and circled the wrecked landing-place, the smouldering city, and the Cut Lands. Reswan had seen to it that the radios were destroyed, and perhaps it was the silence of the radios that had brought the airship from Kushil or Rieshwel, where there were three small towns of yumens. The prisoners in the compound rushed out of the barracks and yelled at the machine whenever it came rattling overhead, and once it dropped an object on a small parachute into the compound: at last it rattled off into the sky.

There were four such winged ships left on Athshe now, three on Kushil and one on Rieshwel, all of the small kind that carried four men; they also carried machine guns and flamethrowers, and they weighed much on the minds of Reswan and the others, while Selver lay lost to them, walking the cryptic ways of the other time.

He woke into the world-time on the third day, thin, dazed, hungry, silent. After he had bathed in the river and had eaten, he listened to Reswan and the headwoman of Berre and the others chosen as leaders. They told him how the world had gone while he dreamed. When he had heard them all, he looked about at them and they saw the god in him. In the sickness of disgust and fear that followed the Night of Eshsen, some of them had come to doubt. Their dreams were uneasy and full of blood and fire; they were surrounded all day by strangers, people come from all over the forests, hundreds of them, thousands, all gathered here like kites to carrion, none knowing another: and it seemed to them as if the end of things had come and nothing would ever be the same, or be right, again. But in Selver's presence they remembered purpose; their distress was quietened, and they waited for him to speak.

"The killing is all done," he said. "Make sure that everyone knows that." He looked round at them. "I have to talk with the ones in the compound. Who is leading them in there?"

"Turkey, Flapfeet, Weteyes," said Reswan, the ex-slave.

"Turkey's alive? Good. Help me get up, Greda, I have eels for bones. . . ."

When he had been afoot a while he was stronger, and within the hour he set off for Eshsen, two hours' walk from Endtor.

When they came Reswan mounted a ladder set against the compound wall and bawled in the pidgin-English taught the slaves, "Dong-a come to gate hurry-up-quick!"

Down in the alleys between the squat cement barracks, some of the yumens yelled and threw clods of dirt at him. He ducked, and waited.

The old Colonel did not come out, but Gosse, whom they called Weteyes, came limping out of a hut and called up to Reswan, "Colonel Dongh is ill, he cannot come out."

"Ill what kind?"

"Bowels, water-illness. What you want?"

"Talk-talk. —My lord god," Reswan said in his own language, looking down at Selver, "the Turkey's hiding, do you want to talk with Weteyes?"

"All right."

"Watch the gate there, you bowmen! —To gate, Mis-ter Goss-a, hurry-up-quick!"

The gate was opened just wide enough and long enough for Gosse to squeeze out. He stood in front of it alone, facing the group led by Selver. He favored one leg, injured on the Night of Eshsen. He was wearing torn pajamas, mudstained and rain-sodden. His greying hair hung in lank festoons around his ears and over his forehead. Twice the height of his captors, he held himself very stiff, and stared at them in courageous, angry misery. "What you want?"

"We must talk, Mr Gosse," said Selver, who had learned plain English from Lyubov. "I'm Selver of the Ash Tree of Eshreth. I'm Lyubov's friend."

"Yes, I know you. What have you to say?"

"I have to say that the killing is over, if that be made a promise kept by your people and my people. You may all go free, if you will gather in your people from the logging camps in South Sornol, Kushil, and Rieshwel, and make them all stay together here. You may live here where the forest is dead, where you grow your seed-grasses. There must not be any more cutting of trees."

Gosse's face had grown eager: "The camps weren't attacked?"

"No."

Gosse said nothing.

Selver watched his face, and presently spoke again: "There are less than two thousand of your people left living in the world, I think. Your women are all dead. In the other camps there are still weapons; you could kill many of us. But we have some of your weapons. And there are more of us than you could kill. I suppose you know that, and that's why you have not tried to have the flying ships bring you fire-throwers, and kill the guards, and escape. It would be no good; there really are so many of us. If you make the promise with us it will be much the best, and then you can wait without harm until one of your Great Ships comes, and you can leave the world. That will be in three years, I think."

"Yes, three local years— How do you know that?"

"Well, slaves have ears, Mr Gosse."

Gosse looked straight at him at last. He looked away,

fidgeted, tried to ease his leg. He looked back at Selver, and away again. "We had already 'promised' not to hurt any of your people. It's why the workers were sent home. It did no good, you didn't listen—"

"It was not a promise made to us."

"How can we make any sort of agreement or treaty with a people who have no government, no central authority?"

"I don't know. I'm not sure you know what a promise is. This one was soon broken."

"What do you mean? By whom, how?"

"In Rieshwel, New Java. Fourteen days ago. A town was burned and its people killed by yumens of the Camp in Rieshwel."

"What are you talking about?"

"About news brought us by messengers from Rieshwel."

"It's a lie. We were in radio contact with New Java right along, until the massacre. Nobody was killing natives there or anywhere else."

"You're speaking the truth you know," Selver said, "I the truth I know. I accept your ignorance of the killings on Rieshwel; but you must accept my telling you that they were done. This remains: the promise must be made to us and with us, and it must be kept. You'll wish to talk about these matters with Colonel Dongh and the others."

Gosse moved as if to re-enter the gate, then turned back and said in his deep, hoarse voice, "Who are you, Selver? Did you—was it you that organised the attack? Did you lead them?"

"Yes, I did."

"Then all this blood is on your head," Gosse said, and with sudden savagery, "Lyubov's too, you know. He's dead—your 'friend Lyubov.'"

Selver did not understand the idiom. He had learned murder, but of guilt he knew little beyond the name. As his gaze locked for a moment with Gosse's pale, resentful stare, he felt afraid. A sickness rose up in him, a mortal chill. He tried to put it away from him, shutting his eyes a moment. At last he said, "Lyubov is my friend, and so not dead."

"You're children," Gosse said with hatred. "Children, savages. You have no conception of reality. This is no dream, this is real! You killed Lyubov. He's dead. You killed the women

—the *women*—you burned them alive, slaughtered them like animals!"

"Should we have let them live?" said Selver with vehemence equal to Gosse's, but softly, his voice singing a little. "To breed like insects in the carcase of the World? To overrun us? We killed them to sterilise you. I know what a realist is, Mr Gosse. Lyubov and I have talked about these words. A realist is a man who knows both the world and his own dreams. You're not sane: there's not one man in a thousand of you who knows how to dream. Not even Lyubov and he was the best among you. You sleep, you wake and forget your dreams, you sleep again and wake again, and so you spend your whole lives, and you think that is being, life, reality! You are not children, you are grown men, but insane. And that's why we had to kill you, before you drove us mad. Now go back and talk about reality with the other insane men. Talk long, and well!"

The guards opened the gate, threatening the crowding yumens inside with their spears; Gosse re-entered the compound, his big shoulders hunched as if against the rain.

Selver was very tired. The headwoman of Berre and another woman came to him and walked with him, his arms over their shoulders so that if he stumbled he should not fall. The young hunter Greda, a cousin of his Tree, joked with him, and Selver answered light-headedly, laughing. The walk back to Endtor seemed to go on for days.

He was too weary to eat. He drank a little hot broth and lay down by the Men's Fire. Endtor was no town but a mere camp by the great river, a favorite fishing place for all the cities that had once been in the forest round about, before the yumens came. There was no Lodge. Two fire-rings of black stone and a long grassy bank over the river where tents of hide and plaited rush could be set up, that was Endtor. The river Menend, the master river of Sornol, spoke ceaselessly in the world and in the dream at Endtor.

There were many old men at the fire, some whom he knew from Broter and Tuntar and his own destroyed city Eshreth, some whom he did not know; he could see in their eyes and gestures, and hear in their voices, that they were Great Dreamers; more dreamers than had ever been gathered in one place before, perhaps. Lying stretched out full length, his head raised on his hands, gazing at the fire, he said, "I have called the yumens mad. Am I mad myself?"

"You don't know one time from the other," said old Tubab, laying a pine-knot on the fire, "because you did not dream either sleeping or waking for far too long. The price for that takes long to pay."

"The poisons the yumens take do much the same as does the lack of sleep and dream," said Heben, who had been a slave both at Central and at Smith Camp. "The yumens poison themselves in order to dream. I saw the dreamer's look in them after they took the poisons. But they couldn't call the dreams, nor control them, nor weave nor shape nor cease to dream; they were driven, overpowered. They did not know what was within them at all. So it is with a man who hasn't dreamed for many days. Though he be the wisest of his Lodge, still he'll be mad, now and then, here and there, for a long time after. He'll be driven, enslaved. He will not understand himself."

A very old man with the accent of South Sornol laid his hand on Selver's shoulder, caressing him, and said, "My dear young god, you need to sing, that would do you good."

"I can't. Sing for me."

The old man sang; others joined in, their voices high and reedy, almost tuneless, like the wind blowing in the water-reeds of Endtor. They sang one of the songs of the ash-tree, about the delicate parted leaves that turn yellow in autumn when the berries turn red, and one night the first frost silvers them.

While Selver was listening to the song of the Ash, Lyubov lay down beside him. Lying down he did not seem so monstrously tall and large-limbed. Behind him was the half-collapsed, fire-gutted building, black against the stars. "I am like you," he said, not looking at Selver, in that dream-voice which tries to reveal its own untruth. Selver's heart was heavy with sorrow for his friend. "I've got a headache," Lyubov said in his own voice, rubbing the back of his neck as he always did, and at that Selver reached out to touch him, to console him. But he was shadow and firelight in the world-time, and the old men were singing the song of the Ash, about the small white flowers on the black branches in spring among the parted leaves.

The next day the yumens imprisoned in the compound sent for Selver. He came to Eshsen in the afternoon, and met with them outside the compound, under the branches of an oak tree, for all Selver's people felt a little uneasy under the bare open sky. Eshsen had been an oak grove; this tree was the largest of the few the colonists had left standing. It was on the long slope behind Lyubov's bungalow, one of the six or eight houses that had come through the night of the burning undamaged. With Selver under the oak were Reswan, the headwoman of Berre, Greda of Cadast, and others who wished to be in on the parley, a dozen or so in all. Many bowmen kept guard, fearing the yumens might have hidden weapons, but they sat behind bushes or bits of wreckage left from the burning, so as not to dominate the scene with the hint of threat. With Gosse and Colonel Dongh were three of the yumens called officers and two from the logging camp, at the sight of one of whom, Benton, the ex-slaves drew in their breaths. Benton had used to punish "lazy creechies" by castrating them in public.

The Colonel looked thin, his normally yellow-brown skin a muddy yellow-grey; his illness had been no sham. "Now the first thing is," he said when they were all settled, the yumens standing, Selver's people squatting or sitting on the damp, soft oak-leaf mould, "the first thing is that I want first to have a working definition of just precisely what these terms of yours mean and what they mean in terms of guaranteed safety of my personnel under my command here."

There was a silence.

"You understand English, don't you, some of you?"

"Yes. I don't understand your question, Mr Dongh."

"Colonel Dongh, if you please!"

"Then you'll call me Colonel Selver, if you please." A singing note came into Selver's voice; he stood up, ready for the contest, tunes running in his mind like rivers.

But the old yumen just stood there, huge and heavy, angry yet not meeting the challenge. "I did not come here to be insulted by you little humanoids," he said. But his lips trembled as he said it. He was old, and bewildered, and humiliated. All anticipation of triumph went out of Selver. There was no triumph in the world any more, only death. He sat down again. "I didn't intend insult, Colonel Dongh," he said resignedly. "Will you repeat your question, please?"

"I want to hear your terms, and then you'll hear ours, that's all there is to it."

Selver repeated what he had said to Gosse.

Dongh listened with apparent impatience. "All right. Now you don't realise that we've had a functioning radio in the prison compound for three days now." Selver did know this, as Reswan had at once checked on the object dropped by the helicopter, lest it be a weapon; the guards reported it was a radio, and he let the yumens keep it. Selver merely nodded. "So we've been in contact with the three outlying camps, the two on King Land and one on New Java, right along, and if we had decided to make a break for it and escape from that prison compound then it would have been very simple for us to do that, with the helicopters to drop us weapons and covering our movements with their mounted weapons, one flamethrower could have got us out of the compound and in case of need they also have the bombs that can blow up an entire area. You haven't seen those in action of course."

"If you'd left the compound, where would you have gone?"

"The point is, without introducing into this any beside the point or erroneous factors, now we are certainly greatly out-numbered by your forces, but we have the four helicopters at the camps, which there's no use you trying to disable as they are under fully armed guard at all times now, and also all the seri-ous fire-power, so that the cold reality of the situation is we can pretty much call it a draw and speak in positions of mutual equality. This of course is a temporary situation. If necessary we are enabled to maintain a defensive police action to prevent all-out war. Moreover we have behind us the entire fire-power of the Terran Interstellar Fleet, which could blow your entire planet right out of the sky. But these ideas are pretty intangible to you, so let's just put it as plainly and simply as I can, that we're prepared to negotiate with you, for the present time, in terms of an equal frame of reference."

Selver's patience was short; he knew his ill-temper was a symptom of his deteriorated mental state, but he could no longer control it. "Go on, then!"

"Well, first I want it clearly understood that as soon as we got the radio we told the men at the other camps not to bring us weapons and not to try any airlift or rescue attempts, and reprisals were strictly out of order—"

"That was prudent. What next?"

Colonel Dongh began an angry retort, then stopped; he turned very pale. "Isn't there anything to sit down on," he said.

Selver went around the yumen group, up the slope, into the empty two-room bungalow, and took the folding desk-chair. Before he left the silent room he leaned down and laid his cheek on the scarred, raw wood of the desk, where Lyubov had always sat when he worked with Selver or alone; some of his papers were lying there now; Selver touched them lightly. He carried the chair out and set it in the rainwet dirt for Dongh. The old man sat down, biting his lips, his almond-shaped eyes narrow with pain.

"Mr Gosse, perhaps you can speak for the Colonel," Selver said. "He isn't well."

"I'll do the talking," Benton said, stepping forward, but Dongh shook his head and muttered, "Gosse."

With the Colonel as auditor rather than speaker it went more easily. The yumens were accepting Selver's terms. With a mutual promise of peace, they would withdraw all their outposts and live in one area, the region they had deforested in Middle Sornol: about 1700 square miles of rolling land, well watered. They undertook not to enter the forest; the forest people undertook not to trespass on the Cut Lands.

The four remaining airships were the cause of some argument. The yumens insisted they needed them to bring their people from the other islands to Sornol. Since the machines carried only four men and would take several hours for each trip, it appeared to Selver that the yumens could get to Eshsen rather sooner by walking, and he offered them ferry service across the straits; but it appeared that yumens never walked far. Very well, they could keep the hoppers for what they called the "Airlift Operation." After that, they were to destroy them. — Refusal. Anger. They were more protective of their machines than of their bodies. Selver gave in, saying they could keep the hoppers if they flew them only over the Cut Lands and if the weapons in them were destroyed. Over this they argued, but with one another, while Selver waited, occasionally repeating the terms of his demand, for he was not giving in on this point.

"What's the difference, Benton," the old Colonel said at last, furious and shaky, "can't you see that we can't use the damned weapons? There's three million of these aliens all scattered out all over every damned island, all covered with trees and undergrowth, no cities, no vital network, no centralised control. You can't disable a guerrilla type structure with bombs, it's been proved, in fact my own part of the world where I was born proved it for about thirty years fighting off major super-powers one after the other in the twentieth century. And we're not in a position until a ship comes to prove our superiority. Let the big stuff go, if we can hold on to the side-arms for hunting and self-defense!"

He was their Old Man, and his opinion prevailed in the end, as it might have done in a Men's Lodge. Benton sulked. Gosse started to talk about what would happen if the truce was broken, but Selver stopped him. "These are possibilities, we aren't yet done with certainties. Your Great Ship is to return in three years, that is three and a half years of your count. Until that time you are free here. It will not be very hard for you. Nothing more will be taken away from Centralville, except some of Lyubov's work that I wish to keep. You still have most of your tools of tree-cutting and ground-moving; if you need more tools, the iron-mines of Peldel are in your territory. I think all this is clear. What remains to be known is this: When that ship comes, what will they seek to do with you, and with us?"

"We don't know," Gosse said. Dongh amplified: "If you hadn't destroyed the ansible communicator first thing off, we might be receiving some current information on these matters, and our reports would of course influence the decisions that may be made concerning a finalised decision on the status of this planet, which we might then expect to begin to implement before the ship returns from Prestno. But due to wanton destruction due to your ignorance of your own interests, we haven't even got a radio left that will transmit over a few hundred miles."

"What is the ansible?" The word had come up before in this talk; it was a new one to Selver.

"ICD," the Colonel said, morose.

"A kind of radio," Gosse said, arrogant. "It put us in instant touch with our home-world."

"Without the 27-year waiting?"

Gosse stared down at Selver. "Right. Quite right. You learned a great deal from Lyubov, didn't you?"

"Didn't he just," said Benton. "He was Lyubov's little green buddyboy. He picked up everything worth knowing and a bit more besides. Like all the vital points to sabotage, and where the guards would be posted, and how to get into the weapon stockpile. They must have been in touch right up to the moment the massacre started."

Gosse looked uneasy. "Raj is dead. All that's irrelevant now, Benton. We've got to establish—"

"Are you trying to infer in some way that Captain Lyubov was involved in some activity that could be called treachery to the Colony, Benton?" said Dongh, glaring and pressing his hands against his belly. "There were no spies or treachers on my staff, it was absolutely handpicked before we ever left Terra and I know the kind of men I have to deal with."

"I'm not inferring anything, Colonel. I'm saying straight out that it was Lyubov stirred up the creechies, and if orders hadn't been changed on us after that Fleet ship was here, it never would have happened."

Gosse and Dongh both started to speak at once. "You are all very ill," Selver observed, getting up and dusting himself off, for the damp brown oak-leaves clung to his short body-fur as to silk. "I'm sorry we've had to hold you in the creechie-pen, it is not a good place for the mind. Please send for your men from the camps. When all are here and the large weapons have been destroyed, and the promise has been spoken by all of us, then we shall leave you alone. The gates of the compound will be opened when I leave here today. Is there more to be said?"

None of them said anything. They looked down at him. Seven big men, with tan or brown hairless skin, cloth-covered, dark-eyed, grim-faced; twelve small men, green or brownish-green, fur-covered, with the large eyes of the seminocturnal creature, with dreamy faces; between the two groups, Selver, the translator, frail, disfigured, holding all their destinies in his empty hands. Rain fell softly on the brown earth about them.

"Farewell then," Selver said, and led his people away.

"They're not so stupid," said the headwoman of Berre as she accompanied Selver back to Endtor. "I thought such giants must be stupid, but they saw that you're a god, I saw it in their faces at the end of the talking. How well you talk that gobble-gubble. Ugly they are, do you think even their children are hairless?"

"That we shall never know, I hope."

"Ugh, think of nursing a child that wasn't furry. Like trying to suckle a fish."

"They are all insane," said old Tubab, looking deeply distressed. "Lyubov wasn't like that, when he used to come to Tuntar. He was ignorant, but sensible. But these ones, they argue, and sneer at the old man, and hate each other, like this," and he contorted his grey-furred face to imitate the expressions of the Terrans, whose words of course he had not been able to follow. "Was that what you said to them, Selver, that they're mad?"

"I told them that they were ill. But then, they've been defeated, and hurt, and locked in that stone cage. After that anyone might be ill and need healing."

"Who's to heal them," said the headwoman of Berre, "their women are all dead. Too bad for them. Poor ugly things—great naked spiders they are, ugh!"

"They are men, men, like us, men," Selver said, his voice shrill and edged like a knife.

"Oh, my dear lord god, I know it, I only meant they *look* like spiders," said the old woman, caressing his cheek. "Look here, you people, Selver is worn out with this going back and forth between Endtor and Eshsen, let's sit down and rest a bit."

"Not here," Selver said. They were still in the Cut Lands, among stumps and grassy slopes, under the bare sky. "When we come under the trees. . . ." He stumbled, and those who were not gods helped him to walk along the road.

7

Davidson found a good use for Major Muhamed's tape recorder. Somebody had to make a record of events on New Tahiti, a history of the crucifixion of the Terran Colony. So that when the ships came from Mother Earth they could learn the truth. So that future generations could learn how much treachery and cowardice and folly humans were capable of, and how much courage against all odds. During his free moments —not much more than moments since he had assumed command—he recorded the whole story of the Smith Camp Massacre, and brought the record up to date for New Java, and for King and Central also, as well as he could with the garbled hysterical stuff that was all he got by way of news from Central HQ.

Exactly what had happened there nobody would ever know, except the creechies, for the humans were trying to cover up their own betrayals and mistakes. The outlines were clear, though. An organised bunch of creechies, led by Selver, had been let into the Arsenal and the Hangars, and turned loose with dynamite, grenades, guns, and flamethrowers to totally destruct the city and slaughter the humans. It was an inside job, the fact that HQ was the first place blown up proved that. Lyubov of course had been in on it, and his little green buddies had proved just as grateful as you might expect, and cut his throat like the others. At least, Gosse and Benton claimed to have seen him dead the morning after the massacre. But could you believe any of them, actually? You could assume that any human left alive in Central after that night was more or less of a traitor. A traitor to his race.

The women were all dead, they claimed. That was bad enough, but what was worse, there was no reason to believe it. It was easy for the creechies to take prisoners in the woods, and nothing would be easier to catch than a terrified girl running out of a burning town. And wouldn't the little green devils like to get hold of a human girl and try experiments on her? God knows how many of the women were still alive in the creechie warrens, tied down underground in one of those stinking holes, being touched and felt and crawled over and defiled by the filthy, hairy little monkeymen. It was unthinkable. But by God sometimes you have to be able to think about the unthinkable.

A hopper from King had dropped the prisoners at Central a receiver-transmitter the day after the massacre, and Muhamed had taped all his exchanges with Central starting that day. The most incredible one was a conversation between him and

Colonel Dongh. The first time he played it Davidson had torn the thing right off the reel and burned it. Now he wished he had kept it, for the records, as a perfect proof of the total incompetence of the C.O.'s at both Central and New Java. He had given in to his own hotbloodedness, destroying it. But how could he sit there and listen to the recording of the Colonel and the Major discussing total surrender to the creechies, agreeing not to try retaliation, not to defend themselves, to give up all their big weapons, to all squeeze together onto a bit of land picked out for them by the creechies, a reservation conceded to them by their generous conquerors, the little green beasts. It was incredible. Literally incredible.

Probably old Ding Dong and Moo were not actually traitors by intent. They had just gone spla, lost their nerve. It was this damned planet that did it to them. It took a very strong personality to withstand it. There was something in the air, maybe pollens from all those trees, acting as some kind of drug maybe, that made ordinary humans begin to get as stupid and out of touch with reality as the creechies were. Then, being so outnumbered, they were pushovers for the creechies to wipe out.

It was too bad Muhamed had had to be put out of the way, but he would never have agreed to accept Davidson's plans, that was clear; he'd been too far gone. Anyone who'd heard that incredible tape would agree. So it was better he got shot before he really knew what was going on, and now no shame would attach to his name, as it would to Dongh's and all the other officers left alive at Central.

Dongh hadn't come on the radio lately. Usually it was Juju Sereng, in Engineering. Davidson had used to pal around a lot with Juju and had thought of him as a friend, but now you couldn't trust anybody any more. And Juju was another asiatiform. It was really queer how many of them had survived the Centralville Massacre; of those he'd talked to, the only non-asio was Gosse. Here in Java the fifty-five loyal men remaining after the reorganization were mostly eurafs like himself, some afros and afrasians, not one pure asio. Blood tells, after all. You couldn't be fully human without some blood in your veins from the Cradle of Man. But that wouldn't stop him from saving those poor yellow bastards at Central, it just helped explain their moral collapse under stress.

"Can't you realise what kind of trouble you're making for us, Don?" Juju Sereng had demanded in his flat voice. "We've made a formal truce with the creechies. And we're under direct orders from Earth not to interfere with the hilfs and not to retaliate. Anyhow how the hell can we retaliate? Now all the fellows from King Land and South Central are here with us we're still less than two thousand, and what have you got there on Java, about sixty-five men isn't it? Do you really think two thousand men can take on three million intelligent enemies, Don?"

"Juju, fifty men can do it. It's a matter of will, skill, and weaponry."

"Batshit! But the point is, Don, a truce has been made. And if it's broken, we've had it. It's all that keeps us afloat, now. Maybe when the ship gets back from Prestno and sees what happened, they'll decide to wipe out the creechies. We don't know. But it does look like the creechies intend to keep the truce, after all it was their idea, and we have got to. They can wipe us out by sheer numbers, any time, the way they did Centralville. There were thousands of them. Can't you understand that, Don?"

"Listen, Juju, sure I understand. If you're scared to use the three hoppers you've still got there, you could send 'em over here, with a few fellows who see things like we do here. If I'm going to liberate you fellows singlehanded, I sure could use some more hoppers for the job."

"You aren't going to liberate us, you're going to incinerate us, you damned fool. Get that last hopper over here to Central now: that's the Colonel's personal order to you as Acting C.O. Use it to fly your men here; twelve trips, you won't need more than four local dayperiods. Now act on those orders, and get to it." Ponk, off the air—afraid to argue with him any more.

At first he worried that they might send their three hoppers over and actually bomb or strafe New Java Camp; for he was, technically, disobeying orders, and old Dongh wasn't tolerant of independent elements. Look how he'd taken it out on Davidson already, for that tiny reprisal-raid on Smith. Initiative got punished. What Ding Dong liked was submission, like most officers. The danger with that is that it can make the officer get submissive himself. Davidson finally realized, with a real shock, that the hoppers were no threat to him, because Dongh, Sereng, Gosse, even Benton were *afraid* to send them. The creechies had ordered them to keep the hoppers inside the Human Reservation: and they were obeying orders.

Christ, it made him sick. It was time to act. They'd been waiting around nearly two weeks now. He had his camp well defended; they had strengthened the stockade fence and built it up so that no little green monkeymen could possibly get over it, and that clever kid Aabi had made lots of neat home-made land mines and sown 'em all around the stockade in a hundred-meter belt. Now it was time to show the creechies that they might push around those sheep on Central but on New Java it was men they had to deal with. He took the hopper up and with it guided an infantry squad of fifteen to a creechie-warren south of camp. He'd learned how to spot the things from the air; the giveaway was the orchards, concentrations of certain kinds of tree, though not planted in rows like humans would. It was incredible how many warrens there were once you learned to spot them. The forest was crawling with the things. The raiding party burned up that warren by hand, and then flying back with a couple of his boys he spotted another, less than four kilos from camp. On that one, just to write his signature real clear and plain for everybody to read, he dropped a bomb. Just a firebomb, not a big one, but baby did it make the green fur fly. It left a big hole in the forest, and the edges of the hole were burning.

Of course that was his real weapon when it actually came to setting up massive retaliation. Forest fire. He could set one of these whole islands on fire, with bombs and firejelly dropped from the hopper. Have to wait a month or two, till the rainy season was over. Should he burn King or Smith or Central? King first, maybe, as a little warning, since there were no humans left there. Then Central, if they didn't get in line.

"What are you trying to do?" said the voice on the radio, and it made him grin, it was so agonised, like some old woman being held up. "Do you know what you're doing, Davidson?"

"Yep."

"Do you think you're going to subdue the creechies?" It wasn't Juju this time, it might be that bigdome Gosse, or any of them; no difference; they all bleated baa.

"Yes, that's right," he said with ironic mildness.

"You think if you keep burning up villages they'll come to you and surrender—three million of them. Right?"

"Maybe."

"Look, Davidson," the radio said after a while, whining and buzzing; they were using some kind of emergency rig, having lost the big transmitter, along with that phoney ansible which was no loss. "Look, is there somebody else standing by there we can talk to?"

"No; they're all pretty busy. Say, we're doing great here, but we're out of dessert stuff, you know, fruit cocktail, peaches, crap like that. Some of the fellows really miss it. And we were due for a load of maryjanes when you fellows got blown up. If I sent the hopper over, could you spare us a few crates of sweet stuff and grass?"

A pause. "Yes, send it on over."

"Great. Have the stuff in a net, and the boys can hook it without landing." He grinned.

There was some fussing around at the Central end, and all of a sudden old Dongh was on, the first time he'd talked to Davidson. He sounded feeble and out of breath on the whining shortwave. "Listen, Captain, I want to know if you fully realize what form of action your actions on New Java are going to be forcing me into taking. If you continue to disobey your orders. I am trying to reason with you as a reasonable and loyal soldier. In order to ensure the safety of my personnel here at Central I'm going to be put into the position of being forced to tell the natives here that we can't assume any responsibility at all for your actions."

"That's correct, sir."

"What I'm trying to make clear to you is that means that we are going to be put into the position of having to tell them that we can't stop you from breaking the truce there on Java. Your personnel there is sixty-six men, is that correct, well I want those men safe and sound here at Central with us to wait for the *Shackleton* and keep the Colony together. You're on a suicide course and I'm responsible for those men you have there with you."

"No, you're not, sir. I am. You just relax. Only when you see the jungle burning, pick up and get out into the middle of a

Strip, because we don't want to roast you folks along with the creechies."

"Now listen, Davidson, I order you to hand your command over to Lt. Temba at once and report to me here," said the distant whining voice, and Davidson suddenly cut off the radio, sickened. They were all spla, playing at still being soldiers, in full retreat from reality. There were actually very few men who could face reality when the going got tough.

As he expected, the local creechies did absolutely nothing about his raids on the warrens. The only way to handle them, as he'd known from the start, was to terrorise them and never let up on them. If you did that, they knew who was boss, and knuckled under. A lot of the villages within a thirty-kilo radius seemed to be deserted now before he got to them, but he kept his men going out to burn them up every few days.

The fellows were getting rather jumpy. He had kept them logging, since that's what forty-eight of the fifty-five loyal survivors were, loggers. But they knew that the robo-freighters from Earth wouldn't be called down to load up the lumber, but would just keep coming in and circling in orbit waiting for the signal that didn't come. No use cutting trees just for the hell of it; it was hard work. Might as well burn them. He exercised the men in teams, developing fire-setting techniques. It was still too rainy for them to do much, but it kept their minds busy. If only he had the other three hoppers, he'd really be able to hit and run. He considered a raid on Central to liberate the hoppers, but did not yet mention this idea even to Aabi and Temba, his best men. Some of the boys would get cold feet at the idea of an armed raid on their own HQ. They kept talking about "when we get back with the others." They didn't know those others had abandoned them, betrayed them, sold their skins to the creechies. He didn't tell them that, they couldn't take it.

One day he and Aabi and Temba and another good sound man would just take the hopper over, then three of them jump out with machine guns, take a hopper apiece, and so home again, home again, jiggety jog. With four nice egg-beaters to beat eggs with. Can't make an omelet without beating eggs. Davidson laughed aloud, in the darkness of his bungalow. He kept that plan hidden just a little longer, because it tickled him so much to think about it.

After two more weeks they had pretty well closed out the creechie-warrens within walking distance, and the forest was neat and tidy. No vermin. No smoke-puffs over the trees. Nobody hopping out of bushes and flopping down on the ground with their eyes shut, waiting for you to stomp them. No little green men. Just a mess of trees and some burned places. The boys were getting really edgy and mean; it was time to make the hopper-raid. He told his plan one night to Aabi, Temba, and Post.

None of them said anything for a minute, then Aabi said, "What about fuel, Captain?"

"We got enough fuel."

"Not for four hoppers; wouldn't last a week."

"You mean there's only a month's supply left for this one?" Aabi nodded.

"Well then, we pick up a little fuel too, looks like."

"How?"

"Put your minds to it."

They all sat there looking stupid. It annoyed him. They looked to him for everything. He was a natural leader, but he liked men who thought for themselves too. "Figure it out, it's your line of work, Aabi," he said, and went out for a smoke, sick of the way everybody acted, like they'd lost their nerve. They just couldn't face the cold hard facts.

They were low on maryjanes now and he hadn't had one for a couple of days. It didn't do anything for him. The night was overcast and black, damp, warm, smelling like spring. Ngenene went by walking like an ice-skater, or almost like a robot on treads; he turned slowly through a gliding step and gazed at Davidson, who stood on the bungalow porch in the dim light from the doorway. He was a power-saw operator, a huge man. "The source of my energy is connected to the Great Generator I cannot be switched off," he said in a level tone, gazing at Davidson.

"Get to your barracks and sleep it off!" Davidson said in the whipcrack voice that nobody ever disobeyed, and after a moment Ngenene skated carefully on, ponderous and graceful. Too many of the men were using hallies more and more heavily. There was plenty, but the stuff was for loggers relaxing on Sundays, not for soldiers of a tiny outpost marooned on a hostile world. They had no time for getting high, for dreaming. He'd have to lock the stuff up. Then some of the boys might crack. Well, let 'em crack. Can't make an omelet without cracking eggs. Maybe he could send them back to Central in exchange for some fuel. You give me two, three tanks of gas and I'll give you two, three warm bodies, loyal soldiers, good loggers, just your type, a little far gone in bye-bye dreamland. . . .

He grinned, and was going back inside to try this one out on Temba and the others, when the guard posted up on the lumberyard smoke stack yelled. "They're coming!" he screeched out in a high voice, like a kid playing Blacks and Rhodesians. Somebody else over on the west side of the stockade began yelling too. A gun went off.

And they came. Christ, they came. It was incredible. There were thousands of them, thousands. No sound, no noise at all, until that screech from the guard; then one gunshot; then an explosion—a land mine going up—and another, one after another, and hundreds and hundreds of torches flaring up lit one from another and being thrown and soaring through the black wet air like rockets, and the walls of the stockade coming alive with creechies, pouring in, pouring over, pushing, swarming, thousands of them. It was like an army of rats Davidson had seen once when he was a little kid, in the last Famine, in the streets of Cleveland, Ohio, where he grew up. Something had driven the rats out of their holes and they had come up in daylight, seething up over the wall, a pulsing blanket of fur and eyes and little hands and teeth, and he had yelled for his mom and run like crazy, or was that only a dream he'd had when he was a kid? It was important to keep cool. The hopper was parked in the creechie-pen; it was still dark over on that side and he got there at once. The gate was locked, he always kept it locked in case one of the weak sisters got a notion of flying off to Papa Ding Dong some dark night. It seemed to take a long time to get the key out and fit it in the lock and turn it right, but it was just a matter of keeping cool, and then it took a long time to sprint to the hopper and unlock it. Post and Aabi were with him now. At last came the huge rattle of the rotors, beating eggs, covering up all the weird noises, the high voices yelling and screeching and singing. Up they went, and hell dropped away below them: a pen full of rats, burning.

"It takes a cool head to size up an emergency situation quickly," Davidson said. "You men thought fast and acted fast. Good work. Where's Temba?"

"Got a spear in his belly," Post said.

Aabi, the pilot, seemed to want to fly the hopper, so Davidson let him. He clambered into one of the rear seats and sat back, letting his muscles relax. The forest flowed beneath them, black under black.

"Where you heading, Aabi?"

"Central."

"No. We don't want to go to Central."

"Where do we want to go to?" Aabi said with a kind of womanish giggle. "New York? Peking?"

"Just keep her up a while, Aabi, and circle camp. Big circles. Out of earshot."

"Captain, there isn't any Java Camp any more by now," said Post, a logging-crew foreman, a stocky, steady man.

"When the creechies are through burning the camp, we'll come in and burn creechies. There must be four thousand of them all in one place there. There's six flamethrowers in the back of this helicopter. Let's give 'em about twenty minutes. Start with the jelly bombs and then catch the ones that run with the flamethrowers."

"Christ," Aabi said violently, "some of our guys might be there, the creechies might take prisoners, we don't know. I'm not going back there and burn up humans, maybe." He had not turned the hopper.

Davidson put the nose of his revolver against the back of Aabi's skull and said, "Yes, we're going back; so pull yourself together, baby, and don't give me a lot of trouble."

"There's enough fuel in the tank to get us to Central, Captain," the pilot said. He kept trying to duck his head away from the touch of the gun, like it was a fly bothering him. "But that's all. That's all we got."

"Then we'll get a lot of mileage out of it. Turn her, Aabi."

"I think we better go on to Central, Captain," Post said in his stolid voice, and this ganging up against him enraged Davidson so much that reversing the gun in his hand he struck out fast as a snake and clipped Post over the ear with the gun-butt. The logger just folded over like a Christmas card, and sat there in the front seat with his head between his knees and his hands hanging to the floor. "Turn her, Aabi," Davidson said, the whiplash in his voice. The helicopter swung around in a wide arc. "Hell, where's camp, I never had this hopper up at night without any signal to follow," Aabi said, sounding dull and snuffly like he had a cold.

"Go east and look for the fire," Davidson said, cold and quiet. None of them had any real stamina, not even Temba. None of them had stood by him when the going got really tough. Sooner or later they all joined up against him, because they just couldn't take it the way he could. The weak conspire against the strong, the strong man has to stand alone and look out for himself. It just happened to be the way things are. Where was the camp?

They should have been able to see the burning buildings for miles in this blank dark, even in the rain. Nothing showed. Grey-black sky, black ground. The fires must have gone out. Been put out. Could the humans have driven off the creechies? After he'd escaped? The thought went like a spray of icewater through his mind. No, of course not, not fifty against thousands. But by God there must be a lot of pieces of blown-up creechie lying around on the minefields, anyway. It was just that they'd come so damned thick. Nothing could have stopped them. He couldn't have planned for that. Where had they come from? There hadn't been any creechies in the forest anywhere around for days and days. They must have poured in from somewhere, from all directions, sneaking along in the woods, coming up out of their holes like rats. There wasn't any way to stop thousands and thousands of them like that. Where the hell was camp? Aabi was tricking, faking course. "Find the camp, Aabi," he said softly.

"For Christ's sake I'm trying to," the boy said.

Post never moved, folded over there by the pilot.

"It couldn't just disappear, could it, Aabi. You got seven minutes to find it."

"Find it yourself," Aabi said, shrill and sullen.

"Not till you and Post get in line, baby. Take her down lower."

After a minute Aabi said, "That looks like the river."

There was a river, and a big clearing; but where was Java

Camp? It didn't show up as they flew north over the clearing. "This must be it, there isn't any other big clearing is there," Aabi said, coming back over the treeless area. Their landing-lights glared but you couldn't see anything outside the tunnels of the lights; it would be better to have them off. Davidson reached over the pilot's shoulder and switched the lights off. Blank wet dark was like black towels slapped on their eyes. "For Christ's sake!" Aabi screamed, and flipping the lights back on slewed the hopper left and up, but not fast enough. Trees leaned hugely out of the night and caught the machine.

The vanes screamed, hurling leaves and twigs in a cyclone through the bright lanes of the lights, but the boles of the trees were very old and strong. The little winged machine plunged, seemed to lurch and tear itself free, and went down sideways into the trees. The lights went out. The noise stopped.

"I don't feel so good," Davidson said. He said it again. Then he stopped saying it, for there was nobody to say it to. Then he realised he hadn't said it anyway. He felt groggy. Must have hit his head. Aabi wasn't there. Where was he? This was the hop-per. It was all slewed around, but he was still in his seat. It was so dark, like being blind. He felt around, and so found Post, inert, still doubled up, crammed in between the front seat and the control panel. The hopper trembled whenever Davidson moved, and he figured out at last that it wasn't on the ground but wedged in between trees, stuck like a kite. His head was feeling better, and he wanted more and more to get out of the black, tilted-over cabin. He squirmed over into the pilot's seat and got his legs out, hung by his hands, and could not feel ground, only branches scraping his dangling legs. Finally he let go, not knowing how far he'd fall, but he had to get out of that cabin. It was only a few feet down. It jolted his head, but he felt better standing up. If only it wasn't so dark, so black. He had a torch in his belt, he always carried one at night around camp. But it wasn't there. That was funny. It must have fallen out. He'd better get back into the hopper and get it. Maybe Aabi had taken it. Aabi had intentionally crashed the hopper, taken Davidson's torch, and made a break for it. The slimy lit-tle bastard, he was like all the rest of them. The air was black and full of moisture, and you couldn't tell where to put your feet, it was all roots and bushes and tangles. There were noises all around, water dripping, rustling, tiny noises, little things sneaking around in the darkness. He'd better get back up into the hopper, get his torch. But he couldn't see how to climb back up. The bottom edge of the doorway was just out of reach of his fingers.

There was a light, a faint gleam seen and gone away off in the trees. Aabi had taken the torch and gone off to reconnoiter, get orientated, smart boy. "Aabi!" he called in a piercing whisper. He stepped on something queer while he was trying to see the light among the trees again. He kicked at it with his boots, then put a hand down on it, cautiously, for it wasn't wise to go feeling things you couldn't see. A lot of wet stuff, slick, like a dead rat. He withdrew his hand quickly. He felt in another place after a while; it was a boot under his hand, he could feel the crossings of the laces. It must be Aabi lying there right under his feet. He'd got thrown out of the hopper when it came down. Well, he'd deserved it with his Judas trick, trying to run off to Central. Davidson did not like the wet feel of the unseen clothes and hair. He straightened up. There was the light again, black-barred by near and distant tree-trunks, a distant glow that moved.

Davidson put his hand to his holster. The revolver was not in it.

He'd had it in his hand, in case Post or Aabi acted up. It was not in his hand. It must be up in the helicopter with his torch.

He stood crouching, immobile; then abruptly began to run. He could not see where he was going. Tree-trunks jolted him from side to side as he knocked into them, and roots tripped up his feet. He fell full length, crashing down among bushes. Getting to hands and knees he tried to hide. Bare, wet twigs dragged and scraped over his face. He squirmed farther into the bushes. His brain was entirely occupied by the complex smells of rot and growth, dead leaves, decay, new shoots, fronds, flowers, the smells of night and spring and rain. The light shone full on him. He saw the creechies.

He remembered what they did when cornered, and what Lyubov had said about it. He turned over on his back and lay with his head tipped back, his eyes shut. His heart stuttered in his chest.

Nothing happened.

It was hard to open his eyes, but finally he managed to. They just stood there: a lot of them, ten or twenty. They carried those spears they had for hunting, little toy-looking things but the iron blades were sharp, they could cut right through your guts. He shut his eyes and just kept lying there.

And nothing happened.

His heart quieted down, and it seemed like he could think better. Something stirred down inside him, something almost like laughter. By God they couldn't get him down! If his own men betrayed him, and human intelligence couldn't do any more for him, then he used their own trick against them— played dead like this, and triggered this instinct reflex that kept them from killing anybody who took that position. They just stood around him, muttering at each other. *They couldn't hurt him.* It was as if he was a god.

"Davidson."

He had to open his eyes again. The resin-flare carried by one of the creechies still burned, but it had grown pale, and the forest was dim grey now, not pitch-black. How had that happened? Only five or ten minutes had gone by. It was still hard to see but it wasn't night any more. He could see the leaves and branches, the forest. He could see the face looking down at him. It had no color in this toneless twilight of dawn. The scarred features looked like a man's. The eyes were like dark holes.

"Let me get up," Davidson said suddenly in a loud, hoarse voice. He was shaking with cold from lying on the wet ground. He could not lie there with Selver looking down at him.

Selver was emptyhanded, but a lot of the little devils around him had not only spears but revolvers. Stolen from his stockpile at camp. He struggled to his feet. His clothes clung icy to his shoulders and the backs of his legs, and he could not stop shaking.

"Get it over with," he said. "Hurry-up-quick!"

Selver just looked at him. At least now he had to look up, way up, to meet Davidson's eyes.

"Do you wish me to kill you now?" he inquired. He had learned that way of talking from Lyubov, of course; even his voice, it could have been Lyubov talking. It was uncanny.

"It's my choice, is it?"

"Well, you have lain all night in the way that means you wished us to let you live; now do you want to die?"

The pain in his head and stomach, and his hatred for this horrible little freak that talked like Lyubov and that had got him at its mercy, the pain and the hatred combined and set his belly churning, so he retched and was nearly sick. He shook with cold and nausea. He tried to hold on to courage. He suddenly stepped forward a pace and spat in Selver's face.

There was a little pause, and then Selver, with a kind of dancing movement, spat back. And laughed. And made no move to kill Davidson. Davidson wiped the cold spittle off his lips.

"Look, Captain Davidson," the creechie said in that quiet little voice that made Davidson go dizzy and sick, "we're both gods, you and I. You're an insane one, and I'm not sure whether I'm sane or not. But we are gods. There will never be another meeting in the forest like this meeting now between us. We bring each other such gifts as gods bring. You gave me a gift, the killing of one's kind, murder. Now, as well as I can, I give you my people's gift, which is not killing. I think we each find each other's gift heavy to carry. However, you must carry it alone. Your people at Eshsen tell me that if I bring you there, they have to make a judgment on you and kill you, it's their law to do so. So, wishing to give you life, I can't take you with the other prisoners to Eshsen; and I can't leave you to wander in the forest, for you do too much harm. So you'll be treated like one of us when we go mad. You'll be taken to Rendlep where nobody lives any more, and left there."

Davidson stared at the creechie, could not take his eyes off it. It was as if it had some hypnotic power over him. He couldn't stand this. Nobody had any power over him. Nobody could hurt him. "I should have broken your neck right away, that day you tried to jump me," he said, his voice still hoarse and thick.

"It might have been best," Selver answered. "But Lyubov prevented you. As he now prevents me from killing you. —All the killing is done now. And the cutting of trees. There aren't trees to cut on Rendlep. That's the place you call Dump Island. Your people left no trees there, so you can't make a boat and sail from it. Nothing much grows there any more, so we shall have to bring you food and wood to burn. There's nothing to kill on Rendlep. No trees, no people. There were trees and people, but now there are only the dreams of them. It seems to me a fitting place for you to live, since you must live. You might learn how to dream there, but more likely you will follow your madness through to its proper end, at last."

"Kill me now and quit your damned gloating."

"Kill you?" Selver said, and his eyes looking up at Davidson seemed to shine, very clear and terrible, in the twilight of the forest. "I can't kill you, Davidson. You're a god. You must do it yourself."

He turned and walked away, light and quick, vanishing among the grey trees within a few steps.

A noose slipped over Davidson's head and tightened a little on his throat. Small spears approached his back and sides. They did not try to hurt him. He could run away, make a break for it, they didn't dare kill him. The blades were polished, leaf-shaped, sharp as razors. The noose tugged gently at his neck. He followed where they led him.

8

Selver had not seen Lyubov for a long time. That dream had gone with him to Rieshwel. It had been with him when he spoke the last time to Davidson. Then it had gone, and perhaps it slept now in the grave of Lyubov's death at Eshsen, for it never came to Selver in the town of Broter where he now lived.

But when the great ship returned, and he went to Eshsen, Lyubov met him there. He was silent and tenuous, very sad, so that the old carking grief awoke in Selver.

Lyubov stayed with him, a shadow in the mind, even when he met the yumens from the ship. These were people of power; they were very different from all yumens he had known, except his friend, but they were much stronger men than Lyubov had been.

His yumen speech had gone rusty, and at first he mostly let them talk. When he was fairly certain what kind of people they were, he brought forward the heavy box he had carried from Broter. "Inside this there is Lyubov's work," he said, groping for the words. "He knew more about us than the others do.

He learned my language and the Men's Tongue; we wrote all that down. He understood somewhat how we live and dream. The others do not. I'll give you the work, if you'll take it to the place he wished."

The tall, white-skinned one, Lepennon, looked happy, and thanked Selver, telling him that the papers would indeed be taken where Lyubov wished, and would be highly valued. That pleased Selver. But it had been painful to him to speak his friend's name aloud, for Lyubov's face was still bitterly sad when he turned to it in his mind. He withdrew a little from the yumens, and watched them. Dongh and Gosse and others of Eshsen were there along with the five from the ship. The new ones looked clean and polished as new iron. The old ones had let the hair grow on their faces, so that they looked a little like huge, black-furred Athsheans. They still wore clothes, but the clothes were old and not kept clean. They were not thin, except for the Old Man, who had been ill ever since the Night of Eshsen; but they all looked a little like men who are lost or mad.

This meeting was at the edge of the forest, in that zone where by tacit agreement neither the forest people nor the yumens had built dwellings or camped for these past years. Selver and his companions settled down in the shade of a big ash-tree that stood out away from the forest eaves. Its berries were only small green knots against the twigs as yet, its leaves were long and soft, labile, summer-green. The light beneath the great tree was soft, complex with shadows.

The yumens consulted and came and went, and at last one came over to the ash-tree. It was the hard one from the ship, the Commander. He squatted down on his heels near Selver, not asking permission but not with any evident intention of rudeness. He said, "Can we talk a little?"

"Certainly."

"You know that we'll be taking all the Terrans away with us. We brought a second ship with us to carry them. Your world will no longer be used as a colony."

"This was the message I heard at Broter, when you came three days ago."

"I wanted to be sure that you understand that this is a permanent arrangement. We're not coming back. Your world has been placed under the League Ban. What that means in your terms is this: I can promise you that no one will come here to cut the trees or take your lands, so long as the League lasts."

"None of you will ever come back," Selver said, statement or question.

"Not for five generations. None. Then perhaps a few men, ten or twenty, no more than twenty, might come to talk to your people, and study your world, as some of the men here were doing."

"The scientists, the Speshes," Selver said. He brooded. "You decide matters all at once, your people," he said, again between statement and question.

"How do you mean?" The Commander looked wary.

"Well, you say that none of you shall cut the trees of Athshe: and all of you stop. And yet you live in many places. Now if a headwoman in Karach gave an order, it would not be obeyed by the people of the next village, and surely not by all the people in the world at once. . . ."

"No, because you haven't one government over all. But we do—now—and I assure you its orders are obeyed. By all of us at once. But, as a matter of fact, it seems to me from the story we've been told by the colonists here, that when *you* gave an order, Selver, it was obeyed by everybody on every island here at once. How did you manage that?"

"At that time I was a god," Selver said, expressionless.

After the Commander had left him, the long white one came sauntering over and asked if he might sit down in the shade of the tree. He had tact, this one, and was extremely clever. Selver was uneasy with him. Like Lyubov, this one would be gentle; he would understand, and yet would himself be utterly beyond understanding. For the kindest of them was as far out of touch, as unreachable, as the cruellest. That was why the presence of Lyubov in his mind remained painful to him, while the dreams in which he saw and touched his dead wife Thele were precious and full of peace.

"When I was here before," Lepennon said, "I met this man, Raj Lyubov. I had very little chance to speak with him, but I remember what he said; and I've had time to read some of his studies of your people, since. His work, as you say. It's largely because of that work of his that Athshe is now free of the

Terran Colony. This freedom had become the direction of Lyubov's life, I think. You, being his friend, will see that his death did not stop him from arriving at his goal, from finishing his journey."

Selver sat still. Uneasiness turned to fear in his mind. This one spoke like a Great Dreamer.

He made no response at all.

"Will you tell me one thing, Selver. If the question doesn't offend you. There will be no more questions after it. . . . There were the killings: at Smith Camp, then at this place, Eshsen, then finally at New Java Camp where Davidson led the rebel group. That was all. No more since then. . . . Is that true? Have there been no more killings?"

"I did not kill Davidson."

"That does not matter," Lepennon said, misunderstanding; Selver meant that Davidson was not dead, but Lepennon took him to mean that someone else had killed Davidson. Relieved to see that the yumen could err, Selver did not correct him.

"There has been no more killing, then?"

"None. They will tell you," Selver said, nodding towards the Colonel and Gosse.

"Among your own people, I mean. Athsheans killing Athsheans."

Selver was silent.

He looked up at Lepennon, at the strange face, white as the mask of the Ash Spirit, that changed as it met his gaze.

"Sometimes a god comes," Selver said. "He brings a new way to do a thing, or a new thing to be done. A new kind of singing, or a new kind of death. He brings this across the bridge between the dream-time and the world-time. When he has done this, it is done. You cannot take things that exist in the world and try to drive them back into the dream, to hold them inside the dream with walls and pretenses. That is insanity. What is, is. There is no use pretending, now, that we do not know how to kill one another."

Lepennon laid his long hand on Selver's hand, so quickly and gently that Selver accepted the touch as if the hand were not a stranger's. The green-gold shadows of the ash leaves flickered over them.

"But you must not pretend to have reasons to kill one

another. Murder has no reason," Lepennon said, his face as anxious and sad as Lyubov's face. "We shall go. Within two days we shall be gone. All of us. Forever. Then the forests of Athshe will be as they were before."

Lyubov came out of the shadows of Selver's mind and said, "I shall be here."

"Lyubov will be here," Selver said. "And Davidson will be here. Both of them. Maybe after I die people will be as they were before I was born, and before you came. But I do not think they will."

STORIES

The Shobies' Story

THEY MET at Ve Port more than a month before their first flight together, and there, calling themselves after their ship as most crews did, became the Shobies. Their first consensual decision was to spend their isyeye in the coastal village of Liden, on Hain, where the negative ions could do their thing.

Liden was a fishing port with an eighty-thousand-year history and a population of four hundred. Its fisherfolk farmed the rich shoal waters of their bay, shipped the catch inland to the cities, and managed the Liden Resort for vacationers and tourists and new space crews on isyeye (the word is Hainish and means "making a beginning together," or "beginning to be together," or, used technically, "the period of time and area of space in which a group forms if it is going to form." A honeymoon is an isyeye of two). The fisherwomen and fishermen of Liden were as weathered as driftwood and about as talkative. Six-year-old Asten, who had misunderstood slightly, asked one of them if they were all eighty thousand years old. "Nope," she said.

Like most crews, the Shobies used Hainish as their common language. So the name of the one Hainish crew member, Sweet Today, carried its meaning as words as well as name, and at first seemed a silly thing to call a big, tall, heavy woman in her late fifties, imposing of carriage and almost as taciturn as the villagers. But her reserve proved to be a deep well of congeniality and tact, to be called upon as needed, and her name soon began to sound quite right. She had family—all Hainish have family—kinfolk of all denominations, grandchildren and cross-cousins, affines and cosines, scattered all over the Ekumen, but no relatives in this crew. She asked to be Grandmother to Rig, Asten, and Betton, and was accepted.

The only Shoby older than Sweet Today was the Terran Lidi, who was seventy-two EYs and not interested in grandmothering. Lidi had been navigating for fifty years, and there was nothing she didn't know about NAFAL ships, although occasionally she forgot that their ship was the *Shoby* and called

it the *Soso* or the *Alterra*. And there were things she didn't
know, none of them knew, about the *Shoby*.

They talked, as human beings do, about what they didn't
know.

Churten theory was the main topic of conversation, evenings
at the driftwood fire on the beach after dinner. The adults had
read whatever there was to read about it, of course, before they
ever volunteered for the test mission. Gveter had more recent
information and presumably a better understanding of it than
the others, but it had to be pried out of him. Only twenty-five,
the only Cetian in the crew, much hairier than the others, and
not gifted in language, he spent a lot of time on the defensive.
Assuming that as an Anarresti he was more proficient at mutual
aid and more adept at cooperation than the others, he lectured
them about their propertarian habits; but he held tight to his
knowledge, because he needed the advantage it gave him. For a
while he would speak only in negatives: don't call it the churten
"drive," it isn't a drive, don't call it the churten "effect," it isn't
an effect. What is it, then? A long lecture ensued, beginning
with the rebirth of Cetian physics since the revision of Shevekian
temporalism by the Intervalists, and ending with the general
conceptual framework of the churten. Everyone listened very
carefully, and finally Sweet Today spoke, carefully. "So the ship
will be moved," she said, "by ideas?"

"No, no, no, no," said Gveter. But he hesitated for the next
word so long that Karth asked a question: "Well, you haven't
actually talked about any physical, material events or effects at
all." The question was characteristically indirect. Karth and
Oreth, the Gethenians who with their two children were the
affective focus of the crew, the "hearth" of it, in their terms,
came from a not very theoretically minded subculture, and
knew it. Gveter could run rings round them with his Cetian
physico-philosophico-techno-natter. He did so at once. His
accent did not make his explanations any clearer. He went on
about coherence and meta-intervals, and at last demanded,
with gestures of despair, "Khow can I say it in Khainish? No! It
is not physical, it is not not physical, these are the categories
our minds must discard entirely, this is the khole point!"

"Buth-buth-buth-buth-buth-buth," went Asten, softly, passing behind the half circle of adults at the driftwood fire on the

wide, twilit beach. Rig followed, also going, "Buth-buth-buth-buth," but louder. They were being spaceships, to judge from their maneuvers around a dune and their communications— "Locked in orbit, Navigator!" —But the noise they were imitating was the noise of the little fishing boats of Liden putt-putting out to sea.

"I crashed!" Rig shouted, flailing in the sand. "Help! Help! I crashed!"

"Hold on, Ship Two!" Asten cried. "I'll rescue you! Don't breathe! Oh, oh, trouble with the Churten Drive! Buth-buth-ack! Ack! Brrrrmmm-ack-ack-ack-rrrrrmmmmm, buth-buth-buth-buth. . . ."

They were six and four EYs old. Tai's son Betton, who was eleven, sat at the driftwood fire with the adults, though at the moment he was watching Rig and Asten as if he wouldn't mind taking off to help rescue Ship Two. The little Gethenians had spent more time on ships than on planet, and Asten liked to boast about being "actually fifty-eight," but this was Betton's first crew, and his only NAFAL flight had been from Terra to Hain. He and his biomother, Tai, had lived in a reclamation commune on Terra. When she had drawn the lot for Ekumenical service, and requested training for ship duty, he had asked her to bring him as family. She had agreed; but after training, when she volunteered for this test flight, she had tried to get Betton to withdraw, to stay in training or go home. He had refused. Shan, who had trained with them, told the others this, because the tension between the mother and son had to be understood to be used effectively in group formation. Betton had requested to come, and Tai had given in, but plainly not with an undivided will. Her relationship to the boy was cool and mannered. Shan offered him fatherly-brotherly warmth, but Betton accepted it sparingly, coolly, and sought no formal crew relation with him or anyone.

Ship Two was being rescued, and attention returned to the discussion. "All right," said Lidi. "We know that anything that goes faster than light, any *thing* that goes faster than light, by so doing transcends the material/immaterial category—that's how we got the ansible, by distinguishing the message from the medium. But if we, the crew, are going to travel as messages, I want to understand *how*."

Gveter tore his hair. There was plenty to tear. It grew fine and thick, a mane on his head, a pelt on his limbs and body, a silvery nimbus on his hands and face. The fuzz on his feet was, at the moment, full of sand. "Khow!" he cried. "I'm trying to tell you khow! Message, information, no no no, that's old, that's ansible technology. This is transilience! Because the field is to be conceived as the virtual field, in which the unreal interval becomes virtually effective through the mediary coherence —don't you see?"

"No," Lidi said. "What do you mean by mediary?"

After several more bonfires on the beach, the consensus opinion was that churten theory was accessible only to minds very highly trained in Cetian temporal physics. There was a less freely voiced conviction that the engineers who had built the *Shoby*'s churten apparatus did not entirely understand how it worked. Or, more precisely, what it did when it worked. That it worked was certain. The *Shoby* was the fourth ship it had been tested with, using robot crew; so far sixty-two instantaneous trips, or transiliences, had been effected between points from four hundred kilometers to twenty-seven light-years apart, with stopovers of varying lengths. Gveter and Lidi steadfastly maintained that this proved that the engineers knew perfectly well what they were doing, and that for the rest of them the seeming difficulty of the theory was only the difficulty human minds had in grasping a genuinely new concept.

"Like the circulation of the blood," said Tai. "People went around with their hearts beating for a long time before they understood why." She did not look satisfied with her own analogy, and when Shan said, "The heart has its reasons, which reason does not know," she looked offended. "Mysticism," she said, in the tone of voice of one warning a companion about dog-shit on the path.

"Surely there's nothing *beyond* understanding in this process," Oreth said, somewhat tentatively. "Nothing that can't be understood, and reproduced."

"And quantified," Gveter said stoutly.

"But, even if people understand the process, nobody knows the human response to it—the *experience* of it. Right? So we are to report on that."

"Why shouldn't it be just like NAFAL flight, only even faster?" Betton asked.

"Because it is totally different," said Gveter.

"What could happen to us?"

Some of the adults had discussed possibilities, all of them had considered them; Karth and Oreth had talked it over in appropriate terms with their children; but evidently Betton had not been included in such discussions.

"We don't know," Tai said sharply. "I told you that at the start, Betton."

"Most likely it will be like NAFAL flight," said Shan, "but the first people who flew NAFAL didn't know what it would be like, and had to find out the physical and psychic effects—"

"The worst thing," said Sweet Today in her slow, comfortable voice, "would be that we would die. Other living beings have been on some of the test flights. Crickets. And intelligent ritual animals on the last two *Shoby* tests. They were all right." It was a very long statement for Sweet Today, and carried proportional weight.

"We are almost certain," said Gveter, "that no temporal rearrangement is involved in churten, as it is in NAFAL. And mass is involved only in terms of needing a certain core mass, just as for ansible transmission, but not in itself. So maybe even a pregnant person could be a transilient."

"They can't go on ships," Asten said. "The unborn dies if they do."

Asten was half lying across Oreth's lap; Rig, thumb in mouth, was asleep on Karth's lap.

"When we were Oneblins," Asten went on, sitting up, "there were ritual animals with our crew. Some fish and some Terran cats and a whole lot of Hainish gholes. We got to play with them. And we helped thank the ghole that they tested for lithovirus. But it didn't die. It bit Shapi. The cats slept with us. But one of them went into kemmer and got pregnant, and then the *Oneblin* had to go to Hain, and she had to have an abortion, or all her unborns would have died inside her and killed her too. Nobody knew a ritual for her, to explain to her. But I fed her some extra food. And Rig cried."

"Other people I know cried too," Karth said, stroking the child's hair.

"You tell good stories, Asten," Sweet Today observed.

"So we're sort of ritual humans," said Betton.

"Volunteers," Tai said.

"Experimenters," said Lidi.

"Experiencers," said Shan.

"Explorers," Oreth said.

"Gamblers," said Karth.

The boy looked from one face to the next.

"You know," Shan said, "back in the time of the League, early in NAFAL flight, they were sending out ships to really distant systems—trying to explore everything—crews that wouldn't come back for centuries. Maybe some of them are still out there. But some of them came back after four, five, six hundred years, and they were all mad. Crazy!" He paused dramatically. "But they were all crazy when they started. Unstable people. They had to be crazy to volunteer for a time dilation like that. What a way to pick a crew, eh?" He laughed.

"Are we stable?" said Oreth. "I like instability. I like this job. I like the risk, taking the risk together. High stakes! That's the edge of it, the sweetness of it."

Karth looked down at their children, and smiled.

"Yes. Together," Gveter said. "You aren't crazy. You are good. I love you. We are ammari."

"Ammar," the others said to him, confirming this unexpected declaration. The young man scowled with pleasure, jumped up, and pulled off his shirt. "I want to swim. Come on, Betton. Come on swimming!" he said, and ran off towards the dark, vast waters that moved softly beyond the ruddy haze of their fire. The boy hesitated, then shed his shirt and sandals and followed. Shan pulled up Tai, and they followed; and finally the two old women went off into the night and the breakers, rolling up their pants legs, laughing at themselves.

To Gethenians, even on a warm summer night on a warm summer world, the sea is no friend. The fire is where you stay. Oreth and Asten moved closer to Karth and watched the flames, listening to the faint voices out in the glimmering surf, now and then talking quietly in their own tongue, while the little sisterbrother slept on.

After thirty lazy days at Liden the Shobies caught the fish train inland to the city, where a Fleet lander picked them up at the train station and took them to the spaceport on Ve, the next planet out from Hain. They were rested, tanned, bonded, and ready to go.

One of Sweet Today's hemi-affiliate cousins once removed was on ansible duty in Ve Port. She urged the Shobies to ask the inventors of the churten on Urras and Anarres any questions they had about churten operation. "The purpose of the experimental flight is understanding," she insisted, "and your full intellectual participation is essential. They've been very anxious about that."

Lidi snorted.

"Now for the ritual," said Shan, as they went to the ansible room in the sunward bubble. "They'll explain to the animals what they're going to do and why, and ask them to help."

"The animals don't understand that," Betton said in his cold, angelic treble. "It's just to make the humans feel better."

"The humans understand?" Sweet Today asked.

"We all use each other," Oreth said. "The ritual says: we have no right to do so; therefore, we accept the responsibility for the suffering we cause."

Betton listened and brooded.

Gveter addressed the ansible first and talked to it for half an hour, mostly in Pravic and mathematics. Finally, apologizing, and looking a little unnerved, he invited the others to use the instrument. There was a pause. Lidi activated it, introduced herself, and said, "We have agreed that none of us, except Gveter, has the theoretical background to grasp the principles of the churten."

A scientist twenty-two light-years away responded in Hainish via the rather flat auto-translator voice, but with unmistakable hopefulness, "The churten, in lay terms, may be seen as displacing the virtual field in order to realize relational coherence in terms of the transiliential experientiality."

"Quite," said Lidi.

"As you know, the material effects have been nil, and negative effect on low-intelligence sentients also nil; but there is considered to be a possibility that the participation of high intelligence in the process might affect the displacement in one way or another. And that such displacement would reciprocally affect the participant."

"What has the level of our intelligence got to do with how the churten functions?" Tai asked.

A pause. Their interlocutor was trying to find the words, to accept the responsibility.

"We have been using 'intelligence' as shorthand for the psychic complexity and cultural dependence of our species," said the translator voice at last. "The presence of the transilient as conscious mind nonduring transilience is the untested factor."

"But if the process is instantaneous, how can we be conscious of it?" Oreth asked.

"Precisely," said the ansible, and after another pause continued: "As the experimenter is an element of the experiment, so we assume that the transilient may be an element or agent of transilience. This is why we asked for a crew to test the process, rather than one or two volunteers. The psychic interbalance of a bonded social group is a margin of strength against disintegrative or incomprehensible experience, if any such occurs. Also, the separate observations of the group members will mutually interverify."

"Who programs this translator?" Shan snarled in a whisper. "Interverify! Shit!"

Lidi looked around at the others, inviting questions.

"How long will the trip actually take?" Betton asked.

"No long," the translator voice said, then self-corrected: "No time."

Another pause.

"Thank you," said Sweet Today, and the scientist on a planet twenty-two years of time-dilated travel from Ve Port answered, "We are grateful for your generous courage, and our hope is with you."

They went directly from the ansible room to the *Shoby*.

The churten equipment, which was not very space-consuming and the controls of which consisted essentially of an on-off switch, had been installed alongside the Nearly As Fast As Light motivators and controls of an ordinary interstellar ship of the Ekumenical Fleet. The *Shoby* had been built on Hain about four hundred years ago, and was thirty-two years old. Most of its early runs had been exploratory, with a Hainish-Chiffewarian crew. Since in such runs a ship might spend years in orbit in a planetary system, the Hainish and Chiffewarians, feeling that it might as well be lived in rather than endured, had arranged and furnished it like a very large, very comfortable house. Three of its residential modules had been disconnected and left in the hangars on Ve, and still there was more than enough room for a crew of only ten. Tai, Betton, and Shan, new from Terra, and Gveter from Anarres, accustomed to the barracks and the communal austerities of their marginally habitable worlds, stalked about the *Shoby*, disapproving it. "Excremental," Gveter growled. "Luxury!" Tai sneered. Sweet Today, Lidi, and the Gethenians, more used to the amenities of shipboard life, settled right in and made themselves at home. And Gveter and the younger Terrans found it hard to maintain ethical discomfort in the spacious, high-ceilinged, well-furnished, slightly shabby living rooms and bedrooms, studies, high- and low-G gyms, the dining room, library, kitchen, and bridge of the *Shoby*. The carpet in the bridge was a genuine Henyekaulil, soft deep blues and purples woven in the patterns of the constellations of the Hainish sky. There was a large, healthy plantation of Terran bamboo in the meditation gym, part of the ship's self-contained vegetal/respiratory system. The windows of any room could be programmed by the homesick to a view of Abbenay or New Cairo or the beach at Liden, or cleared to look out on the suns nearer and farther and the darkness between the suns.

Rig and Asten discovered that as well as the elevators there was a stately staircase with a curving banister, leading from the reception hall up to the library. They slid down the banister shrieking wildly, until Shan threatened to apply a local gravity field and force them to slide up it, which they besought him to do. Betton watched the little ones with a superior gaze, and took the elevator; but the next day he slid down the banister, going a good deal faster than Rig and Asten because he could push off harder and had greater mass, and nearly broke his tailbone. It was Betton who organized the tray-sliding races, but Rig generally won them, being small enough to stay on the tray all the way down the stairs. None of the children had had any lessons at the beach, except in swimming and being Shobies; but while they waited through an unexpected five-day delay at Ve Port, Gveter did physics with Betton and math with all three daily in the library, and they did some history with Shan and Oreth, and danced with Tai in the low-G gym.

When she danced, Tai became light, free, laughing. Rig and Asten loved her then, and her son danced with her like a colt, like a kid, awkward and blissful. Shan often joined them; he was a dark and elegant dancer, and she would dance with him, but even then was shy, would not touch. She had been celibate since Betton's birth. She did not want Shan's patient, urgent desire, did not want to cope with it, with him. She would turn from him to Betton, and son and mother would dance wholly absorbed in the steps, the airy pattern they made together. Watching them, the afternoon before the test flight, Sweet Today began to wipe tears from her eyes, smiling, never saying a word.

"Life is good," said Gveter very seriously to Lidi.

"It'll do," she said.

Oreth, who was just coming out of female kemmer, having thus triggered Karth's male kemmer, all of which, by coming on unexpectedly early, had delayed the test flight for these past five days, enjoyable days for all—Oreth watched Rig, whom she had fathered, dance with Asten, whom she had borne, and watched Karth watch them, and said in Karhidish, "Tomorrow . . ." The edge was very sweet.

Anthropologists solemnly agree that we must not attribute "cultural constants" to the human population of any planet; but certain cultural traits or expectations do seem to run deep. Before dinner that last night in port, Shan and Tai appeared in black-and-silver uniforms of the Terran Ekumen, which had cost them—Terra also still had a money economy—a half-year's allowance.

Asten and Rig clamored at once for equal grandeur. Karth and Oreth suggested their party clothes, and Sweet Today brought out silver lace scarves, but Asten sulked, and Rig imitated. The idea of a *uniform*, Asten told them, was that it was the *same*.

"Why?" Oreth inquired.

Old Lidi answered sharply: "So that no one is responsible."

She then went off and changed into a black velvet evening suit that wasn't a uniform but that didn't leave Tai and Shan sticking out like sore thumbs. She had left Terra at age eighteen and never been back nor wanted to, but Tai and Shan were shipmates.

Karth and Oreth got the idea and put on their finest fur-trimmed hiebs, and the children were appeased with their own party clothes plus all of Karth's hereditary and massive gold jewelry. Sweet Today appeared in a pure white robe which she claimed was in fact ultraviolet. Gveter braided his mane. Betton had no uniform, but needed none, sitting beside his mother at table in a visible glory of pride.

Meals, sent up from the Port kitchens, were very good, and this one was superb: a delicate Hainish iyanwi with all seven sauces, followed by a pudding flavored with Terran chocolate. A lively evening ended quietly at the big fireplace in the library. The logs were fake, of course, but good fakes; no use having a fireplace on a ship and then burning plastic in it. The neocellulose logs and kindling smelled right, resisted catching, caught with spits and sparks and smoke billows, flared up bright. Oreth had laid the fire, Karth lit it. Everybody gathered round.

"Tell bedtime stories," Rig said.

Oreth told about the Ice Caves of Kerm Land, how a ship sailed into the great blue sea-cave and disappeared and was never found by the boats that entered the caves in search; but seventy years later that ship was found drifting—not a living soul aboard nor any sign of what had become of them—off the coast of Osemyet, a thousand miles overland from Kerm. . . .

Another story?

Lidi told about the little desert wolf who lost his wife and went to the land of the dead for her, and found her there dancing with the dead, and nearly brought her back to the land of the living, but spoiled it by trying to touch her before they got all the way back to life, and she vanished, and he could never find the way back to the place where the dead danced, no matter how he looked, and howled, and cried. . . .

Another story!

Shan told about the boy who sprouted a feather every time he told a lie, until his commune had to use him for a duster.

Another!

Gveter told about the winged people called gluns, who were so stupid that they died out because they kept hitting each other head-on in midair. "They weren't real," he added conscientiously. "Only a story."

Another— No. Bedtime now.

Rig and Asten went round as usual for a good-night hug, and this time Betton followed them. When he came to Tai he did not stop, for she did not like to be touched; but she put out her hand, drew the child to her, and kissed his cheek. He fled in joy.

"Stories," said Sweet Today. "Ours begins tomorrow, eh?"

A chain of command is easy to describe; a network of response isn't. To those who live by mutual empowerment, "thick" description, complex and open-ended, is normal and comprehensible, but to those whose only model is hierarchic control, such description seems a muddle, a mess, along with what it describes. Who's in charge here? Get rid of all these petty details. How many cooks spoil a soup? Let's get this perfectly clear now. Take me to your leader!

The old navigator was at the NAFAL console, of course, and Gveter at the paltry churten console; Oreth was wired into the AI; Tai, Shan, and Karth were their respective Support, and what Sweet Today did might be called supervising or overseeing if that didn't suggest a hierarchic function. Interseeing, maybe, or subvising. Rig and Asten always naffled (to use Rig's word) in the ship's library, where, during the boring and disorienting experience of travel at near lightspeed, Asten could try to look at pictures or listen to a music tape, and Rig could curl up on and under a certain furry blanket and go to sleep. Betton's crew function during flight was Elder Sib; he stayed with the little ones, provided himself with a barf bag since he was one of those whom NAFAL flight made queasy, and focused the intervid on Lidi and Gveter so he could watch what they did.

So they all knew what they were doing, as regards NAFAL flight. As regards the churten process, they knew that it was supposed to effectuate their transilience to a solar system seventeen light-years from Ve Port without temporal interval; but nobody, anywhere, knew what they were doing.

So Lidi looked around, like the violinist who raises her bow to poise the chamber group for the first chord, a flicker of eye contact, and sent the *Shoby* into NAFAL mode, as Gveter, like the cellist whose bow comes down in that same instant to ground the chord, sent the *Shoby* into churten mode. They entered unduration. They churtened. No long, as the ansible had said.

"What's wrong?" Shan whispered.

"By damn!" said Gveter.

"What?" said Lidi, blinking and shaking her head.

"That's it," Tai said, flicking readouts.

"That's not A-sixty-whatsit," Lidi said, still blinking.

Sweet Today was gestalting them, all ten at once, the seven on the bridge and by intervid the three in the library. Betton had cleared a window, and the children were looking out at the murky, brownish convexity that filled half of it. Rig was holding a dirty, furry blanket. Karth was taking the electrodes off Oreth's temples, disengaging the AI link. "There was no interval," Oreth said.

"We aren't anywhere," Lidi said.

"There was no interval," Gveter repeated, scowling at the console. "That's right."

"Nothing happened," Karth said, skimming through the AI flight report.

Oreth got up, went to the window, and stood motionless looking out.

"That's it. M-60-340-nolo," Tai said.

All their words fell dead, had a false sound.

"Well! We did it, Shobies!" said Shan.

Nobody answered.

"Buzz Ve Port on the ansible," Shan said with determined jollity. "Tell 'em we're all here in one piece."

"All where?" Oreth asked.

"Yes, of course," Sweet Today said, but did nothing.

"Right," said Tai, going to the ship's ansible. She opened the field, centered to Ve, and sent a signal. Ships' ansibles worked only in the visual mode; she waited, watching the screen. She resignaled. They were all watching the screen.

"Nothing going through," she said.

Nobody told her to check the centering coordinates; in a network system nobody gets to dump their anxieties that easily. She checked the coordinates. She signaled; rechecked, reset, resignaled; opened the field and centered to Abbenay on Anarres and signaled. The ansible screen was blank.

"Check the—" Shan said, and stopped himself.

"The ansible is not functioning," Tai reported formally to her crew.

"Do you find malfunction?" Sweet Today asked.

"No. Nonfunction."

"We're going back now," said Lidi, still seated at the NAFAL console.

Her words, her tone, shook them, shook them apart.

"No, we're not!" Betton said on the intervid while Oreth said, "Back where?"

Tai, Lidi's Support, moved towards her as if to prevent her from activating the NAFAL drive, but then hastily moved back to the ansible to prevent Gveter from getting access to it. He stopped, taken aback, and said, "Perhaps the churten affected ansible function?"

"*I'm* checking it out," Tai said. "Why should it? Robot-operated ansible transmission functioned in all the test flights."

"Where are the AI reports?" Shan demanded.

"I told you, there are none," Karth answered sharply.

"Oreth was plugged in."

Oreth, still at the window, spoke without turning. "Nothing happened."

Sweet Today came over beside the Gethenian. Oreth looked at her and said, slowly, "Yes. Sweet Today. We cannot . . . do this. I think. I can't think."

Shan had cleared a second window, and stood looking out it. "Ugly," he said.

"What is?" said Lidi.

Gveter said, as if reading from the Ekumenical Atlas, "Thick, stable atmosphere, near the bottom of the temperature window for life. Micro-organisms. Bacterial clouds, bacterial reefs."

"Germ stew," Shan said. "Lovely place to send us."

"So that if we arrived as a neutron bomb or a black hole event we'd only take bacteria with us," Tai said. "But we didn't."

"Didn't what?" said Lidi.

"Didn't arrive?" Karth asked.

"Hey," Betton said, "is everybody going to stay on the bridge?"

"I want to come there," said Rig's little pipe, and then Asten's voice, clear but shaky, "Maba, I'd like to go back to Liden now."

"Come on," Karth said, and went to meet the children. Oreth did not turn from the window, even when Asten came close and took Oreth's hand.

"What are you looking at, Maba?"

"The planet, Asten."

"What planet?"

Oreth looked at the child then.

"There isn't anything," Asten said.

"That brown color—that's the surface, the atmosphere of a planet."

"There isn't any brown color. There isn't *anything*. I want to go back to Liden. You said we could when we were done with the test."

Oreth looked around, at last, at the others.

"Perception variation," Gveter said.

"I think," Tai said, "that we must establish that we are—that we got here—and then get here."

"You mean, go back," Betton said.

"The readings are perfectly clear," Lidi said, holding on to the rim of her seat with both hands and speaking very distinctly. "Every coordinate in order. That's M-60-Etcetera down there. What more do you want? Bacteria samples?"

"Yes," Tai said. "Instrument function's been affected, so we can't rely on instrumental records."

"Oh, shitsake!" said Lidi. "What a farce! All right. Suit up, go down, get some goo, and then let's get out. Go home. By NAFAL."

"By NAFAL?" Shan and Tai echoed, and Gveter said, "But we would spend seventeen years, Ve time, and no ansible to explain why."

"Why, Lidi?" Sweet Today asked.

Lidi stared at the Hainishwoman. "You want to churten again?" she demanded, raucous. She looked round at them all. "Are you people made of stone?" Her face was ashy, crumpled, shrunken. "It doesn't bother you, seeing through the walls?"

No one spoke, until Shan said cautiously, "How do you mean?"

"I can see the stars through the walls!" She stared round at them again, pointing at the carpet with its woven constellations. "You can't?" When no one answered, her jaw trembled in a little spasm, and she said, "All right. All right. I'm off duty. Sorry. Be in my room." She stood up. "Maybe you should lock me in," she said.

"Nonsense," said Sweet Today.

"If I fall through . . ." Lidi began, and did not finish. She walked to the door, stiffly and cautiously, as if through a thick fog. She said something they did not understand, "Cause," or perhaps, "Gauze."

Sweet Today followed her.

"I can see the stars too!" Rig announced.

"Hush," Karth said, putting an arm around the child.

"I can! I can see all the stars everywhere. And I can see Ve Port. And I can see anything I want!"

"Yes, of course, but hush now," the mother murmured, at which the child pulled free, stamped, and shrilled, "I can! I can too! I can see *everything*! And Asten can't! And there *is* a planet, there is too! No, don't hold me! Don't! Let me go!"

Grim, Karth carried the screaming child off to their quarters. Asten turned around to yell after Rig, "There is *not* any planet! You're just making it up!"

Grim, Oreth said, "Go to our room, please, Asten."

Asten burst into tears and obeyed. Oreth, with a glance of apology to the others, followed the short, weeping figure across the bridge and out into the corridor.

The four remaining on the bridge stood silent.

"Canaries," Shan said.

"Khallucinations?" Gveter proposed, subdued. "An effect of the churten on extrasensitive organisms—maybe?"

Tai nodded.

"Then is the ansible not functioning, or are we hallucinating nonfunction?" Shan asked after a pause.

Gveter went to the ansible; this time Tai walked away from it, leaving it to him. "I want to go down," she said.

"No reason not to, I suppose," Shan said unenthusiastically.

"Khwat reason to?" Gveter asked over his shoulder.

"It's what we're here for, isn't it? It's what we volunteered to do, isn't it? To test instantaneous—transilience—prove that it worked, that we are here! With the ansible out, it'll be seventeen years before Ve gets our radio signal!"

"We can just churten back to Ve and *tell* them," Shan said.

"If we did that now, we'd have been . . . here . . . about eight minutes."

"Tell them—tell them what? What kind of evidence is that?"

"Anecdotal," said Sweet Today, who had come back quietly to the bridge; she moved like a big sailing ship, imposingly silent.

"Is Lidi all right?" Shan asked.

"No," Sweet Today answered. She sat down where Lidi had sat, at the NAFAL console.

"I ask a consensus about going down onplanet," Tai said.

"I'll ask the others," Gveter said, and went out, returning presently with Karth. "Go down, if you want," the Gethenian said. "Oreth's staying with the children for a bit. They are— We are extremely disoriented."

"I will come down," Gveter said.

"Can I come?" Betton asked, almost in a whisper, not raising his eyes to any adult face.

"No," Tai said, as Gveter said, "Yes."

Betton looked at his mother, one quick glance.

"Khwy not?" Gveter asked her.

"We don't know the risks."

"The planet was surveyed."

"By robot ships—"

"We'll wear suits." Gveter was honestly puzzled.

"I don't want the responsibility," Tai said through her teeth.

"Khwy is it yours?" Gveter asked, more puzzled still. "We all share it; Betton is crew. I don't understand."

"I know you don't understand," Tai said, turned her back on them both, and went out. The man and the boy stood staring, Gveter after Tai, Betton at the carpet.

"I'm sorry," Betton said.

"Not to be," Gveter told him.

"What is . . . what is going on?" Shan asked in an over-controlled voice. "Why are we— We keep crossing, we keep— coming and going—"

"Confusion due to the churten experience," Gveter said.

Sweet Today turned from the console. "I have sent a distress signal," she said. "I am unable to operate the NAFAL system. The radio—" She cleared her throat. "Radio function seems erratic."

There was a pause.

"This is not happening," Shan said, or Oreth said, but Oreth had stayed with the children in another part of the ship, so it could not have been Oreth who said, "This is not happening," it must have been Shan.

A chain of cause and effect is an easy thing to describe; a cessation of cause and effect is not. To those who live in time, sequency is the norm, the only model, and simultaneity seems a muddle, a mess, a hopeless confusion, and the description of that confusion hopelessly confusing. As the members of the crew network no longer perceived the network steadily and were unable to communicate their perceptions, an individual perception is the only clue to follow through the labyrinth of their dislocation. Gveter perceived himself as being on the bridge with Shan, Sweet Today, Betton, Karth, and Tai. He perceived himself as methodically checking out the ship's systems. The NAFAL he found dead, the radio functioning in erratic bursts, the internal electrical and mechanical systems of the ship all in order. He sent out a lander unmanned and brought it back, and perceived it as functioning normally. He perceived himself discussing with Tai her determination to go down onplanet. Since he admitted his unwillingness to trust any instrumental reading on the ship, he had to admit her point that only material evidence would show that they had actually arrived at their destination, M-60-340-nolo. If they were going to have to spend the next seventeen years traveling back to Ve in real time, it would be nice to have something to show for it, even if only a handful of slime.

He perceived this discussion as perfectly rational.

It was, however, interrupted by outbursts of egoizing not characteristic of the crew.

"If you're going, go!" Shan said.

"Don't give me orders," Tai said.

"Somebody's got to stay in control here," Shan said.

"Not the men!" Tai said.

"Not the Terrans," Karth said. "Have you people no self-respect?"

"Stress," Gveter said. "Come on, Tai, Betton, all right, let's go, all right?"

In the lander, everything was clear to Gveter. One thing happened after another just as it should. Lander operation is very simple, and he asked Betton to take them down. The boy did so. Tai sat, tense and compact as always, her strong fists clenched on her knees. Betton managed the little ship with aplomb, and sat back, tense also, but dignified: "We're down," he said.

"No, we're not," Tai said.

"It—it says contact," Betton said, losing his assurance.

"An excellent landing," Gveter said. "Never even felt it." He was running the usual tests. Everything was in order. Outside the lander ports pressed a brownish darkness, a gloom. When Betton put on the outside lights the atmosphere, like a dark fog, diffused the light into a useless glare.

"Tests all tally with survey reports," Gveter said. "Will you go out, Tai, or use the servos?"

"Out," she said.

"Out," Betton echoed.

Gveter, assuming the formal crew role of Support, which one of them would have assumed if he had been going out, assisted them to lock their helmets and decontaminate their suits; he opened the hatch series for them, and watched them on the vid and from the port as they climbed down from the outer hatch. Betton went first. His slight figure, elongated by the whitish suit, was luminous in the weak glare of the lights. He walked a few steps from the ship, turned, and waited. Tai was stepping off the ladder. She seemed to grow very short— did she kneel down? Gveter looked from the port to the vid screen and back. She was shrinking? sinking—she must be sinking into the surface—which could not be solid, then, but bog, or some suspension like quicksand—but Betton had walked on it and was walking back to her, two steps, three steps, on the ground which Gveter could not see clearly but which must be solid, and which must be holding Betton up because he was lighter—but no, Tai must have stepped into a hole, a trench of some kind, for he could see her only from the waist up now, her legs hidden in the dark bog or fog, but she was moving, moving quickly, going right away from the lander and from Betton.

"Bring them back," Shan said, and Gveter said on the suit

intercom, "Please return to the lander, Betton and Tai." Betton at once started up the ladder, then turned to look for his mother. A dim blotch that might be her helmet showed in the brown gloom, almost beyond the suffusion of light from the lander.

"Please come in, Betton. Please return, Tai."

The whitish suit flickered up the ladder, while Betton's voice in the intercom pleaded, "Tai—Tai, come back— Gveter, should I go after her?"

"No. Tai, please return at once to lander."

The boy's crew-integrity held; he came up into the lander and watched from the outer hatch, as Gveter watched from the port. The vid had lost her. The pallid blotch sank into the formless murk.

Gveter perceived that the instruments recorded that the lander had sunk 3.2 meters since contact with planet surface and was continuing to sink at an increasing rate.

"What is the surface, Betton?"

"Like muddy ground— Where is she?"

"Please return at once, Tai!"

"Please return to *Shoby*, Lander One and all crew," said the ship intercom; it was Tai's voice. "This is Tai," it said. "Please return at once to ship, lander and all crew."

"Stay in suit, in decon, please, Betton," Gveter said. "I'm sealing the hatch."

"But— All right," said the boy's voice.

Gveter took the lander up, decontaminating it and Betton's suit on the way. He perceived that Betton and Shan came with him through the hatch series into the *Shoby* and along the halls to the bridge, and that Karth, Sweet Today, Shan, and Tai were on the bridge.

Betton ran to his mother and stopped; he did not put out his hands to her. His face was immobile, as if made of wax or wood.

"Were you frightened?" she asked. "What happened down there?" And she looked to Gveter for an explanation.

Gveter perceived nothing. Unduring a nonperiod of no long, he perceived nothing was had happening happened that had not happened. Lost, he groped, lost, he found the word, the word that saved— "You—" he said, his tongue thick, dumb— "You called us."

It seemed that she denied, but it did not matter. What mattered? Shan was talking. Shan could tell. "Nobody called, Gveter," he said. "You and Betton went out, I was Support; when I realized I couldn't get the lander stable, that there's something funny about that surface, I called you back into the lander, and we came up."

All Gveter could say was, "Insubstantial . . ."

"But Tai came—" Betton began, and stopped. Gveter perceived that the boy moved away from his mother's denying touch. What mattered?

"Nobody went down," Sweet Today said. After a silence and before it, she said, "There is no down to go to."

Gveter tried to find another word, but there was none. He perceived outside the main port a brownish, murky convexity, through which, as he looked intently, he saw small stars shining.

He found a word then, the wrong word. "Lost," he said, and speaking perceived how the ship's lights dimmed slowly into a brownish murk, faded, darkened, were gone, while all the soft hum and busyness of the ship's systems died away into the real silence that was always there. But there was nothing there. Nothing had happened. We are at Ve Port! he tried with all his will to say; but there was no saying.

The suns burn through my flesh, Lidi said.

I am the suns, said Sweet Today. Not I, all is.

Don't breathe! cried Oreth.

It is death, Shan said. What I feared, is: nothing.

Nothing, they said.

Unbreathing, the ghosts flitted, shifted, in the ghost shell of a cold, dark hull floating near a world of brown fog, an unreal planet. They spoke, but there were no voices. There is no sound in vacuum, nor in nontime.

In her cabined solitude, Lidi felt the gravity lighten to the half-G of the ship's core-mass; she saw them, the nearer and the farther suns, burn through the dark gauze of the walls and hulls and the bedding and her body. The brightest, the sun of this system, floated directly under her navel. She did not know its name.

I am the darkness between the suns, one said.

I am nothing, one said.

I am you, one said.

You—one said— You—

And breathed, and reached out, and spoke: "Listen!" Crying out to the other, to the others, "Listen!"

"We have always known this. This is where we have always been, will always be, at the hearth, at the center. There is nothing to be afraid of, after all."

"I can't breathe," one said.

"I am not breathing," one said.

"There is nothing to breathe," one said.

"You are, you are breathing, please breathe!" said another.

"We're here, at the hearth," said another.

Oreth had laid the fire, Karth lit it. As it caught they both said softly, in Karhidish, "Praise also the light, and creation unfinished."

The fire caught with spark-spits, crackles, sudden flares. It did not go out. It burned. The others grouped round.

They were nowhere, but they were nowhere together; the ship was dead, but they were in the ship. A dead ship cools off fairly quickly, but not immediately. Close the doors, come in by the fire; keep the cold night out, before we go to bed.

Karth went with Rig to persuade Lidi from her starry vault. The navigator would not get up. "It's my fault," she said.

"Don't egoize," Karth said mildly. "How could it be?"

"I don't know. I want to stay here," Lidi muttered. Then Karth begged her: "Oh, Lidi, not alone!"

"How else?" the old woman asked, coldly.

But she was ashamed of herself, then, and ashamed of her guilt trip, and growled, "Oh, all right." She heaved herself up and wrapped a blanket around her body and followed Karth and Rig. The child carried a little biolume; it glowed in the black corridors, just as the plants of the aerobic tanks lived on, metabolizing, making an air to breathe, for a while. The light moved before her like a star among the stars through darkness to the room full of books, where the fire burned in the stone hearth. "Hello, children," Lidi said. "What are we doing here?"

"Telling stories," Sweet Today replied.

Shan had a little voice-recorder notebook in his hand.

"Does it work?" Lidi inquired.

"Seems to. We thought we'd tell . . . what happened," Shan said, squinting the narrow black eyes in his narrow black face at the firelight. "Each of us. What we—what it seemed like, seems like, to us. So that . . ."

"As a record, yes. In case . . . How funny that it works, though, your notebook. When nothing else does."

"It's voice-activated," Shan said absently. "So. Go on, Gveter."

Gveter finished telling his version of the expedition to the planet's surface. "We didn't even bring back samples," he ended. "I never thought of them."

"Shan went with you, not me," Tai said.

"You did go, and I did," the boy said with a certainty that stopped her. "And we did go outside. And Shan and Gveter were Support, in the lander. And I took samples. They're in the Stasis closet."

"I don't know if Shan was in the lander or not," Gveter said, rubbing his forehead painfully.

"Where would the lander have gone?" Shan said. "Nothing is out there—we're nowhere—outside time, is all I can think— But when one of you tells how they saw it, it seems as if it was that way, but then the next one changes the story, and I . . ."

Oreth shivered, drawing closer to the fire.

"I never believed this damn thing would work," said Lidi, bearlike in the dark cave of her blanket.

"Not understanding it was the trouble," Karth said. "None of us understood how it would work, not even Gveter. Isn't that true?"

"Yes," Gveter said.

"So that if our psychic interaction with it affected the process—"

"Or *is* the process," said Sweet Today, "so far as we're concerned."

"Do you mean," Lidi said in a tone of deep existential disgust, "that we have to *believe* in it to make it work?"

"You have to believe in yourself in order to act, don't you?" Tai said.

"No," the navigator said. "Absolutely not. I don't believe in myself. I *know* some things. Enough to go on."

"An analogy," Gveter offered. "The effective action of a crew depends on the members perceiving themselves as a crew—you could call it believing in the crew, or just *being* it— Right? So, maybe, to churten, we—we conscious ones—maybe it depends on our consciously perceiving ourselves as . . . as transilient —as being in the other place—the destination?"

"We lost our crewness, certainly, for a— Are there whiles?" Karth said. "We fell apart."

"We lost the thread," Shan said.

"Lost," Oreth said meditatively, laying another massive, half-weightless log on the fire, volleying sparks up into the chimney, slow stars.

"We lost—what?" Sweet Today asked.

No one answered for a while.

"When I can see the sun through the carpet . . ." Lidi said.

"So can I," Betton said, very low.

"I can see Ve Port," said Rig. "And everything. I can tell you what I can see. I can see Liden if I look. And my room on the *Oneblin*. And—"

"First, Rig," said Sweet Today, "tell us what happened."

"All right," Rig said agreeably. "Hold on to me harder, maba, I start floating. Well, we went to the liberry, me and Asten and Betton, and Betton was Elder Sib, and the adults were on the bridge, and I was going to go to sleep like I do when we naffle-fly, but before I even lay down there was the brown planet and Ve Port and both the suns and everywhere else, and you could see through everything, but Asten couldn't. But I can."

"We never went *anywhere*," Asten said. "Rig tells stories all the time."

"We all tell stories all the time, Asten," Karth said.

"Not dumb ones like Rig's!"

"Even dumber," said Oreth. "What we need . . . What we need is . . ."

"We need to know," Shan said, "what transilience is, and we don't, because we never did it before, nobody ever did it before."

"Not in the flesh," said Lidi.

"We need to know what's—real—what happened, *whether*

anything happened—" Tai gestured at the cave of firelight around them and the dark beyond it. "Where are we? Are we here? Where is here? What's the story?"

"We have to tell it," Sweet Today said. "Recount it. Relate it. . . . Like Rig. Asten, how does a story begin?"

"A thousand winters ago, a thousand miles away," the child said; and Shan murmured, "Once upon a time . . ."

"There was a ship called the *Shoby*," said Sweet Today, "on a test flight, trying out the churten, with a crew of ten.

"Their names were Rig, Asten, Betton, Karth, Oreth, Lidi, Tai, Shan, Gveter, and Sweet Today. And they related their story, each one and together. . . ."

There was silence, the silence that was always there, except for the stir and crackle of the fire and the small sounds of their breathing, their movements, until one of them spoke at last, telling the story.

"The boy and his mother," said the light, pure voice, "were the first human beings ever to set foot on that world."

Again the silence; and again a voice.

"Although she wished . . . she realized that she really hoped the thing wouldn't work, because it would make her skills, her whole life, obsolete . . . all the same she really wanted to learn how to use it, too, if she could, if she wasn't too old to learn. . . ."

A long, softly throbbing pause, and another voice.

"They went from world to world, and each time they lost the world they left, lost it in time dilation, their friends getting old and dying while they were in NAFAL flight. If there were a way to live in one's own time, and yet move among the worlds, they wanted to try it. . . ."

"Staking everything on it," the next voice took up the story, "because nothing works except what we give our souls to, nothing's safe except what we put at risk."

A while, a little while; and a voice.

"It was like a game. It was like we were still in the *Shoby* at Ve Port just waiting before we went into NAFAL flight. But it was like we were at the brown planet too. At the same time. And one of them was just pretend, and the other one wasn't, but I didn't know which. So it was like when you pretend in a game. But I didn't want to play. I didn't know how."

Another voice.

"If the churten principle were proved to be applicable to actual transilience of living, conscious beings, it would be a great event in the mind of his people—for all people. A new understanding. A new partnership. A new way of being in the universe. A wider freedom. . . . He wanted that very much. He wanted to be one of the crew that first formed that partnership, the first people to be able to think this thought, and to . . . to relate it. But also he was afraid of it. Maybe it wasn't a true relation, maybe false, maybe only a dream. He didn't know."

It was not so cold, so dark, at their backs, as they sat round the fire. Was it the waves of Liden, hushing on the sand?

Another voice.

"She thought a lot about her people, too. About guilt, and expiation, and sacrifice. She wanted a lot to be on this flight that might give people—more freedom. But it was different from what she thought it would be. What happened— What *happened* wasn't what mattered. What mattered was that she came to be with people who gave *her* freedom. Without guilt. She wanted to stay with them, to be crew with them. . . . And with her son. Who was the first human being to set foot on an unknown world."

A long silence; but not deep, only as deep as the soft drum of the ship's systems, steady and unconscious as the circulation of the blood.

Another voice.

"They were thoughts in the mind; what else had they ever been? So they could be in Ve and at the brown planet, and desiring flesh and entire spirit, and illusion and reality, all at once, as they'd always been. When he remembered this, his confusion and fear ceased, for he knew that they couldn't be lost."

"They got lost. But they found the way," said another voice, soft above the hum and hushing of the ship's systems, in the warm fresh air and light inside the solid walls and hulls.

Only nine voices had spoken, and they looked for the tenth; but the tenth had gone to sleep, thumb in mouth.

"That story was told and is yet to be told," the mother said. "Go on. I'll churten here with Rig."

They left those two by the fire, and went to the bridge, and then to the hatches to invite on board a crowd of anxious scientists, engineers, and officials of Ve Port and the Ekumen, whose instruments had been assuring them that the *Shoby* had vanished, forty-four minutes ago, into non-existence, into silence. "What happened?" they asked. "What happened?" And the Shobies looked at one another and said, "Well, it's quite a story. . . ."

Dancing to Ganam

"POWER IS the great drumming," Aketa said. "The thunder. The noise of the waterfall that makes the electricity. It fills you till there's no room for anything else."

Ket poured a few drops of water onto the ground, murmuring, "Drink, traveler." She sprinkled pollen meal over the ground, murmuring, "Eat, traveler." She looked up at Iyananam, the mountain of power. "Maybe he only listened to the thunder, and couldn't hear anything else," she said. "Do you think he knew what he was doing?"

"I think he knew what he was doing," Aketa said.

Since the successful though problematic transilience of the *Shoby* to and from a nasty little planet called M-60-340-nolo, a whole wing of Ve Port had been given over to churten technology. The originators of churten theory on Anarres and the engineers of transilience on Urras communicated constantly by ansible with the theorists and engineers on Ve, who set up experiments and investigations designed to find out what, in fact, happened when a ship and its crew went from one place in the universe to another without taking any time at all to do so. "You cannot say 'went,' you cannot say 'happened,'" the Cetians chided. "It is here not there in one moment and in that same moment it is there not here. The non-interval is called, in our language, churten."

Interlocking with these circles of Cetian temporalists were circles of Hainish psychologists, investigating and arguing about what, in fact, happened when intelligent life-forms experienced the churten. "You cannot say 'in fact,' you cannot say 'experienced,'" they chided. "The reality point of 'arrival' for a churten crew is obtained by mutual perception-comparison and adjustment, so that for thinking beings construction of event is essential to effective transilience," and so on, and on, for the Hainish have been talking for a million years and have never got tired of it. But they are also fond of listening, and they listened to what the crew of the *Shoby* had to tell them. And when Commander Dalzul arrived, they listened to him.

"You have to send one man alone," he said. "The problem is interference. There were ten people on the *Shoby*. Send one man. Send me."

"You ought to go with Shan," Betton said.

His mother shook her head.

"It's dumb not to go!"

"If they don't want you, they don't get me," she said.

The boy knew better than to hug her, or say anything much. But he did something he seldom did: he made a joke. "You'd be back in no time," he said.

"Oh, get along," Tai said.

Shan knew that the Hainish did not wear uniforms and did not use status indicators such as "Commander." But he put on his black-and-silver uniform of the Terran Ekumen to meet Commander Dalzul.

Born in the barracks of Alberta in the earliest years of Terra's membership in the Ekumen, Dalzul took a degree in temporal physics at the University of A-Io on Urras and trained with the Stabiles on Hain before returning to his native planet as a Mobile of the Ekumen of the Worlds. During the sixty-seven years of his near-lightspeed journey, a troublesome religious movement escalated into the horrors of the Unist Revolution. Dalzul got the situation under control within months, by a combination of acumen and tactics that won him the respect of those he worked for, and the worship of those he had worked against—for the Unist Fathers decided he was God. The worldwide slaughter of unbelievers devolved into a worldwide novena of adoration of the New Manifestation, before devolving further into schisms and sects intent mainly on killing one another. Dalzul had defused the worst resurgence of theocratic violence since the Time of Pollution. He had acted with grace, with wit, with patience, reliability, resilience, trickiness, and good humor, with all the means the Ekumen most honored.

As he could not work on Terra, being prey to deification, he was given obscure but significant tasks on obscure but significant planets; one of them was Orint, the only world from which the Ekumen had yet withdrawn. They did so on Dalzul's advice, shortly before the Orintians destroyed sentient life on their world by the use of pathogens in war. Dalzul had foretold the event with terrible and compassionate accuracy. He had set up the secret, last-minute rescue of a few thousand children whose parents were willing to let them go; Dalzul's Children, these last of the Orintians were called.

Shan knew that heroes were phenomena of primitive cultures; but Terra's culture was primitive, and Dalzul was his hero.

Tai read the message from Ve Port with disbelief. "What kind of crew is that?" she said. "Who asks parents to leave their kid?"

Then she looked up at Shan, and saw his face.

"It's Dalzul," he said. "He wants us. In his crew."

"Go," Tai said.

He argued, of course, but Tai was on the hero's side. He went. And for the reception at which he was to meet Dalzul, he wore the black uniform with the silver thread down the sleeves and the one silver circle over the heart.

The commander wore the same uniform. When he saw him Shan's heart leaped and thudded. Inevitably, Dalzul was shorter than Shan had imagined him: he was not three meters tall. But otherwise he was as he should be, erect and lithe, the long, light hair going grey pulled back from a magnificent, vivid face, the eyes as clear as water. Shan had not realized how white-skinned Dalzul was, but the deformity or atavism was minor and could even be seen as having its own beauty. Dalzul's voice was warm and quiet; he laughed as he talked to a group of excited Anarresti. He saw Shan, turned, came straight to him. "At last! You're Shan, I'm Dalzul, we're shipmates. I am truly sorry your partner couldn't be one of us. But her replacements are old friends of yours, I think—Forest and Riel."

Shan was delighted to see the two familiar faces, Forest's an obsidian knife with watchful eyes, Riel's round and shining as a copper sun. He had been in training on Ollul with them. They greeted him with equal pleasure. "This is wonderful," he said, and then, "So we're all Terrans?"—a stupid question, since the fact was obvious; but the Ekumen generally favored mixing cultures in a crew.

"Come on out of this," Dalzul said, "and I'll explain." He signaled a mezklete, which trotted over, proudly pushing a little cart laden with drinks and food. They filled trays, thanked the mezklete, and found themselves a deep windowseat well away from the noisy throng. There they sat and ate and drank and talked and listened. Dalzul did not try to hide his passionate conviction that he was on the right track to solve the "churten problem."

"I've gone out twice alone," he said. He lowered his voice slightly as he spoke, and Shan began naively, "Without—?" and stopped.

Dalzul grinned. "No, no. With the permission of the Churten Research Group. But not really with their blessing. That's why I tend to whisper and look over my shoulder. There are still some CRG people here who make me feel as if I'd stolen their ship—scoffed at their theories—violated their shifgrethor— peed on their shoes—even after the ship and I round-tripped with no churten problems, no perceptual dissonances at all."

"Where?" Forest asked, blade-sharp face intent.

"First trip, inside this system, from Ve to Hain and back. A bus trip. Everything known, expectable. It was absolutely without incident—as expected. I'm here: I'm there. I leave the ship to check in with the Stabiles, get back in the ship, and I'm here. Hey presto! It is magic, you know. And yet it seems so natural. Where one is, one is. Did you feel that, Shan?"

The clear eyes were amazing in their intensity. It was like being looked at by lightning. Shan wanted to be able to agree, but had to stammer, "I—we, you know, we had some trouble deciding where we were."

"I think that that's unnecessary, that confusion. Transilience is a non-experience. I think that normally, *nothing happens*. Literally nothing. Extraneous events got mixed into it in the *Shoby* experiment—your interval was queered. This time, I think we can have a non-experience." He looked at Forest and Riel and laughed. "You'll not-see what I don't mean," he said. "Anyhow, after the bus trip, I hung about annoying them persistently until Gvonesh agreed to let me do a solo exploratory."

The mezklete bustled up to them, pushing its little cart with its furry paws. Mezkletes love parties, love to give food, love to serve drinks and watch their humans get weird. It stayed about hopefully for a while to see if they would get weird, then bustled back to the Anarresti theorists, who were always weird.

"An exploratory—a first contact?"

Dalzul nodded. His strength and unconscious dignity were daunting, and yet his delight, his simple glee, in what he had done was irresistible. Shan had met brilliant people and wise people, but never one whose energy shone so bright, so clear, so vulnerable.

"We chose a distant one. G-14-214-yomo; it was Tadkla on the maps of the Expansion; the people I met there call it Ganam. A preliminary Ekumen mission is actually on its way there at NAFAL speed. Left Ollul eight years ago, and will get there thirteen years from herenow. Of course there was no way to communicate with them while they're in transit, to tell them I was going to be there ahead of them. The CRG thought it a good idea that somebody would be dropping in after thirteen years. In case I didn't report back, maybe they could find out what happened. But it looks now as if the mission will arrive to find Ganam already a member of the Ekumen!" He looked at them all, alight with passion and intention. "You know, churten is going to change everything. When transilience replaces space travel—all travel—when there is no distance between worlds—when we control interval—I keep trying to imagine, to understand what it will mean, to the Ekumen, to us. We'll be able to make the household of humankind truly one house, one place. But then it goes still deeper! In transilience what we do is to rejoin, restore the primal moment, the beat that is the rhythm. . . . To rejoin unity. To escape time. To use eternity! You've been there, Shan—you felt what I'm trying to say?"

"I don't know," Shan said, "yes—"

"Do you want to see the tape of my trip?" Dalzul asked abruptly, his eyes shining with a flicker of mischief. "I brought a handview."

"Yes!" Forest and Riel said, and they crowded in around him in the windowseat like a bunch of conspirators. The mezklete tried in vain to see what they were doing, but was too short, even when it got up on its cart.

While he programmed the little viewer, Dalzul told them briefly about Ganam. One of the outermost seedings of the Hainish Expansion, the world had been lost from the human community for five hundred millennia; nothing was known about it except that it might have a population descended from human ancestors. If it did, the Ekumenical ship on its way to it would in the normal way have observed from orbit for a long time before sending down a few observers, to hide, or to pass if possible, or to reveal their mission if necessary, while gathering information, learning languages and customs, and so on—a process usually of many years. All this had been short-circuited by the unpredictability of the new technology. Dalzul's small ship had come out of churten not in the stratosphere as intended, but in the atmosphere, about a hundred meters above the ground.

"I didn't have the chance to make an unobtrusive entrance on the scene," he said. The audiovisual record his ship's instruments had made came up on the little screen as he spoke. They saw the grey plains of Ve Port dropping away as the ship left the planet. "Now," Dalzul said, and in one instant they saw the stars blaze in black space and the yellow walls and orange roofs of a city, the blaze of sunlight on a canal.

"You see?" Dalzul murmured. "Nothing happens."

The city tilted and settled, sunny streets and squares full of people, all of them looking up and pointing, unmistakably shouting, "Look! Look!"

"Decided I might as well accept the situation," Dalzul said. Trees and grass rose up around the ship as he brought it on down. People were already hurrying out of the city, human people: terra-cotta-colored, rather massively built, with broad faces, bare-armed, barefoot, wearing kilts and gilets in splendid colors, men with great gold earrings, headdresses of basketry, gold wire, feather plumes.

"The Gaman," Dalzul said. "The people of Ganam. . . . Grand, aren't they? And they don't waste time. They were there within half an hour—there, that's Ket, see her, that stunning woman? —Since the ship was obviously fairly alarming, I decided that the first point to make was my defenselessness."

They saw what he meant, as the ship's camera recorded his exit. He walked slowly out on the grass and stood still, facing the gathering crowd. He was naked. Unarmed, unclothed, alone, he stood there, the fierce sun bright on his white skin and silvery hair, his hands held wide and open in the gesture of offering.

The pause was very long. Talk and exclamation among the

Gaman died out as people came near the front of the crowd. Dalzul, in the center of the camera's field, stood easily, motionless. Then—Shan drew breath sharply as he watched—a woman came forward towards him. She was tall and strongly built, with round arms, black eyes above high cheekbones. Her hair was braided with gold into a coronet on her head. She stood before Dalzul and spoke, her voice clear and full. The words sounded like poetry, like ritual questions, Shan thought. Dalzul responded by bringing his hands toward his heart, then opening them again wide, palm up.

The woman gazed at him a while, then spoke one resonant word. Slowly, with a grave formality, she slipped the dark red gilet from her breasts and shoulders, untied her kilt and dropped it aside with a splendid, conscious gesture, and stood naked before the naked man.

She reached out her hand. Dalzul took it.

They walked away from the ship, towards the city. The crowd closed in behind them and followed them, still quiet, without haste or confusion, as if performing actions they had performed before.

A few people, mostly adolescents, stayed behind, looking at the ship, daring each other to come closer, curious, cautious, but not frightened.

Dalzul stopped the tape.

"You see," he said to Shan, "the difference?"

Shan, awed, did not speak.

"What the *Shoby*'s crew discovered," Dalzul said to the three of them, "is that individual experiences of transilience can be made coherent only by a concerted effort. An effort to synchronize —to entrain. When they realized that, they were able to pull out of an increasingly dangerously fragmented perception of where they were and what was happening. Right, Shan?"

"They call it the chaos experience now," Shan said, subdued by the memory of it, and by the difference of Dalzul's experience.

"The temporalists and psychologists have sweated a lot of theory out of the *Shoby* trip," Dalzul said. "My reading of it is pitifully simple: that a great deal of the perceptual dissonance, the anguish and incoherence, was an effect of the disparity of the *Shoby* crew. No matter how well you had crew-bonded, Shan, you were ten people from four worlds—four different cultures—two very old women, and three young children! If the answer to coherent transilience is entrainment, functioning in rhythm, then we've got to make entrainment easy. That you achieved it at all was miraculous. The simplest way to achieve it, of course, is to bypass it: to go alone."

"Then how do you get a cross-check on the experience?" Forest said.

"You just saw it: the ship's record of the landing."

"But our instruments on the *Shoby* went out, or were totally erratic," Shan said. "The readings are as incoherent as our perceptions were."

"Exactly! You and the instruments were all in one entrainment field, fouling each other up. But when just two or three of you went down onto the planet's surface, things were better: the lander functioned perfectly, and its tapes of the surface are clear. Although very ugly."

Shan laughed. "Ugly, yes. A sort of shit-planet. But, Commander, even on the tapes it never is clear who actually went out onto the surface. And that was one of the most chaotic parts of the whole experience. I went down with Gveter and Betton. The surface under the ship was unstable, so I called them back to the lander and we went back up to the ship. That all seems coherent. But Gveter's perception was that he went down with Betton and Tai, not me, heard Tai call him from the ship, and came back with Betton and me. As for Betton, he went down with Tai and me. He saw his mother walk away from the lander, ignore the order to return, and be left on the surface. Gveter saw that too. They came back without her and found her waiting for them on the bridge. Tai herself has no memory of going down in the lander. Those four stories are all our evidence. They seem to be equally true, equally untrue. And the tapes don't help—don't show who was in the suits. They all look alike in that shit soup on the surface."

"That's it—exactly—" Dalzul said, leaning forward, his face alight. "That murk, that shit, that chaos you saw, which the cameras in your field saw— Think of the difference between that and the tapes we just watched! Sunlight, vivid faces, bright colors, everything brilliant, clear— Because there was no interference, Shan. The Cetians say that in the churten field there is nothing but the deep rhythms, the vibration of the ultimate wave-particles. Transilience is a function of the rhythm that makes being. According to Cetian spiritual physics, it's access to that rhythm which allows the individual to participate in eternity and ubiquity. My extrapolation from that is that individuals in transilience have to be in nearly perfect synchrony to arrive at the same place with a harmonious—that is, an accurate —perception of it. My intuition, as far as we've tested it, has been confirmed: one person can churten sanely. Until we learn what we're doing, ten persons will inevitably experience chaos, or worse."

"And four persons?" Forest inquired, drily.

"—are the control," said Dalzul. "Frankly, I'd rather have started out by going on more solos, or with one companion at most. But our friends from Anarres, as you know, are very distrustful of what they call egoizing. To them, morality isn't accessible to individuals, only to groups. Also, they say, maybe something else went wrong on the *Shoby* experiment, maybe a group can churten just as well as one person, how do we know till we try? So I compromised. I said, send me with two or three highly compatible and highly motivated companions. Send us back to Ganam and let's see what we see!"

"'Motivated' is inadequate," Shan said. "I am committed. I belong to this crew."

Riel was nodding; Forest, wary and saturnine, said only, "Are we going to practice entrainment, Commander?"

"As long as you like," Dalzul said. "But there are things more important than practice. Do you sing, Forest, or play an instrument?"

"I can sing," Forest said, and Riel and Shan nodded as Dalzul looked at them.

"You know this," he said, and began softly to sing an old song, a song everybody from the barracks and camps of Terra knew, "Going to the Western Sea." Riel joined in, then Shan, then Forest in an unexpectedly deep, resonant voice. A few people near them turned to hear the harmonies strike through the gabble of speaking voices. The mezklete came hurrying over, abandoning its cart, its eyes large and bright. They ended the song, smiling, on a long soft chord.

"That is entrainment," Dalzul said. "All we need to get to Ganam is music. All there is, in the end, is music."

Smiling, Forest and then Riel raised their glasses.

"To music!" said Shan, feeling drunk and wildly happy.

"To the crew of the *Galba*," said Dalzul, and they drank.

The minimum crew-bonding period of isyeye was of course observed, and during it they had plenty of time to discuss the churten problem, both with Dalzul and among themselves. They watched the ship's tapes and reread Dalzul's records of his brief stay on Ganam till they had them memorized, and then argued about the wisdom of doing so. "We're simply accepting everything he saw and said as objective fact," Forest pointed out. "What sort of control can we provide?"

"His report and the ship's tapes agree completely," Shan said.

"Because, if his theory is correct, he and the instruments were entrained. The reality of the ship and the instruments may be perceivable to us only as perceived by the person, the intelligent being, in transilience. If the Cetians are sure of one thing about churten, it's that when intelligence is involved in the process they don't understand it any more. Send out a robot ship, no problem. Send out amoebas and crickets, no problem. Send out high-intelligence beings and all the bets are off. Your ship was part of your reality—your ten different realities. Its instruments obediently recorded the dissonances, or were affected by them to the point of malfunction and nonfunction. Only when you all worked together to construct a joint, coherent reality could the ship begin to respond to it and record it. Right?"

"Yes. But it's very difficult," Shan said, "to live without the notion that there is, somewhere, if one could just find it, a fact."

"Only fiction," said Forest, unrelenting. "Fact is one of our finest fictions."

"But music comes first," Shan said. "And dancing is people being music. I think what Dalzul sees is that we can . . . we can dance to Ganam."

"I like that," said Riel. "And look: on the fiction theory, we should be careful not to 'believe' Dalzul's records, or his ship's tapes. They're fictions. But, unless we accept the assumption, based only on the *Shoby* experiment, that the churten experience necessarily skews perception or judgment of perception, we have no reason to *dis*believe them. He's a seasoned observer and a superb gestalter."

"There are elements of a rather familiar kind of fiction in his report," Forest said. "The princess who has apparently been waiting for him, expecting him, and leads him naked to her palace, where after due ceremonies and amenities she has sex with him—and very good sex too—? I'm not saying I disbelieve it. I don't. It looks and rings true. But it would be interesting to know how the princess perceived these events."

"We can't know that till we get there and talk to her," said Riel. "What are we waiting for, anyhow?"

The *Galba* was a Hainish in-system glass ship, newly fitted with churten controls. It was a pretty little bubble, not much bigger than the *Shoby*'s lander. Entering it, Shan had a few rather bad moments. The chaos, the senseless and centerless experience of churten, returned vividly to him: must he go through that again? Could he? Very sharp and aching was the thought of Tai, Tai who should be here now as she had been there then, Tai whom he had come to love aboard the *Shoby*, and Betton, the clear-hearted child—he needed them, they should be here.

Forest and Riel slipped through the hatch, and after them came Dalzul, the concentration of his energy almost visible around him as an aura or halo, a brightness of being. No wonder the Unists thought he was God, Shan thought, and thought also of the ceremonial, almost reverent welcome shown Dalzul by the Gaman. Dalzul was charged, full of mana, a power to which others responded, by which they were entrained. Shan's anxiety slipped from him. He knew that with Dalzul there would be no chaos.

"They thought we'd be able to control a bubble easier than the ship I had. I'll try not to bring her out right over the roofs this time. No wonder they thought I was a god, materializing in full view like that!" Shan had got used to the way Dalzul seemed to echo his thoughts, and Riel's and Forest's, and had come to expect it; they were in synchrony, it was their strength.

They took their places, Dalzul at the churten console, Riel plugged into the AI, Shan at the flight controls, and Forest as gestalt and Support. Dalzul looked round and nodded, and

Shan took them out a few hundred kilometers from Ve Port. The curve of the planet fell away and the stars shone under his feet, around, above.

Dalzul began to sing, not a melody but a held note, a full, deep A. Riel joined in, an octave above, then Forest on the F between, and Shan found himself pouring out a steady middle C as if he were a church organ. Riel shifted to the C above, Dalzul and Forest sang the triad, and as the chord changed Shan did not know who sang which note, hearing and being only the sphere of the stars and the sweet frequencies swelling and fading in one long-held unison as Dalzul touched the console and the yellow sun was high in the blue sky above the city.

Shan had not stopped flying. Red and orange roofs, dusty plazas tilted under the ship. "How about over there, Shan," Dalzul said, pointing to a green strip by a canal, and Shan brought the *Galba* effortlessly down in a long glide and touched it onto grass, soft as a soap bubble.

He looked round at the others and out through the walls.

"Blue sky, green grass, near noon, natives approaching," said Dalzul. "Right?"

"Right," said Riel, and Shan laughed. No conflict of sensations, no chaos of perceptions, no terror of uncertainty, this time. "We churtened," he said. "We did it. We danced it!"

The field workers down by the canal got into a group and watched, evidently afraid to approach, but very soon people could be seen on the dusty road leading out from the city. "The welcoming committee, I trust," said Dalzul.

The four of them waited beside the bubble ship. The tension of the moment only heightened the extraordinary vividness of emotion and sensation. Shan felt that he knew the beautiful, harsh outlines of the two volcanoes that bounded the city's valley, knew them and would never forget them, knew the smell of the air and the fall of the light and the blackness of shadow under leaves; this is herenow, he said to himself with joyous certainty, I am herenow and there is no distance, no separation.

Tension without fear. Plumed and crested men, broad-chested and strong-armed, walked towards them steadily, their faces impassive, and stopped in front of them. One elderly man nodded his head slightly and said, "Sem Dazu." Dalzul made the gesture from heart to open embrace, saying, "Viaka!" The other men said, "Dazu, Sem Dazu," and some of them imitated Dalzul's gesture.

"Viaka," Dalzul said, "beya,"—friend—and he introduced his companions to them, repeating their names and the word friend.

"Foyes," said old Viaka. "Shan. Yeh." He knew he hadn't come very close to "Riel," and frowned slightly. "Friends. Be welcome. Come, come in Ganam." During his brief first stay, Dalzul had not been able to record much of the language for the Hainish linguists to work on; from his meager tapes they and their clever analoguers had produced a little manual of vocabulary and grammar, full of [?]s, which Shan had dutifully studied. He remembered beya, and kiyugi, be welcome [?], be at home [?]. Riel, a hilfer/linguist, would have liked longer to study the manual. "Better to learn the language from the speakers," Dalzul had said.

As they walked the dusty road to Ganam city the vividness of impression began to overload on Shan, becoming a blur and glory of heat and radiance, red and yellow clay walls, pottery-red bare breasts and shoulders, purple and red and orange and umber striped and embroidered cloaks and vests and kilts, the gleam of gold and nod of feathers, the smells of oil and incense and dust and smoke and food and sweat, the sounds of many voices, slap of sandals and sluff of bare feet on stone and earth, bells, gongs, the difference of light, the touch and smell and beat of a world where nothing was known and everything was as it was, as it should be, this little city of stone and mud and splendid carvings, fiery in the light of its gold sun, crude, magnificent, and human. It was stranger than anything Shan had known and it was as if he had been away and come home again. Tears blurred his eyes. We are all one, he thought. There is no distance, no time between us; all we need do is step across, and we are here, together. He walked beside Dalzul and heard the people greet him, grave and quiet: Sem Dazu, they said, Sem Dazu, kiyugi. You have come home.

The first days were all overload. There were moments when Shan thought that he had stopped thinking—was merely experiencing, receiving, not processing. "Process later," Dalzul said with a laugh, when Shan told him. "How often does one get to be a child?" It was indeed like being a child, having no control over events and no responsibility for them. Expectable or incredible, they happened, and he was part of the happening and watched it happening at the same time. They were going to make Dalzul their king. It was ridiculous and it was perfectly natural. Your king dies without an heir; a silver man drops out of your sky and your princess says, "This is the man"; the silver man vanishes and returns with three strange companions who can work various miracles; you make him king. What else can you do with him?

Riel and Forest were, of course, reluctant, dubious about so deep an involvement with a native culture, but had no alternative to offer Dalzul. Since the kingship was evidently more honorary than authoritative, they admitted that he had probably better go along with what the Gaman wanted. Trying to keep some perspective on Dalzul's situation, they had separated themselves early on, living in a house near the market, where they could be with common people and enjoy a freedom of movement Dalzul did not have. The trouble with being king-to-be, he told Shan, was that he was expected to hang around the palace all day observing taboos.

Shan stayed with Dalzul. Viaka gave him one of the many wings of the rambling clay palace to himself. He shared it with a relative of Viaka's wife called Abud, who helped him keep house. Nothing was expected of him, either by Dalzul or by his native hosts; his time was free. The CRG had asked them to spend thirty days in Ganam. The days flowed by like shining water. He tried to keep his journal for the Ekumen, but found he hated to break the continuity of experience by talking about it, analyzing it. The whole point was that nothing happened, he thought, smiling.

The only experience that stood out as in some way different was a day he spent with old Viaka's niece [?] and her husband [?]—he had tried to get the kinship system straight, but the question marks remained, and for some reason this young couple seemed not to use their names. They took him on a long and beautiful walk to a waterfall up on the slope of the larger volcano, Iyananam. He understood that it was a sacred place they wanted him to see. He was very much surprised to find that the sacred waterfall was employed to power a sacred dynamo. The Gaman, as far as his companions could explain and he could understand, had a quite adequate grasp of the principles of hydroelectricity, though they were woefully short of conductors, and had no particular practical use for the power they generated. Their discussion seemed to be about the nature of electricity rather than the application of it, but he could follow very little of it. He tried to ask if there was any place they used electricity, but all he could say was, "somewhere come out?" At such moments he did not find it so agreeable to feel like a child, or a half-wit. Yes, the young woman said, it comes out at the ishkanem when the basemmiak vada. Shan nodded and made notes. Like all Gaman, his companions enjoyed watching him talk into his noter and seeing the tiny symbols appear on the tiny screen, an amiable magic.

They took him onto a terrace built out from the little dynamo building, which was built of dressed stone laid in marvelously intricate courses. They tried to explain something, pointing downstream. He saw something shining in the quick glitter of the water, but could not make out what it was. Heda, taboo, they said, a word he knew well from Dalzul, though he had not himself run into anything heda till now. As they went on, he caught the name "Dazu" in their conversation with each other, but again could not follow. They passed a little earth shrine, where in the informal worship of the Gaman each of them laid a leaf from a nearby tree, and then set off down the mountainside in the long light of late afternoon.

As they rounded a turn of the steep trail, he could see in the hazy golden distance down the great valley two other settlements, towns or cities. He was surprised to see them, and then surprised by his surprise. He realized that he had been so absorbed in being in Ganam that he had forgotten it was not the only place in the world. Pointing, he asked his companions, "Belong Gaman?" After some discussion, probably of what on earth he meant, they said no, only Ganam belonged to the Gaman; those cities were other cities.

Was Dalzul, then, right in thinking the world was called Ganam, or did that name mean just the city and its lands? "Tegud ao? What you call?" he asked, patting the ground, sweeping his arms around the circle of valley, the mountain at their backs, the other mountain facing them. "Nanam tegudyeh," said Viaka's niece [?], tentatively, but her husband [?] disagreed, and they discussed it impenetrably for a mile or more. Shan gave up, put away his noter, and enjoyed the walk in the cool of the evening down towards the golden walls of Ganam.

The next day, or maybe it was the day after, Dalzul came by while Shan was pruning the fruit tree in the walled courtyard of his bit of the palace. The pruning knife was a thin, slightly curved steel blade with a gracefully carved, well-worn wooden handle; it was sharp as a razor. "This is a lovely tool," he said to Dalzul. "My grandmother taught me to prune. It's not an art I've been able to practice much since I joined the Ekumen. They're good orcharders here. I was out talking with some of them yesterday." Had it been yesterday? Not that it mattered. Time is not duration but intensity; time is the beat and the interval, Shan had been thinking as he studied the tree, learning the inner rhythm of its growth, the patterned intervals of its branches. The years are flowers, the worlds are fruit . . . "Pruning makes me poetical," he said, and then, looking at Dalzul, said, "Is something wrong?" It was like a skipped pulse, a wrong note, a step mistaken in the dance.

"I don't know," Dalzul said. "Let's sit down a minute." They went to the shade under the balcony and settled down cross-legged on the flagstones. "Probably," Dalzul said, "I've relied too far on my intuitive understanding of these people— followed my nose, instead of holding back, learning the language word by word, going by the book. . . . I don't know. But something is amiss."

Shan watched the strong, vivid face as Dalzul spoke. The fierce sunlight had tanned his white skin to a more human color. He wore his own shirt and trousers, but had let his grey hair fall loose as Gaman men did, wearing a narrow headband interwoven with gold, which gave him a regal and barbaric look.

"These are a barbaric people," he said. "More violent, more primitive perhaps, than I wanted to admit. This kingship they're determined to invest me with—I'm afraid I have to see it as something more than an honor or a sacral gesture. It is political, after all. At least, it would seem that by being chosen to be king, I've made a rival. An enemy."

"Who?"

"Aketa."

"I don't know him. He's not in the palace here?"

"No. He's not one of Viaka's people. He seems to have been away when I first came. As I understand Viaka, this man considers himself the heir to the throne and the legitimate mate of the princess."

"Princess Ket?" Shan had never yet spoken to the princess, who kept herself aloof, staying always in her part of the palace, though she allowed Dalzul to visit her there. "What does she say about this Aketa? Isn't she on your side? She chose you, after all."

"She says I am to be king. That hasn't changed. But she has. She's left the palace. In fact she's gone to live, as well as I can tell, in this Aketa's household! My God, Shan, is there any world in this universe where men can understand women?"

"Gethen," Shan said.

Dalzul laughed, but his face remained intense, pondering. "You have a partner," he said after a while. "Maybe that's the answer. I never came to a place with a woman where I knew, really knew, what she wanted, who she was. If you stick it out, do you finally get there?"

Shan was touched at the older man, the brilliant man, asking him such questions. "I don't know," he said. "Tai and I—we know each other in a way that— But it's not easy— I don't know. . . . But about the princess— Riel and Forest have been talking with people, learning the language. As women, maybe they'd have some insights?"

"Women yes and no," Dalzul said. "It's why I chose them, Shan. With two real women, the psychological dynamics might have been too complicated."

Shan said nothing, feeling again that something was missing or he was missing something, misunderstanding. He wondered if Dalzul knew that most of Shan's sexuality had been with men until he met Tai.

"Consider," Dalzul said, "for instance, if the princess thought she should be jealous of one or both of them, thought they were my sexual partners. That could be a snake's nest! As it is, they're no threat. Of course, seeking consonance, I'd have preferred all men. But the Elders on Hain are mostly old women, and I knew I had to suit them. So I asked you and your partner, a married couple. When your partner couldn't come, these two seemed the best solution. And they've performed admirably. But I don't think they're equipped to tell me what's going on in the mind, or the hormones, of a very fully sexed woman such as the princess."

The beat skipped again. Shan rubbed one hand against the rough stone of the terrace, puzzled at his own sense of confusion. Trying to return to the original subject, he asked, "If it is a political kingship, not a sacral one, can you possibly—just withdraw your candidacy, as it were?"

"Oh, it's sacred. The only way I could withdraw is to run away. Churten back to Ve Port."

"We could fly the *Galba* to another part of the planet," Shan suggested. "Observe somewhere else."

"From what Viaka tells me, leaving's not really an option. Ket's defection has apparently caused a schism, and if Aketa gains power, his supporters will wreak vengeance on Viaka and all his people. Blood sacrifice for offense to the true and sacred king's person. . . . Religion and politics! How could I of all men be so blind? I let my longings persuade me that we'd found a rather primitive idyll. But what we're in the middle of here is a factional and sexual competition among intelligent barbarians who keep their pruning hooks and their swords extremely sharp." Dalzul smiled suddenly, and his light eyes flashed. "They are wonderful, these people. They are everything we lost with our literacy, our industry, our science. Directly sensual—utterly passionate—primally real. I love them. If they want to make me their king, then by God I'll put a basket of feathers on my head and be their king! But before that, I've got to figure out how to handle Aketa and his crew. And the only key to Aketa seems to be our moody Princess Ket. Whatever you can find out, tell me, Shan. I need your advice and your help."

"You have it, sir," Shan said, touched again. After Dalzul had left, he decided that what he should do was what Dalzul's unexpected male-heterosexual defensiveness prevented him from doing: go ask advice and help of Forest and Riel.

He set off for their house. As he made his way through the marvelously noisy and aromatic market, he asked himself when he had seen them last, and realized it had been several days. What had he been doing? He had been in the orchards. He had been up on the mountain, on Iyananam, where there was a dynamo . . . where he had seen other cities. . . . The pruning hook was steel. How did the Gaman make their steel? Did they have a foundry? Did they get it in trade? His mind was sluggishly, laboriously turning over these matters as he came into the courtyard, where Forest sat on a cushion on the terrace, reading a book.

"Well," she said. "A visitor from another planet!"

It had been quite a long time since he had been here—eight, ten days?

"Where've you been?" he asked, confused.

"Right here. Riel!" Forest called up to the balcony. Several heads looked over the carved railing, and the one with curly hair said, "Shan! I'll be right down!"

Riel arrived with a pot of tipu seeds, the ubiquitous munchy of Ganam. The three of them sat around on the terrace, half in the sun and half out of it, and cracked seeds; typical anthropoids, Riel remarked. She greeted Shan with real warmth, and yet she and Forest were unmistakably cautious: they watched him, they asked nothing, they waited to see . . . what? How long had it been, then, since he had seen them? He felt a sudden tremor of unease, a missed beat so profound that he put his hands flat on the warm sandstone, bracing himself. Was it an earthquake? Built between two sleepy volcanoes, the city shuddered a little now and then, bits of clay fell off the walls, little orange tiles off the roofs. . . . Forest and Riel watched him. Nothing was shaking, nothing was falling.

"Dalzul has run into some kind of problem in the palace," he said.

"Has he," said Forest in a perfectly neutral tone.

"A native claimant to the throne, a pretender or heir, has turned up. And the princess is staying with him, now. But she still tells Dalzul that he's to be king. If this pretender gets power, apparently he threatens reprisals against all Viaka's people, anybody who backed Dalzul. It's just the kind of sticky situation Dalzul was hoping to avoid."

"And is matchless at resolving," said Forest.

"I think he feels pretty much at an impasse. He doesn't un-derstand what role the princess is playing. I think that troubles him most. I thought you might have some idea why, after more or less hurling herself into his arms, she's gone off to stay with his rival."

"It's Ket you're talking about," Riel said, cautious.

"Yes. He calls her the princess. That's not what she is?"

"I don't know what Dalzul means by the word. It has a lot of connotations. If the denotation is 'a king's daughter,' then it doesn't fit. There is no king."

"Not at present—"

"Not ever," Forest said.

Shan suppressed a flash of anger. He was getting tired of being the half-wit child, and Forest could be abrasively gno-mic. "Look," he said, "I—I've been sort of out of it. Bear with me. I thought their king was dead. And given Dalzul's appar-ently miraculous descent from heaven during the search for a new king, they saw him as divinely appointed, 'the one who will hold the scepter.' Is that all wrong?"

"Divinely appointed seems to be right," Riel said. "These are certainly sacred matters." She hesitated and looked at For-est. They worked as a team, Shan thought, but not, at the moment, a team that included him. What had become of the wonderful oneness?

"Who is this rival, this claimant?" Forest asked him.

"A man named Aketa."

"Aketa!"

"You know him?"

Again the glance between the two; then Forest turned to face him and looked directly into his eyes. "Shan," she said, "we are seriously out of sync. I wonder if we're having the churten problem. The chaos experience you had on the *Shoby*."

"Here, now? When we've been here for days, weeks—"

"Where's here?" Forest asked, serious and intent.

Shan slapped his hand on the flagstone. "Here! Now! In this courtyard of your house in Ganam! This is nothing like the chaos experience. We're sharing this—it's coherent, it's conso-nant, we're here together! Eating tipu seeds!"

"I think so too," Forest said, so gently that Shan realized she was trying to calm him, reassure him. "But we may be . . . reading the experience quite differently."

"People always do, everywhere," he said rather desperately.

She had moved so that he could see more clearly the book she had been reading when he came. It was an ordinary bound book, but they had brought no books with them on the *Galba*, a thick book on some kind of heavy brownish paper, hand-lettered, a Terran antique book from New Cairo Library, it was not a book but a pillow, a brick, a basket, not a book, it was a book. In a strange writing. In a strange language. A book with covers of carved wood, hinged with gold.

"What is that?" he asked almost inaudibly.

"The sacred history of the Cities Under Iyananam, we think," Forest said.

"A book," Riel said.

"They're illiterate," Shan said.

"Some of them are," said Forest.

"Quite a lot of them are, actually," said Riel. "But some of the merchants and the priests can read. Aketa gave us this. We've been studying with him. He's a marvelous teacher."

"He's a kind of scholar priest, we think," said Forest. "There are these positions, we're calling them priesthoods because they're basically sacred, but they're really more like jobs, or vocations, callings. Very important to the Gaman, to the whole structure of society, we think. They have to be filled; things go out of whack if they aren't. And if you have the vocation, the talent, you go out of whack if you don't do it, too. A lot of them are kind of occasional, like a person that officiates at an annual festival, but some of them seem to be really demanding, and very prestigious. Most of them are for men. Our feeling is that probably the way a man gets prestige is to fill one of the priesthoods."

"But men run the whole city," Shan protested.

"I don't know," Forest said, still with the uncharacteristic gentleness that told Shan he was not in full control. "We'd describe it as a non-gender-dominant society. Not much division of labor on sexual lines. All kinds of marriages—polyandry may be the most common, two or three husbands. A good many women are out of heterosexual circulation because they have homosexual group marriages, the iyeha, three or four or more women. We haven't found a male equivalent yet—"

"Anyhow," said Riel, "Aketa is one of Ket's husbands. His name means something like Ket's-kin-first-husband. Kin, meaning they're in the same volcano lineage. He was down the valley in Sponta when we first arrived."

"And he's a priest, a high one, we think. Maybe because he's Ket's husband, and she's certainly an important one. But most of the really prestigious priesthoods seem to be for men. Probably to compensate for lack of childbearing."

The anger rose up again in Shan. Who were these women to lecture him on gender and womb envy? Like a sea wave the hatred filled him with salt bitterness, and sank away, and was gone. He sat with his fragile sisters in the sunlight on the stone, and looked at the heavy, impossible book open on Forest's lap.

After a long time he said, "What does it say?"

"I only know a word here and there. Aketa wanted me to have it for a while. He's been teaching us. Mostly I look at the pictures. Like a baby." She showed him the small, brightly painted, gilded picture on the open page: men in wonderful robes and headdresses, dancing, under the purple slopes of Iyananam.

"Dalzul thought they were preliterate," he said. "He has to see this."

"He has seen it," Riel said.

"But—" Shan began, and was silent.

"Long long ago on Terra," Riel said, "one of the first anthropologists took a man from a tiny, remote, isolated Arctic tribe to a huge city, New York City. The thing that most impressed this very intelligent tribesman about New York City were the knobs on the bottom posts of staircases. He studied them with deep interest. He wasn't interested in the vast buildings, the streets full of crowds, the machines. . . ."

"We wonder if the churten problem centers not on impressions only, but expectations," Forest said. "We make sense of the world intentionally. Faced with chaos, we seek or make the familiar, and build up the world with it. Babies do it, we all do it; we filter out most of what our senses report. We're conscious only of what we need to be or want to be conscious of. In churten, the universe dissolves. As we come out, we reconstruct it—frantically. Grabbing at things we recognize. And once one part of it is there, the rest gets built on that."

"I say 'I,'" said Riel, "and an infinite number of sentences could follow. But the next word begins to build the immutable syntax. 'I want—' By the last word of the sentence, there may be no choice at all. And also, you can only use words you know."

"That's how we came out of the chaos experience on the *Shoby*," Shan said. His head had begun suddenly to ache, a painful, irregular throb at the temples. "We talked. We constructed the syntax of the experience. We told our story."

"And tried very hard to tell it truly," Forest said.

After a pause, pressing the pressure points on his temples, Shan said, "You're saying that Dalzul has been lying?"

"No. But is he telling the Ganam story or the Dalzul story? The childlike, simple people acclaiming him king, the beautiful princess offering herself . . ."

"But she did—"

"It's her job. Her vocation. She's one of these priests, an important one. Her title is Anam. Dalzul translated it princess. We think it means earth. The earth, the ground, the world. She is Ganam's earth, receiving the stranger in honor. But there's more to it—this reciprocal function, which Dalzul interprets as kingship. They simply don't have kings. It must be some kind of priesthood role as Anam's mate. Not Ket's husband, but her mate when she's Anam. But we don't know. We don't know what responsibility he's taken on."

"And we may be inventing just as much of it as Dalzul is," Riel said. "How can we be sure?"

"If we have you back to compare notes with, it'll be a big relief," said Forest. "We need you."

So does he, Shan thought. He needs my help, they need my help. What help have I to give? I don't know where I am. I know nothing about this place. I know the stone is warm and rough under the palm of my hand.

I know these two women are sympathetic, intelligent, trying to be honest.

I know Dalzul is a great man, not a foolish egoist, not a liar.

I know the stone is rough, the sun is warm, the shadow cool. I know the slight, sweet taste of tipu seeds, the crunch between the teeth.

I know that when he was thirty, Dalzul was worshiped as

God. No matter how he disavowed that worship, it must have changed him. Growing old, he would remember what it was to be a king. . . .

"Do we know anything at all about this priesthood he's supposed to fill, then?" he asked harshly.

"The key word seems to be 'todok,' stick or staff or scepter. Todoghay, the one who holds the scepter, is the title. Dalzul got that right. It does sound like a king. But we don't think it means ruling people."

"Day-to-day decisions are made by the councils," Riel said. "The priests educate and lead ceremony and—keep the city in spiritual balance?"

"Sometimes, possibly, by blood sacrifice," Forest said. "We don't know what they've asked him to do! But it does seem he'd better find out."

After a while Shan sighed. "I feel like a fool," he said.

"Because you fell in love with Dalzul?" Forest's black eyes gazed straight into his. "I honor you for it. But I think he needs your help."

When he left, walking slowly, he felt Forest and Riel watch him go, felt their affectionate concern following him, staying with him.

He headed back for the big market square. We must tell our story together, he told himself. But the words were hollow.

I must listen, he thought. Not talk, not tell. Be still.

He listened as he walked in the streets of Ganam. He tried to look, to see with his eyes, to feel, to be in his own skin in this world, in this world, itself. Not his world, not Dalzul's, or Forest's or Riel's, but this world as it was in its recalcitrant and irreducible earth and stone and clay, its dry bright air, its breathing bodies and thinking minds. A vendor was calling wares in a brief musical phrase, five beats, tataBANaba, and an equal pause, and the call again, sweet and endless. A woman passed him and Shan saw her, saw her absolutely for a moment: short, with muscular arms and hands, a preoccupied look on her wide face with its thousand tiny wrinkles etched by the sun on the pottery smoothness of the skin. She strode past him, purposeful, not noticing him, and was gone. She left behind her an indubitable sense of being. Of being herself. Unconstructed, unreadable, unreachable. The other. Not his to understand.

All right then. Rough stone warm against the palm, and a five-beat measure, and a short old woman going about her business. It was a beginning.

I've been dreaming, he thought. Ever since we got here. Not a nightmare like the *Shoby*. A good dream, a sweet dream. But was it my dream or his? Following him around, seeing through his eyes, meeting Viaka and the others, being feasted, listening to the music . . . Learning their dances, learning to drum with them . . . Learning to cook . . . Pruning orchards . . . Sitting on my terrace, eating tipu seeds . . . A sunny dream, full of music and trees and simple companionship and peaceful solitude. My good dream, he thought, surprised and wry. No kingship, no beautiful princess, no rivals for the throne. I'm a lazy man. With lazy dreams. I need Tai to wake me up, make me vibrate, irritate me. I need my angry woman, my unforgiving friend.

Forest and Riel weren't a bad substitute. They were certainly friends, and though they forgave his laziness, they had jolted him out of it.

An odd question appeared in his mind: Does Dalzul know we're here? Apparently Forest and Riel don't exist for him as women; do I exist for him as a man?

He did not try to answer the question. My job, he thought, is to try to jolt him. To put a bit of dissonance in the harmony, to syncopate the beat. I'll ask him to dinner and talk to him, he thought.

Middle-aged, majestic, hawk-nosed, fierce-faced, Aketa was the most mild and patient of teachers. "Todokyu nkenes ebegebyu," he repeated for the fifth or sixth time, smiling.

"The scepter—something—is full of? has mastery over? represents?" said Forest.

"Is connected with—symbolizes?" said Riel.

"Kenes!" Shan said. "Electric! That's the word they kept using at the generator. Power!"

"The scepter symbolizes power?" said Forest. "Well, what a revelation. Shit!"

"Shit," Aketa repeated, evidently liking the sound of the word. "Shit!"

Shan went into mime, dancing a waterfall, imitating the motion of wheels, the hum and buzz of the little dynamo up on the volcano. The two women stared at him as he roared, turned, hummed, buzzed, and crackled, shouting "Kenes?" at intervals like a demented chicken. But Aketa's smile broadened. "Soha, kenes," he agreed, and mimicked the leap of a spark from one fingertip to another. "Todokyu nkenes ebegebyu."

"The scepter signifies, symbolizes electricity! It must mean something like—if you take up the scepter you're the Electricity Priest—like Aketa's the Library Priest and Agot's the Calendar Priest—right?"

"It would make sense," Forest said.

"Why would they pick Dalzul straight off as their chief electrician?" Riel asked.

"Because he came out of the sky, like lightning!" said Shan.

"Did they pick him?" Forest asked.

There was a pause. Aketa looked from one to the other, alert and patient.

"What's 'choose'?" Forest asked Riel, who said, "Sotot."

Forest turned to their teacher. "Aketa: Dazu . . . ntodok . . . sotot?"

Aketa was silent for some time and then said, gravely and clearly, "Soha. Todok nDazu oyo sotot."

"'Yes. And also the scepter chooses Dalzul,'" Riel murmured.

"Aheo?" Shan demanded—why? But of Aketa's answer they could understand only a few words: priesthood or vocation, sacredness, the earth.

"Anam," Riel said—"Ket? Anam Ket?"

Aketa's pitch-black eyes met hers. Again he was silent, and the quality of his silence held them all still. When he spoke it was with sorrow. "Ai Dazu!" he said. "Ai Dazu kesemmas!"

He stood up, and knowing what was expected, they too rose, thanked him quietly for his teaching, and filed out. Obedient children, Shan thought. Good pupils. Learning what knowledge?

That evening he looked up from his practice on the little Gaman finger-drum, to which Abud liked to listen, sitting with him on the terrace, sometimes singing a soft chant when he caught a familiar beat.

"Abud," he said, "metu?"—a word?

Abud, who had got used to the inquiry in the last few days, said, "Soha." He was a humorless, even-natured young man; he tolerated all Shan's peculiarities, perhaps, Shan thought, because he really hardly noticed them.

"'Kesemmas.'" Shan said.

"Ah," said Abud, and repeated the word, and then went off slowly and relentlessly into the incomprehensible. Shan had learned to watch him rather than trying to catch the words. He listened to the tone, saw the gestures, the expressions. The earth, down, low, digging? The Gaman buried their dead. Dead, death? He mimed dying, a corpse; but Abud never understood his charades, and stared blankly. Shan gave up, and pattered out the dance rhythm of yesterday's festival on the drum. "Soha, soha," said Abud.

"I've never actually spoken to Ket," Shan said to Dalzul.

It had been a good dinner. He had cooked it, with considerable assistance from Abud, who had prevented him just in time from frying the fezuni. Eaten raw, dipped in fiery pepperjuice, the fezuni had been delicious. Abud had eaten with them, respectfully silent as he always was in Dalzul's presence, and then excused himself. Shan and Dalzul were now nibbling tipu seeds and drinking nut beer, sitting on little carpets on the terrace in the purple twilight, watching the stars slowly clot the sky with brilliance.

"All men except the chosen king are taboo to her," Dalzul said.

"But she's married," Shan said—"isn't she?"

"No, no. The princess must remain virgin until the king is chosen. Then she belongs only to him. The sacred marriage, the hierogamy."

"They do practice polyandry," Shan said uncertainly.

"Her union with him is probably the fundamental event of the kingship ceremonial. Neither has any real choice in the matter. That's why her defection is so troubling. She's breaking her own society's rules." Dalzul took a long draft of beer. "What made me their choice in the first place—my dramatic appearance out of the sky—may be working against me now. I broke the rules by going away, and then coming back, and not coming back alone. One supernatural person pops out of the sky, all right, but four of them, male and female, all eating and drinking and shitting like everybody else, and asking stupid questions in baby talk all the time? We aren't behaving in a properly sacred manner. And they respond by impropriety of the same order, rule-breaking. Primitive worldviews are rigid, they break when strained. We're having a disintegrative effect on this society. And I am responsible."

Shan took a breath. "It isn't your world, sir," he said. "It's theirs. They're responsible for it." He cleared his throat. "And they don't seem all that primitive—they make steel, their grasp of the principles of electricity is impressive—and they are literate, and the social system seems to be very flexible and stable, if what Forest and—"

"I still call her the princess, but as I learn the language better I've realized that that's inaccurate," Dalzul said, setting down his cup and speaking musingly. "Queen is probably nearer: queen of Ganam, of the Gaman. She is identified as Ganam, as the soil of the planet itself."

"Yes," Shan said. "Riel says—"

"So that in a sense she is the Earth. As, in a sense, I am Space, the sky. Coming alone to this world, a conjunction. A mystic union: fire and air with soil and water. The old mythologies enacted yet again in living flesh. She cannot turn away from me. It dislocates the very order of things. The father and the mother are joined, their children are obedient, happy, secure. But if the mother rebels, disorder, distress, failure ensue. These responsibilities are absolute. We don't choose them. They choose us. She must be brought back to her duty to her people."

"As Forest and Riel understand it, she's been married to Aketa for several years, and her second husband is the father of her daughter." Shan heard the harshness of his voice; his mouth was dry and his heart pounding as if he was afraid, of what? of being disobedient?

"Viaka says he can bring her back to the palace," Dalzul said, "but at risk of retaliation from the pretender's faction."

"Dalzul!" Shan said. "Ket is a married woman! She went back to her family. Her duty to you as Earth Priestess or whatever it is is done. Aketa is her husband, not your rival. He doesn't want the scepter, the crown, whatever it is!"

Dalzul made no reply and his expression was unreadable in the deepening twilight.

Shan went on, desperately: "Until we understand this society better, maybe you should hold back—certainly not let Viaka kidnap Ket—"

"I'm glad you see that," Dalzul said. "Although I can't help my involvement, we certainly must try not to interfere with these people's belief systems. Power is responsibility, alas! Well, I should be off. Thank you for a very pleasant evening, Shan. We can still sing a tune together, eh, shipmates?" He stood up and patted the air on the back, saying, "Good night, Forest; good night, Riel," before he patted Shan on the back and said, "Good night and thanks, Shan!" He strode out of the courtyard, a lithe, erect figure, a white glimmer in the starlit dark.

"I think we've got to get him onto the ship, Forest. He's increasingly delusional." Shan squeezed his hands together till the knuckles cracked. "I think he's delusional. Maybe I am. But you and Riel and I, we seem to be in the same general reality —fiction—are we?"

Forest nodded grimly. "Increasingly so," she said. "And if kesemmas does mean dying, or murder—Riel thinks it's murder, it involves violence. . . . I have this horrible vision of poor Dalzul committing some awful ritual sacrifice, cutting somebody's throat while convinced that he's pouring out oil or cutting cloth or something harmless. I'd be glad to get him out of this! I'd be glad to get out myself. But how?"

"Surely if the three of us—"

"Reason with him?" Forest asked, sardonic.

When they went to what he called the palace, they had to wait a long time to see Dalzul. Old Viaka, anxious and nervous, tried to send them away, but they waited. Dalzul came out into his courtyard at last and greeted Shan. He did not acknowledge or did not perceive Riel and Forest. If he was acting, it was a consummate performance; he moved without awareness of their physical presence and talked through their speech. When at last Shan said, "Forest and Riel are here, Dalzul— here—look at them!"—Dalzul looked where he gestured and then looked back at Shan with such shocked compassion that

Shan lost his own bearings and turned to see if the women were still there.

Dalzul, watching him, spoke very gently: "It's about time we went back, Shan."

"Yes— Yes, I think so— I think we ought to." Tears of pity, relief, shame jammed in Shan's throat for a moment. "We should go back. It isn't working."

"Very soon," Dalzul said, "very soon now. Don't worry, Shan. Anxiety increases the perceptual anomalies. Just take it easy, as you did at first, and remember that you've done nothing wrong. As soon as the coronation has—"

"No! We should go now—"

"Shan, whether I asked for it or not, I have an obligation here, and I will fulfill it. If I run out on them, Aketa's faction will have their swords out—"

"Aketa doesn't have a sword," Riel said, her voice high and loud as Shan had never heard it. "These people don't have swords, they don't make them!"

Dalzul talked on through her voice: "As soon as the ceremony is over and the kingship is filled, we'll go. After all, I can go and be back within an hour, if need be. I'll take you back to Ve Port. In no time at all, as the joke is. So stop worrying about what never was your problem. I got you into this. It's my responsibility."

"How can—" Shan began, but Forest's long, black hand was on his arm.

"Don't try, Shan," she said. "The mad reason much better than the sane. Come on. This is very hard to take."

Dalzul was turning serenely away, as if they had left him already.

"Either we have to wait for this ceremony with him," Forest said as they went out into the hot, bright street, "or we knock him on the head and stick him in the ship."

"I'd *like* to knock him on the head," Riel said.

"If we do get him onto the ship," Shan said, "how do we know he'll take us back to Ve? And if he turns round and comes right back, how do we know what he'll do? He could destroy Ganam instead of saving it—"

"Shan!" Riel said, "Stop it! Is Ganam a world? Is Dalzul a god?"

He stared at her. A couple of women going by looked at them, and one nodded a greeting, "Ha, Foyes! Ha, Yeh!"

"Ha, Tasasap!" Forest said to her, while Riel, her eyes blazing, faced Shan: "Ganam is one little city-state on a large planet, which the Gaman call Anam, and the people in the next valley call something else entirely. We've seen one tiny corner of it. It'll take us years to know anything about it. Dalzul, because he's crazy or because churtening made him crazy or made us all crazy, I don't know which, I don't care just now—Dalzul barged in and got mixed up in sacred stuff and maybe is causing some trouble and confusion. But these people *live* here. This is their place. One man can't destroy them and one man can't save them! They have their own story, and *they're* telling it! How we'll figure in it I don't know—maybe as some idiots that fell out of the sky once!"

Forest put a peaceable arm around Riel's shoulders. "When she gets excited she gets excited. Come on, Shan. Aketa certainly isn't planning to slaughter Viaka's household. I don't see these people letting us mess up anything in a big way. They're in control. We'll go through this ceremony. It probably isn't a big deal, except in Dalzul's mind. And as soon as it's over and his mind's at rest, ask him to take us home. He'll do it. He's—" She paused. "He's fatherly," she said, without sarcasm.

They did not see Dalzul again until the day of the ceremony. He stayed holed up in his palace, and Viaka sternly forbade them entrance. Aketa evidently had no power to interfere in another sacred jurisdiction, and no wish to. "Tezyeme," he said, which meant something on the order of "it is happening the way it is supposed to happen." He did not look happy about it, but he was not going to interfere.

On the morning of the Ceremony of the Scepter, there was no buying and selling in the marketplace. People came out in their finest kilts and gorgeous vests; all the men of the priesthoods wore the high, plumed, basketry headdresses and massive gold earrings. Babies' and children's heads were rubbed with red ocher. But it was not a festivity, such as the Star-Rising ceremony of a few days earlier; nobody danced, nobody cooked tipu-bread, there was no music. Only a large, rather

subdued crowd kept gathering in the marketplace. At last the
doors of Aketa's house—Ket's house, actually, Riel reminded
them—swung open, and a procession came forth, walking to
the complex, thrilling, somber beat of drums. The drummers
had been waiting in the streets behind the house, and came
forward to walk behind the procession. The whole city seemed
to shake to the steady, heavy rhythms.

Shan had never seen Ket except on the ship's tape of Dalzul's
first arrival, but he recognized her at once in the procession: a
stern, splendid woman. She wore a headdress less elaborate than
most of the men's, but ornate with gold, balancing it proudly as
she walked. Beside her walked Aketa, red plumes nodding above
his wicker crown, and another man to her left—"Ketketa, second husband," Riel murmured. "That's their daughter." The
child was four or five, very dignified, pacing along with her parents, her dark hair rough and red with ocher. "All the priests in
Ket's volcano lineage are here," Riel went on. "There's the
Earth-Turner. That old one, that's the Calendar Priest. There's a
lot of them I don't know. This is a *big* ceremony. . . ." Her
whisper was a little shaky.

The procession turned left out of the marketplace and
moved on to the heavy beating of the drums until Ket came
abreast of the main entrance of Viaka's rambling, yellow-walled
house. There, with no visible signal, everyone stopped walking
at once. The drums maintained the heavy, complex beat; but
one by one they dropped out, till one throbbed alone like a
heart and then stopped, leaving a terrifying silence.

A man with a towering headdress of woven feathers stepped
forward and called out a summons: "Sem ayatan! Sem Dazu!"

The door opened slowly. Dalzul stood framed in the sunlit
doorway, darkness behind him. He wore his black-and-silver
uniform. His hair shone silver.

In the absolute silence of the crowd, Ket walked forward to
face him. She knelt down on both knees, bowed her head, and
said, "Dazu, sototiyu!"

"'Dalzul, you chose,'" Riel whispered.

Dalzul smiled. He stepped forward and reached out his
hands to lift Ket to her feet.

A whisper ran like wind in the crowd, a hiss or gasp or sigh of shock. Ket's gold-burdened head came up, startled, then she was on her feet, fiercely erect, her hands at her sides. "Sototiyu!" she said, and turned, and strode back to her husbands.

The drums took up a soft patter, a rain sound.

A gap opened in the procession just in front of the door of the house. Quiet and self-possessed, walking with great dignity, Dalzul came forward and took the place left open for him. The rain sound of the drums grew louder, turning to thunder, thunder rolling near and far, loud and low. With the perfect unanimity of a school of fish or flock of birds the procession moved forward.

The people of the city followed, Shan, Riel, and Forest among them.

"Where are they going?" Forest said as they left the last street and struck out on the narrow road between the orchards.

"This road goes up Iyananam," Shan said.

"Onto the volcano? Maybe that's where the ritual will be."

The drums beat, the sunlight beat, Shan's heart beat, his feet struck the dust of the road, all in one huge pulse. Entrained. Thought and speech lost in the one great beat, beat, beat.

The procession had halted. The followers were stopping. The three Terrans kept on until they came up alongside the procession itself. It was re-forming, the drummers drawing off to one side, a few of them softly playing the thunder roll. Some of the crowd, people with children, were beginning to go back down the steep trail beside the mountain stream. Nobody spoke, and the noise of the waterfall uphill from them and the noisy torrent nearby almost drowned out the drums.

They were a hundred paces or so downhill from the little stone building that housed the dynamo. The plumed priests, Ket and her husbands and household, all had drawn aside, leaving the way clear to the bank of the stream. Stone steps were built down right to the water, and at their foot lay a terrace, paved with light-colored stone, over which the clear water washed in quick-moving, shallow sheets. Amidst the shine and motion of the water stood an altar or low pedestal, blinding bright in the noon sun: gilt or solid gold, carved and drawn into intricate and fantastic figures of crowned men, dancing men, men with diamond eyes. On the pedestal lay a wand, not gold, unornamented, of dark wood or tarnished metal.

Dalzul began to walk towards the pedestal.

Aketa stepped forward suddenly and stood at the head of the stone steps, blocking Dalzul's way. He spoke in a ringing voice, a few words. Riel shook her head, not understanding. Dalzul stood silent, motionless, and made no reply. When Aketa fell silent, Dalzul strode straight forward, as if to walk through him.

Aketa held his ground. He pointed to Dalzul's feet. "Tediad!" he said sharply— "'Shoes,'" Riel murmured. Aketa and all the Gaman in the procession were barefoot. After a moment, with no loss of dignity, Dalzul knelt, took off his shoes and stockings, set them aside, and stood up, barefoot in his black uniform.

"Stand aside now," he said quietly, and, as if understanding him, Aketa stepped back among the watchers.

"Ai Dazu," he said as Dalzul passed him, and Ket said softly, "Ai Dazu!" The soft murmur followed Dalzul as he paced down the steps and out onto the terrace, walking through the shallow water that broke in bright drops around his ankles. Unhesitating, he walked to the pedestal and around it, so that he faced the procession and the watching people. He smiled, and put out his hand, and seized the scepter.

"No," Shan said. "No, we had no spy-eye with us. Yes, he died instantly. No, I have no idea what voltage. Underground wires from the generator, we assume. Yes, of course it was deliberate, intentional, arranged. They thought he had chosen that death. He chose it when he chose to have sex with Ket, with the Earth Priestess, with the Earth. They thought he knew; how could they know he didn't know? If you lie with the Earth, you die by the Lightning. Men come from a long way to Ganam for that death. Dalzul came from a very long way. No, we none of us understood. No, I don't know if it had anything to do with the churten effect, with perceptual dissonance, with chaos. We came to see things differently, but which of us knew the truth? He knew he had to be a god again."

Another Story or A Fisherman
of the Inland Sea

*To the Stabiles of the Ekumen on Hain, and to Gvonesh,
Director of the Churten Field Laboratories at Ve Port: from
Tiokunan'n Hideo, Farmholder of the Second Sedoretu of
Udan, Derdan'nad, Oket, on O.*

I shall make my report as if I told a story, this having been the
tradition for some time now. You may, however, wonder why a
farmer on the planet O is reporting to you as if he were a
Mobile of the Ekumen. My story will explain that. But it does
not explain itself. Story is our only boat for sailing on the river
of time, but in the great rapids and the winding shallows, no
boat is safe.

So: once upon a time when I was twenty-one years old I left
my home and came on the NAFAL ship *Terraces of Darranda*
to study at the Ekumenical Schools on Hain.

The distance between Hain and my home world is just over
four light-years, and there has been traffic between O and the
Hainish system for twenty centuries. Even before the Nearly
As Fast As Light drive, when ships spent a hundred years of
planetary time instead of four to make the crossing, there were
people who would give up their old life to come to a new
world. Sometimes they returned; not often. There were tales
of such sad returns to a world that had forgotten the voyager.
I knew also from my mother a very old story called "The
Fisherman of the Inland Sea," which came from her home
world, Terra. The life of a ki'O child is full of stories, but of all
I heard told by her and my othermother and my fathers and
grandparents and uncles and aunts and teachers, that one was
my favorite. Perhaps I liked it so well because my mother told
it with deep feeling, though very plainly, and always in the
same words (and I would not let her change the words if she
ever tried to).

The story tells of a poor fisherman, Urashima, who went out
daily in his boat alone on the quiet sea that lay between his
home island and the mainland. He was a beautiful young man

with long, black hair, and the daughter of the king of the sea saw him as he leaned over the side of the boat and she gazed up to see the floating shadow cross the wide circle of the sky.

Rising from the waves, she begged him to come to her palace under the sea with him. At first he refused, saying, "My children wait for me at home." But how could he resist the sea king's daughter? "One night," he said. She drew him down with her under the water, and they spent a night of love in her green palace, served by strange undersea beings. Urashima came to love her dearly, and maybe he stayed more than one night only. But at last he said, "My dear, I must go. My children wait for me at home."

"If you go, you go forever," she said.

"I will come back," he promised.

She shook her head. She grieved, but did not plead with him. "Take this with you," she said, giving him a little box, wonderfully carved, and sealed shut. "Do not open it, Urashima."

So he went up onto the land, and ran up the shore to his village, to his house: but the garden was a wilderness, the windows were blank, the roof had fallen in. People came and went among the familiar houses of the village, but he did not know a single face. "Where are my children?" he cried. An old woman stopped and spoke to him: "What is your trouble, young stranger?"

"I am Urashima, of this village, but I see no one here I know!"

"Urashima!" the woman said—and my mother would look far away, and her voice as she said the name made me shiver, tears starting to my eyes—"Urashima! My grandfather told me a fisherman named Urashima was lost at sea, in the time of his grandfather's grandfather. There has been no one of that family alive for a hundred years."

So Urashima went back down to the shore; and there he opened the box, the gift of the sea king's daughter. A little white smoke came out of it and drifted away on the sea wind. In that moment Urashima's black hair turned white, and he grew old, old, old; and he lay down on the sand and died.

Once, I remember, a traveling teacher asked my mother about the fable, as he called it. She smiled and said, "In the Annals of the Emperors of my nation of Terra it is recorded that a young man named Urashima, of the Yosa district, went away in the year 477, and came back to his village in the year

825, but soon departed again. And I have heard that the box was kept in a shrine for many centuries." Then they talked about something else.

My mother, Isako, would not tell the story as often as I demanded it. "That one is so sad," she would say, and tell instead about Grandmother and the rice dumpling that rolled away, or the painted cat who came alive and killed the demon rats, or the peach boy who floated down the river. My sister and my germanes, and older people, too, listened to her tales as closely as I did. They were new stories on O, and a new story is always a treasure. The painted cat story was the general favorite, especially when my mother would take out her brush and the block of strange, black, dry ink from Terra, and sketch the animals—cat, rat—that none of us had ever seen: the wonderful cat with arched back and brave round eyes, the fanged and skulking rats, "pointed at both ends" as my sister said. But I waited always, through all other stories, for her to catch my eye, look away, smile a little and sigh, and begin, "Long, long ago, on the shore of the Inland Sea there lived a fisherman . . ."

Did I know then what that story meant to her? that it was her story? that if she were to return to her village, her world, all the people she had known would have been dead for centuries?

Certainly I knew that she "came from another world," but what that meant to me as a five-, or seven-, or ten-year-old, is hard for me now to imagine, impossible to remember. I knew that she was a Terran and had lived on Hain; that was something to be proud of. I knew that she had come to O as a Mobile of the Ekumen (more pride, vague and grandiose) and that "your father and I fell in love at the Festival of Plays in Sudiran." I knew also that arranging the marriage had been a tricky business. Getting permission to resign her duties had not been difficult —the Ekumen is used to Mobiles going native. But as a foreigner, Isako did not belong to a ki'O moiety, and that was only the first problem. I heard all about it from my othermother, Tubdu, an endless source of family history, anecdote, and scandal. "You know," Tubdu told me when I was eleven or twelve, her eyes shining and her irrepressible, slightly wheezing, almost silent laugh beginning to shake her from the inside out—"you know, she didn't even know women got married? Where she came from, she said, women don't marry."

I could and did correct Tubdu: "Only in her part of it. She told me there's lots of parts of it where they do." I felt obscurely defensive of my mother, though Tubdu spoke without a shadow of malice or contempt; she adored Isako. She had fallen in love with her "the moment I saw her—that black hair! that mouth!"—and simply found it endearingly funny that such a woman could have expected to marry only a man.

"I understand," Tubdu hastened to assure me. "I know—on Terra it's different, their fertility was damaged, they have to think about marrying for children. And they marry in twos, too. Oh, poor Isako! How strange it must have seemed to her! I remember how she looked at me—" And off she went again into what we children called The Great Giggle, her joyous, silent, seismic laughter.

To those unfamiliar with our customs I should explain that on O, a world with a low, stable human population and an ancient climax technology, certain social arrangements are almost universal. The dispersed village, an association of farms, rather than the city or state, is the basic social unit. The population consists of two halves or moieties. A child is born into its mother's moiety, so that all ki'O (except the mountain folk of Ennik) belong either to the Morning People, whose time is from midnight to noon, or the Evening People, whose time is from noon to midnight. The sacred origins and functions of the moieties are recalled in the Discussions and the Plays and in the services at every farm shrine. The original social function of the moiety was probably to structure exogamy into marriage and so discourage inbreeding in isolated farmholds, since one can have sex with or marry only a person of the other moiety. The rule is severely reinforced. Transgressions, which of course occur, are met with shame, contempt, and ostracism. One's identity as a Morning or an Evening Person is as deeply and intimately part of oneself as one's gender, and has quite as much to do with one's sexual life.

A ki'O marriage, called a sedoretu, consists of a Morning woman and man and an Evening woman and man; the heterosexual pairs are called Morning and Evening according to the woman's moiety; the homosexual pairs are called Day—the two women—and Night—the two men.

So rigidly structured a marriage, where each of four people

must be sexually compatible with two of the others while never having sex with the fourth—clearly this takes some arranging. Making sedoretu is a major occupation of my people. Experimenting is encouraged; foursomes form and dissolve, couples "try on" other couples, mixing and matching. Brokers, traditionally elderly widowers, go about among the farmholds of the dispersed villages, arranging meetings, setting up field dances, serving as universal confidants. Many marriages begin as a love match of one couple, either homosexual or heterosexual, to which another pair or two separate people become attached. Many marriages are brokered or arranged by the village elders from beginning to end. To listen to the old people under the village great tree making a sedoretu is like watching a master game of chess or tidhe. "If that Evening boy at Erdup were to meet young Tobo during the flour-processing at Gad'd . . . " "Isn't Hodin'n of the Oto Morning a programmer? They could use a programmer at Erdup. . . ." The dowry a prospective bride or groom can offer is their skill, or their home farm. Otherwise undesired people may be chosen and honored for the knowledge or the property they bring to a marriage. The farmhold, in turn, wants its new members to be agreeable and useful. There is no end to the making of marriages on O. I should say that all in all they give as much satisfaction as any other arrangement to the participants, and a good deal more to the marriage-makers.

Of course many people never marry. Scholars, wandering Discussers, itinerant artists and experts, and specialists in the Centers seldom want to fit themselves into the massive permanence of a farmhold sedoretu. Many people attach themselves to a brother's or sister's marriage as aunt or uncle, a position with limited, clearly defined responsibilities; they can have sex with either or both spouses of the other moiety, thus sometimes increasing the sedoretu from four to seven or eight. Children of that relationship are called cousins. The children of one mother are brothers or sisters to one another; the children of the Morning and the children of the Evening are germanes. Brothers, sisters, and first cousins may not marry, but germanes may. In some less conservative parts of O germane marriages are looked at askance, but they are common and respected in my region.

My father was a Morning man of Udan Farmhold of Derdan'nad Village in the hill region of the Northwest Watershed
of the Saduun River, on Oket, the smallest of the six continents
of O. The village comprises seventy-seven farmholds, in a
deeply rolling, stream-cut region of fields and forests on the
watershed of the Oro, a tributary of the wide Saduun. It is
fertile, pleasant country, with views west to the Coast Range
and south to the great floodplains of the Saduun and the gleam
of the sea beyond. The Oro is a wide, lively, noisy river full of
fish and children. I spent my childhood in or on or by the Oro,
which runs through Udan so near the house that you can hear
its voice all night, the rush and hiss of the water and the deep
drumbeats of rocks rolled in its current. It is shallow and quite
dangerous. We all learned to swim very young in a quiet bay
dug out as a swimming pool, and later to handle rowboats and
kayaks in the swift current full of rocks and rapids. Fishing was
one of the children's responsibilities. I liked to spear the fat,
beady-eyed, blue ochid; I would stand heroic on a slippery
boulder in midstream, the long spear poised to strike. I was
good at it. But my germane Isidri, while I was prancing about
with my spear, would slip into the water and catch six or seven
ochid with her bare hands. She could catch eels and even the
darting ei. I never could do it. "You just sort of move with the
water and get transparent," she said. She could stay underwater
longer than any of us, so long you were sure she had drowned.
"She's too bad to drown," her mother, Tubdu, proclaimed.
"You can't drown really bad people. They always bob up again."

Tubdu, the Morning wife, had two children with her husband Kap: Isidri, a year older than me, and Suudi, three years
younger. Children of the Morning, they were my germanes, as
was Cousin Had'd, Tubdu's son with Kap's brother Uncle
Tobo. On the Evening side there were two children, myself
and my younger sister. She was named Koneko, an old name in
Oket, which has also a meaning in my mother's Terran language: "kitten," the young of the wonderful animal "cat" with
the round back and the round eyes. Koneko, four years
younger than me, was indeed round and silky like a baby animal, but her eyes were like my mother's, long, with lids that
went up towards the temple, like the soft sheaths of flowers
before they open. She staggered around after me, calling, "Deo!

Deo! Wait!"—while I ran after fleet, fearless, ever-vanishing Isidri, calling, "Sidi! Sidi! Wait!"

When we were older, Isidri and I were inseparable companions, while Suudi, Koneko, and Cousin Had'd made a trinity, usually coated with mud, splotched with scabs, and in some kind of trouble—gates left open so the yamas got into the crops, hay spoiled by being jumped on, fruit stolen, battles with the children from Drehe Farmhold. "Bad, bad," Tubdu would say. "None of 'em will ever drown!" And she would shake with her silent laughter.

My father Dohedri was a hardworking man, handsome, silent, and aloof. I think his insistence on bringing a foreigner into the tight-woven fabric of village and farm life, conservative and suspicious and full of old knots and tangles of passions and jealousies, had added anxiety to a temperament already serious. Other ki'O had married foreigners, of course, but almost always in a "foreign marriage," a pairing; and such couples usually lived in one of the Centers, where all kinds of untraditional arrangements were common, even (so the village gossips hissed under the great tree) incestuous couplings between two Morning people! two Evening people! —Or such pairs would leave O to live on Hain, or would cut all ties to all homes and become Mobiles on the NAFAL ships, only touching different worlds at different moments and then off again into an endless future with no past.

None of this would do for my father, a man rooted to the knees in the dirt of Udan Farmhold. He brought his beloved to his home, and persuaded the Evening People of Derdan'nad to take her into their moiety, in a ceremony so rare and ancient that a Caretaker had to come by ship and train from Noratan to perform it. Then he had persuaded Tubdu to join the sedoretu. As regards her Day marriage, this was no trouble at all, as soon as Tubdu met my mother; but it presented some difficulty as regards her Morning marriage. Kap and my father had been lovers for years; Kap was the obvious and willing candidate to complete the sedoretu; but Tubdu did not like him. Kap's long love for my father led him to woo Tubdu earnestly and well, and she was far too good-natured to hold out against the interlocking wishes of three people, plus her own lively desire for Isako. She always found Kap a boring husband, I think; but his

younger brother, Uncle Tobo, was a bonus. And Tubdu's relation to my mother was infinitely tender, full of honor, of delicacy, of restraint. Once my mother spoke of it. "She knew how
strange it all was to me," she said. "She knows how strange it
all is."

"This world? our ways?" I asked.

My mother shook her head very slightly. "Not so much that,"
she said in her quiet voice with the faint foreign accent. "But men
and women, women and women, together—love— It is always
very strange. Nothing you know ever prepares you. Ever."

The saying is, "a marriage is made by Day," that is, the relationship of the two women makes or breaks it. Though my
mother and father loved each other deeply, it was a love always
on the edge of pain, never easy. I have no doubt that the radiant childhood we had in that household was founded on the
unshakable joy and strength Isako and Tubdu found in each
other.

So, then: twelve-year-old Isidri went off on the suntrain to
school at Herhot, our district educational Center, and I wept
aloud, standing in the morning sunlight in the dust of Derdan'nad Station. My friend, my playmate, my life was gone. I
was bereft, deserted, alone forever. Seeing her mighty eleven-
year-old elder brother weeping, Kaneko set up a howl too,
tears rolling down her cheeks in dusty balls like raindrops on a
dirt road. She threw her arms about me, roaring, "Hideo!
She'll come back! She'll come back!"

I have never forgotten that. I can hear her hoarse little voice,
and feel her arms round me and the hot morning sunlight on
my neck.

By afternoon we were all swimming in the Oro, Koneko and
I and Suudi and Had'd. As their elder, I resolved on a course of
duty and stern virtue, and led the troop off to help Second-
Cousin Topi at the irrigation control station, until she drove
us away like a swarm of flies, saying, "Go help somebody else
and let me get some work done!" We went and built a mud
palace.

So, then: a year later, twelve-year-old Hideo and thirteen-
year-old Isidri went off on the suntrain to school, leaving
Koneko on the dusty siding, not in tears, but silent, the way
our mother was silent when she grieved.

I loved school. I know that the first days I was achingly homesick, but I cannot recall that misery, buried under my memories of the full, rich years at Herhot, and later at Ran'n, the Advanced Education Center, where I studied temporal physics and engineering.

Isidri finished the First Courses at Herhot, took a year of Second in literature, hydrology, and oenology, and went home to Udan Farmhold of Derdan'nad Village in the hill region of the Northwest Watershed of the Saduun.

The three younger ones all came to school, took a year or two of Second, and carried their learning home to Udan. When she was fifteen or sixteen, Koneko talked of following me to Ran'n; but she was wanted at home because of her excellence in the discipline we call "thick planning"—farm management is the usual translation, but the words have no hint of the complexity of factors involved in thick planning, ecology politics profit tradition aesthetics honor and spirit all functioning in an intensely practical and practically invisible balance of preservation and renewal, like the homeostasis of a vigorous organism. Our "kitten" had the knack for it, and the Planners of Udan and Derdan'nad took her into their councils before she was twenty. But by then, I was gone.

Every winter of my school years I came back to the farm for the long holidays. The moment I was home I dropped school like a book bag and became pure farm boy overnight—working, swimming, fishing, hiking, putting on Plays and farces in the barn, going to field dances and house dances all over the village, falling in and out of love with lovely boys and girls of the Morning from Derdan'nad and other villages.

In my last couple of years at Ran'n, my visits home changed mood. Instead of hiking off all over the country by day and going to a different dance every night, I often stayed home. Careful not to fall in love, I pulled away from my old, dear relationship with Sota of Drehe Farmhold, gradually letting it lapse, trying not to hurt him. I sat whole hours by the Oro, a fishing line in my hand, memorizing the run of the water in a certain place just outside the entrance to our old swimming bay. There, as the water rises in clear strands racing towards two mossy, almost-submerged boulders, it surges and whirls in spirals, and while some of these spin away, grow faint, and disappear, one knots itself on a deep center, becoming a little whirlpool, which spins slowly downstream until, reaching the quick, bright race between the boulders, it loosens and unties itself, released into the body of the river, as another spiral is forming and knotting itself round a deep center upstream where the water rises in clear strands above the boulders. . . . Sometimes that winter the river rose right over the rocks and poured smooth, swollen with rain; but always it would drop, and the whirlpools would appear again.

In the winter evenings I talked with my sister and Suudi, serious, long talks by the fire. I watched my mother's beautiful hands work on the embroidery of new curtains for the wide windows of the dining room, which my father had sewn on the four-hundred-year-old sewing machine of Udan. I worked with him on reprogramming the fertilizer systems for the east fields and the yama rotations, according to our thick-planning council's directives. Now and then he and I talked a little, never very much. In the evenings we had music; Cousin Had'd was a drummer, much in demand for dances, who could always gather a group. Or I would play Word-Thief with Tubdu, a game she adored and always lost at because she was so intent to steal my words that she forgot to protect her own. "Got you, got you!" she would cry, and melt into The Great Giggle, seizing my letterblocks with her fat, tapering, brown fingers; and next move I would take all my letters back along with most of hers. "How did you see that?" she would ask, amazed, studying the scattered words. Sometimes my otherfather Kap played with us, methodical, a bit mechanical, with a small smile for both triumph and defeat.

Then I would go up to my room under the eaves, my room of dark wood walls and dark red curtains, the smell of rain coming in the window, the sound of rain on the tiles of the roof. I would lie there in the mild darkness and luxuriate in sorrow, in great, aching, sweet, youthful sorrow for this ancient home that I was going to leave, to lose forever, to sail away from on the dark river of time. For I knew, from my eighteenth birthday on, that I would leave Udan, leave O, and go out to the other worlds. It was my ambition. It was my destiny.

I have not said anything about Isidri, as I described those

winter holidays. She was there. She played in the Plays, worked on the farm, went to the dances, sang the choruses, joined the hiking parties, swam in the river in the warm rain with the rest of us. My first winter home from Ran'n, as I swung off the train at Derdan'nad Station, she greeted me with a cry of delight and a great embrace, then broke away with a strange, startled laugh and stood back, a tall, dark, thin girl with an intent, watchful face. She was quite awkward with me that evening. I felt that it was because she had always seen me as a little boy, a child, and now, eighteen and a student at Ran'n, I was a man. I was complacent with Isidri, putting her at her ease, patronizing her. In the days that followed, she remained awkward, laughing inappropriately, never opening her heart to me in the kind of long talks we used to have, and even, I thought, avoiding me. My whole last tenday at home that year, Isidri spent visiting her father's relatives in Sabtodiu Village. I was offended that she had not put off her visit till I was gone.

The next year she was not awkward, but not intimate. She had become interested in religion, attending the shrine daily, studying the Discussions with the elders. She was kind, friendly, busy. I do not remember that she and I ever touched that winter until she kissed me good-bye. Among my people a kiss is not with the mouth; we lay our cheeks together for a moment, or for longer. Her kiss was as light as the touch of a leaf, lingering yet barely perceptible.

My third and last winter home, I told them I was leaving: going to Hain, and that from Hain I wanted to go on farther and forever.

How cruel we are to our parents! All I needed to say was that I was going to Hain. After her half-anguished, half-exultant cry of "I knew it!" my mother said in her usual soft voice, suggesting not stating, "After that, you might come back, for a while." I could have said, "Yes." That was all she asked. Yes, I might come back, for a while. With the impenetrable self-centeredness of youth, which mistakes itself for honesty, I refused to give her what she asked. I took from her the modest hope of seeing me after ten years, and gave her the desolation of believing that when I left she would never see me again. "If I qualify, I want to be a Mobile," I said. I had steeled myself to speak without palliations. I prided myself on my truthfulness. And all the time, though I didn't know it, nor did they, it was not the truth at all. The truth is rarely so simple, though not many truths are as complicated as mine turned out to be.

She took my brutality without the least complaint. She had left her own people, after all. She said that evening, "We can talk by ansible, sometimes, as long as you're on Hain." She said it as if reassuring me, not herself. I think she was remembering how she had said good-bye to her people and boarded the ship on Terra, and when she landed a few seeming hours later on Hain, her mother had been dead for fifty years. She could have talked to Terra on the ansible; but who was there for her to talk to? I did not know that pain, but she did. She took comfort in knowing I would be spared it, for a while.

Everything now was "for a while." Oh, the bitter sweetness of those days! How I enjoyed myself—standing, again, poised on the slick boulder amidst the roaring water, spear raised, the hero! How ready, how willing I was to crush all that long, slow, deep, rich life of Udan in my hand and toss it away!

Only for one moment was I told what I was doing, and then so briefly that I could deny it.

I was down in the boathouse workshop, on the rainy, warm afternoon of a day late in the last month of winter. The constant, hissing thunder of the swollen river was the matrix of my thoughts as I set a new thwart in the little red rowboat we used to fish from, taking pleasure in the task, indulging my anticipatory nostalgia to the full by imagining myself on another planet a hundred years away remembering this hour in the boathouse, the smell of wood and water, the river's incessant roar. A knock at the workshop door. Isidri looked in. The thin, dark, watchful face, the long braid of dark hair, not as black as mine, the intent, clear eyes. "Hideo," she said, "I want to talk to you for a minute."

"Come on in!" I said, pretending ease and gladness, though half-aware that in fact I shrank from talking with Isidri, that I was afraid of her—why?

She perched on the vise bench and watched me work in silence for a little while. I began to say something commonplace, but she spoke: "Do you know why I've been staying away from you?"

Liar, self-protective liar, I said, "Staying away from me?"

At that she sighed. She had hoped I would say I understood, and spare her the rest. But I couldn't. I was lying only in pretending that I hadn't noticed that she had kept away from me. I truly had never, never until she told me, imagined why.

"I found out I was in love with you, winter before last," she said. "I wasn't going to say anything about it because—well, you know. If you'd felt anything like that for me, you'd have known I did. But it wasn't both of us. So there was no good in it. But then, when you told us you're leaving . . . At first I thought, all the more reason to say nothing. But then I thought, that wouldn't be fair. To me, partly. Love has a right to be spoken. And you have a right to know that somebody loves you. That somebody has loved you, could love you. We all need to know that. Maybe it's what we need most. So I wanted to tell you. And because I was afraid you thought I'd kept away from you because I didn't love you, or care about you, you know. It might have looked like that. But it wasn't that." She had slipped down off the table and was at the door.

"Sidi!" I said, her name breaking from me in a strange, hoarse cry, the name only, no words—I had no words. I had no feelings, no compassion, no more nostalgia, no more luxurious suffering. Shocked out of emotion, bewildered, blank, I stood there. Our eyes met. For four or five breaths we stood staring into each other's soul. Then Isidri looked away with a wincing, desolate smile, and slipped out.

I did not follow her. I had nothing to say to her: literally. I felt that it would take me a month, a year, years, to find the words I needed to say to her. I had been so rich, so comfortably complete in myself and my ambition and my destiny, five minutes ago; and now I stood empty, silent, poor, looking at the world I had thrown away.

That ability to look at the truth lasted an hour or so. All my life since I have thought of it as "the hour in the boathouse." I sat on the high bench where Isidri had sat. The rain fell and the river roared and the early night came on. When at last I moved, I turned on a light, and began to try to defend my purpose, my planned future, from the terrible plain reality. I began to build up a screen of emotions and evasions and versions; to look away from what Isidri had shown me; to look away from Isidri's eyes.

By the time I went up to the house for dinner I was in control of myself. By the time I went to bed I was master of my destiny again, sure of my decision, almost able to indulge myself in feeling sorry for Isidri—but not quite. Never did I dishonor her with that. I will say that much for myself. I had had the pity that is self-pity knocked out of me in the hour in the boathouse. When I parted from my family at the muddy little station in the village, a few days after, I wept, not luxuriously for them, but for myself, in honest, hopeless pain. It was too much for me to bear. I had had so little practice in pain! I said to my mother, "I will come back. When I finish the course— six years, maybe seven—I'll come back, I'll stay a while."

"If your way brings you," she whispered. She held me close to her, and then released me.

So, then: I have come to the time I chose to begin my story, when I was twenty-one and left my home on the ship *Terraces of Darranda* to study at the Schools on Hain.

Of the journey itself I have no memory whatever. I think I remember entering the ship, yet no details come to mind, visual or kinetic; I cannot recollect being on the ship. My memory of leaving it is only of an overwhelming physical sensation, dizziness. I staggered and felt sick, and was so unsteady on my feet I had to be supported until I had taken several steps on the soil of Hain.

Troubled by this lapse of consciousness, I asked about it at the Ekumenical School. I was told that it is one of the many different ways in which travel at near-lightspeed affects the mind. To most people it seems merely that a few hours pass in a kind of perceptual limbo; others have curious perceptions of space and time and event, which can be seriously disturbing; a few simply feel they have been asleep when they "wake up" on arrival. I did not even have that experience. I had no experience at all. I felt cheated. I wanted to have felt the voyage, to have known, in some way, the great interval of space: but as far as I was concerned, there was no interval. I was at the spaceport on O, and then I was at Ve Port, dizzy, bewildered, and at last, when I was able to believe that I was there, excited.

My studies and work during those years are of no interest now. I will mention only one event, which may or may not be on record in the ansible reception file at Fourth Beck Tower,

EY 21-11-93/1645. (The last time I checked, it was on record in the ansible transmission file at Ran'n, ET date 30-11-93/1645. Urashima's coming and going was on record, too, in the Annals of the Emperors.) 1645 was my first year on Hain. Early in the term I was asked to come to the ansible center, where they explained that they had received a garbled screen transmission, apparently from O, and hoped I could help them reconstitute it. After a date nine days later than the date of reception, it read:

> *les oku n hike problem netru emit it hurt di it may*
> *not be salv devir*

The words were gapped and fragmented. Some were standard Hainish, but *oku* and *netru* mean "north" and "symmetrical" in Sio, my native language. The ansible centers on O had reported no record of the transmission, but the Receivers thought the message might be from O because of these two words and because the Hainish phrase "it may not be salvageable" occurred in a transmission received almost simultaneously from one of the Stabiles on O, concerning a wave-damaged desalinization plant. "We call this a creased message," the Receiver told me, when I confessed I could make nothing of it and asked how often ansible messages came through so garbled. "Not often, fortunately. We can't be certain where or when they originated, or will originate. They may be effects of a double field—interference phenomena, perhaps. One of my colleagues here calls them ghost messages."

Instantaneous transmission had always fascinated me, and though I was then only a beginner in ansible principle, I developed this fortuitous acquaintance with the Receivers into a friendship with several of them. And I took all the courses in ansible theory that were offered.

When I was in my final year in the school of temporal physics, and considering going on to the Cetian Worlds for further study—after my promised visit home, which seemed sometimes a remote, irrelevant daydream and sometimes a yearning and yet fearful need—the first reports came over the ansible from Anarres of the new theory of transilience. Not only information, but matter, bodies, people might be transported from place to place without lapse of time. "Churten technology" was suddenly a reality, although a very strange reality, an implausible fact.

I was crazy to work on it. I was about to go promise my soul and body to the School if they would let me work on churten theory when they came and asked me if I'd consider postponing my training as a Mobile for a year or so to work on churten theory. Judiciously and graciously, I consented. I celebrated all over town that night. I remember showing all my friends how to dance the fen'n, and I remember setting off fireworks in the Great Plaza of the Schools, and I think I remember singing under the Director's windows, a little before dawn. I remember what I felt like next day, too; but it didn't keep me from dragging myself over to the Ti-Phy building to see where they were installing the Churten Field Laboratory.

Ansible transmission is, of course, enormously expensive, and I had only been able to talk to my family twice during my years on Hain; but my friends in the ansible center would occasionally "ride" a screen message for me on a transmission to O. I sent a message thus to Ran'n to be posted on to the First Sedoretu of Udan Farmhold of Derdan'nad Village of the hill district of the Northwest Watershed of the Saduun, Oket, on O, telling them that "although this research will delay my visit home, it may save me four years' travel." The flippant message revealed my guilty feeling; but we did really think then that we would have the technology within a few months.

The Field Laboratories were soon moved out to Ve Port, and I went with them. The joint work of the Cetian and Hainish churten research teams in those first three years was a succession of triumphs, postponements, promises, defeats, breakthroughs, setbacks, all happening so fast that anybody who took a week off was out-of-date. "Clarity hiding mystery," Gvonesh called it. Every time it all came clear it all grew more mysterious. The theory was beautiful and maddening. The experiments were exciting and inscrutable. The technology worked best when it was most preposterous. Four years went by in that laboratory like no time at all, as they say.

I had now spent ten years on Hain and Ve, and was thirty-one. On O, four years had passed while my NAFAL ship passed a few minutes of dilated time going to Hain, and four more would pass while I returned: so when I returned I would have been gone eighteen of their years. My parents were all still alive. It was high time for my promised visit home.

But though churten research had hit a frustrating setback in the Spring Snow Paradox, a problem the Cetians thought might be insoluble, I couldn't stand the thought of being eight years out-of-date when I got back to Hain. What if they broke the paradox? It was bad enough knowing I must lose four years going to O. Tentatively, not too hopefully, I proposed to the Director that I carry some experimental materials with me to O and set up a fixed double-field auxiliary to the ansible link between Ve Port and Ran'n. Thus I could stay in touch with Ve, as Ve stayed in touch with Urras and Anarres; and the fixed ansible link might be preparatory to a churten link. I remember I said, "If you break the paradox, we might eventually send some mice."

To my surprise my idea caught on; the temporal engineers wanted a receiving field. Even our Director, who could be as brilliantly inscrutable as churten theory itself, said it was a good idea. "Mouses, bugs, gholes, who knows what we send you?" she said.

So, then: when I was thirty-one years old I left Ve Port on the NAFAL transport *Lady of Sorra* and returned to O. This time I experienced the near-lightspeed flight the way most people do, as an unnerving interlude in which one cannot think consecutively, read a clockface, or follow a story. Speech and movement become difficult or impossible. Other people appear as unreal half presences, inexplicably there or not there. I did not hallucinate, but everything seemed hallucination. It is like a high fever—confusing, miserably boring, seeming endless, yet very difficult to recall once it is over, as if it were an episode outside one's life, encapsulated. I wonder now if its resemblance to the "churten experience" has yet been seriously investigated.

I went straight to Ran'n, where I was given rooms in the New Quadrangle, fancier than my old student room in the Shrine Quadrangle, and some nice lab space in Tower Hall to set up an experimental transilience field station. I got in touch with my family right away and talked to all my parents; my mother had been ill, but was fine now, she said. I told them I would be home as soon as I had got things going at Ran'n. Every tenday I called again and talked to them and said I'd be along very soon now. I was genuinely very busy, having to catch up the lost four years and to learn Gvonesh's solution to the Spring Snow Paradox. It was, fortunately, the only major advance in theory. Technology had advanced a good deal. I had to retrain myself, and to train my assistants almost from scratch. I had had an idea about an aspect of double-field theory that I wanted to work out before I left. Five months went by before I called them up and said at last, "I'll be there tomorrow." And when I did so, I realized that all along I had been afraid.

I don't know if I was afraid of seeing them after eighteen years, of the changes, the strangeness, or if it was myself I feared.

Eighteen years had made no difference at all to the hills beside the wide Saduun, the farmlands, the dusty little station in Derdan'nad, the old, old houses on the quiet streets. The village great tree was gone, but its replacement had a pretty wide spread of shade already. The aviary at Udan had been enlarged. The yama stared haughtily, timidly at me across the fence. A road gate that I had hung on my last visit home was decrepit, needing its post reset and new hinges, but the weeds that grew beside it were the same dusty, sweet-smelling summer weeds. The tiny dams of the irrigation runnels made their multiple, soft click and thump as they closed and opened. Everything was the same, itself. Timeless, Udan in its dream of work stood over the river that ran timeless in its dream of movement.

But the faces and bodies of the people waiting for me at the station in the hot sunlight were not the same. My mother, forty-seven when I left, was sixty-five, a beautiful and fragile elderly woman. Tubdu had lost weight; she looked shrunken and wistful. My father was still handsome and bore himself proudly, but his movements were slow and he scarcely spoke at all. My otherfather Kap, seventy now, was a precise, fidgety, little old man. They were still the First Sedoretu of Udan, but the vigor of the farmhold now lay in the Second and Third Sedoretu.

I knew of all the changes, of course, but being there among them was a different matter from hearing about them in letters and transmissions. The old house was much fuller than it had been when I lived there. The south wing had been re-opened, and children ran in and out of its doors and across courtyards that in my childhood had been silent and ivied and mysterious.

My sister Koneko was now four years older than I instead of four years younger. She looked very like my early memory of my mother. As the train drew in to Derdan'nad Station, she had been the first of them I recognized, holding up a child of three or four and saying, "Look, look, it's your Uncle Hideo!"

The Second Sedoretu had been married for eleven years: Koneko and Isidri, sister-germanes, were the partners of the Day. Koneko's husband was my old friend Sota, a Morning man of Drehe Farmhold. Sota and I had loved each other dearly when we were adolescents, and I had been grieved to grieve him when I left. When I heard that he and Koneko were in love I had been very surprised, so self-centered am I, but at least I am not jealous: it pleased me very deeply. Isidri's husband, a man nearly twenty years older than herself, named Hedran, had been a traveling scholar of the Discussions. Udan had given him hospitality, and his visits had led to the marriage. He and Isidri had no children. Sota and Koneko had two Evening children, a boy of ten called Murmi, and Lasako, Little Isako, who was four.

The Third Sedoretu had been brought to Udan by Suudi, my brother-germane, who had married a woman from Aster Village; their Morning pair also came from farmholds of Aster. There were six children in that sedoretu. A cousin whose sedoretu at Ekke had broken had also come to live at Udan with her two children; so the coming and going and dressing and undressing and washing and slamming and running and shouting and weeping and laughing and eating was prodigious. Tubdu would sit at work in the sunny kitchen courtyard and watch a wave of children pass. "Bad!" she would cry. "They'll never drown, not a one of 'em!" And she would shake with silent laughter that became a wheezing cough.

My mother, who had after all been a Mobile of the Ekumen, and had traveled from Terra to Hain and from Hain to O, was impatient to hear about my research. "What is it, this churtening? How does it work, what does it do? Is it an ansible for matter?"

"That's the idea," I said. "Transilience: instantaneous transference of being from one s-tc point to another."

"No interval?"

"No interval."

Isako frowned. "It sounds wrong," she said. "Explain."

I had forgotten how direct my soft-spoken mother could be; I had forgotten that she was an intellectual. I did my best to explain the incomprehensible.

"So," she said at last, "you don't really understand how it works."

"No. Nor even what it does. Except that—as a rule—when the field is in operation, the mice in Building One are instantaneously in Building Two, perfectly cheerful and unharmed. Inside their cage, if we remembered to keep their cage inside the initiating churten field. We used to forget. Loose mice everywhere."

"What's *mice?*" said a little Morning boy of the Third Sedoretu, who had stopped to listen to what sounded like a story.

"Ah," I said in a laugh, surprised. I had forgotten that at Udan mice were unknown, and rats were fanged, demon enemies of the painted cat. "Tiny, pretty, furry animals," I said, "that come from Grandmother Isako's world. They are friends of scientists. They have traveled all over the Known Worlds."

"In tiny little spaceships?" the child said hopefully.

"In large ones, mostly," I said. He was satisfied, and went away.

"Hideo," said my mother, in the terrifying way women have of passing without interval from one subject to another because they have them all present in their mind at once, "you haven't found any kind of relationship?"

I shook my head, smiling.

"None at all?"

"A man from Alterra and I lived together for a couple of years," I said. "It was a good friendship; but he's a Mobile now. And . . . oh, you know . . . people here and there. Just recently, at Ran'n, I've been with a very nice woman from East Oket."

"I hoped, if you intend to be a Mobile, that you might make a couple-marriage with another Mobile. It's easier, I think," she said. Easier than what? I thought, and knew the answer before I asked.

"Mother, I doubt now that I'll travel farther than Hain. This churten business is too interesting; I want to be in on it. And if we do learn to control the technology, you know, then travel will be nothing. There'll be no need for the kind of sac-rifice you made. Things will be different. Unimaginably differ-ent! You could go to Terra for an hour and come back here: and only an hour would have passed."

She thought about that. "If you do it, then," she said, speaking slowly, almost shaking with the intensity of comprehension, "you will . . . you will shrink the galaxy—the universe?—to . . ." and she held up her left hand, thumb and fingers all drawn to-gether to a point.

I nodded. "A mile or a light-year will be the same. There will be no distance."

"It can't be right," she said after a while. "To have event without interval . . . Where is the dancing? Where is the way? I don't think you'll be able to control it, Hideo." She smiled. "But of course you must try."

And after that we talked about who was coming to the field dance at Drehe tomorrow.

I did not tell my mother that I had invited Tasi, the nice woman from East Oket, to come to Udan with me and that she had refused, had, in fact, gently informed me that she thought this was a good time for us to part. Tasi was tall, with a braid of dark hair, not coarse, bright black like mine but soft, fine, dark, like the shadows in a forest. A typical ki'O woman, I thought. She had deflated my protestations of love skillfully and without shaming me. "I think you're in love with somebody, though," she said. "Somebody on Hain, maybe. Maybe the man from Alterra you told me about?" No, I said. No, I'd never been in love. I wasn't capable of an intense relationship, that was clear by now. I'd dreamed too long of traveling the galaxy with no at-tachments anywhere, and then worked too long in the churten lab, married to a damned theory that couldn't find its technol-ogy. No room for love, no time.

But why had I wanted to bring Tasi home with me?

Tall but no longer thin, a woman of forty, not a girl, not typical, not comparable, not like anyone anywhere, Isidri had greeted me quietly at the door of the house. Some farm emer-gency had kept her from coming to the village station to meet me. She was wearing an old smock and leggings like any field worker, and her hair, dark beginning to grey, was in a rough braid. As she stood in that wide doorway of polished wood she was Udan itself, the body and soul of that thirty-century-old farmhold, its continuity, its life. All my childhood was in her hands, and she held them out to me.

"Welcome home, Hideo," she said, with a smile as radiant as the summer light on the river. As she brought me in, she said, "I cleared the kids out of your old room. I thought you'd like to be there—would you?" Again she smiled, and I felt her warmth, the solar generosity of a woman in the prime of life, married, settled, rich in her work and being. I had not needed Tasi as a defense. I had nothing to fear from Isidri. She felt no rancor, no embarrassment. She had loved me when she was young, another person. It would be altogether inappropriate for me to feel embarrassment, or shame, or anything but the old affectionate loyalty of the years when we played and worked and fished and dreamed together, children of Udan.

So, then: I settled down in my old room under the tiles. There were new curtains, rust and brown. I found a stray toy under the chair, in the closet, as if I as a child had left my playthings there and found them now. At fourteen, after my entry ceremony in the shrine, I had carved my name on the deep window jamb among the tangled patterns of names and symbols that had been cut into it for centuries. I looked for it now. There had been some additions. Beside my careful, clear *Hideo*, surrounded by my ideogram, the cloudflower, a younger child had hacked a straggling *Dohedri*, and nearby was carved a delicate three-roofs ideogram. The sense of being a bubble in Udan's river, a moment in the permanence of life in this house on this land on this quiet world, was almost crushing, denying my identity, and profoundly reassuring, confirming my identity. Those nights of my visit home I slept as I had not slept for years, lost, drowned in the waters of sleep and darkness, and woke to the summer mornings as if reborn, very hungry.

The children were still all under twelve, going to school at home. Isidri, who taught them literature and religion and was the school planner, invited me to tell them about Hain, about NAFAL travel, about temporal physics, whatever I pleased. Visitors to ki'O farmholds are always put to use. Evening-Uncle Hideo became rather a favorite among the children, always good for hitching up the yama-cart or taking them fishing in the big boat, which they couldn't yet handle, or telling a story about his magic mice who could be in two places at the same time. I asked them if Evening-Grandmother Isako had told them about the painted cat who came alive and killed the demon rats—"And his mouf was all BLUGGY in the morning!" shouted Lasako, her eyes shining. But they didn't know the tale of Urashima.

"Why haven't you told them 'The Fisherman of the Inland Sea'?" I asked my mother.

She smiled and said, "Oh, that was your story. You always wanted it."

I saw Isidri's eyes on us, clear and tranquil, yet watchful still.

I knew my mother had had repair and healing to her heart a year before, and I asked Isidri later, as we supervised some work the older children were doing, "Has Isako recovered, do you think?"

"She seems wonderfully well since you came. I don't know. It's damage from her childhood, from the poisons in the Terran biosphere; they say her immune system is easily depressed. She was very patient about being ill. Almost too patient."

"And Tubdu—does she need new lungs?"

"Probably. All four of them are getting older, and stubborner. . . . But you look at Isako for me. See if you see what I mean."

I tried to observe my mother. After a few days I reported back that she seemed energetic and decisive, even imperative, and that I hadn't seen much of the patient endurance that worried Isidri. She laughed.

"Isako told me once," she said, "that a mother is connected to her child by a very fine, thin cord, like the umbilical cord, that can stretch light-years without any difficulty. I asked her if it was painful, and she said, 'Oh, no, it's just there, you know, it stretches and stretches and never breaks.' It seems to me it must be painful. But I don't know. I have no child, and I've never been more than two days' travel from my mothers." She smiled and said in her soft, deep voice, "I think I love Isako more than anyone, more even than my mother, more even than Koneko. . . ."

Then she had to show one of Suudi's children how to reprogram the timer on the irrigation control. She was the hydrologist for the village and the oenologist for the farm. Her life was thick-planned, very rich in necessary work and wide relationships, a serene and steady succession of days, seasons, years. She swam in life as she had swum in the river, like a fish, at home. She had borne no child, but all the children of the farmhold were hers. She and Koneko were as deeply attached as their mothers had been. Her relation with her rather fragile, scholarly husband seemed peaceful and respectful. I thought his Night marriage with my old friend Sota might be the stronger sexual link, but Isidri clearly admired and depended on his intellectual and spiritual guidance. I thought his teaching a bit dry and disputatious; but what did I know about religion? I had not given worship for years, and felt strange, out of place, even in the home shrine. I felt strange, out of place, in my home. I did not acknowledge it to myself.

I was conscious of the month as pleasant, uneventful, even a little boring. My emotions were mild and dull. The wild nostalgia, the romantic sense of standing on the brink of my destiny, all that was gone with the Hideo of twenty-one. Though now the youngest of my generation, I was a grown man, knowing his way, content with his work, past emotional self-indulgence. I wrote a little poem for the house album about the peacefulness of following a chosen course. When I had to go, I embraced and kissed everyone, dozens of soft or harsh cheek-touches. I told them that if I stayed on O, as it seemed I might be asked to do for a year or so, I would come back next winter for another visit. On the train going back through the hills to Ran'n, I thought with a complacent gravity how I might return to the farm next winter, finding them all just the same; and how, if I came back after another eighteen years or even longer, some of them would be gone and some would be new to me and yet it would be always my home, Udan with its wide dark roofs riding time like a dark-sailed ship. I always grow poetic when I am lying to myself.

I got back to Ran'n, checked in with my people at the lab in Tower Hall, and had dinner with colleagues, good food and drink—I brought them a bottle of wine from Udan, for Isidri was making splendid wines, and had given me a case of the fifteen-year-old Kedun. We talked about the latest breakthrough in churten technology, "continuous-field sending," reported from Anarres just yesterday on the ansible. I went to my rooms in the New Quadrangle through the summer night, my head full of physics, read a little, and went to bed. I turned out the light and darkness filled me as it filled the room. Where was I? Alone in a room among strangers. As I had been for ten years and would always be. On one planet or another, what did it matter? Alone, part of nothing, part of no one. Udan was not my home. I had no home, no people. I had no future, no destiny, any more than a bubble of foam or a whirlpool in a current has a destiny. It is and it isn't. Nothing more.

I turned the light on because I could not bear the darkness, but the light was worse. I sat huddled up in the bed and began to cry. I could not stop crying. I became frightened at how the sobs racked and shook me till I was sick and weak and still could not stop sobbing. After a long time I calmed myself gradually by clinging to an imagination, a childish idea: in the morning I would call Isidri and talk to her, telling her that I needed instruction in religion, that I wanted to give worship at the shrines again, but it had been so long, and I had never listened to the Discussions, but now I needed to, and I would ask her, Isidri, to help me. So, holding fast to that, I could at last stop the terrible sobbing and lie spent, exhausted, until the day came.

I did not call Isidri. In daylight the thought which had saved me from the dark seemed foolish; and I thought if I called her she would ask advice of her husband, the religious scholar. But I knew I needed help. I went to the shrine in the Old School and gave worship. I asked for a copy of the First Discussions, and read it. I joined a Discussion group, and we read and talked together. My religion is godless, argumentative, and mystical. The name of our world is the first word of its first prayer. For human beings its vehicle is the human voice and mind. As I began to rediscover it, I found it quite as strange as churten theory and in some respects complementary to it. I knew, but had never understood, that Cetian physics and religion are aspects of one knowledge. I wondered if all physics and religion are aspects of one knowledge.

At night I never slept well and often could not sleep at all. After the bountiful tables of Udan, college food seemed poor stuff; I had no appetite. But our work, my work went well—wonderfully well.

"No more mouses," said Gvonesh on the voice ansible from Hain. "Peoples."

"What people?" I demanded.

"Me," said Gvonesh.

So our Director of Research churtened from one corner of Laboratory One to another, and then from Building One to Building Two—vanishing in one laboratory and appearing in the other, smiling, in the same instant, in no time.

"What did it feel like?" they asked, of course, and Gvonesh answered, of course, "Like nothing."

Many experiments followed; mice and gholes churtened halfway around Ve and back; robot crews churtened from Anarres to Urras, from Hain to Ve, and then from Anarres to Ve, twenty-two light-years. So, then, eventually the *Shoby* and her crew of ten human beings churtened into orbit around a miserable planet seventeen light-years from Ve and returned (but words that imply coming and going, that imply distance traveled, are not appropriate) thanks only to their intelligent use of entrainment, rescuing themselves from a kind of chaos of dissolution, a death by unreality, that horrified us all. Experiments with high-intelligence life-forms came to a halt.

"The rhythm is wrong," Gvonesh said on the ansible (she said it "rithkhom"). For a moment I thought of my mother saying, "It can't be right to have event without interval." What else had Isako said? Something about dancing. But I did not want to think about Udan. I did not think about Udan. When I did I felt, far down deeper inside me than my bones, the knowledge of being no one, no where, and a shaking like a frightened animal.

My religion reassured me that I was part of the Way, and my physics absorbed my despair in work. Experiments, cautiously resumed, succeeded beyond hope. The Terran Dalzul and his psychophysics took everyone at the research station on Ve by storm; I am sorry I never met him. As he predicted, using the continuity field he churtened without a hint of trouble, alone, first locally, then from Ve to Hain, then the great jump to Tadkla and back. From the second journey to Tadkla, his three companions returned without him. He died on that far world. It did not seem to us in the laboratories that his death was in any way caused by the churten field or by what had come to be known as "the churten experience," though his three companions were not so sure.

"Maybe Dalzul was right. One people at a time," said Gvonesh; and she made herself again the subject, the "ritual animal," as the Hainish say, of the next experiment. Using continuity technology she churtened right round Ve in four skips, which took thirty-two seconds because of the time needed to set up the coordinates. We had taken to calling the non-interval in time/real interval in space a "skip." It sounded light, trivial. Scientists like to trivialize.

I wanted to try the improvement to double-field stability that I had been working on ever since I came to Ran'n. It was time to give it a test; my patience was short, life was too short to fiddle with figures forever. Talking to Gvonesh on the ansible I said, "I'll skip over to Ve Port. And then back here to Ran'n. I promised a visit to my home farm this winter." Scientists like to trivialize.

"You still got that wrinkle in your field?" Gvonesh asked. "Some kind, you know, like a fold?"

"It's ironed out, ammar," I assured her.

"Good, fine," said Gvonesh, who never questioned what one said. "Come."

So, then: we set up the fields in a constant stable churten link with ansible connection; and I was standing inside a chalked circle in the Churten Field Laboratory of Ran'n Center on a late autumn afternoon and standing inside a chalked circle in the Churten Research Station Field Laboratory in Ve Port on a late summer day at a distance of 4.2 light-years and no interval of time.

"Feel nothing?" Gvonesh inquired, shaking my hand heartily. "Good fellow, good fellow, welcome, ammar, Hideo. Good to see. No wrinkle, hah?"

I laughed with the shock and queerness of it, and gave Gvonesh the bottle of Udan Kedun '49 that I had picked up a moment ago from the laboratory table on O.

I had expected, if I arrived at all, to churten promptly back again, but Gvonesh and others wanted me on Ve for a while for discussions and tests of the field. I think now that the Director's extraordinary intuition was at work; the "wrinkle," the "fold" in the Tiokunan'n Field still bothered her. "Is unaes-thetical," she said.

"But it works," I said.

"It worked," said Gvonesh.

Except to retest my field, to prove its reliability, I had no desire to return to O. I was sleeping somewhat better here on Ve, although food was still unpalatable to me, and when I was not working I felt shaky and drained, a disagreeable reminder of my exhaustion after the night which I tried not to remember when for some reason or other I had cried so much. But the work went very well.

"You got no sex, Hideo?" Gvonesh asked me when we were alone in the Lab one day, I playing with a new set of calcula-tions and she finishing her box lunch.

The question took me utterly aback. I knew it was not as impertinent as Gvonesh's peculiar usage of the language made it sound. But Gvonesh never asked questions like that. Her own sex life was as much a mystery as the rest of her existence. No one had ever heard her mention the word, let alone sug-gest the act.

When I sat with my mouth open, stumped, she said, "You used to, hah," as she chewed on a cold varvet.

I stammered something. I knew she was not proposing that she and I have sex, but inquiring after my well-being. But I did not know what to say.

"You got some kind of wrinkle in your life, hah," Gvonesh said. "Sorry. Not my business."

Wanting to assure her I had taken no offense I said, as we say on O, "I honor your intent."

She looked directly at me, something she rarely did. Her eyes were clear as water in her long, bony face softened by a fine, thick, colorless down. "Maybe is time you go back to O?" she asked.

"I don't know. The facilities here—"

She nodded. She always accepted what one said. "You read Harraven's report?" she asked, changing one subject for an-other as quickly and definitively as my mother.

All right, I thought, the challenge was issued. She was ready for me to test my field again. Why not? After all, I could chur-ten to Ran'n and churten right back again to Ve within a minute, if I chose, and if the Lab could afford it. Like ansible transmission, churtening draws essentially on inertial mass, but setting up the field, disinfecting it, and holding it stable in size uses a good deal of local energy. But it was Gvonesh's suggestion, which meant we had the money. I said, "How about a skip over and back?"

"Fine," Gvonesh said. "Tomorrow."

So the next day, on a morning of late autumn, I stood inside a chalked circle in the Field Laboratory on Ve and stood—

A shimmer, a shivering of everything—a missed beat—skipped—

in darkness. A darkness. A dark room. The lab? A lab—I found the light panel. In the darkness I was sure it was the laboratory on Ve. In the light I saw it was not. I didn't know where it was. I didn't know where I was. It seemed familiar yet I could not place it. What was it? A biology lab? There were specimens, an old subparticle microscope, the maker's ideogram on the battered brass casing, the lyre ideogram. . . . I was on O. In some laboratory in some building of the Center at Ran'n? It smelled like the old buildings of Ran'n, it smelled like a rainy night on O. But how could I have not arrived in the receiving field, the circle carefully chalked on the wood floor of the lab in Tower Hall? The field itself must have moved. An appalling, an impossible thought.

I was alarmed and felt rather dizzy, as if my body had skipped that beat, but I was not yet frightened. I was all right, all here, all the pieces in the right places, and the mind working. A slight spatial displacement? said the mind.

I went out into the corridor. Perhaps I had myself been disoriented and left the Churten Field Laboratory and come to full consciousness somewhere else. But my crew would have been there; where were they? And that would have been hours ago; it should have been just past noon on O when I arrived. A slight temporal displacement? said the mind, working away. I went down the corridor looking for my lab, and that is when it became like one of those dreams in which you cannot find the room which you must find. It was that dream. The building was perfectly familiar: it was Tower Hall, the second floor of Tower, but there was no Churten Lab. All the labs were biology and biophysics, and all were deserted. It was evidently late at night. Nobody around. At last I saw a light under a door and knocked and opened it on a student reading at a library terminal.

"I'm sorry," I said. "I'm looking for the Churten Field Lab—"

"The what lab?"

She had never heard of it, and apologized. "I'm not in Ti Phy, just Bi Phy," she said humbly.

I apologized too. Something was making me shakier, increasing my sense of dizziness and disorientation. Was this the "chaos effect" the crew of the *Shoby* and perhaps the crew of the *Galba* had experienced? Would I begin to see the stars through the walls, or turn around and see Gvonesh here on O?

I asked her what time it was. "I should have got here at noon," I said, though that of course meant nothing to her.

"It's about one," she said, glancing at the clock on the terminal. I looked at it too. It gave the time, the tenday, the month, the year.

"That's wrong," I said.

She looked worried.

"That's not right," I said. "The date. It's not right." But I knew from the steady glow of the numbers on the clock, from the girl's round, worried face, from the beat of my heart, from the smell of the rain, that it was right, that it was an hour after midnight eighteen years ago, that I was here, now, on the day after the day I called "once upon a time" when I began to tell this story.

A major temporal displacement, said the mind, working, laboring.

"I don't belong here," I said, and turned to hurry back to what seemed a refuge, Biology Lab 6, which would be the Churten Field Lab eighteen years from now, as if I could re-enter the field, which had existed or would exist for .004 second.

The girl saw that something was wrong, made me sit down, and gave me a cup of hot tea from her insulated bottle.

"Where are you from?" I asked her, the kind, serious student.

"Herdud Farmhold of Deada Village on the South Watershed of the Saduun," she said.

"I'm from downriver," I said. "Udan of Derdan'nad." I

suddenly broke into tears. I managed to control myself, apologized again, drank my tea, and set the cup down. She was not overly troubled by my fit of weeping. Students are intense people, they laugh and cry, they break down and rebuild. She asked if I had a place to spend the night: a perceptive question. I said I did, thanked her, and left.

I did not go back to the biology laboratory, but went downstairs and started to cut through the gardens to my rooms in the New Quadrangle. As I walked the mind kept working; it worked out that somebody else had been/would be in those rooms then/now.

I turned back towards the Shrine Quadrangle, where I had lived my last two years as a student before I left for Hain. If this was in fact, as the clock had indicated, the night after I had left, my room might still be empty and unlocked. It proved to be so, to be as I had left it, the mattress bare, the cyclebasket unemptied.

That was the most frightening moment. I stared at that cyclebasket for a long time before I took a crumpled bit of outprint from it and carefully smoothed it on the desk. It was a set of temporal equations scribbled on my old pocketscreen in my own handwriting, notes from Sedharad's class in Interval, from my last term at Ran'n, day before yesterday, eighteen years ago.

I was now very shaky indeed. You are caught in a chaos field, said the mind, and I believed it. Fear and stress, and nothing to do about it, not till the long night was past. I lay down on the bare bunk-mattress, ready for the stars to burn through the walls and my eyelids if I shut them. I meant to try and plan what I should do in the morning, if there was a morning. I fell asleep instantly and slept like a stone till broad daylight, when I woke up on the bare bed in the familiar room, alert, hungry, and without a moment of doubt as to who or where or when I was.

I went down into the village for breakfast. I didn't want to meet any colleagues—no, fellow students—who might know me and say, "Hideo! What are you doing here? You left on the *Terraces of Darranda* yesterday!"

I had little hope they would not recognize me. I was thirty-one now, not twenty-one, much thinner and not as fit as I had been; but my half-Terran features were unmistakable. I did not want to be recognized, to have to try to explain. I wanted to get out of Ran'n. I wanted to go home.

O is a good world to time-travel in. Things don't change. Our trains run on the same schedule to the same places for centuries. We sign for payment and pay in contracted barter or cash monthly, so I did not have to produce mysterious coins from the future. I signed at the station and took the morning train to Saduun Delta.

The little suntrain glided through the plains and hills of the South Watershed and then the Northwest Watershed, following the ever-widening river, stopping at each village. I got off in the late afternoon at the station in Derdan'nad. Since it was very early spring, the station was muddy, not dusty.

I walked out the road to Udan. I opened the road gate that I had rehung a few days/eighteen years ago; it moved easily on its new hinges. That gave me a little gleam of pleasure. The she-yamas were all in the nursery pasture. Birthing would start any day; their woolly sides stuck out, and they moved like sailboats in a slow breeze, turning their elegant, scornful heads to look distrustfully at me as I passed. Rain clouds hung over the hills. I crossed the Oro on the humpbacked wooden bridge. Four or five great blue ochid hung in a backwater by the bridgefoot; I stopped to watch them; if I'd had a spear . . . The clouds drifted overhead trailing a fine, faint drizzle. I strode on. My face felt hot and stiff as the cool rain touched it. I followed the river road and saw the house come into view, the dark, wide roofs low on the tree-crowned hill. I came past the aviary and the collectors, past the irrigation center, under the avenue of tall bare trees, up the steps of the deep porch, to the door, the wide door of Udan. I went in.

Tubdu was crossing the hall—not the woman I had last seen, in her sixties, grey-haired and tired and fragile, but Tubdu of The Great Giggle, Tubdu at forty-five, fat and rosy-brown and brisk, crossing the hall with short, quick steps, stopping, looking at me at first with mere recognition, there's Hideo, then with puzzlement, is that Hideo? and then with shock—that can't be Hideo!

"Ombu," I said, the baby word for othermother, "Ombu, it's me, Hideo, don't worry, it's all right, I came back." I embraced her, pressed my cheek to hers.

"But, but—" She held me off, looked up at my face. "But what has happened to you, darling boy?" she cried, and then, turning, called out in a high voice, "Isako! Isako!"

When my mother saw me she thought, of course, that I had not left on the ship to Hain, that my courage or my intent had failed me; and in her first embrace there was an involuntary reserve, a withholding. Had I thrown away the destiny for which I had been so ready to throw away everything else? I knew what was in her mind. I laid my cheek to hers and whispered, "I did go, mother, and I came back. I'm thirty-one years old. I came back—"

She held me away a little just as Tubdu had done, and saw my face. "Oh Hideo!" she said, and held me to her with all her strength. "My dear, my dear!"

We held each other in silence, till I said at last, "I need to see Isidri."

My mother looked up at me intently but asked no questions. "She's in the shrine, I think."

"I'll be right back."

I left her and Tubdu side by side and hurried through the halls to the central room, in the oldest part of the house, rebuilt seven centuries ago on the foundations that go back three thousand years. The walls are stone and clay, the roof is thick glass, curved. It is always cool and still there. Books line the walls, the Discussions, the discussions of the Discussions, poetry, texts and versions of the Plays; there are drums and whispersticks for meditation and ceremony; the small, round pool which is the shrine itself wells up from clay pipes and brims its blue-green basin, reflecting the rainy sky above the skylight. Isidri was there. She had brought in fresh boughs for the vase beside the shrine, and was kneeling to arrange them.

I went straight to her and said, "Isidri, I came back. Listen—"

Her face was utterly open, startled, scared, defenseless, the soft, thin face of a woman of twenty-two, the dark eyes gazing into me.

"Listen, Isidri: I went to Hain, I studied there, I worked on a new kind of temporal physics, a new theory—transilience—I spent ten years there. Then we began experiments, I was in Ran'n and crossed over to the Hainish system in no time, using that technology, in no time, you understand me, literally, like the ansible—not at lightspeed, not faster than light, but in no time. In one place and in another place instantaneously, you understand? And it went fine, it worked, but coming back there was . . . there was a fold, a crease, in my field. I was in the same place in a different time. I came back eighteen of your years, ten of mine. I came back to the day I left, but I didn't leave, I came back, I came back to you."

I was holding her hands, kneeling to face her as she knelt by the silent pool. She searched my face with her watchful eyes, silent. On her cheekbone there was a fresh scratch and a little bruise; a branch had lashed her as she gathered the evergreen boughs.

"Let me come back to you," I said in a whisper.

She touched my face with her hand. "You look so tired," she said. "Hideo . . . Are you all right?"

"Yes," I said. "Oh, yes. I'm all right."

And there my story, so far as it has any interest to the Ekumen or to research in transilience, comes to an end. I have lived now for eighteen years as a farmholder of Udan Farm of Derdan'nad Village of the hill region of the Northwest Watershed of the Saduun, on Oket, on O. I am fifty years old. I am the Morning husband of the Second Sedoretu of Udan; my wife is Isidri; my Night marriage is to Sota of Drehe, whose Evening wife is my sister Koneko. My children of the Morning with Isidri are Latubdu and Tadri; the Evening children are Murmi and Lasako. But none of this is of much interest to the Stabiles of the Ekumen.

My mother, who had had some training in temporal engineering, asked for my story, listened to it carefully, and accepted it without question; so did Isidri. Most of the people of my farmhold chose a simpler and far more plausible story, which explained everything fairly well, even my severe loss of weight and ten-year age gain overnight. At the very last moment, just before the space ship left, they said, Hideo decided not to go to the Ekumenical School on Hain after all. He came back to Udan, because he was in love with Isidri. But it had made him quite ill, because it was a very hard decision and he was very much in love.

Maybe that is indeed the true story. But Isidri and Isako chose a stranger truth.

Later, when we were forming our sedoretu, Sota asked me for that truth. "You aren't the same man, Hideo, though you are the man I always loved," he said. I told him why, as best I could. He was sure that Koneko would understand it better than he could, and indeed she listened gravely, and asked several keen questions which I could not answer.

I did attempt to send a message to the temporal physics department of the Ekumenical Schools on Hain. I had not been home long before my mother, with her strong sense of duty and her obligation to the Ekumen, became insistent that I do so.

"Mother," I said, "what can I tell them? They haven't invented churten theory yet!"

"Apologize for not coming to study, as you said you would. And explain it to the Director, the Anarresti woman. Maybe she would understand."

"Even Gvonesh doesn't know about churten yet. They'll begin telling her about it on the ansible from Urras and Anarres about three years from now. Anyhow, Gvonesh didn't know me the first couple of years I was there." The past tense was inevitable but ridiculous; it would have been more accurate to say, "she won't know me the first couple of years I won't be there."

Or *was* I there on Hain, now? That paradoxical idea of two simultaneous existences on two different worlds disturbed me exceedingly. It was one of the points Koneko had asked about. No matter how I discounted it as impossible under every law of temporality, I could not keep from imagining that it was possible, that another I was living on Hain, and would come to Udan in eighteen years and meet myself. After all, my present existence was also and equally impossible.

When such notions haunted and troubled me I learned to replace them with a different image: the little whorls of water that slid down between the two big rocks, where the current ran strong, just above the swimming bay in the Oro. I would imagine those whirlpools forming and dissolving, or I would go down to the river and sit and watch them. And they seemed to hold a solution to my question, to dissolve it as they endlessly dissolved and formed.

But my mother's sense of duty and obligation was unmoved by such trifles as a life impossibly lived twice.

"You should try to tell them," she said.

She was right. If my double transilience field had established itself permanently, it was a matter of real importance to temporal science, not only to myself. So I tried. I borrowed a staggering sum in cash from the farm reserves, went up to Ran'n, bought a five-thousand-word ansible screen transmission, and sent a message to my director of studies at the Ekumenical School, trying to explain why, after being accepted at the School, I had not arrived—if in fact I had not arrived.

I take it that this was the "creased message" or "ghost" they asked me to try to interpret, my first year there. Some of it is gibberish, and some words probably came from the other, nearly simultaneous transmission, but parts of my name are in it, and other words may be fragments or reversals from my long message—problem, churten, return, arrived, time.

It is interesting, I think, that at the ansible center the Receivers used the word "creased" for a temporally disturbed transilient, as Gvonesh would use it for the anomaly, the "wrinkle" in my churten field. In fact, the ansible field was meeting a resonance resistance, caused by the ten-year anomaly in the churten field, which did fold the message back into itself, crumple it up, inverting and erasing. At that point, within the implication of the Tiokunan'n Double Field, my existence on O as I sent the message was simultaneous with my existence on Hain when the message was received. There was an I who sent and an I who received. Yet, so long as the encapsulated field anomaly existed, the simultaneity was literally a point, an instant, a crossing without further implication in either the ansible or the churten field.

An image for the churten field in this case might be a river winding in its floodplain, winding in deep, redoubling curves, folding back upon itself so closely that at last the current breaks through the double banks of the S and runs straight, leaving a whole reach of the water aside as a curving lake, cut off from the current, unconnected. In this analogy, my ansible message would have been the one link, other than my memory, between the current and the lake.

But I think a truer image is the whirlpools of the current itself, occurring and recurring, the same? or not the same?

I worked at the mathematics of an explanation in the early years of my marriage, while my physics was still in good working order. See the "Notes toward a Theory of Resonance Interference in Doubled Ansible and Churten Fields," appended to this document. I realize that the explanation is probably irrelevant, since, on this stretch of the river, there is no Tiokunan'n Field. But independent research from an odd direction can be useful. And I am attached to it, since it is the last temporal physics I did. I have followed churten research with intense interest, but my life's work has been concerned with vineyards, drainage, the care of yamas, the care and education of children, the Discussions, and trying to learn how to catch fish with my bare hands.

Working on that paper, I satisfied myself in terms of mathematics and physics that the existence in which I went to Hain and became a temporal physicist specializing in transilience was in fact encapsulated (enfolded, erased) by the churten effect. But no amount of theory or proof could quite allay my anxiety, my fear—which increased after my marriage and with the birth of each of my children—that there was a crossing point yet to come. For all my images of rivers and whirlpools, I could not prove that the encapsulation might not reverse at the instant of transilience. It was possible that on the day I churtened from Ve to Ran'n I might undo, lose, erase my marriage, our children, all my life at Udan, crumple it up like a bit of paper tossed into a basket. I could not endure that thought.

I spoke of it at last to Isidri, from whom I have only ever kept one secret.

"No," she said, after thinking a long time, "I don't think that can be. There was a reason, wasn't there, that you came back—here."

"You," I said.

She smiled wonderfully. "Yes," she said. She added after a while, "And Sota, and Koneko, and the farmhold . . . But there'd be no reason for you to go back there, would there?"

She was holding our sleeping baby as she spoke; she laid her cheek against the small silky head.

"Except maybe your work there," she said. She looked at me with a little yearning in her eyes. Her honesty required equal honesty of me.

"I miss it sometimes," I said. "I know that. I didn't know that I was missing you. But I was dying of it. I would have died and never known why, Isidri. And anyhow, it was all wrong— my work was wrong."

"How could it have been wrong, if it brought you back?" she said, and to that I had no answer at all.

When information on churten theory began to be published I subscribed to whatever the Center Library of O received, particularly the work done at the Ekumenical Schools and on Ve. The general progress of research was just as I remembered, racing along for three years, then hitting the hard places. But there was no reference to a Tiokunan'n Hideo doing research in the field. Nobody worked on a theory of a stabilized double field. No churten field research station was set up at Ran'n.

At last it was the winter of my visit home, and then the very day; and I will admit that, all reason to the contrary, it was a bad day. I felt waves of guilt, of nausea. I grew very shaky, thinking of the Udan of that visit, when Isidri had been married to He-dran, and I a mere visitor.

Hedran, a respected traveling scholar of the Discussions, had in fact come to teach several times in the village. Isidri had sug-gested inviting him to stay at Udan. I had vetoed the suggestion, saying that though he was a brilliant teacher there was some-thing I disliked about him. I got a sidelong flash from Sidi's clear dark eyes: *Is he jealous?* She suppressed a smile. When I told her and my mother about my "other life," the one thing I had left out, the one secret I kept, was my visit to Udan. I did not want to tell my mother that in that "other life" she had been very ill. I did not want to tell Isidri that in that "other life" He-dran had been her Evening husband and she had had no chil-dren of her body. Perhaps I was wrong, but it seemed to me that I had no right to tell these things, that they were not mine to tell.

So Isidri could not know that what I felt was less jealousy than guilt. I had kept knowledge from her. And I had deprived Hedran of a life with Isidri, the dear joy, the center, the life of my own life.

Or had I shared it with him? I didn't know. I don't know.

That day passed like any other, except that one of Suudi's children broke her elbow falling out of a tree. "At least we know she won't drown," said Tubdu, wheezing.

Next came the date of the night in my rooms in the New Quadrangle, when I had wept and not known why I wept. And a while after that, the day of my return, transilient, to Ve, carrying a bottle of Isidri's wine for Gvonesh. And finally, yesterday, I entered the churten field on Ve, and left it eighteen years ago on O. I spent the night, as I sometimes do, in the shrine. The hours went by quietly; I wrote, gave worship, meditated, and slept. And I woke beside the pool of silent water.

So, now: I hope the Stabiles will accept this report from a farmer they never heard of, and that the engineers of transilience may see it as at least a footnote to their experiments. Certainly it is difficult to verify, the only evidence for it being my word, and my otherwise almost inexplicable knowledge of churten theory. To Gvonesh, who does not know me, I send my respect, my gratitude, and my hope that she will honor my intent.

Unchosen Love

By Heokad'd Arhe of Inanan Farmhold of Tag Village on the Southwest Watershed of the Budran River on Okets on the Planet O.

INTRODUCTION

S EX, FOR EVERYBODY, on every world, is a complicated business, but nobody seems to have complicated marriage quite as much as my people have. To us, of course, it seems simple, and so natural that it's foolish to describe it, like trying to describe how we walk, how we breathe. Well, you know, you stand on one leg and move the other one forward . . . you let the air come into your lungs and then you let it out . . . you marry a man and woman from the other moiety. . . .

What is a moiety? a Gethenian asked me, and I realised that it's easier for me to imagine not knowing which sex I'll be tomorrow morning, like the Gethenian, than to imagine not knowing whether I was a Morning person or an Evening person. So complete, so universal a division of humanity—how can there be a society without it? How do you know who anyone is? How can you give worship without the one to ask and the other to answer, the one to pour and the other to drink? How can you couple indiscriminately without regard to incest? I have to admit that in the unswept, unenlightened basements of my hindbrain I agree with my great-uncle Gambat, who said, "Those people from off the world, they all try to stand on one leg. Two legs, two sexes, two moieties—it only makes sense!"

A moiety is half a population. We call our two halves the Morning and the Evening. If your mother's a Morning woman, you're a Morning person; and all Morning people are in certain respects your brothers or sisters. You have sex, marry, have children only with Evening people.

When I explained our concept of incest to a fellow student on Hain, she said, shocked, "But that means you can't have sex with half the population!" And I in turn said, shocked, "Do you *want* sex with half the population?"

Moieties are in fact not an uncommon social structure within the Ekumen. I have had comfortable conversations with people from several bipartite societies. One of them, a Nadir Woman of the Umna on lthsh, nodded and laughed when I told her my great-uncle's opinion. "But you ki'O," she said, "you marry on all fours."

Few people from other worlds are willing to believe that our form of marriage works. They prefer to think that we endure it. They forget that human beings, while whining after the simple life, thrive on complexity.

When I marry—for love, for stability, for children—I marry three people. I am a Morning man: I marry an Evening woman and an Evening man, with both of whom I have a sexual relationship, and a Morning woman, with whom I have no sexual relationship. Her sexual relationships are with the Evening man and the Evening woman. The whole marriage is called a sedoretu. Within it there are four submarriages; the two heterosexual pairs are called Morning and Evening, according to the woman's moiety; the male homosexual pair is called the Night marriage, and the female homosexual pair is called the Day.

Brothers and sisters of the four primary people can join the sedoretu, so that the number of people in the marriage sometimes gets to six or seven. The children are variously related as siblings, germanes, and cousins.

Clearly a sedoretu takes some arranging. We spend a lot of our time arranging them. How much of a marriage is founded on love and in which couples the love is strongest, how much of it is founded on convenience, custom, profit, friendship, will depend on regional tradition, personal character, and so on. The complexities are so evident that I am always surprised when an offworlder sees, in the multiple relationship, only the forbidden, the illicit one. "How can you be married to three people and never have sex with one of them?" they ask.

The question makes me uncomfortable; it seems to assume that sexuality is a force so dominant that it cannot be contained or shaped by any other relationship. Most societies expect a father and daughter, or a brother and sister, to have a nonsexual family relationship, though I gather that in some the incest ban is often violated by people empowered by age and gender to ignore it. Evidently such societies see human beings as divided into two kinds, the fundamental division being power, and they grant one gender superior power. To us, the fundamental division is moiety; gender is a great but secondary difference; and in the search for power no one starts from a position of innate privilege. It certainly leads to our looking at things differently.

The fact is, the people of O admire the simple life as much as anyone else, and we have found our own peculiar way of achieving it. We are conservative, conventional, self-righteous, and dull. We suspect change and resist it blindly. Many houses, farms, and shrines on O have been in the same place and called by the same name for fifty or sixty centuries, some for hundreds of centuries. We have mostly been doing the same things in the same way for longer than that. Evidently, we do things carefully. We honor self-restraint, often to the point of harboring demons, and are fierce in defense of our privacy. We despise the outstanding. The wise among us do not live in solitude on mountain tops; they live in houses on farms, have many relatives, and keep careful accounts. We have no cities, only dispersed villages composed of a group of farmholds and a community center; educational and technological centers are supported by each region. We do without gods and, for a long time now, without wars. The question strangers most often ask us is, "In those marriages of yours, do you all go to bed together?" and the answer we give is, "No."

That is in fact how we tend to answer any question from a stranger. It is amazing that we ever got into the Ekumen. We are near Hain—sidereally near, 4.2 light years—and the Hainish simply kept coming here and talking to us for centuries, until we got used to them and were able to say Yes. The Hainish, of course, are our ancestral race, but the stolid longevity of our customs makes them feel young and rootless and dashing. That is probably why they like us.

UNCHOSEN LOVE

There was a hold down near the mouths of the Saduun, built on a rock island that stands up out of the great tidal plain south of where the river meets the sea. The sea used to come in and swirl around the island, but as the Saduun slowly built up its delta over the centuries, only the great tides reached it, and then only the storm tides, and at last the sea never came so far, but lay shining all along the west.

Meruo was never a farmhold; built on rock in a salt marsh, it was a seahold, and lived by fishing. When the sea withdrew, the people dug a channel from the foot of the rock to the tideline. Over the years, as the sea withdrew farther, the channel grew longer and longer, till it was a broad canal three miles long. Up and down it fishing boats and trading ships went to and from the docks of Meruo that sprawled over the rocky base of the island. Right beside the docks and the netyards and the drying and freezing plants began the prairies of saltgrass, where vast flocks of yama and flightless baro grazed. Meruo rented out those pastures to farmholds of Sadahun Village in the coastal hills. None of the flocks belonged to Meruo, whose people looked only to the sea, and farmed only the sea, and never walked if they could sail. More than the fishing, it was the prairies that had made them rich, but they spent their wealth on boats and on digging and dredging the great canal. We throw our money in the sea, they said.

They were known as a stiff-necked lot, holding themselves apart from the village. Meruo was a big hold, often with a hundred people living in it, so they seldom made sedoretu with village people, but married one another. They're all germanes at Meruo, the villagers said.

A Morning man from eastern Oket came to stay in Sadahun, studying saltmarsh grazing for his farmhold on the other coast. He chanced to meet an Evening man of Meruo named Suord, in town for a village meeting. The next day, there came Suord again, to see him; and the next day too; and by the fourth night Suord was making love to him, sweeping him off his feet like a storm-wave. The Easterner, whose name was Hadri, was a modest, inexperienced young man to whom the journey and the unfamiliar places and the strangers he met had been a considerable adventure. Now he found one of the strangers wildly in love with him, beseeching him to come out to Meruo and stay there, live there—"We'll make a sedoretu," Suord said. "There's half a dozen Evening girls. Any, any of the Morning women, I'd marry any one of them to keep you.

Come out, come out with me, come out onto the Rock!" For so the people of Meruo called their hold.

Hadri thought he owed it to Suord to do what he asked, since Suord loved him so passionately. He got up his courage, packed his bag, and went out across the wide, flat prairies to the place he had seen all along dark against the sky far off, the high roofs of Meruo, hunched up on its rock above its docks and warehouses and boat-basin, its windows looking away from the land, staring always down the long canal to the sea that had forsaken it.

Suord brought him in and introduced him to the household, and Hadri was terrified. They were all like Suord, dark people, handsome, fierce, abrupt, intransigent—so much alike that he could not tell one from the other and mistook daughter for mother, brother for cousin, Evening for Morning. They were barely polite to him. He was an interloper. They were afraid Suord would bring him in among them for good. And so was he.

Suord's passion was so intense that Hadri, a moderate soul, assumed it must burn out soon. "Hot fires don't last," he said to himself, and took comfort in the adage. "He'll get tired of me and I can go," he thought, not in words. But he stayed a tenday at Meruo, and a month, and Suord burned as hot as ever. Hadri saw too that among the sedoretu of the household there were many passionate matings, sexual tensions running among them like a network of ungrounded wires, filling the air with the crackle and spark of electricity; and some of these marriages were many years old.

He was flattered and amazed at Suord's insatiable, yearning, worshipping desire for a person Hadri himself was used to considering as quite ordinary. He felt his response to such passion was never enough. Suord's dark beauty filled his mind, and his mind turned away, looking for emptiness, a space to be alone. Some nights, when Suord lay flung out across the bed in deep sleep after lovemaking, Hadri would get up, naked, silent; he would sit in the windowseat across the room, gazing down the shining of the long canal under the stars. Sometimes he wept silently. He cried because he was in pain, but he did not know what the pain was.

One such night in early winter his feeling of being chafed,

rubbed raw, like an animal fretting in a trap, all his nerve-ends exposed, was too much to endure. He dressed, very quietly for fear of waking Suord, and went barefoot out of their room, to get outdoors—anywhere out from under the roofs, he thought. He felt that he could not breathe.

The immense house was bewildering in the dark. The seven sedoretu living there now had each their own wing or floor or suite of rooms, all spacious. He had never even been into the regions of the First and Second Sedoretu, way off in the south wing, and always got confused in the ancient central part of the house, but he thought he knew his way around these floors in the north wing. This corridor, he thought, led to the land-ward stairs. It led only to narrow stairs going up. He went up them into a great shadowy attic, and found a door out onto the roof itself.

A long railed walk led along the south edge. He followed it, the peaks of the roofs rising up like black mountains to his left, and the prairies, the marshes, and then as he came round to the west side, the canal, all lying vast and dim in starlight below. The air was soft and damp, smelling of rain to come. A low mist was coming up from the marshes. As he watched, his arms on the rail, the mist thickened and whitened, hiding the marshes and the canal. He welcomed that softness, that slow-ness of the blurring, healing, concealing fog. A little peace and solace came into him. He breathed deep and thought, "Why, why am I so sad? Why don't I love Suord as much as he loves me? Why does he love me?"

He felt somebody was near him, and looked round. A woman had come out onto the roof and stood only a few yards away, her arms on the railing like his, barefoot like him, in a long dressing-gown. When he turned his head, she turned hers, looking at him.

She was one of the women of the Rock, no mistaking the dark skin and straight black hair and a certain fine cut of brow, cheekbone, jaw; but which one he was not sure. At the dining rooms of the north wing he had met a number of Evening women in their twenties, all sisters, cousins, or germanes, all unmarried. He was afraid of them all, because Suord might propose one of them as his wife in sedoretu. Hadri was a little shy sexually and found the gender difference hard to cross; he had found his pleasure and solace mostly with other young men, though some women attracted him very much. These women of Meruo were powerfully attractive, but he could not imagine himself touching one of them. Some of the pain he suffered here was caused by the distrustful coldness of the Evening women, always making it clear to him that he was the outsider. They scorned him and he avoided them. And so he was not perfectly certain which one was Sasni, which one was Lamateo, or Saval, or Esbuai.

He thought this was Esbuai, because she was tall, but he wasn't sure. The darkness might excuse him, for one could barely make out the features of a face. He murmured, "Good evening," and said no name.

There was a long pause, and he thought resignedly that a woman of Meruo would snub him even in the dead of night on a rooftop.

But then she said, "Good evening," softly, with a laugh in her voice, and it was a soft voice, that lay on his mind the way the fog did, mild and cool. "Who is that?" she said.

"Hadri," he said, resigned again. Now she knew him and would snub him.

"Hadri? You aren't from here."

Who was she, then?

He said his farmhold name. "I'm from the east, from the Fadan'n Watershed. Visiting."

"I've been away," she said. "I just came back. Tonight. Isn't it a lovely night? I like these nights best of all, when the fog comes up, like a sea of its own . . ."

Indeed the mists had joined and risen, so that Meruo on its rock seemed to float suspended in darkness over a faintly luminous void.

"I like it too," he said. "I was thinking. . . ." Then he stopped.

"What?" she said after a minute, so gently that he took courage and went on.

"That being unhappy in a room is worse than being unhappy out of doors," he said, with a self-conscious and unhappy laugh. "I wonder why that is."

"I knew," she said. "By the way you were standing. I'm sorry. What do you . . . what would you need to make you happier?" At first he had thought her older than himself, but now she spoke like a quite young girl, shy and bold at the same time, awkwardly, with sweetness. It was the dark and the fog that made them both bold, released them, so they could speak truly.

"I don't know," he said. "I think I don't know how to be in love."

"Why do you think so?"

"Because I— It's Suord, he brought me here," he told her, trying to go on speaking truly. "I do love him, but not—not the way he deserves—"

"Suord," she said thoughtfully.

"He is strong. Generous. He gives me everything he is, his whole life. But I'm not, I'm not able to . . ."

"Why do you stay?" she asked, not accusingly, but asking for an answer.

"I love him," Hadri said. "I don't want to hurt him. If I run away I'll be a coward. I want to be worth him." They were four separate answers, each spoken separately, painfully.

"Unchosen love," she said with a dry, rough tenderness. "Oh, it's hard."

She did not sound like a girl now, but like a woman who knew what love is. While they talked they had both looked out westward over the sea of mist, because it was easier to talk that way. She turned now to look at him again. He was aware of her quiet gaze in the darkness. A great star shone bright between the line of the roof and her head. When she moved again her round, dark head occulted the star, and then it shone tangled in her hair, as if she was wearing it. It was a lovely thing to see.

"I always thought I'd choose love," he said at last, her words working in his mind. "Choose a sedoretu, settle down, some day, somewhere near my farm. I never imagined anything else. And then I came out here, to the edge of the world. . . . And I don't know what to do. I was chosen, I can't choose. . . ."

There was a little self-mockery in his voice.

"This is a strange place," he said.

"It is," she said. "Once you've seen the great tide. . . ."

He had seen it once. Suord had taken him to a headland that stood above the southern floodplain. Though it was only a few miles southwest of Meruo, they had to go a long way round inland and then back out west again, and Hadri asked, "Why can't we just go down the coast?"

"You'll see why," Suord said. They sat up on the rocky headland eating their picnic, Suord always with an eye on the brown-grey mud flats stretching off to the western horizon, endless and dreary, cut by a few worming, silted channels. "Here it comes," he said, standing up; and Hadri stood up to see the gleam and hear the distant thunder, see the advancing bright line, the incredible rush of the tide across the immense plain for seven miles till it crashed in foam on the rocks below them and flooded on round the headland.

"A good deal faster than you could run," Suord said, his dark face keen and intense. "That's how it used to come in around our Rock. In the old days."

"Are we cut off here?" Hadri had asked, and Suord had answered, "No, but I wish we were."

Thinking of it now, Hadri imagined the broad sea lying under the fog all around Meruo, lapping on the rocks, under the walls. As it had been in the old days.

"I suppose the tides cut Meruo off from the mainland," he said, and she said, "Twice every day."

"Strange," he murmured, and heard her slight intaken breath of laughter.

"Not at all," she said. "Not if you were born here. . . . Do you know that babies are born and the dying die on what they call the lull? The low point of the low tide of morning."

Her voice and words made his heart clench within him, they were so soft and seemed so strange. "I come from inland, from the hills, I never saw the sea before," he said. "I don't know anything about the tides."

"Well," she said, "there's their true love." She was looking behind him. He turned and saw the waning moon just above the sea of mist, only its darkest, scarred crescent showing. He stared at it, unable to say anything more.

"Hadri," she said, "don't be sad. It's only the moon. Come up here again if you are sad, though. I liked talking with you. There's nobody here to talk to. . . . Good night," she whispered. She went away from him along the walk and vanished in the shadows.

He stayed a while watching the mist rise and the moon rise; the mist won the slow race, blotting out moon and all in a cold dimness at last. Shivering, but no longer tense and anguished, he found his way back to Suord's room and slid into the wide, warm bed. As he stretched out to sleep, he thought, I don't know her name.

Suord woke in an unhappy mood. He insisted that Hadri come out in the sailboat with him down the canal, to check the locks on the side-canals, he said; but what he wanted was to get Hadri alone, in a boat, where Hadri was not only useless but slightly uneasy and had no escape at all. They drifted in the mild sunshine on the glassy side-canal. "You want to leave, don't you," Suord said, speaking as if the sentence was a knife that cut his tongue as he spoke it.

"No," Hadri said, not knowing if it was true, but unable to say any other word.

"You don't want to get married here."

"I don't know, Suord."

"What do you mean, you don't know?"

"I don't think any of the Evening women want a marriage with me," he said, and trying to speak true, "I know they don't. They want you to find somebody from around here. I'm a foreigner."

"They don't know you," Suord said with a sudden, pleading gentleness. "People here, they take a long time to get to know people. We've lived too long on our Rock. Seawater in our veins instead of blood. But they'll see—they'll come to know you if you—If you'll stay—" He looked out over the side of the boat and after a while said almost inaudibly, "If you leave, can I come with you?"

"I'm not leaving," Hadri said. He went and stroked Suord's hair and face and kissed him. He knew that Suord could not follow him, couldn't live in Oket, inland; it wouldn't work, it wouldn't do. But that meant he must stay here with Suord. There was a numb coldness in him, under his heart.

"Sasni and Duun are germanes," Suord said presently, sounding like himself again, controlled, intense. "They've been lovers ever since they were thirteen. Sasni would marry me if I asked her, if she can have Duun in the Day marriage. We can make a sedoretu with them, Hadri."

The numbness kept Hadri from reacting to this for some time; he did not know what he was feeling, what he thought. What he finally said was, "Who is Duun?" There was a vague hope in him that it was the woman he had talked with on the roof, last night—in a different world, it seemed, a realm of fog and darkness and truth.

"You know Duun."

"Did she just come back from somewhere else?"

"No," Suord said, too intent to be puzzled by Hadri's stupidity. "Sasni's germane, Lasudu's daughter of the Fourth Sedoretu. She's short, very thin, doesn't talk much."

"I don't know her," Hadri said in despair, "I can't tell them apart, they don't talk to me," and he bit his lip and stalked over to the other end of the boat and stood with his hands in his pockets and his shoulders hunched.

Suord's mood had quite changed; he splashed about happily in the water and mud when they got to the lock, making sure the mechanisms were in order, then sailed them back to the great canal with a fine following wind. Shouting, "Time you got your sea legs!" to Hadri, he took the boat west down the canal and out onto the open sea. The misty sunlight, the breeze full of salt spray, the fear of the depths, the exertion of working the boat under Suord's capable directions, the triumph of steering it back into the canal at sunset, when the light lay red-gold on the water and vast flocks of stilts and marshbirds rose crying and circling around them—it made a great day, after all, for Hadri.

But the glory dropped away as soon as he came under the roofs of Meruo again, into the dark corridors and the low, wide, dark rooms that all looked west. They took meals with the Fourth and Fifth Sedoretu. In Hadri's farmhold there would have been a good deal of teasing when they came in just in time for dinner, having been out all day without notice and done none of the work of it; here nobody ever teased or joked. If there was resentment it stayed hidden. Maybe there was no resentment, maybe they all knew each other so well and were so much of a piece that they trusted one another the way you trust your own hands, without question. Even the children joked and quarrelled less than Hadri was used to. Conversation at the long table was always quiet, many not speaking a word.

As he served himself, Hadri looked around among them for the woman of last night. Had it in fact been Esbuai? He thought not; the height was like, but Esbuai was very thin, and had a particularly arrogant carriage to her head. The woman was not here. Maybe she was First Sedoretu. Which of these women was Duun?

That one, the little one, with Sasni; he recalled her now. She was always with Sasni. He had never spoken to her, because Sasni of them all had snubbed him most hatefully, and Duun was her shadow.

"Come on," said Suord, and went round the table to sit down beside Sasni, gesturing Hadri to sit beside Duun. He did so. I'm Suord's shadow, he thought.

"Hadri says he's never talked to you," Suord said to Duun. The girl hunched up a bit and muttered something meaningless. Hadri saw Sasni's face flash with anger, and yet there was a hint of a challenging smile in it, as she looked straight at Suord. They were very much alike. They were well matched.

Suord and Sasni talked—about the fishing, about the locks—while Hadri ate his dinner. He was ravenous after the day on the water. Duun, having finished her meal, sat and said nothing. These people had a capacity for remaining perfectly motionless and silent, like predatory animals, or fishing birds. The dinner was fish, of course; it was always fish. Meruo had been wealthy once and still had the manners of wealth, but few of the means. Dredging out the great canal took more of their income every year, as the sea relentlessly pulled back from the delta. Their fishing fleet was large, but the boats were old, often rebuilt. Hadri had asked why they did not build new ones, for a big shipyard loomed above the drydocks; Suord explained that the cost of the wood alone was prohibitive. Having only the one crop, fish and shellfish, they had to pay for all other food, for clothing, for wood, even for water. The wells for miles around Meruo were salt. An aqueduct led to the seahold from the village in the hills.

They drank their expensive water from silver cups, however, and ate their eternal fish from bowls of ancient, translucent blue Edia ware, which Hadri was always afraid of breaking when he washed them.

Sasni and Suord went on talking, and Hadri felt stupid and sullen, sitting there saying nothing to the girl who said nothing.

"I was out on the sea for the first time today," he said, feeling the blood flush his face.

She made some kind of noise, mhm, and gazed at her empty bowl.

"Can I get you some soup?" Hadri asked. They ended the meal with broth, here, fish broth of course.

"No," she said, with a scowl.

"In my farmhold," he said, "people often bring dishes to each other; it's a minor kind of courtesy; I am sorry if you find it offensive." He stood up and strode off to the sideboard, where with shaking hands he served himself a bowl of soup. When he got back Suord was looking at him with a speculative eye and a faint smile, which he resented. What did they take him for? Did they think he had no standards, no people, no place of his own? Let them marry each other, he would have no part of it. He gulped his soup, got up without waiting for Suord, and went to the kitchen, where he spent an hour in the washing-up crew to make up for missing his time in the cooking crew. Maybe they had no standards about things, but he did.

Suord was waiting for him in their room—Suord's room—Hadri had no room of his own here. That in itself was insulting, unnatural. In a decent hold, a guest was always given a room.

Whatever Suord said—he could not remember later what it was—was a spark to blasting-powder. "I will not be treated this way!" he cried passionately, and Suord firing up at once demanded what he meant, and they had at it, an explosion of rage and frustration and accusation that left them staring grey-faced at each other, appalled. "Hadri," Suord said, the name a sob; he was shivering, his whole body shaking. They came together, clinging to each other. Suord's small, rough, strong hands held Hadri close. The taste of Suord's skin was salt as the sea. Hadri sank, sank and was drowned.

But in the morning everything was as it had been. He did not dare ask for a room to himself, knowing it would hurt Suord. If they do make this sedoretu, then at least I'll have a room, said a small, unworthy voice in his head. But it was wrong, wrong. . . .

He looked for the woman he had met on the roof, and saw half a dozen who might have been her and none he was certain was her. Would she not look at him, speak to him? Not in daylight, not in front of the others? Well, so much for her, then.

It occurred to him only now that he did not know whether she was a woman of the Morning or the Evening. But what did it matter?

That night the fog came in. Waking suddenly, deep in the night, he saw out the window only a formless grey, glowing very dimly with diffused light from a window somewhere in another wing of the house. Suord slept, as he always did, flat out, lying like a bit of jetsam flung on the beach of the night, utterly absent and abandoned. Hadri watched him with an aching tenderness for a while. Then he got up, pulled on clothes, and found the corridor to the stairs that led up to the roof.

The mist hid even the roof-peaks. Nothing at all was visible over the railing. He had to feel his way along, touching the railing. The wooden walkway was damp and cold to the soles of his feet. Yet a kind of happiness had started in him as he went up the attic stairs, and it grew as he breathed the foggy air, and as he turned the corner to the west side of the house. He stood still a while and then spoke, almost in a whisper. "Are you there?" he said.

There was a pause, as there had been the first time he spoke to her, and then she answered, the laugh just hidden in her voice, "Yes, I'm here. Are you there?"

The next moment they could see each other, though only as shapes bulking in the mist.

"I'm here," he said. His happiness was absurd. He took a step closer to her, so that he could make out her dark hair, the darkness of her eyes in the lighter oval of her face. "I wanted to talk to you again," he said.

"I wanted to talk to you again," she said.

"I couldn't find you. I hoped you'd speak to me."

"Not down there," she said, her voice turning light and cold.

"Are you in the First Sedoretu?"

"Yes," she said. "The Morning wife of the First Sedoretu of

Meruo. My name is An'nad. I wanted to know if you're still unhappy."

"Yes," he said, "no—" He tried to see her face more clearly, but there was little light. "Why is it that you talk to me, and I can talk to you, and not to anybody else in this household?" he said. "Why are you the only kind one?"

"Is—Suord unkind?" she asked, with a little hesitation on the name.

"He never means to be. He never is. Only he—he drags me, he pushes me, he . . . He's stronger than I am."

"Maybe not," said An'nad, "maybe only more used to getting his way."

"Or more in love," Hadri said, low-voiced, with shame.

"You're not in love with him?"

"Oh yes!"

She laughed.

"I never knew anyone like him—he's more than—his feelings are so deep, he's— I'm out of my depth," Hadri stammered. "But I love him—immensely—"

"So what's wrong?"

"He wants to marry," Hadri said, and then stopped. He was talking about her household, probably her blood kin; as a wife of the First Sedoretu she was part of all the network of relationships of Meruo. What was he blundering into?

"Who does he want to marry?" she asked. "Don't worry. I won't interfere. Is the trouble that you don't want to marry him?"

"No, no," Hadri said. "It's only— I never meant to stay here, I thought I'd go home. . . . Marrying Suord seems—more than I, than I deserve— But it would be amazing, it would be wonderful! But . . . the marriage itself, the sedoretu, it's not right. He says that Sasni will marry him, and Duun will marry me, so that she and Duun can be married."

"Suord and Sasni," again the faint pause on the name, "don't love each other, then?"

"No," he said, a little hesitant, remembering that challenge between them, like a spark struck.

"And you and Duun?"

"I don't even know her."

"Oh, no, that is dishonest," An'nad said. "One should

choose love, but not that way. . . . Whose plan is it? All three of them?"

"I suppose so. Suord and Sasni have talked about it. The girl, Duun, she never says anything."

"Talk to her," said the soft voice. "Talk to her, Hadri." She was looking at him; they stood quite close together, close enough that he felt the warmth of her arm on his arm though they did not touch.

"I'd rather talk to you," he said, turning to face her. She moved back, seeming to grow insubstantial even in that slight movement, the fog was so dense and dark. She put out her hand, but again did not quite touch him. He knew she was smiling.

"Then stay and talk with me," she said, leaning again on the rail. "Tell me . . . oh, tell me anything. What do you do, you and Suord, when you're not making love?"

"We went out sailing," he said, and found himself telling her what it had been like for him out on the open sea for the first time, his terror and delight. "Can you swim?" she asked, and he laughed and said, "In the lake at home, it's not the same," and she laughed and said, "No, I imagine not." They talked a long time, and he asked her what she did—"in daylight. I haven't seen you yet, down there."

"No," she said. "What do I do? Oh, I worry about Meruo, I suppose. I worry about my children. . . . I don't want to think about that now. How did you come to meet Suord?"

Before they were done talking the mist had begun to lighten very faintly with moonrise. It had grown piercingly cold. Hadri was shivering. "Go on," she said. "I'm used to it. Go on to bed."

"There's frost," he said, "look," touching the silvered wooden rail. "You should go down too."

"I will. Good night, Hadri." As he turned she said, or he thought she said, "I'll wait for the tide."

"Good night, An'nad." He spoke her name huskily, tenderly. If only the others were like her. . . .

He stretched himself out close to Suord's inert, delicious warmth, and slept.

The next day Suord had to work in the records office, where Hadri was utterly useless and in the way. Hadri took his chance, and by asking several sullen, snappish women, found where

Duun was: in the fish-drying plant. He went down to the docks and found her, by luck, if it was luck, eating her lunch alone in the misty sunshine at the edge of the boat basin.

"I want to talk with you," he said.

"What for?" she said. She would not look at him.

"Is it honest to marry a person you don't even like in order to marry a person you love?"

"No," she said fiercely. She kept looking down. She tried to fold up the bag she had carried her lunch in, but her hands shook too much.

"Why are you willing to do it, then?"

"Why are *you* willing to do it?"

"I'm not," he said. "It's Suord. And Sasni."

She nodded.

"Not you?"

She shook her head violently. Her thin, dark face was a very young face, he realised.

"But you love Sasni," he said a little uncertainly.

"Yes! I love Sasni! I always did, I always will! That doesn't mean I, I, I have to do everything she says, everything she wants, that I have to, that I have to—" She was looking at him now, right at him, her face burning like a coal, her voice quivering and breaking. "I don't *belong* to Sasni!"

"Well," he said, "I don't belong to Suord, either."

"I don't know anything about men," Duun said, still glaring at him. "Or any other women. Or anything. I never was with anybody but Sasni, all my life! She thinks she *owns* me."

"She and Suord are a lot alike," Hadri said cautiously.

There was a silence. Duun, though tears had spouted out of her eyes in the most childlike fashion, did not deign to wipe them away. She sat straight-backed, cloaked in the dignity of the women of Meruo, and managed to get her lunch-bag folded.

"I don't know very much about women," Hadri said. His was perhaps a simpler dignity. "Or men. I know I love Suord. But I . . . I need freedom."

"Freedom!" she said, and he thought at first she was mocking him, but quite the opposite—she burst right into tears, and put her head down on her knees, sobbing aloud. "I do too," she cried, "I do too."

Hadri put out a timid hand and stroked her shoulder. "I didn't mean to make you cry," he said. "Don't cry, Duun. Look. If we, if we feel the same way, we can work something out. We don't have to get married. We can be friends."

She nodded, though she went on sobbing for a while. At last she raised her swollen face and looked at him with wet-lidded, luminous eyes. "I would like to have a friend," she said. "I never had one."

"I only have one other one here," he said, thinking how right she had been in telling him to talk to Duun. "An'nad."

She stared at him. "Who?"

"An'nad. The Morning woman of the First Sedoretu."

"What do you mean?" She was not scornful, merely very surprised. "That's Teheo."

"Then who is An'nad?"

"She was the Morning woman of the First Sedoretu four hundred years ago," the girl said, her eyes still on Hadri's, clear and puzzled.

"Tell me," he said.

"She was drowned—here, at the foot of the Rock. They were all down on the sands, her sedoretu, with the children. That was when the tides had begun not to come in as far as Meruo. They were all out on the sands, planning the canal, and she was up in the house. She saw there was a storm in the west, and the wind might bring one of the great tides. She ran down to warn them. And the tide did come in, all the way round the Rock, the way it used to. They all kept ahead of it, except An'nad. She was drowned. . . ."

With all he had to wonder about then, about An'nad, and about Duun, he did not wonder why Duun answered his question and asked him none.

It was not until much later, half a year later, that he said, "Do you remember when I said I'd met An'nad—that first time we talked—by the boat basin?"

"I remember," she said.

They were in Hadri's room, a beautiful, high room with windows looking east, traditionally occupied by a member of the Eighth Sedoretu. Summer morning sunlight warmed their bed, and a soft, earth-scented land-wind blew in the windows.

"Didn't it seem strange?" he asked. His head was pillowed

on her shoulder. When she spoke he felt her warm breath in his hair.

"Everything was so strange then . . . I don't know. And anyhow, if you've heard the tide. . . ."

"The tide?"

"Winter nights. Up high in the house, in the attics. You can hear the tide come in, and crash around the Rock, and run on inland to the hills. At the true high tide. But the sea is miles away. . . ."

Suord knocked, waited for their invitation, and came in, already dressed. "Are you still in bed? Are we going into town or not?" he demanded, splendid in his white summer coat, imperious. "Sasni's already down in the courtyard."

"Yes, yes, we're just getting up," they said, secretly entwining further.

"Now!" he said, and went out.

Hadri sat up, but Duun pulled him back down. "You saw her? You talked with her?"

"Twice. I never went back after you told me who she was. I was afraid. . . . Not of her. Only afraid she wouldn't be there."

"What did she do?" Duun asked softly.

"She saved us from drowning," Hadri said.

Mountain Ways

I N THE stony uplands of the Deka Mountains the farmholds are few and far between. Farmers scrape a living out of that cold earth, planting on sheltered slopes facing south, combing the yama for fleece, carding and spinning and weaving the prime wool, selling pelts to the carpet-factories. The mountain yama, called ariu, are a small wiry breed; they run wild, without shelter, and are not fenced in, since they never cross the invisible, immemorial boundaries of the herd territory. Each farmhold is in fact a herd territory. The animals are the true farmholders. Tolerant and aloof, they allow the farmers to comb out their thick fleeces, to assist them in difficult births, and to skin them when they die. The farmers are dependent on the ariu; the ariu are not dependent on the farmers. The question of ownership is moot. At Danro Farmhold they don't say, "We have nine hundred ariu," they say, "The herd has nine hundred."

Danro is the farthest farm of Oro Village in the High Watershed of the Mane River on Oniasu on O. The people up there in the mountains are civilised but not very civilised. Like most ki'O they pride themselves on doing things the way they've always been done, but in fact they are a wilful, stubborn lot who change the rules to suit themselves and then say the people "down there" don't know the rules, don't honor the old ways, the true ki'O ways, the mountain ways.

Some years ago, the First Sedoretu of Danro was broken by a landslide up on the Farren that killed the Morning woman and her husband. The widowed Evening couple, who had both married in from other farmholds, fell into a habit of mourning and grew old early, letting the daughter of the Morning manage the farm and all its business.

Her name was Shahes. At thirty, she was a straight-backed, strong, short woman with rough red cheeks, a mountaineer's long stride, and a mountaineer's deep lungs. She could walk down the road to the village center in deep snow with a sixty-pound pack of pelts on her back, sell the pelts, pay her taxes and visit a bit at the village hearth, and stride back up the steep zigzags to be home before nightfall, forty kilometers round trip and six hundred meters of altitude each way. If she or anyone else at Danro wanted to see a new face they had to go down the mountain to other farms or to the village center. There was nothing to bring anybody up the hard road to Danro. Shahes seldom hired help, and the family wasn't sociable. Their hospitality, like their road, had grown stony through lack of use.

But a travelling scholar from the lowlands who came up the Mane all the way to Oro was not daunted by another near-vertical stretch of ruts and rubble. Having visited the other farms, the scholar climbed on around the Farren from Ked'din and up to Danro, and there made the honorable and traditional offer: to share worship at the house shrine, to lead conversation about the Discussions, to instruct the children of the farmhold in spiritual matters, for as long as the farmers wished to lodge and keep her.

This scholar was an Evening woman, over forty, tall and long-limbed, with cropped dark-brown hair as fine and curly as a yama's. She was quite fearless, expected nothing in the way of luxury or even comfort, and had no small talk at all. She was not one of the subtle and eloquent expounders of the great Centers. She was a farm woman who had gone to school. She read and talked about the Discussions in a plain way that suited her hearers, sang the Offerings and the praise songs to the oldest tunes, and gave brief, undemanding lessons to Danro's one child, a ten-year-old Morning half-nephew. Otherwise she was as silent as her hosts, and as hardworking. They were up at dawn; she was up before dawn to sit in meditation. She studied her few books and wrote for an hour or two after that. The rest of the day she worked alongside the farm people at whatever job they gave her.

It was fleecing season, midsummer, and the people were all out every day, all over the vast mountain territory of the herd, following the scattered groups, combing the animals when they lay down to chew the cud.

The old ariu knew and liked the combing. They lay with their legs folded under them or stood still for it, leaning into the combstrokes a little, sometimes making a small, shivering whisper-cough of enjoyment. The yearlings, whose fleece was the finest and brought the best price raw or woven, were ticklish and frisky; they sidled, bit, and bolted. Fleecing yearlings called for a profound and resolute patience. To this the young ariu would at last respond, growing quiet and even drowsing as the long, fine teeth of the comb bit in and stroked through, over and over again, in the rhythm of the comber's soft monotonous tune, "Hunna, hunna, na, na. . . ."

The travelling scholar, whose religious name was Enno, showed such a knack for handling newborn ariu that Shahes took her out to try her hand at fleecing yearlings. Enno proved to be as good with them as with the infants, and soon she and Shahes, the best fine-fleecer of Oro, were working daily side by side. After her meditation and reading, Enno would come out and find Shahes on the great slopes where the yearlings still ran with their dams and the newborns. Together the two women could fill a forty-pound sack a day with the airy, silky, milk-colored clouds of combings. Often they would pick out a pair of twins, of which there had been an unusual number this mild year. If Shahes led out one twin the other would follow it, as yama twins will do all their lives; and so the women could work side by side in a silent, absorbed companionship. They talked only to the animals. "Move your fool leg," Shahes would say to the yearling she was combing, as it gazed at her with its great, dark, dreaming eyes. Enno would murmur "Hunna, hunna, hunna, na," or hum a fragment of an Offering, to soothe her beast when it shook its disdainful, elegant head and showed its teeth at her for tickling its belly. Then for half an hour nothing but the crisp whisper of the combs, the flutter of the unceasing wind over stones, the soft bleat of a calf, the faint rhythmical sound of the nearby beasts biting the thin, dry grass. Always one old female stood watch, the alert head poised on the long neck, the large eyes watching up and down the vast, tilted planes of the mountain from the river miles below to the hanging glaciers miles above. Far peaks of stone and snow stood distinct against the dark-blue, sun-filled sky, blurred off into cloud and blowing mists, then shone out again across the gulfs of air.

Enno took up the big clot of milky fleece she had combed, and Shahes held open the long, loose-woven, double-ended sack.

Enno stuffed the fleece down into the sack. Shahes took her hands.

Leaning across the half-filled sack they held each other's hands, and Shahes said, "I want—" and Enno said, "Yes, yes!"

Neither of them had had much love, neither had had much pleasure in sex. Enno, when she was a rough farm girl named Akal, had the misfortune to attract and be attracted by a man whose pleasure was in cruelty. When she finally understood that she did not have to endure what he did to her, she ran away, not knowing how else to escape him. She took refuge at the school in Asta, and there found the work and learning much to her liking, as she did the spiritual discipline, and later the wandering life. She had been an itinerant scholar with no family, no close attachments, for twenty years. Now Shahes's passion opened to her a spirituality of the body, a revelation that transformed the world and made her feel she had never lived in it before.

As for Shahes, she'd given very little thought to love and not much more to sex, except as it entered into the question of marriage. Marriage was an urgent matter of business. She was thirty years old. Danro had no whole sedoretu, no childbearing women, and only one child. Her duty was plain. She had gone courting in a grim, reluctant fashion to a couple of neighboring farms where there were Evening men. She was too late for the man at Beha Farm, who ran off with a lowlander. The widower at Upper Ked'd was receptive, but he also was nearly sixty and smelled like piss. She tried to force herself to accept the advances of Uncle Mika's half-cousin from Okba Farm down the river, but his desire to own a share of Danro was clearly the sole substance of his desire for Shahes, and he was even lazier and more shiftless than Uncle Mika.

Ever since they were girls, Shahes had met now and then with Temly, the Evening daughter of the nearest farmhold, Ked'din, round on the other side of the Farren. Temly and Shahes had a sexual friendship that was a true and reliable pleasure to them both. They both wished it could be permanent. Every now and then they talked, lying in Shahes's bed at Danro or Temly's bed at Ked'din, of getting married, making a sedoretu. There was no use going to the village matchmakers;

they knew everybody the matchmakers knew. One by one they would name the men of Oro and the very few men they knew from outside the Oro Valley, and one by one they would dismiss them as either impossible or inaccessible. The only name that always stayed on the list was Otorra, a Morning man who worked at the carding sheds down in the village center. Shahes liked his reputation as a steady worker; Temly liked his looks and conversation. He evidently liked Temly's looks and conversation too, and would certainly have come courting her if there were any chance of a marriage at Ked'din, but it was a poor farmhold, and there was the same problem there as at Danro: there wasn't an eligible Evening man. To make a sedoretu, Shahes and Temly and Otorra would have to marry the shiftless, shameless fellow at Okba or the sour old widower at Ked'd. To Shahes the idea of sharing her farm and her bed with either of them was intolerable.

"If I could only meet a man who was a match for me!" she said with bitter energy.

"I wonder if you'd like him if you did," said Temly.

"I don't know that I would."

"Maybe next autumn at Manebo . . ."

Shahes sighed. Every autumn she trekked down sixty kilometers to Manebo Fair with a train of pack-yama laden with pelts and wool, and looked for a man; but those she looked at twice never looked at her once. Even though Danro offered a steady living, nobody wanted to live way up there, on the roof, as they called it. And Shahes had no prettiness or nice ways to interest a man. Hard work, hard weather, and the habit of command had made her tough; solitude had made her shy. She was like a wild animal among the jovial, easy-talking dealers and buyers. Last autumn once more she had gone to the fair and once more strode back up into her mountains, sore and dour, and said to Temly, "I wouldn't touch a one of 'em."

Enno woke in the ringing silence of the mountain night. She saw the small square of the window ablaze with stars and felt Shahes's warm body beside her shake with sobs.

"What is it? What is it, my dear love?"

"You'll go away. You're going to go away!"

"But not now—not soon—"

"You can't stay here. You have a calling. A resp—" the word broken by a gasp and sob—"responsibility to your school, to your work, and I can't keep you. I can't give you the farm. I haven't anything to give you, anything at all!"

Enno—or Akal, as she had asked Shahes to call her when they were alone, going back to the girl-name she had given up—Akal knew only too well what Shahes meant. It was the farmholder's duty to provide continuity. As Shahes owed life to her ancestors she owed life to her descendants. Akal did not question this; she had grown up on a farmhold. Since then, at school, she had learned about the joys and duties of the soul, and with Shahes she had learned the joys and duties of love. Neither of them in any way invalidated the duty of a farmholder. Shahes need not bear children herself, but she must see to it that Danro had children. If Temly and Otorra made the Evening marriage, Temly would bear the children of Danro. But a sedoretu must have a Morning marriage; Shahes must find an Evening man. Shahes was not free to keep Akal at Danro, nor was Akal justified in staying there, for she was in the way, an irrelevance, ultimately an obstacle, a spoiler. As long as she stayed on as a lover, she was neglecting her religious obligations while compromising Shahes's obligation to her farmhold. Shahes had said the truth: she had to go.

She got out of bed and went over to the window. Cold as it was she stood there naked in the starlight, gazing at the stars that flared and dazzled from the far grey slopes up to the zenith. She had to go and she could not go. Life was here, life was Shahes's body, her breasts, her mouth, her breath. She had found life and she could not go down to death. She could not go and she had to go.

Shahes said across the dark room, "Marry me."

Akal came back to the bed, her bare feet silent on the bare floor. She slipped under the bedfleece, shivering, feeling Shahes's warmth against her, and turned to her to hold her; but Shahes took her hand in a strong grip and said again, "Marry me."

"Oh if I could!"

"You can."

After a moment Akal sighed and stretched out, her hands behind her head on the pillow. "There's no Evening men here;

you've said so yourself. So how can we marry? What can I do? Go fishing for a husband down in the lowlands, I suppose. With the farmhold as bait. What kind of man would that turn up? Nobody I'd let share you with me for a moment. I won't do it."

Shahes was following her own train of thought. "I can't leave Temly in the lurch," she said.

"And that's the other obstacle," Akal said. "It's not fair to Temly. If we do find an Evening man, then she'll get left out."

"No, she won't."

"Two Day marriages and no Morning marriage? Two Evening women in one sedoretu? There's a fine notion!"

"Listen," Shahes said, still not listening. She sat up with the bedfleece round her shoulders and spoke low and quick. "You go away. Back down there. The winter goes by. Late in the spring, people come up the Mane looking for summer work. A man comes to Oro and says, is anybody asking for a good finefleecer? At the sheds they tell him, yes, Shahes from Danro was down here looking for a hand. So he comes on up here, he knocks at the door here. My name is Akal, he says, I hear you need a fleecer. Yes, I say, yes, we do. Come in. Oh come in, come in and stay forever!"

Her hand was like iron on Akal's wrist, and her voice shook with exultation. Akal listened as to a fairytale.

"Who's to know, Akal? Who'd ever know you? You're taller than most men up here—you can grow your hair, and dress like a man—you said you liked men's clothes once. Nobody will know. Who ever comes here anyway?"

"Oh, come on, Shahes! The people here, Magel and Madu —Shest—"

"The old people won't see anything. Mika's a halfwit. The child won't know. Temly can bring old Barres from Ked'din to marry us. He never knew a tit from a toe anyhow. But he can say the marriage ceremony."

"And Temly?" Akal said, laughing but disturbed; the idea was so wild and Shahes was so serious about it.

"Don't worry about Temly. She'd do anything to get out of Ked'din. She wants to come here, she and I have wanted to marry for years. Now we can. All we need is a Morning man for her. She likes Otorra well enough. And he'd like a share of Danro."

"No doubt, but he gets a share of me with it, you know! A woman in a Night marriage?"

"He doesn't have to know."

"You're crazy, of course he'll know!"

"Only after we're married."

Akal stared through the dark at Shahes, speechless. Finally she said, "What you're proposing is that I go away now and come back after half a year dressed as a man. And marry you and Temly and a man I never met. And live here the rest of my life pretending to be a man. And nobody is going to guess who I am or see through it or object to it. Least of all my husband."

"He doesn't matter."

"Yes he does," said Akal. "It's wicked and unfair. It would desecrate the marriage sacrament. And anyway it wouldn't work. I couldn't fool everybody! Certainly not for the rest of my life!"

"What other way have we to marry?"

"Find an Evening husband—somewhere—"

"But I want you! I want you for my husband and my wife. I don't want any man, ever. I want you, only you till the end of life, and nobody between us, and nobody to part us. Akal, think, think about it, maybe it's against religion, but who does it hurt? Why is it unfair? Temly likes men, and she'll have Otorra. He'll have her, and Danro. And Danro will have their children. And I will have you, I'll have you forever and ever, my soul, my life and soul."

"Oh don't, oh don't," Akal said with a great sob.

Shahes held her.

"I never was much good at being a woman," Akal said. "Till I met you. You can't make me into a man now! I'd be even worse at that, no good at all!"

"You won't be a man, you'll be my Akal, my love, and nothing and nobody will ever come between us."

They rocked back and forth together, laughing and crying, with the fleece around them and the stars blazing at them. "We'll do it, we'll do it!" Shahes said, and Akal said, "We're crazy, we're crazy!"

Gossips in Oro had begun to ask if that scholar woman was going to spend the winter up in the high farmholds, where was she now, Danro was it or Ked'din?—when she came walking down the zigzag road. She spent the night and sang the Offerings for the mayor's family, and caught the daily freighter to the suntrain station down at Dermane. The first of the autumn blizzards followed her down from the peaks.

Shahes and Akal sent no message to each other all through the winter. In the early spring Akal telephoned the farm. "When are you coming?" Shahes asked, and the distant voice replied, "In time for the fleecing."

For Shahes the winter passed in a long dream of Akal. Her voice sounded in the empty next room. Her tall body moved beside Shahes through the wind and snow. Shahes's sleep was peaceful, rocked in a certainty of love known and love to come.

For Akal, or Enno as she became again in the lowlands, the winter passed in a long misery of guilt and indecision. Marriage was a sacrament, and surely what they planned was a mockery of that sacrament. Yet as surely it was a marriage of love. And as Shahes had said, it harmed no one—unless to deceive them was to harm them. It could not be right to fool the man, Otorra, into a marriage where his Night partner would turn out to be a woman. But surely no man knowing the scheme beforehand would agree to it; deception was the only means at hand. They must cheat him.

The religion of the ki'O lacks priests and pundits who tell the common folk what to do. The common folk have to make their own moral and spiritual choices, which is why they spend a good deal of time discussing the Discussions. As a scholar of the Discussions, Enno knew more questions than most people, but fewer answers.

She sat all the dark winter mornings wrestling with her soul. When she called Shahes, it was to tell her that she could not come. When she heard Shahes's voice her misery and guilt ceased to exist, were gone, as a dream is gone on waking. She said, "I'll be there in time for the fleecing."

In the spring, while she worked with a crew rebuilding and repainting a wing of her old school at Asta, she let her hair grow. When it was long enough, she clubbed it back, as men often did. In the summer, having saved a little money working for the school, she bought men's clothes. She put them on and looked at herself in the mirror in the shop. She saw Akal. Akal was a tall, thin man with a thin face, a bony nose, and a slow, brilliant smile. She liked him.

Akal got off the High Deka freighter at its last stop, Oro, went to the village center, and asked if anybody was looking for a fleecer.

"Danro." —"The farmer was down from Danro, twice already." —"Wants a finefleecer." —"Coarsefleecer, wasn't it?" —It took a while, but the elders and gossips agreed at last: a finefleecer was wanted at Danro.

"Where's Danro?" asked the tall man.

"Up," said an elder succinctly. "You ever handled ariu yearlings?"

"Yes," said the tall man. "Up west or up east?"

They told him the road to Danro, and he went off up the zigzags, whistling a familiar praise song.

As Akal went on he stopped whistling, and stopped being a man, and wondered how she could pretend not to know anybody in the household, and how she could imagine they wouldn't know her. How could she deceive Shest, the child whom she had taught the water rite and the praise-songs? A pang of fear and dismay and shame shook her when she saw Shest come running to the gate to let the stranger in.

Akal spoke little, keeping her voice down in her chest, not meeting the child's eyes. She was sure he recognised her. But his stare was simply that of a child who saw strangers so seldom that for all he knew they all looked alike. He ran in to fetch the old people, Magel and Madu. They came out to offer Akal the customary hospitality, a religious duty, and Akal accepted, feeling mean and low at deceiving these people, who had always been kind to her in their rusty, stingy way, and at the same time feeling a wild impulse of laughter, of triumph. They did not see Enno in her, they did not know her. That meant that she was Akal, and Akal was free.

She was sitting in the kitchen drinking a thin and sour soup of summer greens when Shahes came in—grim, stocky, weatherbeaten, wet. A summer thunderstorm had broken over the Farren soon after Akal reached the farm. "Who's that?" said Shahes, doffing her wet coat.

"Come up from the village." Old Magel lowered his voice to

address Shahes confidentially: "He said they said you said you wanted a hand with the yearlings."

"Where've you worked?" Shahes demanded, her back turned, as she ladled herself a bowl of soup.

Akal had no life history, at least not a recent one. She groped a long time. No one took any notice, prompt answers and quick talk being unusual and suspect practices in the mountains. At last she said the name of the farm she had run away from twenty years ago. "Bredde Hold, of Abba Village, on the Oriso."

"And you've finefleeced? Handled yearlings? Ariu yearlings?"

Akal nodded, dumb. Was it possible that Shahes did not recognise her? Her voice was flat and unfriendly, and the one glance she had given Akal was dismissive. She had sat down with her soupbowl and was eating hungrily.

"You can come out with me this afternoon and I'll see how you work," Shahes said. "What's your name, then?"

"Akal."

Shahes grunted and went on eating. She glanced up across the table at Akal again, one flick of the eyes, like a stab of light.

Out on the high hills, in the mud of rain and snowmelt, in the stinging wind and the flashing sunlight, they held each other so tight neither could breathe, they laughed and wept and talked and kissed and coupled in a rock shelter, and came back so dirty and with such a sorry little sack of combings that old Magel told Madu that he couldn't understand why Shahes was going to hire the tall fellow from down there at all, if that's all the work was in him, and Madu said what's more he eats for six.

But after a month or so, when Shahes and Akal weren't hiding the fact that they slept together, and Shahes began to talk about making a sedoretu, the old couple grudgingly approved. They had no other kind of approval to give. Maybe Akal was ignorant, didn't know a hassel-bit from a cold-chisel; but they were all like that down there. Remember that travelling scholar, Enno, stayed here last year, she was just the same, too tall for her own good and ignorant, but willing to learn, same as Akal. Akal was a prime hand with the beasts, or had the makings of it anyhow. Shahes could look farther and do worse. And it meant she and Temly could be the Day marriage of a sedoretu, as they would have been long since if there'd been any kind of men around worth taking into the farmhold, what's wrong with this generation, plenty of good men around in my day.

Shahes had spoken to the village matchmakers down in Oro. They spoke to Otorra, now a foreman at the carding sheds; he accepted a formal invitation to Danro. Such invitations included meals and an overnight stay, necessarily, in such a remote place, but the invitation was to share worship with the farm family at the house shrine, and its significance was known to all.

So they all gathered at the house shrine, which at Danro was a low, cold, inner room walled with stone, with a floor of earth and stones that was the unlevelled ground of the mountainside. A tiny spring, rising at the higher end of the room, trickled in a channel of cut granite. It was the reason why the house stood where it did, and had stood there for six hundred years. They offered water and accepted water, one to another, one from another, the old Evening couple, Uncle Mika, his son Shest, Asbi who had worked as a pack-trainer and handyman at Danro for thirty years, Akal the new hand, Shahes the farmholder, and the guests: Otorra from Oro and Temly from Ked'din.

Temly smiled across the spring at Otorra, but he did not meet her eyes, or anyone else's.

Temly was a short, stocky woman, the same type as Shahes, but fairer-skinned and a bit lighter all round, not as solid, not as hard. She had a surprising, clear singing voice that soared up in the praise-songs. Otorra was also rather short and broad-shouldered, with good features, a competent-looking man, but just now extremely ill at ease; he looked as if he had robbed the shrine or murdered the mayor, Akal thought, studying him with interest, as well she might. He looked furtive; he looked guilty.

Akal observed him with curiosity and dispassion. She would share water with Otorra, but not guilt. As soon as she had seen Shahes, touched Shahes, all her scruples and moral anxieties had dropped away, as if they could not breathe up here in the mountains. Akal had been born for Shahes and Shahes for Akal; that was all there was to it. Whatever made it possible for them to be together was right.

Once or twice she did ask herself, what if I'd been born into the Morning instead of the Evening moiety?—a perverse and terrible thought. But perversity and sacrilege were not asked of her. All she had to do was change sex. And that only in appearance, in public. With Shahes she was a woman, and more truly a woman and herself than she had ever been in her life. With everybody else she was Akal, whom they took to be a man. That was no trouble at all. She was Akal; she liked being Akal. It was not like acting a part. She never had been herself with other people, had always felt a falsity in her relationships with them; she had never known who she was at all, except sometimes for a moment in meditation, when her *I am* became *It is*, and she breathed the stars. But with Shahes she was herself utterly, in time and in the body, Akal, a soul consumed in love and blessed by intimacy.

So it was that she had agreed with Shahes that they should say nothing to Otorra, nothing even to Temly. "Let's see what Temly makes of you," Shahes said, and Akal agreed.

Last year Temly had entertained the scholar Enno overnight at her farmhold for instruction and worship, and had met her two or three times at Danro. When she came to share worship today she met Akal for the first time. Did she see Enno? She gave no sign of it. She greeted Akal with a kind of brusque goodwill, and they talked about breeding ariu. She quite evidently studied the newcomer, judging, sizing up; but that was natural enough in a woman meeting a stranger she might be going to marry. "You don't know much about mountain farming, do you?" she said kindly after they had talked a while. "Different from down there. What did you raise? Those big flatland yama?" And Akal told her about the farm where she grew up, and the three crops a year they got, which made Temly nod in amazement.

As for Otorra, Shahes and Akal colluded to deceive him without ever saying a word more about it to each other. Akal's mind shied away from the subject. They would get to know each other during the engagement period, she thought vaguely. She would have to tell him, eventually, that she did not want to have sex with him, of course, and the only way to do that without insulting and humiliating him was to say that she, that Akal, was averse to having sex with other men, and hoped he would forgive her. But Shahes had made it clear that she mustn't tell him that till they were married. If he knew it beforehand he would refuse to enter the sedoretu. And even worse, he might talk about it, expose Akal as a woman, in revenge. Then they would never be able to marry. When Shahes had spoken about this, Akal had felt distressed and trapped, anxious, guilty again; but Shahes was serenely confident and untroubled, and somehow Akal's guilty feelings would not stick. They dropped off. She simply hadn't thought much about it. She watched Otorra now with sympathy and curiosity, wondering what made him look so hangdog. He was scared of something, she thought.

After the water was poured and the blessing said, Shahes read from the Fourth Discussion; she closed the old boxbook very carefully, put it on its shelf and put its cloth over it, and then, speaking to Magel and Madu as was proper, they being what was left of the First Sedoretu of Danro, she said, "My Othermother and my Otherfather, I propose that a new sedoretu be made in this house."

Madu nudged Magel. He fidgeted and grimaced and muttered inaudibly. Finally Madu said in her weak, resigned voice, "Daughter of the Morning, tell us the marriages."

"If all be well and willing, the marriage of the Morning will be Shahes and Akal, and the marriage of the Evening will be Temly and Otorra, and the marriage of the Day will be Shahes and Temly, and the marriage of the Night will be Akal and Otorra."

There was a long pause. Magel hunched his shoulders. Madu said at last, rather fretfully, "Well, is that all right with everybody?"—which gave the gist, if not the glory, of the formal request for consent, usually couched in antique and ornate language.

"Yes," said Shahes, clearly.

"Yes," said Akal, manfully.

"Yes," said Temly, cheerfully.

A pause.

Everybody looked at Otorra, of course. He had blushed purple and, as they watched, turned greyish.

"I am willing," he said at last in a forced mumble, and cleared his throat. "Only—" He stuck there.

Nobody said anything.

The silence was horribly painful.

Akal finally said, "We don't have to decide now. We can talk. And, and come back to the shrine later, if . . ."

"Yes," Otorra said, glancing at Akal with a look in which so much emotion was compressed that she could not read it at all—terror, hate, gratitude, despair?—"I want to—I need to talk—to Akal."

"I'd like to get to know my brother of the Evening too," said Temly in her clear voice.

"Yes, that's it, yes, that is—" Otorra stuck again, and blushed again. He was in such an agony of discomfort that Akal said, "Let's go on outside for a bit, then," and led Otorra out into the yard, while the others went to the kitchen.

Akal knew Otorra had seen through her pretense. She was dismayed, and dreaded what he might say; but he had not made a scene, he had not humiliated her before the others, and she was grateful to him for that.

"This is what it is," Otorra said in a stiff, forced voice, coming to a stop at the gate. "It's the Night marriage." He came to a stop there, too.

Akal nodded. Reluctantly, she spoke, to help Otorra do what he had to do. "You don't have to—" she began, but he was speaking again:

"The Night marriage. Us. You and me. See, I don't— There's some— See, with men, I—"

The whine of delusion and the buzz of incredulity kept Akal from hearing what the man was trying to tell her. He had to stammer on even more painfully before she began to listen. When his words came clear to her she could not trust them, but she had to. He had stopped trying to talk.

Very hesitantly, she said, "Well, I . . . I was going to tell you. . . . The only man I ever had sex with, it was . . . It wasn't good. He made me— He did things— I don't know what was wrong. But I never have— I have never had any sex with men. Since that. I can't. I can't make myself want to."

"Neither can I," Otorra said.

They stood side by side leaning on the gate, contemplating the miracle, the simple truth.

"I just only ever want women," Otorra said in a shaking voice.

"A lot of people are like that," Akal said.

"They are?"

She was touched and grieved by his humility. Was it men's boastfulness with other men, or the hardness of the mountain people, that had burdened him with this ignorance, this shame?

"Yes," she said. "Everywhere I've been. There's quite a lot of men who only want sex with women. And women who only want sex with men. And the other way round, too. Most people want both, but there's always some who don't. It's like the two ends of," she was about to say "a spectrum," but it wasn't the language of Akal the fleecer or Otorra the carder, and with the adroitness of the old teacher she substituted "a sack. If you pack it right, most of the fleece is in the middle. But there's some at both ends where you tie off, too. That's us. There's not as many of us. But there's nothing wrong with us." As she said this last it did not sound like what a man would say to a man. But it was said; and Otorra did not seem to think it peculiar, though he did not look entirely convinced. He pondered. He had a pleasant face, blunt, unguarded, now that his unhappy secret was out. He was only about thirty, younger than she had expected.

"But in a marriage," he said. "It's different from just . . . A marriage is— Well, if I don't—and you don't—"

"Marriage isn't just sex," Akal said, but said it in Enno's voice, Enno the scholar discussing questions of ethics, and Akal cringed.

"A lot of it is," said Otorra, reasonably.

"All right," Akal said in a consciously deeper, slower voice. "But if I don't want it with you and you don't want it with me why can't we have a good marriage?" It came out so improbable and so banal at the same time that she nearly broke into a fit of laughter. Controlling herself, she thought, rather shocked, that Otorra was laughing at her, until she realised that he was crying.

"I never could tell anybody," he said.

"We don't ever have to," she said. She put her arm around his shoulders without thinking about it at all. He wiped his eyes with his fists like a child, cleared his throat, and stood thinking. Obviously he was thinking about what she had just said.

"Think," she said, also thinking about it, "how lucky we are!"

"Yes. Yes, we are." He hesitated. "But . . . but is it religious . . . to marry each other knowing . . . Without really meaning to. . . ." He stuck again.

After a long time, Akal said, in a voice as soft and nearly as deep as his, "I don't know."

She had withdrawn her comforting, patronising arm from his shoulders. She leaned her hands on the top bar of the gate. She looked at her hands, long and strong, hardened and dirt-engrained from farm work, though the oil of the fleeces kept them supple. A farmer's hands. She had given up the religious life for love's sake and never looked back. But now she was ashamed.

She wanted to tell this honest man the truth, to be worthy of his honesty.

But it would do no good, unless not to make the sedoretu was the only good.

"I don't know," she said again. "I think what matters is if we try to give each other love and honor. However we do that, that's how we do it. That's how we're married. The marriage—the religion is in the love, in the honoring."

"I wish there was somebody to ask," Otorra said, unsatisfied. "Like that travelling scholar that was here last summer. Somebody who knows about religion."

Akal was silent.

"I guess the thing is to do your best," Otorra said after a while. It sounded sententious, but he added, plainly, "I would do that."

"So would I," Akal said.

A mountain farmhouse like Danro is a dark, damp, bare, grim place to live in, sparsely furnished, with no luxuries except the warmth of the big kitchen and the splendid bedfleeces. But it offers privacy, which may be the greatest luxury of all, though the ki'O consider it a necessity. "A three-room sedoretu" is a common expression in Okets, meaning an enterprise doomed to fail.

At Danro, everyone had their own room and bathroom. The two old members of the First Sedoretu, and Uncle Mika and his child, had rooms in the center and west wing; Asbi, when he wasn't sleeping out on the mountain, had a cozy, dirty nest behind the kitchen. The new Second Sedoretu had the whole east side of the house. Temly chose a little attic room, up a half-flight of stairs from the others, with a fine view. Shahes kept her room, and Akal hers, adjoining; and Otorra chose the southeast corner, the sunniest room in the house.

The conduct of a new sedoretu is to some extent, and wisely, prescribed by custom and sanctioned by religion. The first night after the ceremony of marriage belongs to the Morning and Evening couples; the second night to the Day and Night couples. Thereafter the four spouses may join as and when they please, but always and only by invitation given and accepted, and the arrangements are to be known to all four. Four souls and bodies and all the years of their four lives to come are in the balance in each of those decisions and invitations; passion, negative and positive, must find its channels, and trust must be established, lest the whole structure fail to found itself solidly, or destroy itself in selfishness and jealousy and grief.

Akal knew all the customs and sanctions, and she insisted that they be followed to the letter. Her wedding night with Shahes was tender and a little tense. Her wedding night with Otorra was also tender; they sat in his room and talked softly, shy with each other but each very grateful; then Otorra slept in the deep windowseat, insisting that Akal have the bed.

Within a few weeks Akal knew that Shahes was more intent on having her way, on having Akal as her partner, than on maintaining any kind of sexual balance or even a pretense of it. As far as Shahes was concerned, Otorra and Temly could look after each other and that was that. Akal had of course known many sedoretu where one or two of the partnerships dominated the others completely, through passion or the power of an ego. To balance all four relationships perfectly was an ideal seldom realised. But this sedoretu, already built on a deception, a disguise, was more fragile than most. Shahes wanted what she wanted and consequences be damned. Akal had followed her far up the mountain, but would not follow her over a precipice.

It was a clear autumn night, the window full of stars, like that night last year when Shahes had said, "Marry me."

"You have to give Temly tomorrow night," Akal repeated.

"She's got Otorra," Shahes repeated.

"She wants you. Why do you think she married you?"

"She's got what she wants. I hope she gets pregnant soon," Shahes said, stretching luxuriously, and running her hand over Akal's breasts and belly. Akal stopped her hand and held it.

"It isn't fair, Shahes. It isn't right."

"A fine one you are to talk!"

"But Otorra doesn't want me, you know that. And Temly does want you. And we owe it to her."

"Owe her what?"

"Love and honor."

"She's got what she wanted," Shahes said, and freed her hand from Akal's grasp with a harsh twist. "Don't preach at me."

"I'm going back to my room," Akal said, slipping lithely from the bed and stalking naked through the starry dark. "Good night."

She was with Temly in the old dye room, unused for years until Temly, an expert dyer, came to the farm. Weavers down in the Centers would pay well for fleece dyed the true Deka red. Her skill had been Temly's dowry. Akal was her assistant and apprentice now.

"Eighteen minutes. Timer set?"

"Set."

Temly nodded, checked the vents on the great dye-boiler, checked the read-out again, and went outside to catch the morning sun. Akal joined her on the stone bench by the stone doorway. The smell of the vegetable dye, pungent and acid-sweet, clung to them, and their clothes and hands and arms were raddled pink and crimson.

Akal had become attached to Temly very soon, finding her reliably good-tempered and unexpectedly thoughtful—both qualities that had been in rather short supply at Danro. Without knowing it, Akal had formed her expectation of the mountain people on Shahes—powerful, wilful, undeviating, rough. Temly was strong and quite self-contained, but open to impressions as Shahes was not. Relationships within her moiety meant little to Shahes; she called Otorra brother because it was customary, but did not see a brother in him. Temly called Akal brother and meant it, and Akal, who had had no family for so long, welcomed the relationship, returning Temly's warmth. They talked easily together, though Akal had constantly to guard herself from becoming too easy and letting her woman-self speak out. Mostly it was no trouble at all being Akal and she gave little thought to it, but sometimes with Temly it was very hard to keep up the pretense, to prevent herself from saying what a woman would say to her sister. In general she had found that the main drawback in being a man was that conversations were less interesting.

They talked about the next step in the dyeing process, and then Temly said, looking off over the low stone wall of the yard to the huge purple slant of the Farren, "You know Enno, don't you?"

The question seemed innocent and Akal almost answered automatically with some kind of deceit—"The scholar that was here . . . ?"

But there was no reason why Akal the fleecer should know Enno the scholar. And Temly had not asked, do you remember Enno, or did you know Enno, but, "You know Enno, don't you?" She knew the answer.

"Yes."

Temly nodded, smiling a little. She said nothing more.

Akal was amazed by her subtlety, her restraint. There was no difficulty in honoring so honorable a woman.

"I lived alone for a long time," Akal said. "Even on the farm where I grew up I was mostly alone. I never had a sister. I'm glad to have one at last."

"So am I," said Temly.

Their eyes met briefly, a flicker of recognition, a glance planting trust deep and silent as a tree-root.

"She knows who I am, Shahes."

Shahes said nothing, trudging up the steep slope.

"Now I wonder if she knew from the start. From the first water-sharing. . . ."

"Ask her if you like," Shahes said, indifferent.

"I can't. The deceiver has no right to ask for the truth."

"Humbug!" Shahes said, turning on her, halting her in midstride. They were up on the Farren looking for an old beast that Asbi had reported missing from the herd. The keen autumn wind had blown Shahes's cheeks red, and as she stood staring up at Akal she squinted her watering eyes so that they glinted like knifeblades. "Quit preaching! Is that who you are? 'The deceiver'? I thought you were my wife!"

"I am, and Otorra's too, and you're Temly's—you can't leave them out, Shahes!"

"Are they complaining?"

"Do you want them to complain?" Akal shouted, losing her temper. "Is that the kind of marriage you want? —Look, there she is," she added in a suddenly quiet voice, pointing up the great rocky mountainside. Farsighted, led by a bird's circling, she had caught the movement of the yama's head near an outcrop of boulders. The quarrel was postponed. They both set off at a cautious trot towards the boulders.

The old yama had broken a leg in a slip from the rocks. She lay neatly collected, though the broken foreleg would not double under her white breast but stuck out forward, and her whole body had a lurch to that side. Her disdainful head was erect on the long neck, and she gazed at the women, watching her death approach, with clear, unfathomable, uninterested eyes.

"Is she in pain?" Akal asked, daunted by that great serenity.

"Of course," Shahes said, sitting down several paces away from the yama to sharpen her knife on its emery-stone. "Wouldn't you be?"

She took a long time getting the knife as sharp as she could get it, patiently retesting and rewhetting the blade. At last she tested it again and then sat completely still. She stood up quietly, walked over to the yama, pressed its head up against her breast and cut its throat in one long fast slash. Blood leaped out in a brilliant arc. Shahes slowly lowered the head with its gazing eyes down to the ground.

Akal found that she was speaking the words of the ceremony for the dead, *Now all that was owed is repaid and all that was owned, returned. Now all that was lost is found and all that was bound, free.* Shahes stood silent, listening till the end.

Then came the work of skinning. They would leave the carcass to be cleaned by the scavengers of the mountain; it was a carrion-bird circling over the yama that had first caught Akal's eye, and there were now three of them riding the wind. Skinning was fussy, dirty work, in the stink of meat and blood. Akal was inexpert, clumsy, cutting the hide more than once. In penance she insisted on carrying the pelt, rolled as best they could and strapped with their belts. She felt like a grave robber, carrying away the white-and-dun fleece, leaving the thin, broken corpse sprawled among the rocks in the indignity of its nakedness. Yet in her mind as she lugged the heavy fleece along was Shahes standing up and taking the yama's beautiful head against her breast and slashing its throat, all one long movement, in which the woman and the animal were utterly one.

It is need that answers need, Akal thought, as it is question that answers question. The pelt reeked of death and dung. Her hands were caked with blood, and ached, gripping the stiff belt, as she followed Shahes down the steep rocky path homeward.

"I'm going down to the village," Otorra said, getting up from the breakfast table.

"When are you going to card those four sacks?" Shahes said.

He ignored her, carrying his dishes to the washer-rack. "Any errands?" he asked of them all.

"Everybody done?" Madu asked, and took the cheese out to the pantry.

"No use going into town till you can take the carded fleece," said Shahes.

Otorra turned to her, stared at her, and said, "I'll card it when I choose and take it when I choose and I don't take orders at my own work, will you understand that?"

Stop, stop now! Akal cried silently, for Shahes, stunned by the uprising of the meek, was listening to him. But he went on, firing grievance with grievance, blazing out in recriminations. "You can't give all the orders, we're your sedoretu, we're your household, not a lot of hired hands, yes it's your farm but it's ours too, you married us, you can't make all the decisions, and you can't have it all your way either," and at this point Shahes unhurriedly walked out of the room.

"Shahes!" Akal called after her, loud and imperative. Though Otorra's outburst was undignified it was completely justified, and his anger was both real and dangerous. He was a man who had been used, and he knew it. As he had let himself be used and had colluded in that misuse, so now his anger threatened destruction. Shahes could not run away from it.

She did not come back. Madu had wisely disappeared. Akal told Shest to run out and see to the pack-beasts' feed and water.

The three remaining in the kitchen sat or stood silent. Temly looked at Otorra. He looked at Akal.

"You're right," Akal said to him.

He gave a kind of satisfied snarl. He looked handsome in his anger, flushed and reckless. "Damn right I'm right. I've let this go on for too long. Just because she owned the farmhold—"

"And managed it since she was fourteen," Akal cut in. "You think she can quit managing just like that? She's always run things here. She had to. She never had anybody to share power with. Everybody has to learn how to be married."

"That's right," Otorra flashed back, "and a marriage isn't two pairs. It's four pairs!"

That brought Akal up short. Instinctively she looked to Temly for help. Temly was sitting, quiet as usual, her elbows on the table, gathering up crumbs with one hand and pushing them into a little pyramid.

"Temly and me, you and Shahes, Evening and Morning, fine," Otorra said. "What about Temly and her? What about you and me?"

Akal was now completely at a loss. "I thought . . . When we talked . . ."

"I said I didn't like sex with men," said Otorra.

She looked up and saw a gleam in his eye. Spite? Triumph? Laughter?

"Yes. You did," Akal said after a long pause. "And I said the same thing."

Another pause.

"It's a religious duty," Otorra said.

Enno suddenly said very loudly in Akal's voice, "Don't come on to me with your religious duty! I studied religious duty for twenty years and where did it get me? Here! With you! In this mess!"

At this, Temly made a strange noise and put her face in her hands. Akal thought she had burst into tears, and then saw she was laughing, the painful, helpless, jolting laugh of a person who hasn't had much practice at it.

"There's nothing to laugh about," Otorra said fiercely, but then had no more to say; his anger had blown up leaving nothing but smoke. He groped for words for a while longer. He looked at Temly, who was indeed in tears now, tears of laughter. He made a despairing gesture. He sat down beside Temly and said, "I suppose it is funny if you look at it. It's just that I feel like a chump." He laughed, ruefully, and then, looking up at Akal, he laughed genuinely. "Who's the biggest chump?" he asked her.

"Not you," she said. "How long. . . ."

"How long do you think?"

It was what Shahes, standing in the passageway, heard: their laughter. The three of them laughing. She listened to it with dismay, fear, shame, and terrible envy. She hated them for laughing. She wanted to be with them, she wanted to laugh with them, she wanted to silence them. Akal, Akal was laughing at her.

She went out to the workshed and stood in the dark behind the door and tried to cry and did not know how. She had not cried when her parents were killed; there had been too much to do. She thought the others were laughing at her for loving Akal, for wanting her, for needing her. She thought Akal was laughing at her for being such a fool, for loving her. She thought Akal would sleep with the man and they would laugh together at her. She drew her knife and tested its edge. She had made it very sharp yesterday on the Farren to kill the yama. She came back to the house, to the kitchen.

They were all still there. Shest had come back and was pestering Otorra to take him into town and Otorra was saying, "Maybe, maybe," in his soft lazy voice.

Temly looked up, and Akal looked round at Shahes—the small head on the graceful neck, the clear eyes gazing.

Nobody spoke.

"I'll walk down with you, then," Shahes said to Otorra, and sheathed her knife. She looked at the women and the child. "We might as well all go," she said sourly. "If you like."

The Matter of Seggri

The first recorded contact with Seggri was in year 242 of Hainish Cycle 93. A Wandership six generations out from Iao (4-Taurus) came down on the planet, and the captain entered this report in his ship's log.

CAPTAIN AOLAO-OLAO'S REPORT

WE HAVE SPENT near forty days on this world they call Se-ri or Ye-ha-ri, well entertained, and leave with as good an estimation of the natives as is consonant with their unregenerate state. They live in fine great buildings they call castles, with large parks all about. Outside the walls of the parks lie well-tilled fields and abundant orchards, reclaimed by diligence from the parched and arid desert of stone that makes up the greatest part of the land. Their women live in villages and towns huddled outside the walls. All the common work of farm and mill is performed by the women, of whom there is a vast superabundance. They are ordinary drudges, living in towns which belong to the lords of the castle. They live amongst the cattle and brute animals of all kinds, who are permitted into the houses, some of which are of fair size. These women go about drably clothed, always in groups and bands. They are never allowed within the walls of the park, leaving the food and necessaries with which they provide the men at the outer gate of the castle. They evinced great fear and distrust of us. A few of my men following some girls on the road, women rushed from the town like a pack of wild beasts, so that the men thought it best to return forthwith to the castle. Our hosts advised us that it were best for us to keep away from their towns, which we did.

The men go freely about their great parks, playing at one sport or another. At night they go to certain houses which they own in the town, where they may have their pick among the women and satisfy their lust upon them as they will. The women pay them, we were told, in their money, which is copper, for a night of pleasure, and pay them yet more if they get a child on them. Their nights thus are spent in carnal satisfaction as often as they desire, and their days in a diversity of sports and games, notably a kind of wrestling, in which they throw each other through the air so that we marveled that they seemed never to take hurt, but rose up and returned to the combat with wonderful dexterity of hand and foot. Also they fence with blunt swords, and combat with long light sticks. Also they play a game with balls on a great field, using the arms to catch or throw the ball and the legs to kick the ball and trip or catch or kick the men of the other team, so that many are bruised and lamed in the passion of the sport, which was very fine to see, the teams in their contrasted garments of bright colors much gauded out with gold and finery seething now this way, now that, up and down the field in a mass, from which the balls were flung up and caught by runners breaking free of the struggling crowd and fleeting towards the one or the other goal with all the rest in hot pursuit. There is a "battlefield" as they call it of this game lying without the walls of the castle park, near to the town, so that the women may come watch and cheer, which they do heartily, calling out the names of favorite players and urging them with many uncouth cries to victory.

Boys are taken from the women at the age of eleven and brought to the castle to be educated as befits a man. We saw such a child brought into the castle with much ceremony and rejoicing. It is said that the women find it difficult to bring a pregnancy of a manchild to term, and that of those born many die in infancy despite the care lavished upon them, so that there are far more women than men. In this we see the curse of GOD laid upon this race as upon all those who acknowledge HIM not, unrepentant heathens whose ears are stopped to true discourse and blind to the light.

These men know little of art, only a kind of leaping dance, and their science is little beyond that of savages. One great man of a castle to whom I talked, who was dressed out in cloth of gold and crimson and whom all called Prince and Grandsire with much respect and deference, yet was so ignorant he believed the stars to be worlds full of people and beasts, asking us from which star we descended. They have only vessels driven by steam along the surface of the land and water, and no notion of flight either in the air or in space, nor any curiosity about such things, saying with disdain, "That is all women's work," and indeed I found that if I asked these great men about matters of common knowledge such as the working of machinery, the weaving of cloth, the transmission of holovision, they would soon chide me for taking interest in womanish things as they called them, desiring me to talk as befit a man.

In the breeding of their fierce cattle within the parks they are very knowledgeable, as in the sewing up of their clothing, which they make from cloth the women weave in their factories. The men vie in the ornamentation and magnificence of their costumes to an extent which we might indeed have thought scarcely manly, were they not withal such proper men, strong and ready for any game or sport, and full of pride and a most delicate and fiery honor.

> *The log including Captain Aolao-olao's entries was (after a 12-generation journey) returned to the Sacred Archives of the Universe on Iao, which were dispersed during the period called The Tumult, and eventually preserved in fragmentary form on Hain. There is no record of further contact with Seggri until the First Observers were sent by the Ekumen in 93/1333: an Alterran man and a Hainish woman, Kaza Agad and G. Merriment. After a year in orbit mapping, photographing, recording and studying broadcasts, and analysing and learning a major regional language, the Observers landed. Acting upon a strong persuasion of the vulnerability of the planetary culture, they presented themselves as survivors of the wreck of a fishing boat, blown far off course, from a remote island. They were, as they had anticipated, separated at once, Kaza Agad being taken to the Castle and Merriment into the town. Kaza kept his name, which was plausible in the native context; Merriment called herself Yude. We have only her report, from which three excerpts follow.*

FROM MOBILE GERINDU'UTTAHAYUDETWE'MENRADE
MERRIMENT'S NOTES FOR A REPORT TO THE
EKUMEN, 93/1334

34/223. Their network of trade and information, hence their awareness of what goes on elsewhere in their world, is too sophisticated for me to maintain my Stupid Foreign Castaway act any longer. Ekhaw called me in today and said, "If we had a sire here who was worth buying or if our teams were winning their games, I'd think you were a spy. Who are you, anyhow?"

I said, "Would you let me go to the College at Hagka?"

She said, "Why?"

"There are scientists there, I think? I need to talk with them."

This made sense to her; she made their "Mh" noise of assent.

"Could my friend go there with me?"

"Shask, you mean?"

We were both puzzled for a moment She didn't expect a woman to call a man "friend," and I hadn't thought of Shask as a friend. She's very young, and I haven't taken her very seriously.

"I mean Kaza, the man I came with."

"A man—to the college?" she said, incredulous. She looked at me and said, "Where *do* you come from?"

It was a fair question, not asked in enmity or challenge. I wish I could have answered it, but I am increasingly convinced that we can do great damage to these people; we are facing Resehavanar's Choice here, I fear.

Ekhaw paid for my journey to Hagka, and Shask came along with me. As I thought about it I saw that of course Shask was my friend. It was she who brought me into the motherhouse, persuading Ekhaw and Azman of their duty to be hospitable; it was she who had looked out for me all along. Only she was so conventional in everything she did and said that I hadn't realised how radical her compassion was. When I tried to thank her, as our little jitney-bus purred along the road to Hagka, she said things like she always says—"Oh, we're all family," and "People have to help each other," and "Nobody can live alone."

"Don't women ever live alone?" I asked her, for all the ones I've met belong to a motherhouse or a daughterhouse, whether a couple or a big family like Ekhaw's, which is three generations: five older women, three of their daughters living at home, and four children—the boy they all coddle and spoil so, and three girls.

"Oh yes," Shask said. "If they don't want wives, they can be singlewomen. And old women, when their wives die, sometimes they just live alone till they die. Usually they go live at a daughterhouse. In the colleges, the *vev* always have a place to be alone." Conventional she may be, but Shask always tries to answer a question seriously and completely; she thinks about her answer. She has been an invaluable informant. She has also made life easy for me by not asking questions about where I come from. I took this for the incuriosity of a person securely embedded in an unquestioned way of life, and for the self-centeredness of the young. Now I see it as delicacy.

"A vev is a teacher?"

"Mh."

"And the teachers at the college are very respected?"

"That's what vev means. That's why we call Eckaw's mother Vev Kakaw. She didn't go to college, but she's a thoughtful person, she's learned from life, she has a lot to teach us."

So respect and teaching are the same thing, and the only term of respect I've heard women use for women means teacher. And so in teaching me, young Shask respects herself? And/or earns my respect? This casts a different light on what I've been seeing as a society in which wealth is the important thing. Zadedr, the current mayor of Reha, is certainly admired for her very ostentatious display of possessions; but they don't call her Vev.

I said to Shask, "You have taught me so much, may I call you Vev Shask?"

She was equally embarrassed and pleased, and squirmed and said, "Oh no no no no." Then she said, "If you ever come back to Reha I would like very much to have love with you, Yude."

"I thought you were in love with Sire Zadr!" I blurted out.

"Oh, I am," she said, with that eye-roll and melted look they have when they speak of the sires, "aren't you? Just think of him fucking you, oh! Oh, I get all wet thinking about it!" She smiled and wriggled. I felt embarrassed in my turn and probably showed it. "Don't you like him?" she inquired with a na-ivety I found hard to bear. She was acting like a silly adolescent, and I know she's not a silly adolescent. "But I'll never be able to afford him," she said, and sighed.

So you want to make do with me, I thought nastily.

"I'm going to save my money," she announced after a minute. "I think I want to have a baby next year. Of course I can't afford Sire Zadr, he's a Great Champion, but if I don't go to the Games at Kadaki this year I can save up enough for a really good sire at our fuckery, maybe Master Rosra. I wish, I know this is silly, I'm going to say it anyway, I've been wishing you could be its lovemother. I know you can't, you have to go to the college. I just wanted to tell you. I love you." She took my hands, drew them to her face, pressed my palms on her eyes for a moment, and then released me. She was smiling, but her tears were on my hands.

"Oh, Shask," I said, floored.

"It's all right!" she said. "I have to cry a minute." And she did. She wept openly, bending over, wringing her hands, and wailing softly. I patted her arm and felt unutterably ashamed of myself. Other passengers looked round and made little sympathetic grunting noises. One old woman said, "That's it, that's right, lovey!" In a few minutes Shask stopped crying, wiped her nose and face on her sleeve, drew a long, deep breath, and said, "All right." She smiled at me. "Driver," she called, "I have to piss, can we stop?"

The driver, a tense-looking woman, growled something, but stopped the bus on the wide, weedy roadside; and Shask and another woman got off and pissed in the weeds. There is an enviable simplicity to many acts in a society which has, in all its daily life, only one gender. And which, perhaps—I don't know this but it occurred to me then, while I was ashamed of myself —has no shame?

34/245. (Dictated) Still nothing from Kaza. I think I was right to give him the ansible. I hope he's in touch with somebody. I wish it was me. I need to know what goes on in the castles.

Anyhow I understand better now what I was seeing at the Games in Reha. There are sixteen adult women for every adult man. One conception in six or so is male, but a lot of nonviable male fetuses and defective male births bring it down to one in sixteen by puberty. My ancestors must have really had fun playing with these people's chromosomes. I feel guilty, even if it was a million years ago. I have to learn to do without shame but had better not forget the one good use of guilt. Anyhow. A fairly small town like Reha shares its castle with other towns. That confusing spectacle I was taken to on my tenth day down was Awaga Castle trying to keep its place in the Maingame against a castle from up north, and losing. Which means Awaga's team can't play in the big game this year in Fadrga, the city south of here, from which the winners go on to compete in the *big* big game at Zask, where people come from all over the continent—hundreds of contestants and thousands of spectators. I saw some holos of last year's Maingame at Zask. There were 1,280 players, the comment said, and forty balls in play. It looked to me like a total mess, my idea of a battle between two unarmed armies, but I gather that great skill and strategy is involved. All the members of the winning team get a special title for the year, and another one for life, and bring glory back to their various castles and the towns that support them.

I can now get some sense of how this works, see the system from outside it, because the college doesn't support a castle. People here aren't obsessed with sports and athletes and sexy sires the way the young women in Reha were, and some of the older ones. It's a kind of obligatory obsession. Cheer your team, support your brave men, adore your local hero. It makes sense. Given their situation, they need strong, healthy men at their fuckery; it's social selection reinforcing natural selection. But I'm glad to get away from the rah-rah and the swooning and the posters of fellows with swelling muscles and huge penises and bedroom eyes.

I have made Resehavanar's Choice. I chose the option: Less than the truth. Shoggrad and Skodr and the other teachers, professors we'd call them, are intelligent, enlightened people, perfectly capable of understanding the concept of space travel, etc., making decisions about technological innovation, etc. I limit my answers to their questions to technology. I let them assume, as most people naturally assume, particularly people from a monoculture, that our society is pretty much like theirs. When they find how it differs, the effect will be revolutionary, and I have no mandate, reason, or wish to cause such a revolution on Seggri.

Their gender imbalance has produced a society in which, as far as I can tell, the men have all the privilege and the women have all the power. It's obviously a stable arrangement. According to their histories, it's lasted at least two millennia, and probably in some form or another much longer than that. But it could be quickly and disastrously destabilised by contact with us, by their experiencing the human norm. I don't know if the men would cling to their privileged status or demand freedom, but surely the women would resist giving up their power, and their sexual system and affectional relationships would break down. Even if they learned to undo the genetic program that was inflicted on them, it would take several generations to restore normal gender distribution. I can't be the whisper that starts that avalanche.

34/266. (Dictated) Skodr got nowhere with the men of Awaga Castle. She had to make her inquiries very cautiously, since it would endanger Kaza if she told them he was an alien or in any way unique. They'd take it as a claim of superiority, which he'd have to defend in trials of strength and skill. I gather that the hierarchies within the castles are a rigid framework, within which a man moves up or down issuing challenges and winning or losing obligatory and optional trials. The sports and games the women watch are only the showpieces of an endless series of competitions going on inside the castles. As an untrained, grown man Kaza would be at a total disadvantage in such trials. The only way he might get out of them, she said, would be by feigning illness or idiocy. She thinks he must have done so, since he is at least alive; but that's all she could find out—"The man who was cast away at Taha-Reha is alive."

Although the women feed, house, clothe, and support the lords of the castle, they evidently take their noncooperation for granted. She seemed glad to get even that scrap of information. As I am.

But we have to get Kaza out of there. The more I hear about it from Skodr the more dangerous it sounds. I keep thinking "spoiled brats!" but actually these men must be more like soldiers in the training camps that militarists have. Only the training never ends. As they win trials they gain all kinds of titles and ranks you could translate as "generals" and the other names militarists have for all their power-grades. Some of the "generals," the Lords and Masters and so on, are the sports idols, the darlings of the fuckeries, like the one poor Shask adored; but as they get older apparently they often trade glory among the women for power among the men, and become tyrants within their castle, bossing the "lesser" men around, until they're overthrown, kicked out. Old sires often live alone, it seems, in little houses away from the main castle, and are considered crazy and dangerous—rogue males.

It sounds like a miserable life. All they're allowed to do after age eleven is compete at games and sports inside the castle, and compete in the fuckeries, after they're fifteen or so, for money and number of fucks and so on. Nothing else. No options. No trades. No skills of making. No travel unless they play in the big games. They aren't allowed into the colleges to gain any kind of freedom of mind. I asked Skodr why an intelligent man couldn't at least come study in the college, and she told me that learning was very bad for men: it weakens a man's sense of honor, makes his muscles flabby, and leaves him impotent. "'What goes to the brain takes from the testicles,'" she said. "Men have to be sheltered from education for their own good."

I tried to "be water," as I was taught, but I was disgusted. Probably she felt it, because after a while she told me about "the secret college." Some women in colleges do smuggle information to men in castles. The poor things meet secretly and teach each other. In the castles, homosexual relationships are encouraged among boys under fifteen, but not officially tolerated among grown men; she says the "secret colleges" often are run by the homosexual men. They have to be secret because if they're caught reading or talking about ideas they may be punished by their Lords and Masters. There have been some interesting works from the "secret colleges," Skodr said, but she had to think to come up with examples. One was a man who had smuggled out an interesting mathematical theorem, and one was a painter whose landscapes, though primitive in technique, were admired by professionals of the art. She couldn't remember his name.

Arts, sciences, all learning, all professional techniques, are *baggyad*, skilled work. They're all taught at the colleges, and there are no divisions and few specialists. Teachers and students cross and mix fields all the time, and being a famous scholar in one field doesn't keep you from being a student in another. Skodr is a vev of physiology, writes plays, and is currently studying history with one of the history vevs. Her thinking is informed and lively and fearless. My School on Hain could learn from this college. It's a wonderful place, full of free minds. But only minds of one gender. A hedged freedom.

I hope Kaza has found a secret college or something, some way to fit in at the castle. He's strong, but these men have trained for years for the games they play. And a lot of the games are violent. The women say don't worry, we don't let the men kill each other, we protect them, they're our treasures. But I've seen men carried off with concussions, on the holos of their martial-art fights, where they throw each other around spectacularly. "Only inexperienced fighters get hurt." Very reassuring. And they wrestle bulls. And in that melee they call the Maingame they break each other's legs and ankles deliberately. "What's a hero without a limp?" the women say. Maybe that's the safe thing to do, get your leg broken so you don't have to prove you're a hero any more. But what else might Kaza have to prove?

I asked Shask to let me know if she ever heard of him being at the Reha fuckery. But Awaga Castle services (that's their word, the same word they use for their bulls) four towns, so he might get sent to one of the others. But probably not, because men who don't win at things aren't allowed to go to the fuckeries. Only the champions. And boys between fifteen and nineteen, the ones the older women call *dippida*, baby animals —puppy, kitty, lamby. They use the dippida for pleasure. They only pay for a champion when they go to the fuckery to get pregnant. But Kaza's thirty-six, he isn't a puppy or a kitten or a lamb. He's a man, and this is a terrible place to be a man.

Kaza Agad had been killed; the Lords of Awaga Castle finally disclosed the fact, but not the circumstances. A year later, Merriment radioed her lander and left Seggri for Hain. Her recommendation was to observe and avoid. The Stabiles, however, decided to send another pair of observers; these were both women, Mobiles Alee Iyoo and Zerin Wu. They lived for eight years on Seggri, after the third year as First Mobiles; Iyoo stayed as Ambassador another fifteen years. They made Resehavanar's Choice as "all the truth slowly." A limit of two hundred visitors from offworld was set. During the next several generations the people of Seggri, becoming accustomed to the alien presence, considered their own options as members of the Ekumen. Proposals for a planetwide referendum on genetic alteration were abandoned, since the men's vote would be insignificant unless the women's vote were handicapped. As of the date of this report the Seggri have not undertaken major genetic alteration, though they have learned and applied various repair techniques, which have resulted in a higher proportion of full-term male infants; the gender balance now stands at about 12:1.

The following is a memoir given to Ambassador Eritho te Ves in 93/1569 by a woman in Ush on Seggri.

You asked me, dear friend, to tell you anything I might like people on other worlds to know about my life and my world. That's not easy! Do I want anybody anywhere else to know anything about my life? I know how strange we seem to all the others, the half-and-half races; I know they think us backward, provincial, even perverse. Maybe in a few more decades we'll decide that we should remake ourselves. I won't be alive then; I don't think I'd want to be. I like my people. I like our fierce, proud, beautiful men, I don't want them to become like women. I like our trustful, powerful, generous women, I don't want them to become like men. And yet I see that among you each man has his own being and nature, each woman has hers, and I can hardly say what it is I think we would lose.

When I was a child I had a brother a year and a half younger than me. His name was Ittu. My mother had gone to the city and paid five years' savings for my sire, a Master Champion in the Dancing. Ittu's sire was an old fellow at our village fuckery; they called him "Master Fallback." He'd never been a champion at anything, hadn't sired a child for years, and was only too glad to fuck for free. My mother always laughed about it—she was still suckling me, she didn't even use a preventive, and she tipped him two coppers! When she found herself pregnant she was furious. When they tested and found it was a male fetus she was even more disgusted at having, as they say, to wait for the miscarriage. But when Ittu was born sound and healthy, she gave the old sire two hundred coppers, all the cash she had.

He wasn't delicate like so many boy babies, but how can you keep from protecting and cherishing a boy? I don't remember when I wasn't looking after Ittu, with it all very clear in my head what Little Brother should do and shouldn't do and all the perils I must keep him from. I was proud of my responsibility, and vain, too, because I had a brother to look after. Not one other motherhouse in my village had a son still living at home.

Ittu was a lovely child, a star. He had the fleecy soft hair that's common in my part of Ush, and big eyes; his nature was sweet and cheerful, and he was very bright. The other children loved him and always wanted to play with him, but he and I were happiest playing by ourselves, long elaborate games of make-believe. We had a herd of twelve cattle an old woman of the village had carved from gourdshell for Ittu—people always gave him presents—and they were the actors in our dearest game. Our cattle lived in a country called Shush, where they had great adventures, climbing mountains, discovering new lands, sailing on rivers, and so on. Like any herd, like our village herd, the old cows were the leaders; the bull lived apart; the other males were gelded; and the heifers were the adventurers. Our bull would make ceremonial visits to service the cows, and then he might have to go fight with men at Shush Castle. We made the castle of clay and the men of sticks, and the bull always won, knocking the stick-men to pieces. Then sometimes he knocked the castle to pieces too. But the best of our stories were told with two of the heifers. Mine was named Op and my brother's was Utti. Once our hero heifers were having a great adventure on the stream that runs past our village, and their boat got away from us. We found it caught against a log far downstream where the stream was deep and quick. My heifer was still in it. We both dived and dived, but we never found Utti. She had drowned. The Cattle of Shush had a great funeral for her, and Ittu cried very bitterly.

He mourned his brave little toy cow so long that I asked Djerdji the cattleherd if we could work for her, because I thought being with the real cattle might cheer Ittu up. She was glad to get two cowhands for free (when Mother found out we were really working, she made Djerdji pay us a quarter-copper a day). We rode two big, goodnatured old cows, on saddles so big Ittu could lie down on his. We took a herd of two-year-old calves out onto the desert every day to forage for the *edta* that grows best when it's grazed. We were supposed to keep them from wandering off and from trampling stream-banks, and when they wanted to settle down and chew the cud we were supposed to gather them in a place where their droppings would nourish useful plants. Our old mounts did most of the work. Mother came out and checked on what we were doing and decided it was all right, and being out in the desert all day was certainly keeping us fit and healthy.

We loved our riding cows, but they were serious-minded and responsible, rather like the grown-ups in our motherhouse. The calves were something else; they were all riding breed, not fine animals of course, just villagebred; but living on edta they were fat and had plenty of spirit. Ittu and I rode them bareback with a rope rein. At first we always ended up on our own backs watching a calf's heels and tail flying off. By the end of a year we were good riders, and took to training our mounts to tricks, trading mounts at a full run, and hornvaulting. Ittu was a marvelous hornvaulter. He trained a big three-year-old roan ox with lyre horns, and the two of them danced like the finest vaulters of the great castles that we saw on the holos. We couldn't keep our excellence to ourselves out in the desert; we started showing off to the other children, inviting them to come out to Salt Springs to see our Great Trick Riding Show. And so of course the adults got to hear of it.

My mother was a brave woman, but that was too much for even her, and she said to me in cold fury, "I trusted you to look after Ittu. You let me down."

All the others had been going on and on about endangering the precious life of a boy, the Vial of Hope, the Treasurehouse of Life, and so on, but it was what my mother said that hurt.

"I do look after Ittu, and he looks after me," I said to her, in that passion of justice that children know, the birthright we seldom honor. "We both know what's dangerous and we don't do stupid things and we know our cattle and we do everything together. When he has to go to the castle he'll have to do lots more dangerous things, but at least he'll already know how to do one of them. And there he has to do them alone, but we did everything together. And I didn't let you down."

My mother looked at us. I was nearly twelve, Ittu was ten. She burst into tears, she sat down on the dirt and wept aloud. Ittu and I both went to her and hugged her and cried. Ittu said, "I won't go. I won't go to the damned castle. They can't make me!"

And I believed him. He believed himself. My mother knew better.

Maybe some day it will be possible for a boy to choose his life. Among your peoples a man's body does not shape his fate, does it? Maybe some day that will be so here.

Our Castle, Hidjegga, had of course been keeping their eye on Ittu ever since he was born; once a year Mother would send them the doctor's report on him, and when he was five Mother and her wives took him out there for the ceremony of Confirmation. Ittu had been embarrassed, disgusted, and flattered. He told me in secret, "There were all these old *men* that smelled funny and they made me take off my clothes and they had these measuring things and they measured my peepee! And they said it was very good. They said it was a good one. What happens when you descend?" It wasn't the first question he had ever asked me that I couldn't answer, and as usual I made up the answer. "Descend means you can have babies," I said, which, in a way, wasn't so far off the mark.

Some castles, I am told, prepare boys of nine and ten for the Severance, woo them with visits from older boys, tickets to games, tours of the park and the buildings, so that they may be quite eager to go to the castle when they turn eleven. But we "outyonders," villagers of the edge of the desert, kept to the harsh old-fashioned ways. Aside from Confirmation, a boy had no contact at all with men until his eleventh birthday. On that day everybody he had ever known brought him to the Gate and gave him to the strangers with whom he would live the rest of his life. Men and women alike believed and still believe that this absolute severance makes the man.

Vev Ushiggi, who had borne a son and had a grandson, and had been mayor five or six times, and was held in great esteem even though she'd never had much money, heard Ittu say that he wouldn't go to the damned Castle. She came next day to our motherhouse and asked to talk to him. He told me what she said. She didn't do any wooing or sweetening. She told him that he was born to the service of his people and had one responsibility, to sire children when he got old enough; and one duty, to be a strong, brave man, stronger and braver than other men, so that women would choose him to sire their children. She said he had to live in the Castle because men could not live among women. At this, Ittu asked her, "Why can't they?"

"You did?" I said, awed by his courage, for Vev Ushiggi was a formidable old woman.

"Yes. And she didn't really answer. She took a long time. She looked at me and then she looked off somewhere and then she stared at me for a long time and then finally she said, 'Because we would destroy them.'"

"But that's crazy," I said. "Men are our treasures. What did she say that for?"

Ittu, of course, didn't know. But he thought hard about what she had said, and I think nothing she could have said would have so impressed him.

After discussion, the village elders and my mother and her wives decided that lttu could go on practicing hornvaulting, because it really would be a useful skill for him in the Castle; but he could not herd cattle any longer, nor go with me when I did, nor join in any of the work children of the village did, nor their games. "You've done everything together with Po," they told him, "but she should be doing things together with the other girls, and you should be doing things by yourself, the way men do."

They were always very kind to Ittu, but they were stern with us girls; if they saw us even talking with Ittu they'd tell us to go on about our work, leave the boy alone. When we disobeyed— when Ittu and I sneaked off and met at Salt Springs to ride together, or just hid out in our old playplace down in the draw by the stream to talk—he got treated with cold silence to shame him, but I got punished. A day locked in the cellar of the old fiber-processing mill, which was what my village used for a jail; next time it was two days; and the third time they caught us alone together, they locked me in that cellar for ten days. A young woman called Fersk brought me food once a day and made sure I had enough water and wasn't sick, but she didn't speak; that's how they always used to punish people in the villages. I could hear the other children going by up on the street in the evening. It would get dark at last and I could sleep. All day I had nothing to do, no work, nothing to think about except the scorn and contempt they held me in for betraying their trust, and the injustice of my getting punished when Ittu didn't.

When I came out, I felt different. I felt like something had closed up inside me while I was closed up in that cellar.

When we ate at the motherhouse they made sure Ittu and I didn't sit near each other. For a while we didn't even talk to each other. I went back to school and work. I didn't know what Ittu was doing all day. I didn't think about it. It was only fifty days to his birthday.

One night I got into bed and found a note under my clay pillow: *in the draw to-nt.* Ittu never could spell; what writing he knew I had taught him in secret. I was frightened and angry, but I waited an hour till everybody was asleep, and got up and crept outside into the windy, starry night, and ran to the draw. It was late in the dry season and the stream was barely running. Ittu was there, hunched up with his arms round his knees, a little lump of shadow on the pale, cracked clay at the waterside.

The first thing I said was, "You want to get me locked up again? They said next time it would be thirty days!"

"They're going to lock me up for fifty years," Ittu said, not looking at me.

"What am I supposed to do about it? It's the way it has to be! You're a man. You have to do what men do. They won't lock you up, anyway, you get to play games and come to town to do service and all that. You don't even know what being locked up is!"

"I want to go to Seradda," Ittu said, talking very fast, his eyes shining as he looked up at me. "We could take the riding cows to the bus station in Redang, I saved my money, I have twenty-three coppers, we could take the bus to Seradda. The cows would come back home if we turned them loose."

"What do you think you'd do in Seradda?" I asked, disdainful but curious. Nobody from our village had ever been to the capital.

"The Ekkamen people are there," he said.

"The Ekumen," I corrected him. "So what?"

"They could take me away," Ittu said.

I felt very strange when he said that. I was still angry and still disdainful but a sorrow was rising in me like dark water. "Why would they do that? What would they talk to some little boy for? How would you find them? Twenty-three coppers isn't enough anyway. Seradda's way far off. That's a really stupid idea. You can't do that."

"I thought you'd come with me," Ittu said. His voice was softer, but didn't shake.

"I wouldn't do a stupid thing like that," I said furiously.

"All right," he said. "But you won't tell. Will you?"

"No, I won't tell!" I said. "But you can't run away, Ittu. You can't. It would be—it would be dishonorable."

This time when he answered his voice shook. "I don't care," he said. "I don't care about honor. I want to be free!"

We were both in tears. I sat down by him and we leaned together the way we used to, and cried a while; not long; we weren't used to crying.

"You can't do it," I whispered to him. "It won't work, Ittu."

He nodded, accepting my wisdom.

"It won't be so bad at the Castle," I said.

After a minute he drew away from me very slightly.

"We'll see each other," I said.

He said only, "When?"

"At games. I can watch you. I bet you'll be the best rider and hornvaulter there. I bet you win all the prizes and get to be a Champion."

He nodded, dutiful. He knew and I knew that I had betrayed our love and our birthright of justice. He knew he had no hope.

That was the last time we talked together alone, and almost the last time we talked together.

Ittu ran away about ten days after that, taking the riding cow and heading for Redang; they tracked him easily and had him back in the village before nightfall. I don't know if he thought I had told them where he would be going. I was so ashamed of not having gone with him that I could not look at him. I kept away from him; they didn't have to keep me away any more. He made no effort to speak to me.

I was beginning my puberty, and my first blood was the night before Ittu's birthday. Menstruating women are not allowed to come near the Gates at conservative castles like ours, so when Ittu was made a man I stood far back among a few other girls and women, and could not see much of the ceremony. I stood silent while they sang, and looked down at the dirt and my new sandals and my feet in the sandals, and felt the ache and tug of my womb and the secret movement of the blood, and grieved. I knew even then that this grief would be with me all my life.

Ittu went in and the Gates closed.

He became a Young Champion Hornvaulter, and for two years, when he was eighteen and nineteen, came a few times to service in our village, but I never saw him. One of my friends fucked with him and started to tell me about it, how nice he was, thinking I'd like to hear, but I shut her up and walked away in a blind rage which neither of us understood.

He was traded away to a castle on the east coast when he was twenty. When my daughter was born I wrote him, and several times after that, but he never answered my letters.

I don't know what I've told you about my life and my world. I don't know if it's what I want you to know. It is what I had to tell.

The following is a short story written in 93/1586 by a popular writer of the city of Adr, Sem Gridji. The classic literature of Seggri was the narrative poem and the drama. Classical poems and plays were written collaboratively, in the original version and also by re-writers of subsequent generations, usually anonymous. Small value was placed on preserving a "true" text, since the work was seen as an ongoing process. Probably under Ekumenical influence, individual writers in the late sixteenth century began writing short prose narratives, historical and fictional. The genre became popular, particularly in the cities, though it never obtained the immense audience of the great classical epics and plays. Literally everyone knew the plots and many quotations from the epics and plays, from books and holo, and almost every adult woman had seen or participated in a staged performance of several of them. They were one of the principal unifying influences of the Seggrian monoculture. The prose narrative, read in silence, served rather as a device by which the culture might question itself, and a tool for individual moral self-examination. Conservative Seggrian women disapproved of the genre as antagonistic to the intensely cooperative, collaborative structure of their society. Fiction was not included in the curriculum of the literature departments of the colleges, and was often dismissed contemptuously—"fiction is for men."

Sem Gridji published three books of stories. Her bare, blunt style is characteristic of the Seggrian short story.

LOVE OUT OF PLACE

by Sem Gridji

Azak grew up in a motherhouse in the Downriver Quarter, near the textile mills. She was a bright girl, and her family and neighborhood were proud to gather the money to send her to college. She came back to the city as a starting manager at one of the mills. Azak worked well with other people; she prospered. She had a clear idea of what she wanted to do in the next few years: to find two or three partners with whom to found a daughterhouse and a business.

A beautiful woman in the prime of youth, Azak took great pleasure in sex, especially liking intercourse with men. Though she saved money for her plan of founding a business, she also spent a good deal at the fuckery, going there often, sometimes hiring two men at once. She liked to see how they incited each other to prowess beyond what they would have achieved alone, and shamed each other when they failed. She found a flaccid penis very disgusting, and did not hesitate to send away a man who could not penetrate her three or four times an evening.

The castle of her district bought a Young Champion at the Southeast Castles Dance Tournament, and soon sent him to the fuckery. Having seen him dance in the finals on the holovision and been captivated by his flowing, graceful style and his beauty, Azak was eager to have him service her. His price was twice that of any other man there, but she did not hesitate to pay it. She found him handsome and amiable, eager and gentle, skillful and compliant. In their first evening they came to orgasm together five times. When she left she gave him a large tip. Within the week she was back, asking for Toddra. The pleasure he gave her was exquisite, and soon she was quite obsessed with him.

"I wish I had you all to myself," she said to him one night as they lay still conjoined, languorous and fulfilled.

"That is my heart's desire," he said. "I wish I were your servant. None of the other women that come here arouse me. I don't want them. I want only you."

She wondered if he was telling the truth. The next time she came, she inquired casually of the manager if Toddra were as popular as they had hoped. "No," the manager said. "Everybody else reports that he takes a lot of arousing, and is sullen and careless towards them."

"How strange," Azak said.

"Not at all," said the manager. "He's in love with you."

"A man in love with a woman?" Azak said, and laughed.

"It happens all too often," the manager said.

"I thought only women fell in love," said Azak.

"Women fall in love with a man, sometimes, and that's bad too," said the manager. "May I warn you, Azak? Love should be between women. It's out of place here. It can never come to any good end. I hate to lose the money, but I wish you'd fuck with some of the other men and not always ask for Toddra. You're encouraging him, you see, in something that does harm to him."

"But he and you are making lots of money from me!" said Azak, still taking it as a joke.

"He'd make more from other women if he wasn't in love with you," said the manager. To Azak that seemed a weak argument against the pleasure she had in Toddra, and she said, "Well, he can fuck them all when I've done with him, but for now, I want him."

After their intercourse that evening, she said to Toddra, "The manager here says you're in love with me."

"I told you I was," Toddra said. "I told you I wanted to belong to you, to serve you, you alone. I would die for you, Azak."

"That's foolish," she said.

"Don't you like me? Don't I please you?"

"More than any man I ever knew," she said, kissing him. "You are beautiful and utterly satisfying, my sweet Toddra."

"You don't want any of the other men here, do you?" he asked.

"No. They're all ugly fumblers, compared to my beautiful dancer."

"Listen, then," he said, sitting up and speaking very seriously. He was a slender man of twenty-two, with long, smooth-muscled limbs, wide-set eyes, and a thin-lipped, sensitive mouth. Azak lay stroking his thigh, thinking how lovely and lovable he was. "I have a plan," he said. "When I dance, you know, in the story-dances, I play a woman, of course; I've done it since I was twelve. People always say they can't believe I really am a man, I play a woman so well. If I escaped—from here, from the Castle—as a woman—I could come to your house as a servant—"

"What?" cried Azak, astounded.

"I could live there," he said urgently, bending over her.

"With you. I would always be there. You could have me every night. It would cost you nothing, except my food. I would serve you, service you, sweep your house, do anything, anything, Azak, please, my beloved, my mistress, let me be yours!" He saw that she was still incredulous, and hurried on, "You could send me away when you got tired of me—"

"If you tried to go back to the Castle after an escapade like that they'd whip you to death, you idiot!"

"I'm valuable," he said. "They'd punish me, but they wouldn't damage me."

"You're wrong. You haven't been dancing, and your value here has slipped because you don't perform well with anybody but me. The manager told me so."

Tears stood in Toddra's eyes. Azak disliked giving him pain, but she was genuinely shocked at his wild plan. "And if you were discovered, my dear," she said more gently, "I would be utterly disgraced. It is a very childish plan, Toddra. Please never dream of such a thing again. But I am truly, truly fond of you, I adore you and want no other man but you. Do you believe that, Toddra?"

He nodded. Restraining his tears, he said, "For now."

"For now and for a long, long, long time! My dear, sweet, beautiful dancer, we have each other as long as we want, years and years! Only do your duty by the other women that come, so that you don't get sold away by your Castle, please! I couldn't bear to lose you, Toddra." And she clasped him passionately in her arms, and arousing him at once, opened to him, and soon both were crying out in the throes of delight.

Though she could not take his love entirely seriously, since what could come of such a misplaced emotion, except such foolish schemes as he had proposed?—still he touched her heart, and she felt a tenderness towards him that greatly enhanced the pleasure of their intercourse. So for more than a year she spent two or three nights a week with him at the fuckery, which was as much as she could afford. The manager, trying still to discourage his love, would not lower Toddra's fee, even though he was unpopular among the other clients of the fuckery; so Azak spent a great deal of money on him, although he would never, after the first night, accept a tip from her.

Then a woman who had not been able to conceive with any of the sires at the fuckery tried Toddra, and at once conceived, and being tested found the fetus to be male. Another woman conceived by him, again a male fetus. At once Toddra was in demand as a sire. Women began coming from all over the city to be serviced by him. This meant, of course, that he must be free during their period of ovulation. There were now many evenings that he could not meet Azak, for the manager was not to be bribed. Toddra disliked his popularity, but Azak soothed and reassured him, telling him how proud she was of him, and how his work would never interfere with their love. In fact, she was not altogether sorry that he was so much in demand, for she had found another person with whom she wanted to spend her evenings.

This was a young woman named Zedr, who worked in the mill as a machine-repair specialist. She was tall and handsome; Azak noticed first how freely and strongly she walked and how proudly she stood. She found a pretext to make her acquaintance. It seemed to Azak that Zedr admired her; but for a long time each behaved to the other as a friend only, making no sexual advances. They were much in each other's company, going to games and dances together, and Azak found that she enjoyed this open and sociable life better than always being in the fuckery alone with Toddra. They talked about how they might set up a machine-repair service in partnership. As time went on, Azak found that Zedr's beautiful body was always in her thoughts. At last, one evening in her singlewoman's flat, she told her friend that she loved her, but did not wish to burden their friendship with an unwelcome desire.

Zedr replied, "I have wanted you ever since I first saw you, but I didn't want to embarrass you with my desire. I thought you preferred men."

"Until now I did, but I want to make love with you," Azak said.

She found herself quite timid at first, but Zedr was expert and subtle, and could prolong Azak's orgasms till she found such consummation as she had not dreamed of. She said to Zedr, "You have made me a woman."

"Then let's make each other wives," said Zedr joyfully.

They married, moved to a house in the west of the city, and left the mill, setting up in business together.

All this time, Azak had said nothing of her new love to Toddra, whom she had seen less and less often. A little ashamed of her cowardice, she reassured herself that he was so busy performing as a sire that he would not really miss her. After all, despite his romantic talk of love, he was a man, and to a man fucking is the most important thing, instead of being merely one element of love and life as it is to a woman.

When she married Zedr, she sent Toddra a letter, saying that their lives had drifted apart, and she was now moving away and would not see him again, but would always remember him fondly.

She received an immediate answer from Toddra, a letter begging her to come and talk with him, full of avowals of unchanging love, badly spelled and almost illegible. The letter touched, embarrassed, and shamed her, and she did not answer it.

He wrote again and again, and tried to reach her on the holonet at her new business. Zedr urged her not to make any response, saying, "It would be cruel to encourage him."

Their new business went well from the start. They were home one evening busy chopping vegetables for dinner when there was a knock at the door. "Come in," Zedr called, thinking it was Chochi, a friend they were considering as a third partner. A stranger entered, a tall, beautiful woman with a scarf over her hair. The stranger went straight to Azak, saying in a strangled voice, "Azak, Azak, please, please let me stay with you." The scarf fell back from his long hair. Azak recognised Toddra.

She was astonished and a little frightened, but she had known Toddra a long time and been very fond of him, and this habit of affection made her put out her hands to him in greeting. She saw fear and despair in his face, and was sorry for him.

But Zedr, guessing who he was, was both alarmed and angry. She kept the chopping knife in her hand. She slipped from the room and called the city police.

When she returned she saw the man pleading with Azak to let him stay hidden in their household as a servant. "I will do anything," he said. "Please, Azak, my only love, please! I can't live without you. I can't service those women, those strangers who only want to be impregnated. I can't dance any more. I think only of you, you are my only hope. I will be a woman, no one will know. I'll cut my hair, no one will know!" So he went on, almost threatening in his passion, but pitiful also. Zedr listened coldly, thinking he was mad. Azak listened with pain and shame. "No, no, it is not possible," she said over and over, but he would not hear.

When the police came to the door and he realised who they were, he bolted to the back of the house seeking escape. The policewomen caught him in the bedroom; he fought them desperately, and they subdued him brutally. Azak shouted at them not to hurt him, but they paid no heed, twisting his arms and hitting him about the head till he stopped resisting. They dragged him out. The chief of the troop stayed to take evidence. Azak tried to plead for Toddra, but Zedr stated the facts and added that she thought he was insane and dangerous.

After some days, Azak inquired at the police office and was told that Toddra had been returned to his Castle with a warning not to send him to the fuckery again for a year or until the Lords of the Castle found him capable of responsible behavior. She was uneasy thinking of how he might be punished. Zedr said, "They won't hurt him, he's too valuable," just as he himself had said. Azak was glad to believe this. She was, in fact, much relieved to know that he was out of the way.

She and Zedr took Chochi first into their business and then into their household. Chochi was a woman from the dockside quarter, tough and humorous, a hard worker and an undemanding, comfortable lovemaker. They were happy with one another, and prospered.

A year went by, and another year. Azak went to her old quarter to arrange a contract for repair work with two women from the mill where she had first worked. She asked them about Toddra. He was back at the fuckery from time to time, they told her. He had been named the year's Champion Sire of his Castle, and was much in demand, bringing an even higher price, because he impregnated so many women and so many of the conceptions were male. He was not in demand for pleasure, they said, as he had a reputation for roughness and even cruelty. Women asked for him only if they wanted to conceive. Thinking of his gentleness with her, Azak found it hard to imagine him behaving brutally. Harsh punishment at the Castle, she thought, must have altered him. But she could not believe that he had truly changed.

Another year passed. The business was doing very well, and Azak and Chochi both began talking seriously about having children. Zedr was not interested in bearing, though happy to be a mother. Chochi had a favorite man at their local fuckery to whom she went now and then for pleasure; she began going to him at ovulation, for he had a good reputation as a sire.

Azak had not been to a fuckery since she and Zedr married. She honored fidelity highly, and made love with no one but Zedr and Chochi. When she thought of being impregnated, she found that her old interest in fucking with men had quite died out or even turned to distaste. She did not like the idea of self-impregnation from the sperm bank, but the idea of letting a strange man penetrate her was even more repulsive. Thinking what to do, she thought of Toddra, whom she had truly loved and had pleasure with. He was again a Champion Sire, known throughout the city as a reliable impregnator. There was certainly no other man with whom she could take any pleasure. And he had loved her so much he had put his career and even his life in danger, trying to be with her. That irresponsibility was over and done with. He had never written to her again, and the Castle and the managers of the fuckery would never have let him service women if they thought him mad or untrustworthy. After all this time, she thought, she could go back to him and give him the pleasure he had so desired.

She notified the fuckery of the expected period of her next ovulation, requesting Toddra. He was already engaged for that period, and they offered her another sire; but she preferred to wait till the next month.

Chochi had conceived, and was elated. "Hurry up, hurry up!" she said to Azak. "We want twins!"

Azak found herself looking forward to being with Toddra. Regretting the violence of their last encounter and the pain it must have given him, she wrote the following letter to him:

"My dear, I hope our long separation and the distress of our last meeting will be forgotten in the joy of being together again, and that you still love me as I still love you. I shall be very proud to bear your

child, and let us hope it may be a son! I am impatient to see you again, my beautiful dancer. Your Azak."

There had not been time for him to answer this letter when her ovulation period began. She dressed in her best clothes. Zedr still distrusted Toddra and had tried to dissuade her from going to him; she bade her "Good luck!" rather sulkily. Chochi hung a mothercharm around her neck, and she went off.

There was a new manager on duty at the fuckery, a coarse-faced young woman who told her, "Call out if he gives you any trouble. He may be a Champion but he's rough, and we don't let him get away with hurting anybody."

"He won't hurt me," Azak said, smiling, and went eagerly into the familiar room where she and Toddra had enjoyed each other so often. He was standing waiting at the window just as he had used to stand. When he turned he looked just as she remembered, long-limbed, his silky hair flowing like water down his back, his wide-set eyes gazing at her.

"Toddra!" she said, coming to him with outstretched hands.

He took her hands and said her name.

"Did you get my letter? Are you happy?"

"Yes," he said, smiling.

"And all that unhappiness, all that foolishness about love, is it over? I am so sorry you were hurt, Toddra, I don't want any more of that. Can we just be ourselves and be happy together as we used to be?"

"Yes, all that is over," he said. "And I am happy to see you." He drew her gently to him. Gently he began to undress her and caress her body, just as he had used to, knowing what gave her pleasure, and she remembering what gave him pleasure. They lay down naked together. She was fondling his erect penis, aroused and yet a little reluctant to be penetrated after so long, when he moved his arm as if uncomfortable. Drawing away from him a little, she saw that he had a knife in his hand, which he must have hidden in the bed. He was holding it concealed behind his back.

Her womb went cold, but she continued to fondle his penis and testicles, not daring to say anything and not able to pull away, for he was holding her close with the other hand.

Suddenly he moved onto her and forced his penis into her

vagina with a thrust so painful that for an instant she thought it was the knife. He ejaculated instantly. As his body arched she writhed out from under him, scrambled to the door, and ran from the room crying for help.

He pursued her, striking with the knife, stabbing her in the shoulderblade before the manager and other women and men seized him. The men were very angry and treated him with a violence which the manager's protests did not lessen. Naked, bloody, and half-conscious, he was bound and taken away immediately to the Castle.

Everyone now gathered around Azak, and her wound, which was slight, was cleaned and covered. Shaken and confused, she could ask only, "What will they do to him?"

"What do you think they do to a murdering rapist? Give him a prize?" the manager said. "They'll geld him."

"But it was my fault," Azak said.

The manager stared at her and said, "Are you mad? Go home."

She went back into the room and mechanically put on her clothes. She looked at the bed where they had lain. She stood at the window where Toddra had stood. She remembered how she had seen him dance long ago in the contest where he had first been made champion. She thought, "My life is wrong." But she did not know how to make it right.

Alteration in Seggrian social and cultural institutions did not take the disastrous course Merriment feared. It has been slow and its direction is not clear. In 93/1602 Terhada College invited men from two neighboring castles to apply as students, and three men did so. In the next decades, most colleges opened their doors to men. Once they were graduated, male students had to return to their castle, unless they left the planet, since native men were not allowed to live anywhere but as students in a college or in a castle, until the Open Gate Law was passed in 93/1662.

Even after passage of that law, the castles remained closed to women; and the exodus of men from the castles was much slower than opponents of the measure feared. Social adjustment to the Open Gate Law has been slow. In several regions programs to train men in basic skills such as farming and construction have met with moderate success; the men work in competitive teams, separate from and managed by the women's companies. A good many Seggri have come to Hain

*to study in recent years—more men than women, despite the great
numerical imbalance that still exists.*

*The following autobiographical sketch by one of these men is of
particular interest, since he was involved in the event which directly
precipitated the Open Gate Law.*

AUTOBIOGRAPHICAL SKETCH BY MOBILE ARDAR DEZ

I was born in Ekumenical Cycle 93, Year 1641, in Rakedr on
Seggri. Rakedr was a placid, prosperous, conservative town,
and I was brought up in the old way, the petted boychild of a
big motherhouse. Altogether there were seventeen of us, not
counting the kitchen staff—a great-grandmother, two grandmothers, four mothers, nine daughters, and me. We were well
off; all the women were or had been managers or skilled workers in the Rakedr Pottery, the principal industry of the town.
We kept all the holidays with pomp and energy, decorating the
house from roof to foundation with banners for Hillalli, making fantastic costumes for the Harvest Festival, and celebrating
somebody's birthday every few weeks with gifts all round. I
was petted, as I said, but not, I think, spoiled. My birthday was
no grander than my sisters', and I was allowed to run and play
with them just as if I were a girl. Yet I was always aware, as
were they, that our mothers' eyes rested on me with a different
look, brooding, reserved, and sometimes, as I grew older,
desolate.

After my Confirmation, my birthmother or her mother took
me to Rakedr Castle every spring on Visiting Day. The gates of
the park, which had opened to admit me alone (and terrified)
for my Confirmation, remained shut, but rolling stairs were
placed against the park walls. Up these I and a few other little
boys from the town climbed, to sit on top of the park wall in
great state, on cushions, under awnings, and watch demonstration dancing, bull-dancing, wrestling, and other sports on
the great gamefield inside the wall. Our mothers waited below,
outside, in the bleachers of the public field. Men and youths
from the Castle sat with us, explaining the rules of the games
and pointing out the fine points of a dancer or wrestler, treat-
ing us seriously, making us feel important. I enjoyed that very

much, but as soon as I came down off the wall and started home it all fell away like a costume shrugged off, a part played in a play; and I went on with my work and play in the mother-house with my family, my real life.

When I was ten I went to Boys' Class downtown. The class had been set up forty or fifty years before as a bridge between the motherhouses and the Castle, but the Castle, under in-creasingly reactionary governance, had recently withdrawn from the project. Lord Fassaw forbade his men to go anywhere outside the walls but directly to the fuckery, in a closed car, returning at first light; and so no men were able to teach the class. The townswomen who tried to tell me what to expect when I went to the Castle did not really know much more than I did. However well-meaning they were, they mostly frightened and confused me. But fear and confusion were an appropriate preparation.

I cannot describe the ceremony of Severance. I really cannot describe it. Men on Seggri, in those days, had this advantage: they knew what death is. They had all died once before their body's death. They had turned and looked back at their whole life, every place and face they had loved, and turned away from it as the gate closed.

At the time of my Severance, our small Castle was internally divided into "collegials" and "traditionals," a liberal faction left from the regime of Lord Ishog and a younger, highly conservative faction. The split was already disastrously wide when I came to the Castle. Lord Fassaw's rule had grown in-creasingly harsh and irrational. He governed by corruption, brutality, and cruelty. All of us who lived there were of course infected, and would have been destroyed if there had not been a strong, constant, moral resistance, centered around Ragaz and Kohadrat, who had been protégés of Lord Ishog. The two men were open partners; their followers were all the homosex-uals in the Castle, and a good number of other men and older boys.

My first days and months in the Scrubs' dormitory were a bewildering alternation: terror, hatred, shame, as the boys who had been there a few months or years longer than I were in-cited to humiliate and abuse the newcomer, in order to make a man of him—and comfort, gratitude, love, as boys who had come under the influence of the collegials offered me secret friendship and protection. They helped me in the games and competitions and took me into their beds at night, not for sex but to keep me from the sexual bullies. Lord Fassaw detested adult homosexuality and would have reinstituted the death penalty if the Town Council had allowed it. Though he did not dare punish Ragaz and Kohadrat, he punished consenting love between older boys with bizarre and appalling physical mutilations—ears cut into fringes, fingers branded with red-hot iron rings. Yet he encouraged the older boys to rape the eleven- and twelve-year-olds, as a manly practice. None of us escaped. We particularly dreaded four youths, seventeen or eighteen years old when I came there, who called themselves the Lordsmen. Every few nights they raided the Scrubs' dormitory for a victim, whom they raped as a group. The collegials protected us as best they could by ordering us to their beds, where we wept and protested loudly, while they pretended to abuse us, laughing and jeering. Later, in the dark and silence, they comforted us with candy, and sometimes, as we grew older, with a desired love, gentle and exquisite in its secrecy.

There was no privacy at all in the Castle. I have said that to women who asked me to describe life there, and they thought they understood me. "Well, everybody shares everything in a motherhouse," they would say, "everybody's in and out of the rooms all the time. You're never really alone unless you have a singlewoman's flat." I could not tell them how different the loose, warm commonality of the motherhouse was from the rigid, deliberate publicity of the forty-bed, brightly-lighted Castle dormitories. Nothing in Rakedr was private: only secret, only silent. We ate our tears.

I grew up; I take some pride in that, along with my profound gratitude to the boys and men who made it possible. I did not kill myself, as several boys did during those years, nor did I kill my mind and soul, as some did so their body could survive. Thanks to the maternal care of the collegials—the resistance, as we came to call ourselves—I grew up.

Why do I say maternal, not paternal? Because there were no fathers in my world. There were only sires. I knew no such word as father or paternal. I thought of Ragaz and Kohadrat as my mothers. I still do.

Fassaw grew quite mad as the years went on, and his hold over the Castle tightened to a deathgrip. The Lordsmen now ruled us all. They were lucky in that we still had a strong Maingame team, the pride of Fassaw's heart, which kept us in the First League, as well as two Champion Sires in steady demand at the town fuckeries. Any protest the resistance tried to bring to the Town Council could be dismissed as typical male whining, or laid to the demoralising influence of the aliens. From the outside Rakedr Castle seemed all right. Look at our great team! Look at our champion studs! The women looked no further.

How could they abandon us?—the cry every Seggrian boy must make in his heart. How could she leave me here? Doesn't she know what it's like? Why doesn't she know? Doesn't she want to know?

"Of course not," Ragaz said to me when I came to him in a passion of righteous indignation, the Town Council having denied our petition to be heard. "Of course they don't want to know how we live. Why do they never come into the castles? Oh, we keep them out, yes; but do you think we could keep them out if they wanted to enter? My dear, we collude with them and they with us in maintaining the great foundation of ignorance and lies on which our civilisation rests."

"Our own mothers abandon us," I said.

"Abandon us? Who feeds us, clothes us, houses us, pays us? We're utterly dependent on them. If ever we made ourselves independent, perhaps we could rebuild society on a foundation of truth."

Independence was as far as his vision could reach. Yet I think his mind groped further, towards what he could not see, the body's obscure, inalterable dream of mutuality.

Our effort to make our case heard at the Council had no effect except within the Castle. Lord Fassaw saw his power threatened. Within a few days Ragaz was seized by the Lordsmen and their bully boys, accused of repeated homosexual acts and treasonable plots, arraigned, and sentenced by the Lord of the Castle. Everyone was summoned to the Gamefield to witness the punishment. A man of fifty with a heart ailment—he had been a Maingame racer in his twenties and had overtrained—Ragaz was tied naked across a bench and beaten with "Lord Long," a heavy leather tube filled with lead weights. The Lordsman Berhed, who wielded it, struck repeatedly at the head, the kidneys, and the genitals. Ragaz died an hour or two later in the infirmary.

The Rakedr Mutiny took shape that night. Kohadrat, older than Ragaz and devastated by his loss, could not restrain or guide us. His vision had been of a true resistance, longlasting and nonviolent, through which the Lordsmen would in time destroy themselves. We had been following that vision. Now we let it go. We dropped the truth and grabbed weapons. "How you play is what you win," Kohadrat said, but we had heard all those old saws. We would not play the patience game any more. We would win, now, once for all.

And we did. We won. We had our victory. Lord Fassaw, the Lordsmen and their bullies had been slaughtered by the time the police got to the Gate.

I remember how those tough women strode in among us, staring at the rooms of the Castle which they had never seen, staring at the mutilated bodies, eviscerated, castrated, headless—at Lordsman Berhed, who had been nailed to the floor with "Lord Long" stuffed down his throat—at us, the rebels, the victors, with our bloody hands and defiant faces—at Kohadrat, whom we thrust forward as our leader, our spokesman.

He stood silent. He ate his tears.

The women drew closer to one another, clutching their guns, staring around. They were appalled, they thought us all insane. Their utter incomprehension drove one of us at last to speak—a young man, Tarsk, who wore the iron ring that had been forced onto his finger when it was red-hot. "They killed Ragaz," he said. "They were all mad. Look." He held out his crippled hand.

The chief of the troop, after a pause, said, "No one will leave here till this is looked into," and marched her women out of the Castle, out of the park, locking the gate behind them, leaving us with our victory.

The hearings and judgments on the Rakedr Mutiny were all broadcast, of course, and the event has been studied and discussed ever since. My own part in it was the murder of the Lordsman Tatiddi. Three of us set on him and beat him to death with exercise-clubs in the gymnasium where we had cornered him.

How we played was what we won.

We were not punished. Men were sent from several castles to form a government over Rakedr Castle. They learned enough of Fassaw's behavior to see the cause of our rebellion, but the contempt of even the most liberal of them for us was absolute. They treated us not as men, but as irrational, irresponsible creatures, untamable cattle. If we spoke they did not answer.

I do not know how long we could have endured that cold regime of shame. It was only two months after the Mutiny that the World Council enacted the Open Gate Law. We told one another that that was our victory, we had made that happen. None of us believed it. We told one another we were free. For the first time in history, any man who wanted to leave his castle could walk out the gate. We were free!

What happened to the free man outside the gate? Nobody had given it much thought.

I was one who walked out the gate, on the morning of the day the law came into force. Eleven of us walked into town together.

Several of us, men not from Rakedr, went to one or another of the fuckeries, hoping to be allowed to stay there; they had nowhere else to go. Hotels and inns of course would not accept men. Those of us who had been children in the town went to our motherhouses.

What is it like to return from the dead? Not easy. Not for the one who returns, nor for his people. The place he occupied in their world has closed up, ceased to be, filled with accumulated change, habit, the doings and needs of others. He has been replaced. To return from the dead is to be a ghost: a person for whom there is no room.

Neither I nor my family understood that, at first. I came back to them at twenty-one as trustingly as if I were the eleven-year-old who had left them, and they opened their arms to their child. But he did not exist. Who was I?

For a long time, months, we refugees from the Castle hid in our motherhouses. The men from other towns all made their way home, usually by begging a ride with teams on tour. There were seven or eight of us in Rakedr, but we scarcely ever saw one another. Men had no place on the street; for hundreds of

years a man seen alone on the street had been arrested immediately. If we went out, women ran from us, or reported us, or
surrounded and threatened us—"Get back into your Castle
where you belong! Get back to the fuckery where you belong!
Get out of our city!" They called us drones, and in fact we had
no work, no function at all in the community. The fuckeries
would not accept us for service, because we had no guarantee
of health and good behavior from a castle.

This was our freedom: we were all ghosts, useless, frightened, frightening intruders, shadows in the corners of life. We
watched life going on around us—work, love, childbearing,
childrearing, getting and spending, making and shaping, gov-
erning and adventuring—the women's world, the bright, full,
real world—and there was no room in it for us. All we had ever
learned to do was play games and destroy one another.

My mothers and sisters racked their brains, I know, to find
some place and use for me in their lively, industrious household. Two old live-in cooks had run our kitchen since long
before I was born, so cooking, the one practical art I had been
taught in the Castle, was superfluous. They found household
tasks for me, but they were all make-work, and they and I
knew it. I was perfectly willing to look after the babies, but
one of the grandmothers was very jealous of that privilege, and
also some of my sisters' wives were uneasy about a man touching their baby. My sister Pado broached the possibility of an
apprenticeship in the clayworks, and I leaped at the chance;
but the managers of the Pottery, after long discussion, were
unable to agree to accept men as employees. Their hormones
would make male workers unreliable, and female workers
would be uncomfortable, and so on.

The holonews was full of such proposals and discussions, of
course, and orations about the unforeseen consequences of the
Open Gate Law, the proper place of men, male capacities and
limitations, gender as destiny. Feeling against the Open Gate
policy ran very strong, and it seemed that every time I watched
the holo there was a woman talking grimly about the inherent
violence and irresponsibility of the male, his biological unfit-
ness to participate in social and political decision-making.
Often it was a man saying the same things. Opposition to the
new law had the fervent support of all the conservatives in the

castles, who pleaded eloquently for the gates to be closed and men to return to their proper station, pursuing the true, masculine glory of the games and the fuckeries.

Glory did not tempt me, after the years at Rakedr Castle; the word itself had come to mean degradation to me. I ranted against the games and competitions, puzzling most of my family, who loved to watch the Maingames and wrestling, and complained only that the level of excellence of most of the teams had declined since the gates were opened. And I ranted against the fuckeries, where, I said, men were used as cattle, stud bulls, not as human beings. I would never go there again.

"But my dear boy," my mother said at last, alone with me one evening, "will you live the rest of your life celibate?"

"I hope not," I said.

"Then . . . ?"

"I want to get married."

Her eyes widened. She brooded a bit, and finally ventured, "To a man."

"No. To a woman. I want a normal, ordinary marriage. I want to have a wife and be a wife."

Shocking as the idea was, she tried to absorb it. She pondered, frowning.

"All it means," I said, for I had had a long time with nothing to do but ponder, "is that we'd live together just like any married pair. We'd set up our own daughterhouse, and be faithful to each other, and if she had a child I'd be its lovemother along with her. There isn't any reason why it wouldn't work!"

"Well, I don't know—I don't know of any," said my mother, gentle and judicious, and never happy at saying no to me. "But you do have to find the woman, you know."

"I know," I said glumly.

"It's such a problem for you to meet people," she said. "Perhaps if you went to the fuckery . . . ? I don't see why your own motherhouse couldn't guarantee you just as well as a castle. We could try—?"

But I passionately refused. Not being one of Fassaw's sycophants, I had seldom been allowed to go to the fuckery; and my few experiences there had been unfortunate. Young, inexperienced, and without recommendation, I had been selected by older women who wanted a plaything. Their practiced skill at arousing me had left me humiliated and enraged. They patted and tipped me as they left. That elaborate, mechanical excitation and their condescending coldness were vile to me, after the tenderness of my lover-protectors in the Castle. Yet women attracted me physically as men never had; the beautiful bodies of my sisters and their wives, all around me constantly now, clothed and naked, innocent and sensual, the wonderful heaviness and strength and softness of women's bodies, kept me continually aroused. Every night I masturbated, fantasising my sisters in my arms. It was unendurable. Again I was a ghost, a raging, yearning impotence in the midst of untouchable reality.

I began to think I would have to go back to the Castle. I sank into a deep depression, an inertia, a chill darkness of the mind.

My family, anxious, affectionate, busy, had no idea what to do for me or with me. I think most of them thought in their hearts that it would be best if I went back through the gate.

One afternoon my sister Pado, with whom I had been closest as a child, came to my room—they had cleared out a dormer attic for me, so that I had room at least in the literal sense. She found me in my now constant lethargy, lying on the bed doing nothing at all. She breezed in, and with the indifference women often show to moods and signals, plumped down on the foot of the bed and said, "Hey, what do you know about the man who's here from the Ekumen?"

I shrugged and shut my eyes. I had been having rape fantasies lately. I was afraid of her.

She talked on about the offworlder, who was apparently in Rakedr to study the Mutiny. "He wants to talk to the resistance," she said. "Men like you. The men who opened the gates. He says they won't come forward, as if they were ashamed of being heroes."

"Heroes!" I said. The word in my language is gendered female. It refers to the semi-divine, semi-historic protagonists of the Epics.

"It's what you are," Pado said, intensity breaking through her assumed breeziness. "You took responsibility in a great act. Maybe you did it wrong. Sassume did it wrong in the *Founding of Emmo*, didn't she, she let Faradr get killed. But she was still a hero. She took the responsibility. So did you. You ought to go talk to this Alien. Tell him what happened. Nobody really knows what happened at the Castle. You owe us the story."

That was a powerful phrase, among my people. "The untold story mothers the lie," was the saying. The doer of any notable act was held literally *accountable* for it to the community.

"So why should I tell it to an Alien?" I said, defensive of my inertia.

"Because he'll listen," my sister said drily. "We're all too damned busy."

It was profoundly true. Pado had seen a gate for me and opened it; and I went through it, having just enough strength and sanity left to do so.

Mobile Noem was a man in his forties, born some centuries earlier on Terra, trained on Hain, widely travelled; a small, yellow-brown, quick-eyed person, very easy to talk to. He did not seem at all masculine to me, at first; I kept thinking he was a woman, because he acted like one. He got right to business, with none of the maneuvering to assert his authority or jockeying for position that men of my society felt obligatory in any relationship with another man. I was used to men being wary, indirect, and competitive. Noem, like a woman, was direct and receptive. He was also as subtle and powerful as any man or woman I had known, even Ragaz. His authority was in fact immense; but he never stood on it. He sat down on it, comfortably, and invited you to sit down with him.

I was the first of the Rakedr mutineers to come forward and tell our story to him. He recorded it, with my permission, to use in making his report to the Stabiles on the condition of our society, "the matter of Seggri," as he called it. My first description of the Mutiny took less than an hour. I thought I was done. I didn't know, then, the inexhaustible desire to learn, to understand, to hear *all* the story, that characterises the Mobiles of the Ekumen. Noem asked questions, I answered; he speculated and extrapolated, I corrected; he wanted details, I furnished them—telling the story of the Mutiny, of the years before it, of the men of the Castle, of the women of the Town, of my people, of my life—little by little, bit by bit, all in fragments, a muddle. I talked to Noem daily for a month. I learned that the story has no beginning, and no story has an end. That the story is all muddle, all middle. That the story is never true, but that the lie is indeed a child of silence.

By the end of the month I had come to love and trust Noem, and of course to depend on him. Talking to him had become my reason for being. I tried to face the fact that he would not stay in Rakedr much longer. I must learn to do without him. Do what? There were things for men to do, ways for men to live, he proved it by his mere existence; but could I find them?

He was keenly aware of my situation, and would not let me withdraw, as I began to do, into the lethargy of fear again; he would not let me be silent. He asked me impossible questions. "What would you be if you could be anything?" he asked me, a question children ask each other.

I answered at once, passionately—"A wife!"

I know now what the flicker that crossed his face was. His quick, kind eyes watched me, looked away, looked back.

"I want my own family," I said. "Not to live in my mothers' house, where I'm always a child. Work. A wife, wives—children —to be a mother. I want life, not games!"

"You can't bear a child," he said gently.

"No, but I can mother one!"

"We gender the word," he said. "I like it better your way. . . . But tell me, Ardar, what are the chances of your marrying —meeting a woman willing to marry a man? It hasn't happened, here, has it?"

I had to say no, not to my knowledge.

"It will happen, certainly, I think," he said (his certainties were always uncertain). "But the personal cost, at first, is likely to be high. Relationships formed against the negative pressure of a society are under terrible strain; they tend to become defensive, overintense, unpeaceful. They have no room to grow."

"Room!" I said. And I tried to tell him my feeling of having no room in my world, no air to breathe.

He looked at me, scratching his nose; he laughed. "There's plenty of room in the galaxy, you know," he said.

"Do you mean . . . I could . . . That the Ekumen . . ." I didn't even know what the question I wanted to ask was. Noem did. He began to answer it thoughtfully and in detail. My education so far had been so limited, even as regards the culture of my own people, that I would have to attend a college for at least two or three years, in order to be ready to apply to an offworld institution such as the Ekumenical Schools on Hain. Of course, he went on, where I went and what kind of training I chose would depend on my interests, which I would go to a college to discover, since neither my schooling as a child nor my training at the Castle had really given me any idea of what there was to be interested in. The choices offered me had been unbelievably limited, addressing neither the needs of a normally intelligent person nor the needs of my society. And so the Open Gate Law instead of giving me freedom had left me "with no air to breathe but airless Space," said Noem, quoting some poet from some planet somewhere. My head was spinning, full of stars. "Hagka College is quite near Rakedr," Noem said, "did you never think of applying? If only to escape from your terrible Castle?"

I shook my head. "Lord Fassaw always destroyed the application forms when they were sent to his office. If any of us had tried to apply. . . ."

"You would have been punished. Tortured, I suppose. Yes. Well, from the little I know of your colleges, I think your life there would be better than it is here, but not altogether pleasant. You will have work to do, a place to be; but you will be made to feel marginal, inferior. Even highly educated, enlightened women have difficulty accepting men as their intellectual equals. Believe me, I have experienced it myself! And because you were trained at the Castle to compete, to want to excel, you may find it hard to be among people who either believe you incapable of excellence, or to whom the concept of competition, of winning and defeating, is valueless. But just there, there is where you will find air to breathe."

Noem recommended me to women he knew on the faculty of Hagka College, and I was enrolled on probation. My family were delighted to pay my tuition. I was the first of us to go to college, and they were genuinely proud of me.

As Noem had predicted, it was not always easy, but there were enough other men there that I found friends and was not caught in the paralysing isolation of the motherhouse. And as I took courage, I made friends among the women students, finding many of them unprejudiced and companionable. In my third year, one of them and I managed, tentatively and warily, to fall in love. It did not work very well or last very long, yet it was a great liberation for both of us, our liberation from the belief that the only communication or commonality possible between us was sexual, that an adult man and woman had nothing to join them but their genitals. Emadr loathed the professionalism of the fuckery as I did, and our lovemaking was always shy and brief. Its true significance was not as a consummation of desire, but as proof that we could trust each other. Where our real passion broke loose was when we lay together talking, telling each other what our lives had been, how we felt about men and women and each other and ourselves, what our nightmares were, what our dreams were. We talked endlessly, in a communion that I will cherish and honor all my life, two young souls finding their wings, flying together, not for long, but high. The first flight is the highest.

Emadr has been dead two hundred years; she stayed on Seggri, married into a motherhouse, bore two children, taught at Hagka, and died in her seventies. I went to Hain, to the Ekumenical Schools, and later to Werel and Yeowe as part of the Mobile's staff; my record is herewith enclosed. I have written this sketch of my life as part of my application to return to Seggri as a Mobile of the Ekumen. I want very much to live among my people, to learn who they are, now that I know with at least an uncertain certainty who I am.

Solitude

An addition to "POVERTY: The Second Report on Eleven-Soro" by Mobile Entselenne'temharyonoterregwis Leaf, by her daughter, Serenity.

M Y MOTHER, a field ethnologist, took the difficulty of learning anything about the people of Eleven-Soro as a personal challenge. The fact that she used her children to meet that challenge might be seen as selfishness or as selflessness. Now that I have read her report I know that she finally thought she had done wrong. Knowing what it cost her, I wish she knew my gratitude to her for allowing me to grow up as a person.

Shortly after a robot probe reported people of the Hainish Descent on the eleventh planet of the Soro system, she joined the orbital crew as backup for the three First Observers down onplanet. She had spent four years in the tree-cities of nearby Huthu. My brother In Joy Born was eight years old and I was five; she wanted a year or two of ship duty so we could spend some time in a Hainish-style school. My brother had enjoyed the rainforests of Huthu very much, but though he could brachiate he could barely read, and we were all bright blue with skin fungus. While Borny learned to read and I learned to wear clothes and we all had anti-fungus treatments, my mother became as intrigued by Eleven-Soro as the Observers were frustrated by it.

All this is in her report, but I will say it as I learned it from her, which helps me remember and understand. The language had been recorded by the probe and the Observers had spent a year learning it. The many dialectical variations excused their accents and errors, and they reported that language was not a problem. Yet there was a communication problem. The two men found themselves isolated, faced with suspicion or hostility, unable to form any connection with the native men, all of whom lived in solitary houses as hermits, or in pairs. Finding communities of adolescent males, they tried to make contact with them, but when they entered the territory of such a group the boys either fled or rushed desperately at them trying to kill them. The women, who lived in what they called "dispersed villages," drove them away with volleys of stones as soon as they came anywhere near the houses. "I believe," one of them reported, "that the only community activity of the Sorovians is throwing rocks at men."

Neither of them succeeded in having a conversation of more than three exchanges with a man. One of them mated with a woman who came by his camp; he reported that though she made unmistakable and insistent advances, she seemed disturbed by his attempts to converse, refused to answer his questions, and left him, he said, "as soon as she got what she came for."

The woman Observer was allowed to settle in an unused house in a "village" (auntring) of seven houses. She made excellent observations of daily life, insofar as she could see any of it, and had several conversations with adult women and many with children; but she found that she was never asked into another woman's house, nor expected to help or ask for help in any work. Conversation concerning normal activities was unwelcome to the other women; the children, her only informants, called her Aunt Crazy-Jabber. Her aberrant behavior caused increasing distrust and dislike among the women, and they began to keep their children away from her. She left. "There's no way," she told my mother, "for an adult to learn anything. They don't ask questions, they don't answer questions. Whatever they learn, they learn when they're children."

Aha! said my mother to herself, looking at Borny and me. And she requested a family transfer to Eleven-Soro with Observer status. The Stabiles interviewed her extensively by ansible, and talked with Borny and even with me—I don't remember it, but she told me I told the Stabiles all about my new stockings —and agreed to her request. The ship was to stay in close orbit, with the previous Observers in the crew, and she was to keep radio contact with it, daily if possible.

I have a dim memory of the tree-city, and of playing with what must have been a kitten or a ghole-kit on the ship; but my first clear memories are of our house in the auntring. It is half underground, half aboveground, with wattle-and-daub walls. Mother and I are standing outside it in the warm sunshine. Between us is a big mud puddle, into which Borny pours water from a basket; then he runs off to the creek to get more water. I muddle the mud with my hands, deliciously, till it is thick and smooth. I pick up a big double handful and slap it onto the walls where the sticks show through. Mother says, "That's good! That's right!" in our new language, and I realise that this is work, and I am doing it. I am repairing the house. I am making it right, doing it right. I am a competent person.

I have never doubted that, so long as I lived there.

We are inside the house at night, and Borny is talking to the ship on the radio, because he misses talking the old language, and anyway he is supposed to tell them stuff. Mother is making a basket and swearing at the split reeds. I am singing a song to drown out Borny so nobody in the auntring hears him talking funny, and anyway I like singing. I learned this song this afternoon in Hyuru's house. I play every day with Hyuru. "Be aware, listen, listen, be aware," I sing. When Mother stops swearing she listens, and then she turns on the recorder. There is a little fire still left from cooking dinner, which was lovely pigi root, I never get tired of pigi. It is dark and warm and smells of pigi and of burning duhur, which is a strong, sacred smell to drive out magic and bad feelings, and as I sing "Listen, be aware," I get sleepier and sleepier and lean against Mother, who is dark and warm and smells like Mother, strong and sacred, full of good feelings.

Our daily life in the auntring was repetitive. On the ship, later, I learned that people who live in artificially complicated situations call such a life "simple." I never knew anybody, anywhere I have been, who found life simple. I think a life or a time looks simple when you leave out the details, the way a planet looks smooth, from orbit.

Certainly our life in the auntring was easy, in the sense that our needs came easily to hand. There was plenty of food to be gathered or grown and prepared and cooked, plenty of temas to pick and rett and spin and weave for clothes and bedding, plenty of reeds to make baskets and thatch with; we children had other children to play with, mothers to look after us, and a great deal to learn. None of this is simple, though it's all easy enough, when you know how to do it, when you are aware of the details.

It was not easy for my mother. It was hard for her, and

complicated. She had to pretend she knew the details while she was learning them, and had to think how to report and explain this way of living to people in another place who didn't understand it. For Borny it was easy until it got hard because he was a boy. For me it was all easy. I learned the work and played with the children and listened to the mothers sing.

The First Observer had been quite right: there was no way for a grown woman to learn how to make her soul. Mother couldn't go listen to another mother sing, it would have been too strange. The aunts all knew she hadn't been brought up well, and some of them taught her a good deal without her realising it. They had decided her mother must have been irresponsible and had gone on scouting instead of settling in an auntring, so that her daughter didn't get educated properly. That's why even the most aloof of the aunts always let me listen with their children, so that I could become an educated person. But of course they couldn't ask another adult into their houses. Borny and I had to tell her all the songs and stories we learned, and then she would tell them to the radio, or we told them to the radio while she listened to us. But she never got it right, not really. How could she, trying to learn it after she'd grown up, and after she'd always lived with magicians?

"Be aware!" She would imitate my solemn and probably irritating imitation of the aunts and the big girls. "Be aware! How many times a day do they say that? Be aware of what? They aren't aware of *what* the ruins are, their own history—they aren't aware of each other! They don't even talk to each other! Be aware, indeed!"

When I told her the stories of the Before Time that Aunt Sadne and Aunt Noyit told their daughters and me, she often heard the wrong things in them. I told her about the People, and she said, "Those are the ancestors of the people here now." When I said, "There aren't any people here now," she didn't understand. "There are persons here now," I said, but she still didn't understand.

Borny liked the story about the Man Who Lived with Women, how he kept some women in a pen, the way some persons keep rats in a pen for eating, and all of them got pregnant, and they each had a hundred babies, and the babies grew up as horrible monsters and ate the man and the mothers and each other. Mother explained to us that that was a parable of the human overpopulation of this planet thousands of years ago. "No, it's not," I said, "it's a moral story." —"Well, yes," Mother said. "The moral is, don't have too many babies." —"No, it's not," I said. "Who could have a hundred babies even if they wanted to? The man was a sorcerer. He did magic. The women did it with him. So their children were monsters."

The key, of course, is the word "tekell," which translates so nicely into the Hainish word "magic," an art or power that violates natural law. It was hard for Mother to understand that some persons truly consider most human relationships unnatural; that marriage, for instance, or government, can be seen as an evil spell woven by sorcerers. It is hard for her people to believe magic.

The ship kept asking if we were all right, and every now and then a Stabile would hook up the ansible to our radio and grill Mother and us. She always convinced them that she wanted to stay, for despite her frustrations, she was doing the work the First Observers had not been able to do, and Borny and I were happy as mudfish, all those first years. I think Mother was happy too, once she got used to the slow pace and the indirect way she had to learn things. She was lonely, missing other grown-ups to talk to, and told us that she would have gone crazy without us. If she missed sex she never showed it. I think, though, that her report is not very complete about sexual matters, perhaps because she was troubled by them. I know that when we first lived in the auntring, two of the aunts, Hedimi and Behyu, used to meet to make love, and Behyu courted my mother; but Mother didn't understand, because Behyu wouldn't talk the way Mother wanted to talk. She couldn't understand having sex with a person whose house you wouldn't enter.

Once when I was nine or so, and had been listening to some of the older girls, I asked her why didn't she go out scouting. "Aunt Sadne would look after us," I said hopefully. I was tired of being the uneducated woman's daughter. I wanted to live in Aunt Sadne's house and be just like the other children.

"Mothers don't scout," she said, scornfully, like an aunt.

"Yes, they do, sometimes," I insisted. "They have to, or how could they have more than one baby?"

"They go to settled men near the auntring. Behyu went back to the Red Knob Hill Man when she wanted a second child. Sadne goes and sees Downriver Lame Man when she wants to have sex. They know the men around here. None of the mothers scout."

I realised that in this case she was right and I was wrong, but I stuck to my point. "Well, why don't you go see Downriver Lame Man? Don't you ever want sex? Migi says she wants it all the time."

"Migi is seventeen," Mother said drily. "Mind your own nose." She sounded exactly like all the other mothers.

Men, during my childhood, were a kind of uninteresting mystery to me. They turned up a lot in the Before Time stories, and the singing-circle girls talked about them; but I seldom saw any of them. Sometimes I'd glimpse one when I was foraging, but they never came near the auntring. In summer the Downriver Lame Man would get lonesome waiting for Aunt Sadne and would come lurking around, not very far from the auntring—not in the bush or down by the river, of course, where he might be mistaken for a rogue and stoned—but out in the open, on the hillsides, where we could all see who he was. Hyuru and Didsu, Aunt Sadne's daughters, said she had had sex with him when she went out scouting the first time, and always had sex with him and never tried any of the other men of the settlement.

She had told them, too, that the first child she bore was a boy, and she drowned it, because she didn't want to bring up a boy and send him away. They felt queer about that and so did I, but it wasn't an uncommon thing. One of the stories we learned was about a drowned boy who grew up underwater, and seized his mother when she came to bathe, and tried to hold her under till she too drowned; but she escaped.

At any rate, after the Downriver Lame Man had sat around for several days on the hillsides, singing long songs and braiding and unbraiding his hair, which was long too, and shone black in the sun, Aunt Sadne always went off for a night or two with him, and came back looking cross and self-conscious.

Aunt Noyit explained to me that Downriver Lame Man's songs were magic; not the usual bad magic, but what she called the great good spells. Aunt Sadne never could resist his spells.

"But he hasn't half the charm of some men I've known," said Aunt Noyit, smiling reminiscently.

Our diet, though excellent, was very low in fat, which Mother thought might explain the rather late onset of puberty; girls seldom menstruated before they were fifteen, and boys often weren't mature till they were considerably older than that. But the women began looking askance at boys as soon as they showed any signs at all of adolescence. First Aunt Hedimi, who was always grim, then Aunt Noyit, then even Aunt Sadne began to turn away from Borny, to leave him out, not answering when he spoke. "What are you doing playing with the children?" old Aunt Dnemi asked him so fiercely that he came home in tears. He was not quite fourteen.

Sadne's younger daughter Hyuru was my soulmate, my best friend, you would say. Her elder sister Didsu, who was in the singing-circle now, came and talked to me one day, looking serious. "Borny is very handsome," she said. I agreed proudly.

"Very big, very strong," she said, "stronger than I am."

I agreed proudly again, and then I began to back away from her.

"I'm not doing magic, Ren," she said.

"Yes you are," I said. "I'll tell your mother!"

Didsu shook her head. "I'm trying to speak truly. If my fear causes your fear, I can't help it. It has to be so. We talked about it in the singing-circle. I don't like it," she said, and I knew she meant it; she had a soft face, soft eyes, she had always been the gentlest of us children. "I wish he could be a child," she said. "I wish I could. But we can't."

"Go be a stupid old woman, then," I said, and ran away from her. I went to my secret place down by the river and cried. I took the holies out of my soulbag and arranged them. One holy—it doesn't matter if I tell you—was a crystal that Borny had given me, clear at the top, cloudy purple at the base. I held it a long time and then I gave it back. I dug a hole under a boulder, and wrapped the holy in duhur leaves inside a square of cloth I tore out of my kilt, beautiful, fine cloth Hyuru had woven and sewn for me. I tore the square right from the front, where it would show. I gave the crystal back, and then sat a long time there near it. When I went home I said nothing of what Didsu had said. But Borny was very silent, and my mother had a worried look. "What have you done to your kilt, Ren?" she asked. I raised my head a little and did not answer; she started to speak again, and then did not. She had finally learned not to talk to a person who chose to be silent.

Borny didn't have a soulmate, but he had been playing more and more often with the two boys nearest his age, Ednede who was a year or two older, a slight, quiet boy, and Bit who was only eleven, but boisterous and reckless. The three of them went off somewhere all the time. I hadn't paid much attention, partly because I was glad to be rid of Bit. Hyuru and I had been practising being aware, and it was tiresome to always have to be aware of Bit yelling and jumping around. He never could leave anyone quiet, as if their quietness took something from him. His mother, Hedimi, had educated him, but she wasn't a good singer or storyteller like Sadne and Noyit, and Bit was too restless to listen even to them. Whenever he saw me and Hyuru trying to slow-walk or sitting being aware, he hung around making noise till we got mad and told him to go, and then he jeered, "Dumb girls!"

I asked Borny what he and Bit and Ednede did, and he said, "Boy stuff."

"Like what?"

"Practising?"

"Being aware?"

After a while he said, "No."

"Practising what, then?"

"Wrestling. Getting strong. For the boygroup." He looked gloomy, but after a while he said, "Look," and showed me a knife he had hidden under his mattress. "Ednede says you have to have a knife, then nobody will challenge you. Isn't it a beauty?" It was metal, old metal from the People, shaped like a reed, pounded out and sharpened down both edges, with a sharp point. A piece of polished flintshrub wood had been bored and fitted on the handle to protect the hand. "I found it in an empty man's-house," he said. "I made the wooden part." He brooded over it lovingly. Yet he did not keep it in his soulbag.

"What do you *do* with it?" I asked, wondering why both edges were sharp, so you'd cut your hand if you used it.

"Keep off attackers," he said.

"Where was the empty man's-house?"

"Way over across Rocky Top."

"Can I go with you if you go back?"

"No," he said, not unkindly, but absolutely.

"What happened to the man? Did he die?"

"There was a skull in the creek. We think he slipped and drowned."

He didn't sound quite like Borny. There was something in his voice like a grown-up; melancholy; reserved. I had gone to him for reassurance, but came away more deeply anxious. I went to Mother and asked her, "What do they do in the boygroups?"

"Perform natural selection," she said, not in my language but in hers, in a strained tone. I didn't always understand Hainish any more and had no idea what she meant, but the tone of her voice upset me; and to my horror I saw she had begun to cry silently. "We have to move, Serenity," she said—she was still talking Hainish without realising it. "There isn't any reason why a family can't move, is there? Women just move in and move out as they please. Nobody cares what anybody does. Nothing is anybody's business. Except hounding the boys out of town!"

I understood most of what she said, but got her to say it in my language; and then I said, "But anywhere we went, Borny would be the same age, and size, and everything."

"Then we'll leave," she said fiercely. "Go back to the ship."

I drew away from her. I had never been afraid of her before: she had never used magic on me. A mother has great power, but there is nothing unnatural in it, unless it is used against the child's soul.

Borny had no fear of her. He had his own magic. When she told him she intended leaving, he persuaded her out of it. He wanted to go join the boygroup, he said; he'd been wanting to for a year now. He didn't belong in the auntring any more, all women and girls and little kids. He wanted to go live with other boys. Bit's older brother Yit was a member of the boygroup in the Four Rivers Territory, and would look after a boy from his auntring. And Ednede was getting ready to go. And Borny and Ednede and Bit had been talking to some men, recently. Men weren't all ignorant and crazy, the way Mother thought. They didn't talk much, but they knew a lot.

"What do they know?" Mother asked grimly.

"They know how to be men," Borny said. "It's what I'm going to be."

"Not that kind of man—not if I can help it! In Joy Born, you must remember the men on the ship, real men—nothing like these poor, filthy hermits. I can't let you grow up thinking that that's what you have to be!"

"They're not like that," Borny said. "You ought to go talk to some of them, Mother."

"Don't be naive," she said with an edgy laugh. "You know perfectly well that women don't go to men to *talk*."

I knew she was wrong; all the women in the auntring knew all the settled men for three days' walk around. They did talk with them, when they were out foraging. They only kept away from the ones they didn't trust; and usually those men disappeared before long. Noyit had told me, "Their magic turns on them." She meant the other men drove them away or killed them. But I didn't say any of this, and Borny said only, "Well, Cave Cliff Man is really nice. And he took us to the place where I found those People things"—some ancient artifacts that Mother had been excited about. "The men know things the women don't," Borny went on. "At least I could go to the boygroup for a while, maybe. I ought to. I could learn a lot! We don't have any solid information on them at all. All we know anything about is this auntring. I'll go and stay long enough to get material for our report. I can't ever come back to either the auntring or the boygroup once I leave them. I'll have to go to the ship, or else try to be a man. So let me have a real go at it, please, Mother?"

"I don't know why you think you have to learn how to be a man," she said after a while. "You know how already."

He really smiled then, and she put her arm around him.

What about me? I thought. I don't even know what the ship is. I want to be here, where my soul is. I want to go on learning to be in the world.

But I was afraid of Mother and Borny, who were both working magic, and so I said nothing and was still, as I had been taught.

Ednede and Borny went off together. Noyit, Ednede's mother, was as glad as Mother was about their keeping company, though she said nothing. The evening before they left, the two boys went to every house in the auntring. It took a long time. The houses were each just within sight or hearing of one or two of the others, with bush and gardens and irrigation ditches and paths in between. In each house the mother and the children were waiting to say goodbye, only they didn't say it; my language has no word for hello or goodbye. They asked the boys in and gave them something to eat, something they could take with them on the way to the Territory. When the boys went to the door everybody in the household came and touched their hand or cheek. I remembered when Yit had gone around the auntring that way. I had cried then, because even though I didn't much like Yit, it seemed so strange for somebody to leave forever, like they were dying. This time I didn't cry; but I kept waking and waking again, until I heard Borny get up before the first light and pick up his things and leave quietly. I know Mother was awake too, but we did as we should do, and lay still while he left, and for a long time after.

I have read her description of what she calls "An Adolescent Male leaves the Auntring: a Vestigial Survival of Ceremony."

She had wanted him to put a radio in his soulbag and get in touch with her at least occasionally. He had been unwilling. "I want to do it right, Mother. There's no use doing it if I don't do it right."

"I simply can't handle not hearing from you at all, Borny," she had said in Hainish.

"But if the radio got broken or taken or something, you'd worry a lot more, maybe with no reason at all."

She finally agreed to wait half a year, till the first rain; then she would go to a landmark, a huge ruin near the river that marked the southern end of the Territory, and he would try and come to her there. "But only wait ten days," he said. "If I can't come, I can't." She agreed. She was like a mother with a little baby, I thought, saying yes to everything. That seemed wrong to me; but I thought Borny was right. Nobody ever came back to their mother from boygroup.

But Borny did.

Summer was long, clear, beautiful. I was learning to star-watch; that is when you lie down outside on the open hills in the dry season at night, and find a certain star in the eastern sky, and watch it cross the sky till it sets. You can look away, of course, to rest your eyes, and doze, but you try to keep looking back at the star and the stars around it, until you feel the earth turning, until you become aware of how the stars and the world and the soul move together. After the certain star sets you sleep until dawn wakes you. Then as always you greet the sunrise with aware silence. I was very happy on the hills those warm great nights, those clear dawns. The first time or two Hyuru and I starwatched together, but after that we went alone, and it was better alone.

I was coming back from such a night, along the narrow valley between Rocky Top and Over Home Hill in the first sunlight, when a man came crashing through the bush down onto the path and stood in front of me. "Don't be afraid," he said. "Listen!" He was heavyset, half-naked; he stank. I stood still as a stick. He had said "Listen!" just as the aunts did, and I listened. "Your brother and his friend are all right. Your mother shouldn't go there. Some of the boys are in a gang. They'd rape her. I and some others are killing the leaders. It takes a while. Your brother is with the other gang. He's all right. Tell her. Tell me what I said."

I repeated it word for word, as I had learned to do when I listened.

"Right. Good," he said, and took off up the steep slope on his short, powerful legs, and was gone.

Mother would have gone to the Territory right then, but I told the man's message to Noyit, too, and she came to the porch of our house to speak to Mother. I listened to her, because she was telling things I didn't know well and Mother didn't know at all. Noyit was a small, mild woman, very like her son Ednede; she liked teaching and singing, so the children were always around her place. She saw Mother was getting ready for a journey. She said, "House on the Skyline Man says the boys are all right." When she saw Mother wasn't listening, she went on; she pretended to be talking to me, because women don't teach women: "He says some of the men are breaking up the gang. They do that, when the boygroups get wicked. Sometimes there are magicians among them, leaders, older boys, even men who want to make a gang. The settled men will kill the magicians and make sure none of the boys gets hurt. When gangs come out of the Territories, nobody is safe. The settled men don't like that. They see to it that the auntring is safe. So your brother will be all right."

My mother went on packing pigi-roots into her net.

"A rape is a very, very bad thing for the settled men," said Noyit to me. "It means the women won't come to them. If the boys raped some woman, probably the men would kill *all* the boys."

My mother was finally listening.

She did not go to the rendezvous with Borny, but all through the rainy season she was utterly miserable. She got sick, and old Dnemi sent Didsu over to dose her with gagberry syrup. She made notes while she was sick, lying on her mattress, about illnesses and medicines and how the older girls had to look after sick women, since grown women did not enter one another's houses. She never stopped working and never stopped worrying about Borny.

Late in the rainy season, when the warm wind had come and the yellow honey-flowers were in bloom on all the hills, the Golden World time, Noyit came by while Mother was working in the garden. "House on the Skyline Man says things are all right in the boygroup," she said, and went on.

Mother began to realise then that although no adult ever entered another's house, and adults seldom spoke to one another, and men and women had only brief, often casual relationships, and men lived all their lives in real solitude, still there was a kind of community, a wide, thin, fine network of delicate and certain intention and restraint: a social order. Her reports to the ship were filled with this new understanding. But she still found Sorovian life impoverished, seeing these persons as mere survivors, poor fragments of the wreck of something great.

"My dear," she said, in Hainish; there is no way to say "my dear" in my language. She was speaking Hainish with me in the house so that I wouldn't forget it entirely. "My dear, the explanation of an uncomprehended technology as magic *is* primitivism. It's not a criticism, merely a description."

"But technology isn't magic," I said.

"Yes, it is, in their minds; look at the story you just recorded.

Before-Time sorcerers who could fly in the air and undersea and underground in magic boxes!"

"In *metal* boxes," I corrected.

"In other words, airplanes, tunnels, submarines; a lost technology explained as supernatural."

"The *boxes* weren't magic," I said. "The *people* were. They were sorcerers. They used their power to get power over other persons. To live rightly a person has to keep away from magic."

"That's a cultural imperative, because a few thousand years ago uncontrolled technological expansion led to disaster. Exactly. There's a perfectly rational reason for the irrational taboo."

I did not know what "rational" and "irrational" meant in my language; I could not find words for them. "Taboo" was the same as "poisonous." I listened to my mother because a daughter must learn from her mother, and my mother knew many, many things no other person knew; but my education was very difficult, sometimes. If only there were more stories and songs in her teaching, and not so many words, words that slipped away from me like water through a net!

The Golden Time passed, and the beautiful summer; the Silver Time returned, when the mists lie in the valleys between the hills, before the rains begin; and the rains began, and fell long and slow and warm, day after day after day. We had heard nothing of Borny and Ednede for over a year. Then in the night the soft thrum of rain on the reed roof turned into a scratching at the door and a whisper, "Shh—it's all right—it's all right."

We wakened the fire and crouched at it in the dark to talk. Borny had got tall and very thin, like a skeleton with the skin dried on it. A cut across his upper lip had drawn it up into a kind of snarl that bared his teeth, and he could not say *p*, *b*, or *m*. His voice was a man's voice. He huddled at the fire trying to get warmth into his bones. His clothes were wet rags. The knife hung on a cord around his neck. "It was all right," he kept saying. "I don't want to go on there, though."

He would not tell us much about the year and a half in the boygroup, insisting that he would record a full description when he got to the ship. He did tell us what he would have to

do if he stayed on Soro. He would have to go back to the
Territory and hold his own among the older boys, by fear and
sorcery, always proving his strength, until he was old enough
to walk away—that is, to leave the Territory and wander alone
till he found a place where the men would let him settle.
Ednede and another boy had paired, and were going to walk
away together when the rains stopped. It was easier for a pair,
he said, if their bond was sexual; so long as they offered no
competition for women, settled men wouldn't challenge them.
But a new man in the region anywhere within three days' walk
of an auntring had to prove himself against the settled men
there. "It would 'e three or four years of the sa'e thing," he
said, "challenging, fighting, always watching the others, on
guard, showing how strong you are, staying alert all night, all
day. To go on living alone your whole life. I can't do it." He
looked at me. "I'ne not a 'erson," he said. "I want to go ho'e."

"I'll radio the ship now," Mother said quietly, with infinite
relief.

"No," I said.

Borny was watching Mother, and raised his hand when she
turned to speak to me.

"I'll go," he said. "She doesn't have to. Why should she?"
Like me, he had learned not to use names without some reason to.

Mother looked from him to me and finally gave a kind of
laugh. "I can't leave her here, Borny!"

"Why should you go?"

"Because I want to," she said. "I've had enough. More than
enough. We've got a tremendous amount of material on the
women, over seven years of it, and now you can fill the information gaps on the men's side. That's enough. It's time, past
time, that we all got back to our own people. All of us."

"I have no people," I said. "I don't belong to people. I am
trying to be a person. Why do you want to take me away from
my soul? You want me to do magic! I won't. I won't do magic.
I won't speak your language. I won't go with you!"

My mother was still not listening; she started to answer angrily. Borny put up his hand again, the way a woman does
when she is going to sing, and she looked at him.

"We can talk later," he said. "We can decide. I need to slee'."

He hid in our house for two days while we decided what to do and how to do it. That was a miserable time. I stayed home as if I were sick so that I would not lie to the other persons, and Borny and Mother and I talked and talked. Borny asked Mother to stay with me; I asked her to leave me with Sadne or Noyit, either of whom would certainly take me into their household. She refused. She was the mother and I the child and her power was sacred. She radioed the ship and arranged for a lander to pick us up in a barren area two days' walk from the auntring. We left at night, sneaking away. I carried nothing but my soulbag. We walked all next day, slept a little when it stopped raining, walked on and came to the desert. The ground was all lumps and hollows and caves, Before-Time ruins; the soil was tiny bits of glass and hard grains and fragments, the way it is in the deserts. Nothing grew there. We waited there.

The sky broke open and a shining thing fell down and stood before us on the rocks, bigger than any house, though not as big as the ruins of the Before Time. My mother looked at me with a queer, vengeful smile. "Is it magic?" she said. And it was very hard for me not to think that it was. Yet I knew it was only a thing, and there is no magic in things, only in minds. I said nothing. I had not spoken since we left my home.

I had resolved never to speak to anybody until I got home again; but I was still a child, used to listening and obeying. In the ship, that utterly strange new world, I held out only for a few hours, and then began to cry and ask to go home. Please, please, can I go home now.

Everyone on the ship was very kind to me.

Even then I thought about what Borny had been through and what I was going through, comparing our ordeals. The difference seemed total. He had been alone, without food, without shelter, a frightened boy trying to survive among equally frightened rivals against the brutality of older youths intent on having and keeping power, which they saw as manhood. I was cared for, clothed, fed so richly I got sick, kept so warm I felt feverish, guided, reasoned with, praised, befriended by citizens of a very great city, offered a share in their power, which they saw as humanity. He and I had both fallen among sorcerers. Both he and I could see the good in the people we were among, but neither he nor I could live with them.

Borny told me he had spent many desolate nights in the Territory crouched in a fireless shelter, telling over the stories he had learned from the aunts, singing the songs in his head. I did the same thing every night on the ship. But I refused to tell the stories or sing to the people there. I would not speak my language, there. It was the only way I had to be silent.

My mother was enraged, and for a long time unforgiving. "You owe your knowledge to our people," she said. I did not answer, because all I had to say was that they were not my people, that I had no people. I was a person. I had a language that I did not speak. I had my silence. I had nothing else.

I went to school; there were children of different ages on the ship, like an auntring, and many of the adults taught us. I learned Ekumenical history and geography, mostly, and Mother gave me a report to learn about the history of Eleven-Soro, what my language calls the Before Time. I read that the cities of my world had been the greatest cities ever built on any world, covering two of the continents entirely, with small areas set aside for farming; there had been 120 billion people living in the cities, while the animals and the sea and the air and the dirt died, until the people began dying too. It was a hideous story. I was ashamed of it and wished nobody else on the ship or in the Ekumen knew about it. And yet, I thought, if they knew the stories I knew about the Before Time, they would understand how magic turns on itself, and that it must be so.

After less than a year, Mother told us we were going to Hain. The ship's doctor and his clever machines had repaired Borny's lip; he and Mother had put all the information they had into the records; he was old enough to begin training for the Ekumenical Schools, as he wanted to do. I was not flourishing, and the doctor's machines were not able to repair me. I kept losing weight, I slept badly, I had terrible headaches. Almost as soon as we came aboard the ship, I had begun to menstruate; each time the cramps were agonizing. "This is no good, this ship life," Mother said. "You need to be outdoors. On a planet. On a civilised planet."

"If I went to Hain," I said, "when I came back, the persons I know would all be dead hundreds of years ago."

"Serenity," she said, "you must stop thinking in terms of Soro. We have left Soro. You must stop deluding and tormenting yourself, and look forward, not back. Your whole life is ahead of you. Hain is where you will learn to live it."

I summoned up my courage and spoke in my own language: "I am not a child now. You have no power over me. I will not go. Go without me. You have no power over me!"

Those are the words I had been taught to say to a magician, a sorcerer. I don't know if my mother fully understood them, but she did understand that I was deathly afraid of her, and it struck her into silence.

After a long time she said in Hainish, "I agree. I have no power over you. But I have certain rights; the right of loyalty; of love."

"Nothing is right that puts me in your power," I said, still in my language.

She stared at me. "You are like one of them," she said. "You are one of them. You don't know what love is. You're closed into yourself like a rock. I should never have taken you there. People crouching in the ruins of a society—brutal, rigid, ignorant, superstitious—each one in a terrible solitude—and I let them make you into one of them!"

"You educated me," I said, and my voice began to tremble and my mouth to shake around the words, "and so does the school here, but my aunts educated me, and I want to finish my education." I was weeping, but I kept standing with my hands clenched. "I'm not a woman yet. I want to be a woman."

"But Ren, you will be!—ten times the woman you could ever be on Soro—you must try to understand, to believe me—"

"You have no power over me," I said, shutting my eyes and putting my hands over my ears. She came to me then and held me, but I stood stiff, enduring her touch, until she let me go.

The ship's crew had changed entirely while we were on-planet. The First Observers had gone on to other worlds; our backup was now a Gethenian archeologist named Arrem, a mild, watchful person, not young. Arrem had gone down on-planet only on the two desert continents, and welcomed the chance to talk with us, who had "lived with the living," as heshe said. I felt easy when I was with Arrem, who was so unlike anybody else. Arrem was not a man—I could not get used to having men around all the time—yet not a woman; and so not exactly an adult, yet not a child: a person, alone, like me. Heshe did not know my language well, but always tried to talk it with me. When this crisis came, Arrem came to my mother and took counsel with her, suggesting that she let me go back down on-planet. Borny was in on some of these talks, and told me about them.

"Arrem says if you go to Hain you'll probably die," he said. "Your soul will. Heshe says some of what we learned is like what they learn on Gethen, in their religion. That kind of stopped Mother from ranting about primitive superstition. . . . And Arrem says you could be useful to the Ekumen, if you stay and finish your education on Soro. You'll be an invaluable resource." Borny sniggered, and after a minute I did too. "They'll mine you like an asteroid," he said. Then he said, "You know, if you stay and I go, we'll be dead."

That was how the young people of the ships said it, when one was going to cross the lightyears and the other was going to stay. Goodbye, we're dead. It was the truth.

"I know," I said. I felt my throat get tight, and was afraid. I had never seen an adult at home cry, except when Sut's baby died. Sut howled all night. Howled like a dog, Mother said, but I had never seen or heard a dog; I heard a woman terribly crying. I was afraid of sounding like that. "If I can go home, when I finish making my soul, who knows, I might come to Hain for a while," I said, in Hainish.

"Scouting?" Borny said in my language, and laughed, and made me laugh again.

Nobody gets to keep a brother. I knew that. But Borny had come back from being dead to me, so I might come back from being dead to him; at least I could pretend I might.

My mother came to a decision. She and I would stay on the ship for another year while Borny went to Hain. I would keep going to school; if at the end of the year I was still determined to go back on-planet, I could do so. With me or without me, she would go on to Hain then and join Borny. If I ever wanted to see them again, I could follow them. It was a compromise that satisfied no one, but it was the best we could do, and we all consented.

When he left, Borny gave me his knife.

After he left, I tried not to be sick. I worked hard at learning everything they taught me in the ship school, and I tried to teach Arrem how to be aware and how to avoid witchcraft. We did slow walking together in the ship's garden, and the first hour of the Untrance movements from the Handdara of Karhide on Gethen. We agreed that they were alike.

The ship was staying in the Soro system not only because of my family, but because the crew was now mostly zoologists who had come to study a sea animal on Eleven-Soro, a kind of cephalopod that had mutated towards high intelligence, or maybe it already was highly intelligent; but there was a communication problem. "Almost as bad as with the local humans," said Steadiness, the zoologist who taught and teased us mercilessly. She took us down twice by lander to the uninhabited islands in the Northern Hemisphere where her station was. It was very strange to go down to my world and yet be a world away from my aunts and sisters and my soulmate; but I said nothing.

I saw the great, pale, shy creature come slowly up out of the deep waters with a running ripple of colors along its long coiling tentacles and a ringing shimmer of sound, all so quick it was over before you could follow the colors or hear the tune. The zoologist's machine produced a pink glow and a mechanically speeded-up twitter, tinny and feeble in the immensity of the sea. The cephalopod patiently responded in its beautiful silvery shadowy language. "CP," Steadiness said to us, ironic—Communication Problem. "We don't know what we're talking about."

I said, "I learned something in my education here. In one of the songs, it says," and I hesitated, trying to translate it into Hainish, "it says, thinking is one way of doing, and words are one way of thinking."

Steadiness stared at me, in disapproval I thought, but probably only because I had never said anything to her before except "Yes." Finally she said, "Are you suggesting that it doesn't speak in words?"

"Maybe it's not speaking at all. Maybe it's thinking."

Steadiness stared at me some more and then said, "Thank you." She looked as if she too might be thinking. I wished I could sink into the water, the way the cephalopod was doing.

The other young people on the ship were friendly and mannerly. Those are words that have no translation in my language. I was unfriendly and unmannerly, and they let me be. I was grateful. But there was no place to be alone on the ship. Of course we each had a room; though small, the *Heyho* was a Hainish-built explorer, designed to give its people room and privacy and comfort and variety and beauty while they hung around in a solar system for years on end. But it was designed. It was all human-made—everything was human. I had much more privacy than I had ever had at home in our one-room house; yet there I had been free and here I was in a trap. I felt the pressure of people all around me, all the time. People around me, people with me, people pressing on me, pressing me to be one of them, to be one of them, one of the people. How could I make my soul? I could barely cling to it. I was in terror that I would lose it altogether.

One of the rocks in my soulbag, a little ugly grey rock that I had picked up on a certain day in a certain place in the hills above the river in the Silver Time, a little piece of my world, that became my world. Every night I took it out and held it in my hand while I lay in bed waiting to sleep, thinking of the sunlight on the hills above the river, listening to the soft hushing of the ship's systems, like a mechanical sea.

The doctor hopefully fed me various tonics. Mother and I ate breakfast together every morning. She kept at work, making our notes from all the years on Eleven-Soro into her report to the Ekumen, but I knew the work did not go well. Her soul was in as much danger as mine was.

"You will never give in, will you, Ren?" she said to me one morning out of the silence of our breakfast. I had not intended the silence as a message. I had only rested in it.

"Mother, I want to go home and you want to go home," I said. "Can't we?"

Her expression was strange for a moment, while she misunderstood me; then it cleared to grief, defeat, relief.

"Will we be dead?" she asked me, her mouth twisting.

"I don't know. I have to make my soul. Then I can know if I can come."

"You know I can't come back. It's up to you."

"I know. Go see Borny," I said. "Go home. Here we're both dying." Then noises began to come out of me, sobbing, howling. Mother was crying. She came to me and held me, and I could hold my mother, cling to her and cry with her, because her spell was broken.

From the lander approaching I saw the oceans of Eleven-Soro, and in the greatness of my joy I thought that when I was grown and went out alone I would go to the sea shore and watch the sea-beasts shimmering their colors and tunes till I knew what they were thinking. I would listen, I would learn, till my soul was as large as the shining world. The scarred barrens whirled beneath us, ruins as wide as the continent, endless desolations. We touched down. I had my soulbag, and Borny's knife around my neck on its string, a communicator implant behind my right earlobe, and a medicine kit Mother had made for me. "No use dying of an infected finger, after all," she had said. The people on the lander said goodbye, but I forgot to. I set off out of the desert, home.

It was summer; the night was short and warm; I walked most of it. I got to the auntring about the middle of the second day. I went to my house cautiously, in case somebody had moved in while I was gone; but it was just as we had left it. The mattresses were moldy, and I put them and the bedding out in the sun, and started going over the garden to see what had kept growing by itself. The pigi had got small and seedy, but there were some good roots. A little boy came by and stared; he had to be Migi's baby. After a while Hyuru came by. She squatted down near me in the garden in the sunshine. I smiled when I saw her, and she smiled, but it took us a while to find something to say.

"Your mother didn't come back," she said.

"She's dead," I said.

"I'm sorry," Hyuru said.

She watched me dig up another root.

"Will you come to the singing circle?" she asked.

I nodded.

She smiled again. With her rose-brown skin and wide-set eyes, Hyuru had become very beautiful, but her smile was exactly the same as when we were little girls. "Hi, ya!" she sighed in deep contentment, lying down on the dirt with her chin on her arms. "This is good!"

I went on blissfully digging.

That year and the next two, I was in the singing circle with Hyuru and two other girls. Didsu still came to it often, and Han, a woman who settled in our auntring to have her first baby, joined it too. In the singing circle the older girls pass around the stories, songs, knowledge they learned from their own mother, and young women who have lived in other auntrings teach what they learned there; so women make each other's souls, learning how to make their children's souls.

Han lived in the house where old Dnemi had died. Nobody in the auntring except Sut's baby had died while my family lived there. My mother had complained that she didn't have any data on death and burial. Sut had gone away with her dead baby and never came back, and nobody talked about it. I think that turned my mother against the others more than anything else. She was angry and ashamed that she could not go and try to comfort Sut and that nobody else did. "It is not human," she said. "It is pure animal behavior. Nothing could be clearer evidence that this is a broken culture—not a society, but the remains of one. A terrible, an appalling poverty."

I don't know if Dnemi's death would have changed her mind. Dnemi was dying for a long time, of kidney failure I think; she turned a kind of dark orange color, jaundice. While she could get around, nobody helped her. When she didn't come out of her house for a day or two, the women would send the children in with water and a little food and firewood. It went on so through the winter; then one morning little Rashi told his mother Aunt Dnemi was "staring." Several of the women went to Dnemi's house, and entered it for the first and last time. They sent for all the girls in the singing circle, so that we could learn what to do. We took turns sitting by the body or in the porch of the house, singing soft songs, child-songs, giving the soul a day and a night to leave the body and the house; then the older women wrapped the body in the bedding, strapped it on a kind of litter, and set off with it towards the barren lands. There it would be given back, under a rock cairn or inside one of the ruins of the ancient city. "Those are the lands of the dead," Sadne said. "What dies stays there."

Han settled down in that house a year later. When her baby began to be born she asked Didsu to help her, and Hyuru and I stayed in the porch and watched, so that we could learn. It was a wonderful thing to see, and quite altered the course of my thinking, and Hyuru's too. Hyuru said, "I'd like to do that!" I said nothing, but thought, So do I, but not for a long time, because once you have a child you're never alone.

And though it is of the others, of relationships, that I write, the heart of my life has been my being alone.

I think there is no way to write about being alone. To write is to tell something to somebody, to communicate to others. CP, as Steadiness would say. Solitude is noncommunication, the absence of others, the presence of a self sufficient to itself.

A woman's solitude in the auntring is, of course, based firmly on the presence of others at a little distance. It is a contingent, and therefore human, solitude. The settled men are connected as stringently to the women, though not to one another; the settlement is an integral though distant element of the aunt-ring. Even a scouting woman is part of the society—a moving part, connecting the settled parts. Only the isolation of a woman or man who chooses to live outside the settlements is absolute. They are outside the network altogether. There are worlds where such persons are called saints, holy people. Since isolation is a sure way to prevent magic, on my world the assumption is that they are sorcerers, outcast by others or by their own will, their conscience.

I knew I was strong with magic, how could I help it? and I began to long to get away. It would be so much easier and safer to be alone. But at the same time, and increasingly, I wanted to know something about the great harmless magic, the spells cast between men and women.

I preferred foraging to gardening, and was out on the hills a good deal; and these days, instead of keeping away from the man's-houses, I wandered by them, and looked at them, and looked at the men if they were outside. The men looked back. Downriver Lame Man's long, shining hair was getting a little white in it now, but when he sat singing his long, long songs I found myself sitting down and listening, as if my legs had lost their bones. He was very handsome. So was the man I remembered as a boy named Tret in the auntring, when I was little, Behyu's son. He had come back from the boygroup and from wandering, and had built a house and made a fine garden in the valley of Red Stone Creek. He had a big nose and big eyes, long arms and legs, long hands; he moved very quietly, almost like Arrem doing the Untrance. I went often to pick lowberries in Red Stone Creek valley.

He came along the path and spoke. "You were Borny's sister," he said. He had a low voice, quiet.

"He's dead," I said.

Red Stone Man nodded. "That's his knife."

In my world, I had never talked with a man. I felt extremely strange. I kept picking berries.

"You're picking green ones," Red Stone Man said.

His soft, smiling voice made my legs lose their bones again.

"I think nobody's touched you," he said. "I'd touch you gently. I think about it, about you, ever since you came by here early in the summer. Look, here's a bush full of ripe ones. Those are green. Come over here."

I came closer to him, to the bush of ripe berries.

When I was on the ship, Arrem told me that many languages have a single word for sexual desire and the bond between mother and child and the bond between soulmates and the feeling for one's home and worship of the sacred; they are all called love. There is no word that great in my language. Maybe my mother is right, and human greatness perished in my world with the people of the Before Time, leaving only small, poor, broken things and thoughts. In my language, love is many different words. I learned one of them with Red Stone Man. We sang it together to each other.

We made a brush house on a little cove of the creek, and neglected our gardens, but gathered many, many sweet berries.

Mother had put a lifetime's worth of nonconceptives in the little medicine kit. She had no faith in Sorovian herbals. I did, and they worked.

But when a year or so later, in the Golden Time, I decided to go out scouting, I thought I might go places where the right herbs were scarce; and so I stuck the little noncon jewel on the back of my left earlobe. Then I wished I hadn't, because it seemed like witchcraft. Then I told myself I was being superstitious; the noncon wasn't any more witchcraft than the herbs were, it just worked longer. I had promised my mother in my soul that I would never be superstitious. The skin grew over the noncon, and I took my soulbag and Borny's knife and the medicine kit, and set off across the world.

I had told Hyuru and Red Stone Man I would be leaving. Hyuru and I sang and talked together all one night down by the river. Red Stone Man said in his soft voice, "Why do you want to go?" and I said, "To get away from your magic, sorcerer," which was true in part. If I kept going to him I might always go to him. I wanted to give my soul and body a larger world to be in.

Now to tell of my scouting years is more difficult than ever. CP! A woman scouting is entirely alone, unless she chooses to ask a settled man for sex, or camps in an auntring for a while to sing and listen with the singing circle. If she goes anywhere near the territory of a boygroup, she is in danger; and if she comes on a rogue she is in danger; and if she hurts herself or gets into polluted country, she is in danger. She has no responsibility except to herself, and so much freedom is very dangerous.

In my right earlobe was the tiny communicator; every forty days, as I had promised, I sent a signal to the ship that meant "all well." If I wanted to leave, I would send another signal. I could have called for the lander to rescue me from a bad situation, but though I was in bad situations a couple of times I never thought of using it. My signal was the mere fulfilment of a promise to my mother and her people, the network I was no longer part of, a meaningless communication.

Life in the auntring, or for a settled man, is repetitive, as I said; and so it can be dull. Nothing new happens. The mind always wants new happenings. So for the young soul there is wandering and scouting, travel, danger, change. But of course travel and danger and change have their own dullness. It is finally always the same otherness over again; another hill, another river, another man, another day. The feet begin to turn in a long, long circle. The body begins to think of what it learned back home, when it learned to be still. To be aware. To be aware of the grain of dust beneath the sole of the foot, and the skin of the sole of the foot, and the touch and scent of the air on the cheek, and the fall and motion of the light across the air, and the color of the grass on the high hill across the river, and the thoughts of the body, of the soul, the shimmer and ripple of colors and sounds in the clear darkness of the depths, endlessly moving, endlessly changing, endlessly new.

So at last I came back home. I had been gone about four years.

Hyuru had moved into my old house when she left her mother's house. She had not gone scouting, but had taken to going to Red Stone Creek valley; and she was pregnant. I was glad to see her living there. The only house empty was an old half-ruined one too close to Hedimi's. I decided to make a new house. I dug out the circle as deep as my chest; the digging took most of the summer. I cut the sticks, braced and wove them, and then daubed the framework solidly with mud inside and out. I remembered when I had done that with my mother long, long ago, and how she had said, "That's right. That's good." I left the roof open, and the hot sun of late summer baked the mud into clay. Before the rains came, I thatched the house with reeds, a triple thatching, for I'd had enough of being wet all winter.

My auntring was more a string than a ring, stretching along the north bank of the river for about three kilos; my house lengthened the string a good bit, upstream from all the others. I could just see the smoke from Hyuru's fireplace. I dug the house into a sunny slope with good drainage. It is still a good house.

I settled down. Some of my time went to gathering and gardening and mending and all the dull, repetitive actions of primitive life, and some went to singing and thinking the songs and stories I had learned here at home and while scouting, and the things I had learned on the ship, also. Soon enough I found why women are glad to have children come to listen to them, for songs and stories are meant to be heard, listened to. "Listen!" I would say to the children. The children of the auntring came and went, like the little fish in the river, one or two or five of them, little ones, big ones. When they came, I sang or told stories to them. When they left, I went on in silence. Sometimes I joined the singing circle to give what I had learned travelling to the older girls. And that was all I did; except that I worked, always, to be aware of all I did.

By solitude the soul escapes from doing or suffering magic; it escapes from dullness, from boredom, by being aware. Nothing is boring if you are aware of it. It may be irritating, but it is not boring. If it is pleasant the pleasure will not fail so long as you are aware of it. Being aware is the hardest work the soul can do, I think.

I helped Hyuru have her baby, a girl, and played with the baby. Then after a couple of years I took the noncon out of my left earlobe. Since it left a little hole, I made the hole go all the way through with a burnt needle, and when it healed I hung in it a tiny jewel I had found in a ruin when I was scouting. I had seen a man on the ship with a jewel hung in his ear that way. I wore it when I went out foraging. I kept clear of Red Stone Valley. The man there behaved as if he had a claim on me, a right to me. I liked him still, but I did not like that smell of magic about him, his imagination of power over me. I went up into the hills, northward.

A pair of young men had settled in old North House about the time I came home. Often boys got through boygroup by pairing, and often they stayed paired when they left the Territory. It helped their chances of survival. Some of them were sexually paired, others weren't; some stayed paired, others didn't. One of this pair had gone off with another man last summer. The one that stayed wasn't a handsome man, but I had noticed him. He had a kind of solidness I liked. His body and hands were short and strong. I had courted him a little, but he was very shy. This day, a day in the Silver Time when the mist lay on the river, he saw the jewel swinging in my ear, and his eyes widened.

"It's pretty, isn't it?" I said.

He nodded.

"I wore it to make you look at me," I said.

He was so shy that I finally said, "If you only like sex with men, you know, just tell me." I really was not sure.

"Oh, no," he said, "no. No." He stammered and then bolted back down the path. But he looked back; and I followed him slowly, still not certain whether he wanted me or wanted to be rid of me.

He waited for me in front of a little house in a grove of redroot, a lovely little bower, all leaves outside, so that you would walk within arm's length of it and not see it. Inside he had laid sweet grass, deep and dry and soft, smelling of summer. I went in, crawling because the door was very low, and sat in the summer-smelling grass. He stood outside. "Come in," I said, and he came in very slowly.

"I made it for you," he said.

"Now make a child for me," I said.

And we did that; maybe that day, maybe another.

Now I will tell you why after all these years I called the ship, not knowing even if it was still there in the space between the planets, asking for the lander to meet me in the barren land.

When my daughter was born, that was my heart's desire and the fulfilment of my soul. When my son was born, last year, I knew there is no fulfilment. He will grow towards manhood, and go, and fight and endure, and live or die as a man must. My daughter, whose name is Yedneke, Leaf, like my mother, will grow to womanhood and go or stay as she chooses. I will live alone. This is as it should be, and my desire. But I am of two worlds; I am a person of this world, and a woman of my mother's people. I owe my knowledge to the children of her people. So I asked the lander to come, and spoke to the people on it. They gave me my mother's report to read, and I have written my story in their machine, making a record for those who want to learn one of the ways to make a soul. To them, to the children I say: Listen! Avoid magic! Be aware!

FIVE WAYS TO FORGIVENESS

CONTENTS

Betrayals

"ON THE planet O there has not been a war for five thousand years," she read, "and on Gethen there has never been a war." She stopped reading, to rest her eyes and because she was trying to train herself to read slowly, not gobble words down in chunks the way Tikuli gulped his food. "There has never been a war": in her mind the words stood clear and bright, surrounded by and sinking into an infinite, dark, soft incredulity. What would that world be, a world without war? It would be the real world. Peace was the true life, the life of working and learning and bringing up children to work and learn. War, which devoured work, learning, and children, was the denial of reality. But my people, she thought, know only how to deny. Born in the dark shadow of power misused, we set peace outside our world, a guiding and unattainable light. All we know to do is fight. Any peace one of us can make in our life is only a denial that the war is going on, a shadow of the shadow, a doubled unbelief.

So as the cloud-shadows swept over the marshes and the page of the book open on her lap, she sighed and closed her eyes, thinking, "I am a liar." Then she opened her eyes and read more about the other worlds, the far realities.

Tikuli, sleeping curled up around his tail in the weak sunshine, sighed as if imitating her, and scratched a dreamflea. Gubu was out in the reeds, hunting; she could not see him, but now and then the plume of a reed quivered, and once a marsh hen flew up cackling in indignation.

Absorbed in a description of the peculiar social customs of the Ithsh, she did not see Wada till he was at the gate letting himself in. "Oh, you're here already," she said, taken by surprise and feeling unready, incompetent, old, as she always felt with other people. Alone, she only felt old when she was overtired or ill. Maybe living alone was the right thing for her after all. "Come on in," she said, getting up and dropping her book and picking it up and feeling her back hair where the knot was coming loose. "I'll just get my bag and be off, then."

"No hurry," the young man said in his soft voice. "Eyid won't be here for a while yet."

Very kind of you to tell me I don't have to hurry to leave my own house, Yoss thought, but said nothing, obedient to the insufferable, adorable selfishness of the young. She went in and got her shopping bag, reknotted her hair, tied a scarf over it, and came out onto the little open porch. Wada had sat down in her chair; he jumped up when she came out. He was a shy boy, the gentler, she thought, of the two lovers. "Have fun," she said with a smile, knowing she embarrassed him. "I'll be back in a couple of hours—before sunset." She went down to her gate, let herself out, and set off the way Wada had come, along the path up to the winding wooden causeway across the marshes to the village.

She would not meet Eyid on the way. The girl would be coming from the north on one of the bog-paths, having left the village at a different time and in a different direction than Wada, so that nobody would notice that for a few hours every week or so the two young people were gone at the same time. They were madly in love, had been in love for three years, and would have lived in partnership long since if Wada's father and Eyid's father's brother hadn't quarreled over a piece of reallocated Corporation land and set up a feud between the families that had so far stopped short of bloodshed, but put a love match out of the question. The land was valuable; the families, though poor, each aspired to be leaders of the village. Nothing would heal the grudge. The whole village took sides in it. Eyid and Wada had nowhere to go, no skills to keep them alive in the cities, no tribal relations in another village who might take them in. Their passion was trapped in the hatred of the old. Yoss had come on them, a year ago now, in each other's arms on the cold ground of an island in the marshes—blundering onto them as once she had blundered onto a pair of fendeer fawns holding utterly still in the nest of grass where the doe had left them. This pair had been as frightened, as beautiful and vulnerable as the fawns, and they had begged her "not to tell" so humbly, what could she do? They were shivering with cold, Eyid's bare legs were muddy, they clung to each other like children. "Come to my house," she said sternly. "For mercy sake!" She stalked off. Timidly, they followed her. "I will be back in an hour or so," she said when she had got them indoors, into her one room with the bed alcove right beside the chimney. "Don't get things muddy!"

That time she had roamed the paths keeping watch, in case anybody was out looking for them. Nowadays she mostly went into the village while "the fawns" were in her house having their sweet hour.

They were too ignorant to think of any way to thank her. Wada, a peat-cutter, might have supplied her fire without anyone being suspicious, but they never left so much as a flower, though they always made up the bed very neat and tight. Perhaps indeed they were not very grateful. Why should they be? She gave them only what was their due: a bed, an hour of pleasure, a moment of peace. It wasn't their fault, or her virtue, that nobody else would give it to them.

Her errand today took her in to Eyid's uncle's shop. He was the village sweets-seller. All the holy abstinence she had intended when she came here two years ago, the single bowl of unflavored grain, the draft of pure water, she'd given that up in no time. She got diarrhea from a cereal diet, and the water of the marshes was undrinkable. She ate every fresh vegetable she could buy or grow, drank wine or bottled water or fruit juice from the city, and kept a large supply of sweets—dried fruits, raisins, sugar-brittle, even the cakes Eyid's mother and aunts made, fat disks with a nutmeat squashed onto the top, dry, greasy, tasteless, but curiously satisfying. She bought a bagful of them and a brown wheel of sugar-brittle, and gossiped with the aunts, dark, darting-eyed little women who had been at old Uad's wake last night and wanted to talk about it. "Those people"—Wada's family, indicated by a glance, a shrug, a sneer —had misbehaved as usual, got drunk, picked fights, boasted, got sick, and vomited all over the place, greedy upstart louts that they were. When she stopped by the newsstand to pick up a paper (another vow long since broken; she had been going to read only the *Arkamye* and learn it by heart), Wada's mother was there, and she heard how "those people"—Eyid's family— had boasted and picked fights and vomited all over the place at the wake last night. She did not merely hear; she asked for details, she drew the gossip out; she loved it.

What a fool, she thought, starting slowly home on the

causeway path, what a fool I was to think I could ever drink water and be silent! I'll never, never be able to let anything go, anything at all. I'll never be free, never be worthy of freedom. Even old age can't make me let go. Even losing Safnan can't make me let go.

Before the Five Armies they stood. Holding up his sword, Enar said to Kamye: My hands hold your death, my Lord! Kamye answered: Brother, it is your death they hold.

She knew those lines, anyway. Everybody knew those lines. And so then Enar dropped his sword, because he was a hero and a holy man, the Lord's younger brother. But I can't drop my death. I'll hold it to the end, I'll cherish it, hate it, eat it, drink it, listen to it, give it my bed, mourn it, everything but let it go.

She looked up out of her thoughts into the afternoon on the marshes: the sky a cloudless misty blue, reflected in one distant curving channel of water, and the sunlight golden over the dun levels of the reedbeds and among the stems of the reeds. The rare, soft west wind blew. A perfect day. The beauty of the world, the beauty of the world! A sword in my hand, turned against me. Why do you make beauty to kill us, my Lord?

She trudged on, pulling her headscarf tighter with a little dissatisfied jerk. At this rate she would soon be wandering around the marshes shouting aloud, like Abberkam.

And there he was, the thought had summoned him: lurching along in the blind way he had as if he never saw anything but his thoughts, striking at the roadway with his big stick as if he was killing a snake. Long grey hair blowing around his face. He wasn't shouting, he only shouted at night, and not for a long time now, but he was talking, she saw his lips move; then he saw her, and shut his mouth, and drew himself into himself, wary as a wild animal. They approached each other on the narrow causeway path, not another human being in all the wilderness of reeds and mud and water and wind.

"Good evening, Chief Abberkam," Yoss said when there were only a few paces between them. What a big man he was; she never could believe how tall and broad and heavy he was till she saw him again, his dark skin still smooth as a young man's, but his head stooped and his hair grey and wild. A huge hook nose and the mistrustful, unseeing eyes. He muttered some kind of greeting, hardly slowing his gait.

The mischief was in Yoss today; she was sick of her own thoughts and sorrows and shortcomings. She stopped, so that he had to stop or else run right into her, and said, "Were you at the wake last night?"

He stared down at her; she felt he was getting her into focus, or part of her; he finally said, "Wake?"

"They buried old Uad last night. All the men got drunk, and it's a mercy the feud didn't finally break out."

"Feud?" he repeated in his deep voice.

Maybe he wasn't capable of focusing any more, but she was driven to talk to him, to get through to him. "The Dewis and Kamanners. They're quarreling over that arable island just north of the village. And the two poor children, they want to be partners, and their fathers threaten to kill them if they look at each other. What idiocy! Why don't they divide the island and let the children pair and let their children share it? It'll come to blood one of these days, I think."

"To blood," the Chief said, repeating again like a half-wit, and then slowly, in that great, deep voice, the voice she had heard crying out in agony in the night across the marshes, "Those men. Those shopkeepers. They have the souls of owners. They won't kill. But they won't share. If it's property, they won't let go. Never."

She saw again the lifted sword.

"Ah," she said with a shudder. "So then the children must wait . . . till the old people die . . ."

"Too late," he said. His eyes met hers for one instant, keen and strange; then he pushed back his hair impatiently, growled something by way of good-bye, and started on so abruptly that she almost crouched aside to make way for him. That's how a chief walks, she thought wryly, as she went on. Big, wide, taking up space, stamping the earth down. And this, this is how an old woman walks, narrowly, narrowly.

There was a strange noise behind her—gunshots, she thought, for city usages stay in the nerves—and she turned sharp round. Abberkam had stopped and was coughing explosively, tremendously, his big frame hunched around the spasms that nearly wracked him off his feet. Yoss knew that kind of coughing. The Ekumen was supposed to have medicine for it, but she'd left the city before any of it came. She went to Abberkam and when the paroxysm was over and he stood gasping, grey-faced, she said, "That's berlot: are you getting over it or are you getting it?"

He shook his head.

She waited.

While she waited she thought, what do I care if he's sick or not? Does he care? He came here to die. I heard him howling out on the marshes in the dark, last winter. Howling in agony. Eaten out with shame, like a man with cancer who's been all eaten out by the cancer but can't die.

"It's all right," he said, hoarse, angry, wanting her only to get away from him; and she nodded and went on her way. Let him die. How could he want to live knowing what he'd lost, his power, his honor, and what he'd done? Lied, betrayed his supporters, embezzled. The perfect politician. Big Chief Abberkam, hero of the Liberation, leader of the World Party, who had destroyed the World Party by his greed and folly.

She glanced back once. He was moving very slowly or perhaps had stopped, she was not sure. She went on, taking the right-hand way where the causeway forked, going down onto the bog-path that led to her little house.

Three hundred years ago these marshlands had been a vast, rich agricultural valley, one of the first to be irrigated and cultivated by the Agricultural Plantation Corporation when they brought their slaves from Werel to the Yeowe Colony. Too well irrigated, too well cultivated; fertilizing chemicals and salts of the soil had accumulated till nothing would grow, and the Owners went elsewhere for their profit. The banks of the irrigation canals slumped here and there and the waters of the river wandered free again, pooling and meandering, slowly washing the lands clean. The reeds grew, miles and miles of reeds bowing a little under the wind, under the cloud-shadows and the wings of long-legged birds. Here and there on an island of rockier soil a few fields and a slave-village remained, a few sharecroppers left behind, useless people on useless land. The freedom of desolation. And all through the marshes there were lonely houses.

Growing old, the people of Werel and Yeowe might turn to silence, as their religion recommended them to do: when their children were grown, when they had done their work as householder and citizen, when as their body weakened their soul might make itself strong, they left their life behind and came empty-handed to lonely places. Even on the Plantations, the Bosses had let old slaves go out into the wilderness, go free. Here in the North, freedmen from the cities had come out to the marshlands and lived as recluses in the lonely houses. Now, since the Liberation, even women came.

Some of the houses were derelict, and any soulmaker might claim them; most, like Yoss's thatched cabin, were owned by villagers who maintained them and gave them to a recluse rent-free as a religious duty, a means of enriching the soul. Yoss liked knowing that she was a source of spiritual profit to her landlord, a grasping man whose account with Providence was probably otherwise all on the debit side. She liked to feel useful. She took it for another sign of her incapacity to let the world go, as the Lord Kamye bade her do. *You are no longer useful*, he had told her in a hundred ways, over and over, since she was sixty; but she would not listen. She left the noisy world and came out to the marshes, but she let the world go on chattering and gossiping and singing and crying in her ears. She would not hear the low voice of the Lord.

Eyid and Wada were gone when she got home; the bed was made up very tight, and the foxdog Tikuli was sleeping on it, curled up around his tail. Gubu the spotted cat was prancing around asking about dinner. She picked him up and petted his silken, speckled back while he nuzzled under her ear, making his steady roo-roo-roo of pleasure and affection; then she fed him. Tikuli took no notice, which was odd. Tikuli was sleeping too much. She sat on the bed and scratched the roots of his stiff, red-furred ears. He woke and yawned and looked at her with soft amber eyes, his red plume of tail stirring. "Aren't you hungry?" she asked him. I will eat to please you, Tikuli answered, getting down off the bed rather stiffly. "Oh, Tikuli, you're getting old," Yoss said, and the sword stirred in her heart. Her daughter Safnan had given her Tikuli, a tiny red cub, a scurry of paws and plume-tail—how long ago? Eight years. A long time. A lifetime for a foxdog.

More than a lifetime for Safnan. More than a lifetime for her children, Yoss's grandchildren, Enkamma and Uye.

If I am alive, they are dead, Yoss thought, as she always

thought; if they are alive, I am dead. They went on the ship that goes like light; they are translated into the light. When they return into life, when they step off the ship on the world called Hain, it will be eighty years from the day they left, and I will be dead, long dead; I am dead. They left me and I am dead. Let them be alive, Lord, sweet Lord, let them be alive, I will be dead. I came here to be dead. For them. I cannot, I cannot let them be dead for me.

Tikuli's cold nose touched her hand. She looked intently at him. The amber of his eyes was dimmed, bluish. She stroked his head, scratched the roots of his ears, silent.

He ate a few bites to please her, and climbed back up onto the bed. She made her own dinner, soup and rewarmed soda cakes, and ate it, not tasting it. She washed the three dishes she had used, made up the fire, and sat by it trying to read her book slowly, while Tikuli slept on the bed and Gubu lay on the hearth gazing into the fire with round golden eyes, going roo-roo-roo very softly. Once he sat up and made his battlecall, "Hoooo!" at some noise he heard out in the marshes, and stalked about a bit; then he settled down again to staring and roo-ing. Later, when the fire was out and the house utterly dark in the starless darkness, he joined Yoss and Tikuli in the warm bed, where earlier the young lovers had had their brief, sharp joy.

She found she was thinking about Abberkam, the next couple of days, as she worked in her little vegetable garden, cleaning it up for the winter. When the Chief first came, the villagers had been all abuzz with excitement about his living in a house that belonged to the headman of their village. Disgraced, dishonored, he was still a very famous man. An elected Chief of the Heyend, one of the principal Tribes of Yeowe, he had come to prominence during the last years of the War of Liberation, leading a great movement for what he called Racial Freedom. Even some of the villagers had embraced the main principle of the World Party: No one was to live on Yeowe but its own people. No Werelians, the hated ancestral colonizers, the Bosses and Owners. The War had ended slavery; and in the last few years the diplomats of the Ekumen had negotiated an end to Werel's economic power over its former colony-planet. The Bosses and

Owners, even those whose families had lived on Yeowe for centuries, had all withdrawn to Werel, the Old World, next outward from the sun. They had run, and their soldiers had been driven after them. They must never return, said the World Party. Not as traders, not as visitors, they would never again pollute the soil and soul of Yeowe. Nor would any other foreigner, any other Power. The Aliens of the Ekumen had helped Yeowe free itself; now they too must go. There was no place for them here. "This is our world. This is the free world. Here we will make our souls in the image of Kamye the Swordsman," Abberkam had said over and over, and that image, the curved sword, was the symbol of the World Party.

And blood had been shed. From the Uprising at Nadami on, thirty years of fighting, rebellions, retaliations, half her lifetime, and even after Liberation, after all the Werelians were gone, the fighting went on. Always, always, the young men were ready to rush out and kill whoever the old men told them to kill, each other, women, old people, children; always there was a war to be fought in the name of Peace, Freedom, Justice, the Lord. Newly freed tribes fought over land, the city chiefs fought for power. All Yoss had worked for all her life as an educator in the capital had come to pieces not only during the War of Liberation but after it, as the city disintegrated in one ward-war after another.

In all fairness, she thought, despite his waving Kamye's sword, Abberkam, in leading the World Party, had tried to avoid war and had partly succeeded. His preference was for the winning of power by policy and persuasion, and he was a master of it. He had come very near success. The curved sword was everywhere, the rallies cheering his speeches were immense. ABBERKAM AND RACIAL FREEDOM! said huge posters stretched across the city avenues. He was certain to win the first free election ever held on Yeowe, to be Chief of the World Council. And then, nothing much at first, the rumors. The defections. His son's suicide. His son's mother's accusations of debauchery and gross luxury. The proof that he had embezzled great sums of money given his party for relief of districts left in poverty by the withdrawal of Werelian capital. The revelation of the secret plan to assassinate the Envoy of the Ekumen and put the blame on Abberkam's old friend and supporter Demeye. . . . That was what brought him down. A chief could indulge himself sexually, misuse power, grow rich off his people and be admired for it, but a chief who betrayed a companion was not forgiven. It was, Yoss thought, the code of the slave.

Mobs of his own supporters turned against him, attacking the old APCY Manager's Residency, which he had taken over. Supporters of the Ekumen joined with forces still loyal to him to defend him and restore order to the capital city. After days of street warfare, hundreds of men killed fighting and thousands more in riots around the continent, Abberkam surrendered. The Ekumen supported a provisional government in declaring amnesty. Their people walked him through the bloodstained, bombed-out streets in absolute silence. People watched, people who had trusted him, people who had revered him, people who had hated him, watched him walk past in silence, guarded by the foreigners, the Aliens he had tried to drive from their world.

She had read about it in the paper. She had been living in the marshes for over a year then. "Serve him right," she had thought, and not much more. Whether the Ekumen was a true ally or a new set of Owners in disguise, she didn't know, but she liked to see any chief go down. Werelian Bosses, strutting tribal headmen, or ranting demagogues, let them taste dirt. She'd eaten enough of their dirt in her life.

When a few months later they told her in the village that Abberkam was coming to the marshlands as a recluse, a soulmaker, she had been surprised and for a moment ashamed at having assumed his talk had all been empty rhetoric. Was he a religious man, then? —Through all the luxury, the orgies, the thefts, the powermongering, the murders? No! Since he'd lost his money and power, he'd stay in view by making a spectacle of his poverty and piety. He was utterly shameless. She was surprised at the bitterness of her indignation. The first time she saw him she felt like spitting at the big, thick-toed, sandaled feet, which were all she saw of him; she refused to look at his face.

But then in the winter she had heard the howling out on the marshes, at night, in the freezing wind. Tikuli and Gubu had pricked an ear but been unfrightened by the awful noise. That led her after a minute to recognize it as a human voice—a man shouting aloud, drunk? mad?—howling, beseeching, so that she had got up to go to him, despite her terror; but he was not calling out for human aid. "Lord, my Lord, Kamye!" he shouted, and looking out her door she saw him up on the causeway, a shadow against the pale night clouds, striding and tearing at his hair and crying like an animal, like a soul in pain.

After that night she did not judge him. They were equals. When she next met him she looked him in the face and spoke, forcing him to speak to her.

That was not often; he lived in true seclusion. No one came across the marshes to see him. People in the village often enriched their souls by giving her food, harvest surplus, leftovers, sometimes at the holy days a dish cooked for her; but she saw no one take anything out to Abberkam's house. Maybe they had offered and he was too proud to take. Maybe they were afraid to offer.

She dug up her root bed with the miserable short-handled spade Em Dewi had given her, and thought about Abberkam howling, and about the way he had coughed. Safnan had nearly died of the berlot when she was four. Yoss had heard that terrible cough for weeks. Had Abberkam been going to the village to get medicine, the other day? Had he got there, or turned back?

She put on her shawl, for the wind had turned cold again, the autumn was getting on. She went up to the causeway and took the right-hand turn.

Abberkam's house was of wood, riding a raft of tree trunks sunk in the peaty water of the marsh. Such houses were very old, going back two hundred years or more to when there had been trees growing in the valley. It had been a farmhouse and was much larger than her hut, a rambling, dark place, the roof in ill repair, some windows boarded over, planks on the porch loose as she stepped up on it. She said his name, then said it again louder. The wind whined in the reeds. She knocked, waited, pushed the heavy door open. It was dark indoors. She was in a kind of vestibule. She heard him talking in the next room. "Never down to the adit, in the intent, take it out, take it out," the deep, hoarse voice said, and then he coughed. She opened the door; she had to let her eyes adjust to the darkness for a minute before she could see where she was. It was the old front room of the house. The windows were shuttered, the fire dead. There was a sideboard, a table, a couch, but a bed stood near the fireplace. The tangled covers had slid to the floor, and Abberkam was naked on the bed, writhing and raving in fever. "Oh, Lord!" Yoss said. That huge, black, sweat-oiled breast and belly whorled with grey hair, those powerful arms and groping hands, how was she going to get near him?

She managed it, growing less timid and cautious as she found him weak in his fever, and, when he was lucid, obedient to her requests. She got him covered up, piled up all the blankets he had and a rug from the floor of an unused room on top; she built up the fire as hot as she could make it; and after a couple of hours he began to sweat, sweat pouring out of him till the sheets and mattress were soaked. "You are immoderate," she railed at him in the depths of the night, shoving and hauling at him, making him stagger over to the decrepit couch and lie there wrapped in the rug so she could get his bedding dry at the fire. He shivered and coughed, and she brewed up the herbals she had brought, and drank the scalding tea along with him. He fell suddenly asleep and slept like death, not wakened even by the cough that wracked him. She fell as suddenly asleep and woke to find herself lying on bare hearthstones, the fire dying, the day white in the windows.

Abberkam lay like a mountain range under the rug, which she saw now to be filthy; his breath wheezed but was deep and regular. She got up piece by piece, all ache and pain, made up the fire and got warm, made tea, investigated the pantry. It was stocked with essentials; evidently the Chief ordered in supplies from Veo, the nearest town of any size. She made herself a good breakfast, and when Abberkam roused, got some more herbal tea into him. The fever had broken. The danger now was water in the lungs, she thought; they had warned her about that with Safnan, and this was a man of sixty. If he stopped coughing, that would be a danger sign. She made him lie propped up. "Cough," she told him.

"Hurts," he growled.

"You have to," she said, and he coughed, hak-hak.

"More!" she ordered, and he coughed till his body was shaken with the spasms.

"Good," she said. "Now sleep." He slept.

Tikuli, Gubu would be starving! She fled home, fed her pets, petted them, changed her underclothes, sat down in her own chair by her own fireside for half an hour with Gubu going roo-roo under her ear. Then she went back across the marshes to the Chief's house.

She got his bed dried out by nightfall and moved him back into it. She stayed that night, but left him in the morning, saying, "I'll be back in the evening." He was silent, still very sick, indifferent to his own plight or hers.

The next day he was clearly better: the cough was phlegmy and rough, a good cough; she well remembered when Safnan had finally begun coughing a good cough. He was fully awake from time to time, and when she brought him the bottle she had made serve as a bedpan he took it from her and turned away from her to piss in it. Modesty, a good sign in a Chief, she thought. She felt pleased with him and with herself. She had been useful. "I'm going to leave you tonight; don't let the covers slip off. I'll be back in the morning," she told him, pleased with herself, her decisiveness, her unanswerability.

But when she got home in the clear, cold evening, Tikuli was curled up in a corner of the room where he had never slept before. He would not eat, and crept back to his corner when she tried to move him, pet him, make him sleep on the bed. Let me be, he said, looking away from her, turning his eyes away, tucking his dry, black, sharp nose into the curve of his foreleg. Let me be, he said patiently, let me die, that is what I am doing now.

She slept, because she was very tired. Gubu stayed out in the marshes all night. In the morning Tikuli was just the same, curled up on the floor in the place where he had never slept, waiting.

"I have to go," she told him, "I'll be back soon—very soon. Wait for me, Tikuli."

He said nothing, gazing away from her with dim amber eyes. It was not her he waited for.

She strode across the marshes, dry-eyed, angry, useless. Abberkam was much the same as he had been; she fed him some grain pap, looked to his needs, and said, "I can't stay. My kit is sick, I have to go back."

"Kit," the big man said in his rumble of voice.

"A foxdog. My daughter gave him to me." Why was she explaining, excusing herself? She left; when she got home Tikuli was where she had left him. She did some mending, cooked up some food she thought Abberkam might eat, tried to read the book about the worlds of the Ekumen, about the world that had no war, where it was always winter, where people were both men and women. In the middle of the afternoon she thought she must go back to Abberkam, and was just getting up when Tikuli too stood up. He walked very slowly over to her. She sat down again in her chair and stooped to pick him up, but he put his sharp muzzle into her hand, sighed, and lay down with his head on his paws. He sighed again.

She sat and wept aloud for a while, not long; then she got up and got the gardening spade and went outdoors. She made the grave at the corner of the stone chimney, in a sunny nook. When she went in and picked Tikuli up she thought with a thrill like terror, "He is not dead!" He was dead, only he was not cold yet; the thick red fur kept the body's warmth in. She wrapped him in her blue scarf and took him in her arms, carried him to his grave, feeling that faint warmth still through the cloth, and the light rigidity of the body, like a wooden statue. She filled the grave and set a stone that had fallen from the chimney on it. She could not say anything, but she had an image in her mind like a prayer, of Tikuli running in the sunlight somewhere.

She put out food on the porch for Gubu, who had kept out of the house all day, and set off up the causeway. It was a silent, overcast evening. The reeds stood grey and the pools had a leaden gleam.

Abberkam was sitting up in bed, certainly better, perhaps with a touch of fever but nothing serious; he was hungry, a good sign. When she brought him his tray he said, "The kit, it's all right?"

"No," she said and turned away, able only after a minute to say, "Dead."

"In the Lord's hands," said the hoarse, deep voice, and she saw Tikuli in the sunlight again, in some presence, some kind presence like the sunlight.

"Yes," she said. "Thank you." Her lips quivered and her

throat closed up. She kept seeing the design on her blue scarf, leaves printed in a darker blue. She made herself busy. Presently she came back to see to the fire and sit down beside it. She felt very tired.

"Before the Lord Kamye took up the sword, he was a herdsman," Abberkam said. "And they called him Lord of the Beasts, and Deer-Herd, because when he went into the forest he came among the deer, and lions also walked with him among the deer, offering no harm. None were afraid."

He spoke so quietly that it was a while before she realised he was saying lines from the *Arkamye*.

She put another block of peat on the fire and sat down again. "Tell me where you come from, Chief Abberkam," she said.

"Gebba Plantation."

"In the east?"

He nodded.

"What was it like?"

The fire smouldered, making its pungent smoke. The night was intensely silent. When she first came out here from the city the silence had wakened her, night after night.

"What was it like," he said almost in a whisper. Like most people of their race, the dark iris filled his eyes, but she saw the white flash as he glanced over at her. "Sixty years ago," he said. "We lived in the Plantation compound. The canebrakes; some of us worked there, cut cane, worked in the mill. Most of the women, the little children. Most men and the boys over nine or ten went down the mines. Some of the girls, too, they wanted them small, to work the shafts a man couldn't get into. I was big. They sent me down the mines when I was eight years old."

"What was it like?"

"Dark," he said. Again she saw the flash of his eyes. "I look back and think how did we live? how did we stay living in that place? The air down the mine was so thick with the dust that it was black. Black air. Your lantern light didn't go five feet into that air. There was water in most of the workings, up to a man's knees. There was one shaft where a soft-coal face had caught fire and was burning so the whole system was full of smoke. They went on working it, because the lodes ran behind that coke. We wore masks, filters. They didn't do much good. We breathed the smoke. I always wheeze some like I do now.

It's not just the berlot. It's the old smoke. The men died of the black lung. All the men. Forty, forty-five years old, they died. The Bosses gave your tribe money when a man died. A death bonus. Some men thought that made it worth while dying."

"How did you get out?"

"My mother," he said. "She was a chief's daughter from the village. She taught me. She taught me religion and freedom."

He has said that before, Yoss thought. It has become his stock answer, his standard myth.

"How? What did she say?"

A pause. "She taught me the Holy Word," Abberkam said. "And she said to me, 'You and your brother, you are the true people, you are the Lord's people, his servants, his warriors, his lions: only you. Lord Kamye came with us from the Old World and he is ours now, he lives among us.' She named us Abberkam, Tongue of the Lord, and Domerkam, Arm of the Lord. To speak the truth and fight to be free."

"What became of your brother?" Yoss asked after a time.

"Killed at Nadami," Abberkam said, and again both were silent for a while.

Nadami had been the first great outbreak of the Uprising which finally brought the Liberation to Yeowe. At Nadami plantation slaves and city freedpeople had first fought side by side against the owners. If the slaves had been able to hold together against the owners, the Corporations, they might have won their freedom years sooner. But the liberation movement had constantly splintered into tribal rivalries, chiefs vying for power in the newly freed territories, bargaining with the Bosses to consolidate their gains. Thirty years of war and destruction before the vastly outnumbered Werelians were defeated, driven offworld, leaving the Yeowans free to turn upon one another.

"Your brother was lucky," said Yoss.

Then she looked across at the Chief, wondering how he would take this challenge. His big, dark face had a softened look in the firelight. His grey, coarse hair had escaped from the loose braid she had made of it to keep it from his eyes, and straggled around his face. He said slowly and softly, "He was my younger brother. He was Enar on the Field of the Five Armies."

Oh, so then you're the Lord Kamye himself? Yoss retorted in her mind, moved, indignant, cynical. What an ego! —But, to be sure, there was another implication. Enar had taken up his sword to kill his Elder Brother on that battlefield, to keep him from becoming Lord of the World. And Kamye had told him that the sword he held was his own death; that there is no lordship and no freedom in life, only in the letting go of life, of longing, of desire. Enar had laid down his sword and gone into the wilderness, into the silence, saying only, "Brother, I am thou." And Kamye had taken up that sword to fight the Armies of Desolation, knowing there is no victory.

So who was he, this man? this big fellow? this sick old man, this little boy down in the mines in the dark, this bully, thief, and liar who thought he could speak for the Lord?

"We're talking too much," Yoss said, though neither of them had said a word for five minutes. She poured a cup of tea for him and set the kettle off the fire, where she had kept it simmering to keep the air moist. She took up her shawl. He watched her with that same soft look in his face, an expression almost of confusion.

"It was freedom I wanted," he said. "Our freedom."

His conscience was none of her concern. "Keep warm," she said.

"You're going out now?"

"I can't get lost on the causeway."

It was a strange walk, though, for she had no lantern, and the night was very black. She thought, feeling her way along the causeway, of that black air he had told her of down in the mines, swallowing light. She thought of Abberkam's black, heavy body. She thought how seldom she had walked alone at night. When she was a child on Banni Plantation, the slaves were locked in the compound at night. Women stayed on the women's side and never went alone. Before the War, when she came to the city as a freedwoman, studying at the training school, she'd had a taste of freedom; but in the bad years of the War and even since the Liberation a woman couldn't go safely in the streets at night. There were no police in the working quarters, no streetlights; district warlords sent their gangs out raiding; even in daylight you had to look out, try to stay in the crowd, always be sure there was a street you could escape by.

She grew anxious that she would miss her turning, but her eyes had grown used to the dark by the time she came to it, and she could even make out the blot of her house down in the formlessness of the reedbeds. The Aliens had poor night vision, she had heard. They had little eyes, little dots with white all round them, like a scared calf. She didn't like their eyes, though she liked the colors of their skin, mostly dark brown or ruddy brown, warmer than her greyish-brown slave skin or the blue-black hide Abberkam had got from the owner who had raped his mother. Cyanid skins, the Aliens said politely, and ocular adaptation to the radiation spectrum of the Werelian System sun.

Gubu danced about her on the pathway down, silent, tickling her legs with his tail. "Look out," she scolded him, "I'm going to walk on you." She was grateful to him, picked him up as soon as they were indoors. No dignified and joyous greeting from Tikuli, not this night, not ever. Roo-roo-roo, Gubu went under her ear, listen to me, I'm here, life goes on, where's dinner?

The Chief got a touch of pneumonia after all, and she went into the village to call the clinic in Veo. They sent out a practitioner, who said he was doing fine, just keep him sitting up and coughing, the herbal teas were fine, just keep an eye on him, that's right, and went away, thanks very much. So she spent her afternoons with him. The house without Tikuli seemed very drab, the late autumn days seemed very cold, and anyhow what else did she have to do? She liked the big, dark raft-house. She wasn't going to clean house for the Chief or any man who didn't do it for himself, but she poked about in it, in rooms Abberkam evidently hadn't used or even looked at. She found one upstairs, with long low windows all along the west wall, that she liked. She swept it out and cleaned the windows with their small, greenish panes. When he was asleep she would go up to that room and sit on a ragged wool rug, its only furnishing. The fireplace had been sealed up with loose bricks, but heat came up it from the peat fire burning below, and with her back against the warm bricks and the sunlight slanting in, she was warm. She felt a peacefulness there that seemed to belong to the room, the shape of its air, the greenish, wavery glass of the windows. There she would sit in silence, unoccupied, content, as she had never sat in her own house.

The Chief was slow to get his strength back. Often he was sullen, dour, the uncouth man she had first thought him, sunk in a stupor of self-centered shame and rage. Other days he was ready to talk; even to listen, sometimes.

"I've been reading a book about the worlds of the Ekumen," Yoss said, waiting for their bean-cakes to be ready to turn and fry on the other side. For the last several days she had made and eaten dinner with him in the late afternoon, washed up, and gone home before dark. "It's very interesting. There isn't any question that we're descended from the people of Hain, all of us. Us and the Aliens too. Even our animals have the same ancestors."

"So they say," he grunted.

"It isn't a matter of who says it," she said. "Anybody who will look at the evidence sees it; it's a genetic fact. That you don't like it doesn't alter it."

"What is a 'fact' a million years old?" he said. "What has it to do with you, with me, with us? This is our world. We are ourselves. We have nothing to do with them."

"We do now," she said rather fliply, flipping the bean-cakes.

"Not if I had had my way," he said.

She laughed. "You don't give up, do you?"

"No," he said.

After they were eating, he in bed with his tray, she at a stool on the hearth, she went on, with a sense of teasing a bull, daring the avalanche to fall; for all he was still sick and weak, there was that menace in him, his size, not of body only. "Is that what it was all about, really?" she asked. "The World Party. Having the planet for ourselves, no Aliens? Just that?"

"Yes," he said, the dark rumble.

"Why? The Ekumen has so much to share with us. They broke the Corporations' hold over us. They're on our side."

"We were brought to this world as slaves," he said, "but it is our world to find our own way in. Kamye came with us, the Herdsman, the Bondsman, Kamye of the Sword. This is his world. Our earth. No one can give it to us. We don't need to share other peoples' knowledge or follow their gods. This is where we live, this earth. This is where we die to rejoin the Lord."

After a while she said, "I have a daughter, and a grandson and granddaughter. They left this world four years ago. They're on a ship that is going to Hain. All these years I live till I die are like a few minutes, an hour to them. They'll be there in eighty years—seventy-six years, now. On that other earth. They'll live and die there. Not here."

"Were you willing for them to go?"

"It was her choice."

"Not yours."

"I don't live her life."

"But you grieve," he said.

The silence between them was heavy.

"It is wrong, wrong, wrong!" he said, his voice strong and loud. "We had our own destiny, our own way to the Lord, and they've taken it from us—we're slaves again! The wise Aliens, the scientists with all their great knowledge and inventions, our ancestors, they say they are— 'Do this!' they say, and we do it. 'Do that!' and we do it. 'Take your children on the wonderful ship and fly to our wonderful worlds!' And the children are taken, and they'll never come home. Never know their home. Never know who they are. Never know whose hands might have held them."

He was orating; for all she knew it was a speech he had made once or a hundred times, ranting and magnificent; there were tears in his eyes. There were tears in her eyes also. She would not let him use her, play on her, have power over her.

"If I agreed with you," she said, "still, still, why did you cheat, Abberkam? You lied to your own people, you stole!"

"Never," he said. "Everything I did, always, every breath I took, was for the World Party. Yes, I spent money, all the money I could get, what was it for except the cause? Yes, I threatened the Envoy, I wanted to drive him and all the rest of them off this world! Yes, I lied to them, because they want to control us, to own us, and I will do anything to save my people from slavery—anything!"

He beat his great fists on the mound of his knees, and gasped for breath, sobbing.

"And there is nothing I can do, O Kamye!" he cried, and hid his face in his arms.

She sat silent, sick at heart.

After a long time he wiped his hands over his face, like a child, wiping the coarse, straggling hair back, rubbing his eyes and nose. He picked up the tray and set it on his knees, picked up the fork, cut a piece of bean-cake, put it in his mouth, chewed, swallowed. If he can, I can, Yoss thought, and did the same. They finished their dinner. She got up and came to take his tray. "I'm sorry," she said.

"It was gone then," he said very quietly. He looked up at her directly, seeing her, as she felt he seldom did.

She stood, not understanding, waiting.

"It was gone then. Years before. What I believed at Nadami. That all we needed was to drive them out and we would be free. We lost our way as the war went on and on. I knew it was a lie. What did it matter if I lied more?"

She understood only that he was deeply upset and probably somewhat mad, and that she had been wrong to goad him. They were both old, both defeated, they had both lost their child. Why did she want to hurt him? She put her hand on his hand for a moment, in silence, before she picked up his tray.

As she washed up the dishes in the scullery, he called her, "Come here, please!" He had never done so before, and she hurried into the room.

"Who were you?" he asked.

She stood staring.

"Before you came here," he said impatiently.

"I went from the plantation to education school," she said. "I lived in the city. I taught physics. I administered the teaching of science in the schools. I brought up my daughter."

"What is your name?"

"Yoss. Seddewi Tribe, from Banni."

He nodded, and after a moment more she went back to the scullery. He didn't even know my name, she thought.

Every day she made him get up, walk a little, sit in a chair; he was obedient, but it tired him. The next afternoon she made him walk about a good while, and when he got back to bed he closed his eyes at once. She slipped up the rickety stairs to the west-window room and sat there a long time in perfect peace.

She had him sit up in the chair while she made their dinner. She talked to cheer him up, for he never complained at her demands, but he looked gloomy and bleak, and she blamed herself for upsetting him yesterday. Were they not both here to leave all that behind them, all their mistakes and failures as well as their loves and victories? She told him about Wada and Eyid, spinning out the story of the star-crossed lovers, who were, in fact, in bed in her house that afternoon. "I didn't use to have anywhere to go when they came," she said. "It could be rather inconvenient, cold days like today. I'd have to hang around the shops in the village. This is better, I must say. I like this house."

He only grunted, but she felt he was listening intently, almost that he was trying to understand, like a foreigner who did not know the language.

"You don't care about the house, do you?" she said, and laughed, serving up their soup. "You're honest, at least. Here I am pretending to be holy, to be making my soul, and I get fond of things, attached to them, I love things." She sat down by the fire to eat her soup. "There's a beautiful room upstairs," she said, "the front corner room, looking west. Something good happened in that room, lovers lived there once, maybe. I like to look out at the marshes from there."

When she made ready to go he asked, "Will they be gone?"

"The fawns? Oh yes. Long since. Back to their hateful families. I suppose if they could live together, they'd soon be just as hateful. They're very ignorant. How can they help it? The village is narrow-minded, they're so poor. But they cling to their love for each other, as if they knew it . . . it was their truth . . ."

"'Hold fast to the noble thing,'" Abberkam said. She knew the quotation.

"Would you like me to read to you?" she asked. "I have the *Arkamye*, I could bring it."

He shook his head, with a sudden, broad smile. "No need," he said. "I know it."

"All of it?"

He nodded.

"I meant to learn it—part of it anyway—when I came here," she said, awed. "But I never did. There never seems to be time. Did you learn it here?"

"Long ago. In the jail, in Gebba City," he said. "Plenty of time there. . . . These days, I lie here and say it to myself." His smile lingered as he looked up at her. "It gives me company in your absence."

She stood wordless.

"Your presence is sweet to me," he said.

She wrapped herself in her shawl and hurried out with scarcely a word of good-bye.

She walked home in a crowd of confused, conflicted feelings. What a monster the man was! He had been flirting with her: there was no doubt about it. Coming on to her, was more like it. Lying in bed like a great felled ox, with his wheezing and his grey hair! That soft, deep voice, that smile, he knew the uses of that smile, he knew how to keep it rare. He knew how to get round a woman, he'd got round a thousand if the stories were true, round them and into them and out again, here's a little semen to remember your Chief by, and bye-bye, baby. Lord!

So, why had she taken it into her head to tell him about Eyid and Wada being in her bed? Stupid woman, she told herself, striding into the mean east wind that scoured the greying reeds. Stupid, stupid, old, old woman.

Gubu came to meet her, dancing and batting with soft paws at her legs and hands, waving his short, end-knotted, black-spotted tail. She had left the door unlatched for him, and he could push it open. It was ajar. Feathers of some kind of small bird were strewn all over the room and there was a little blood and a bit of entrail on the hearthrug. "Monster," she told him. "Murder outside!" He danced his battle dance and cried Hoo! Hoo! He slept all night curled up in the small of her back, obligingly getting up, stepping over her, and curling up on the other side each time she turned over.

She turned over frequently, imagining or dreaming the weight and heat of a massive body, the weight of hands on her breasts, the tug of lips at her nipples, sucking life.

She shortened her visits to Abberkam. He was able to get up, see to his needs, get his own breakfast; she kept his peatbox by the chimney filled and his larder supplied, and she now brought him dinner but did not stay to eat it with him. He was mostly grave and silent, and she watched her tongue. They were wary with each other. She missed her hours upstairs in the western room; but that was done with, a kind of dream, a sweetness gone.

Eyid came to Yoss's house alone one afternoon, sullen-faced. "I guess I won't come back out here," she said.

"What's wrong?"

The girl shrugged.

"Are they watching you?"

"No. I don't know. I might, you know. I might get stuffed." She used the old slave word for pregnant.

"You used the contraceptives, didn't you?" She had bought them for the pair in Veo, a good supply.

Eyid nodded vaguely. "I guess it's wrong," she said, pursing her mouth.

"Making love? Using contraceptives?"

"I guess it's wrong," the girl repeated, with a quick, vengeful glance.

"All right," Yoss said.

Eyid turned away.

"Good-bye, Eyid."

Without speaking, Eyid went off by the bog-path.

"Hold fast to the noble thing," Yoss thought, bitterly.

She went round the house to Tikuli's grave, but it was too cold to stand outside for long, a still, aching, midwinter cold. She went in and shut the door. The room seemed small and dark and low. The dull peat fire smoked and smouldered. It made no noise burning. There was no noise outside the house. The wind was down, the ice-bound reeds were still.

I want some wood, I want a wood fire, Yoss thought. A flame leaping and crackling, a story-telling fire, like we used to have in the grandmothers' house on the plantation.

The next day she went off one of the bog-paths to a ruined house half a mile away and pulled some loose boards off the fallen-in porch. She had a roaring blaze in her fireplace that night. She took to going to the ruined house once or more daily, and built up a sizeable woodpile next to the stacked peat in the nook on the other side of the chimney from her bed nook. She was no longer going to Abberkam's house; he was recovered, and she wanted a goal to walk to. She had no way to cut the longer boards, and so shoved them into the fireplace a bit at a time; that way one would last all the evening. She sat by the bright fire and tried to learn the First Book of the *Arkamye*. Gubu lay on the hearthstone sometimes watching the flames and whispering roo, roo, sometimes asleep. He hated so to go out into the icy reeds that she made him a little dirt-box in the scullery, and he used it very neatly.

The deep cold continued, the worst winter she had known on the marshes. Fierce drafts led her to cracks in the wood walls she had not known about; she had no rags to stuff them with and used mud and wadded reeds. If she let the fire go out, the little house grew icy within an hour. The peat fire, banked, got her through the nights. In the daytime often she put on a piece of wood for the flare, the brightness, the company of it.

She had to go into the village. She had put off going for days, hoping that the cold might relent, and had run out of practically everything. It was colder than ever. The peat blocks now on the fire were earthy and burned poorly, smouldering, so she put a piece of wood in with them to keep the fire lively and the house warm. She wrapped every jacket and shawl she had around her and set off with her sack. Gubu blinked at her from the hearth. "Lazy lout," she told him. "Wise beast."

The cold was frightening. If I slipped on the ice and broke a leg, no one might come by for days, she thought. I'd lie here and be frozen dead in a few hours. Well, well, well, I'm in the Lord's hands, and dead in a few years one way or the other. Only, dear Lord, let me get to the village and get warm!

She got there, and spent a good while at the sweet-shop stove catching up on gossip, and at the news vendor's woodstove, reading old newspapers about a new war in the eastern province. Eyid's aunts and Wada's father, mother, and aunts all asked her how the Chief was. They also all told her to go by her landlord's house, Kebi had something for her. He had a packet of cheap nasty tea for her. Perfectly willing to let him enrich his soul, she thanked him for the tea. He asked her about Abberkam. The Chief had been ill? He was better now? He pried; she replied indifferently. It's easy to live in silence, she thought; what I could not do is live with these voices.

She was loath to leave the warm room, but her bag was heavier than she liked to carry, and the icy spots on the road would be hard to see as the light failed. She took her leave and set off across the village again and up onto the causeway. It was later than she had thought. The sun was quite low, hiding behind one bar of cloud in an otherwise stark sky, as if grudging even a half hour's warmth and brightness. She wanted to get home to her fire, and stepped right along.

Keeping her eyes on the way ahead for fear of ice, at first she only heard the voice. She knew it, and she thought, Abberkam has gone mad again! For he was running towards her, shouting. She stopped, afraid of him, but it was her name he was shouting. "Yoss! Yoss! It's all right!" he shouted, coming up right on her, a huge wild man, all dirty, muddy, ice and mud in his grey hair, his hands black, his clothes black, and she could see the whites all round his eyes.

"Get back!" she said, "get away, get away from me!"

"It's all right," he said, "but the house, but the house—"

"What house?"

"Your house, it burned. I saw it, I was coming to the village, I saw the smoke down in the marsh—"

He went on, but Yoss stood paralysed, unhearing. She had shut the door, let the latch fall. She never locked it, but she had let the latch fall, and Gubu would not be able to get out. He was in the house. Locked in: the bright, desperate eyes: the little voice crying—

She started forward. Abberkam blocked her way.

"Let me get by," she said. "I have to get by." She set down her bag and began to run.

Her arm was caught, she was stopped as if by a sea wave, swung right round. The huge body and voice were all around her. "It's all right, the kit is all right, it's in my house," he was saying. "Listen, listen to me, Yoss! The house burned. The kit is all right."

"What happened?" she said, shouting, furious. "Let me go! I don't understand! What happened?"

"Please, please be quiet," he begged her, releasing her. "We'll go by there. You'll see it. There isn't much to see."

Very shakily, she walked along with him while he told her what had happened. "But how did it start?" she said, "how could it?"

"A spark; you left the fire burning? Of course, of course you

did, it's cold. But there were stones out of the chimney, I could
see that. Sparks, if there was any wood on the fire—maybe a
floorboard caught—the thatch, maybe. Then it would all go, in
this dry weather, everything dried out, no rain. Oh my Lord,
my sweet Lord, I thought you were in there. I thought you
were in the house. I saw the fire, I was up on the causeway—
then I was down at the door of the house, I don't know how, did
I fly, I don't know—I pushed, it was latched, I pushed it in, and
I saw the whole back wall and ceiling burning, blazing. There
was so much smoke, I couldn't tell if you were there, I went in,
the little animal was hiding in a corner—I thought how you
cried when the other one died, I tried to catch it, and it went
out the door like a flash, and I saw no one was there, and made
for the door, and the roof fell in." He laughed, wild, triumphant.
"Hit me on the head, see?" He stooped, but she still was not tall
enough to see the top of his head. "I saw your bucket and tried
to throw water on the front wall, to save something, then I saw
that was crazy, it was all on fire, nothing left. And I went up the
path, and the little animal, your pet, was waiting there, all shaking. It let me pick it up, and I didn't know what to do with it, so
I ran back to my house, and left it there. I shut the door. It's safe
there. Then I thought you must be in the village, so I came back
to find you."

They had come to the turnoff. She went to the side of the
causeway and looked down. A smear of smoke, a huddle of
black. Black sticks. Ice. She shook all over and felt so sick she
had to crouch down, swallowing cold saliva. The sky and the
reeds went from left to right, spinning, in her eyes; she could
not stop them spinning.

"Come, come on now, it's all right. Come on with me." She
was aware of the voice, the hands and arms, a large warmth
supporting her. She walked along with her eyes shut. After a
while she could open them and look down at the road,
carefully.

"Oh, my bag—I left it— It's all I have," she said suddenly
with a kind of laugh, turning around and nearly falling over
because the turn started the spinning again.

"I have it here. Come on, it's just a short way now." He
carried the bag oddly, in the crook of his arm. The other arm
was around her, helping her stand up and walk. They came to

his house, the dark raft-house. It faced a tremendous orange-and-yellow sky, with pink streaks going up the sky from where the sun had set; the sun's hair, they used to call that, when she was a child. They turned from the glory, entering the dark house.

"Gubu?" she said.

It took a while to find him. He was cowering under the couch. She had to haul him out, he would not come to her. His fur was full of dust and came out in her hands as she stroked it. There was a little foam on his mouth, and he shivered and was silent in her arms. She stroked and stroked the silvery, speckled back, the spotted sides, the silken white belly fur. He closed his eyes finally; but the instant she moved a little, he leapt, and ran back under the couch.

She sat and said, "I'm sorry, I'm sorry, Gubu, I'm sorry."

Hearing her speak, the Chief came back into the room. He had been in the scullery. He held his wet hands in front of him and she wondered why he didn't dry them. "Is he all right?" he asked.

"It'll take a while," she said. "The fire. And a strange house. They're . . . cats are territorial. Don't like strange places."

She could not arrange her thoughts or words, they came in pieces, unattached.

"That is a cat, then?"

"A spotted cat, yes."

"Those pet animals, they belonged to the Bosses, they were in the Bosses' houses," he said. "We never had any around."

She thought it was an accusation. "They came from Werel with the Bosses," she said, "yes. So did we." After the sharp words were out she thought that maybe what he had said was an apology for ignorance.

He still stood there holding out his hands stiffly. "I'm sorry," he said. "I need some kind of bandage, I think."

She focused slowly on his hands.

"You burned them," she said.

"Not much. I don't know when."

"Let me see." He came nearer and turned the big hands palm up: a fierce red blistered bar across the bluish inner skin of the fingers of one, and a raw bloody wound in the base of the thumb of the other.

"I didn't notice till I was washing," he said. "It didn't hurt."

"Let me see your head," she said, remembering; and he knelt and presented her a matted shaggy sooty object with a red-and-black burn right across the top of it. "Oh, Lord," she said.

His big nose and eyes appeared under the grey tangle, close to her, looking up at her, anxious. "I know the roof fell onto me," he said, and she began to laugh.

"It would take more than a roof falling onto you!" she said. "Have you got anything—any clean cloths— I know I left some clean dish towels in the scullery closet— Any disinfectant?"

She talked as she cleaned the head wound. "I don't know anything about burns except try to keep them clean and leave them open and dry. We should call the clinic in Veo. I can go into the village, tomorrow."

"I thought you were a doctor or a nurse," he said.

"I'm a school administrator!"

"You looked after me."

"I knew what you had. I don't know anything about burns. I'll go into the village and call. Not tonight, though."

"Not tonight," he agreed. He flexed his hands, wincing. "I was going to make us dinner," he said. "I didn't know there was anything wrong with my hands. I don't know when it happened."

"When you rescued Gubu," Yoss said in a matter-of-fact voice, and then began crying. "Show me what you were going to eat, I'll put it on," she said through tears.

"I'm sorry about your things," he said.

"Nothing mattered. I'm wearing almost all my clothes," she said, weeping. "There wasn't anything. Hardly any food there even. Only the *Arkamye*. And my book about the worlds." She thought of the pages blackening and curling as the fire read them. "A friend sent me that from the city, she never approved of me coming here, pretending to drink water and be silent. She was right, too, I should go back, I should never have come. What a liar I am, what a fool! Stealing wood! Stealing wood so I could have a nice fire! So I could be warm and cheerful! So I set the house on fire, so everything's gone, ruined, Kebi's house, my poor little cat, your hands, it's my fault. I forgot about sparks from wood fires, the chimney was built for peat fires, I forgot. I forget everything, my mind betrays me, my memory lies, I lie. I dishonor my Lord, pretending to turn to him when I can't turn to him, when I can't let go the world. So I burn it! So the sword cuts your hands." She took his hands in hers and bent her head over them. "Tears are disinfectant," she said. "Oh I'm sorry, I am sorry!"

His big, burned hands rested in hers. He leaned forward and kissed her hair, caressing it with his lips and cheek. "I will say you the *Arkamye*," he said. "Be still now. We need to eat something. You feel very cold. I think you have some shock, maybe. You sit there. I can put a pot on to heat, anyhow."

She obeyed. He was right, she felt very cold. She huddled closer to the fire. "Gubu?" she whispered. "Gubu, it's all right. Come on, come on, little one." But nothing moved under the couch.

Abberkam stood by her, offering her something: a glass: it was wine, red wine.

"You have wine?" she said, startled.

"Mostly I drink water and am silent," he said. "Sometimes I drink wine and talk. Take it."

She took it humbly. "I wasn't shocked," she said.

"Nothing shocks a city woman," he said gravely. "Now I need you to open up this jar."

"How did you get the wine open?" she asked as she unscrewed the lid of a jar of fish stew.

"It was already open," he said, deep-voiced, imperturbable.

They sat across the hearth from each other to eat, helping themselves from the pot hung on the firehook. She held bits of fish down low so they could be seen from under the couch and whispered to Gubu, but he would not come out.

"When he's very hungry, he will," she said. She was tired of the teary quaver in her voice, the knot in her throat, the sense of shame. "Thank you for the food," she said. "I feel better."

She got up and washed the pot and the spoons; she had told him not to get his hands wet, and he did not offer to help her, but sat on by the fire, motionless, like a great dark lump of stone.

"I'll go upstairs," she said when she was done. "Maybe I can get hold of Gubu and take him with me. Let me have a blanket or two."

He nodded. "They're up there. I lighted the fire," he said. She did not know what he meant; she had knelt to peer under the couch. She knew as she did so that she was grotesque, an old woman bundled up in shawls with her rear end in the air, whispering, "Gubu, Gubu!" to a piece of furniture. But there was a little scrabbling, and then Gubu came straight into her hands. He clung to her shoulder with his nose hidden under her ear. She sat up on her heels and looked at Abberkam, radiant. "Here he is!" she said. She got to her feet with some difficulty, and said, "Good night."

"Good night, Yoss," he said. She dared not try to carry the oil lamp, and made her way up the stairs in the dark, holding Gubu close with both hands till she was in the west room and had shut the door. Then she stood staring. Abberkam had unsealed the fireplace, and some time this evening he had lighted the peat laid ready in it; the ruddy glow flickered in the long, low windows black with night, and the scent of it was sweet. A bedstead that had been in another unused room now stood in this one, made up, with mattress and blankets and a new white wool rug thrown over it. A jug and basin stood on the shelf by the chimney. The old rug she had used to sit on had been beaten and scrubbed, and lay clean and threadbare on the hearth.

Gubu pushed at her arms; she set him down, and he ran straight under the bed. He would be all right there. She poured a little water from the jug into the basin and set it on the hearth in case he was thirsty. He could use the ashes for his box. Everything we need is here, she thought, still looking with a sense of bewilderment at the shadowy room, the soft light that struck the windows from within.

She went out, closing the door behind her, and went downstairs. Abberkam sat still by the fire. His eyes flashed at her. She did not know what to say.

"You liked that room," he said.

She nodded.

"You said maybe it was a lovers' room once. I thought maybe it was a lovers' room to be."

After a while she said, "Maybe."

"Not tonight," he said, with a low rumble: a laugh, she realised. She had seen him smile once, now she had heard him laugh.

"No. Not tonight," she said stiffly.

"I need my hands," he said, "I need everything, for that, for you."

She said nothing, watching him.

"Sit down, Yoss, please," he said. She sat down in the hearth-seat facing him.

"When I was ill I thought about these things," he said, always a touch of the orator in his voice. "I betrayed my cause, I lied and stole in its name, because I could not admit I had lost faith in it. I feared the Aliens because I feared their gods. So many gods! I feared that they would diminish my Lord. Diminish him!" He was silent for a minute, and drew breath; she could hear the deep rasp in his chest. "I betrayed my son's mother many times, many times. Her, other women, myself. I did not hold to the one noble thing." He opened up his hands, wincing a little, looking at the burns across them. "I think you did," he said.

After a while she said, "I only stayed with Safnan's father a few years. I had some other men. What does it matter, now?"

"That's not what I mean," he said. "I mean that you did not betray your men, your child, yourself. All right, all that's past. You say, what does it matter now, nothing matters. But you give me this chance even now, this beautiful chance, to me, to hold you, hold you fast."

She said nothing.

"I came here in shame," he said, "and you honored me."

"Why not? Who am I to judge you?"

"'Brother, I am thou.'"

She looked at him in terror, one glance, then looked into the fire. The peat burned low and warm, sending up one faint curl of smoke. She thought of the warmth, the darkness of his body.

"Would there be any peace between us?" she said at last.

"Do you need peace?"

After a while she smiled a little.

"I will do my best," he said. "Stay in this house a while."

She nodded.

Forgiveness Day

SOLLY HAD been a space brat, a Mobile's child, living on this ship and that, this world and that; she'd traveled five hundred light-years by the time she was ten. At twenty-five she had been through a revolution on Alterra, learned *aiji* on Terra and farthinking from an old hilfer on Rokanan, breezed through the Schools on Hain, and survived an assignment as Observer in murderous, dying Kheakh, skipping another half millennium at near-lightspeed in the process. She was young, but she'd been around.

She got bored with the Embassy people in Voe Deo telling her to watch out for this, remember that; she was a Mobile herself now, after all. Werel had its quirks—what world didn't? She'd done her homework, she knew when to curtsy and when not to belch, and vice versa. It was a relief to get on her own at last, in this gorgeous little city, on this gorgeous little continent, the first and only Envoy of the Ekumen to the Divine Kingdom of Gatay.

She was high for days on the altitude, the tiny, brilliant sun pouring vertical light into the noisy streets, the peaks soaring up incredibly behind every building, the dark blue sky where great near stars burned all day, the dazzling nights under six or seven lolloping bits of moon, the tall black people with their black eyes, narrow heads, long, narrow hands and feet, gorgeous people, her people! She loved them all. Even if she saw a little too much of them.

The last time she had had completely to herself was a few hours in the passenger cabin of the airskimmer sent by Gatay to bring her across the ocean from Voe Deo. On the airstrip she was met by a delegation of priests and officials from the King and the Council, magnificent in scarlet and brown and turquoise, and swept off to the Palace, where there was a lot of curtsying and no belching, of course, for hours—an introduction to his little shrunken old majesty, introductions to High Muckamucks and Lord Hooziwhats, speeches, a banquet—all completely predictable, no problems at all, not even the impenetrable giant fried flower on her plate at the banquet. But with her, from that first moment on the airstrip and at every moment thereafter, discreetly behind or beside or very near her, were two men: her Guide and her Guard.

The Guide, whose name was San Ubattat, was provided by her hosts in Gatay; of course he was reporting on her to the government, but he was a most obliging spy, endlessly smoothing the way for her, showing her with a bare hint what was expected or what would be a gaffe, and an excellent linguist, ready with a translation when she needed one. San was all right. But the Guard was something else.

He had been attached to her by the Ekumen's hosts on this world, the dominant power on Werel, the big nation of Voe Deo. She had promptly protested to the Embassy back in Voe Deo that she didn't need or want a bodyguard. Nobody in Gatay was out to get her and even if they were, she preferred to look after herself. The Embassy sighed. Sorry, they said. You're stuck with him. Voe Deo has a military presence in Gatay, which after all is a client state, economically dependent. It's in Voe Deo's interest to protect the legitimate government of Gatay against the native terrorist factions, and you get protected as one of their interests. We can't argue with that.

She knew better than to argue with the Embassy, but she could not resign herself to the Major. His military title, rega, she translated by the archaic word "Major," from a skit she'd seen on Terra. That Major had been a stuffed uniform, covered with medals and insignia. It puffed and strutted and commanded, and finally blew up into bits of stuffing. If only this Major would blow up! Not that he strutted, exactly, or even commanded, directly. He was stonily polite, woodenly silent, stiff and cold as rigor mortis. She soon gave up any effort to talk to him; whatever she said, he replied Yessum or Nomum with the prompt stupidity of a man who does not and will not actually listen, an officer officially incapable of humanity. And he was with her in every public situation, day and night, on the street, shopping, meeting with businessmen and officials, sightseeing, at court, in the balloon ascent above the mountains— with her everywhere, everywhere but bed.

Even in bed she wasn't quite as alone as she would often have liked; for the Guide and the Guard went home at night, but in the anteroom of her bedroom slept the Maid—a gift from His Majesty, her own private asset.

She remembered her incredulity when she first learned that word, years ago, in a text about slavery. "On Werel, members of the dominant caste are called *owners*; members of the serving class are called *assets*. Only owners are referred to as men or women; assets are called bondsmen, bondswomen."

So here she was, the owner of an asset. You don't turn down a king's gift. Her asset's name was Rewe. Rewe was probably a spy too, but it was hard to believe. She was a dignified, handsome woman some years older than Solly and about the same intensity of skin color, though Solly was pinkish brown and Rewe was bluish brown. The palms of her hands were a delicate azure. Rewe's manners were exquisite and she had tact, astuteness, an infallible sense of when she was wanted and when not. Solly of course treated her as an equal, stating right out at the beginning that she believed no human being had a right to dominate, much less own, another, that she would give Rewe no orders, and that she hoped they might become friends. Rewe accepted this, unfortunately, as a new set of orders. She smiled and said yes. She was infinitely yielding. Whatever Solly said or did sank into that acceptance and was lost, leaving Rewe unchanged: an attentive, obliging, gentle physical presence, just out of reach. She smiled, and said yes, and was untouchable.

And Solly began to think, after the first fizz of the first days in Gatay, that she needed Rewe, really needed her as a woman to talk with. There was no way to meet owner women, who lived hidden away in their bezas, women's quarters, "at home," they called it. All bondswomen but Rewe were somebody else's property, not hers to talk to. All she ever met was men. And eunuchs.

That had been another thing hard to believe, that a man would voluntarily trade his virility for a little social standing; but she met such men all the time in King Hotat's court. Born assets, they earned partial independence by becoming eunuchs, and as such often rose to positions of considerable power and trust among their owners. The eunuch Tayandan, majordomo of the palace, ruled the King, who didn't rule, but figureheaded for the Council. The Council was made up of various kinds of lord but only one kind of priest, Tualites. Only assets worshiped Kamye, and the original religion of Gatay had been suppressed when the monarchy became Tualite a century or so ago. If there was one thing she really disliked about Werel, aside from slavery and gender-dominance, it was the religions. The songs about Lady Tual were beautiful, and the statues of her and the great temples in Voe Deo were wonderful, and the *Arkamye* seemed to be a good story though long-winded; but the deadly self-righteousness, the intolerance, the stupidity of the priests, the hideous doctrines that justified every cruelty in the name of the faith! As a matter of fact, Solly said to herself, was there anything she *did* like about Werel?

And answered herself instantly: I love it, I love it. I love this weird little bright sun and all the broken bits of moons and the mountains going up like ice walls and the people—the people with their black eyes without whites like animals' eyes, eyes like dark glass, like dark water, mysterious—I want to love them, I want to know them, I want to reach them!

But she had to admit that the pissants at the Embassy had been right about one thing: being a woman was tough on Werel. She fit nowhere. She went about alone, she had a public position, and so was a contradiction in terms: proper women stayed at home, invisible. Only bondswomen went out in the streets, or met strangers, or worked at any public job. She behaved like an asset, not like an owner. Yet she was something very grand, an envoy of the Ekumen, and Gatay very much wanted to join the Ekumen and not to offend its envoys. So the officials and courtiers and businessmen she talked to on the business of the Ekumen did the best they could: they treated her as if she were a man.

The pretense was never complete and often broke right down. The poor old King groped her industriously, under the vague impression that she was one of his bedwarmers. When she contradicted Lord Gatuyo in a discussion, he stared with the blank disbelief of a man who has been talked back to by his shoe. He had been thinking of her as a woman. But in general the disgenderment worked, allowing her to work with them; and she began to fit herself into the game, enlisting Rewe's help in making clothes that resembled what male owners wore in Gatay, avoiding anything that to them would be specifically feminine. Rewe was a quick, intelligent seamstress. The bright, heavy, close-fitted trousers were practical and becoming, the embroidered jackets were splendidly warm. She liked wearing them. But she felt unsexed by these men who could not accept her for what she was. She needed to talk to a woman.

She tried to meet some of the hidden owner women through the owner men, and met a wall of politeness without a door, without a peephole. What a wonderful idea; we will certainly arrange a visit when the weather is better! I should be overwhelmed with the honor if the Envoy were to entertain Lady Mayoyo and my daughters, but my foolish, provincial girls are so unforgivably timid—I'm sure you understand. Oh, surely, surely, a tour of the inner gardens—but not at present, when the vines are not in flower! We must wait until the vines are in flower!

There was nobody to talk to, nobody, until she met Batikam the Makil.

It was an event: a touring troupe from Voe Deo. There wasn't much going on in Gatay's little mountain capital by way of entertainment, except for temple dancers—all men, of course—and the soppy fluff that passed as drama on the Werelian network. Solly had doggedly entered some of these wet pastels, hoping for a glimpse into the life "at home," but she couldn't stomach the swooning maidens who died of love while the stiff-necked jackass heroes, who all looked like the Major, died nobly in battle, and Tual the Merciful leaned out of the clouds smiling upon their deaths with her eyes slightly crossed and the whites showing, a sign of divinity. Solly had noticed that Werelian men never entered the network for drama. Now she knew why. But the receptions at the palace and the parties in her honor given by various lords and businessmen were pretty dull stuff: all men, always, because they wouldn't have the slave girls in while the Envoy was there; and she couldn't flirt even with the nicest men, couldn't remind them that they were men, since that would remind them that she was a woman not behaving like a lady. The fizz had definitely gone flat by the time the makil troupe came.

She asked San, a reliable etiquette advisor, if it would be all right for her to attend the performance. He hemmed and hawed and finally, with more than usually oily delicacy, gave her to understand that it would be all right so long as she went dressed as a man. "Women, you know, don't go in public. But sometimes, they want so much to see the entertainers, you know? Lady Amatay used to go with Lord Amatay, dressed in his clothes, every year; everybody knew, nobody said anything —you know. For you, such a great person, it would be all right. Nobody will say anything. Quite, quite all right. Of course, I come with you, the rega comes with you. Like friends, ha? You know, three good men friends going to the entertainment, ha? Ha?"

Ha, ha, she said obediently. What fun! —But it was worth it, she thought, to see the makils.

They were never on the network. Young girls at home were not to be exposed to their performances, some of which, San gravely informed her, were unseemly. They played only in theaters. Clowns, dancers, prostitutes, actors, musicians, the makils formed a kind of subclass, the only assets not personally owned. A talented slave boy bought by the Entertainment Corporation from his owner was thenceforth the property of the Corporation, which trained and looked after him the rest of his life.

They walked to the theater, six or seven streets away. She had forgotten that the makils were all transvestites, indeed she did not remember it when she first saw them, a troop of tall slender dancers sweeping out onto the stage with the precision and power and grace of great birds wheeling, flocking, soaring. She watched unthinking, enthralled by their beauty, until suddenly the music changed and the clowns came in, black as night, black as owners, wearing fantastic trailing skirts, with fantastic jutting jeweled breasts, singing in tiny, swoony voices, "Oh do not rape me please kind Sir, no no, not now!" They're men, they're men! Solly realized then, already laughing helplessly. By the time Batikam finished his star turn, a marvelous dramatic monologue, she was a fan. "I want to meet him," she said to San at a pause between acts. "The actor—Batikam."

San got the bland expression that signified he was thinking how it could be arranged and how to make a little money out of it. But the Major was on guard, as ever. Stiff as a stick, he barely turned his head to glance at San. And San's expression began to alter.

If her proposal was out of line, San would have signaled or said so. The Stuffed Major was simply controlling her, trying to keep her as tied down as one of "his" women. It was time to challenge him. She turned to him and stared straight at him. "Rega Teyeo," she said, "I quite comprehend that you're under orders to keep me in order. But if you give orders to San or to me, they must be spoken aloud, and they must be justified. I will not be managed by your winks or your whims."

There was a considerable pause, a truly delicious and rewarding pause. It was difficult to see if the Major's expression changed; the dim theater light showed no detail in his blueblack face. But there was something frozen about his stillness that told her she'd stopped him. At last he said, "I'm charged to protect you, Envoy."

"Am I endangered by the makils? Is there impropriety in an envoy of the Ekumen congratulating a great artist of Werel?"

Again the frozen silence. "No," he said.

"Then I request you to accompany me when I go backstage after the performance to speak to Batikam."

One stiff nod. One stiff, stuffy, defeated nod. Score one! Solly thought, and sat back cheerfully to watch the lightpainters, the erotic dances, and the curiously touching little drama with which the evening ended. It was in archaic poetry, hard to understand, but the actors were so beautiful, their voices so tender that she found tears in her eyes and hardly knew why.

"A pity the makils always draw on the *Arkamye*," said San, with smug, pious disapproval. He was not a very high-class owner, in fact he owned no assets; but he was an owner, and a bigoted Tualite, and liked to remind himself of it. "Scenes from the *Incarnations of Tual* would be more befitting such an audience."

"I'm sure you agree, Rega," she said, enjoying her own irony.

"Not at all," he said, with such toneless politeness that at first she did not realise what he had said; and then forgot the minor puzzle in the bustle of finding their way and gaining admittance to the backstage and to the performers' dressing room.

When they realised who she was, the managers tried to clear all the other performers out, leaving her alone with Batikam (and San and the Major, of course); but she said no, no, no, these wonderful artists must not be disturbed, just let me talk a moment with Batikam. She stood there in the bustle of doffed costumes, half-naked people, smeared makeup, laughter, dissolving tension after the show, any backstage on any world, talking with the clever, intense man in elaborate archaic woman's costume. They hit it off at once. "Can you come to my house?" she asked. "With pleasure," Batikam said, and his eyes did not flick to San's or the Major's face: the first bondsman she had yet met who did not glance to her Guard or her Guide for permission to say or do anything, anything at all. She glanced at them only to see if they were shocked. San looked collusive, the Major looked rigid. "I'll come in a little while," Batikam said. "I must change."

They exchanged smiles, and she left. The fizz was back in the air. The huge close stars hung clustered like grapes of fire. A moon tumbled over the icy peaks, another jigged like a lop-sided lantern above the curlicue pinnacles of the palace. She strode along the dark street, enjoying the freedom of the male robe she wore and its warmth, making San trot to keep up; the Major, long-legged, kept pace with her. A high, trilling voice called, "Envoy!" and she turned with a smile, then swung round, seeing the Major grappling momentarily with someone in the shadow of a portico. He broke free, caught up to her without a word, seized her arm in an iron grip, and dragged her into a run. "Let go!" she said, struggling; she did not want to use an aiji break on him, but nothing less was going to get her free.

He pulled her nearly off-balance with a sudden dodge into an alley; she ran with him, letting him keep hold on her arm. They came unexpectedly out into her street and to her gate, through it, into the house, which he unlocked with a word—how did he do that?—"What is all this?" she demanded, breaking away easily, holding her arm where his grip had bruised it.

She saw, outraged, the last flicker of an exhilarated smile on his face. Breathing hard, he asked, "Are you hurt?"

"Hurt? Where you yanked me, yes—what do you think you were doing?"

"Keeping the fellow away."

"What fellow?"

He said nothing.

"The one who called out? Maybe he wanted to talk to me!"

After a moment the Major said, "Possibly. He was in the shadow. I thought he might be armed. I must go out and look for San Ubattat. Please keep the door locked until I come back." He was out the door as he gave the order; it never occurred to him that she would not obey, and she did obey, raging. Did he think she couldn't look after herself? that she needed him interfering in her life, kicking slaves around, "protecting" her? Maybe it was time he saw what an aiji fall looked like. He was strong and quick, but had no real training. This kind of amateur interference was intolerable, really intolerable; she must protest to the Embassy again.

As soon as she let him back in with a nervous, shamefaced San in tow, she said, "You opened my door with a password. I was not informed that you had right of entrance day and night."

He was back to his military blankness. "Nomum," he said.

"You are not to do so again. You are not to seize hold of me ever again. I must tell you that if you do, I will injure you. If something alarms you, tell me what it is and I will respond as I see fit. Now will you please go."

"With pleasure, mum," he said, wheeled, and marched out.

"Oh, Lady— Oh, Envoy," San said, "that was a dangerous person, extremely dangerous people, I am so sorry, disgraceful," and he babbled on. She finally got him to say who he thought it was, a religious dissident, one of the Old Believers who held to the original religion of Gatay and wanted to cast out or kill all foreigners and unbelievers. "A bondsman?" she asked with interest, and he was shocked— "Oh, no, no, a real person, a man—but most misguided, a fanatic, a heathen fanatic! Knifemen, they call themselves. But a man, Lady—Envoy, certainly a man!"

The thought that she might think that an asset might touch her upset him as much as the attempted assault. If such it had been.

As she considered it, she began to wonder if, since she had put the Major in his place at the theater, he had found an excuse to put her in her place by "protecting" her. Well, if he tried it again, he'd find himself upside down against the opposite wall.

"Rewe!" she called, and the bondswoman appeared instantly as always. "One of the actors is coming. Would you like to make us a little tea, something like that?" Rewe smiled, said, "Yes," and vanished. There was a knock at the door. The Major opened it—he must be standing guard outside—and Batikam came in.

It had not occurred to her that the makil would still be in
women's clothing, but it was how he dressed offstage too, not
so magnificently, but with elegance, in the delicate, flowing
materials and dark, subtle hues that the swoony ladies in the
dramas wore. It gave considerable piquancy, she felt, to her
own male costume. Batikam was not as handsome as the
Major, who was a stunning-looking man till he opened his
mouth; but the makil was magnetic, you had to look at him.
He was a dark greyish brown, not the blue-black that the
owners were so vain of (though there were plenty of black assets too, Solly had noticed: of course, when every bondswoman
was her owner's sexual servant). Intense, vivid intelligence and
sympathy shone in his face through the makil's stardust black
makeup, as he looked around with a slow, lovely laugh at her,
at San, and at the Major standing at the door. He laughed like
a woman, a warm ripple, not the ha, ha of a man. He held out
his hands to Solly, and she came forward and took them.
"Thank you for coming, Batikam!" she said, and he said, "Thank
you for asking me, Alien Envoy!"

"San," she said, "I think this is your cue?"

Only indecision about what he ought to do could have
slowed San down till she had to speak. He still hesitated a
moment, then smiled with unction and said, "Yes, so sorry, a
very good night to you, Envoy! Noon hour at the Office of
Mines, tomorrow, I believe?" Backing away, he backed right
into the Major, who stood like a post in the doorway. She
looked at the Major, ready to order him out without ceremony,
how dare he shove back in!—and saw the expression on his
face. For once his blank mask had cracked, and what was revealed was contempt. Incredulous, sickened contempt. As if he
was obliged to watch someone eat a turd.

"Get out," she said. She turned her back on both of them.
"Come on, Batikam; the only privacy I have is in here," she
said, and led the makil to her bedroom.

He was born where his fathers before him were born, in the
old, cold house in the foothills above Noeha. His mother did
not cry out as she bore him, since she was a soldier's wife, and
a soldier's mother, now. He was named for his great-uncle,

killed on duty in the Sosa. He grew up in the stark discipline of a poor household of pure veot lineage. His father, when he was on leave, taught him the arts a soldier must know; when his father was on duty the old Asset-Sergeant Habbakam took over the lessons, which began at five in the morning, summer or winter, with worship, shortsword practice, and a cross-country run. His mother and grandmother taught him the other arts a man must know, beginning with good manners before he was two, and after his second birthday going on to history, poetry, and sitting still without talking.

The child's day was filled with lessons and fenced with disciplines; but a child's day is long. There was room and time for freedom, the freedom of the farmyard and the open hills. There was the companionship of pets, foxdogs, running dogs, spotted cats, hunting cats, and the farm cattle and the greathorses; not much companionship otherwise. The family's assets, other than Habbakam and the two housewomen, were sharecroppers, working the stony foothill land that they and their owners had lived on forever. Their children were light-skinned, shy, already stooped to their lifelong work, ignorant of anything beyond their fields and hills. Sometimes they swam with Teyeo, summers, in the pools of the river. Sometimes he rounded up a couple of them to play soldiers with him. They stood awkward, uncouth, smirking when he shouted "Charge!" and rushed at the invisible enemy. "Follow me!" he cried shrilly, and they lumbered after him, firing their tree-branch guns at random, pow, pow. Mostly he went alone, riding his good mare Tasi or afoot with a hunting cat pacing by his side.

A few times a year visitors came to the estate, relatives or fellow officers of Teyeo's father, bringing their children and their housepeople. Teyeo silently and politely showed the child guests about, introduced them to the animals, took them on rides. Silently and politely, he and his cousin Gemat came to hate each other; at age fourteen they fought for an hour in a glade behind the house, punctiliously following the rules of wrestling, relentlessly hurting each other, getting bloodier and wearier and more desperate, until by unspoken consent they called it off and returned in silence to the house, where everyone was gathering for dinner. Everyone looked at them and said nothing. They washed up hurriedly, hurried to table. Gemat's nose leaked blood all through the meal; Teyeo's jaw was so sore he could not open it to eat. No one commented.

Silently and politely, when they were both fifteen, Teyeo and Rega Toebawe's daughter fell in love. On the last day of her visit they escaped by unspoken collusion and rode out side by side, rode for hours, too shy to talk. He had given her Tasi to ride. They dismounted to water and rest the horses in a wild valley of the hills. They sat near each other, not very near, by the side of the little quiet-running stream. "I love you," Teyeo said. "I love you," Emdu said, bending her shining black face down. They did not touch or look at each other. They rode back over the hills, joyous, silent.

When he was sixteen Teyeo was sent to the Officers' Academy in the capital of his province. There he continued to learn and practice the arts of war and the arts of peace. His province was the most rural in Voe Deo; its ways were conservative, and his training was in some ways anachronistic. He was of course taught the technologies of modern warfare, becoming a first-rate pod pilot and an expert in telereconnaissance; but he was not taught the modern ways of thinking that accompanied the technologies in other schools. He learned the poetry and history of Voe Deo, not the history and politics of the Ekumen. The Alien presence on Werel remained remote, theoretical to him. His reality was the old reality of the veot class, whose men held themselves apart from all men not soldiers and in brotherhood with all soldiers, whether owners, assets, or enemies. As for women, Teyeo considered his rights over them absolute, binding him absolutely to responsible chivalry to women of his own class and protective, merciful treatment of bondswomen. He believed all foreigners to be basically hostile, untrustworthy heathens. He honored the Lady Tual, but worshiped the Lord Kamye. He expected no justice, looked for no reward, and valued above all competence, courage, and self-respect. In some respects he was utterly unsuited to the world he was to enter, in others well prepared for it, since he was to spend seven years on Yeowe fighting a war in which there was no justice, no reward, and never even an illusion of ultimate victory.

Rank among veot officers was hereditary. Teyeo entered active service as a rega, the highest of the three veot ranks. No degree of ineptitude or distinction could lower or raise his status or his pay. Material ambition was no use to a veot. But honor and responsibility were to be earned, and he earned them quickly. He loved service, loved the life, knew he was good at it, intelligently obedient, effective in command; he had come out of the Academy with the highest recommendations, and being posted to the capital, drew notice as a promising officer as well as a likable young man. At twenty-four he was absolutely fit, his body would do anything he asked of it. His austere upbringing had given him little taste for indulgence but an intense appreciation of pleasure, so the luxuries and entertainments of the capital were a discovery of delight to him. He was reserved and rather shy, but companionable and cheerful. A handsome young man, in with a set of other young men very like him, for a year he knew what it is to live a completely privileged life with complete enjoyment of it. The brilliant intensity of that enjoyment stood against the dark background of the war in Yeowe, the slave revolution on the colony planet, which had gone on all his lifetime, and was now intensifying. Without that background, he could not have been so happy. A whole life of games and diversions had no interest for him; and when his orders came, posted as a pilot and division commander to Yeowe, his happiness was pretty nearly complete.

He went home for his thirty-day leave. Having received his parents' approbation, he rode over the hills to Rega Toebawe's estate and asked for his daughter's hand in marriage. The rega and his wife told their daughter that they approved his offer and asked her, for they were not strict parents, if she would like to marry Teyeo. "Yes," she said. As a grown, unmarried woman, she lived in seclusion in the women's side of the house, but she and Teyeo were allowed to meet and even to walk together, the chaperone remaining at some distance. Teyeo told her it was a three-year posting; would she marry in haste now, or wait three years and have a proper wedding? "Now," she said, bending down her narrow, shining face. Teyeo gave a laugh of delight, and she laughed at him. They were married nine days later—it couldn't be sooner, there had to be some fuss and ceremony, even if it was a soldier's wedding—and for seventeen days Teyeo and Emdu made love, walked together, made love, rode together, made love, came to know each other, came to love each other, quarreled, made up, made love, slept in each other's arms. Then he left for the war on another world, and she moved to the women's side of her husband's house.

His three-year posting was extended year by year, as his value as an officer was recognised and as the war on Yeowe changed from scattered containing actions to an increasingly desperate retreat. In his seventh year of service an order for compassionate leave was sent out to Yeowe Headquarters for Rega Teyeo, whose wife was dying of complications of berlot fever. At that point, there was no headquarters on Yeowe; the Army was retreating from three directions towards the old colonial capital; Teyeo's division was fighting a rear-guard defense in the sea marshes; communications had collapsed.

Command on Werel continued to find it inconceivable that a mass of ignorant slaves with the crudest kind of weapons could be defeating the Army of Voe Deo, a disciplined, trained body of soldiers with an infallible communications network, skimmers, pods, every armament and device permitted by the Ekumenical Convention Agreement. A strong faction in Voe Deo blamed the setbacks on this submissive adherence to Alien rules. The hell with Ekumenical Conventions. Bomb the damned dusties back to the mud they were made of. Use the biobomb, what was it for, anyway? Get our men off the foul planet and wipe it clean. Start fresh. If we don't win the war on Yeowe, the next revolution's going to be right here on Werel, in our own cities, in our own homes! The jittery government held on against this pressure. Werel was on probation, and Voe Deo wanted to lead the planet to Ekumenical status. Defeats were minimised, losses were not made up, skimmers, pods, weapons, men were not replaced. By the end of Teyeo's seventh year, the Army on Yeowe had been essentially written off by its government. Early in the eighth year, when the Ekumen was at last permitted to send its Envoys to Yeowe, Voe Deo and the other countries that had supplied auxiliary troops finally began to bring their soldiers home.

It was not until he got back to Werel that Teyeo learned his wife was dead.

He went home to Noeha. He and his father greeted each other with a silent embrace, but his mother wept as she embraced him. He knelt to her in apology for having brought her more grief than she could bear.

He lay that night in the cold room in the silent house, listening to his heart beat like a slow drum. He was not unhappy, the relief of being at peace and the sweetness of being home were too great for that; but it was a desolate calm, and somewhere in it was anger. Not used to anger, he was not sure what he felt. It was as if a faint, sullen red flare colored every image in his mind, as he lay trying to think through the seven years on Yeowe, first as a pilot, then the ground war, then the long retreat, the killing and the being killed. Why had they been left there to be hunted down and slaughtered? Why had the government not sent them reinforcements? The questions had not been worth asking then, they were not worth asking now. They had only one answer: We do what they ask us to do, and we don't complain. I fought every step of the way, he thought without pride. The new knowledge sliced keen as a knife through all other knowledge— And while I was fighting, she was dying. All a waste, there on Yeowe. All a waste, here on Werel. He sat up in the dark, the cold, silent, sweet dark of night in the hills. "Lord Kamye," he said aloud, "help me. My mind betrays me."

During the long leave home he sat often with his mother. She wanted to talk about Emdu, and at first he had to force himself to listen. It would be easy to forget the girl he had known for seventeen days seven years ago, if only his mother would let him forget. Gradually he learned to take what she wanted to give him, the knowledge of who his wife had been. His mother wanted to share all she could with him of the joy she had had in Emdu, her beloved child and friend. Even his father, retired now, a quenched, silent man, was able to say, "She was the light of the house." They were thanking him for her. They were telling him that it had not all been a waste.

But what lay ahead of them? Old age, the empty house. They did not complain, of course, and seemed content in their severe, placid round of daily work; but for them the continuity of the past with the future was broken.

"I should remarry," Teyeo said to his mother. "Is there anyone you've noticed . . . ?"

It was raining, a grey light through the wet windows, a soft thrumming on the eaves. His mother's face was indistinct as she bent to her mending.

"No," she said. "Not really." She looked up at him, and after a pause asked, "Where do you think you'll be posted?"

"I don't know."

"There's no war now," she said, in her soft, even voice.

"No," Teyeo said. "There's no war."

"Will there be . . . ever? do you think?"

He stood up, walked down the room and back, sat down again on the cushioned platform near her; they both sat straight-backed, still except for the slight motion of her hands as she sewed; his hands lay lightly one in the other, as he had been taught when he was two.

"I don't know," he said. "It's strange. It's as if there hadn't been a war. As if we'd never been on Yeowe—the Colony, the Uprising, all of it. They don't talk about it. It didn't happen. We don't fight wars. This is a new age. They say that often on the net. The age of peace, brotherhood across the stars. So, are we brothers with Yeowe, now? Are we brothers with Gatay and Bambur and the Forty States? Are we brothers with our assets? I can't make sense of it. I don't know what they mean. I don't know where I fit in." His voice too was quiet and even.

"Not here, I think," she said. "Not yet."

After a while he said, "I thought . . . children . . ."

"Of course. When the time comes." She smiled at him. "You never could sit still for half an hour. . . . Wait. Wait and see."

She was right, of course; and yet what he saw in the net and in town tried his patience and his pride. It seemed that to be a soldier now was a disgrace. Government reports, the news and the analyses, constantly referred to the Army and particularly the veot class as fossils, costly and useless, Voe Deo's principal obstacle to full admission to the Ekumen. His own uselessness was made clear to him when his request for a posting was met by an indefinite extension of his leave on half pay. At thirty-two, they appeared to be telling him, he was superannuated.

Again he suggested to his mother that he should accept the situation, settle down, and look for a wife. "Talk to your father," she said. He did so; his father said, "Of course your help is welcome, but I can run the farm well enough for a while yet.

Your mother thinks you should go to the capital, to Command. They can't ignore you if you're there. After all. After seven years' combat—your record—"

Teyeo knew what that was worth, now. But he was certainly not needed here, and probably irritated his father with his ideas of changing this or that way things were done. They were right: he should go to the capital and find out for himself what part he could play in the new world of peace.

His first half-year there was grim. He knew almost no one at Command or in the barracks; his generation was dead, or invalided out, or home on half pay. The younger officers, who had not been on Yeowe, seemed to him a cold, buttoned-up lot, always talking money and politics. Little businessmen, he privately thought them. He knew they were afraid of him—of his record, of his reputation. Whether he wanted to or not he reminded them that there had been a war that Werel had fought and lost, a civil war, their own race fighting against itself, class against class. They wanted to dismiss it as a meaningless quarrel on another world, nothing to do with them.

Teyeo walked the streets of the capital, watched the thousands of bondsmen and bondswomen hurrying about their owners' business, and wondered what they were waiting for.

"The Ekumen does not interfere with the social, cultural, or economic arrangements and affairs of any people," the Embassy and the government spokesmen repeated. "Full membership for any nation or people that wishes it is contingent only on absence, or renunciation, of certain specific methods and devices of warfare," and there followed the list of terrible weapons, most of them mere names to Teyeo, but a few of them inventions of his own country: the biobomb, as they called it, and the neuronics.

He personally agreed with the Ekumen's judgment on such devices, and respected their patience in waiting for Voe Deo and the rest of Werel to prove not only compliance with the ban, but acceptance of the principle. But he very deeply resented their condescension. They sat in judgment on everything Werelian, viewing from above. The less they said about the division of classes, the clearer their disapproval was. "Slavery is of very rare occurrence in Ekumenical worlds," said their books, "and disappears completely with full participation in the Ekumenical polity." Was that what the Alien Embassy was really waiting for?

"By our Lady!" said one of the young officers—many of them were Tualites, as well as businessmen—"the Aliens are going to admit the dusties before they admit us!" He was sputtering with indignant rage, like a red-faced old rega faced with an insolent bondsoldier. "Yeowe—a damned planet of savages, tribesmen, regressed into barbarism—preferred over us!"

"They fought well," Teyeo observed, knowing he should not say it as he said it, but not liking to hear the men and women he had fought against called dusties. Assets, rebels, enemies, yes.

The young man stared at him and after a moment said, "I suppose you love 'em, eh? The dusties?"

"I killed as many as I could," Teyeo replied politely, and then changed the conversation. The young man, though nominally Teyeo's superior at Command, was an oga, the lowest rank of veot, and to snub him further would be ill-bred.

They were stuffy, he was touchy; the old days of cheerful good fellowship were a faint, incredible memory. The bureau chiefs at Command listened to his request to be put back on active service and sent him endlessly on to another department. He could not live in barracks, but had to find an apartment, like a civilian. His half pay did not permit him indulgence in the expensive pleasures of the city. While waiting for appointments to see this or that official, he spent his days in the library net of the Officers' Academy. He knew his education had been incomplete and was out of date. If his country was going to join the Ekumen, in order to be useful he must know more about the Alien ways of thinking and the new technologies. Not sure what he needed to know, he floundered about in the network, bewildered by the endless information available, increasingly aware that he was no intellectual and no scholar and would never understand Alien minds, but doggedly driving himself on out of his depth.

A man from the Embassy was offering an introductory course in Ekumenical history in the public net. Teyeo joined it, and sat through eight or ten lecture-and-discussion periods, straight-backed and still, only his hands moving slightly as he took full and methodical notes. The lecturer, a Hainishman who translated his extremely long Hainish name as Old Music, watched Teyeo, tried to draw him out in discussion, and at last asked him to stay in after session. "I should like to meet you, Rega," he said, when the others had dropped out.

They met at a café. They met again. Teyeo did not like the Alien's manners, which he found effusive; he did not trust his quick, clever mind; he felt Old Music was using him, studying him as a specimen of The Veot, The Soldier, probably The Barbarian. The Alien, secure in his superiority, was indifferent to Teyeo's coldness, ignored his distrust, insisted on helping him with information and guidance, and shamelessly repeated questions Teyeo had avoided answering. One of these was, "Why are you sitting around here on half pay?"

"It's not by my own choice, Mr. Old Music," Teyeo finally answered, the third time it was asked. He was very angry at the man's impudence, and so spoke with particular mildness. He kept his eyes away from Old Music's eyes, bluish, with the whites showing like a scared horse. He could not get used to Aliens' eyes.

"They won't put you back on active service?"

Teyeo assented politely. Could the man, however alien, really be oblivious to the fact that his questions were grossly humiliating?

"Would you be willing to serve in the Embassy Guard?"

That question left Teyeo speechless for a moment; then he committed the extreme rudeness of answering a question with a question. "Why do you ask?"

"I'd like very much to have a man of your capacity in that corps," said Old Music, adding with his appalling candor, "Most of them are spies or blockheads. It would be wonderful to have a man I knew was neither. It's not just sentry duty, you know. I imagine you'd be asked by your government to give information; that's to be expected. And we would use you, once you had experience and if you were willing, as a liaison officer. Here or in other countries. We would not, however, ask you to give information to us. Am I clear, Teyeo? I want no misunderstanding between us as to what I am and am not asking of you."

"You would be able . . . ?" Teyeo asked cautiously.

Old Music laughed and said, "Yes. I have a string to pull in your Command. A favor owed. Will you think it over?"

Teyeo was silent a minute. He had been nearly a year now in the capital and his requests for posting had met only bureaucratic evasion and, recently, hints that they were considered insubordinate. "I'll accept now, if I may," he said, with a cold deference.

The Hainishman looked at him, his smile changing to a thoughtful, steady gaze. "Thank you," he said. "You should hear from Command in a few days."

So Teyeo put his uniform back on, moved back to the City Barracks, and served for another seven years on alien ground. The Ekumenical Embassy was, by diplomatic agreement, a part not of Werel but of the Ekumen—a piece of the planet that no longer belonged to it. The Guardsmen furnished by Voe Deo were protective and decorative, a highly visible presence on the Embassy grounds in their white-and-gold dress uniform. They were also visibly armed, since protest against the Alien presence still broke out erratically in violence.

Rega Teyeo, at first assigned to command a troop of these guards, soon was transferred to a different duty, that of accompanying members of the Embassy staff about the city and on journeys. He served as a bodyguard, in undress uniform. The Embassy much preferred not to use their own people and weapons, but to request and trust Voe Deo to protect them. Often he was also called upon to be a guide and interpreter, and sometimes a companion. He did not like it when visitors from somewhere in space wanted to be chummy and confiding, asked him about himself, invited him to come drinking with them. With perfectly concealed distaste, with perfect civility, he refused such offers. He did his job and kept his distance. He knew that that was precisely what the Embassy valued him for. Their confidence in him gave him a cold satisfaction.

His own government had never approached him to give information, though he certainly learned things that would have interested them. Voe Dean intelligence did not recruit their agents among veots. He knew who the agents in the Embassy Guard were; some of them tried to get information from him, but he had no intention of spying for spies.

Old Music, whom he now surmised to be the head of the

Embassy's intelligence system, called him in on his return from a winter leave at home. The Hainishman had learned not to make emotional demands on Teyeo, but could not hide a note of affection in his voice greeting him. "Hullo, Rega! I hope your family's well? Good. I've got a particularly tricky job for you. Kingdom of Gatay. You were there with Kemehan two years ago, weren't you? Well, now they want us to send an Envoy. They say they want to join. Of course the old King's a puppet of your government; but there's a lot else going on there. A strong religious separatist movement. A Patriotic Cause, kick out all the foreigners, Voe Deans and Aliens alike. But the King and Council requested an Envoy, and all we've got to send them is a new arrival. She may give you some problems till she learns the ropes. I judge her a bit headstrong. Excellent material, but young, very young. And she's only been here a few weeks. I requested you, because she needs your experience. Be patient with her, Rega. I think you'll find her likable."

He did not. In seven years he had got accustomed to the Aliens' eyes and their various smells and colors and manners. Protected by his flawless courtesy and his stoical code, he endured or ignored their strange or shocking or troubling behavior, their ignorance and their different knowledge. Serving and protecting the foreigners entrusted to him, he kept himself aloof from them, neither touched nor touching. His charges learned to count on him and not to presume on him. Women were often quicker to see and respond to his Keep Out signs than men; he had an easy, almost friendly relationship with an old Terran Observer whom he had accompanied on several long investigatory tours. "You are as peaceful to be with as a cat, Rega," she told him once, and he valued the compliment. But the Envoy to Gatay was another matter.

She was physically splendid, with clear red-brown skin like that of a baby, glossy swinging hair, a free walk—too free: she flaunted her ripe, slender body at men who had no access to it, thrusting it at him, at everyone, insistent, shameless. She expressed her opinion on everything with coarse self-confidence. She could not hear a hint and refused to take an order. She was an aggressive, spoiled child with the sexuality of an adult, given the responsibility of a diplomat in a dangerously unstable country. Teyeo knew as soon as he met her that this was an impossible assignment. He could not trust her or himself. Her sexual immodesty aroused him as it disgusted him; she was a whore whom he must treat as a princess. Forced to endure and unable to ignore her, he hated her.

He was more familiar with anger than he had used to be, but not used to hating. It troubled him extremely. He had never in his life asked for a reposting, but on the morning after she had taken the makil into her room, he sent a stiff little appeal to the Embassy. Old Music responded to him with a sealed voice-message through the diplomatic link: "Love of god and country is like fire, a wonderful friend, a terrible enemy; only children play with fire. I don't like the situation. There's nobody here I can replace either of you with. Will you hang on a while longer?"

He did not know how to refuse. A veot did not refuse duty. He was ashamed at having even thought of doing so, and hated her again for causing him that shame.

The first sentence of the message was enigmatic, not in Old Music's usual style but flowery, indirect, like a coded warning. Teyeo of course knew none of the intelligence codes either of his country or of the Ekumen. Old Music would have to use hints and indirection with him. "Love of god and country" could well mean the Old Believers and the Patriots, the two subversive groups in Gatay, both of them fanatically opposed to foreign influence; the Envoy could be the child playing with fire. Was she being approached by one group or the other? He had seen no evidence of it, unless the man in the shadows that night had been not a knifeman but a messenger. She was under his eyes all day, her house watched all night by soldiers under his command. Surely the makil, Batikam, was not acting for either of those groups. He might well be a member of the Hame, the asset liberation underground of Voe Deo, but as such would not endanger the Envoy, since the Hame saw the Ekumen as their ticket to Yeowe and to freedom.

Teyeo puzzled over the words, replaying them over and over, knowing his own stupidity faced with this kind of subtlety, the ins and outs of the political labyrinth. At last he erased the message and yawned, for it was late; bathed, lay down, turned off the light, said under his breath, "Lord Kamye, let me hold with courage to the one noble thing!" and slept like a stone.

The makil came to her house every night after the theater. Teyeo tried to tell himself there was nothing wrong in it. He himself had spent nights with the makils, back in the palmy days before the war. Expert, artistic sex was part of their business. He knew by hearsay that rich city women often hired them to come supply a husband's deficiencies. But even such women did so secretly, discreetly, not in this vulgar, shameless way, utterly careless of decency, flouting the moral code, as if she had some kind of right to do whatever she wanted wherever and whenever she wanted it. Of course Batikam colluded eagerly with her, playing on her infatuation, mocking the Gatayans, mocking Teyeo—and mocking her, though she didn't know it. What a chance for an asset to make fools of all the owners at once!

Watching Batikam, Teyeo felt sure he was a member of the Hame. His mockery was very subtle; he was not trying to disgrace the Envoy. Indeed his discretion was far greater than hers. He was trying to keep her from disgracing herself. The makil returned Teyeo's cold courtesy in kind, but once or twice their eyes met and some brief, involuntary understanding passed between them, fraternal, ironic.

There was to be a public festival, an observation of the Tualite Feast of Forgiveness, to which the Envoy was pressingly invited by the King and Council. She was put on show at many such events. Teyeo thought nothing about it except how to provide security in an excited holiday crowd, until San told him that the festival day was the highest holy day of the old religion of Gatay, and that the Old Believers fiercely resented the imposition of the foreign rites over their own. The little man seemed genuinely worried. Teyeo worried too when next day San was suddenly replaced by an elderly man who spoke little but Gatayan and was quite unable to explain what had become of San Ubattat. "Other duties, other duties call," he said in very bad Voe Dean, smiling and bobbing, "very great relishes time, aha? Relishes duties call."

During the days that preceded the festival tension rose in

the city; graffiti appeared, symbols of the old religion smeared across walls; a Tualite temple was desecrated, after which the Royal Guard was much in evidence in the streets. Teyeo went to the palace and requested, on his own authority, that the Envoy not be asked to appear in public during a ceremony that was "likely to be troubled by inappropriate demonstrations." He was called in and treated by a Court official with a mixture of dismissive insolence and conniving nods and winks, which left him really uneasy. He left four men on duty at the Envoy's house that night. Returning to his quarters, a little barracks down the street which had been handed over to the Embassy Guard, he found the window of his room open and a scrap of writing, in his own language, on his table: *Fest F is set up for assasnation.*

He was at the Envoy's house promptly the next morning and asked her asset to tell her he must speak to her. She came out of her bedroom pulling a white wrap around her naked body. Batikam followed her, half-dressed, sleepy, and amused. Teyeo gave him the eye-signal *go*, which he received with a serene, patronising smile, murmuring to the woman, "I'll go have some breakfast. Rewe? have you got something to feed me?" He followed the bondswoman out of the room. Teyeo faced the Envoy and held out the scrap of paper.

"I received this last night, ma'am," he said. "I must ask you not to attend the festival tomorrow."

She considered the paper, read the writing, and yawned. "Who's it from?"

"I don't know, ma'am."

"What's it mean? *Assassination?* They can't spell, can they?"

After a moment, he said, "There are a number of other indications—enough that I must ask you—"

"Not to attend the festival of Forgiveness, yes. I heard you." She went to a window seat and sat down, her robe falling wide to reveal her legs; her bare, brown feet were short and supple, the soles pink, the toes small and orderly. Teyeo looked fixedly at the air beside her head. She twiddled the bit of paper. "If you think it's dangerous, Rega, bring a guardsman or two with you," she said, with the faintest tone of scorn. "I really have to be there. The King requested it, you know. And I'm to light the big fire, or something. One of the few things women are allowed to do in public here. . . . I can't back out of it." She held out the paper, and after a moment he came close enough to take it. She looked up at him smiling; when she defeated him she always smiled at him. "Who do you think would want to blow me away, anyhow? The Patriots?"

"Or the Old Believers, ma'am. Tomorrow is one of their holidays."

"And your Tualites have taken it away from them? Well, they can't exactly blame the Ekumen, can they?"

"I think it possible that the government might permit violence in order to excuse retaliation, ma'am."

She started to answer carelessly, realised what he had said, and frowned. "You think the Council's setting me up? What evidence have you?"

After a pause he said, "Very little, ma'am. San Ubattat—"

"San's been ill. The old fellow they sent isn't much use, but he's scarcely dangerous! Is that all?" He said nothing, and she went on, "Until you have real evidence, Rega, don't interfere with my obligations. Your militaristic paranoia isn't acceptable when it spreads to the people I'm dealing with here. Control it, please! I'll expect an extra guardsman or two tomorrow; and that's enough."

"Yes, ma'am," he said, and went out. His head sang with anger. It occurred to him now that her new guide had told him San Ubattat had been kept away by religious duties, not by illness. He did not turn back. What was the use? "Stay on for an hour or so, will you, Seyem?" he said to the guard at her gate, and strode off down the street, trying to walk away from her, from her soft brown thighs and the pink soles of her feet and her stupid, insolent, whorish voice giving him orders. He tried to let the bright icy sunlit air, the stepped streets snapping with banners for the festival, the glitter of the great mountains and the clamor of the markets fill him, dazzle and distract him; but he walked seeing his own shadow fall in front of him like a knife across the stones, knowing the futility of his life.

"The veot looked worried," Batikam said in his velvet voice, and she laughed, spearing a preserved fruit from the dish and popping it, dripping, into his mouth.

"I'm ready for breakfast now, Rewe," she called, and sat

down across from Batikam. "I'm starving! He was having one of his phallocratic fits. He hasn't saved me from anything lately. It's his only function, after all. So he has to invent occasions. I wish, I wish he was out of my hair. It's so nice not to have poor little old San crawling around like some kind of pubic infestation. If only I could get rid of the Major now!"

"He's a man of honor," the makil said; his tone did not seem ironical.

"How can an owner of slaves be an honorable man?"

Batikam watched her from his long, dark eyes. She could not read Werelian eyes, beautiful as they were, filling their lids with darkness.

"Male hierarchy members always yatter about their precious honor," she said. "And 'their' women's honor, of course."

"Honor is a great privilege," Batikam said. "I envy it. I envy him."

"Oh, the hell with all that phony dignity, it's just pissing to mark your territory. All you need envy him, Batikam, is his freedom."

He smiled. "You're the only person I've ever known who was neither owned nor owner. That is freedom. *That* is freedom. I wonder if you know it?"

"Of course I do," she said. He smiled, and went on eating his breakfast, but there had been something in his voice she had not heard before. Moved and a little troubled, she said after a while, "You're going away soon."

"Mind reader. Yes. In ten days, the troupe goes on to tour the Forty States."

"Oh, Batikam, I'll miss you! You're the only man, the only person here I can talk to—let alone the sex—"

"Did we ever?"

"Not often," she said, laughing, but her voice shook a little. He held out his hand; she came to him and sat on his lap, the robe dropping open. "Little pretty Envoy breasts," he said, lipping and stroking, "little soft Envoy belly . . ." Rewe came in with a tray and softly set it down. "Eat your breakfast, little Envoy," Batikam said, and she disengaged herself and returned to her chair, grinning.

"Because you're free you can be honest," he said, fastidiously peeling a pini fruit. "Don't be too hard on those of us who aren't and can't." He cut a slice and fed it to her across the table. "It has been a taste of freedom to know you," he said. "A hint, a shadow . . ."

"In a few years at most, Batikam, you *will* be free. This whole idiotic structure of masters and slaves will collapse completely when Werel comes into the Ekumen."

"If it does."

"Of course it will."

He shrugged. "My home is Yeowe," he said.

She stared, confused. "You come from Yeowe?"

"I've never been there," he said. "I'll probably never go there. What use have they got for makils? But it is my home. Those are my people. That is my freedom. When will you see . . ." His fist was clenched; he opened it with a soft gesture of letting something go. He smiled and returned to his breakfast. "I've got to get back to the theater," he said. "We're rehearsing an act for the Day of Forgiveness."

She wasted all day at court. She had made persistent attempts to obtain permission to visit the mines and the huge government-run farms on the far side of the mountains, from which Gatay's wealth flowed. She had been as persistently foiled—by the protocol and bureaucracy of the government, she had thought at first, their unwillingness to let a diplomat do anything but run round to meaningless events; but some businessmen had let something slip about conditions in the mines and on the farms that made her think they might be hiding a more brutal kind of slavery than any visible in the capital. Today she got nowhere, waiting for appointments that had not been made. The old fellow who was standing in for San misunderstood most of what she said in Voe Dean, and when she tried to speak Gatayan he misunderstood it all, through stupidity or intent. The Major was blessedly absent most of the morning, replaced by one of his soldiers, but turned up at court, stiff and silent and set-jawed, and attended her until she gave up and went home for an early bath.

Batikam came late that night. In the middle of one of the elaborate fantasy games and role reversals she had learned from him and found so exciting, his caresses grew slower and slower, soft, dragging across her like feathers, so that she shivered with unappeased desire and, pressing her body against his, realised that he had gone to sleep. "Wake up," she said, laughing and yet chilled, and shook him a little. The dark eyes opened, bewildered, full of fear.

"I'm sorry," she said at once, "go back to sleep, you're tired. No, no, it's all right, it's late." But he went on with what she now, whatever his skill and tenderness, had to see was his job.

In the morning at breakfast she said, "Can you see me as an equal, do you, Batikam?"

He looked tired, older than he usually did. He did not smile. After a while he said, "What do you want me to say?"

"That you do."

"I do," he said quietly.

"You don't trust me," she said, bitter.

After a while he said, "This is Forgiveness Day. The Lady Tual came to the men of Asdok, who had set their hunting cats upon her followers. She came among them riding on a great hunting cat with a fiery tongue, and they fell down in terror, but she blessed them, forgiving them." His voice and hands enacted the story as he told it. "Forgive me," he said.

"You don't need any forgiveness!"

"Oh, we all do. It's why we Kamyites borrow the Lady Tual now and then. When we need her. So, today you'll be the Lady Tual, at the rites?"

"All I have to do is light a fire, they said," she said anxiously, and he laughed. When he left she told him she would come to the theater to see him, tonight, after the festival.

The horse-race course, the only flat area of any size anywhere near the city, was thronged, vendors calling, banners waving; the Royal motorcars drove straight into the crowd, which parted like water and closed behind. Some rickety-looking bleachers had been erected for lords and owners, with a curtained section for ladies. She saw a motorcar drive up to the bleachers; a figure swathed in red cloth was bundled out of it and hurried between the curtains, vanishing. Were there peepholes for them to watch the ceremony through? There were women in the crowds, but bondswomen only, assets. She realised that she, too, would be kept hidden until her moment of the ceremony arrived: a red tent awaited her, alongside the bleachers, not far from the roped enclosure where priests were chanting. She was rushed out of the car and into the tent by obsequious and determined courtiers.

Bondswomen in the tent offered her tea, sweets, mirrors, makeup, and hair oil, and helped her put on the complex swathing of fine red-and-yellow cloth, her costume for her brief enactment of Lady Tual. Nobody had told her very clearly what she was to do, and to her questions the women said, "The priests will show you, Lady, you just go with them. You just light the fire. They have it all ready." She had the impression that they knew no more than she did; they were pretty girls, court assets, excited at being part of the show, indifferent to the religion. She knew the symbolism of the fire she was to light: into it faults and transgressions could be cast and burnt up, forgotten. It was a nice idea.

The priests were whooping it up out there; she peeked out—there were indeed peepholes in the tent fabric—and saw the crowd had thickened. Nobody except in the bleachers and right against the enclosure ropes could possibly see anything, but everybody was waving red-and-yellow banners, munching fried food, and making a day of it, while the priests kept up their deep chanting. In the far right of the little, blurred field of vision through the peephole was a familiar arm: the Major's, of course. They had not let him get into the motorcar with her. He must have been furious. He had got here, though, and stationed himself on guard. "Lady, Lady," the court girls were saying, "here come the priests now," and they buzzed around her making sure her headdress was on straight and the damnable, hobbling skirts fell in the right folds. They were still plucking and patting as she stepped out of the tent, dazzled by the daylight, smiling and trying to hold herself very straight and dignified as a Goddess ought to do. She really didn't want to fuck up their ceremony.

Two men in priestly regalia were waiting for her right outside the tent door. They stepped forward immediately, taking her by the elbows and saying, "This way, this way, Lady." Evidently she really wouldn't have to figure out what to do. No doubt they considered women incapable of it, but in the circumstances it was a relief. The priests hurried her along faster than she could comfortably walk in the tight-drawn skirt. They were behind the bleachers now; wasn't the enclosure in the other direction? A car was coming straight at them, scattering the few people who were in its way. Somebody was shouting; the priests suddenly began yanking her, trying to run; one of them yelled and let go her arm, felled by a flying darkness that had hit him with a jolt—she was in the middle of a melee, unable to break the iron hold on her arm, her legs imprisoned in the skirt, and there was a noise, an enormous noise, that hit her head and bent it down, she couldn't see or hear, blinded, struggling, shoved face first into some dark place with her face pressed into a stifling, scratchy darkness and her arms held locked behind her.

A car, moving. A long time. Men, talking low. They talked in Gatayan. It was very hard to breathe. She did not struggle; it was no use. They had taped her arms and legs, bagged her head. After a long time she was hauled out like a corpse and carried quickly, indoors, down stairs, set down on a bed or couch, not roughly though with the same desperate haste. She lay still. The men talked, still almost in whispers. It made no sense to her. Her head was still hearing that enormous noise, had it been real? had she been struck? She felt deaf, as if inside a wall of cotton. The cloth of the bag kept getting stuck on her mouth, sucked against her nostrils as she tried to breathe.

It was plucked off; a man stooping over her turned her so he could untape her arms, then her legs, murmuring as he did so, "Don't to be scared, Lady, we don't to hurt you," in Voe Dean. He backed away from her quickly. There were four or five of them; it was hard to see, there was very little light. "To wait here," another said, "everything all right. Just to keep happy." She was trying to sit up, and it made her dizzy. When her head stopped spinning, they were all gone. As if by magic. Just to keep happy.

A small very high room. Dark brick walls, earthy air. The light was from a little biolume plaque stuck on the ceiling, a weak, shadowless glow. Probably quite sufficient for Werelian eyes. Just to keep happy. I have been kidnapped. How about that. She inventoried: the thick mattress she was on; a blanket; a door; a small pitcher and a cup; a drainhole, was it, over in the corner? She swung her legs off the mattress and her feet struck something lying on the floor at the foot of it—she coiled up, peered at the dark mass, the body lying there. A man. The uniform, the skin so black she could not see the features, but she knew him. Even here, even here, the Major was with her.

She stood up unsteadily and went to investigate the drainhole, which was simply that, a cement-lined hole in the floor, smelling slightly chemical, slightly foul. Her head hurt, and she sat down on the bed again to massage her arms and ankles, easing the tension and pain and getting herself back into herself by touching and confirming herself, rhythmically, methodically. I have been kidnapped. How about that. Just to keep happy. What about him?

Suddenly knowing that he was dead, she shuddered and held still.

After a while she leaned over slowly, trying to see his face, listening. Again she had the sense of being deaf. She heard no breath. She reached out, sick and shaking, and put the back of her hand against his face. It was cool, cold. But warmth breathed across her fingers, once, again. She crouched on the mattress and studied him. He lay absolutely still, but when she put her hand on his chest she felt the slow heartbeat.

"Teyeo," she said in a whisper. Her voice would not go above a whisper.

She put her hand on his chest again. She wanted to feel that slow, steady beat, the faint warmth; it was reassuring. Just to keep happy.

What else had they said? Just to wait. Yes. That seemed to be the program. Maybe she could sleep. Maybe she could sleep and when she woke up the ransom would have come. Or whatever it was they wanted.

She woke up with the thought that she still had her watch, and after sleepily studying the tiny silver readout for a while decided she had slept three hours; it was still the day of the Festival, too soon for ransom probably, and she wouldn't be able to go to the theater to see the makils tonight. Her eyes had grown accustomed to the low light and when she looked she could see, now, that there was dried blood all over one side of the man's head. Exploring, she found a hot lump like a fist above his temple, and her fingers came away smeared. He had got himself crowned. That must have been him, launching

himself at the priest, the fake priest, all she could remember
was a flying shadow and a hard thump and an ooof! like an aiji
attack, and then there had been the huge noise that confused
everything. She clicked her tongue, tapped the wall, to check
her hearing. It seemed to be all right; the wall of cotton had
disappeared. Maybe she had been crowned herself? She felt
her head, but found no lumps. The man must have a concussion, if he was still out after three hours. How bad? When
would the men come back?

She got up and nearly fell over, entangled in the damned
Goddess skirts. If only she was in her own clothes, not this
fancy dress, three pieces of flimsy stuff you had to have servants
to put on you! She got out of the skirt piece, and used the
scarf piece to make a kind of tied skirt that came to her knees.
It wasn't warm in this basement or whatever it was; it was dank
and rather cold. She walked up and down, four steps turn, four
steps turn, four steps turn, and did some warm-ups. They had
dumped the man onto the floor. How cold was it? Was shock
part of concussion? People in shock needed to be kept warm.
She dithered a long time, puzzled at her own indecision, at not
knowing what to do. Should she try to heave him up onto the
mattress? Was it better not to move him? Where the hell were
the men? Was he going to die?

She stooped over him and said sharply, "Rega! Teyeo!" and
after a moment he caught his breath.

"Wake up!" She remembered now, she thought she remembered, that it was important not to let concussed people lapse
into a coma. Except he already had.

He caught his breath again, and his face changed, came out
of the rigid immobility, softened; his eyes opened and closed,
blinked, unfocused. "Oh Kamye," he said very softly.

She couldn't believe how glad she was to see him. Just to
keep happy. He evidently had a blinding headache, and admitted that he was seeing double. She helped him haul himself up
onto the mattress and covered him with the blanket. He asked
no questions, and lay mute, lapsing back to sleep soon. Once
he was settled she went back to her exercises, and did an hour
of them. She looked at her watch. It was two hours later, the
same day, the Festival day. It wasn't evening yet. When were
the men going to come?

They came early in the morning, after the endless night that was the same as the afternoon and the morning. The metal door was unlocked and thrown clanging open, and one of them came in with a tray while two of them stood with raised, aimed guns in the doorway. There was nowhere to put the tray but the floor, so he shoved it at Solly, said, "Sorry, Lady!" and backed out; the door clanged shut, the bolts banged home. She stood holding the tray. "Wait!" she said.

The man had waked up and was looking groggily around. After finding him in this place with her she had somehow lost his nickname, did not think of him as the Major, yet shied away from his name. "Here's breakfast, I guess," she said, and sat down on the edge of the mattress. A cloth was thrown over the wicker tray; under it was a pile of Gatayan grainrolls stuffed with meat and greens, several pieces of fruit, and a capped water carafe of thin, fancily beaded metal alloy. "Breakfast, lunch, and dinner, maybe," she said. "Shit. Oh well. It looks good. Can you eat? Can you sit up?"

He worked himself up to sit with his back against the wall, and then shut his eyes.

"You're still seeing double?"

He made a small noise of assent.

"Are you thirsty?"

Small noise of assent.

"Here." She passed him the cup. By holding it in both hands he got it to his mouth, and drank the water slowly, a swallow at a time. She meanwhile devoured three grainrolls one after the other, then forced herself to stop, and ate a pini fruit. "Could you eat some fruit?" she asked him, feeling guilty. He did not answer. She thought of Batikam feeding her the slice of pini at breakfast, when, yesterday, a hundred years ago.

The food in her stomach made her feel sick. She took the cup from the man's relaxed hand—he was asleep again—and poured herself water, and drank it slowly, a swallow at a time.

When she felt better she went to the door and explored its hinges, lock, and surface. She felt and peered around the brick walls, the poured concrete floor, seeking she knew not what, something to escape with, something. . . . She should do exercises. She forced herself to do some, but the queasiness returned, and a lethargy with it. She went back to the mattress and sat down. After a while she found she was crying. After a while she found she had been asleep. She needed to piss. She squatted over the hole and listened to her urine fall into it. There was nothing to clean herself with. She came back to the bed and sat down on it, stretching out her legs, holding her ankles in her hands. It was utterly silent.

She turned to look at the man; he was watching her. It made her start. He looked away at once. He still lay half-propped up against the wall, uncomfortably, but relaxed.

"Are you thirsty?" she asked.

"Thank you," he said. Here where nothing was familiar and time was broken off from the past, his soft, light voice was welcome in its familiarity. She poured him a cup full and gave it to him. He managed it much more steadily, sitting up to drink. "Thank you," he whispered again, giving her back the cup.

"How's your head?"

He put up his hand to the swelling, winced, and sat back.

"One of them had a stick," she said, seeing it in a flash in the jumble of her memories—"a priest's staff. You jumped the other one."

"They took my gun," he said. "Festival." He kept his eyes closed.

"I got tangled in those damn clothes. I couldn't help you at all. Listen. Was there a noise, an explosion?"

"Yes. Diversion, maybe."

"Who do you think these boys are?"

"Revolutionaries. Or . . ."

"You said you thought the Gatayan government was in on it."

"I don't know," he murmured.

"You were right, I was wrong, I'm sorry," she said with a sense of virtue at remembering to make amends.

He moved his hand very slightly in an it-doesn't-matter gesture.

"Are you still seeing double?"

He did not answer; he was phasing out again.

She was standing, trying to remember Selish breathing exercises, when the door crashed and clanged, and the same three men were there, two with guns, all young, black-skinned, short-haired, very nervous. The lead one stooped to set a tray down on the floor, and without the least premeditation Solly stepped on his hand and brought her weight down on it. "You wait!" she said. She was staring straight into the faces and gun muzzles of the other two. "Just wait a moment, listen! He has a head injury, we need a doctor, we need more water, I can't even clean his wound, there's no toilet paper, who the hell are you people anyway?"

The one she had stomped was shouting, "Get off! Lady to get off my hand!" but the others heard her. She lifted her foot and got out of his way as he came up fast, backing into his buddies with the guns. "All right, Lady, we are sorry to have trouble," he said, tears in his eyes, cradling his hand. "We are Patriots. You send messish to this Pretender, like our messish. Nobody is to hurt. All right?" He kept backing up, and one of the gunmen swung the door to. Crash, rattle.

She drew a deep breath and turned. Teyeo was watching her. "That was dangerous," he said, smiling very slightly.

"I know it was," she said, breathing hard. "It was stupid. I can't get hold of myself. I feel like pieces of me. But they shove stuff in and run, damn it! We have to have some water!" She was in tears, the way she always was for a moment after violence or a quarrel. "Let's see, what have they brought this time." She lifted the tray up onto the mattress; like the other, in a ridiculous semblance of service in a hotel or a house with slaves, it was covered with a cloth. "All the comforts," she murmured. Under the cloth was a heap of sweet pastries, a little plastic hand mirror, a comb, a tiny pot of something that smelled like decayed flowers, and a box of what she identified after a while as Gatayan tampons.

"It's things for the lady," she said, "God damn them, the stupid Goddamn pricks! A mirror!" She flung the thing across the room. "Of course I can't last a day without looking in the mirror! God *damn* them!" She flung everything else but the pastries after the mirror, knowing as she did so that she would pick up the tampons and keep them under the mattress and, oh, God forbid, use them if she had to, if they had to stay here, how long would it be? ten days or more— "Oh, God," she said again. She got up and picked everything up, put the mirror and the little pot, the empty water jug and the fruit skins from the last meal, onto one of the trays and set it beside the door.

"Garbage," she said in Voe Dean. Her outburst, she realised, had been in another language; Alterran, probably. "Have you any idea," she said, sitting down on the mattress again, "how hard you people make it to be a woman? You could turn a woman against being one!"

"I think they meant well," Teyeo said. She realised that there was not the faintest shade of mockery, even of amusement in his voice. If he was enjoying her shame, he was ashamed to show her that he was. "I think they're amateurs," he said.

After a while she said, "That could be bad."

"It might." He had sat up and was gingerly feeling the knot on his head. His coarse, heavy hair was blood-caked all around it. "Kidnapping," he said. "Ransom demands. Not assassins. They didn't have guns. Couldn't have got in with guns. I had to give up mine."

"You mean these aren't the ones you were warned about?"

"I don't know." His explorations caused him a shiver of pain, and he desisted. "Are we very short of water?"

She brought him another cupful. "Too short for washing. A stupid Goddamn mirror when what we need is water!"

He thanked her and drank and sat back, nursing the last swallows in the cup. "They didn't plan to take me," he said.

She thought about it and nodded. "Afraid you'd identify them?"

"If they had a place for me, they wouldn't put me in with a lady." He spoke without irony. "They had this ready for you. It must be somewhere in the city."

She nodded. "The car ride was half an hour or less. My head was in a bag, though."

"They've sent a message to the Palace. They got no reply, or an unsatisfactory one. They want a message from you."

"To convince the government they really have me? Why do they need convincing?"

They were both silent.

"I'm sorry," he said, "I can't think." He lay back. Feeling tired, low, edgy after her adrenaline rush, she lay down alongside him. She had rolled up the Goddess's skirt to make a pillow; he had none. The blanket lay across their legs.

"Pillow," she said. "More blankets. Soap. What else?"

"Key," he murmured.

They lay side by side in the silence and the faint unvarying light.

Next morning about eight, according to Solly's watch, the Patriots came into the room, four of them. Two stood on guard at the door with their guns ready; the other two stood uncomfortably in what floor space was left, looking down at their captives, both of whom sat cross-legged on the mattress. The new spokesman spoke better Voe Dean than the others. He said they were very sorry to cause the lady discomfort and would do what they could to make it comfortable for her, and she must be patient and write a message by hand to the Pretender King, explaining that she would be set free unharmed as soon as the King commanded the Council to rescind their treaty with Voe Deo.

"He won't," she said. "They won't let him."

"Please do not discuss," the man said with frantic harshness. "This is writing materials. This is the message." He set the papers and a stylo down on the mattress, nervously, as if afraid to get close to her.

She was aware of how Teyeo effaced himself, sitting without a motion, his head lowered, his eyes lowered; the men ignored him.

"If I write this for you, I want water, a lot of water, and soap and blankets and toilet paper and pillows and a doctor, and I want somebody to come when I knock on that door, and I want some decent clothes. Warm clothes. Men's clothes."

"No doctor!" the man said. "Write it! Please! Now!" He was jumpy, twitchy, she dared push him no further. She read their statement, copied it out in her large, childish scrawl—she seldom handwrote anything—and handed both to the spokesman. He glanced over it and without a word hurried the other men out. Clash went the door.

"Should I have refused?"

"I don't think so," Teyeo said. He stood up and stretched, but sat down again looking dizzy. "You bargain well," he said.

"We'll see what we get. Oh, God. What is going *on*?"

"Maybe," he said slowly, "Gatay is unwilling to yield to these demands. But when Voe Deo—and your Ekumen—get word of it, they'll put pressure on Gatay."

"I wish they'd get moving. I suppose Gatay is horribly embarrassed, saving face by trying to conceal the whole thing—is that likely? How long can they keep it up? What about your people? Won't they be hunting for you?"

"No doubt," he said, in his polite way.

It was curious how his stiff manner, his manners, which had always shunted her aside, cut her out, here had quite another effect: his restraint and formality reassured her that she was still part of the world outside this room, from which they came and to which they would return, a world where people lived long lives.

What did long life matter? she asked herself, and didn't know. It was nothing she had ever thought about before. But these young Patriots lived in a world of short lives. Demands, violence, immediacy, and death, for what? for a bigotry, a hatred, a rush of power.

"Whenever they leave," she said in a low voice, "I get really frightened."

Teyeo cleared his throat and said, "So do I."

Exercises.

"Take hold—no, take *hold*, I'm not made of glass!—Now—"

"Ha!" he said, with his flashing grin of excitement, as she showed him the break, and he in turn repeated it, breaking from her.

"All right, now you'd be waiting—here"—thump—"see?"

"Ai!"

"I'm sorry— I'm sorry, Teyeo— I didn't think about your head— Are you all right? I'm really sorry—"

"Oh, Kamye," he said, sitting up and holding his black, narrow head between his hands. He drew several deep breaths. She knelt penitent and anxious.

"That's," he said, and breathed some more, "that's not, not fair play."

"No of course it's not, it's aiji—all's fair in love and war, they say that on Terra— Really, I'm sorry, I'm terribly sorry, that was so stupid of me!"

He laughed, a kind of broken and desperate laugh, shook his head, shook it again. "Show me," he said. "I don't know what you did."

*

Exercises.

"What do you do with your mind?"

"Nothing."

"You just let it wander?"

"No. Am I and my mind different beings?"

"So . . . you don't focus on something? You just wander with it?"

"No."

"So you *don't* let it wander."

"Who?" he said, rather testily.

A pause.

"Do you think about—"

"No," he said. "Be still."

A very long pause, maybe a quarter hour.

"Teyeo, I can't. I itch. My mind itches. How long have you been doing this?"

A pause, a reluctant answer: "Since I was two."

He broke his utterly relaxed motionless pose, bent his head to stretch his neck and shoulder muscles. She watched him.

"I keep thinking about long life, about living long," she said. "I don't mean just being alive a long time, hell, I've been alive about eleven hundred years, what does that mean, nothing. I mean . . . Something about thinking of life as long makes a difference. Like having kids does. Even thinking about having kids. It's like it changes some balance. It's funny I keep thinking about that now, when my chances for a long life have kind of taken a steep fall. . . ."

He said nothing. He was able to say nothing in a way that allowed her to go on talking. He was one of the least talkative men she had ever known. Most men were so wordy. She was fairly wordy herself. He was quiet. She wished she knew how to be quiet.

"It's just practice, isn't it?" she asked. "Just sitting there."

He nodded.

"Years and years and years of practice. . . . Oh, God. Maybe . . ."

"No, no," he said, taking her thought immediately.

"But why don't they *do* something? What are they *waiting* for? It's been nine *days*!"

*

From the beginning, by unplanned, unspoken agreement, the room had been divided in two: the line ran down the middle of the mattress and across to the facing wall. The door was on her side, the left; the shit-hole was on his side, the right. Any invasion of the other's space was requested by some almost invisible cue and permitted the same way. When one of them used the shit-hole the other unobtrusively faced away. When they had enough water to take cat-baths, which was seldom, the same arrangement held. The line down the middle of the mattress was absolute. Their voices crossed it, and the sounds and smells of their bodies. Sometimes she felt his warmth; Werelian body temperature was somewhat higher than hers, and in the dank, still air she felt that faint radiance as he slept. But they never crossed the line, not by a finger, not in the deepest sleep.

Solly thought about this, finding it, in some moments, quite funny. At other moments it seemed stupid and perverse. Couldn't they both use some human comfort? The only time she had touched him was the first day, when she had helped him get onto the mattress, and then when they had enough water she had cleaned his scalp wound and little by little washed the clotted, stinking blood out of his hair, using the comb, which had after all been a good thing to have, and pieces of the Goddess's skirt, an invaluable source of wash-cloths and bandages. Then once his head healed, they practiced aiji daily; but aiji had an impersonal, ritual purity to its clasps and grips that was a long way from creature comfort. The rest of the time his bodily presence was clearly, invariably uninva-sive and untouchable.

He was only maintaining, under incredibly difficult circum-stances, the rigid restraint he had always shown. Not just he, but Rewe, too; all of them, all of them but Batikam; and yet was Batikam's instant yielding to her whim and desire the true contact she had thought it? She thought of the fear in his eyes, that last night. Not restraint, but constraint.

It was the mentality of a slave society: slaves and masters caught in the same trap of radical distrust and self-protection.

"Teyeo," she said, "I don't understand slavery. Let me say what I mean," though he had shown no sign of interruption or protest, merely civil attention. "I mean, I do understand how a social institution comes about and how an individual is simply part of it—I'm not saying why don't you agree with me in seeing it as wicked and unprofitable, I'm not asking you to defend it or renounce it. I'm trying to understand what it feels like to believe that two-thirds of the human beings in your world are actually, rightfully your property. Five-sixths, in fact, including women of your caste."

After a while he said, "My family owns about twenty-five assets."

"Don't quibble."

He accepted the reproof.

"It seems to me that you cut off human contact. You don't touch slaves and slaves don't touch you, in the way human beings ought to touch, in mutuality. You have to keep yourselves separate, always working to maintain that boundary. Because it isn't a natural boundary—it's totally artificial, man-made. I can't tell owners and assets apart physically. Can you?"

"Mostly."

"By cultural, behavioral clues—right?"

After thinking a while, he nodded.

"You are the same species, race, people, exactly the same in every way, with a slight selection towards color. If you brought up an asset child as an owner it would *be* an owner in every respect, and vice versa. So you spend your lives keeping up this tremendous division that doesn't exist. What I don't understand is how you can fail to see how appallingly wasteful it is. I don't mean economically!"

"In the war," he said, and then there was a very long pause; though Solly had a lot more to say, she waited, curious. "I was on Yeowe," he said, "you know, in the civil war."

That's where you got all those scars and dents, she thought; for however scrupulously she averted her eyes, it was impossible not to be familiar with his spare, onyx body by now, and she knew that in aiji he had to favor his left arm, which had a considerable chunk out of it just above the bicep.

"The slaves of the Colonies revolted, you know, some of them at first, then all of them. Nearly all. So we Army men there were all owners. We couldn't send asset soldiers, they might defect. We were all veots and volunteers. Owners fighting assets. I was fighting my equals. I learned that pretty soon. Later on I learned I was fighting my superiors. They defeated us."

"But that—" Solly said, and stopped; she did not know what to say.

"They defeated us from beginning to end," he said. "Partly because my government didn't understand that they could. That they fought better and harder and more intelligently and more bravely than we did."

"Because they were fighting for their freedom!"

"Maybe so," he said in his polite way.

"So . . ."

"I wanted to tell you that I respect the people I fought."

"I know so little about war, about fighting," she said, with a mixture of contrition and irritation. "Nothing, really. I was on Kheakh, but that wasn't war, it was racial suicide, mass slaughter of a biosphere. I guess there's a difference. . . . That was when the Ekumen finally decided on the Arms Convention, you know. Because of Orint and then Kheakh destroying themselves. The Terrans had been pushing for the Convention for ages. Having nearly committed suicide themselves a while back. I'm half-Terran. My ancestors rushed around their planet slaughtering each other. For millennia. They were masters and slaves, too, some of them, a lot of them. . . . But I don't know if the Arms Convention was a good idea. If it's right. Who are we to tell anybody what to do and not to do? The idea of the Ekumen was to offer a way. To open it. Not to bar it to anybody."

He listened intently, but said nothing until after some while. "We learn to . . . close ranks. Always. You're right, I think, it wastes . . . energy, the spirit. You are open."

His words cost him so much, she thought, not like hers that just came dancing out of the air and went back into it. He spoke from his marrow. It made what he said a solemn compliment, which she accepted gratefully, for as the days went on she realized occasionally how much confidence she had lost and kept losing: self-confidence, confidence that they would be ransomed, rescued, that they would get out of this room, that they would get out of it alive.

"Was the war very brutal?"

"Yes," he said. "I can't . . . I've never been able to—to see it— Only something comes like a flash—" He held his hands up as if to shield his eyes. Then he glanced at her, wary. His apparently cast-iron self-respect was, she knew now, vulnerable in many places.

"Things from Kheakh that I didn't even know I saw, they come that way," she said. "At night." And after a while, "How long were you there?"

"A little over seven years."

She winced. "Were you lucky?"

It was a queer question, not coming out the way she meant, but he took it at value. "Yes," he said. "Always. The men I went there with were killed. Most of them in the first few years. We lost three hundred thousand men on Yeowe. They never talk about it. Two-thirds of the veot men in Voe Deo were killed. If it was lucky to live, I was lucky." He looked down at his clasped hands, locked into himself.

After a while she said softly, "I hope you still are."

He said nothing.

"How long has it been?" he asked, and she said, clearing her throat, after an automatic glance at her watch, "Sixty hours."

Their captors had not come yesterday at what had become a regular time, about eight in the morning. Nor had they come this morning.

With nothing left to eat and now no water left, they had grown increasingly silent and inert. It was hours since either had said anything. He had put off asking the time as long as he could prevent himself.

"This is horrible," she said, "this is so horrible. I keep thinking . . ."

"They won't abandon you," he said. "They feel a responsibility."

"Because I'm a woman?"

"Partly."

"Shit."

He remembered that in the other life her coarseness had offended him.

"They've been taken, shot. Nobody bothered to find out where they were keeping us," she said.

Having thought the same thing several hundred times, he had nothing to say.

"It's just such a horrible *place* to die," she said. "It's sordid. I stink. I've stunk for twenty days. Now I have diarrhea because I'm scared. But I can't shit anything. I'm thirsty and I can't drink."

"Solly," he said sharply. It was the first time he had spoken her name. "Be still. Hold fast."

She stared at him.

"Hold fast to what?"

He did not answer at once and she said, "You won't let me touch you!"

"Not to me—"

"Then to what? There isn't anything!" He thought she was going to cry, but she stood up, took the empty tray, and beat it against the door till it smashed into fragments of wicker and dust. "Come! God damn you! Come, you bastards!" she shouted. "Let us out of here!"

After that she sat down again on the mattress. "Well," she said.

"Listen," he said.

They had heard it before: no city sounds came down to this cellar, wherever it was, but this was something bigger, explosions, they both thought.

The door rattled.

They were both afoot when it opened: not with the usual clash and clang, but slowly. A man waited outside; two men came in. One, armed, they had never seen; the other, the tough-faced young man they called the spokesman, looked as if he had been running or fighting, dusty, worn-out, a little dazed. He closed the door. He had some papers in his hand. The four of them stared at one another in silence for a minute.

"Water," Solly said. "You bastards!"

"Lady," the spokesman said, "I'm sorry." He was not listening to her. His eyes were not on her. He was looking at Teyeo, for the first time. "There is a lot of fighting," he said.

"Who's fighting?" Teyeo asked, hearing himself drop into the even tone of authority, and the young man respond to it as automatically: "Voe Deo. They sent troops. After the funeral, they said they would send troops unless we surrendered. They came yesterday. They go through the city killing. They know all the Old Believer centers. Some of ours." He had a bewildered, accusing note in his voice.

"What funeral?" Solly said.

When he did not answer, Teyeo repeated it: "What funeral?"

"The lady's funeral, yours. Here— I brought net prints— A state funeral. They said you died in the explosion."

"What Goddamned explosion?" Solly said in her hoarse, parched voice, and this time he answered her: "At the Festival. The Old Believers. The fire, Tual's fire, there were explosives in it. Only it went off too soon. We knew their plan. We rescued you from that, Lady," he said, suddenly turning to her with that same accusatory tone.

"Rescued me, you asshole!" she shouted, and Teyeo's dry lips split in a startled laugh, which he repressed at once.

"Give me those," he said, and the young man handed him the papers.

"Get us water!" Solly said.

"Stay here, please. We need to talk," Teyeo said, instinctively holding on to his ascendancy. He sat down on the mattress with the net prints. Within a few minutes he and Solly had scanned the reports of the shocking disruption of the Festival of Forgiveness, the lamentable death of the Envoy of the Ekumen in a terrorist act executed by the cult of Old Believers, the brief mention of the death of a Voe Dean Embassy guard in the explosion, which had killed over seventy priests and onlookers, the long descriptions of the state funeral, reports of unrest, terrorism, reprisals, then reports of the Palace gratefully accepting offers of assistance from Voe Deo in cleaning out the cancer of terrorism. . . .

"So," he said finally. "You never heard from the Palace. Why did you keep us alive?"

Solly looked as if she thought the question lacked tact, but the spokesman answered with equal bluntness, "We thought your country would ransom you."

"They will," Teyeo said. "Only you have to keep your government from knowing we're alive. If you—"

"Wait," Solly said, touching his hand. "Hold on. I want to think about this stuff. You'd better not leave the Ekumen out of the discussion. But getting in touch with them is the tricky bit."

"If there are Voe Dean troops here, all I need is to get a message to anyone in my command, or the Embassy Guards."

Her hand was still on his, with a warning pressure. She shook the other one at the spokesman, finger outstretched: "You kidnapped an Envoy of the Ekumen, you asshole! Now you have to do the thinking you didn't do ahead of time. And I do too, because I don't want to get blown away by your Goddamned little government for turning up alive and embarrassing them. Where are you hiding, anyhow? Is there any chance of us getting out of this room, at least?"

The man, with that edgy, frantic look, shook his head. "We are all down here now," he said. "Most of the time. You stay here safe."

"Yes, you'd better keep your passports safe!" Solly said. "Bring us some water, damn it! Let us talk a while. Come back in an hour."

The young man leaned towards her suddenly, his face contorted. "What the hell kind of lady you are," he said. "You foreign filthy stinking cunt."

Teyeo was on his feet, but her grip on his hand had tightened: after a moment of silence, the spokesman and the other man turned to the door, rattled the lock, and were let out.

"Ouf," she said, looking dazed.

"Don't," he said, "don't—" He did not know how to say it. "They don't understand," he said. "It's better if I talk."

"Of course. Women don't give orders. Women don't talk. Shitheads! I thought you said they felt so responsible for me!"

"They do," he said. "But they're young men. Fanatics. Very frightened." And you talk to them as if they were assets, he thought, but did not say.

"Well so am I frightened!" she said, with a little spurt of tears. She wiped her eyes and sat down again among the papers. "God," she said. "We've been dead for twenty days. Buried for fifteen. Who do you think they buried?"

Her grip was powerful; his wrist and hand hurt. He massaged the place gently, watching her.

"Thank you," he said. "I would have hit him."

"Oh, I know. Goddamn chivalry. And the one with the gun would have blown your head off. Listen, Teyeo. Are you sure all you have to do is get word to somebody in the Army or the Guard?"

"Yes, of course."

"You're sure your country isn't playing the same game as Gatay?"

He stared at her. As he understood her, slowly the anger he had stifled and denied, all these interminable days of imprisonment with her, rose in him, a fiery flood of resentment, hatred, and contempt.

He was unable to speak, afraid he would speak to her as the young Patriot had done.

He went around to his side of the room and sat on his side of the mattress, somewhat turned from her. He sat cross-legged, one hand lying lightly in the other.

She said some other things. He did not listen or reply.

After a while she said, "We're supposed to be talking, Teyeo. We've only got an hour. I think those kids might do what we tell them, if we tell them something plausible—something that'll work."

He would not answer. He bit his lip and held still.

"Teyeo, what did I say? I said something wrong. I don't know what it was. I'm sorry."

"They would—" He struggled to control his lips and voice. "They would not betray us."

"Who? The Patriots?"

He did not answer.

"Voe Deo, you mean? Wouldn't betray us?"

In the pause that followed her gentle, incredulous question, he knew that she was right; that it was all collusion among the powers of the world; that his loyalty to his country and service was wasted, as futile as the rest of his life. She went on talking, palliating, saying he might very well be right. He put his head into his hands, longing for tears, dry as stone.

She crossed the line. He felt her hand on his shoulder.

"Teyeo, I am very sorry," she said. "I didn't mean to insult you! I honor you. You've been all my hope and help."

"It doesn't matter," he said. "If I— If we had some water."

She leapt up and battered on the door with her fists and a sandal.

"Bastards, bastards," she shouted.

Teyeo got up and walked, three steps and turn, three steps and turn, and halted on his side of the room. "If you're right," he said, speaking slowly and formally, "we and our captors are in danger not only from Gatay but from my own people, who may . . . who have been furthering these anti-Government factions, in order to make an excuse to bring troops here . . . to *pacify* Gatay. That's why they know where to find the factionalists. We are . . . we're lucky our group were . . . were genuine."

She watched him with a tenderness that he found irrelevant.

"What we don't know," he said, "is what side the Ekumen will take. That is . . . There really is only one side."

"No, there's ours, too. The underdogs. If the Embassy sees Voe Deo pulling a takeover of Gatay, they won't interfere, but they won't approve. Especially if it involves as much repression as it seems to."

"The violence is only against the anti-Ekumen factions."

"They still won't approve. And if they find out I'm alive, they're going to be quite pissed at the people who claimed I went up in a bonfire. Our problem is how to get word to them. I was the only person representing the Ekumen in Gatay. Who'd be a safe channel?"

"Any of my men. But . . ."

"They'll have been sent back; why keep Embassy Guards here when the Envoy's dead and buried? I suppose we could try. Ask the boys to try, that is." Presently she said wistfully, "I don't suppose they'd just let us go—in disguise? It would be the safest for them."

"There is an ocean," Teyeo said.

She beat her head. "Oh, why don't they bring some *water*. . . ." Her voice was like paper sliding on paper. He was ashamed of his anger, his grief, himself. He wanted to tell her that she had been a help and hope to him too, that he honored her, that she was brave beyond belief; but none of the words would come. He felt empty, worn-out. He felt old. If only they would bring water!

Water was given them at last; some food, not much and not fresh. Clearly their captors were in hiding and under duress. The spokesman—he gave them his war-name, Kergat, Gatayan for Liberty—told them that whole neighborhoods had been cleared out, set afire, that Voe Dean troops were in control of most of the city including the Palace, and that almost none of this was being reported in the net. "When this is over Voe Deo will own my country," he said with disbelieving fury.

"Not for long," Teyeo said.

"Who can defeat them?" the young man said.

"Yeowe. The idea of Yeowe."

Both Kergat and Solly stared at him.

"Revolution," he said. "How long before Werel becomes New Yeowe?"

"The assets?" Kergat said, as if Teyeo had suggested a revolt of cattle or of flies. "They'll never organise."

"Look out when they do," Teyeo said mildly.

"You don't have any assets in your group?" Solly asked Kergat, amazed. He did not bother to answer. He had classed her as an asset, Teyeo saw. He understood why; he had done so himself, in the other life, when such distinctions made sense.

"Your bondswoman, Rewe," he asked Solly—"was she a friend?"

"Yes," Solly said, then, "No. I wanted her to be."

"The makil?"

After a pause she said, "I think so."

"Is he still here?"

She shook her head. "The troupe was going on with their tour, a few days after the Festival."

"Travel has been restricted since the Festival," Kergat said. "Only government and troops."

"He's Voe Dean. If he's still here, they'll probably send him and his troupe home. Try and contact him, Kergat."

"A makil?" the young man said, with that same distaste and incredulity. "One of your Voe Dean homosexual clowns?"

Teyeo shot a glance at Solly: Patience, patience.

"Bisexual actors," Solly said, disregarding him, but fortunately Kergat was determined to disregard her.

"A clever man," Teyeo said, "with connections. He could help us. You and us. It could be worth it. If he's still here. We must make haste."

"Why would he help us? He is Voe Dean."

"An asset, not a citizen," Teyeo said. "And a member of Hame, the asset underground, which works against the government of

Voe Deo. The Ekumen admits the legitimacy of Hame. He'll report to the Embassy that a Patriot group has rescued the Envoy and is holding her safe, in hiding, in extreme danger. The Ekumen, I think, will act promptly and decisively. Correct, Envoy?"

Suddenly reinstated, Solly gave a short, dignified nod. "But discreetly," she said. "They'll avoid violence, if they can use political coercion."

The young man was trying to get it all into his mind and work it through. Sympathetic to his weariness, distrust, and confusion, Teyeo sat quietly waiting. He noticed that Solly was sitting equally quietly, one hand lying in the other. She was thin and dirty and her unwashed, greasy hair was in a lank braid. She was brave, like a brave mare, all nerve. She would break her heart before she quit.

Kergat asked questions; Teyeo answered them, reasoning and reassuring. Occasionally Solly spoke, and Kergat was now listening to her again, uneasily, not wanting to, not after what he had called her. At last he left, not saying what he intended to do; but he had Batikam's name and an identifying message from Teyeo to the Embassy: "Half-pay veots learn to sing old songs quickly."

"What on earth!" Solly said when Kergat was gone.

"Did you know a man named Old Music, in the Embassy?"

"Ah! Is he a friend of yours?"

"He has been kind."

"He's been here on Werel from the start. A First Observer. Rather a powerful man— Yes, and 'quickly,' all right. . . . My mind really isn't working at all. I wish I could lie down beside a little stream, in a meadow, you know, and drink. All day. Every time I wanted to, just stretch my neck out and slup, slup, slup. . . . Running water . . . In the sunshine . . . Oh God, oh God, sunshine. Teyeo, this is very difficult. This is harder than ever. Thinking that there maybe is really a way out of here. Only not knowing. Trying not to hope and not to not hope. Oh, I am so tired of sitting here!"

"What time is it?"

"Half past twenty. Night. Dark out. Oh God, darkness! Just to be in the darkness . . . Is there any way we could cover up that damned biolume? Partly? To pretend we had night, so we could pretend we had day?"

"If you stood on my shoulders, you could reach it. But how could we fasten a cloth?"

They pondered, staring at the plaque.

"I don't know. Did you notice there's a little patch of it that looks like it's dying? Maybe we don't have to worry about making darkness. If we stay here long enough. Oh, God!"

"Well," he said after a while, curiously self-conscious, "I'm tired." He stood up, stretched, glanced for permission to enter her territory, got a drink of water, returned to his territory, took off his jacket and shoes, by which time her back was turned, took off his trousers, lay down, pulled up the blanket, and said in his mind, "Lord Kamye, let me hold fast to the one noble thing." But he did not sleep.

He heard her slight movements; she pissed, poured a little water, took off her sandals, lay down.

A long time passed.

"Teyeo."

"Yes."

"Do you think . . . that it would be a mistake . . . under the circumstances . . . to make love?"

A pause.

"Not under the circumstances," he said, almost inaudibly. "But—in the other life—"

A pause.

"Short life versus long life," she murmured.

"Yes."

A pause.

"No," he said, and turned to her. "No, that's wrong." They reached out to each other. They clasped each other, cleaved together, in blind haste, greed, need, crying out together the name of God in their different languages and then like animals in the wordless voice. They huddled together, spent, sticky, sweaty, exhausted, reviving, rejoined, reborn in the body's tenderness, in the endless exploration, the ancient discovery, the long flight to the new world.

He woke slowly, in ease and luxury. They were entangled, his face was against her arm and breast; she was stroking his hair, sometimes his neck and shoulder. He lay for a long time aware only of that lazy rhythm and the cool of her skin against his face, under his hand, against his leg.

"Now I know," she said, her half whisper deep in her chest, near his ear, "that I don't know you. Now I need to know you." She bent forward to touch his face with her lips and cheek.

"What do you want to know?"

"Everything. Tell me who Teyeo is. . . ."

"I don't know," he said. "A man who holds you dear."

"Oh, God," she said, hiding her face for a moment in the rough, smelly blanket.

"Who is God?" he asked sleepily. They spoke Voe Dean, but she usually swore in Terran or Alterran; in this case it had been Alterran, *Seyt*, so he asked, "Who is Seyt?"

"Oh—Tual—Kamye—what have you. I just say it. It's just bad language. Do you believe in one of them? I'm sorry! I feel like such an oaf with you, Teyeo. Blundering into your soul, invading you— We *are* invaders, no matter how pacifist and priggish we are—"

"Must I love the whole Ekumen?" he asked, beginning to stroke her breasts, feeling her tremor of desire and his own.

"Yes," she said, "yes, yes."

It was curious, Teyeo thought, how little sex changed anything. Everything was the same, a little easier, less embarrassment and inhibition; and there was a certain and lovely source of pleasure for them, when they had enough water and food to have enough vitality to make love. But the only thing that was truly different was something he had no word for. Sex, comfort, tenderness, love, trust, no word was the right word, the whole word. It was utterly intimate, hidden in the mutuality of their bodies, and it changed nothing in their circumstances, nothing in the world, even the tiny wretched world of their imprisonment. They were still trapped. They were getting very tired and were hungry most of the time. They were increasingly afraid of their increasingly desperate captors.

"I will be a lady," Solly said. "A good girl. Tell me how, Teyeo."

"I don't want you to give in," he said, so fiercely, with tears in his eyes, that she went to him and held him in her arms.

"Hold fast," he said.

"I will," she said. But when Kergat or the others came in she was sedate and modest, letting the men talk, keeping her eyes down. He could not bear to see her so, and knew she was right to do so.

The doorlock rattled, the door clashed, bringing him up out of a wretched, thirsty sleep. It was night or very early morning. He and Solly had been sleeping close entangled for the warmth and comfort of it; and seeing Kergat's face now he was deeply afraid. This was what he had feared, to show, to prove her sexual vulnerability. She was still only half-awake, clinging to him.

Another man had come in. Kergat said nothing. It took Teyeo some time to recognize the second man as Batikam.

When he did, his mind remained quite blank. He managed to say the makil's name. Nothing else.

"Batikam?" Solly croaked. "Oh, my God!"

"This is an interesting moment," Batikam said in his warm actor's voice. He was not transvestite, Teyeo saw, but wore Gatayan men's clothing. "I meant to rescue you, not to embarrass you, Envoy, Rega. Shall we get on with it?"

Teyeo had scrambled up and was pulling on his filthy trousers. Solly had slept in the ragged pants their captors had given her. They both had kept on their shirts for warmth.

"Did you contact the Embassy, Batikam?" she was asking, her voice shaking, as she pulled on her sandals.

"Oh, yes. I've been there and come back, indeed. Sorry it took so long. I don't think I quite realised your situation here."

"Kergat has done his best for us," Teyeo said at once, stiffly.

"I can see that. At considerable risk. I think the risk from now on is low. That is . . ." He looked straight at Teyeo. "Rega, how do you feel about putting yourself in the hands of Hame?" he said. "Any problems with that?"

"Don't, Batikam," Solly said. "Trust him!"

Teyeo tied his shoe, straightened up, and said, "We are all in the hands of the Lord Kamye."

Batikam laughed, the beautiful full laugh they remembered.

"In the Lord's hands, then," he said, and led them out of the room.

In the *Arkamye* it is said, "To live simply is most complicated."

Solly requested to stay on Werel, and after a recuperative leave at the seashore was sent as Observer to South Voe Deo.

Teyeo went straight home, being informed that his father was very ill. After his father's death, he asked for indefinite leave from the Embassy Guard, and stayed on the farm with his mother until her death two years later. He and Solly, a continent apart, met only occasionally during those years.

When his mother died, Teyeo freed his family's assets by act of irrevocable manumission, deeded over their farms to them, sold his now almost valueless property at auction, and went to the capital. He knew Solly was temporarily staying at the Embassy. Old Music told him where to find her. He found her in a small office of the palatial building. She looked older, very elegant. She looked at him with a stricken and yet wary face. She did not come forward to greet or touch him. She said, "Teyeo, I've been asked to be the first Ambassador of the Ekumen to Yeowe."

He stood still.

"Just now—I just came from talking on the ansible with Hain—"

She put her face in her hands. "Oh, my God!" she said.

He said, "My congratulations, truly, Solly."

She suddenly ran at him, threw her arms around him, and cried, "Oh, Teyeo, and your mother died, I never thought, I'm so sorry, I never, I never do— I thought we could— What are you going to do? Are you going to stay there?"

"I sold it," he said. He was enduring rather than returning her embrace. "I thought I might return to the service."

"You sold your *farm*? But I never saw it!"

"I never saw where you were born," he said.

There was a pause. She stood away from him, and they looked at each other.

"You would come?" she said.

"I would," he said.

Several years after Yeowe entered the Ekumen, Mobile Solly Agat Terwa was sent as an Ekumenical liaison to Terra; later she went from there to Hain, where she served with great distinction as a Stabile. In all her travels and posts she was accompanied by her husband, a Werelian army officer, a very handsome man, as reserved as she was outgoing. People who

knew them knew their passionate pride and trust in each other. Solly was perhaps the happier person, rewarded and fulfilled in her work; but Teyeo had no regrets. He had lost his world, but he had held fast to the one noble thing.

A Man of the People

H<small>E SAT</small> beside his father by the great irrigation tank. Fire-colored wings soared and dipped through the twilight air. Trembling circles enlarged, interlocked, faded on the still surface of the water. "What makes the water go that way?" he asked, softly because it was mysterious, and his father answered softly, "It's where the araha touch it when they drink." So he understood that in the center of each circle was a desire, a thirst. Then it was time to go home, and he ran before his father, pretending he was an araha flying, back through the dusk into the steep, bright-windowed town.

His name was Mattinyehedarheddyuragamuruskets Havzhiva. The word *havzhiva* means "ringed pebble," a small stone with a quartz inclusion running through it that shows as a stripe round it. The people of Stse are particular about stones and names. Boys of the Sky, the Other Sky, and the Static Interference lineages are traditionally given the names of stones or desirable manly qualities such as courage, patience, and grace. The Yehedarhed family were traditionalists, strong on family and lineage. "If you know who your people are, you know who you are," said Havzhiva's father, Granite. A kind, quiet man who took his paternal responsibility seriously, he spoke often in sayings.

Granite was Havzhiva's mother's brother, of course; that is what a father was. The man who had helped his mother conceive Havzhiva lived on a farm; he stopped in sometimes to say hello when he was in town. Havzhiva's mother was the Heir of the Sun. Sometimes Havzhiva envied his cousin Aloe, whose father was only six years older than she was and played with her like a big brother. Sometimes he envied children whose mothers were unimportant. His mother was always fasting or dancing or traveling, had no husband, and rarely slept at home. It was exciting to be with her, but difficult. He had to be important when he was with her. It was always a relief to be home with nobody there but his father and his undemanding grandmother and her sister the Winter Dancekeeper and her hus-

band and whichever Other Sky relatives from farms and other pueblos were visiting at the moment.

There were only two Other Sky households in Stse, and the Yehedarheds were more hospitable than the Doyefarads, so all the relatives came and stayed with them. They would have been hard put to afford it if the visitors hadn't brought all sorts of farm stuff, and if Tovo hadn't been Heir of the Sun. She got paid richly for teaching and for performing the rituals and handling the protocol at other pueblos. She gave all she earned to her family, who spent it all on their relatives and on ceremonies, festivities, celebrations, and funerals.

"Wealth can't stop," Granite said to Havzhiva. "It has to keep going. Like the blood circulating. You keep it, it gets stopped —that's a heart attack. You die."

"Will Hezhe-old-man die?" the boy asked. Old Hezhe never spent anything on a ritual or a relative; and Havzhiva was an observant child.

"Yes," his father answered. "His araha is already dead."

Araha is enjoyment; honor; the particular quality of one's gender, manhood or womanhood; generosity; the savor of good food or wine.

It is also the name of the plumed, fire-colored, quick-flying mammal that Havzhiva used to see come to drink at the irrigation ponds, tiny flames darting above the darkening water in the evening.

Stse is an almost-island, separated from the mainland of the great south continent by marshes and tidal bogs, where millions of wading birds gather to mate and nest. Ruins of an enormous bridge are visible on the landward side, and another half-sunk fragment of ruin is the basis of the town's boat pier and breakwater. Vast works of other ages encumber all Hain, and are no more and no less venerable or interesting to the Hainish than the rest of the landscape. A child standing on the pier to watch his mother sail off to the mainland might wonder why people had bothered to build a bridge when there were boats and flyers to ride. They must have liked to walk, he thought. I'd rather sail in a boat. Or fly.

But the silver flyers flew over Stse, not landing, going from somewhere else to somewhere else, where historians lived. Plenty of boats came in and out of Stse harbor, but the people of his lineage did not sail them. They lived in the Pueblo of Stse and did the things that their people and their lineage did. They learned what people needed to learn, and lived their knowledge.

"People have to learn to be human," his father said. "Look at Shell's baby. It keeps saying 'Teach me! Teach me!'"

"Teach me," in the language of Stse, is "aowa."

"Sometimes the baby says 'ngaaaaa,'" Havzhiva observed.

Granite nodded. "She can't speak human words very well yet," he said.

Havzhiva hung around the baby that winter, teaching her to say human words. She was one of his Etsahin relatives, his second cousin once removed, visiting with her mother and her father and his wife. The family watched Havzhiva with approval as he patiently said "baba" and "gogo" to the fat, placid, staring baby. Though he had no sister and thus could not be a father, if he went on studying education with such seriousness, he would probably have the honor of being the adopted father of a baby whose mother had no brother.

He also studied at school and in the temple, studied dancing, and studied the local version of soccer. He was a serious student. He was good at soccer but not as good as his best friend, a Buried Cable girl named Iyan Iyan (a traditional name for Buried Cable girls, a seabird name). Until they were twelve, boys and girls were educated together and alike. Iyan Iyan was the best soccer player on the children's team. They always had to put her on the other side at halftime so that the score would even out and they could go home for dinner without anybody having lost or won badly. Part of her advantage was that she had got her height very early, but most of it was pure skill.

"Are you going to work at the temple?" she asked Havzhiva as they sat on the porch roof of her house watching the first day of the Enactment of the Unusual Gods, which took place every eleven years. No unusual things were happening yet, and the amplifiers weren't working well, so the music in the plaza sounded faint and full of static. The two children kicked their heels and talked quietly. "No, I think I'll learn weaving from my father," the boy said.

"Lucky you. Why do only stupid boys get to use looms?" It was a rhetorical question, and Havzhiva paid it no attention.

Women were not weavers. Men did not make bricks. Other
Sky people did not operate boats but did repair electronic devices. Buried Cable people did not castrate animals but did
maintain generators. There were things one could do and
things one could not do; one did those things for people and
people did those things for one. Coming up on puberty, Iyan
Iyan and Havzhiva were making a first choice of their first
profession. Iyan Iyan had already chosen to apprentice in
house-building and repair, although the adult soccer team
would probably claim a good deal of her time.

A globular silver person with spidery legs came down the
street in long bounds, emitting a shower of sparks each time it
landed. Six people in red with tall white masks ran after it,
shouting and throwing speckled beans at it. Havzhiva and Iyan
Iyan joined in the shouting and craned from the roof to see it
go bounding round the corner towards the plaza. They both
knew that this Unusual God was Chert, a young man of the
Sky lineage, a goalkeeper for the adult soccer team; they both
also knew that it was a manifestation of deity. A god called
Zarstsa or Ball-Lighting was using Chert to come into town
for the ceremony, and had just bounded down the street pursued by shouts of fear and praise and showers of fertility.
Amused and entertained by the spectacle, they judged with
some acuteness the quality of the god's costume, the jumping,
and the fireworks, and were awed by the strangeness and
power of the event. They did not say anything for a long time
after the god had passed, but sat dreamily in the foggy sunlight
on the roof. They were children who lived among the daily
gods. Now they had seen one of the unusual gods. They were
content. Another one would come along, before long. Time is
nothing to the gods.

At fifteen, Havzhiva and Iyan Iyan became gods together.

Stse people between twelve and fifteen were vigilantly
watched; there would be a great deal of grief and deep, lasting
shame if a child of the house, the family, the lineage, the people,
should change being prematurely and without ceremony. Virginity was a sacred status, not to be carelessly abandoned; sexual
activity was a sacred status, not to be carelessly undertaken. It
was assumed that a boy would masturbate and make some

homosexual experiments, but not a homosexual pairing; adolescent boys who paired off, and those who incurred suspicion of trying to get alone with a girl, were endlessly lectured and hectored and badgered by older men. A grown man who made sexual advances to a virgin of either sex would forfeit his professional status, his religious offices, and his houseright.

Changing being took a while. Boys and girls had to be taught how to recognise and control their fertility, which in Hainish physiology is a matter of personal decision. Conception does not happen: it is performed. It cannot take place unless both the woman and the man have chosen it. At thirteen, boys began to be taught the technique of deliberately releasing potent sperm. The teachings were full of warnings, threats, and scoldings, though the boys were never actually punished. After a year or two came a series of tests of achieved potency, a threshold ritual, frightening, formal, extremely secret, exclusively male. To have passed the tests was, of course, a matter of intense pride; yet Havzhiva, like most boys, came to his final change-of-being rites very apprehensive, hiding fear under a sullen stoicism.

The girls had been differently taught. The people of Stse believed that a woman's cycle of fertility made it easy for her to learn when and how to conceive, and so the teaching was easy too. Girls' threshold rituals were celebratory, involving praise rather than shame, arousing anticipation rather than fear. Women had been telling them for years, with demonstrations, what a man wants, how to make him stand up tall, how to show him what a woman wants. During this training, most girls asked if they couldn't just go on practicing with each other, and got scolded and lectured. No, they couldn't. Once they had changed status they could do as they pleased, but everybody must go through "the twofold door" once.

The change-of-being rites were held whenever the people in charge of them could get an equal number of fifteen-year-old boys and girls from the pueblo and its farms. Often a boy or girl had to be borrowed from one of the related pueblos to even out the number or to pair the lineages correctly. Magnificently masked and costumed, silent, the participants danced and were honored all day in the plaza and in the house consecrated to the ceremony; in the evening they ate a ritual meal in silence; then they were led off in pairs by masked and silent ritualists. Many of them kept their masks on, hiding their fear and modesty in that sacred anonymity.

Because Other Sky people have sex only with Original and Buried Cable people and they were the only ones of those lineages in the group, Iyan Iyan and Havzhiva had known they must be paired. They had recognised each other as soon as the dancing began. When they were left alone in the consecrated room, they took off their masks at once. Their eyes met. They looked away.

They had been kept apart most of the time for the past couple of years, and completely apart for the last months. Havzhiva had begun to get his growth, and was nearly as tall as she was now. Each saw a stranger. Decorous and serious, they approached each other, each thinking, "Let's get it over with." So they touched, and that god entered them, becoming them; the god for whom they were the doorway; the meaning for which they were the word. It was an awkward god at first, clumsy, but became an increasingly happy one.

When they left the consecrated house the next day, they both went to Iyan Iyan's house. "Havzhiva will live here," Iyan Iyan said, as a woman has a right to say. Everybody in her family made him welcome and none of them seemed surprised.

When he went to get his clothes from his grandmother's house, nobody there seemed surprised, everybody congratulated him, an old woman cousin from Etsahin made some embarrassing jokes, and his father said, "You are a man of this house now; come back for dinner."

So he slept with Iyan Iyan at her house, ate breakfast there, ate dinner at his house, kept his daily clothes at her house, kept his dance clothes at his house, and went on with his education, which now had mostly to do with rug-weaving on the power broadlooms and with the nature of the cosmos. He and Iyan Iyan both played on the adult soccer team.

He began to see more of his mother, because when he was seventeen she asked him if he wanted to learn Sun-stuff with her, the rites and protocols of trade, arranging fair exchange with farmers of Stse and bargaining with other pueblos of the lineages and with foreigners. The rituals were learned by rote, the protocols were learned by practice. Havzhiva went with his mother to the market, to outlying farms, and across the bay to the mainland pueblos. He had been getting restless with weaving, which filled his mind with patterns that left no room outside themselves. The travel was welcome, the work was interesting, and he admired Tovo's authority, wit, and tact. Listening to her and a group of old merchants and Sun people maneuvering around a deal was an education in itself. She did not push him; he played a very minor role in these negotiations. Training in complicated business such as Sun-stuff took years, and there were other, older people in training before him. But she was satisfied with him. "You have a knack for persuading," she told him one afternoon as they were sailing home across the golden water, watching the roofs of Stse solidify out of mist and sunset light. "You could inherit the Sun, if you wanted to."

Do I want to? he thought. There was no response in him but a sense of darkening or softening, which he could not interpret. He knew he liked the work. Its patterns were not closed. It took him out of Stse, among strangers, and he liked that. It gave him something to do which he didn't know how to do, and he liked that.

"The woman who used to live with your father is coming for a visit," Tovo said.

Havzhiva pondered. Granite had never married. The women who had borne the children Granite sired both lived in Stse and always had. He asked nothing, a polite silence being the adult way of signifying that one doesn't understand.

"They were young. No child came," his mother said. "She went away after that. She became a historian."

"Ah," Havzhiva said in pure, blank surprise.

He had never heard of anybody who became a historian. It had never occurred to him that a person could become one, any more than a person could become a Stse. You were born what you were. You were what you were born.

The quality of his polite silence was desperately intense, and Tovo certainly was not unaware of it. Part of her tact as a teacher was knowing when a question needed an answer. She said nothing.

As their sail slackened and the boat slid in toward the pier built on the ancient bridge foundations, he asked, "Is the historian Buried Cable or Original?"

"Buried Cable," his mother said. "Oh, how stiff I am! Boats are such stiff creatures!" The woman who had sailed them across, a ferrywoman of the Grass lineage, rolled her eyes, but said nothing in defense of her sweet, supple little boat.

"A relative of yours is coming?" Havzhiva said to Iyan Iyan that night.

"Oh, yes, she templed in." Iyan Iyan meant a message had been received in the information center of Stse and transmitted to the recorder in her household. "She used to live in your house, my mother said. Who did you see in Etsahin today?"

"Just some Sun people. Your relative is a historian?"

"Crazy people," Iyan Iyan said with indifference, and came to sit naked on naked Havzhiva and massage his back.

The historian arrived, a little short thin woman of fifty or so called Mezha. By the time Havzhiva met her she was wearing Stse clothing and eating breakfast with everybody else. She had bright eyes and was cheerful but not talkative. Nothing about her showed that she had broken the social contract, done things no woman does, ignored her lineage, become another kind of being. For all he knew she was married to the father of her children, and wove at a loom, and castrated animals. But nobody shunned her, and after breakfast the old people of the household took her off for a returning-traveler ceremony, just as if she were still one of them.

He kept wondering about her, wondering what she had done. He asked Iyan Iyan questions about her till Iyan Iyan snapped at him, "I don't know what she does, I don't know what she thinks. Historians are crazy. Ask her yourself!"

When Havzhiva realised that he was afraid to do so, for no reason, he understood that he was in the presence of a god who was requiring something of him. He went up to one of the sitting holes, rock cairns on the heights above the town. Below him the black tile roofs and white walls of Stse nestled under the bluffs, and the irrigation tanks shone silver among fields and orchards. Beyond the tilled land stretched the long sea marshes. He spent a day sitting in silence, looking out to sea and into his soul. He came back down to his own house and slept there. When he turned up for breakfast at Iyan Iyan's house she looked at him and said nothing.

"I was fasting," he said.

She shrugged a little. "So eat," she said, sitting down by him. After breakfast she left for work. He did not, though he was expected at the looms.

"Mother of All Children," he said to the historian, giving her the most respectful title a man of one lineage can give a woman of another, "there are things I do not know, which you know."

"What I know I will teach you with pleasure," she said, as ready with the formula as if she had lived here all her life. She then smiled and forestalled his next oblique question. "What was given me I give," she said, meaning there was no question of payment or obligation. "Come on, let's go to the plaza."

Everybody goes to the plaza in Stse to talk, and sits on the steps or around the fountain or on hot days under the arcades, and watches other people come and go and sit and talk. It was perhaps a little more public than Havzhiva would have liked, but he was obedient to his god and his teacher.

They sat in a niche of the fountain's broad base and conversed, greeting people every sentence or two with a nod or a word.

"Why did—" Havzhiva began, and stuck.

"Why did I leave? Where did I go?" She cocked her head, bright-eyed as an araha, checking that those were the questions he wanted answered. "Yes. Well, I was crazy in love with Granite, but we had no child, and he wanted a child. . . . You look like he did then. I like to look at you. . . . So, I was unhappy. Nothing here was any good to me. And I knew how to do everything here. Or that's what I thought."

Havzhiva nodded once.

"I worked at the temple. I'd read messages that came in or came by and wonder what they were about. I thought, all that's going on in the world! Why should I stay here my whole life? Does my mind have to stay here? So I began to talk with some of them in other places in the temple: who are you, what do you do, what is it like there. . . . Right away they put me in touch with a group of historians who were born in the pueblos, who look out for people like me, to make sure they don't waste time or offend a god."

This language was completely familiar to Havzhiva, and he nodded again, intent.

"I asked them questions. They asked me questions. Historians have to do a lot of that. I found out they have schools, and asked if I could go to one. Some of them came here and talked to me and my family and other people, finding out if there would be trouble if I left. Stse is a conservative pueblo. There hadn't been a historian from here for four hundred years."

She smiled; she had a quick, catching smile, but the young man listened with unchanging, intense seriousness. Her look rested on his face tenderly.

"People here were upset, but nobody was angry. So after they talked about it, I left with those people. We flew to Kathhad. There's a school there. I was twenty-two. I began a new education. I changed being. I learned to be a historian."

"How?" he asked, after a long silence.

She drew a long breath. "By asking hard questions," she said. "Like you're doing now. . . . And by giving up all the knowledge I had—throwing it away."

"How?" he asked again, frowning. "Why?"

"Like this. When I left, I knew I was a Buried Cable woman. When I was there, I had to unknow that knowledge. There, I'm not a Buried Cable woman. I'm a woman. I can have sex with any person I choose. I can take up any profession I choose. Lineage matters, here. It does not matter, there. It has meaning here, and a use. It has no meaning and no use, anywhere else in the universe." She was as intense as he, now. "There are two kinds of knowledge, local and universal. There are two kinds of time, local and historical."

"Are there two kinds of gods?"

"No," she said. "There are no gods there. The gods are here." She saw his face change.

She said after a while, "There are souls, there. Many, many souls, minds, minds full of knowledge and passion. Living and dead. People who lived on this earth a hundred, a thousand, a hundred thousand years ago. Minds and souls of people from worlds a hundred light-years from this one, all of them with their own knowledge, their own history. The world is sacred, Havzhiva. The cosmos is sacred. That's not a knowledge I ever had to give up. All I learned, here and there, only increased it. There's nothing that is not sacred." She spoke slowly and quietly, the way most people talked in the pueblo. "You can choose the local sacredness or the great one. In the end they're the same. But not in the life one lives. 'To know there is a choice is to have to make the choice: change or stay: river or rock.' The Peoples are the rock. The historians are the river."

After a while he said, "Rocks are the river's bed."

She laughed. Her gaze rested on him again, appraising and affectionate. "So I came home," she said. "For a rest."

"But you're not—you're no longer a woman of your lineage?"

"Yes; here. Still. Always."

"But you've changed being. You'll leave again."

"Yes," she said decisively. "One can be more than one kind of being. I have work to do, there."

He shook his head, slower, but equally decisive. "What good is work without the gods? It makes no sense to me, Mother of All Children. I don't have the mind to understand."

She smiled at the double meaning. "I think you'll understand what you choose to understand, Man of my People," she said, addressing him formally to show that he was free to leave when he wanted.

He hesitated, then took his leave. He went to work, filling his mind and world with the great repeated patterns of the broadloom rugs.

That night he made it up to Iyan Iyan so ardently that she was left spent and a bit amazed. The god had come back to them burning, consuming.

"I want a child," Havzhiva said as they lay melded, sweated together, arms and legs and breasts and breath all mingled in the musky dark.

"Oh," Iyan Iyan sighed, not wanting to talk, decide, resist. "Maybe . . . Later . . . Soon . . ."

"Now," he said, "now."

"No," she said softly. "Hush."

He was silent. She slept.

More than a year later, when they were nineteen, Iyan Iyan said to him before he put out the light, "I want a baby."

"It's too soon."

"Why? My brother's nearly thirty. And his wife would like a baby around. After it's weaned I'll come sleep with you at your house. You always said you'd like that."

"It's too soon," he repeated. "I don't want it."

She turned to him, laying aside her coaxing, reasonable tone. "What do you want, Havzhiva?"

"I don't know."

"You're going away. You're going to leave the People. You're going crazy. That woman, that damned witch!"

"There are no witches," he said coldly. "That's stupid talk. Superstition."

They stared at each other, the dear friends, the lovers.

"Then what's wrong with you? If you want to move back home, say so. If you want another woman, go to her. But you could give me my child, first! when I ask you for it! Have you lost your araha?" She gazed at him with tearful eyes, fierce, unyielding.

He put his face in his hands. "Nothing is right," he said. "Nothing is right. Everything I do, I have to do because that's how it's done, but it—it doesn't make sense—there are other ways—"

"There's one way to live rightly," Iyan Iyan said, "that I know of. And this is where I live. There's one way to make a baby. If you know another, you can do it with somebody else!" She cried hard after this, convulsively, the fear and anger of months breaking out at last, and he held her to calm and comfort her.

When she could speak, she leaned her head against him and said miserably, in a small, hoarse voice, "To have when you go, Havzhiva."

At that he wept for shame and pity, and whispered, "Yes, yes." But that night they lay holding each other, trying to console each other, till they fell asleep like children.

"I am ashamed," Granite said painfully.

"Did you make this happen?" his sister asked, dry.

"How do I know? Maybe I did. First Mezha, now my son. Was I too stern with him?"

"No, no."

"Too lax, then. I didn't teach him well. Why is he crazy?"

"He isn't crazy, brother. Let me tell you what I think. As a child he always asked why, why, the way children do. I would answer: That's how it is, that's how it's done. He understood.

But his mind has no peace. My mind is like that, if I don't remind myself. Learning the Sun-stuff, he always asked, why
thus? why this way, not another way? I answered: Because in
what we do daily and in the way we do it, we enact the gods.
He said: Then the gods are only what we do. I said: In what
we do rightly, the gods are: that is the truth. But he wasn't
satisfied by the truth. He isn't crazy, brother, but he is lame.
He can't walk. He can't walk with us. So, if a man can't walk,
what should he do?"

"Sit still and sing," Granite said slowly.

"If he can't sit still? He can fly."

"Fly?"

"They have wings for him, brother."

"I am ashamed," Granite said, and hid his face in his hands.

Tovo went to the temple and sent a message to Mezha at
Kathhad: "Your pupil wishes to join you." There was some
malice in the words. Tovo blamed the historian for upsetting
her son's balance, offcentering him till, as she said, his soul was
lamed. And she was jealous of the woman who in a few days
had outdone the teachings of years. She knew she was jealous
and did not care. What did her jealousy or her brother's humiliation matter? What they had to do was grieve.

As the boat for Daha sailed away, Havzhiva looked back and
saw Stse: a quilt of a thousand shades of green, the sea marshes,
the pastures, fields, hedgerows, orchards; the town clambering
up the bluffs above, pale granite walls, white stucco walls, black
tile roofs, wall above wall and roof above roof. As it diminished
it looked like a seabird perched there, white and black, a bird
on its nest. Above the town the heights of the island came in
view, grey-blue moors and high, wild hills fading into the
clouds, white skeins of marsh birds flying.

At the port in Daha, though he was farther from Stse than
he had ever been and people had a strange accent, he could
understand them and read the signs. He had never seen signs
before, but their usefulness was evident. Using them, he found
his way to the waiting room for the Kathhad flyer. People were
sleeping on the cots provided, in their own blankets. He found
an empty cot and lay on it, wrapped in the blanket Granite had

woven for him years ago. After a short, strange night, people came in with fruit and hot drinks. One of them gave Havzhiva his ticket. None of the passengers knew anyone else; they were all strangers; they kept their eyes down. Announcements were made, and they all went outside and went into the machine, the flyer.

Havzhiva made himself look at the world as it fell out from under him. He whispered the Staying Chant soundlessly, steadily. The stranger in the seat next to him joined in.

When the world began to tilt and rush up towards him he shut his eyes and tried to keep breathing.

One by one they filed out of the flyer onto a flat, black place where it was raining. Mezha came to him through the rain, saying his name. "Havzhiva, Man of my People, welcome! Come on. There's a place for you at the School."

KATHHAD AND VE

By the third year at Kathhad Havzhiva knew a great many things that distressed him. The old knowledge had been difficult but not distressing. It had been all paradox and myth, and it had made sense. The new knowledge was all fact and reason, and it made no sense.

For instance, he knew now that historians did not study history. No human mind could encompass the history of Hain: three million years of it. The events of the first two million years, the Fore-Eras, like layers of metamorphic rock, were so compressed, so distorted by the weight of the succeeding millennia and their infinite events that one could reconstruct only the most sweeping generalities from the tiny surviving details. And if one did chance to find some miraculously preserved document from a thousand millennia ago, what then? A king ruled in Azbahan; the Empire fell to the Infidels; a fusion rocket has landed on Ve. . . . But there had been uncountable kings, empires, inventions, billions of lives lived in millions of countries, monarchies, democracies, oligarchies, anarchies, ages of chaos and ages of order, pantheon upon pantheon of gods, infinite wars and times of peace, incessant discoveries and forgettings, innumerable horrors and triumphs, an endless repetition of unceasing novelty. What is the use trying to describe the flowing of a river at any one moment, and then at the next moment, and then at the next, and the next, and the next? You wear out. You say: There is a great river, and it flows through this land, and we have named it History.

To Havzhiva the knowledge that his life, any life was one flicker of light for one moment on the surface of that river was sometimes distressing, sometimes restful.

What the historians mostly did was explore, in an easy and unhurried fashion, the local reach and moment of the river. Hain itself had been for several thousand years in an unexciting period marked by the coexistence of small, stable, self-contained societies, currently called pueblos, with a high-technology, low-density network of cities and information centers, currently called the temple. Many of the people of the temple, the historians, spent their lives traveling to and gathering knowledge about the other inhabited planets of the nearby Orion Arm, colonised by their ancestors a couple of million years ago during the Fore-Eras. They acknowledged no motive in these contacts and explorations other than curiosity and fellow-feeling. They were getting in touch with their long-lost relatives. They called that greater network of worlds by an alien word, Ekumen, which meant "the household."

By now Havzhiva knew that everything he had learned in Stse, all the knowledge he had had, could be labeled: *typical pueblo culture of northwestern coastal South Continent.* He knew that the beliefs, practices, kinship systems, technologies, and intellectual organising patterns of the different pueblos were entirely different one from another, wildly different, totally bizarre—just as bizarre as the system of Stse—and he knew that such systems were to be met with on every Known World that contained human populations living in small, stable groups with a technology adapted to their environment, a low, constant birth rate, and a political life based on consent.

At first such knowledge had been intensely distressing. It had been painful. It had made him ashamed and angry. First he thought the historians kept their knowledge from the pueblos, then he thought the pueblos kept knowledge from their own people. He accused; his teachers mildly denied. No, they said. You were taught that certain things were true, or necessary;

and those things are true and necessary. They are the local knowledge of Stse.

They are childish, irrational beliefs! he said. They looked at him, and he knew he had said something childish and irrational.

Local knowledge is not partial knowledge, they said. There are different ways of knowing. Each has its own qualities, penalties, rewards. Historical knowledge and scientific knowledge are a way of knowing. Like local knowledge, they must be learned. The way they know in the Household isn't taught in the pueblos, but it wasn't hidden from you, by your people or by us. Everybody anywhere on Hain has access to all the information in the temple.

This was true; he knew it to be true. He could have found out for himself, on the screens of the temple of Stse, what he was learning now. Some of his fellow students from other pueblos had indeed taught themselves how to learn from the screens, and had entered history before they ever met a historian.

Books, however, books that were the body of history, the durable reality of it, barely existed in Stse, and his anger sought justification there. You keep the books from us, all the books in the Library of Hain! No, they said mildly. The pueblos choose not to have many books. They prefer the live knowledge, spoken or passing on the screens, passing from the breath to the breath, from living mind to living mind. Would you give up what you learned that way? Is it less than, is it inferior to what you've learned here from books? There's more than one kind of knowledge, said the historians.

By his third year, Havzhiva had decided that there was more than one kind of people. The pueblans, able to accept that existence is fundamentally arbitrary, enriched the world intellectually and spiritually. Those who couldn't be satisfied with mystery were more likely to be of use as historians, enriching the world intellectually and materially.

Meanwhile he had got quite used to people who had no lineage, no relatives, and no religion. Sometimes he said to himself with a glow of pride, "I am a citizen of all history, of the millions of years of Hainish history, and my country is the whole galaxy!" At other times he felt miserably small, and he would leave his screens or his books and go look for company among his fellow students, especially the young women who were so friendly, so companionable.

At the age of twenty-four Havzhiva, or Zhiv as he was now called, had been at the Ekumenical School on Ve for a year.

Ve, the next planet out from Hain, was colonised eons ago, the first step in the vast Hainish expansion of the Fore-Eras. It has gone through many phases as a satellite or partner of Hainish civilizations; at this period it is inhabited entirely by historians and Aliens.

In their current (that is, for at least the past hundred millennia) mood of not tampering, the Hainish have let Ve return to its own norms of coldness, dryness, and bleakness—a climate within human tolerance, but likely to truly delight only people from the Terran Altiplano or the uplands of Chiffewar. Zhiv was out hiking through this stern landscape with his companion, friend, and lover, Tiu.

They had met two years before, in Kathhad. At that point Zhiv had still been reveling in the availability of all women to himself and himself to all women, a freedom that had only gradually dawned on him, and about which Mezha had warned him gently. "You will think there are no rules," she said. "There are always rules." He had been conscious mainly of his own increasingly fearless and careless transgression of what had been the rules. Not all the women wanted to have sex, and not all the women wanted to have sex with men, as he had soon discovered, but that still left an infinite variety. He found that he was considered attractive. And being Hainish was a definite advantage with the Alien women.

The genetic alteration that made the Hainish able to control their fertility was not a simple bit of gene-splicing; involving a profound and radical reconstruction of human physiology, it had probably taken up to twenty-five generations to establish —so say the historians of Hain, who think they know in general terms the steps such a transformation must have followed. However the ancient Hainish did it, they did not do it for any of their colonists. They left the peoples of their colony worlds to work out their own solutions to the First Heterosexual Problem. These have been, of course, various and ingenious;

but in all cases so far, to avoid conception you have to do something or have done something or take something or use something—unless you have sex with the Hainish.

Zhiv had been outraged when a girl from Beldene asked him if he was sure he wouldn't get her pregnant. "How do you *know*?" she said. "Maybe I should take a zapper just to be *safe*." Insulted in the quick of his manhood, he disentangled himself, said, "Maybe it is only safe not to be with me," and stalked out. Nobody else questioned his integrity, fortunately, and he cruised happily on, until he met Tiu.

She was not an Alien. He had sought out women from off-world; sleeping with Aliens added exoticism to transgression, or, as he put it, was an enrichment of knowledge such as every historian should seek. But Tiu was Hainish. She had been born and brought up in Darranda, as had her ancestors before her. She was a child of the Historians as he was a child of the People. He realised very soon that this bond and division was far greater than any mere foreignness: that their unlikeness was true difference and their likeness was true kinship. She was the country he had left his own country to discover. She was what he sought to be. She was what he sought.

What she had—so it seemed to him—was perfect equilibrium. When he was with her he felt that for the first time in his life he was learning to walk. To walk as she did: effortless, unself-conscious as an animal, and yet conscious, careful, keeping in mind all that might unbalance her and using it as tightrope walkers use their long poles. . . . This, he thought, this is a dweller in true freedom of mind, this is a woman free to be fully human, this perfect measure, this perfect grace.

He was utterly happy when he was with her. For a long time he asked nothing beyond that, to be with her. And for a long time she was wary of him, gentle but distant. He thought she had every right to keep her distance. A pueblo boy, a fellow who couldn't tell his uncle from his father—he knew what he was, here, in the eyes of the ill-natured and the insecure. Despite their vast knowledge of human ways of being, historians retained the vast human capacity for bigotry. Tiu had no such prejudices, but what did he have to offer her? She had and was everything. She was complete. Why should she look at him? If she would only let him look at her, be with her, it was all he wanted.

She looked at him, liked him, found him appealing and a little frightening. She saw how he wanted her, how he needed her, how he had made her into the center of his life and did not even know it. That would not do. She tried to be cold, to turn him away. He obeyed. He did not plead. He stayed away.

But after fifteen days he came to her and said, "Tiu, I cannot live without you," and knowing that he was speaking the plain truth she said, "Then live with me a while." For she had missed the passion his presence filled the air with. Everybody else seemed so tame, so balanced.

Their lovemaking was an immediate, immense, and continual delight. Tiu was amazed at herself, at her obsession with Zhiv, at her letting him pull her out of her orbit so far. She had never expected to adore anybody, let alone to be adored. She had led an orderly life, in which the controls were individual and internal, not social and external as they had been in Zhiv's life in Stse. She knew what she wanted to be and do. There was a direction in her, a true north, that she would always follow. Their first year together was a series of continual shifts and changes in their relationship, a kind of exciting love dance, unpredictable and ecstatic. Very gradually, she began to resist the tension, the intensity, the ecstasy. It was lovely but it wasn't right, she thought. She wanted to go on. That constant direction began to pull her away from him again; and then he fought for his life against it.

That was what he was doing, after a long day's hike in the Desert of Asu Asi on Ve, in their miraculously warm Gethenian-made tent. A dry, icy wind moaned among cliffs of crimson stone above them, polished by the endless winds to a shine like lacquer and carved by a lost civilization with lines of some vast geometry.

They might have been brother and sister, as they sat in the glow of the Chabe stove: their red-bronze coloring was the same, their thick, glossy, black hair, their fine, compact body type. The pueblan decorum and quietness of Zhiv's movements and voice met in her an articulate, quicker, more vivid response.

But she spoke now slowly, almost stiffly.

"Don't force me to choose, Zhiv," she said. "Ever since I started in the Schools I've wanted to go to Terra. Since before.

When I was a kid. All my life. Now they offer me what I want, what I've worked for. How can you ask me to refuse?"

"I don't."

"But you want me to put it off. If I do, I may lose the chance forever. Probably not. But why risk it—for one year? You can follow me next year!"

He said nothing.

"If you want to," she added stiffly. She was always too ready to forgo her claim on him. Perhaps she had never believed fully in his love for her. She did not think of herself as lovable, as worthy of his passionate loyalty. She was frightened by it, felt inadequate, false. Her self-respect was an intellectual thing. "You make a god of me," she had told him, and did not understand when he replied with happy seriousness, "We make the god together."

"I'm sorry," he said now. "It's a different form of reason. Superstition, if you like. I can't help it, Tiu. Terra is a hundred and forty light-years away. If you go, when you get there, I'll be dead."

"You will not! You'll have lived another year here, you'll be on your way there, you'll arrive a year after I do!"

"I know that. Even in Stse we learned that," he said patiently. "But I'm superstitious. We die to each other if you go. Even in Kathhad you learned that."

"I didn't. It's not true. How can you ask me to give up this chance for what you admit is a superstition? Be fair, Zhiv!"

After a long silence, he nodded.

She sat stricken, understanding that she had won. She had won badly.

She reached across to him, trying to comfort him and herself. She was scared by the darkness in him, his grief, his mute acceptance of betrayal. But it wasn't betrayal—she rejected the word at once. She wouldn't betray him. They were in love. They loved each other. He would follow her in a year, two years at the most. They were adults, they must not cling together like children. Adult relationships are based on mutual freedom, mutual trust. She told herself all these things as she said them to him. He said yes, and held her, and comforted her. In the night, in the utter silence of the desert, the blood singing in his ears, he lay awake and thought, "It has died unborn. It was never conceived."

They stayed together in their little apartment at the School for the few more weeks before Tiu left. They made love cautiously, gently, talked about history and economics and ethnology, kept busy. Tiu had to prepare herself to work with the team she was going with, studying the Terran concepts of hierarchy; Zhiv had a paper to write on social-energy generation on Werel. They worked hard. Their friends gave Tiu a big farewell party. The next day Zhiv went with her to Ve Port. She kissed and held him, telling him to hurry, hurry and come to Terra. He saw her board the flyer that would take her up to the NAFAL ship waiting in orbit. He went back to the apartment on the South Campus of the School. There a friend found him three days later sitting at his desk in a curious condition, passive, speaking very slowly if at all, unable to eat or drink. Being pueblo-born, the friend recognised this state and called in the medicine man (the Hainish do not call them doctors). Having ascertained that he was from one of the Southern pueblos, the medicine man said, "Havzhiva! The god cannot die in you here!"

After a long silence the young man said softly in a voice which did not sound like his voice, "I need to go home."

"That is not possible now," said the medicine man. "But we can arrange a Staying Chant while I find a person able to address the god." He promptly put out a call for students who were ex–People of the South. Four responded. They sat all night with Havzhiva singing the Staying Chant in two languages and four dialects, until Havzhiva joined them in a fifth dialect, whispering the words hoarsely, till he collapsed and slept for thirty hours.

He woke in his own room. An old woman was having a conversation with nobody beside him. "You aren't here," she said. "No, you are mistaken. You can't die here. It would not be right, it would be quite wrong. You know that. This is the wrong place. This is the wrong life. You know that! What are you doing here? Are you lost? Do you want to know the way home? Here it is. Listen." She began singing in a thin, high voice, an almost tuneless, almost wordless song that was familiar to Havzhiva, as if he had heard it long ago. He fell asleep again while the old woman went on talking to nobody.

When he woke again she was gone. He never knew who she

was or where she came from; he never asked. She had spoken and sung in his own language, in the dialect of Stse.

He was not going to die now, but he was very unwell. The medicine man ordered him to the Hospital at Tes, the most beautiful place on all Ve, an oasis where hot springs and sheltering hills make a mild local climate and flowers and forests can grow. There are paths endlessly winding under great trees, warm lakes where you can swim forever, little misty ponds from which birds rise crying, steam-shrouded hot springs, and a thousand waterfalls whose voices are the only sound all night. There he was sent to stay till he was recovered.

He began to speak into his noter, after he had been at Tes twenty days or so; he would sit in the sunlight on the doorstep of his cottage in a glade of grasses and ferns and talk quietly to himself by way of the little recording machine. "What you select from, in order to tell your story, is nothing less than everything," he said, watching the branches of the old trees dark against the sky. "What you build up your world from, your local, intelligible, rational, coherent world, is nothing less than everything. And so all selection is arbitrary. All knowledge is partial—infinitesimally partial. Reason is a net thrown out into an ocean. What truth it brings in is a fragment, a glimpse, a scintillation of the whole truth. All human knowledge is local. Every life, each human life, is local, is arbitrary, the infinitesimal momentary glitter of a reflection of . . ." His voice ceased; the silence of the glade among the great trees continued.

After forty-five days he returned to the School. He took a new apartment. He changed fields, leaving social science, Tiu's field, for Ekumenical service training, which was intellectually closely related but led to a different kind of work. The change would lengthen his time at the School by at least a year, after which if he did well he could hope for a post with the Ekumen. He did well, and after two years was asked, in the polite fashion of the Ekumenical councils, if he would care to go to Werel. Yes, he said, he would. His friends gave a big farewell party for him.

"I thought you were aiming for Terra," said one of his less-astute classmates. "All that stuff about war and slavery and class and caste and gender—isn't that Terran history?"

"It's current events in Werel," Havzhiva said.

He was no longer Zhiv. He had come back from the Hospital as Havzhiva.

Somebody else was stepping on the unastute classmate's foot, but she paid no attention. "I thought you were going to follow Tiu," she said. "I thought that's why you never slept with anybody. God, if I'd only known!" The others winced, but Havzhiva smiled and hugged her apologetically.

In his own mind it was quite clear. As he had betrayed and forsaken Iyan Iyan, so Tiu had betrayed and forsaken him. There was no going back and no going forward. So he must turn aside. Though he was one of them, he could no longer live with the People; though he had become one of them, he did not want to live with the historians. So he must go live among Aliens.

He had no hope of joy. He had bungled that, he thought. But he knew that the two long, intense disciplines that had filled his life, that of the gods and that of history, had given him an uncommon knowledge, which might be of use somewhere; and he knew that the right use of knowledge is fulfillment.

The medicine man came to visit him the day before he left, checked him over, and then sat for a while saying nothing. Havzhiva sat with him. He had long been used to silence, and still sometimes forgot that it was not customary among historians.

"What's wrong?" the medicine man said. It seemed to be a rhetorical question, from its meditative tone; at any rate, Havzhiva made no answer.

"Please stand up," the medicine man said, and when Havzhiva had done so, "Now walk a little." He walked a few steps; the medicine man observed him. "You're out of balance," he said. "Did you know it?"

"Yes."

"I could get a Staying Chant together this evening."

"It's all right," Havzhiva said. "I've always been off-balance."

"There's no need to be," the medicine man said. "On the other hand, maybe it's best, since you're going to Werel. So: Good-bye for this life."

They embraced formally, as historians did, especially when as now it was absolutely certain that they would never see one another again. Havzhiva had to give and get a good many formal embraces that day. The next day he boarded the *Terraces of Darranda* and went across the darkness.

YEOWE

During his journey of eighty light-years at NAFAL speed, his mother died, and his father, and Iyan Iyan, everyone he had known in Stse, everyone he knew in Kathhad and on Ve. By the time the ship landed, they had all been dead for years. The child Iyan Iyan had borne had lived and grown old and died.

This was a knowledge he had lived with ever since he saw Tiu board her ship, leaving him to die. Because of the medicine man, the four people who had sung for him, the old woman, and the waterfalls of Tes, he had lived; but he had lived with that knowledge.

Other things had changed as well. At the time he left Ve, Werel's colony planet Yeowe had been a slave world, a huge work camp. By the time he arrived on Werel, the War of Liberation was over, Yeowe had declared its independence, and the institution of slavery on Werel itself was beginning to disintegrate.

Havzhiva longed to observe this terrible and magnificent process, but the Embassy sent him promptly off to Yeowe. A Hainishman called Sohikelwenyanmurkeres Esdardon Aya counseled him before he left. "If you want danger, it's dangerous," he said, "and if you like hope, it's hopeful. Werel is unmaking itself, while Yeowe's trying to make itself. I don't know if it's going to succeed. I tell you what, Yehedarhed Havzhiva: there are great gods loose on these worlds."

Yeowe had got rid of its Bosses, its Owners, the Four Corporations who had run the vast slave plantations for three hundred years; but though the thirty years of the War of Liberation were over, the fighting had not stopped. Chiefs and warlords among the slaves who had risen to power during the Liberation now fought to keep and extend their power. Factions had battled over the question of whether to kick all foreigners off the planet forever or to admit Aliens and join the Ekumen. The isolationists had finally been voted down, and there was a new Ekumenical Embassy in the old colonial capital. Havzhiva spent a while there learning "the language and the table manners," as they said. Then the Ambassador, a clever young Terran named Solly, sent him south to the region called Yotebber, which was clamoring for recognition.

History is infamy, Havzhiva thought as he rode the train through the ruined landscapes of the world.

The Werelian capitalists who colonised the planet had exploited it and their slaves recklessly, mindlessly, in a long orgy of profit-making. It takes a while to spoil a world, but it can be done. Strip-mining and single-crop agriculture had defaced and sterilised the earth. The rivers were polluted, dead. Huge dust storms darkened the eastern horizon.

The Bosses had run their plantations by force and fear. For over a century they had shipped male slaves only, worked them till they died, imported fresh ones as needed. Work gangs in these all-male compounds developed into tribal hierarchies. At last, as the price of slaves on Werel and the cost of shipping rose, the Corporations began to buy bondswomen for Yeowe Colony. So over the next two centuries the slave population grew, and slave-cities were founded, "Assetvilles" and "Dusty-towns" spreading out from the old compounds of the plantations. Havzhiva knew that the Liberation movement had arisen first among the women in the tribal compounds, a rebellion against male domination, before it became a war of all slaves against their owners.

The slow train stopped in city after city: miles of shacks and cabins, treeless, whole tracts bombed or burnt out in the war and not yet rebuilt; factories, some of them gutted ruins, some functioning but ancient-looking, rattletrap, smoke-belching. At each station hundreds of people got off the train and onto it, swarming, crowding, shouting out bribes to the porters, clambering up onto the roofs of the cars, brutally shoved off again by uniformed guards and policemen. In the north of the long continent, as on Werel, he had seen many black-skinned people, blue-black; but as the train went farther south there were fewer of these, until in Yotebber the people in the villages and on the desolate sidings were much paler than he was, a bluish, dusty color. These were the "dust people," the descendants of a hundred generations of Werelian slaves.

Yotebber had been an early center of the Liberation. The Bosses had made reprisal with bombs and poison gas; thousands of people had died. Whole towns had been burned to get rid of the unburied dead, human and animal. The mouth of the great river had been dammed with rotting bodies. But all that was past. Yeowe was free, a new member of the Ekumen of the Worlds, and Havzhiva in the capacity of Sub-Envoy was on his way to help the people of Yotebber Region to begin their new history. Or from the point of view of a Hainishman, to rejoin their ancient history.

He was met at the station in Yotebber City by a large crowd surging and cheering and yelling behind barricades manned by policemen and soldiers; in front of the barricades was a delegation of officials wearing splendid robes and sashes of office and variously ornate uniforms: big men, most of them, dignified, very much public figures. There were speeches of welcome, reporters and photographers for the holonet and the neareal news. It wasn't a circus, however. The big men were definitely in control. They wanted their guest to know he was welcome, he was popular, he was—as the Chief said in his brief, impressive speech—the Envoy from the Future.

That night in his luxurious suite in an Owner's city mansion converted to a hotel, Havzhiva thought: If they knew that their man from the future grew up in a pueblo and never saw a neareal till he came here . . .

He hoped he would not disappoint these people. From the moment he had first met them on Werel he had liked them, despite their monstrous society. They were full of vitality and pride, and here on Yeowe they were full of dreams of justice. Havzhiva thought of justice what an ancient Terran said of another god: I believe in it because it is impossible. He slept well, and woke early in the warm, bright morning, full of anticipation. He walked out to begin to get to know the city, his city.

The doorman—it was disconcerting to find that people who had fought so desperately for their freedom had servants—the doorman tried hard to get him to wait for a car, a guide, evidently distressed at the great man's going out so early, afoot, without a retinue. Havzhiva explained that he wanted to walk and was quite able to walk alone. He set off, leaving the unhappy doorman calling after him, "Oh, sir, please, avoid the City Park, sir!"

Havzhiva obeyed, thinking the park must be closed for a ceremony or replanting. He came on a plaza where a market was in full swing, and there found himself likely to become the center of a crowd; people inevitably noticed him. He wore the handsome Yeowan clothes, singlet, breeches, a light narrow robe, but he was the only person with red-brown skin in a city of four hundred thousand people. As soon as they saw his skin, his eyes, they knew him: the Alien. So he slipped away from the market and kept to quiet residential streets, enjoying the soft, warm air and the decrepit, charming colonial architecture of the houses. He stopped to admire an ornate Tualite temple. It looked rather shabby and desolate, but there was, he saw, a fresh offering of flowers at the feet of the image of the Mother at the doorway. Though her nose had been knocked off during the war, she smiled serenely, a little cross-eyed. People called out behind him. Somebody said close to him, "Foreign shit, get off our world," and his arm was seized as his legs were kicked out from under him. Contorted faces, screaming, closed in around him. An enormous, sickening cramp seized his body, doubling him into a red darkness of struggle and voices and pain, then a dizzy shrinking and dwindling away of light and sound.

An old woman was sitting by him, whispering an almost tuneless song that seemed dimly familiar.

She was knitting. For a long time she did not look at him; when she did she said, "Ah." He had trouble making his eyes focus, but he made out that her face was bluish, a pale bluish tan, and there were no whites to her dark eyes.

She rearranged some kind of apparatus that was attached to him somewhere, and said, "I'm the medicine woman—the nurse. You have a concussion, a slight skull fracture, a bruised kidney, a broken shoulder, and a knife wound in your gut; but you'll be all right; don't worry." All this was in a foreign language, which he seemed to understand. At least he understood "don't worry," and obeyed.

He thought he was on the *Terraces of Darranda* in NAFAL mode. A hundred years passed in a bad dream but did not pass. People and clocks had no faces. He tried to whisper the Staying Chant and it had no words. The words were gone.

The old woman took his hand. She held his hand and slowly, slowly brought him back into time, into local time, into the dim, quiet room where she sat knitting.

It was morning, hot, bright sunlight in the window. The Chief of Yotebber Region stood by his bedside, a tower of a man in white-and-crimson robes.

"I'm very sorry," Havzhiva said, slowly and thickly because his mouth was damaged. "It was stupid of me to go out alone. The fault was entirely mine."

"The villains have been caught and will be tried in a court of justice," said the Chief.

"They were young men," Havzhiva said. "My ignorance and folly caused the incident—"

"They will be punished," the Chief said.

The day nurses always had the holoscreen up and watched the news and the dramas as they sat with him. They kept the sound down, and Havzhiva could ignore it. It was a hot afternoon; he was watching faint clouds move slowly across the sky, when the nurse said, using the formal address to a person of high status, "Oh, quick—if the gentleman will look, he can see the punishment of the bad men who attacked him!"

Havzhiva obeyed. He saw a thin human body suspended by the feet, the arms and hands twitching, the intestines hanging down over the chest and face. He cried out aloud and hid his face in his arm. "Turn it off," he said, "turn it off!" He retched and gasped for air. "You are not people!" he cried in his own language, the dialect of Stse. There was some coming and going in the room. The noise of a yelling crowd ceased abruptly. He got control of his breath and lay with his eyes shut, repeating one phrase of the Staying Chant over and over until his mind and body began to steady and find a little balance somewhere, not much.

They came with food; he asked them to take it away.

The room was dim, lit only by a night-light somewhere low on the wall and the lights of the city outside the window. The old woman, the night nurse, was there, knitting in the half dark.

"I'm sorry," Havzhiva said at random, knowing he didn't know what he had said to them.

"Oh, Mr. Envoy," the old woman said with a long sigh. "I

read about your people. The Hainish people. You don't do things like we do. You don't torture and kill each other. You live in peace. I wonder, I wonder what we seem to you. Like witches, like devils, maybe."

"No," he said, but he swallowed down another wave of nausea.

"When you feel better, when you're stronger, Mr. Envoy, I have a thing I want to speak to you about." Her voice was quiet and full of an absolute, easy authority, which probably could become formal and formidable. He had known people who talked that way all his life.

"I can listen now," he said, but she said, "Not now. Later. You are tired. Would you like me to sing?"

"Yes," he said, and she sat and knitted and sang voicelessly, tunelessly, in a whisper. The names of her gods were in the song: Tual, Kamye. They are not my gods, he thought, but he closed his eyes and slept, safe in the rocking balance.

Her name was Yeron, and she was not old. She was forty-seven. She had been through a thirty-year war and several famines. She had artificial teeth, something Havzhiva had never heard of, and wore eyeglasses with wire frames; body mending was not unknown on Werel, but on Yeowe most people couldn't afford it, she said. She was very thin, and her hair was thin. She had a proud bearing, but moved stiffly from an old wound in the left hip. "Everybody, everybody in this world has a bullet in them, or whipping scars, or a leg blown off, or a dead baby in their heart," she said. "Now you're one of us, Mr. Envoy. You've been through the fire."

He was recovering well. There were five or six medical specialists on his case. The Regional Chief visited every few days and sent officials daily. The Chief was, Havzhiva realised, grateful. The outrageous attack on a representative of the Ekumen had given him the excuse and strong popular support for a strike against the diehard isolationist World Party led by his rival, another warlord hero of the Liberation. He sent glowing reports of his victories to the Sub-Envoy's hospital room. The holonews was all of men in uniforms running, shooting, flyers buzzing over desert hills. As he walked the halls, gaining strength, Havzhiva saw patients lying in bed in the wards wired in to the neareal net, "experiencing" the fighting, from the point of view, of course, of the ones with guns, the ones with cameras, the ones who shot.

At night the screens were dark, the nets were down, and Yeron came and sat by him in the dim light from the window.

"You said there was something you had to tell me," he said. The city night was restless, full of noises, music, voices down in the street below the window she had opened wide to let in the warm, many-scented air.

"Yes, I did." She put her knitting down. "I am your nurse, Mr. Envoy, but also a messenger. When I heard you'd been hurt, forgive me, but I said, 'Praise the Lord Kamye and the Lady of Mercy!' Because I had not known how to bring my message to you, and now I knew how." Her quiet voice paused a minute. "I ran this hospital for fifteen years. During the war. I can still pull a few strings here." Again she paused. Like her voice, her silences were familiar to him. "I'm a messenger to the Ekumen," she said, "from the women. Women here. Women all over Yeowe. We want to make an alliance with you. . . . I know, the government already did that. Yeowe is a member of the Ekumen of the Worlds. We know that. But what does it mean? To us? It means nothing. Do you know what women are, here, in this world? They are nothing. They are not part of the government. Women made the Liberation. They worked and they died for it just like the men. But they weren't generals, they aren't chiefs. They are nobody. In the villages they are less than nobody, they are work animals, breeding stock. Here it's some better. But not good. I was trained in the Medical School at Besso. I am a doctor, not a nurse. Under the Bosses, I ran this hospital. Now a man runs it. Our men are the owners now. And we're what we always were. Property. I don't think that's what we fought the long war for. Do you, Mr. Envoy? I think what we have is a new liberation to make. We have to finish the job."

After a long silence, Havzhiva asked softly, "Are you organised?"

"Oh, yes. Oh, yes! Just like the old days. We can organize in the dark!" She laughed a little. "But I don't think we can win

freedom for ourselves alone by ourselves alone. There has to
be a change. The men think they have to be bosses. They have
to stop thinking that. Well, one thing we have learned in my
lifetime, you don't change a mind with a gun. You kill the boss
and you become the boss. We must change that mind. The old
slave mind, boss mind. We have got to change it, Mr. Envoy.
With your help. The Ekumen's help."

"I'm here to be a link between your people and the Ekumen.
But I'll need time," he said. "I need to learn."

"All the time in the world. We know we can't turn the boss
mind around in a day or a year. This is a matter of education."
She said the word as a sacred word. "It will take a long time.
You take your time. If we just know that you will *listen*."

"I will listen," he said.

She drew a long breath, took up her knitting again. Presently she said, "It won't be easy to hear us."

He was tired. The intensity of her talk was more than he
could yet handle. He did not know what she meant. A polite
silence is the adult way of signifying that one doesn't understand. He said nothing.

She looked at him. "How are we to come to you? You
see, that's a problem. I tell you, we are nothing. We can come
to you only as your nurse. Your housemaid. The woman
who washes your clothes. We don't mix with the chiefs. We
aren't on the councils. We wait on table. We don't eat the
banquet."

"Tell me—" he hesitated. "Tell me how to start. Ask to see
me if you can. Come as you can, as it . . . if it's safe?" He had
always been quick to learn his lessons. "I'll listen. I'll do what
I can." He would never learn much distrust.

She leaned over and kissed him very gently on the mouth.
Her lips were light, dry, soft.

"There," she said, "no chief will give you that."

She took up her knitting again. He was half-asleep when she
asked, "Your mother is living, Mr. Havzhiva?"

"All my people are dead."

She made a little soft sound. "Bereft," she said. "And no
wife?"

"No."

"We will be your mothers, your sisters, your daughters. Your people. I kissed you for that love that will be between us. You will see."

"The list of the persons invited to the reception, Mr. Yehedarhed," said Doranden, the Chief's chief liaison to the Sub-Envoy.

Havzhiva looked through the list on the handscreen carefully, ran it past the end, and said, "Where is the rest?"

"I'm so sorry, Mr. Envoy—are there omissions? This is the entire list."

"But these are all men."

In the infinitesimal silence before Doranden replied, Havzhiva felt the balance of his life poised.

"You wish the guests to bring their wives? Of course! If this is the Ekumenical custom, we shall be delighted to invite the ladies!"

There was something lip-smacking in the way Yeowan men said "the ladies," a word which Havzhiva had thought was applied only to women of the owner class on Werel. The balance dipped. "What ladies?" he asked, frowning. "I'm talking about women. Do they have no part in this society?"

He became very nervous as he spoke, for he now knew his ignorance of what constituted danger here. If a walk on a quiet street could be nearly fatal, embarrassing the Chief's liaison might be completely so. Doranden was certainly embarrassed —floored. He opened his mouth and shut it.

"I'm sorry, Mr. Doranden," Havzhiva said, "please pardon my poor efforts at jocosity. Of course I know that women have all kinds of responsible positions in your society. I was merely saying, in a stupidly unfortunate manner, that I should be very glad to have such women and their husbands, as well as the wives of these guests, attend the reception. Unless I am truly making an enormous blunder concerning your customs? I thought you did not segregate the sexes socially, as they do on Werel. Please, if I was wrong, be so kind as to excuse the ignorant foreigner once again."

Loquacity is half of diplomacy, Havzhiva had already decided. The other half is silence.

Doranden availed himself of the latter option, and with a few earnest reassurances got himself away. Havzhiva remained nervous until the following morning, when Doranden reappeared with a revised list containing eleven new names, all female. There was a school principal and a couple of teachers; the rest were marked "retired."

"Splendid, splendid!" said Havzhiva. "May I add one more name?" —Of course, of course, anyone Your Excellency desires — "Dr. Yeron," he said.

Again the infinitesimal silence, the grain of dust dropping on the scales. Doranden knew that name. "Yes," he said.

"Dr. Yeron nursed me, you know, at your excellent hospital. We became friends. An ordinary nurse might not be an appropriate guest among such very distinguished people; but I see there are several other doctors on our list."

"Quite," said Doranden. He seemed bemused. The Chief and his people had become used to patronising the Sub-Envoy, ever so slightly and politely. An invalid, though now well recovered; a victim; a man of peace, ignorant of attack and even of self-defense; a scholar, a foreigner, unworldly in every sense: they saw him as something like that, he knew. Much as they valued him as a symbol and as a means to their ends, they thought him an insignificant man. He agreed with them as to the fact, but not as to the quality, of his insignificance. He knew that what he did might signify. He had just seen it.

"Surely *you* understand the reason for having a bodyguard, Envoy," the General said with some impatience.

"This is a dangerous city, General Denkam, yes, I understand that. Dangerous for everyone. I see on the net that gangs of young men, such as those who attacked me, roam the streets quite beyond the control of the police. Every child, every woman needs a bodyguard. I should be distressed to know that the safety which is every citizen's right was my special privilege."

The General blinked but stuck to his guns. "We can't let you get assassinated," he said.

Havzhiva loved the bluntness of Yeowan honesty. "I don't want to be assassinated," he said. "I have a suggestion, sir. There are policewomen, female members of the city police force, are there not? Find me bodyguards among them. After all, an armed woman is as dangerous as an armed man, isn't she? And I should like to honor the great part women played in winning Yeowe's freedom, as the Chief said so eloquently in his talk yesterday."

The General departed with a face of cast iron.

Havzhiva did not particularly like his bodyguards. They were hard, tough women, unfriendly, speaking a dialect he could hardly understand. Several of them had children at home, but they refused to talk about their children. They were fiercely efficient. He was well protected. He saw when he went about with these cold-eyed escorts that he began to be looked at differently by the city crowds: with amusement and a kind of fellow-feeling. He heard an old man in the market say, "That fellow has some sense."

Everybody called the Chief the Chief except to his face. "Mr. President," Havzhiva said, "the question really isn't one of Ekumenical principles or Hainish customs at all. None of that is or should be of the least weight, the least importance, here on Yeowe. This is your world."

The Chief nodded once, massively.

"Into which," said Havzhiva, by now insuperably loquacious, "immigrants are beginning to come from Werel now, and many, many more will come, as the Werelian ruling class tries to lessen revolutionary pressure by allowing increasing numbers of the underclass to emigrate. You, sir, know far better than I the opportunities and the problems that this great influx of population will cause here in Yotebber. Now of course at least half the immigrants will be female, and I think it worth considering that there is a very considerable difference between Werel and Yeowe in what is called the construction of gender—the roles, the expectations, the behavior, the relationships of men and women. Among the Werelian immigrants most of the decision-makers, the people of authority, will be female. The Council of the Hame is about nine-tenths women, I believe. Their speakers and negotiators are mostly women. These people are coming into a society governed and represented entirely by men. I think there is the possibility of misunderstandings and conflict, unless the situation is carefully considered beforehand. Perhaps the use of some women as representatives—"

"Among slaves on the Old World," the Chief said, "women were chiefs. Among our people, men are chiefs. That is how it is. The slaves of the Old World will be the free men of the New World."

"And the women, Mr. President?"

"A free man's women are free," said the Chief.

"Well, then," Yeron said, and sighed her deep sigh. "I guess we have to kick up some dust."

"What dust people are good at," said Dobibe.

"Then we better kick up a whole lot," said Tualyan. "Because no matter what we do, they'll get hysterical. They'll yell and scream about castrating dykes who kill boy babies. If there's five of us singing some damn song, it'll get into the neareals as five hundred of us with machine guns and the end of civilisation on Yeowe. So I say let's go for it. Let's have five thousand women out singing. Let's stop the trains. Lie down on the tracks. Fifty thousand women lying on the tracks all over Yotebber. You think?"

The meeting (of the Yotebber City and Regional Educational Aid Association) was in a schoolroom of one of the city schools. Two of Havzhiva's bodyguards, in plain clothes, waited unobtrusively in the hall. Forty women and Havzhiva were jammed into small chairs attached to blank netscreens.

"Asking for?" Havzhiva said.

"The secret ballot!"

"No job discrimination!"

"Pay for our work!"

"The secret ballot!"

"Child care!"

"The secret ballot!"

"Respect!"

Havzhiva's noter scribbled away madly. The women went on shouting for a while and then settled down to talk again.

One of the bodyguards spoke to Havzhiva as she drove him home. "Sir," she said. "Was those all teachers?"

"Yes," he said. "In a way."

"Be damn," she said. "Different from they used to be."

"Yehedarhed! What the hell are you doing down there?"

"Ma'am?"

"You were on the news. Along with about a million women

lying across railroad tracks and all over flyer pads and draped around the President's Residence. You were talking to women and smiling."

"It was hard not to."

"When the Regional Government begins shooting, will you stop smiling?"

"Yes. Will you back us?"

"How?"

"Words of encouragement to the women of Yotebber from the Ambassador of the Ekumen. Yeowe a model of true freedom for immigrants from the Slave World. Words of praise to the Government of Yotebber—Yotebber a model for all Yeowe of restraint, enlightenment, et cetera."

"Sure. I hope it helps. Is this a revolution, Havzhiva?"

"It is education, ma'am."

The gate stood open in its massive frame; there were no walls.

"In the time of the Colony," the Elder said, "this gate was opened twice in the day: to let the people out to work in the morning, to let the people in from work in the evening. At all other times it was locked and barred." He displayed the great broken lock that hung on the outer face of the gate, the massive bolts rusted in their hasps. His gesture was solemn, measured, like his words, and again Havzhiva admired the dignity these people had kept in degradation, the stateliness they had maintained in, or against, their enslavement. He had begun to appreciate the immense influence of their sacred text, the *Arkamye*, preserved in oral tradition. "This was what we had. This was our belonging," an old man in the city had told him, touching the book which, at sixty-five or seventy, he was learning to read.

Havzhiva himself had begun to read the book in its original language. He read it slowly, trying to understand how this tale of fierce courage and abnegation had for three millennia informed and nourished the minds of people in bondage. Often he heard in its cadences the voices he had heard speak that day.

He was staying for a month in Hayawa Tribal Village, which had been the first slave compound of the Agricultural Plantation Corporation of Yeowe in Yotebber, three hundred fifty years ago. In this immense, remote region of the eastern coast, much of the society and culture of plantation slavery had been preserved. Yeron and other women of the Liberation Movement had told him that to know who the Yeowans were he must know the plantations and the tribes.

He knew that the compounds had for the first century been a domain of men without women and without children. They had developed an internal government, a strict hierarchy of force and favoritism. Power was won by tests and ordeals and kept by a nimble balancing of independence and collusion. When women slaves were brought in at last, they entered this rigid system as the slaves of slaves. By bondsmen as by Bosses, they were used as servants and sexual outlets. Sexual loyalty and partnership continued to be recognized only between men, a nexus of passion, negotiation, status, and tribal politics. During the next centuries the presence of children in the compounds had altered and enriched tribal customs, but the system of male dominance, so entirely advantageous to the slave-owners, had not essentially changed.

"We hope to have your presence at the initiation tomorrow," the Elder said in his grave way, and Havzhiva assured him that nothing could please or honor him more than attendance at a ceremony of such importance. The Elder was sedately but visibly gratified. He was a man over fifty, which meant he had been born a slave and had lived as a boy and man through the years of the Liberation. Havzhiva looked for scars, remembering what Yeron had said, and found them: the Elder was thin, meager, lame, and had no upper teeth; he was marked all through by famine and war. Also he was ritually scarred, four parallel ridges running from neck to elbow over the point of the shoulder like long epaulets, and a dark blue open eye tattooed on his forehead, the sign, in this tribe, of assigned, unalterable chiefdom. A slave chief, a chattel master of chattels, till the walls went down.

The Elder walked on a certain path from the gate to the longhouse, and Havzhiva following him observed that no one else used this path: men, women, children trotted along a wider, parallel road that diverged off to a different entrance to the longhouse. This was the chiefs' way, the narrow way.

That night, while the children to be initiated next day fasted and kept vigil over on the women's side, all the chiefs and elders gathered for a feast. There were inordinate amounts of the heavy food Yeowans were accustomed to, spiced and ornately served, the marsh rice that was the basis of everything fancied up with colorings and herbs; above all there was meat. Women slipped in and out serving ever more elaborate platters, each one with more meat on it—cattle flesh, Boss food, the sure and certain sign of freedom.

Havzhiva had not grown up eating meat, and could count on it giving him diarrhea, but he chewed his way manfully through the stews and steaks, knowing the significance of the food and the meaning of plenty to those who had never had enough.

After huge baskets of fruit finally replaced the platters, the women disappeared and the music began. The tribal chief nodded to his leos, a word meaning "sexual favorite/adopted brother/not heir/not son." The young man, a self-assured, good-natured beauty, smiled; he clapped his long hands very softly once, then began to brush the grey-blue palms in a subtle rhythm. As the table fell silent he sang, but in a whisper.

Instruments of music had been forbidden on most plantations; most Bosses had allowed no singing except the ritual hymns to Tual at the tenthday service. A slave caught wasting Corporation time in singing might have acid poured down his throat. So long as he could work there was no need for him to make noise.

On such plantations the slaves had developed this almost silent music, the touch and brush of palm against palm, a barely voiced, barely varied, long line of melody. The words sung were deliberately broken, distorted, fragmented, so that they seemed meaningless. *Shesh*, the owners had called it, rubbish, and slaves were permitted to "pat hands and sing rubbish" so long as they did it so softly it could not be heard outside the compound walls. Having sung so for three hundred years, they sang so now.

To Havzhiva it was unnerving, almost frightening, as voice after voice joined, always at a whisper, increasing the complexity of the rhythms till the cross-beats nearly, but never quite, joined into a single texture of hushing sibilant sound, threaded by the long-held, quarter-tonal melody sung on syllables that seemed always about to make a word but never did. Caught in it, soon almost lost in it, he kept thinking now—now one of them will raise his voice—now the leos will give a shout, a shout of triumph, letting his voice free! —But he did not. None did. The soft, rushing, waterlike music with its infinitely delicate shifting rhythm went on and on. Bottles of the orange Yote wine passed up and down the table. They drank. They drank freely, at least. They got drunk. Laughter and shouts began to interrupt the music. But they never once sang above a whisper.

They all reeled back to the longhouse on the chiefs' path, embracing, peeing companionably, one or two pausing to vomit here and there. A kind, dark man who had been seated next to Havzhiva now joined him in his bed in his alcove of the longhouse.

Earlier in the evening this man had told him that during the night and day of the initiation heterosexual intercourse was forbidden, as it would change the energies. The initiation would go crooked, and the boys might not become good members of the tribe. Only a witch, of course, would deliberately break the taboo, but many women were witches and would try to seduce a man out of malice. Regular, that is, homosexual, intercourse would encourage the energies, keep the initiation straight, and give the boys strength for their ordeal. Hence every man leaving the banquet would have a partner for the night. Havzhiva was glad he had been assigned to this man, not to one of the chiefs, whom he found daunting, and who might have expected a properly energetic performance. As it was, as well as he could remember in the morning, he and his companion had been too drunk to do much but fall asleep amidst well-intended caresses.

Too much Yote wine left a ringing headache, he knew that already, and his whole skull reconfirmed the knowledge when he woke.

At noon his friend brought him to a place of honor in the plaza, which was filling up with men. Behind them were the men's longhouses, in front of them the ditch that separated the women's side, the inside, from the men's or gate side—still so-called, though the compound walls were gone and the gate alone stood, a monument, towering above the huts and longhouses of the compound and the flat grainfields that stretched away in all directions, shimmering in the windless, shadowless heat.

From the women's huts, six boys came at a run to the ditch. It was wider than a thirteen-year-old could jump, Havzhiva thought; but two of the boys made it. The other four leapt valiantly, fell short, clambered out, one of them hobbling, having hurt a leg or foot in his fall. Even the two who had made the jump successfully looked exhausted and frightened, and all six were bluish grey from fasting and staying awake. Elders surrounded them and got them standing in line in the plaza, naked and shivering, facing the crowd of all the men of the tribe.

No women at all were visible, over on the women's side.

A catechism began, chiefs and elders barking questions which must evidently be answered without delay, sometimes by one boy, sometimes by all together, depending on the questioner's pointing or sweeping gesture. They were questions of ritual, protocol, and ethics. The boys had been well drilled, delivering their answers in prompt yelps. The one who had lamed himself in the jump suddenly vomited and then fainted, slipping quietly down in a little heap. Nothing was done, and some questions were still pointed to him, followed by a moment of painful silence. After a while the boy moved, sat up, sat a while shuddering, then struggled to his feet and stood with the others. His bluish lips moved in answer to all the questions, though no voice reached the audience.

Havzhiva kept his apparent attention fixed on the ritual, though his mind wandered back a long time, a long way. We teach what we know, he thought, and all our knowledge is local.

After the inquisition came the marking: a single deep cut from the base of the neck over the point of the shoulder and down the outer arm to the elbow, made with a hard, sharp stake of wood dragged gouging through skin and flesh to leave, when it healed, the furrowed scar that proved the man. Slaves would not have been allowed any metal tools inside the gate, Havzhiva reflected, watching steadily as behooved a visitor and guest. After each arm and each boy, the officiating elders stopped to resharpen the stake, rubbing it on a big grooved stone that sat in the plaza. The boys' pale blue lips drew back, baring their white teeth; they writhed, half-fainting, and one of them screamed aloud, silencing himself by clapping his free hand over his mouth. One bit on his thumb till blood flowed from it as well as from his lacerated arms. As each boy's marking was finished the Tribal Chief washed the wounds and smeared some ointment on them. Dazed and wobbling, the boys stood again in line; and now the old men were tender with them, smiling, calling them "tribesman," "hero." Havzhiva drew a long breath of relief.

But now six more children were being brought into the plaza, led across the ditch-bridge by old women. These were girls, decked with anklets and bracelets, otherwise naked. At the sight of them a great cheer went up from the audience of men. Havzhiva was surprised. Women were to be made members of the tribe too? That at least was a good thing, he thought.

Two of the girls were barely adolescent, the others were younger, one of them surely not more than six. They were lined up, their backs to the audience, facing the boys. Behind each of them stood the veiled woman who had led her across the bridge; behind each boy stood one of the naked elders. As Havzhiva watched, unable to turn his eyes or mind from what he saw, the little girls lay down face up on the bare, greyish ground of the plaza. One of them, slow to lie down, was tugged and forced down by the woman behind her. The old men came around the boys, and each one lay down on one of the girls, to a great noise of cheering, jeering, and laughter and a chant of "ha-ah-ha-ah!" from the spectators. The veiled women crouched at the girls' heads. One of them reached out and held down a thin, flailing arm. The elders' bare buttocks pumped, whether in actual coitus or an imitation Havzhiva could not tell. "That's how you do it, watch, watch!" the spectators shouted to the boys, amid jokes and comments and roars of laughter. The elders one by one stood up, each shielding his penis with curious modesty.

When the last had stood up, the boys stepped forward. Each lay down on a girl and pumped his buttocks up and down, though not one of them, Havzhiva saw, had had an erection. The men around him grasped their own penises, shouting, "Here, try mine!" and cheering and chanting until the last boy scrambled to his feet. The girls lay flat, their legs parted, like little dead lizards. There was a slight, terrible movement towards them in the crowd of men. But the old women were hauling the girls to their feet, yanking them up, hurrying them back across the bridge, followed by a wave of howls and jeers from the audience.

"They're drugged, you know," said the kind, dark man who had shared Havzhiva's bed, looking into his face. "The girls. It doesn't hurt them."

"Yes, I see," said Havzhiva, standing still in his place of honor.

"These ones are lucky, privileged to assist initiation. It's important that girls cease to be virgin as soon as possible, you know. Always more than one man must have them, you know. So that they can't make claims—'this is your son,' 'this baby is the chief's son,' you know. That's all witchcraft. A son is chosen. Being a son has nothing to do with bondswomen's cunts. Bondswomen have to be taught that early. But the girls are given drugs now. It's not like the old days, under the Corporations."

"I understand," Havzhiva said. He looked into his friend's face, thinking that his dark skin meant he must have a good deal of owner blood, perhaps indeed was the son of an owner or a Boss. Nobody's son, begotten on a slave woman. A son is chosen. All knowledge is local, all knowledge is partial. In Stse, in the Schools of the Ekumen, in the compounds of Yeowe.

"You still call them bondswomen," he said. His tact, all his feelings were frozen, and he spoke in mere stupid intellectual curiosity.

"No," the dark man said, "no, I'm sorry, the language I learned as a boy—I apologize—"

"Not to me."

Again Havzhiva spoke only and coldly what was in his head. The man winced and was silent, his head bowed.

"Please, my friend, take me to my room now," Havzhiva said, and the dark man gratefully obeyed him.

He talked softly into his noter in Hainish in the dark. "You can't change anything from outside it. Standing apart, looking down, taking the overview, you see the pattern. What's wrong, what's missing. You want to fix it. But you can't patch it. You have to be in it, weaving it. You have to be part of the weaving." This last phrase was in the dialect of Stse.

Four women squatted on a patch of ground on the women's side, which had roused his curiosity by its untrodden smoothness:

some kind of sacred space, he had thought. He walked towards them. They squatted gracelessly, hunched forward between their knees, with the indifference to their appearance, the carelessness of men's gaze, that he had noticed before on the women's side. Their heads were shaved, their skin chalky and pale. Dust people, dusties, was the old epithet, but to Havzhiva their color was more like clay or ashes. The azure tinge of palms and soles and wherever the skin was fine was almost hidden by the soil they were handling. They had been talking fast and quietly, but went silent as he came near. Two were old, withered up, with knobby, wrinkled knees and feet. Two were young women. They all glanced sidelong from time to time as he squatted down near the edge of the smooth patch of ground.

On it, he saw, they had been spreading dust, colored earth, making some kind of pattern or picture. Following the boundaries between colors he made out a long pale figure a little like a hand or a branch, and a deep curve of earthen red.

Having greeted them, he said nothing more, but simply squatted there. Presently they went back to what they were doing, talking in whispers to one another now and then.

When they stopped working, he said, "Is it sacred?"

The old women looked at him, scowled, and said nothing.

"You can't see it," said the darker of the young women, with a flashing, teasing smile that took Havzhiva by surprise.

"I shouldn't be here, you mean."

"No. You can be here. But you can't see it."

He rose and looked over the earth painting they had made with grey and tan and red and umber dust. The lines and forms were in a definite relationship, rhythmical but puzzling.

"It's not all there," he said.

"This is only a little, little bit of it," said the teasing woman, her dark eyes bright with mockery in her dark face.

"Never all of it at once?"

"No," she said, and the others said, "No," and even the old women smiled.

"Can you tell me what the picture is?"

She did not know the word "picture." She glanced at the others; she pondered, and looked up at him shrewdly.

"We make what we know, here," she said, with a soft gesture

over the softly colored design. A warm evening breeze was already blurring the boundaries between the colors.

"They don't know it," said the other young woman, ashen-skinned, in a whisper.

"The men? —They never see it whole?"

"Nobody does. Only us. We have it here." The dark woman did not touch her head but her heart, covering her breasts with her long, work-hardened hands. She smiled again.

The old women stood up; they muttered together, one said something sharply to the young women, a phrase Havzhiva did not understand; and they stumped off.

"They don't approve of your talking of this work to a man," he said.

"A city man," said the dark woman, and laughed. "They think we'll run away."

"Do you want to run away?"

She shrugged. "Where to?"

She rose to her feet in one graceful movement and looked over the earth painting, a seemingly random, abstract pattern of lines and colors, curves and areas.

"Can you see it?" she asked Havzhiva, with that liquid teasing flash of the eyes.

"Maybe someday I can learn to," he said, meeting her gaze.

"You'll have to find a woman to teach you," said the woman the color of ashes.

"We are a free people now," said the Young Chief, the Son and Heir, the Chosen.

"I haven't yet known a free people," Havzhiva said, polite, ambiguous.

"We won our freedom. We made ourselves free. By courage, by sacrifice, by holding fast to the one noble thing. We are a free people." The Chosen was a strong-faced, handsome, intelligent man of forty. Six gouged lines of scarring ran down his upper arms like a rough mantle, and an open blue eye stared between his eyes, unwinking.

"You are free men," Havzhiva said.

There was a silence.

"Men of the cities do not understand our women," the

Chosen said. "Our women do not want a man's freedom. It is not for them. A woman holds fast to her baby. That is the noble thing for her. That is how the Lord Kamye made woman, and the Merciful Tual is her example. In other places it may be different. There may be another kind of woman, who does not care for her children. That may be. Here it is as I have said."

Havzhiva nodded, the deep, single nod he had learned from the Yeowans, almost a bow. "That is so," he said.

The Chosen looked gratified.

"I have seen a picture," Havzhiva went on.

The Chosen was impassive; he might or might not know the word. "Lines and colors made with earth on earth may hold knowledge in them. All knowledge is local, all truth is partial," Havzhiva said with an easy, colloquial dignity that he knew was an imitation of his mother, the Heir of the Sun, talking to foreign merchants. "No truth can make another truth untrue. All knowledge is a part of the whole knowledge. A true line, a true color. Once you have seen the larger pattern, you cannot go back to seeing the part as the whole."

The Chosen stood like a grey stone. After a while he said, "If we come to live as they live in the cities, all we know will be lost." Under his dogmatic tone was fear and grief.

"Chosen One," Havzhiva said, "you speak the truth. Much will be lost. I know it. The lesser knowledge must be given to gain the greater. And not once only."

"The men of this tribe will not deny our truth," the Chosen said. His unseeing, unwinking central eye was fixed on the sun that hung in a yellow dust-haze above the endless fields, though his own dark eyes gazed downward at the earth.

His guest looked from that alien face to the fierce, white, small sun that still blazed low above the alien land. "I am sure of that," he said.

When he was fifty-five, Stabile Yehedarhed Havzhiva went back to Yotebber for a visit. He had not been there for a long time. His work as Ekumenical Advisor to the Yeowan Ministry of Social Justice had kept him in the north, with frequent trips to the other hemisphere. He had lived for years in the Old Capital with his partner, but often visited the New Capital at the request of a new Ambassador who wanted to draw on his expertise. His partner—they had lived together for eighteen years, but there was no marriage on Yeowe—had a book she was trying to finish, and admitted that she would like to have the apartment to herself for a couple of weeks while she wrote. "Take that trip south you keep mooning about," she said. "I'll fly down as soon as I'm done. I won't tell any damned politicians where you are. Escape! Go, go, go!"

He went. He had never liked flying, though he had had to do a great deal of it, and so he made the long journey by train. They were good, fast trains, terribly crowded, people at every station swarming and rushing and shouting bribes to the conductors, though not trying to ride the roofs of the cars, not at 130 kmh. He had a private room in a through car to Yotebber City. He spent the long hours in silence watching the landscape whirl by, the reclamation projects, the old wastelands, the young forests, the swarming cities, miles of shacks and cabins and cottages and houses and apartment buildings, sprawling Werel-style compounds with connected houses and kitchen gardens and worksheds, factories, huge new plants; and then suddenly the country again, canals and irrigation tanks reflecting the colors of the evening sky, a bare-legged child walking with a great white ox past a field of shadowy grain. The nights were short, a dark, rocking sweetness of sleep.

On the third afternoon he got off the train in Yotebber City Station. No crowds. No chiefs. No bodyguards. He walked through the hot, familiar streets, past the market, through the City Park. A little bravado, there. Gangs, muggers were still about, and he kept his eye alert and his feet on the main pathways. On past the old Tualite temple. He had picked up a white flower that had dropped from a shrub in the park. He set it at the Mother's feet. She smiled, looking cross-eyed at her missing nose. He walked on to the big, rambling new compound where Yeron lived.

She was seventy-four and had retired recently from the hospital where she had taught, practiced, and been an administrator for the last fifteen years. She was little changed from the woman he had first seen sitting by his bedside, only she seemed smaller all over. Her hair was quite gone, and she wore a glittering kerchief tied round her head. They embraced hard and kissed, and she stroked him and patted him, smiling irrepressibly. They had never made love, but there had always been a desire between them, a yearning to the other, a great comfort in touch. "Look at that, look at that grey!" she cried, petting his hair, "how beautiful! Come in and have a glass of wine with me! How is your Araha? When is she coming? You walked right across the city carrying that bag? You're still crazy!"

He gave her the gift he had brought her, a treatise on *Certain Diseases of Werel-Yeowe* by a team of Ekumenical medical researchers, and she seized it greedily. For some while she conversed only between plunges into the table of contents and the chapter on berlot. She poured out the pale orange wine. They had a second glass. "You look fine, Havzhiva," she said, putting the book down and looking at him steadily. Her eyes had faded to an opaque bluish darkness. "Being a saint agrees with you."

"It's not that bad, Yeron."

"A hero, then. You can't deny that you're a hero."

"No," he said with a laugh. "Knowing what a hero is, I won't deny it."

"Where would we be without you?"

"Just where we are now. . . ." He sighed. "Sometimes I think we're losing what little we've ever won. This Tualbeda, in Detake Province, don't underestimate him, Yeron. His speeches are pure misogyny and anti-immigrant prejudice, and people are eating it up—"

She made a gesture that utterly dismissed the demagogue. "There is no end to that," she said. "But I knew what you were going to be to us. Right away. When I heard your name, even. I knew."

"You didn't give me much choice, you know."

"Bah. You chose, man."

"Yes," he said. He savored the wine. "I did." After a while he said, "Not many people have the choices I had. How to live, whom to live with, what work to do. Sometimes I think I was able to choose because I grew up where all choices had been made for me."

"So you rebelled, made your own way," she said, nodding.

He smiled. "I'm no rebel."

"Bah!" she said again. "No rebel? You, in the thick of it, in the heart of our movement all the way?"

"Oh yes," he said. "But not in a rebellious spirit. That had to be your spirit. My job was acceptance. To keep an acceptant spirit. That's what I learned growing up. To accept. Not to change the world. Only to change the soul. So that it can be in the world. Be rightly in the world."

She listened but looked unconvinced. "Sounds like a woman's way of being," she said. "Men generally want to change things to suit."

"Not the men of my people," he said.

She poured them a third glass of wine. "Tell me about your people. I was always afraid to ask. The Hainish are so old! So learned! They know so much history, so many worlds! Us here with our three hundred years of misery and murder and ignorance—you don't know how small you make us feel."

"I think I do," Havzhiva said. After a while he said, "I was born in a town called Stse."

He told her about the pueblo, about the Other Sky people, his father who was his uncle, his mother the Heir of the Sun, the rites, the festivals, the daily gods, the unusual gods; he told her about changing being; he told her about the historian's visit, and how he had changed being again, going to Kathhad.

"All those rules!" Yeron said. "So complicated and unnecessary. Like our tribes. No wonder you ran away."

"All I did was go learn in Kathhad what I wouldn't learn in Stse," he said, smiling. "What the rules are. Ways of needing one another. Human ecology. What have we been doing here, all these years, but trying to find a good set of rules—a pattern that makes sense?" He stood up, stretched his shoulders, and said, "I'm drunk. Come for a walk with me."

They went out into the sunny gardens of the compound and walked slowly along the paths between vegetable plots and flower beds. Yeron nodded to people weeding and hoeing, who looked up and greeted her by name. She held Havzhiva's arm firmly, with pride. He matched his steps to hers.

"When you have to sit still, you want to fly," he said, looking down at her pale, gnarled, delicate hand on his arm. "If you have to fly, you want to sit still. I learned sitting, at home. I learned flying, with the historians. But I still couldn't keep my balance."

"Then you came here," she said.

"Then I came here."

"And learned?"

"How to walk," he said. "How to walk with my people."

A Woman's Liberation

MY DEAR FRIEND has asked me to write the story of my life, thinking it might be of interest to people of other worlds and times. I am an ordinary woman, but I have lived in years of mighty changes and have been advantaged to know with my very flesh the nature of servitude and the nature of freedom.

I did not learn to read or write until I was a grown woman, which is all the excuse I will make for the faults of my narrative.

I was born a slave on the planet Werel. As a child I was called Shomekes' Radosse Rakam. That is, Property of the Shomeke Family, Granddaughter of Dosse, Granddaughter of Kamye. The Shomeke family owned an estate on the eastern coast of Voe Deo. Dosse was my grandmother. Kamye is the Lord God.

The Shomekes possessed over four hundred assets, mostly used to cultivate the fields of gede, to herd the saltgrass cattle, to work in the mills, and as domestics in the House. The Shomeke family had been great in history. Our Owner was an important man politically, often away in the capital.

Assets took their name from their grandmother because it was the grandmother that raised the child. The mother worked all day, and there was no father. Women were always bred to more than one man. Even if a man knew his child he could not care for it. He might be sold or traded away at any time. Young men were seldom kept long on the estates. If they were valuable, they were traded to other estates or sold to the factories. If they were worthless, they were worked to death.

Women were not often sold. The young ones were kept for work and breeding, the old ones to raise the young and keep the compound in order. On some estates women bore a baby a year till they died, but on ours most had only two or three children. The Shomekes valued women as workers. They did not want the men always getting at the women. The grandmothers agreed with them and guarded the young women closely.

I say men, women, children, but you are to understand that

457

we were not called men, women, children. Only our owners were called so. We assets or slaves were called bondsmen, bondswomen, and pups or young. I will use those words, though I have not heard or spoken them for many years, and never before on this blessed world.

The bondsmen's part of the compound, the gateside, was ruled by the Bosses, who were men, some relations of the Shomeke family, others hired by them. On the inside the young and the bondswomen lived. There two cutfrees, castrated bondsmen, were the Bosses in name, but the grandmothers ruled. Indeed nothing in the compound happened without the grandmothers' knowledge.

If the grandmothers said an asset was too sick to work, the Bosses would let that one stay home. Sometimes the grandmothers could save a bondsman from being sold away, sometimes they could protect a girl from being bred by more than one man, or could give a delicate girl a contraceptive. Everybody in the compound obeyed the council of the grandmothers. But if one of them went too far, the Bosses would have her flogged or blinded or her hands cut off. When I was a young child, there lived in our compound a woman we called Great-Grandmother, who had holes for eyes and no tongue. I thought that she was thus because she was so old. I feared that my grandmother Dosse's tongue would wither in her mouth. I told her that. She said, "No. It won't get any shorter, because I don't let it get too long."

I lived in the compound. My mother birthed me there, and was allowed to stay three months to nurse me; then I was weaned to cow's milk, and my mother returned to the House. Her name was Shomekes' Rayowa Yowa. She was light-skinned like most of the assets, but very beautiful, with slender wrists and ankles and delicate features. My grandmother, too, was light, but I was dark, darker than anybody else in the compound.

My mother came to visit, the cutfrees letting her in by their ladder-door. She found me rubbing grey dust on my body. When she scolded me, I told her that I wanted to look like the others.

"Listen, Rakam," she said to me, "they are dust people. They'll never get out of the dust. You're something better. And you will be beautiful. Why do you think you're so black?"

I had no idea what she meant. "Someday I'll tell you who your father is," she said, as if she were promising me a gift. I knew that the Shomekes' stallion, a prized and valuable animal, serviced mares from other estates. I did not know a father could be human.

That evening I boasted to my grandmother: "I'm beautiful because the black stallion is my father!" Dosse struck me across the head so that I fell down and wept. She said, "Never speak of your father."

I knew there was anger between my mother and my grandmother, but it was a long time before I understood why. Even now I am not sure I understand all that lay between them.

We little pups ran around in the compound. We knew nothing outside the walls. All our world was the bondswomen's huts and the bondsmen's longhouses, the kitchens and kitchen gardens, the bare plaza beaten hard by bare feet. To me, the stockade wall seemed a long way off.

When the field and mill hands went out the gate in the early morning I didn't know where they went. They were just gone. All day long the whole compound belonged to us pups, naked in the summer, mostly naked in the winter too, running around playing with sticks and stones and mud, keeping away from the grandmothers, until we begged them for something to eat or they put us to work weeding the gardens for a while.

In the evening or the early night the workers would come back, trooping in the gate guarded by the Bosses. Some were worn out and grim, others would be cheerful and talking and calling back and forth. The great gate was slammed behind the last of them. Smoke went up from all the cooking stoves. The burning cowdung smelled sweet. People gathered on the porches of the huts and longhouses. Bondsmen and bondswomen lingered at the ditch that divided the gateside from the inside, talking across the ditch. After the meal the freedmen led prayers to Tual's statue, and we lifted our own prayers to Kamye, and then people went to their beds, except for those who lingered to "jump the ditch." Some nights, in the summer, there would be singing, or a dance was allowed. In the winter one of the grandfathers—poor old broken men, not strong people like the grandmothers—would "sing the word." That is what we called reciting the *Arkamye*. Every night, always, some of the people were teaching and others were learning the sacred verses. On winter nights one of these old worthless bondsmen kept alive by the grandmothers' charity would begin to sing the word. Then even the pups would be still to listen to that story.

The friend of my heart was Walsu. She was bigger than I, and was my defender when there were fights and quarrels among the young or when older pups called me "Blackie" and "Bossie." I was small but had a fierce temper. Together, Walsu and I did not get bothered much. Then Walsu was sent out the gate. Her mother had been bred and was now stuffed big, so that she needed help in the fields to make her quota. Gede must be hand-harvested. Every day as a new section of the bearing stalk comes ripe it has to be picked, and so gede pickers go through the same field over and over for twenty or thirty days, and then move on to a later planting. Walsu went with her mother to help her pick her rows. When her mother fell ill, Walsu took her place, and with help from other hands she kept up her mother's quota. She was then six years old by owner's count, which gave all assets the same birthday, new year's day at the beginning of spring. She might have truly been seven. Her mother remained ill both before birthing and after, and Walsu took her place in the gede field all that time. She never afterward came back to play, only in the evenings to eat and sleep. I saw her then and we could talk. She was proud of her work. I envied her and longed to go through the gate. I followed her to it and looked through it at the world. Now the walls of the compound seemed very close.

I told my grandmother Dosse that I wanted to go to work in the fields.

"You're too young."

"I'll be seven at the new year."

"Your mother made me promise not to let you go out."

Next time my mother visited the compound, I said, "Grandmother won't let me go out. I want to go work with Walsu."

"Never," my mother said. "You were born for better than that."

"What for?"

"You'll see."

She smiled at me. I knew she meant the House, where she

worked. She had told me often of the wonderful things in the House, things that shone and were colored brightly, things that were thin and delicate, clean things. It was quiet in the House, she said. My mother herself wore a beautiful red scarf, her voice was soft, and her clothing and body were always clean and fresh.

"When will I see?"

I teased her until she said, "All right! I'll ask my lady."

"Ask her what?"

All I knew of my-lady was that she too was delicate and clean, and that my mother belonged to her in some particular way, of which she was proud. I knew my-lady had given my mother the red scarf.

"I'll ask her if you can come begin training at the House."

My mother said "the House" in a way that made me see it as a great sacred place like the place in our prayer: *May I enter in the clear house, in the rooms of peace.*

I was so excited I began to dance and sing, "I'm going to the House, to the House!" My mother slapped me to make me stop and scolded me for being wild. She said, "You are too young! You can't behave! If you get sent away from the House, you can never come back."

I promised to be old enough.

"You must do everything right," Yowa told me. "You must do everything I say when I say it. Never question. Never delay. If my lady sees that you're wild, she'll send you back here. And that will be the end of you forever."

I promised to be tame. I promised to obey at once in everything, and not to speak. The more frightening she made it, the more I desired to see the wonderful, shining House.

When my mother left I did not believe she would speak to my-lady. I was not used to promises being kept. But after some days she returned, and I heard her speaking to my grandmother. Dosse was angry at first, speaking loudly. I crept under the window of the hut to listen. I heard my grandmother weep. I was frightened and amazed. My grandmother was patient with me, always looked after me, and fed me well. It had never entered my mind that there was anything more to it than that, until I heard her crying. Her crying made me cry, as if I were part of her.

"You could let me keep her one more year," she said. "She's just a baby. I would never let her out the gate." She was pleading, as if she were powerless, not a grandmother. "She is my joy, Yowa!"

"Don't you want her to do well, then?"

"Just a year more. She's too wild for the House."

"She's run wild too long. She'll get sent out to the fields if she stays. A year of that and they won't have her at the House. She'll be dust. Anyhow, there's no use crying about it. I asked my lady, and she's expected. I can't go back without her."

"Yowa, don't let her come to harm," Dosse said very low, as if ashamed to say this to her daughter, and yet with strength in her voice.

"I'm taking her to keep her out of harm," my mother said. Then she called me, and I wiped my tears and came.

It is queer, but I do not remember my first walk through the world outside the compound or my first sight of the House. I suppose I was frightened and kept my eyes down, and everything was so strange to me that I did not understand what I saw. I know it was a number of days before my mother took me to show me to Lady Tazeu. She had to scrub me and train me and make sure I would not disgrace her. I was terrified when at last she took my hand, scolding me in a whisper all the time, and brought me out of the bondswomen's quarters, through halls and doorways of painted wood, into a bright, sunny room with no roof, full of flowers growing in pots.

I had hardly ever seen a flower, only the weeds in the kitchen gardens, and I stared and stared at them. My mother had to jerk my hand to make me look at the woman lying in a chair among the flowers, in clothes soft and brightly colored like the flowers. I could hardly tell them apart. The woman's hair was long and shining, and her skin was shining and black. My mother pushed me, and I did what she had made me practice over and over: I went and knelt down beside the chair and waited, and when the woman put out her long, narrow, soft hand, black above and azure on the palm, I touched my forehead to it. I was supposed to say "I am your slave Rakam, ma'am," but my voice would not come out.

"What a pretty little thing," she said. "So dark." Her voice changed a little on the last words.

"The Bosses came in . . . that night," Yowa said in a timid, smiling way, looking down as if embarrassed.

"No doubt about that," the woman said. I was able to glance up at her again. She was beautiful. I did not know a person could be so beautiful. I think she saw my wonder. She put out her long, soft hand again and caressed my cheek and neck. "Very, very pretty, Yowa," she said. "You did quite right to bring her here. Has she been bathed?"

She would not have asked that if she had seen me when I first came, fithy and smelling of the cowdung we made our fires with. She knew nothing of the compound at all. She knew nothing beyond the beza, the women's side of the House. She was kept there just as I had been kept in the compound, ignorant of anything outside. She had never smelled cowdung, as I had never seen flowers.

My mother assured her I was clean, and she said, "Then she can come to bed with me tonight. I'd like that. Will you like to come sleep with me, pretty little—" She glanced at my mother, who murmured, "Rakam." Ma'am pursed her lips at the name. "I don't like that," she murmured. "So ugly. Toti. Yes. You can be my new Toti. Bring her this evening, Yowa."

She had had a foxdog called Toti, my mother told me. Her pet had died. I did not know animals ever had names, and so it did not seem odd to me to be given an animal's name, but it did seem strange at first not to be Rakam. I could not think of myself as Toti.

That night my mother bathed me again and oiled my skin with sweet oil and dressed me in a soft gown, softer even than her red scarf. Again she scolded and warned me, but she was excited, too, and pleased with me, as we went to the beza again, through other halls, meeting some other bondswomen on the way, and to the lady's bedroom. It was a wonderful room, hung with mirrors and draperies and paintings. I did not understand what the mirrors were, or the paintings, and was frightened when I saw people in them. Lady Tazeu saw that I was frightened. "Come, little one," she said, making a place for me in her great, wide, soft bed strewn with pillows, "come and cuddle up." I crawled in beside her, and she stroked my hair and skin and held me in her warm, soft arms until I was comfortable and at ease. "There, there, little Toti," she said, and so we slept.

I became the pet of Lady Tazeu Wehoma Shomeke. I slept with her almost every night. Her husband was seldom home and when he was there did not come to her, preferring bonds-women for his pleasure. Sometimes she had my mother or other, younger bondswomen come into her bed, and she sent me away at those times, until I was older, ten or eleven, when she began to keep me and have me join in with them, teaching me how to be pleasured. She was gentle, but she was the mis-tress in love, and I was her instrument which she played.

I was also trained in household arts and duties. She taught me to sing with her, as I had a true voice. All those years I was never punished and never made to do hard work. I who had been wild in the compound was perfectly obedient in the Great House. I had been rebellious to my grandmother and impatient of her commands, but whatever my lady ordered me to do I gladly did. She held me fast to her by the only kind of love she had to give me. I thought that she was the Merciful Tual come down upon the earth. That is not a way of speaking, that is the truth. I thought she was a higher being, superior to myself.

Perhaps you will say that I could not or should not have had pleasure in being used without my consent by my mistress, and if I did, I should not speak of it, showing even so little good in so great an evil. But I knew nothing of consent or refusal. Those are freedom words.

She had one child, a son, three years older than I. She lived quite alone among us bondswomen. The Wehomas were no-bles of the Islands, old-fashioned people whose women did not travel, so she was cut off from her family. The only com-pany she had was when Owner Shomeke brought friends with him from the capital, but those were all men, and she could be with them only at table.

I seldom saw the Owner and only at a distance. I thought he too was a superior being, but a dangerous one.

As for Erod, the Young Owner, we saw him when he came to visit his mother daily or when he went out riding with his tutors. We girls would peep at him and giggle to each other when we were eleven or twelve, because he was a handsome boy, night-black and slender like his mother. I knew that he was afraid of his father, because I had heard him weep when he was with his mother. She would comfort him with candy and caresses, saying, "He'll be gone again soon, my darling." I too felt sorry for Erod, who was like a shadow, soft and harmless. He was sent off to school for a year at fifteen, but his father brought him back before the year was up. Bondsmen told us the Owner had beaten him cruelly and had forbidden him even to ride off the estate.

Bondswomen whom the Owner used told us how brutal he was, showing us where he had bruised and hurt them. They hated him, but my mother would not speak against him. "Who do you think you are?" she said to a girl who was complaining of his use of her. "A lady to be treated like glass?" And when the girl found herself pregnant, stuffed was the word we used, my mother had her sent back to the compound. I did not understand why. I thought Yowa was hard and jealous. Now I think she was also protecting the girl from our lady's jealousy.

I do not know when I understood that I was the Owner's daughter. Because she had kept that secret from our lady, my mother believed it was a secret from all. But the bondswomen all knew it. I do not know what I heard or overheard, but when I saw Erod, I would study him and think that I looked much more like our father than he did, for by then I knew what a father was. And I wondered that Lady Tazeu did not see it. But she chose to live in ignorance.

During these years I seldom went to the compound. After I had been a halfyear or so at the House, I was eager to go back and see Walsu and my grandmother and show them my fine clothes and clean skin and shining hair; but when I went, the pups I used to play with threw dirt and stones at me and tore my clothes. Walsu was in the fields. I had to hide in my grandmother's hut all day. I never wanted to go back. When my grandmother sent for me, I would go only with my mother and always stayed close by her. The people in the compound, even my grandmother, came to look coarse and foul to me. They were dirty and smelled strongly. They had sores, scars from punishment, lopped fingers, ears, or noses. Their hands and feet were coarse, with deformed nails. I was no longer used to people who looked so. We domestics of the Great House were entirely different from them, I thought. Serving the higher beings, we became like them.

When I was thirteen and fourteen Lady Tazeu still kept me in her bed, making love to me often. But also she had a new pet, the daughter of one of the cooks, a pretty little girl though white as clay. One night she made love to me for a long time in ways that she knew gave me great ecstasy of the body. When I lay exhausted in her arms she whispered "good-bye, good-bye," kissing me all over my face and breasts. I was too spent to wonder at this.

The next morning my lady called in my mother and myself to tell us that she intended to give me to her son for his seven-teenth birthday. "I shall miss you terribly, Toti darling," she said, with tears in her eyes. "You have been my joy. But there isn't another girl on the place that I could let Erod have. You are the cleanest, dearest, sweetest of them all. I know you are a virgin," she meant a virgin to men, "and I know my boy will enjoy you. And he'll be kind to her, Yowa," she said earnestly to my mother. My mother bowed and said nothing. There was nothing she could say. And she said nothing to me. It was too late to speak of the secret she had been so proud of.

Lady Tazeu gave me medicine to prevent conception, but my mother, not trusting the medicine, went to my grandmother and brought me contraceptive herbs. I took both faithfully that week.

If a man in the House visited his wife he came to the beza, but if he wanted a bondswoman she was "sent across." So on the night of the Young Owner's birthday I was dressed all in red and led over, for the first time in my life, to the men's side of the House.

My reverence for my lady extended to her son, and I had been taught that owners were superior by nature to us. But he was a boy whom I had known since childhood, and I knew that his blood and mine were half the same. It gave me a strange feeling towards him.

I thought he was shy, afraid of his manhood. Other girls had tried to tempt him and failed. The women had told me what I was to do, how to offer myself and encourage him, and I was ready to do that. I was brought to him in his great bedroom, all of stone carved like lace, with high, thin windows of violet glass. I stood timidly near the door for a while, and he stood near a table covered with papers and screens. He came forward at last, took my hand, and led me to a chair. He made me sit down, and spoke to me standing, which was all improper, and confused my mind.

"Rakam," he said—"that's your name, isn't it?"—I nodded —"Rakam, my mother means only kindness, and you must not think me ungrateful to her, or blind to your beauty. But I will not take a woman who cannot freely offer herself. Intercourse between owner and slave is rape." And he talked on, talking beautifully, as when my lady read aloud from one of her books. I did not understand much, except that I was to come whenever he sent for me and sleep in his bed, but he would never touch me. And I was not to speak of this to anyone. "I am sorry, I am very sorry to ask you to lie," he said, so earnestly that I wondered if it hurt him to lie. That made him seem more like a god than a human being. If it hurt to lie, how could you stay alive?

"I will do just as you say, Lord Erod," I said.

So, most nights, his bondsmen came to bring me across. I would sleep in his great bed, while he worked at the papers on his table. He slept on a couch beneath the windows. Often he wanted to talk to me, sometimes for a long time, telling me his ideas. When he was in school in the capital he had become a member of a group of owners who wished to abolish slavery, called The Community. Getting wind of this, his father had ordered him out of school, sent him home, and forbidden him to leave the estate. So he too was a prisoner. But he corresponded constantly with others in The Community through the net, which he knew how to operate without his father's knowledge, or the government's.

His head was so full of ideas he had to speak them. Often Geu and Ahas, the young bondsmen who had grown up with him, who always came to fetch me across, stayed with us while he talked to all of us about slavery and freedom and many other things. Often I was sleepy, but I did listen, and heard much I did not know how to understand or even believe. He told us there was an organization among assets, called the Hame, that worked to steal slaves from the plantations. These slaves would be brought to members of The Community, who would make out false papers of ownership and treat them well, renting them to decent work in the cities. He told us about the

cities, and I loved to hear all that. He told us about Yeowe
Colony, saying that there was a revolution there among the
slaves.

Of Yeowe I knew nothing. It was a great blue-green star
that set after the sun or rose before it, brighter than the smallest of the moons. It was a name in an old song they sang in the
compound:

> *O, O, Ye-o-we,*
> *Nobody never comes back.*

I had no idea what a revolution was. When Erod told me that
meant that assets on plantations in this place called Yeowe
were fighting their owners, I did not understand how assets
could do that. From the beginning it was ordained that there
should be higher and lower beings, the Lord and the human,
the man and the woman, the owner and the owned. All my
world was Shomeke Estate and it stood on that one foundation. Who would want to overturn it? Everyone would be
crushed in the ruins.

I did not like Erod to call assets slaves, an ugly word that
took away our value. I decided in my mind that here on Werel
we were assets, and in that other place, Yeowe Colony, there
were slaves, worthless bondspeople, intractables. That was why
they had been sent there. It made good sense.

By this you know how ignorant I was. Sometimes Lady
Tazeu had let us watch shows on the holonet with her, but she
watched only dramas, not the reports of events. Of the world
beyond the estate I knew nothing but what I learned from
Erod, and that I could not understand.

Erod liked us to argue with him. He thought it meant our
minds were growing free. Geu was good at it. He would ask
questions like, "But if there's no assets, who'll do the work?"
Then Erod could answer at length. His eyes shone, his voice
was eloquent. I loved him very much when he talked to us. He
was beautiful and what he said was beautiful. It was like hearing the old men "singing the word," reciting the *Arkamye,*
when I was a little pup in the compound.

I gave the contraceptives my lady gave me every month to
girls who needed them. Lady Tazeu had aroused my sexuality
and accustomed me to being used sexually. I missed her ca-

resses. But I did not know how to approach any of the bonds-women, and they were afraid to approach me, since I belonged to the Young Owner. Being with Erod often, while he talked I yearned to him in my body. I lay in his bed and dreamed that he came and stooped over me and did with me as my lady used to do. But he never touched me.

Geu also was a handsome young man, clean and well mannered, rather dark-skinned, attractive to me. His eyes were always on me. But he would not approach me, until I told him that Erod did not touch me.

Thus I broke my promise to Erod not to tell anyone; but I did not think myself bound to keep promises, as I did not think myself bound to speak the truth. Honor of that kind was for owners, not for us.

After that, Geu used to tell me when to meet him in the attics of the House. He gave me little pleasure. He would not penetrate me, believing that he must save my virginity for our master. He had me take his penis in my mouth instead. He would turn away in his climax, for the slave's sperm must not defile the master's woman. That is the honor of a slave.

Now you may say in disgust that my story is all of such things, and there is far more to life, even a slave's life, than sex. That is very true. I can say only that it may be in our sexuality that we are most easily enslaved, both men and women. It may be there, even as free men and women, that we find freedom hardest to keep. The politics of the flesh are the roots of power.

I was young, full of health and desire for joy. And even now, even here, when I look back across the years from this world to that, to the compound and the House of Shomeke, I see images like those in a bright dream. I see my grandmother's big, hard hands. I see my mother smiling, the red scarf about her neck. I see my lady's black, silky body among the cushions. I smell the smoke of the cowdung fires, and the perfumes of the beza. I feel the soft, fine clothing on my young body, and my lady's hands and lips. I hear the old men singing the word, and my voice twining with my lady's voice in a love song, and Erod telling us of freedom. His face is illuminated with his vision. Behind him the windows of stone lace and violet glass keep out the night. I do not say I would go back. I would die before I would go back to Shomeke. I would die before I left this free world, my world, to go back to the place of slavery. But whatever I knew in my youth of beauty, of love, and of hope, was there.

And there it was betrayed. All that is built upon that foundation in the end betrays itself.

I was sixteen years old in the year the world changed.

The first change I heard about was of no interest to me except that my lord was excited about it, and so were Geu and Ahas and some of the other young bondsmen. Even my grandmother wanted to hear about it when I visited her. "That Yeowe, that slave world," she said, "they made freedom? They sent away their owners? They opened the gates? My lord, my sweet Lord Kamye, how can that be? Praise his name, praise his marvels!" She rocked back and forth as she squatted in the dust, her arms about her knees. She was an old, shrunken woman now. "Tell me!" she said.

I knew little else to tell her. "All the soldiers came back here," I said. "And those other people, those alemens, they're there on Yeowe. Maybe they're the new owners. That's all somewhere way out there," I said, flipping my hand at the sky.

"What's alemens?" my grandmother asked, but I did not know. It was all mere words to me.

But when our Owner, Lord Shomeke, came home sick, that I understood. He came on a flyer to our little port. I saw him carried by on a stretcher, the whites showing in his eyes, his black skin mottled grey. He was dying of a sickness that was ravaging the cities. My mother, sitting with Lady Tazeu, saw a politician on the net who said that the alemens had brought the sickness to Werel. He talked so fearsomely that we thought everybody was going to die. When I told Geu about it he snorted. "Aliens, not alemens," he said, "and they've got nothing to do with it. My lord talked with the doctors. It's just a new kind of pusworm."

That dreadful disease was bad enough. We knew that any asset found to be infected with it was slaughtered at once like an animal and the corpse burned on the spot.

They did not slaughter the Owner. The House filled with doctors, and Lady Tazeu spent day and night by her husband's bed. It was a cruel death. It went on and on. Lord Shomeke in his suffering made terrible sounds, screams, howls. One would not believe a man could cry out hour after hour as he did. His flesh ulcerated and fell away, he went mad, but he did not die.

As Lady Tazeu became like a shadow, worn and silent, Erod filled with strength and excitement. Sometimes when we heard his father howling his eyes would shine. He would whisper, "Lady Tual have mercy on him," but he fed on those cries. I knew from Geu and Ahas, who had been brought up with him, how the father had tormented and despised him, and how Erod had vowed to be everything his father was not and to undo all he did.

But it was Lady Tazeu who ended it. One night she sent away the other attendants, as she often did, and sat alone with the dying man. When he began his moaning howl, she took her little sewing knife and cut his throat. Then she cut the veins in her arms across and across, and lay down by him, and so died. My mother was in the next room all night. She said she wondered a little at the silence, but was so weary that she fell asleep; and in the morning she went in and found them lying in their cold blood.

All I wanted to do was weep for my lady, but everything was in confusion. Everything in the sickroom must be burned, the doctors said, and the bodies must be burned without delay. The House was under quarantine, so only the priests of the House could hold the funeral. No one was to leave the estate for twenty days. But several of the doctors themselves left when Erod, who was now Lord Shomeke, told them what he intended to do. I heard some confused word of it from Ahas, but in my grief I paid little heed.

That evening, all the House assets stood outside the Lady's Chapel during the funeral service to hear the songs and prayers within. The Bosses and cutfrees had brought the people from the compound, and they stood behind us. We saw the procession come out, the white biers carried by, the pyres lighted, and the black smoke go up. Long before the smoke ceased rising, the new Lord Shomeke came to us all where we stood.

Erod stood up on the little rise of ground behind the chapel and spoke in a strong voice such as I had never heard from him. Always in the House it had been whispering in the dark. Now it was broad day and a strong voice. He stood there black and straight in his white mourning clothes. He was not yet twenty years old. He said, "Listen, you people: you have been slaves, you will be free. You have been my property, you will own your own lives now. This morning I sent to the Government the Order of Manumission for every asset on the estate, four hundred and eleven men, women, and children. If you will come to my office in the Counting House in the morning, I will give you your papers. Each of you is named in those papers as a free person. You can never be enslaved again. You are free to do as you please from tomorrow on. There will be money for each one of you to begin your new life with. Not what you deserve, not what you have earned in all your work for us, but what I have to give you. I am leaving Shomeke. I will go to the capital, where I will work for the freedom of every slave on Werel. The Freedom Day that came to Yeowe is coming to us, and soon. Any of you who wish to come with me, come! There's work for us all to do!"

I remember all he said. Those are his words as he spoke them. When one does not read and has not had one's mind filled up by the images on the nets, words spoken strike down deep in the mind.

There was such a silence when he stopped speaking as I had never heard.

One of the doctors began talking, protesting to Erod that he must not break the quarantine.

"The evil has been burned away," Erod said, with a great gesture to the black smoke rising. "This has been an evil place, but no more harm will go forth from Shomeke!"

At that a slow sound began among the compound people standing behind us, and it swelled into a great noise of jubilation mixed with wailing, crying, shouting, singing. "Lord Kamye! Lord Kamye!" the men shouted. An old woman came forward: my grandmother. She strode through us House assets as if we were a field of grain. She stopped a good way from Erod. People fell silent to listen to the grandmother. She said, "Lord Master, are you turning us out of our homes?"

"No," he said. "They are yours. The land is yours to use. The profit of the fields is yours. This is your home, and you are free!"

At that the shouts rose up again so loud I cowered down

and covered my ears, but I was crying and shouting too, praising Lord Erod and Lord Kamye in one voice with the rest of them.

We danced and sang there in sight of the burning pyres until the sun went down. At last the grandmothers and the cutfrees got the people to go back to the compound, saying they did not have their papers yet. We domestics went straggling back to the House, talking about tomorrow, when we would get our freedom and our money and our land.

All that next day Erod sat in the Counting House and made out the papers for each slave and counted out the same amount of money for each: a hundred kue in cash, and a draft for five hundred kue on the district bank, which could not be drawn for forty days. This was, he explained to each one, to save them from exploitation by the unscrupulous before they knew how best to use their money. He advised them to form a cooperative, to pool their funds, to run the estate democratically. "Money in the bank, Lord!" an old crippled man came out crying, jigging on his twisted legs. "Money in the bank, Lord!"

If they wanted, Erod said over and over, they could save their money and contact the Hame, who would help them buy passage to Yeowe with it.

"O, O, Ye-o-we," somebody began singing, and they changed the words:

> *"Everybody's going to go.*
> *O, O, Ye-o-we,*
> *Everybody's going to go!"*

They sang it all day long. Nothing could change the sadness of it. I want to weep now, remembering that song, that day.

The next morning Erod left. He could not wait to get away from the place of his misery and begin his life in the capital working for freedom. He did not say good-bye to me. He took Geu and Ahas with him. The doctors and their aides and assets had all left the day before. We watched his flyer go up into the air.

We went back to the House. It was like something dead. There were no owners in it, no masters, no one to tell us what to do.

My mother and I went in to pack up our clothing. We had

said little to each other, but felt we could not stay there. We heard other women running through the beza, rummaging in Lady Tazeu's rooms, going through her closets, laughing and screaming with excitement, finding jewelry and valuables. We heard men's voices in the hall: Bosses' voices. Without a word my mother and I took what we had in our hands and went out by a back door, slipped through the hedges of the garden, and ran all the way to the compound.

The great gate of the compound stood wide open.

How can I tell you what that was to us, to see that, to see that gate stand open? How can I tell you?

2. ZESKRA

Erod knew nothing about how the estate was run, because the Bosses ran it. He was a prisoner too. He had lived in his screens, his dreams, his visions.

The grandmothers and others in the compound had spent all that night trying to make plans, to draw our people together so they could defend themselves. That morning when my mother and I came, there were bondsmen guarding the compound with weapons made of farm tools. The grandmothers and cutfrees had made an election of a headman, a strong, well-liked field hand. In that way they hoped to keep the young men with them.

By the afternoon that hope was broken. The young men ran wild. They went up to the House to loot it. The Bosses shot them from the windows, killing many; the others fled away. The Bosses stayed holed up in the House, drinking the wine of the Shomekes. Owners of other plantations were flying reinforcements to them. We heard the flyers land, one after another. The bondswomen who had stayed in the House were at their mercy now.

As for us in the compound, the gates were closed again. We had moved the great bars from the outside to the inside, so we thought ourselves safe for the night at least. But in the midnight they came with heavy tractors and pushed down the wall, and a hundred men or more, our Bosses and owners from all the plantations of the region, came swarming in. They were armed with guns. We fought them with farm tools and pieces of wood. One or two of them were hurt or killed. They killed as many of us as they wanted to kill and then began to rape us. It went on all night.

A group of men took all the old women and men and held them and shot them between the eyes, the way they kill cattle. My grandmother was one of them. I do not know what happened to my mother. I did not see any bondsmen living when they took me away in the morning. I saw white papers lying in the blood on the ground. Freedom papers.

Several of us girls and young women still alive were herded into a truck and taken to the port field. There they made us enter a flyer, shoving and using sticks, and we were carried off in the air. I was not then in my right mind. All I know of this is what the others told me later.

We found ourselves in a compound, like our compound in every way. I thought they had brought us back home. They shoved us in by the cutfrees' ladder. It was still morning and the hands were out at work, only the grandmothers and pups and old men in the compound. The grandmothers came to us fierce and scowling. I could not understand at first why they were all strangers. I looked for my grandmother.

They were frightened of us, thinking we must be runaways. Plantation slaves had been running away, the last years, trying to get to the cities. They thought we were intractables and would bring trouble with us. But they helped us clean ourselves, and gave us a place near the cutfrees' tower. There were no huts empty, they said. They told us this was Zeskra Estate. They did not want to hear about what had happened at Shomeke. They did not want us to be there. They did not need our trouble.

We slept there on the ground without shelter. Some of the bondsmen came across the ditch in the night and raped us because there was nothing to prevent them from it, no one to whom we were of any value. We were too weak and sick to fight them. One of us, a girl named Abye, tried to fight. The men beat her insensible. In the morning she could not talk or walk. She was left there when the Bosses came and took us away. Another girl was left behind too, a big farmhand with white scars on her head like parts in her hair. As we were going I looked at her and saw that it was Walsu, who had been my friend. We had not recognised each other. She sat in the dirt, her head bowed down.

Five of us were taken from the compound to the Great House of Zeskra, to the bondswomen's quarters. There for a while I had a little hope, since I knew how to be a good domestic asset. I did not know then how different Zeskra was from Shomeke. The House at Zeskra was full of people, full of owners and bosses. It was a big family, not a single Lord as at Shomeke but a dozen of them with their retainers and relations and visitors, so there might be thirty or forty men staying on the men's side and as many women in the beza, and a House staff of fifty or more. We were not brought as domestics, but as use-women.

After we were bathed we were left in the use-women's quarters, a big room without any private places. There were ten or more use-women already there. Those of them who liked their work were not glad to see us, thinking of us as rivals; others welcomed us, hoping we might take their places and they might be let join the domestic staff. But none were very unkind, and some were kind, giving us clothes, for we had been naked all this time, and comforting the youngest of us, Mio, a little compound girl of ten or eleven whose white body was mottled all over with brown-and-blue bruises.

One of them was a tall woman called Sezi-Tual. She looked at me with an ironic face. Something in her made my soul awaken.

"You're not a dusty," she said. "You're as black as old Lord Devil Zeskra himself. You're a Bossbaby, aren't you?"

"No ma'am," I said. "A lord's child. And the Lord's child. My name is Rakam."

"Your Grandfather hasn't treated you too well lately," she said. "Maybe you should pray to the Merciful Lady Tual."

"I don't look for mercy," I said. From then on Sezi-Tual liked me, and I had her protection, which I needed.

We were sent across to the men's side most nights. When there were dinner parties, after the ladies left the dinner room we were brought in to sit on the owners' knees and drink wine with them. Then they would use us there on the couches or take us to their rooms. The men of Zeskra were not cruel. Some liked to rape, but most preferred to think that we desired them and wanted whatever they wanted. Such men could be satisfied, the one kind if we showed fear or submission, the other kind if we showed yielding and delight. But some of their visitors were another kind of man.

There was no law or rule against damaging or killing a use-woman. Her owner might not like it, but in his pride he could not say so: he was supposed to have so many assets that the loss of one or another did not matter at all. So some men whose pleasure lay in torture came to hospitable estates like Zeskra for their pleasure. Sezi-Tual, a favorite of the Old Lord, could and did protest to him, and such guests were not invited back. But while I was there, Mio, the little girl who had come with us from Shomeke, was murdered by a guest. He tied her down to the bed. He made the knot across her neck so tight that while he used her she strangled to death.

I will say no more of these things. I have told what I must tell. There are truths that are not useful. All knowledge is local, my friend has said. Is it true, where is it true, that that child had to die in that way? Is it true, where is it true, that she did not have to die in that way?

I was often used by Lord Yaseo, a middle-aged man, who liked my dark skin, calling me "My Lady." Also he called me "Rebel," because what had happened at Shomeke they called a rebellion of the slaves. Nights when he did not send for me I served as a common-girl.

After I had been at Zeskra two years Sezi-Tual came to me one morning early. I had come back late from Lord Yaseo's bed. Not many others were there, for there had been a drinking party the night before, and all the common-girls had been sent for. Sezi-Tual woke me. She had strange hair, curly, in a bush. I remember her face above me, that hair curling out all about it. "Rakam," she whispered, "one of the visitor's assets spoke to me last night. He gave me this. He said his name is Suhame."

"Suhame," I repeated. I was sleepy. I looked at what she was holding out to me: some dirty crumpled paper. "I can't read!" I said, yawning, impatient.

But I looked at it and knew it. I knew what it said. It was the freedom paper. It was my freedom paper. I had watched Lord Erod write my name on it. Each time he wrote a name he had spoken it aloud so that we would know what he was writing. I remembered the big flourish of the first letter of both my names: Radosse Rakam. I took the paper in my hand, and my hand was shaking. "Where did you get this?" I whispered.

"Better ask this Suhame," she said. Now I heard what that name meant: "from the Hame." It was a password name. She knew that too. She was watching me, and she bent down suddenly and leaned her forehead against mine, her breath catching in her throat. "If I can, I'll help," she whispered.

I met with "Suhame" in one of the pantries. As soon as I saw him I knew him: Ahas, who had been Lord Erod's favorite along with Geu. A slight, silent young man with dusty skin, he had never been much in my mind. He had watchful eyes, and I had thought when Geu and I spoke that he looked at us with ill will. Now he looked at me with a strange face, still watchful, yet blank.

"Why are you here with that Lord Boeba?" I said. "Aren't you free?"

"I am as free as you are," he said.

I did not understand him, then.

"Didn't Lord Erod protect even you?" I asked.

"Yes. I am a free man." His face began to come alive, losing that dead blankness it had when he first saw me. "Lady Boeba's a member of The Community. I work with the Hame. I've been trying to find people from Shomeke. We heard several of the women were here. Are there others still alive, Rakam?"

His voice was soft, and when he said my name my breath caught and my throat swelled. I said his name and went to him, holding him. "Ratual, Ramayo, Keo are still here," I said. He held me gently. "Walsu is in the compound," I said, "if she's still alive." I wept. I had not wept since Mio's death. He too was in tears.

We talked, then and later. He explained to me that we were indeed, by law, free, but that law meant nothing on the Estates. The government would not interfere between owners and those they claimed as their assets. If we claimed our rights, the Zeskras would probably kill us, since they considered us stolen goods and did not want to be shamed. We must run away or be stolen away, and get to the city, the capital, before we could have any safety at all.

We had to be sure that none of the Zeskra assets would betray us out of jealousy or to gain favor. Sezi-Tual was the only one I trusted entirely.

Ahas arranged our escape with Sezi-Tual's help. I pleaded once with her to join us, but she thought that since she had no papers she would have to live always in hiding, and that would be worse than her life at Zeskra.

"You could go to Yeowe," I said.

She laughed. "All I know about Yeowe is nobody ever came back. Why run from one hell to the next one?"

Ratual chose not to come with us; she was a favorite of one of the young lords and content to remain so. Ramayo, the oldest of us from Shomeke, and Keo, who was now about fifteen, wanted to come. Sezi-Tual went down to the compound and found that Walsu was alive, working as a field hand. Arranging her escape was far more difficult than ours. There was no escape from a compound. She could get away only in daylight, in the fields, under the overseer's and the Boss's eyes. It was difficult even to talk to her, for the grandmothers were distrustful. But Sezi-Tual managed it, and Walsu told her she would do whatever she must do "to see her paper again."

Lady Boeba's flyer waited for us at the edge of a great gede field that had just been harvested. It was late summer. Ramayo, Keo, and I walked away from the House separately at different times of the morning. Nobody watched over us closely, as there was nowhere for us to go. Zeskra lies among other great estates, where a runaway slave would find no friends for hundreds of miles. One by one, taking different ways, we came through the fields and woods, crouching and hiding all the way to the flyer where Ahas waited for us. My heart beat and beat so I could not breathe. There we waited for Walsu.

"There!" said Keo, perched up on the wing of the flyer. She pointed across the wide field of stubble.

Walsu came running from the strip of trees on the far side of the field. She ran heavily, steadily, not as if she were afraid. But all at once she halted. She turned. We did not know why for a moment. Then we saw two men break from the shadow of the trees in pursuit of her.

She did not run from them, leading them towards us. She ran back at them. She leapt at them like a hunting cat. As she made that leap, one of them fired a gun. She bore one man down with her, falling. The other fired again and again. "In," Ahas said, "now." We scrambled into the flyer and it rose into the air, seemingly all in one instant, the same instant in which Walsu made that great leap, she too rising into the air, into her death, into her freedom.

3. THE CITY

I had folded up my freedom paper into a tiny packet. I carried it in my hand all the time we were in the flyer and while we landed and went in a public car through the city streets. When Ahas found what I was clutching, he said I need not worry about it. Our manumission was on record in the Government Office and would be honored, here in the City. We were free people, he said. We were gareots, that is, owners who have no assets. "Just like Lord Erod," he said. That meant nothing to me. There was too much to learn. I kept hold of my freedom paper until I had a place to keep it safe. I have it still.

We walked a little way in the streets and then Ahas led us into one of the huge houses that stood side by side on the pavement. He called it a compound, but we thought it must be an owner's house. There a middle-aged woman welcomed us. She was pale-skinned, but talked and behaved like an owner, so that I did not know what she was. She said she was Ress, a rentswoman and an elderwoman of the house.

Rentspeople were assets rented out by their owners to a company. If they were hired by a big company, they lived in the company compounds, but there were many, many rentspeople in the City who worked for small companies or businesses they managed themselves, and they occupied buildings run for profit, called open compounds. In such places the occupants must keep curfew, the doors being locked at night, but that was all; they were self-governed. This was such an open compound. It was supported by The Community. Some of the occupants were rentspeople, but many were like us, gareots who had been slaves. Over a hundred people lived there in forty apartments. It was supervised by several women, whom I would have called grandmothers, but here they were called elderwomen.

On the estates deep in the country, deep in the past, where the life was protected by miles of land and by the custom of centuries and by determined ignorance, any asset was absolutely at the mercy of any owner. From there we had come into this great crowd of two million people where nothing and nobody was protected from chance or change, where we had to learn as fast as we could how to stay alive, but where our life was in our own hands.

I had never seen a street. I could not read a word. I had much to learn.

Ress made that clear at once. She was a City woman, quick-thinking and quick-talking, impatient, aggressive, sensitive. I could not like or understand her for a long time. She made me feel stupid, slow, a clod. Often I was angry at her.

There was anger in me now. I had not felt anger while I lived at Zeskra. I could not. It would have eaten me. Here there was room for it, but I found no use for it. I lived with it in silence. Keo and Ramayo had a big room together, I had a small one next to theirs. I had never had a room to myself. At first I felt lonely in it and as if ashamed, but soon I came to like it. The first thing I did freely, as a free woman, was to shut my door.

Nights, I would shut my door and study. Days, we had work training in the morning, classes in the afternoon: reading and writing, arithmetic, history. My work training was in a small shop which made boxes of paper and thin wood to hold cosmetics, candies, jewelry, and such things. I was trained in all the different steps and crafts of making and ornamenting the boxes, for that is how most work was done in the City, by artisans who knew all their trade. The shop was owned by a member of The Community. The older workers were rents-people. When my training was finished I too would be paid wages.

Till then Lord Erod supported me as well as Keo and Ramayo and some men from Shomeke compound, who lived in a different house. Erod never came to the house. I think he did not want to see any of the people he had so disastrously freed. Ahas and Geu said he had sold most of the land at Shomeke and used the money for The Community and to make his way in politics, as there was now a Radical Party which favored emancipation.

Geu came a few times to see me. He had become a City man, dapper and knowing. I felt when he looked at me he was thinking I had been a use-woman at Zeskra, and I did not like to see him.

Ahas, whom I had never thought about in the old days, I now admired, knowing him brave, resolute, and kind. It was he who had looked for us, found us, rescued us. Owners had paid the money but Ahas had done it. He came often to see us. He was the only link that had not broken between me and my childhood.

And he came as a friend, a companion, never driving me back into my slave body. I was angry now at every man who looked at me as men look at women. I was angry at women who looked at me seeing me sexually. To Lady Tazeu all I had been was my body. At Zeskra that was all I had been. Even to Erod who would not touch me that was all I had been. Flesh to touch or not to touch, as they pleased. To use or not to use, as they chose. I hated the sexual parts of myself, my genitals and breasts and the swell of my hips and belly. Ever since I was a child, I had been dressed in soft clothing made to display all that sexuality of a woman's body. When I began to be paid and could buy or make my own clothing, I dressed in hard, heavy cloth. What I liked of myself was my hands, clever at their work, and my head, not clever at learning, but still learning, no matter how long it took.

What I loved to learn was history. I had grown up without any history. There was nothing at Shomeke or Zeskra but the way things were. Nobody knew anything about any time when things had been different. Nobody knew there was any place where things might be different. We were enslaved by the present time.

Erod had talked of change, indeed, but the owners were going to make the change. We were to be changed, we were to be freed, just as we had been owned. In history I saw that any freedom has been made, not given.

The first book I read by myself was a history of Yeowe, written very simply. It told about the days of the Colony, of the Four Corporations, of the terrible first century when the ships carried slave men to Yeowe and precious ores back. Slave men were so cheap then they worked them to death in a few years in the mines, bringing in new shipments continually. *O, O, Yeowe, nobody never comes back.* Then the Corporations began to send women slaves to work and breed, and over the years the assets spilled out of the compounds and made cities —whole great cities like this one I was living in. But not run by the owners or Bosses. Run by the assets, the way this house was run by us. On Yeowe the assets had belonged to the Corporations. They could rent their freedom by paying the Corporation a part of what they earned, the way sharecropper assets paid their owners in parts of Voe Deo. On Yeowe they called those assets freedpeople. Not free people, but freedpeople. And then, this history I was reading said, they began to think, why aren't we free people? So they made the revolution, the Liberation. It began on a plantation called Nadami, and spread from there. Thirty years they fought for their freedom. And just three years ago they had won the war, they had driven the Corporations, the owners, the bosses, off their world. They had danced and sung in the streets, freedom, freedom! This book I was reading (slowly, but reading it) had been printed there—there on Yeowe, the Free World. The Aliens had brought it to Werel. To me it was a sacred book.

I asked Ahas what it was like now on Yeowe, and he said they were making their government, writing a perfect Constitution to make all men equal under the Law.

On the net, on the news, they said they were fighting each other on Yeowe, there was no government at all, people were starving, savage tribesmen in the countryside and youth gangs in the cities running amuck, law and order broken down. Corruption, ignorance, a doomed attempt, a dying world, they said.

Ahas said that the Government of Voe Deo, which had fought and lost the war against Yeowe, now was afraid of a Liberation on Werel. "Don't believe any news," he counseled me. "Especially don't believe the neareals. Don't ever go into them. They're just as much lies as the rest, but if you feel and see a thing, you will believe it. And they know that. They don't need guns if they own our minds." The owners had no reporters, no cameras on Yeowe, he said; they invented their "news," using actors. Only some of the Aliens of the Ekumen were allowed on Yeowe, and the Yeowans were debating whether they should send them away, keeping the world they had won for themselves alone.

"But then what about us?" I said, for I had begun dreaming

of going there, going to the Free World, when the Hame could charter ships and send people.

"Some of them say assets can come. Others say they can't feed so many, and would be overwhelmed. They're debating it democratically. It will be decided in the first Yeowan elections, soon." Ahas was dreaming of going there too. We talked to-gether of our dream the way lovers talk of their love.

But there were no ships going to Yeowe now. The Hame could not act openly and The Community was forbidden to act for them. The Ekumen had offered transportation on their own ships to anyone who wanted to go, but the government of Voe Deo refused to let them use any spaceport for that purpose. They could carry only their own people. No Werelian was to leave Werel.

It had been only forty years since Werel had at last allowed the Aliens to land and maintain diplomatic relations. As I went on reading history I began to understand a little of the nature of the dominant people of Werel. The black-skinned race that conquered all the other peoples of the Great Continent, and finally all the world, those who call themselves the owners, have lived in the belief that there is only one way to be. They have believed they are what people should be, do as people should do, and know all the truth that is known. All the other peoples of Werel, even when they resisted them, imitated them, trying to become them, and so became their property. When a people came out of the sky looking differently, doing differently, knowing differently, and would not let themselves be conquered or enslaved, the owner race wanted nothing to do with them. It took them four hundred years to admit that they had equals.

I was in the crowd at a rally of the Radical Party, at which Erod spoke, as beautifully as ever. I noticed a woman beside me in the crowd listening. Her skin was a curious orange-brown, like the rind of a pini, and the whites showed in the corners of her eyes. I thought she was sick—I thought of the pusworm, how Lord Shomeke's skin had changed and his eyes had shown their whites. I shuddered and drew away. She glanced at me, smiling a little, and returned her attention to the speaker. Her hair curled in a bush or cloud, like Sezi-Tual's. Her clothing was of a delicate cloth, a strange fashion. It came upon me very slowly what she was, that she had come here from a world unimaginably far. And the wonder of it was that for all her strange skin and eyes and hair and mind, she was human, as I am human: I had no doubt of that. I felt it. For a moment it disturbed me deeply. Then it ceased to trouble me and I felt a great curiosity, almost a yearning, a drawing to her. I wished to know her, to know what she knew.

In me the owner's soul was struggling with the free soul. So it will do all my life.

Keo and Ramayo stopped going to school after they had learned to read and write and use the calculator, but I kept on. When there were no more classes to take from the school the Hame kept, the teachers helped me find classes in the net. Though the government controlled such courses, there were fine teachers and groups from all over the world, talking about literature and history and the sciences and arts. Always I wanted more history.

Ress, who was a member of the Hame, first took me to the Library of Voe Deo. As it was open only to owners, it was not censored by the government. Freed assets, if they were light-skinned, were kept out by the librarians on one pretext or another. I was dark-skinned, and had learned here in the City to carry myself with an indifferent pride that spared one many insults and offenses. Ress told me to stride in as if I owned the place. I did so, and was given all privileges without question. So I began to read freely, to read any book I wanted in that great library, every book in it if I could. That was my joy, that reading. That was the heart of my freedom.

Beyond my work at the boxmaker's, which was well paid, pleasant, and among pleasant companions, and my learning and reading, there was not much to my life. I did not want more. I was lonely, but felt that loneliness was no high price to pay for what I wanted.

Ress, whom I had disliked, was a friend to me. I went with her to meetings of the Hame, and also to entertainments that I would have known nothing about without her guidance. "Come on, Bumpkin," she would say. "Got to educate the plantation pup." And she would take me to the makil theater, or to asset dance halls where the music was good. She always wanted to dance. I let her teach me, but was not very happy dancing. One night as we were dancing the "slow-go" her hands began pressing me to her, and looking in her face I saw the mask of sexual desire on it, soft and blank. I broke away. "I don't want to dance," I said.

We walked home. She came up to my room with me, and at my door she tried to hold and kiss me. I was sick with anger. "I don't want that!" I said.

"I'm sorry, Rakam," she said, more gently than I had ever heard her speak. "I know how you must feel. But you've got to get over that, you've got to have your own life. I'm not a man, and I do want you."

I broke in—"A woman used me before a man ever did. Did you ask me if I wanted you? I will never be used again!"

That rage and spite came bursting out of me like poison from an infection. If she had tried to touch me again, I would have hurt her. I slammed my door in her face. I went trembling to my desk, sat down, and began to read the book that was open on it.

Next day we were both ashamed and stiff. But Ress had patience under her City quickness and roughness. She did not try to make love to me again, but she got me to trust her and talk to her as I could not talk to anybody else. She listened intently and told me what she thought. She said, "Bumpkin, you have it all wrong. No wonder. How could you have got it right? You think sex is something that gets done to you. It's not. It's something you do. With somebody else. Not to them. You never had any sex. All you ever knew was rape."

"Lord Erod told me all that a long time ago," I said. I was bitter. "I don't care what it's called. I had enough of it. For the rest of my life. And I'm glad to be without it."

Ress made a face. "At twenty-two?" she said. "Maybe for a while. If you're happy, then fine. But think about what I said. It's a big part of life to just cut out."

"If I have to have sex, I can pleasure myself," I said, not caring if I hurt her. "Love has nothing to do with it."

"That's where you're wrong," she said, but I did not listen. I would learn from teachers and books which I chose for myself, but I would not take advice I had not asked for. I refused to be told what to do or what to think. If I was free, I would be free by myself. I was like a baby when it first stands up.

Ahas had been giving me advice too. He said it was foolish to pursue education so far. "There's nothing useful you can do with so much book learning," he said. "It's self-indulgent. We need leaders and members with practical skills."

"We need teachers!"

"Yes," he said, "but you knew enough to teach a year ago. What's the good of ancient history, facts about alien worlds? We have a revolution to make!"

I did not stop my reading, but I felt guilty. I took a class at the Hame school teaching illiterate assets and freedpeople to read and write, as I myself had been taught only three years before. It was hard work. Reading is hard for a grown person to learn, tired, at night, after work all day. It is much easier to let the net take one's mind over.

I kept arguing with Ahas in my mind, and one day I said to him, "Is there a Library on Yeowe?"

"I don't know."

"You know there isn't. The Corporations didn't leave any libraries there. They didn't have any. They were ignorant people who knew nothing but profit. Knowledge is a good in itself. I keep on learning so that I can bring my knowledge to Yeowe. If I could, I'd bring them the whole Library!"

He stared. "What owners thought, what owners did—that's all their books are about. They don't need that on Yeowe."

"Yes they do," I said, certain he was wrong, though again I could not say why.

At the school they soon called on me to teach history, one of the teachers having left. These classes went well. I worked hard preparing them. Presently I was asked to speak to a study group of advanced students, and that, too, went well. People were interested in the ideas I drew from history and the comparisons I had learned to make of our world with other worlds. I had been studying the way various peoples bring up their children, who takes the responsibility for them and how that responsibility is understood, since this seemed to me a place where a people frees or enslaves itself.

To one of these talks a man from the Embassy of the Ekumen came. I was frightened when I saw the alien face in my audience. I was worse frightened when I recognised him. He had taught the first course in Ekumenical History that I had taken in the net. I had listened to it devotedly though I never participated in the discussion. What I learned had had a great influence on me. I thought he would find me presumptuous for talking of things he truly knew. I stammered on through my lecture, trying not to see his white-cornered eyes.

He came up to me afterwards, introduced himself politely, complimented my talk, and asked if I had read such-and-such a book. He engaged me so deftly and kindly in conversation that I had to like and trust him. And he soon earned my trust. I needed his guidance, for much foolishness has been written and spoken, even by wise people, about the balance of power between men and women, on which depend the lives of children and the value of their education. He knew useful books to read, from which I could go on by myself.

His name was Esdardon Aya. He worked in some high position, I was not sure what, at the Embassy. He had been born on Hain, the Old World, humanity's first home, from which all our ancestors came.

Sometimes I thought how strange it was that I knew about such things, such vast and ancient matters, I who had not known anything outside the compound walls till I was six, who had not known the name of the country I lived in till I was eighteen! When I was new to the City someone had spoken of "Voe Deo," and I had asked, "Where is that?" They had all stared at me. A woman, a hard-voiced old City rentswoman, had said, "Here, Dusty. Right here's Voe Deo. Your country and mine!"

I told Esdardon Aya that. He did not laugh. "A country, a people," he said. "Those are strange and very difficult ideas."

"My country was slavery," I said, and he nodded.

By now I seldom saw Ahas. I missed his kind friendship, but it had all turned to scolding. "You're puffed up, publishing, talking to audiences all the time," he said. "You're putting yourself before our cause."

I said, "But I talk to people in the Hame, I write about things we need to know. Everything I do is for freedom."

"The Community is not pleased with that pamphlet of yours," he said, in a serious, counseling way, as if telling me a secret I needed to know. "I've been asked to tell you to submit your writings to the committee before you publish again. That press is run by hotheads. The Hame is causing a good deal of trouble to our candidates."

"Our candidates!" I said in a rage. "No owner is my candidate! Are you still taking orders from the Young Owner?"

That stung him. He said, "If you put yourself first, if you won't cooperate, you bring danger on us all."

"I don't put myself first—politicians and capitalists do that. I put freedom first. Why can't you cooperate with me? It goes two ways, Ahas!"

He left angry, and left me angry.

I think he missed my dependence on him. Perhaps he was jealous, too, of my independence, for he did remain Lord Erod's man. His was a loyal heart. Our disagreement gave us both much bitter pain. I wish I knew what became of him in the troubled times that followed.

There was truth in his accusation. I had found that I had the gift in speaking and writing of moving people's minds and hearts. Nobody told me that such a gift is as dangerous as it is strong. Ahas said I was putting myself first, but I knew I was not doing that. I was wholly in the service of the truth and of liberty. No one told me that the end cannot purify the means, since only the Lord Kamye knows what the end may be. My grandmother could have told me that. The *Arkamye* would have reminded me of it, but I did not often read in it, and in the City there were no old men singing the word, evenings. If there had been, I would not have heard them over the sound of my beautiful voice speaking the beautiful truth.

I believe I did no harm, except as we all did, in bringing it to the attention of the rulers of Voe Deo that the Hame was growing bolder and the Radical Party was growing stronger, and that they must move against us.

The first sign was a divisive one. In the open compounds, as well as the men's side and the women's side there were several apartments for couples. This was a radical thing. Any kind of marriage between assets was illegal. They were allowed to live in pairs only by their owners' indulgence. Assets' only legitimate loyalty was to their owner. The child did not belong to the mother, but to the owner. But since gareots were living in the same place as owned assets, these apartments for couples had been tolerated or ignored. Now suddenly the law was invoked, asset couples were arrested, fined if they were wage earners, separated, and sent to company-run compound houses. Ress and the other elderwomen who ran our house were fined and warned that if "immoral arrangements" were discovered again, they would be held responsible and sent to the labor camps. Two little children of one of the couples were not on the government's list and so were left, abandoned, when their parents were taken off. Keo and Ramayo took them in. They became wards of the women's side, as orphans in the compounds always did.

There were fierce debates about this in meetings of the Hame and The Community. Some said the right of assets to live together and to bring up their children was a cause the Radical Party should support. It was not directly threatening to ownership, and might appeal to the natural instincts of many owners, especially the women, who could not vote but who were valuable allies. Others said that private affections must be overridden by loyalty to the cause of liberty, and that any personal issue must take second place to the great issue of emancipation. Lord Erod spoke thus at a meeting. I rose to answer him. I said that there was no freedom without sexual freedom, and that until women were allowed and men were willing to take responsibility for their children, no woman, whether owner or asset, would be free.

"Men must bear the responsibility for the public side of life, the greater world the child will enter; women, for the domestic side of life, the moral and physical upbringing of the child. This is a division enjoined by God and Nature," Erod answered.

"Then will emancipation for a woman mean she's free to enter the beza, be locked in on the women's side?"

"Of course not," he began, but I broke in again, fearing his golden tongue—"Then what is freedom for a woman? Is it different from freedom for a man? Or is a free person free?"

The moderator was angrily thumping his staff, but some other asset women took up my question. "When will the Radical Party speak for us?" they said, and one elderwoman cried, "Where are your women, you owners who want to abolish slavery? Why aren't they here? Don't you let them out of the beza?"

The moderator pounded and finally got order restored. I was half-triumphant and half-dismayed. I saw Erod and also some of the people from the Hame now looking at me as an open troublemaker. And indeed my words had divided us. But were we not already divided?

A group of us women went home talking through the streets, talking aloud. These were my streets now, with their traffic and lights and dangers and life. I was a City woman, a free woman. That night I was an owner. I owned the City. I owned the future.

The arguments went on. I was asked to speak at many places. As I was leaving one such meeting, the Hainishman Esdardon Aya came to me and said in a casual way, as if discussing my speech, "Rakam, you're in danger of arrest."

I did not understand. He walked along beside me away from the others and went on: "A rumor has come to my attention at the Embassy. . . . The government of Voe Deo is about to change the status of manumitted assets. You're no longer to be considered gareots. You must have an owner-sponsor."

This was bad news, but after thinking it over I said, "I think I can find an owner to sponsor me. Lord Boeba, maybe."

"The owner-sponsor will have to be approved by the government. . . . This will tend to weaken The Community both through the asset and the owner members. It's very clever, in its way," said Esdardon Aya.

"What happens to us if we don't find an approved sponsor?"

"You'll be considered runaways."

That meant death, the labor camps, or auction.

"O Lord Kamye," I said, and took Esdardon Aya's arm, because a curtain of dark had fallen across my eyes.

We had walked some way along the street. When I could see again I saw the street, the high houses of the City, the shining lights I had thought were mine.

"I have some friends," said the Hainishman, walking on with me, "who are planning a trip to the Kingdom of Bambur."

After a while I said, "What would I do there?"

"A ship to Yeowe leaves from there."

"To Yeowe," I said.

"So I hear," he said, as if we were talking about a streetcar line. "In a few years, I expect Voe Deo will begin offering rides to Yeowe. Exporting intractables, troublemakers, members of the Hame. But that will involve recognising Yeowe as a nation state, which they haven't brought themselves to do yet. They are, however, permitting some semilegitimate trade arrangements by their client states. . . . A couple of years ago, the King of Bambur bought one of the old Corporation ships, a genuine old Colony Trader. The King thought he'd like to visit the moons of Werel. But he found the moons boring. So he rented the ship to a consortium of scholars from the University of Bambur and businessmen from his capital. Some manufacturers in Bambur carry on a little trade with Yeowe in it, and some scientists at the university make scientific expeditions in it at the same time. Of course each trip is very expensive, so they carry as many scientists as they can whenever they go."

I heard all this not hearing it, yet understanding it.

"So far," he said, "they've gotten away with it."

He always sounded quiet, a little amused, yet not superior.

"Does The Community know about this ship?" I asked.

"Some members do, I believe. And people in the Hame. But it's very dangerous to know about. If Voe Deo were to find out that a client state was exporting valuable property . . . In fact, we believe they may have some suspicions. So this is a decision that can't be made lightly. It is both dangerous and irrevocable. Because of that danger, I hesitated to speak of it to you. I hesitated so long that you must make it very quickly. In fact, tonight, Rakam."

I looked from the lights of the City up to the sky they hid. "I'll go," I said. I thought of Walsu.

"Good," he said. At the next corner he changed the direction we had been walking, away from my house, towards the Embassy of the Ekumen.

I never wondered why he did this for me. He was a secret man, a man of secret power, but he always spoke truth, and I think he followed his own heart when he could.

As we entered the Embassy grounds, a great park softly illuminated in the winter night by groundlights, I stopped. "My books," I said. He looked his question. "I wanted to take my books to Yeowe," I said. Now my voice shook with a rush of tears, as if everything I was leaving came down to that one thing. "They need books on Yeowe, I think," I said.

After a moment he said, "I'll have them sent on our next ship. I wish I could put you on that ship," he added in a lower voice. "But of course the Ekumen can't give free rides to runaway slaves. . . ."

I turned and took his hand and laid my forehead against it for a moment, the only time in my life I ever did that of my own free will.

He was startled. "Come, come," he said, and hurried me along.

The Embassy hired Werelian guards, mostly veots, men of the old warrior caste. One of them, a grave, courteous, very silent man, went with me on the flyer to Bambur, the island kingdom east of the Great Continent. He had all the papers I needed. From the flyer port he took me to the Royal Space Observatory, which the King had built for his spaceship. There without delay I was taken to the ship, which stood in its great scaffolding ready to depart.

I imagine that they had made comfortable apartments up front for the King when he went to see the moons. The body of the ship, which had belonged to the Agricultural Plantation Corporation, still consisted of great compartments for the produce of the Colony. It would be bringing back grain from Yeowe in four of the cargo bays that now held farm machinery made in Bambur. The fifth compartment held assets.

The cargo bay had no seats. They had laid felt pads on the floor, and we lay down and were strapped to stanchions, as cargo would have been. There were about fifty "scientists." I was the last to come aboard and be strapped in. The crew were hasty and nervous and spoke only the language of Bambur. I could not understand the instructions we were given. I needed very badly to relieve my bladder, but they had shouted "No time, no time!" So I lay in torment while they closed the great doors of the bay, which made me think of the doors of Shomeke compound. Around me people called out to one another in their language. A baby screamed. I knew that language. Then the great noise began, beneath us. Slowly I felt my body pressed down on the floor, as if a huge soft foot were stepping on me, till my shoulder blades felt as if they were cutting into the mat, and my tongue pressed back into my throat as if to choke me, and with a sharp stab of pain and hot relief my bladder released its urine.

Then we began to be weightless—to float in our bonds. Up was down and down was up, either was both or neither. I heard people all around me calling out again, saying one another's names, saying what must be, "Are you all right? Yes, I'm all right." The baby had never ceased its fierce, piercing yells. I began to feel at my restraints, for I saw the woman next to me sitting up and rubbing her arms and chest where the straps had held her. But a great blurry voice came bellowing over the loudspeaker, giving orders in the language of Bambur and then in Voe Dean: "Do not unfasten the straps! Do not attempt to move about! The ship is under attack! The situation is extremely dangerous!"

So I lay floating in my little mist of urine, listening to the strangers around me talk, understanding nothing. I was utterly miserable, and yet fearless as I had never been. I was carefree. It was like dying. It would be foolish to worry about anything while one died.

The ship moved strangely, shuddering, seeming to turn. Several people were sick. The air filled with the smell and tiny droplets of vomit. I freed my hands enough to draw the scarf I was wearing up over my face as a filter, tucking the ends under my head to hold it.

Inside the scarf I could no longer see the huge vault of the cargo bay stretching above or below me, making me feel I was about to fly or fall into it. It smelled of myself, which was comforting. It was the scarf I often wore when I dressed up to give a talk, fine gauze, pale red with a silver thread woven in at intervals. When I bought it at a City market, paying my own earned money for it, I had thought of my mother's red scarf, given her by Lady Tazeu. I thought she would have liked this one, though it was not as bright. Now I lay and looked into the pale red dimness it made of the vault, starred with the lights at the hatches, and thought of my mother, Yowa. She had probably been killed that morning in the compound. Perhaps she had been carried to another estate as a use-woman, but Ahas had never found any trace of her. I thought of the way she had of carrying her head a little to the side, deferent yet alert, gracious. Her eyes had been full and bright, "eyes that hold the seven moons," as the song says. I thought then: But I will never see the moons again.

At that I felt so strange that to comfort myself and distract my mind I began to sing under my breath, there alone in my tent of red gauze warm with my own breath. I sang the freedom songs we sang in the Hame, and then I sang the love songs Lady Tazeu had taught me. Finally I sang "O, O, Yeowe," softly at first, then a little louder. I heard a voice somewhere out in that soft red mist world join in with me, a man's voice, then a woman's. Assets from Voe Deo all know that song. We sang it together. A Bambur man's voice picked it up and put words in his own language to it, and others joined in singing it. Then the singing died away. The baby's crying was weak now. The air was very foul.

We learned many hours later, when at last clean air entered the vents and we were told we could release our bonds, that a ship of the Voe Dean Space Defense Fleet had intercepted the freighter's course just above the atmosphere and ordered it to stop. The captain chose to ignore the signal. The warship had fired, and though nothing hit the freighter the blast had damaged the controls. The freighter had gone on, and had seen and heard nothing more of the warship. We were now about eleven days from Yeowe. The warship, or a group of them, might be in wait for us near Yeowe. The reason they gave for ordering the freighter to halt was "suspected contraband merchandise."

That fleet of warships had been built centuries ago to protect Werel from the attacks they expected from the Alien Empire, which is what they then called the Ekumen. They were so frightened by that imagined threat that they put all their energy into the technology of space flight; and the colonisation of Yeowe was a result. After four hundred years without any threat of attack, Voe Deo had finally let the Ekumen send envoys and ambassadors. They had used the Defense Fleet to transport troops and weapons during the War of Liberation. Now they were using them the way estate owners used hunting dogs and hunting cats, to hunt down runaway slaves.

I found the two other Voe Deans in the cargo bay, and we moved our "bedstraps" together so we could talk. Both of them had been brought to Bambur by the Hame, who had paid their fare. It had not occurred to me that there was a fare to be paid. I knew who had paid mine.

"Can't fly a spaceship on love," the woman said. She was a strange person. She really was a scientist. Highly trained in chemistry by the company that rented her, she had persuaded the Hame to send her to Yeowe because she was sure her skills would be needed and in demand. She had been making higher wages than many gareots did, but she expected to do still better on Yeowe. "I'm going to be rich," she said.

The man, only a boy, a mill hand in a northern city, had simply run away and had the luck to meet people who could save him from death or the labor camps. He was sixteen, ignorant, noisy, rebellious, sweet-natured. He became a general favorite, like a puppy. I was in demand because I knew the history of Yeowe and through a man who knew both our languages I could tell the Bamburs something about where they were going—the centuries of Corporation slavery, Nadami, the War, the Liberation. Some of them were rentspeople from the cities, others were a group of estate slaves bought at auction by the Hame with false money and under a false name and hurried onto this flight, knowing very little of where they were going. It was that trick that had drawn Voe Deo's attention to this flight.

Yoke, the mill boy, speculated endlessly about how the Yeowans would welcome us. He had a story, half a joke, half a dream, about the bands playing and the speeches and the big dinner they would have for us. The dinner grew more and more elaborate as the days went on. They were long, hungry days, floating in the featureless great space of the cargo bay, marked only by the alternation every twelve hours of brighter and dimmer lighting and the issuing of two meals during the "day," food and water in tubes you squeezed into your mouth. I did not think much about what might happen. I was between happenings. If the warships found us, we would probably die. If we got to Yeowe, it would be a new life. Now we were floating.

4. YEOWE

The ship came down safe at the Port of Yeowe. They unloaded the crates of machinery first, then the other cargo. We came out staggering and holding on to one another, not able to stand up to the great pull of this new world drawing us down to its center, blinded by the light of the sun that we were closer to than we had ever been.

"Over here! Over here!" a man shouted. I was grateful to hear my language, but the Bamburs looked apprehensive.

Over here—in here—strip—wait— All we heard when we were first on the Free World was orders. We had to be decontaminated, which was painful and exhausting. We had to be examined by doctors. Anything we had brought with us had to be decontaminated and examined and listed. That did not take long for me. I had brought the clothes I wore and had worn for two weeks now. I was glad to get decontaminated. Finally we were told to stand in line in one of the big empty cargo sheds. The sign over the doors still read APCY—Agricultural Plantation Corporation of Yeowe. One by one we were processed for entry. The man who processed me was short, white, middle-aged, with spectacles, like any clerk asset in the City, but I looked at him with reverence. He was the first Yeowan I had spoken to. He asked me questions from a form and wrote down my answers. "Can you read?" —"Yes." —"Skills?" —I stammered a moment and said, "Teaching—I can teach reading and history." He never looked up at me.

I was glad to be patient. After all, the Yeowans had not asked us to come. We were admitted only because they knew if they sent us back, we would die horribly in a public execution. We were a profitable cargo to Bambur, but to Yeowe we were a problem. But many of us had skills they must need, and I was glad they asked us about them.

When we had all been processed, we were separated into two groups: men and women. Yoke hugged me and went off to the men's side laughing and waving. I stood with the women. We watched all the men led off to the shuttle that went to the Old Capital. Now my patience failed and my hope darkened. I prayed, "Lord Kamye, not here, not here too!" Fear made me angry. When a man came giving us orders again, come on, this way, I went up to him and said, "Who are you? Where are we going? We are free women!"

He was a big fellow with a round, white face and bluish eyes. He looked down at me, huffy at first, then smiling. "Yes, Little Sister, you're free," he said. "But we've all got to work, don't we? You ladies are going south. They need people on the rice plantations. You do a little work, make a little money, look around a little, all right? If you don't like it down there, come on back. We can always use more pretty little ladies round here."

I had never heard the Yeowan country accent, a singing, blurry softening, with long, clear vowels. I had never heard asset women called ladies. No one had ever called me Little Sister. He did not mean the word "use" as I took it, surely. He meant well. I was bewildered and said no more. But the chemist, Tualtak, said, "Listen, I'm no field hand, I'm a trained scientist—"

"Oh, you're all scientists," the Yeowan said with his big smile. "Come on now, ladies!" He strode ahead, and we followed. Tualtak kept talking. He smiled and paid no heed.

We were taken to a train car waiting on a siding. The huge, bright sun was setting. All the sky was orange and pink, full of light. Long shadows ran black along the ground. The warm air was dusty and sweet-smelling. While we stood waiting to climb up into the car I stooped and picked up a little reddish stone from the ground. It was round, with a tiny stripe of white clear through it. It was a piece of Yeowe. I held Yeowe in my hand. That little stone, too, I still have.

Our car was shunted along to the main yards and hooked onto a train. When the train started we were served dinner, soup from great kettles wheeled through the car, bowls of sweet, heavy marsh rice, pini fruit—a luxury on Werel, here a commonplace. We ate and ate. I watched the last light die away from the long, rolling hills that the train was passing through. The stars came out. No moons. Never again. But I saw Werel rising in the east. It was a great blue-green star, looking as Yeowe looks from Werel. But you would never see Yeowe rising after sunset. Yeowe followed the sun.

I'm alive and I'm here, I thought. I'm following the sun. I let the rest go, and fell asleep to the swaying of the train.

We were taken off the train on the second day at a town on the great river Yot. Our group of twenty-three was separated there, and ten of us were taken by oxcart to a village, Hagayot. It had been an APCY compound, growing marsh rice to feed the Colony slaves. Now it was a cooperative village, growing marsh rice to feed the Free People. We were enrolled as members of the cooperative. We lived share and share alike with the villagers until payout, when we could pay them back what we owed the cooperative.

It was a reasonable way to handle immigrants without money who did not know the language or who had no skills. But I did not understand why they had ignored our skills. Why had they sent the men from Bambur plantations, field hands, into the city, not here? Why only women?

I did not understand why, in a village of free people, there was a men's side and a women's side, with a ditch between them.

I did not understand why, as I soon discovered, the men made all the decisions and gave all the orders. But, it being so, I did understand that they were afraid of us Werelian women, who were not used to taking orders from our equals. And I understood that I must take orders and not even look as if I thought of questioning them. The men of Hagayot Village watched us with fierce suspicion and a whip as ready as any Boss's. "Maybe you told men what to do back over there," the foreman told us the first morning in the fields. "Well, that's back over there. That's not here. Here we free people work together. You think you're Bosswomen. There aren't any Boss-women here."

There were grandmothers on the women's side, but they were not the powers our grandmothers had been. Here, where for the first century there had been no slave women at all, the men had had to make their own life, set up their own powers. When women slaves at last were sent into those slave-kingdoms of men, there was no power for them at all. They had no voice. Not till they got away to the cities did they ever have a voice on Yeowe.

I learned silence.

But it was not as bad for me and Tualtak as for our eight Bambur companions. We were the first immigrants any of these villagers had ever seen. They knew only one language. They thought the Bambur women were witches because they did not talk "like human beings." They whipped them for talking to each other in their own language.

I will confess that in my first year on the Free World my heart was as low as it had been at Zeskra. I hated standing all day in the shallow water of the rice paddies. Our feet were always sodden and swollen and full of tiny burrowing worms we had to pick out every night. But it was needed work and not too hard for a healthy woman. It was not the work that bore me down.

Hagayot was not a tribal village, not as conservative as some of the old villages I learned about later. Girls here were not ritually raped, and a woman was safe on the women's side. She "jumped the ditch" only with a man she chose. But if a woman went anywhere alone, or even got separated from the other women working in the paddies, she was supposed to be "asking for it," and any man thought it his right to force himself on her.

I made good friends among the village women and the Bamburs. They were no more ignorant than I had been a few years before and some were wiser than I would ever be. There was no possibility of having a friend among men who thought themselves our owners. I could not see how life here would ever change. My heart was very low, nights, when I lay among the sleeping women and children in our hut and thought, Is this what Walsu died for?

In my second year there, I resolved to do what I could to keep above the misery that threatened me. One of the Bambur women, meek and slow of understanding, whipped and beaten by both women and men for speaking her language, had drowned in one of the great rice paddies. She had lain down there in the warm shallow water not much deeper than her ankles, and had drowned. I feared that yielding, that water of despair. I made up my mind to use my skill, to teach the village women and children to read.

I wrote out some little primers on rice cloth and made a game of it for the little children, first. Some of the older girls and women were curious. Some of them knew that people in the towns and cities could read. They saw it as a mystery, a witchcraft that gave the city people their great power. I did not deny this.

For the women, I first wrote down verses and passages of the *Arkamye*, all I could remember, so that they could have it and not have to wait for one of the men who called themselves "priests" to recite it. They were proud of learning to read these verses. Then I had my friend Seugi tell me a story, her own recollection of meeting a wild hunting cat in the marshes as a child. I wrote it down, entitling it "The Marsh Lion, by Aro Seugi," and read it aloud to the author and a circle of girls and women. They marveled and laughed. Seugi wept, touching the writing that held her voice.

The chief of the village and his headmen and foremen and honorary sons, all the hierarchy and government of the village, were suspicious and not pleased by my teaching, yet did not want to forbid me. The government of Yotebber Region had sent word that they were establishing country schools where village children were to be sent for half the year. The village men knew that their sons would be advantaged if they could already read and write when they went there.

The Chosen Son, a big, mild, pale man, blind in one eye from a war wound, came to me at last. He wore his coat of office, a tight, long coat such as Werelian owners had worn three hundred years ago. He told me that I should not teach girls to read, only boys.

I told him I would teach all the children who wanted to learn or none of them.

"Girls do not want to learn this," he said.

"They do. Fourteen girls have asked to be in my class. Eight boys. Do you say girls do not need religious training, Chosen Son?"

This gave him pause. "They should learn the life of the Merciful Lady," he said.

"I will write the Life of Tual for them," I said at once. He walked away, saving his dignity.

I had little pleasure in my victory, such as it was. At least I went on teaching.

Tualtak was always at me to run away, run away to the city downriver. She had grown very thin, for she could not digest the heavy food. She hated the work and the people. "It's all right for you, you were a plantation pup, a dusty, but I never was, my mother was a rentswoman, we lived in fine rooms on Haba Street, I was the brightest trainee they ever had in the laboratory," and on and on, over and over, living in the world she had lost.

Sometimes I listened to her talk about running away. I tried to remember the maps of Yeowe in my lost books. I remembered the great river, the Yot, running from far inland three thousand kilos to the South Sea. But where were we on its vast length, how far from Yotebber City on its delta? Between Hagayot and the city might be a hundred villages like this one. "Have you been raped?" I asked Tualtak.

She took offense. "I'm a rentswoman, not a use-woman," she snapped.

I said, "I was a use-woman for two years. If I was raped again, I would kill the man or kill myself. I think two Werelian women walking alone here would be raped. I can't do it, Tualtak."

"It can't all be like this place!" she cried, so desperate that I felt my own throat close up with tears.

"Maybe when they open the schools—there will be people from the cities then—" It was all I had to offer her, or myself, as hope. "Maybe if the harvest's good this year, if we can get our money, we can get on the train. . . ."

That indeed was our best hope. The problem was to get our money from the chief and his cohorts. They kept the cooperative's income in a stone hut which they called the Bank of Hagayot, and only they ever saw the money. Each individual had an account, and they kept tally faithfully, the old Banker Headman scratching your account out in the dirt if you asked for it. But women and children could not withdraw money from their account. All we could get was a kind of scrip, clay pieces marked by the Banker Headman, good to buy things from one another, things people in the village made, clothes, sandals, tools, bead necklaces, rice beer. Our real money was safe, we were told, in the bank. I thought of that old lame bondsman at Shomeke, jigging and singing, "Money in the bank, Lord! Money in the bank!"

Before we ever came, the women had resented this system. Now there were nine more women resenting it.

One night I asked my friend Seugi, whose hair was as white as her skin, "Seugi, do you know what happened at a place called Nadami?"

"Yes," she said. "The women opened the door. All the women rose up and then the men rose up against the Bosses. But they needed weapons. And a woman ran in the night and stole the key from the owner's box and opened the door of the strong place where the Bosses kept their guns and bullets, and she held it open with the strength of her body, so that the slaves could arm themselves. And they killed the Corporations and made that place, Nadami, free."

"Even on Werel they tell that story," I said. "Even there women tell about Nadami, where the women began the Liberation. Men tell it too. Do men here tell it? Do they know it?"

Seugi and the other women nodded.

"If a woman freed the men of Nadami," I said, "maybe the women of Hagayot can free their money."

Seugi laughed. She called out to a group of grandmothers, "Listen to Rakam! Listen to this!"

After plenty of talk for days and weeks, it ended in a delegation of women, thirty of us. We crossed the ditch bridge onto the men's side and ceremoniously asked to see the chief. Our principal bargaining counter was shame. Seugi and other village women did the speaking, for they knew how far they could shame the men without goading them into anger and retaliation. Listening to them, I heard dignity speak to dignity, pride speak to pride. For the first time since I came to Yeowe I felt I was one of these people, that this pride and dignity were mine.

Nothing happens fast in a village. But by the next harvest, the women of Hagayot could draw their own earned share out of the bank in cash.

"Now for the vote," I said to Seugi, for there was no secret ballot in the village. When there was a regional election, even in the worldwide Ratification of the Constitution, the chiefs polled the men and filled out the ballots. They did not even poll the women. They wrote in the votes they wanted cast.

But I did not stay to help bring about that change at Hagayot. Tualtak was really ill and half-crazy with her longing to get out of the marshes, to the city. And I too longed for that. So we took our wages, and Seugi and other women drove us in an oxcart on the causeway across the marshes to the freight station. There we raised the flag that signaled the next train to stop for passengers.

It came along in a few hours, a long train of boxcars loaded with marsh rice, heading for the mills of Yotebber City. We rode in the crew car with the train crew and a few other passengers, village men. I had a big knife in my belt, but none of the men showed us any disrespect. Away from their compounds they were timid and shy. I sat up in my bunk in that car watching the great, wild, plumy marshes whirl by, and the villages on the banks of the wide river, and wished the train would go on forever.

But Tualtak lay in the bunk below me, coughing and fretful. When we got to Yotebber City she was so weak I knew I had to get her to a doctor. A man from the train crew was kind, telling us how to get to the hospital on the public cars. As we rattled through the hot, crowded city streets in the crowded car, I was still happy. I could not help it.

At the hospital they demanded our citizen's registration papers.

I had never heard of such papers. Later I found that ours had been given to the chiefs at Hagayot, who had kept them, as they kept all "their" women's papers. At the time, all I could do was stare and say, "I don't know anything about registration papers."

I heard one of the women at the desk say to the other, "Lord, how dusty can you get?"

I knew what we looked like. I knew we looked dirty and low. I knew I seemed ignorant and stupid. But when I heard that word "dusty" my pride and dignity woke up again. I put my hand into my pack and brought out my freedom paper, that old paper with Erod's writing on it, all crumpled and folded, all dusty.

"This is my Citizen's Registration paper," I said in a loud voice, making those women jump and turn. "My mother's blood and my grandmother's blood is on it. My friend here is sick. She needs a doctor. Now bring us to a doctor!"

A thin little woman came forward from the corridor. "Come on this way," she said. One of the deskwomen started to protest. This little woman gave her a look.

We followed her to an examination room.

"I'm Dr. Yeron," she said, then corrected herself. "I'm serving as a nurse," she said. "But I am a doctor. And you—you come from the Old World? from Werel? Sit down there, now, child, take off your shirt. How long have you been here?"

Within a quarter of an hour she had diagnosed Tualtak and got her a bed in a ward for rest and observation, found out our histories, and sent me off with a note to a friend of hers who would help me find a place to live and a job.

"Teaching!" Dr. Yeron said. "A teacher! Oh, woman, you are rain to the dry land!"

Indeed the first school I talked to wanted to hire me at once, to teach anything I wanted. Because I come of a capitalist people, I went to other schools to see if I could make more money at them. But I came back to the first one. I liked the people there.

Before the War of Liberation, the cities of Yeowe, which were cities of Corporation-owned assets who rented their own freedom, had had their own schools and hospitals and many kinds of training programs. There was even a University for assets in the Old Capital. The Corporations, of course, had controlled all the information that came to such institutions, and watched and censored all teaching and writing, keeping everything aimed towards the maximization of their profits. But within that narrow frame the assets had been free to use the information they had as they pleased, and city Yeowans had valued education deeply. During the long war, thirty years, all that system of gathering and teaching knowledge had broken down. A whole generation grew up learning nothing but fighting and hiding, famine and disease. The head of my school said to me, "Our children grew up illiterate, ignorant. Is it any wonder the plantation chiefs just took over where the Corporation Bosses left off? Who was to stop them?"

These men and women believed with a fierce passion that only education would lead to freedom. They were still fighting the War of Liberation.

Yotebber City was a big, poor, sunny, sprawling city with wide streets, low buildings, and huge old shady trees. The traffic was mostly afoot, with cycles tinging and public cars clanging along among the slow crowds. There were miles of shacks and shanties down in the old floodplain of the river behind the levees, where the soil was rich for gardening. The center of the city was on a low rise, the mills and train yards spreading out from it. Downtown it looked like the City of Voe Deo, only older and poorer and gentler. Instead of big stores for owners, people bought and sold everything from stalls in open markets. The air was soft here in the south, a warm, soft sea air full of mist and sunlight. I stayed happy. I have by the grace of the Lord a mind that can leave misfortune behind, and I was happy in Yotebber City.

Tualtak recovered her health and found a good job as a chemist in a factory. I saw her seldom, as our friendship had been a matter of necessity, not choice. Whenever I saw her she talked about Haba Street and her laboratory on Werel and complained about her work and the people here.

Dr. Yeron did not forget me. She wrote a note and told me to come visit her, which I did. Presently, when I was settled, she asked me to come with her to a meeting of an educational society. This, I found, was a group of democrats, mostly teachers, who sought to work against the autocratic power of the tribal and regional chiefs under the new Constitution, and to counteract what they called the slave mind, the rigid, misogynistic hierarchy that I had encountered in Hagayot. My experience was useful to them, for they were all city people who had met the slave mind only when they found themselves governed by it. The women of the group were the angriest. They had lost the most at Liberation and now had less to lose. In general the men were gradualists, the women ready for revolution. As a Werelian, ignorant of politics on Yeowe, I listened and did not talk. It was hard for me not to talk. I am a talker, and sometimes I had plenty to say. But I held my tongue and heard them. They were people worth hearing.

Ignorance defends itself savagely, and illiteracy, as I well knew, can be shrewd. Though the Chief, the President of Yotebber Region, elected by a manipulated ballot, might not understand our counter-manipulations of the school curriculum, he did not waste much energy trying to control the schools, merely sending his inspectors to meddle with our classes and censor our books. But what he saw as important was the fact that, just as the Corporations had, he controlled the net. The news, the information programs, the puppets of the neareals, all danced to his strings. Against that, what harm could a lot of teachers do? Parents who had no schooling had children who entered the net to hear and see and feel what the Chief wanted them to know: that freedom is obedience to leaders, that virtue is violence, that manhood is domination. Against the enactment of such truths in daily life and in the heightened sensational experience of the neareals, what good were words?

"Literacy is irrelevant," one of our group said sorrowfully.

"The chiefs have jumped right over our heads into the postliterate information technology."

I brooded over that, hating her fancy words, irrelevant, postliterate, because I was afraid she was right.

To the next meeting of our group, to my surprise, an Alien came: the Sub-Envoy of the Ekumen. He was supposed to be a great feather in our Chief's cap, sent down from the Old Capital apparently to support the Chief's stand against the World Party, which was still strong down here and still clamoring that Yeowe should keep out all foreigners. I had heard vaguely that such a person was here, but I had not expected to meet him at a gathering of subversive schoolteachers.

He was a short man, red-brown, with white corners to his eyes, but handsome if one could ignore that. He sat in the seat in front of me. He sat perfectly still, as if accustomed to sitting still, and listened without speaking, as if accustomed to listening. At the end of the meeting he turned around and his queer eyes looked straight at me.

"Radosse Rakam?" he said.

I nodded, dumb.

"I'm Yehedarhed Havzhiva," he said. "I have some books for you from old music."

I stared. I said, "Books?"

"From old music," he said again. "Esdardon Aya, on Werel."

"My books?" I said.

He smiled. He had a broad, quick smile.

"Oh, where?" I cried.

"They're at my house. We can get them tonight, if you like. I have a car." There was something ironic and light in how he said that, as if he was a man who did not expect to have a car, though he might enjoy it.

Dr. Yeron came over. "So you found her," she said to the Sub-Envoy. He looked at her with such a bright face that I thought, these two are lovers. Though she was much older than he, there was nothing unlikely in the thought. Dr. Yeron was a magnetic woman. It was odd to me to think it, though, for my mind was not given to speculating about people's sexual affairs. That was no interest of mine.

He put his hand on her arm as they talked, and I saw with peculiar intensity how gentle his touch was, almost hesitant, yet trustful. That is love, I thought. Yet they parted, I saw, without that look of private understanding that lovers often give each other.

He and I rode in his government electric car, his two silent bodyguards, policewomen, sitting in the front seat. We spoke of Esdardon Aya, whose name, he explained to me, meant Old Music. I told him how Esdardon Aya had saved my life by sending me here. He listened in a way that made it easy to talk to him. I said, "I was sick to leave my books, and I've thought about them, missing them, as if they were my family. But I think maybe I'm a fool to feel that way."

"Why a fool?" he asked. He had a foreign accent, but he had the Yeowan lilt already, and his voice was beautiful, low and warm.

I tried to explain everything at once: "Well, they mean so much to me because I was illiterate when I came to the City, and it was the books that gave me freedom, gave me the world—the worlds— But now, here, I see how the net, the holos, the neareals mean so much more to people, giving them the present time. Maybe it's just clinging to the past to cling to books. Yeowans have to go towards the future. And we'll never change people's minds just with words."

He listened intently, as he had done at the meeting, and then answered slowly, "But words are an essential way of thinking. And books keep the words true. . . . I didn't read till I was an adult, either."

"You didn't?"

"I knew how, but I didn't. I lived in a village. It's cities that have to have books," he said, quite decisively, as if he had thought about this matter. "If they don't, we keep on starting over every generation. It's a waste. You have to save the words."

When we got to his house, up at the top end of the old part of town, there were four crates of books in the entrance hall.

"These aren't all mine!" I said.

"Old Music said they were yours," Mr. Yehedarhed said, with his quick smile and a quick glance at me. You can tell where an Alien is looking much better than you can tell with us. With us, except for the few people with bluish eyes, you have to be close enough to see the dark pupil move in the dark eye.

"I haven't got anywhere to put so many," I said, amazed, realising how that strange man, Old Music, had helped me to freedom yet again.

"At your school, maybe? The school library?"

It was a good idea, but I thought at once of the Chief's inspectors pawing through them, perhaps confiscating them. When I spoke of that, the Sub-Envoy said, "What if I present them as a gift from the Embassy? I think that might embarrass the inspectors."

"Oh," I said, and burst out, "Why are you so kind? You, and he— Are you Hainish too?"

"Yes," he said, not answering my other question. "I was. I hope to be Yeowan."

He asked me to sit down and drink a little glass of wine with him before his guard drove me home. He was easy and friendly, but a quiet man. I saw he had been hurt. There were scars on his face and a gap in his hair where he had had a head injury. He asked me what my books were, and I said, "History."

At that he smiled, slowly this time. He said nothing, but he raised his glass to me. I raised mine, imitating him, and we drank.

Next day he had the books delivered to our school. When we opened and shelved them, we realised we had a great treasure. "There's nothing like this at the University," said one of the teachers, who had studied there for a year.

There were histories and anthropologies of Werel and of the worlds of the Ekumen, works of philosophy and politics by Werelians and by people of other worlds, there were compendiums of literature, poetry and stories, encyclopedias, books of science, atlases, dictionaries. In a corner of one of the crates were my own few books, my own treasure, even that first little crude *History of Yeowe, Printed at Yeowe University in the Year One of Liberty.* Most of my books I left in the school library, but I took that one and a few others home for love, for comfort.

I had found another love and comfort not long since. A child at school had brought me a present, a spotted-cat kitten, just weaned. The boy gave it to me with such loving pride that I could not refuse it. When I tried to pass it on to another teacher they all laughed at me. "You're elected, Rakam!" they said. So unwillingly I took the little being home, afraid of its frailty and delicacy and near to feeling a disgust for it. Women in the beza at Zeskra had had pets, spotted cats and foxdogs, spoiled little animals fed better than we were. I had been called by the name of a pet animal once.

I alarmed the kitten taking it out of its basket, and it bit my thumb to the bone. It was tiny and frail but it had teeth. I began to have some respect for it.

That night I put it to sleep in its basket, but it climbed up on my bed and sat on my face until I let it under the covers. There it slept perfectly still all night. In the morning it woke me by dancing on me, chasing dust motes in a sunbeam. It made me laugh, waking, which is a pleasant thing. I felt that I had never laughed very much, and wanted to.

The kitten was all black, its spots showing only in certain lights, black on black. I called it Owner. I found it pleasant to come home evenings to be greeted by my little Owner.

Now for the next half year we were planning the great demonstration of women. There were many meetings, at some of which I met the Sub-Envoy again, so that I began to look for him. I liked to watch him listen to our arguments. There were those who argued that the demonstration must not be limited to the wrongs and rights of women, for equality must be for all. Others argued that it should not depend in any way on the support of foreigners, but should be a purely Yeowan movement. Mr. Yehedarhed listened to them, but I got angry. "I'm a foreigner," I said. "Does that make me no use to you? That's owner talk—as if you were better than other people!" And Dr. Yeron said, "I will believe equality is for all when I see it written in the Constitution of Yeowe." For our Constitution, ratified by a world vote during the time I was at Hagayot, spoke of citizens only as men. That is finally what the demonstration became, a demand that the Constitution be amended to include women as citizens, provide for the secret ballot, and guarantee the right to free speech, freedom of the press and of assembly, and free education for all children.

I lay down on the train tracks along with seventy thousand women, that hot day. I sang with them. I heard what that sounds like, so many women singing together, what a big, deep sound it makes.

I had begun to speak in public again when we were gathering women for the great demonstration. It was a gift I had, and we made use of it. Sometimes gang boys or ignorant men would come to heckle and threaten me, shouting, "Boss-woman, Ownerwoman, black cunt, go back where you came from!" Once when they were yelling that, go back, go back, I leaned into the microphone and said, "I can't go back. We used to sing a song on the plantation where I was a slave," and I sang it,

> *O, O, Ye-o-we,*
> *Nobody never comes back.*

The singing made them be still for a moment. They heard it, that awful grief, that yearning.

After the great demonstration the unrest never died down, but there were times that the energy flagged, the Movement didn't move, as Dr. Yeron said. During one of those times I went to her and proposed that we set up a printing house and publish books. This had been a dream of mine, growing from that day in Hagayot when Seugi had touched her words and wept.

"Talk goes by," I said, "and all the words and images in the net go by, and anybody can change them. But books are there. They last. They are the body of history, Mr. Yehedarhed says."

"Inspectors," said Dr. Yeron. "Until we get the free press amendment, the chiefs aren't going to let anybody print anything they didn't dictate themselves."

I did not want to give up the idea. I knew that in Yotebber Region we could not publish anything political, but I argued that we might print stories and poems by women of the region. Others thought it a waste of time. We discussed it back and forth for a long time. Mr. Yehedarhed came back from a trip to the Embassy, up north in the Old Capital. He listened to our discussions, but said nothing, which disappointed me. I had thought that he might support my project.

One day I was walking home from school to my apartment, which was in a big, old, noisy house not far from the levee. I liked the place because my windows opened into the branches of trees, and through the trees I saw the river, four miles wide here, easing along among sandbars and reedbeds and willow isles in the dry season, brimming up the levees in the wet season when the rainstorms scudded across it. That day as I came near the house, Mr. Yehedarhed appeared, with two sour-faced policewomen close behind him as usual. He greeted me and asked if we might talk. I was confused and did not know what to do but to invite him up to my room.

His guards waited in the lobby. I had just the one big room on the third floor. I sat on the bed and the Sub-Envoy sat in the chair. Owner went round and round his legs, saying roo? roo?

I had observed that the Sub-Envoy took pleasure in disappointing the expectations of the Chief and his cohorts, who were all for pomp and fleets of cars and elaborate badges and uniforms. He and his policewomen went all over the city, all over Yotebber, in his government car or on foot. People liked him for it. They knew, as I knew now, that he had been assaulted and beaten and left for dead by a World Party gang his first day here, when he went out afoot alone. The city people liked his courage and the way he talked with everybody, anywhere. They had adopted him. We in the Liberation Movement thought of him as "our Envoy," but he was theirs, and the Chief's too. The Chief may have hated his popularity, but he profited from it.

"You want to start a publishing house," he said, stroking Owner, who fell over with his paws in the air.

"Dr. Yeron says there's no use until we get the Amendments."

"There's one press on Yeowe not directly controlled by the government," Mr. Yehedarhed said, stroking Owner's belly.

"Look out, he'll bite," I said. "Where is that?"

"At the University. I see," Mr. Yehedarhed said, looking at his thumb. I apologized. He asked me if I was certain that Owner was male. I said I had been told so, but never had thought to look. "My impression is that your Owner is a lady," Mr. Yehedarhed said, in such a way that I began to laugh helplessly.

He laughed along with me, sucked the blood off his thumb, and went on. "The University never amounted to much. It was a Corporation ploy—let the assets pretend they're going to college. During the last years of the War it was closed down. Since Liberation Day it's reopened and crawled along with no one taking much notice of it. The faculty are mostly old. They came back to it after the War. The National Government gives it a subsidy because it sounds well to have a University of Yeowe, but they don't pay it any attention, because it has no prestige. And because many of them are unenlightened men." He said this without scorn, descriptively. "It does have a printing house."

"I know," I said. I reached out for my old book and showed it to him.

He looked through it for a few minutes. His face was curiously tender as he did so. I could not help watching him. It was like watching a woman with a baby, a constant, changing play of attention and response.

"Full of propaganda and errors and hope," he said at last, and his voice too was tender. "Well, I think this could be improved upon. Don't you? All that's needed is an editor. And some authors."

"Inspectors," I warned, imitating Dr. Yeron.

"Academic freedom is an easy issue for the Ekumen to have some influence upon," he said, "because we invite people to attend the Ekumenical Schools on Hain and Ve. We certainly want to invite graduates of the University of Yeowe. But of course, if their education is severely defective because of the lack of books, of information . . ."

I said, "Mr. Yehedarhed, are you *supposed* to subvert government policies?" The question broke out of me unawares.

He did not laugh. He paused for quite a long time before he answered. "I don't know," he said. "So far the Ambassador has backed me. We may both get reprimanded. Or fired. What I'd like to do . . ." His strange eyes were right on me again. He looked down at the book he still held. "What I'd like is to become a Yeowan citizen," he said. "But my usefulness to Yeowe, and to the Liberation Movement, is my position with the Ekumen. So I'll go on using that, or misusing it, till they tell me to stop."

When he left I had to think about what he had asked me to do. That was to go to the University as a teacher of history, and once there to volunteer for the editorship of the press. That all seemed so preposterous, for a woman of my background and my little learning, that I thought I must be

misunderstanding him. When he convinced me that I had understood him, I thought he must have very badly misunderstood who I was and what I was capable of. After we had talked
about that for a little while, he left, evidently feeling that he
was making me uncomfortable, and perhaps feeling uncomfortable himself, though in fact we laughed a good deal and I
did not feel uncomfortable, only a little as if I were crazy.

I tried to think about what he had asked me to do, to step so
far beyond myself. I found it difficult to think about. It was as
if it hung over me, this huge choice I must make, this future I
could not imagine. But what I thought about was him, Yehedarhed Havzhiva. I kept seeing him sitting there in my old
chair, stooping down to stroke Owner. Sucking blood off his
thumb. Laughing. Looking at me with his white-cornered
eyes. I saw his red-brown face and red-brown hands, the color
of pottery. His quiet voice was in my mind.

I picked up the kitten, half-grown now, and looked at its
hinder end. There was no sign of any male parts. The little
black silky body squirmed in my hands. I thought of him saying, "Your Owner is a lady," and I wanted to laugh again, and
to cry. I stroked the kitten and set her down, and she sat sedately beside me, washing her shoulder. "Oh poor little lady,"
I said. I don't know who I meant. The kitten, or Lady Tazeu,
or myself.

He had said to take my time thinking about his proposal, all
the time I wanted. But I had not really thought about it at all
when, the next day but one, there he was, on foot, waiting for
me as I came out of the school. "Would you like to walk on the
levee?" he said.

I looked around.

"There they are," he said, indicating his cold-eyed bodyguards. "Everywhere I am, they are, three to five meters away.
Walking with me is dull, but safe. My virtue is guaranteed."

We walked down through the streets to the levee and up
onto it in the long early evening light, warm and pink-gold,
smelling of river and mud and reeds. The two women with
guns walked along just about four meters behind us.

"If you do go to the University," he said after a long silence,
"I'll be there constantly."

"I haven't yet—" I stammered.

"If you stay here, I'll be here constantly," he said. "That is, if it's all right with you."

I said nothing. He looked at me without turning his head. I said without intending to, "I like it that I can see where you're looking."

"I like it that I can't see where you're looking," he said, looking directly at me.

We walked on. A heron rose up out of a reed islet and its great wings beat over the water, away. We were walking south, downriver. All the western sky was full of light as the sun went down behind the city in smoke and haze.

"Rakam, I would like to know where you came from, what your life on Werel was," he said very softly.

I drew a long breath. "It's all gone," I said. "Past."

"We are our past. Though not only that. I want to know you. Forgive me. I want very much to know you."

After a while I said, "I want to tell you. But it's so bad. It's so ugly. Here, now, it's beautiful. I don't want to lose it."

"Whatever you tell me I will hold valuable," he said, in his quiet voice that went to my heart. So I told him what I could about Shomeke compound, and then hurried on through the rest of my story. Sometimes he asked a question. Mostly he listened. At some time in my telling he had taken my arm, I scarcely noticing at the time. When he let me go, thinking some movement I made meant I wanted to be released, I missed that light touch. His hand was cool. I could feel it on my forearm after it was gone.

"Mr. Yehedarhed," said a voice behind us: one of the body-guards. The sun was down, the sky flushed with gold and red. "Better head back?"

"Yes," he said, "thanks." As we turned I took his arm. I felt him catch his breath.

I had not desired a man or a woman—this is the truth— since Shomeke. I had loved people, and I had touched them with love, but never with desire. My gate was locked.

Now it was open. Now I was so weak that at the touch of his hand I could scarcely walk on.

I said, "It's a good thing walking with you is so safe."

I hardly knew what I meant. I was thirty years old but I was like a young girl. I had never been that girl.

He said nothing. We walked along in silence between the river and the city in a glory of failing light.

"Will you come home with me, Rakam?" he said.

Now I said nothing.

"They don't come in with us," he said, very low, in my ear, so that I felt his breath.

"Don't make me laugh!" I said, and began crying. I wept all the way back along the levee. I sobbed and thought the sobs were ceasing and then sobbed again. I cried for all my sorrows, all my shames. I cried because they were with me now and always would be. I cried because the gate was open and I could go through at last, go into the country on the other side, but I was afraid to.

When we got into the car, up near my school, he took me in his arms and simply held me, silent. The two women in the front seat never looked round.

We went into his house, which I had seen once before, an old mansion of some owner of the Corporation days. He thanked the guards and shut the door. "Dinner," he said. "The cook's out. I meant to take you to a restaurant. I forgot." He led me to the kitchen, where we found cold rice and salad and wine. After we ate he looked at me across the kitchen table and looked down again. His hesitance made me hold still and say nothing. After a long time he said, "Oh, Rakam! will you let me make love to you?"

"I want to make love to you," I said. "I never did. I never made love to anyone."

He got up smiling and took my hand. We went upstairs together, passing what had been the entrance to the men's side of the house. "I live in the beza," he said, "in the harem. I live on the woman's side. I like the view."

We came to his room. There he stood still, looking at me, then looked away. I was so frightened, so bewildered, I thought I could not go to him or touch him. I made myself go to him. I raised my hand and touched his face, the scars by his eye and on his mouth, and put my arms around him. Then I could hold him to me, closer and closer.

Some time in that night as we lay drowsing entangled I said, "Did you sleep with Dr. Yeron?"

I felt Havzhiva laugh, a slow, soft laugh in his belly, which was against my belly. "No," he said. "No one on Yeowe but you. And you, no one on Yeowe but me. We were virgins, Yeowan virgins. . . . Rakam, *araha*. . . ." He rested his head in the hollow of my shoulder and said something else in a foreign language and fell asleep. He slept deeply, silently.

Later that year I came up north to the University, where I was taken on the faculty as a teacher of history. By their standards at that time, I was competent. I have worked there ever since, teaching and as editor of the press.

As he had said he would be, Havzhiva was there constantly, or almost.

The Amendments to the Constitution were voted, by secret ballot, mostly, in the Yeowan Year of Liberty 18. Of the events that led to this, and what has followed, you may read in the new three-volume *History of Yeowe* from the University Press. I have told the story I was asked to tell. I have closed it, as so many stories close, with a joining of two people. What is one man's and one woman's love and desire, against the history of two worlds, the great revolutions of our lifetimes, the hope, the unending cruelty of our species? A little thing. But a key is a little thing, next to the door it opens. If you lose the key, the door may never be unlocked. It is in our bodies that we lose or begin our freedom, in our bodies that we accept or end our slavery. So I wrote this book for my friend, with whom I have lived and will die free.

Old Music and the Slave Women

THE CHIEF intelligence officer of the Ekumenical embassy to Werel, a man who on his home world had the name Sohikelwenyanmurkeres Esdan, and who in Voe Deo was known by a nickname, Esdardon Aya or Old Music, was bored. It had taken a civil war and three years to bore him, but he had got to the point where he referred to himself in ansible reports to the Stabiles on Hain as the embassy's chief stupidity officer.

He had been able, however, to retain a few clandestine links with friends in the Free City even after the Legitimate Government sealed the embassy, allowing no one and no information to enter or leave it. In the third summer of the war, he came to the Ambassador with a request. Cut off from reliable communication with the embassy, Liberation Command had asked him (how? asked the Ambassador; through one of the men who delivered groceries, he explained) if the embassy would let one or two of its people slip across the lines and talk with them, be seen with them, offer proof that despite propaganda and disinformation, and though the embassy was stuck in Jit City, its staff had not been co-opted into supporting the Legitimates, but remained neutral and ready to deal with rightful authority on either side.

"Jit City?" said the Ambassador. "Never mind. But how do you get there?"

"Always the problem with Utopia," Esdan said. "Well, I can pass with contact lenses, if nobody's looking closely. Crossing the Divide is the tricky bit."

Most of the great city was still physically there, the government buildings, factories and warehouses, the university, the tourist attractions: the Great Shrine of Tual, Theater Street, the Old Market with its interesting display rooms and lofty Hall of Auction, disused since the sale and rental of assets had been shifted to the electronic marketplace; the numberless streets, avenues, and boulevards, the dusty parks shaded by purple-flowered beya trees, the miles and miles of shops, sheds, mills, tracks, stations, apartment buildings, houses, compounds, the neighborhoods, the suburbs, the exurbs. Most of it still stood, most of its fifteen million people were still there, but its deep complexity was gone. Connections were broken. Interactions did not take place. A brain after a stroke.

The greatest break was a brutal one, an axe-blow right through the pons, a kilo-wide no-man's-land of blown-up buildings and blocked streets, wreckage and rubble. East of the Divide was Legitimate territory: downtown, government offices, embassies, banks, communications towers, the university, the great parks and wealthy neighborhoods, the roads out to the armory, barracks, airports, and spaceport. West of the Divide was Free City, Dustyville, Liberation territory: factories, union compounds, the rentspeople's quarters, the old gareot residential neighborhoods, endless miles of little streets petering out into the plains at last. Through both ran the great East–West highways, empty.

The Liberation people successfully smuggled him out of the embassy and almost across the Divide. He and they had had a lot of practice in the old days getting runaway assets out to Yeowe and freedom. He found it interesting to be the one smuggled instead of one of the smugglers, finding it far more frightening yet less stressful, since he was not responsible, the package not the postman. But somewhere in the connection there had been a bad link.

They made it on foot into the Divide and partway through it and stopped at a little derelict truck sitting on its wheel rims under a gutted apartment house. A driver sat at the wheel behind the cracked, crazed windshield, and grinned at him. His guide gestured him into the back. The truck took off like a hunting cat, following a crazy route, zigzagging through the ruins. They were nearly across the Divide, jolting across a rubbled stretch which might have been a street or a marketplace, when the truck veered, stopped, there were shouts, shots, the vanback was flung open and men plunged in at him. "Easy," he said, "go easy," for they were manhandling him, hauling him, twisting his arm behind his back. They yanked him out of the truck, pulled off his coat and slapped him down searching for weapons, frogmarched him to a car waiting beside the truck. He tried to see if his driver was dead but could not look around before they shoved him into the car.

It was an old government state-coach, dark red, wide and

long, made for parades, for carrying great estate owners to the Council and ambassadors from the spaceport. Its main section could be curtained to separate men from women passengers, and the driver's compartment was sealed off so the passengers wouldn't be breathing in what a slave breathed out.

One of the men had kept his arm twisted up his back until he shoved him headfirst into the car, and all he thought as he found himself sitting between two men and facing three others and the car starting up was, "I'm getting too old for this."

He held still, letting his fear and pain subside, not ready yet to move even to rub his sharply hurting shoulder, not looking into faces nor too obviously at the streets. Two glances told him they were passing Rei Street, going east, out of the city. He realised then he had been hoping they were taking him back to the embassy. What a fool.

They had the streets to themselves, except for the startled gaze of people on foot as they flashed by. Now they were on a wide boulevard, going very fast, still going east. Although he was in a very bad situation, he still found it absolutely exhilarating just to be out of the embassy, out in the air, in the world, and moving, going fast.

Cautiously he raised his hand and massaged his shoulder. As cautiously, he glanced at the men beside him and facing him. All were dark-skinned, two blue-black. Two of the men facing him were young. Fresh, stolid faces. The third was a veot of the third rank, an oga. His face had the quiet inexpressiveness in which his caste was trained. Looking at him, Esdan caught his eye. Each looked away instantly.

Esdan liked veots. He saw them, soldiers as well as slave-holders, as part of the old Voe Deo, members of a doomed species. Businessmen and bureaucrats would survive and thrive in the Liberation and no doubt find soldiers to fight for them, but the military caste would not. Their code of loyalty, honor, and austerity was too like that of their slaves, with whom they shared the worship of Kamye, the Swordsman, the Bondsman. How long would that mysticism of suffering survive the Liberation? Veots were intransigent vestiges of an intolerable order. He trusted them, and had seldom been disappointed in his trust.

The oga was very black, very handsome, like Teyeo, a veot

Esdan had particularly liked. He had left Werel long before the war, off to Terra and Hain with his wife, who would be a Mobile of the Ekumen one of these days. In a few centuries. Long after the war was over, long after Esdan was dead. Unless he chose to follow them, went back, went home.

Idle thoughts. During a revolution you don't choose. You're carried, a bubble in a cataract, a spark in a bonfire, an unarmed man in a car with seven armed men driving very fast down the broad, blank East Arterial Highway. . . . They were leaving the city. Heading for the East Provinces. The Legitimate Government of Voe Deo was now reduced to half the capital city and two provinces, in which seven out of eight people were what the eighth person, their owner, called assets.

The two men up in the front compartment were talking, though they couldn't be heard in the owner compartment. Now the bullet-headed man to Esdan's right asked a muttered question to the oga facing him, who nodded.

"Oga," Esdan said.

The veot's expressionless eyes met his.

"I need to piss."

The man said nothing and looked away. None of them said anything for a while. They were on a bad stretch of the highway, torn up by fighting during the first summer of the Uprising or merely not maintained since. The jolts and shocks were hard on Esdan's bladder.

"Let the fucking white-eyes piss himself," said one of the two young men facing him to the other, who smiled tightly.

Esdan considered possible replies, good-humored, joking, not offensive, not provocative, and kept his mouth shut. They only wanted an excuse, those two. He closed his eyes and tried to relax, to be aware of the pain in his shoulder, the pain in his bladder, merely aware.

The man to his left, whom he could not see clearly, spoke: "Driver. Pull off up there." He used a speakerphone. The driver nodded. The car slowed, pulled off the road, jolting horribly. They all got out of the car. Esdan saw that the man to his left was also a veot, of the second rank, a zadyo. One of the young men grabbed Esdan's arm as he got out, another shoved a gun against his liver. The others all stood on the dusty roadside and pissed variously on the dust, the gravel, the roots of a row of scruffy trees. Esdan managed to get his fly open but his legs were so cramped and shaky he could barely stand, and the young man with the gun had come around and now stood directly in front of him with the gun aimed at his penis. There was a knot of pain somewhere between his bladder and his cock. "Back up a little," he said with plaintive irritability. "I don't want to wet your shoes." The young man stepped forward instead, bringing his gun right against Esdan's groin.

The zadyo made a slight gesture. The young man backed off a step. Esdan shuddered and suddenly pissed out a fountain. He was pleased, even in the agony of relief, to see he'd driven the young man back two more steps.

"Looks almost human," the young man said.

Esdan tucked his brown alien cock away with discreet promptness and slapped his trousers shut. He was still wearing lenses that hid the whites of his eyes, and was dressed as a rentsman in loose, coarse clothes of dull yellow, the only dye color that had been permitted to urban slaves. The banner of the Liberation was that same dull yellow. The wrong color, here. The body inside the clothes was the wrong color too.

Having lived on Werel for thirty-three years, Esdan was used to being feared and hated, but he had never before been entirely at the mercy of those who feared and hated him. The aegis of the Ekumen had sheltered him. What a fool, to leave the embassy where at least he'd been harmless, and let himself be got hold of by these desperate defenders of a lost cause, who might do a good deal of harm not only to but with him. How much resistance, how much endurance, was he capable of? Fortunately they couldn't torture any information about Liberation plans from him, since he didn't know a damned thing about what his friends were doing. But still, what a fool.

Back in the car, sandwiched in the seat with nothing to see but the young men's scowls and the oga's watchful nonexpression, he shut his eyes again. The highway was smooth here. Rocked in speed and silence he slipped into a post-adrenaline doze.

When he came fully awake the sky was gold, two of the little moons glittering above a cloudless sunset. They were jolting along on a side road, a driveway that wound past fields, orchards, plantations of trees and building-cane, a huge field-worker compound, more fields, another compound. They stopped at a checkpoint guarded by a single armed man, were checked briefly and waved through. The road went through an immense, open, rolling park. Its familiarity troubled him. Lacework of trees against the sky, the swing of the road among groves and glades. He knew the river was over that long hill.

"This is Yaramera," he said aloud.

None of the men spoke.

Years ago, decades ago, when he'd been on Werel only a year or so, they'd invited a party from the embassy down to Yaramera, the greatest estate in Voe Deo. The Jewel of the East. The model of efficient slavery. Thousands of assets working the fields, mills, factories of the estate, living in enormous compounds, walled towns. Everything clean, orderly, industrious, peaceful. And the house on the hill above the river, a palace, three hundred rooms, priceless furnishings, paintings, sculptures, musical instruments— he remembered a private concert hall with walls of gold-backed glass mosaic, a Tualite shrine-room that was one huge flower carved of scented wood.

They were driving up to that house now. The car turned. He caught only a glimpse, jagged black spars against the sky.

The two young men were allowed to handle him again, haul him out of the car, twist his arm, push and shove him up the steps. Trying not to resist, not to feel what they were doing to him, he kept looking about him. The center and the south wing of the immense house were roofless, ruinous. Through the black outline of a window shone the blank clear yellow of the sky. Even here in the heartland of the Law, the slaves had risen. Three years ago, now, in that first terrible summer when thousands of houses had burned, compounds, towns, cities. Four million dead. He had not known the Uprising had reached even to Yaramera. No news came up the river. What toll among the Jewel's slaves for that night of burning? Had the owners been slaughtered, or had they survived to deal out punishment? No news came up the river.

All this went through his mind with unnatural rapidity and clarity as they crowded him up the shallow steps towards the north wing of the house, guarding him with drawn guns as if they thought a man of sixty-two with severe leg cramps from sitting motionless for hours was going to break and run for it, here, three hundred kilos inside their own territory. He thought fast and noticed everything.

This part of the house, joined to the central house by a long arcade, had not burned down. The walls still bore up the roof, but he saw as they came into the front hall that they were bare stone, their carved panelling burnt away. Dirty sheetflooring replaced parquet or covered painted tile. There was no furniture at all. In its ruin and dirt the high hall was beautiful, bare, full of clear evening light. Both veots had left his group and were reporting to some men in the doorway of what had been a reception room. He felt the veots as a safeguard and hoped they would come back, but they did not. One of the young men kept his arm twisted up his back. A heavy-set man came towards him, staring at him.

"You're the alien called Old Music?"

"I am Hainish, and use that name here."

"Mr. Old Music, you're to understand that by leaving your embassy in violation of the protection agreement between your Ambassador and the Government of Voe Deo, you've forfeited diplomatic immunity. You may be held in custody, interrogated, and duly punished for any infractions of civil law or crimes of collusion with insurgents and enemies of the State you're found to have committed."

"I understand that this is your statement of my position," Esdan said. "But you should know, sir, that the Ambassador and the Stabiles of the Ekumen of the Worlds consider me protected both by diplomatic immunity and the laws of the Ekumen."

No harm trying, but his wordy lies weren't listened to. Having recited his litany the man turned away, and the young men grabbed Esdan again. He was hustled through doorways and corridors that he was now in too much pain to see, down stone stairs, across a wide, cobbled courtyard, and into a room where with a final agonising jerk on his arm and his feet knocked from under him so that he fell sprawling, they slammed the door and left him belly-down on stone in darkness.

He dropped his forehead onto his arm and lay shivering, hearing his breath catch in a whimper again and again.

Later on he remembered that night, and other things from the next days and nights. He did not know, then or later, if he was tortured in order to break him down or was merely the handy object of aimless brutality and spite, a sort of plaything for the boys. There were kicks, beatings, a great deal of pain, but none of it was clear in his memory later except the crouchcage.

He had heard of such things, read about them. He had never seen one. He had never been inside a compound. Foreigners, visitors, were not taken into slave quarters on the estates of Voe Deo. They were served by house-slaves in the houses of the owners.

This was a small compound, not more than twenty huts on the women's side, three longhouses on the gateside. It had housed the staff of a couple of hundred slaves who looked after the house and the immense gardens of Yaramera. They would have been a privileged set compared to the fieldhands. But not exempt from punishment. The whipping post still stood near the high gate that sagged open in the high walls.

"There?" said Nemeo, the one who always twisted his arm, but the other one, Alatual, said, "No, come on, it's over here," and ran ahead, excited, to winch the crouchcage down from where it hung below the main sentry station, high up on the inside of the wall.

It was a tube of coarse, rusty steel mesh sealed at one end and closable at the other. It hung suspended by a single hook from a chain. Lying on the ground it looked like a trap for an animal, not a very big animal. The two young men stripped off his clothes and goaded him to crawl into it headfirst, using the fieldhandlers, electric prods to stir up lazy slaves, which they had been playing with the last couple of days. They screamed with laughter, pushing him and jabbing the prods in his anus and scrotum. He writhed into the cage until he was crouching in it head-down, his arms and legs bent and jammed up into his body. They slammed the trap end shut, catching his naked foot between the wires and causing a pain that blinded him while they hoisted the cage back up. It swung about wildly and he clung to the wires with his cramped hands. When he opened his eyes he saw the ground swinging about seven or eight meters below him. After a while the lurching and circling stopped. He could not move his head at all. He could see what was below the crouchcage, and by straining his eyes round he could see most of the inside of the compound.

In the old days there had been people down there to see the moral spectacle, a slave in the crouchcage. There had been children to learn the lesson of what happens to a housemaid who shirked a job, a gardener who spoiled a cutting, a hand who talked back to a boss. Nobody was there now. The dusty ground was bare. The dried-up garden plots, the little grave-yard at the far edge of the women's side, the ditch between the two sides, the pathways, a vague circle of greener grass right underneath him, all were deserted. His torturers stood around for a while laughing and talking, got bored, went off.

He tried to ease his position but could move only very slightly. Any motion made the cage rock and swing so that he grew sick and increasingly fearful of falling. He did not know how securely the cage was balanced on that single hook. His foot, caught in the cage-closure, hurt so sharply that he longed to faint, but though his head swam he kept conscious. He tried to breathe as he had learned how to breathe a long time ago on another world, quietly, easily. He could not do it here now in this world in this cage. His lungs were squeezed in his rib-cage so that each breath was extremely difficult. He tried not to suffocate. He tried not to panic. He tried to be aware, only to be aware, but awareness was unendurable.

When the sun came around to that side of the compound and shone full on him, the dizziness turned to sickness. Some-times then he fainted for a while.

There was night and cold and he tried to imagine water, but there was no water.

He thought later he had been in the crouchcage two days. He could remember the scraping of the wires on his sunburned naked flesh when they pulled him out, the shock of cold water played over him from a hose. He had been fully aware for a moment then, aware of himself, like a doll, lying small, limp, on dirt, while men above him talked and shouted about some-thing. Then he must have been carried back to the cell or stable where he was kept, for there was dark and silence, but also he was still hanging in the crouchcage roasting in the icy fire of the sun, freezing in his burning body, fitted tighter and tighter into the exact mesh of the wires of pain.

At some point he was taken to a bed in a room with a window, but he was still in the crouchcage, swinging high above the dusty ground, the dusties' ground, the circle of green grass.

The zadyo and the heavy-set man were there, were not there. A bondswoman, whey-faced, crouching and trembling, hurt him trying to put salve on his burned arm and leg and back. She was there and not there. The sun shone in the window. He felt the wire snap down on his foot again, and again.

Darkness eased him. He slept most of the time. After a couple of days he could sit up and eat what the scared bondswoman brought him. His sunburn was healing and most of his aches and pains were milder. His foot was swollen hugely; bones were broken; that didn't matter till he had to get up. He dozed, drifted. When Rayaye walked into the room, he recognised him at once.

They had met several times, before the Uprising. Rayaye had been Minister of Foreign Affairs under President Oyo. What position he had now, in the Legitimate Government, Esdan did not know. Rayaye was short for a Werelian but broad and solid, with a blue-black polished-looking face and greying hair, a striking man, a politician.

"Minister Rayaye," Esdan said.

"Mr. Old Music. How kind of you to recall me! I'm sorry you've been unwell. I hope the people here are looking after you satisfactorily?"

"Thank you."

"When I heard you were unwell I inquired for a doctor, but there's no one here but a veterinarian. No staff at all. Not like the old days! What a change! I wish you'd seen Yaramera in its glory."

"I did." His voice was rather weak, but sounded quite natural. "Thirty-two or -three years ago. Lord and Lady Aneo entertained a party from our embassy."

"Really? Then you know what it was," said Rayaye, sitting down in the one chair, a fine old piece missing one arm. "Painful to see it like this, isn't it! The worst of the destruction was here in the house. The whole women's wing and the great rooms burned. But the gardens were spared, may the Lady be praised. Laid out by Meneya himself, you know, four hundred years ago. And the fields are still being worked. I'm told there are still nearly three thousand assets attached to the property. When the trouble's over, it'll be far easier to restore Yaramera than many of the great estates." He gazed out the window. "Beautiful, beautiful. The Aneos' housepeople were famous for their beauty, you know. And training. It'll take a long time to build up to that kind of standard again."

"No doubt."

The Werelian looked at him with bland attentiveness. "I expect you're wondering why you're here."

"Not particularly," Esdan said pleasantly.

"Oh?"

"Since I left the embassy without permission, I suppose the Government wanted to keep an eye on me."

"Some of us were glad to hear you'd left the embassy. Shut up there—a waste of your talents."

"Oh, my talents," Esdan said with a deprecatory shrug, which hurt his shoulder. He would wince later. Just now he was enjoying himself. He liked fencing.

"You're a very talented man, Mr. Old Music. The wisest, canniest alien on Werel, Lord Mehao called you once. You've worked with us—and against us, yes—more effectively than any other offworlder. We understand one another. We can talk. It's my belief that you genuinely wish my people well, and that if I offered you a way of serving them—a hope of bringing this terrible conflict to an end—you'd take it."

"I would hope to be able to."

"Is it important to you that you be identified as a supporter of one side of the conflict, or would you prefer to remain neutral?"

"Any action can bring neutrality into question."

"To have been kidnapped from the embassy by the rebels is no evidence of your sympathy for them."

"It would seem not."

"Rather the opposite."

"It could be so perceived."

"It can be. If you like."

"My preferences are of no weight, Minister."

"They're of very great weight, Mr. Old Music. But here. You've been ill, I'm tiring you. We'll continue our conversation tomorrow, eh? If you like."

"Of course, Minister," Esdan said, with a politeness edging on submissiveness, a tone that he knew suited men like this one, more accustomed to the attention of slaves than the company of equals. Never having equated incivility with pride, Esdan, like most of his people, was disposed to be polite in any circumstance that allowed it, and disliked circumstances that did not. Mere hypocrisy did not trouble him. He was perfectly capable of it himself. If Rayaye's men had tortured him and Rayaye pretended ignorance of the fact, Esdan had nothing to gain by insisting on it.

He was glad, indeed, not to be obliged to talk about it, and hoped not to think about it. His body thought about it for him, remembered it precisely, in every joint and muscle, now. The rest of his thinking about it he would do as long as he lived. He had learned things he had not known. He had thought he understood what it was to be helpless. Now he knew he had not understood.

When the scared woman came in, he asked her to send for the veterinarian. "I need a cast on my foot," he said.

"He does mend the hands, the bondsfolk, master," the woman whispered, shrinking. The assets here spoke an archaic-sounding dialect that was sometimes hard to follow.

"Can he come into the house?"

She shook her head.

"Is there anybody here who can look after it?"

"I will ask, master," she whispered.

An old bondswoman came in that night. She had a wrinkled, seared, stern face, and none of the crouching manner of the other. When she first saw him she whispered, "Mighty Lord!" But she performed the reverence stiffly, and then examined his swollen foot, impersonal as any doctor. She said, "If you do let me bind that, master, it will heal."

"What's broken?"

"These toes. There. Maybe a little bone in here too. Lotsalot bones in feet."

"Please bind it for me."

She did so, firmly, binding cloths round and round until the wrapping was quite thick and kept his foot immobile at one angle. She said, "You do walk, then you use a stick, sir. You put down only that heel to the ground."

He asked her name.

"Gana," she said. Saying her name she shot a sharp glance right at him, full-face, a daring thing for a slave to do. She probably wanted to get a good look at his alien eyes, having found the rest of him, though a strange color, pretty commonplace, bones in the feet and all.

"Thank you, Gana. I'm grateful for your skill and kindness."

She bobbed, but did not reverence, and left the room. She herself walked lame, but upright. "All the grandmothers are rebels," somebody had told him long ago, before the Uprising.

The next day he was able to get up and hobble to the broken-armed chair. He sat for a while looking out the window.

The room looked out from the second floor over the gardens of Yaramera, terraced slopes and flowerbeds, walks, lawns, and a series of ornamental lakes and pools that descended gradually to the river: a vast pattern of curves and planes, plants and paths, earth and still water, embraced by the broad living curve of the river. All the plots and walks and terraces formed a soft geometry centered very subtly on an enormous tree down at the riverside. It must have been a great tree when the garden was laid out four hundred years ago. It stood above and well back from the bank, but its branches reached far out over the water and a village could have been built in its shade. The grass of the terraces had dried to soft gold. The river and the lakes and pools were all the misty blue of the summer sky. The flowerbeds and shrubberies were untended, overgrown, but not yet gone wild. The gardens of Yaramera were utterly beautiful in their desolation. Desolate, forlorn, forsaken, all such romantic words befitted them, yet they were also rational and noble, full of peace. They had been built by the labor of slaves. Their dignity and peace were founded on cruelty, misery, pain. Esdan was Hainish, from a very old people, people who had built and destroyed Yaramera a thousand times. His mind contained the beauty and the terrible grief of the place, assured that the existence of one cannot justify the other, the destruction of one cannot destroy the other. He was aware of both, only aware.

And aware also, sitting in some comfort of body at last, that the lovely sorrowful terraces of Yaramera may contain within them the terraces of Darranda on Hain, roof below red roof, garden below green garden, dropping steep down to the shining harbor, the promenades and piers and sailboats. Out past the harbor the sea rises up, stands up as high as his house, as high as his eyes. Esi knows that books say the sea lies down. "The sea lies calm tonight," says the poem, but he knows better. The sea stands, a wall, the blue-grey wall at the end of the world. If you sail out on it it will seem flat, but if you see it truly it's as tall as the hills of Darranda, and if you sail truly on it you will sail through that wall to the other side, beyond the end of the world.

The sky is the roof that wall holds up. At night the stars shine through the glass air roof. You can sail to them, too, to the worlds beyond the world.

"Esi," somebody calls from indoors, and he turns away from the sea and the sky, leaves the balcony, goes in to meet the guests, or for his music lesson, or to have lunch with the family. He's a nice little boy, Esi: obedient, cheerful, not talkative but quite sociable, interested in people. With very good manners, of course; after all he's a Kelwen and the older generation wouldn't stand for anything less in a child of the family, but good manners come easy to him, perhaps because he's never seen any bad ones. Not a dreamy child. Alert, present, noticing. But thoughtful, and given to explaining things to himself, such as the wall of the sea and the roof of the air. Esi isn't as clear and close to Esdan as he used to be; he's a little boy a long time ago and very far away, left behind, left at home. Only rarely now does Esdan see through his eyes, or breathe the marvelous intricate smell of the house in Darranda—wood, the resinous oil used to polish the wood, sweetgrass matting, fresh flowers, kitchen herbs, the sea wind—or hear his mother's voice: "Esi? Come on in now, love. The cousins are here from Dorased!"

Esi runs in to meet the cousins, old Iliawad with crazy eyebrows and hair in his nostrils, who can do magic with bits of sticky tape, and Tuitui who's better at catch than Esi even though she's younger, while Esdan falls asleep in the broken chair by the window looking out on the terrible, beautiful gardens.

Further conversations with Rayaye were deferred. The zadyo came with his apologies. The Minister had been called back to speak with the President, would return within three or four days. Esdan realised he had heard a flyer take off early in the morning, not far away. It was a reprieve. He enjoyed fencing, but was still very tired, very shaken, and welcomed the rest. No one came into his room but the scared woman, Heo, and the zadyo who came once a day to ask if he had all he needed.

When he could he was permitted to leave his room, go outside if he wished. By using a stick and strapping his bound foot onto a stiff old sandal-sole Gana brought him, he could walk, and so get out into the gardens and sit in the sun, which was growing milder daily as the summer grew old. The two veots were his guards, or more exactly guardians. He saw the two young men who had tortured him; they kept at a distance, evidently under orders not to approach him. One of the veots was usually in view, but never crowded him.

He could not go far. Sometimes he felt like a bug on a beach. The part of the house that was still usable was huge, the gardens were vast, the people were very few. There were the six men who had brought him, and five or six more who had been here, commanded by the heavy-set man Tualenem. Of the original asset population of the house and estate there were ten or twelve, a tiny remnant of the house-staff of cooks, cooks' helpers, washwomen, chambermaids, ladies' maids, bodyservants, shoe-polishers, window-cleaners, gardeners, path-rakers, waiters, footmen, errandboys, stablemen, drivers, usewomen and useboys who had served the owners and their guests in the old days. These few were no longer locked up at night in the old house-asset compound where the crouchcage was, but slept in the courtyard warren of stables for horses and people where he had been kept at first, or in the complex of rooms around the kitchens. Most of these remaining few were women, two of them young, and two or three old, frail-looking men.

He was cautious of speaking to any of them at first lest he get them into trouble, but his captors ignored them except to give orders, evidently considering them trustworthy, with good reason. Troublemakers, the assets who had broken out of the compounds, burned the great house, killed the bosses and owners, were long gone: dead, escaped, or re-enslaved with a cross branded deep on both cheeks. These were good dusties. Very likely they had been loyal all along. Many bonds-

people, especially personal slaves, as terrified by the Uprising as
their owners, had tried to defend them or had fled with them.
They were no more traitors than were owners who had freed
their assets and fought on the Liberation side. As much, and
no more.

Girls, young fieldhands, were brought in one at a time as
usewomen for the men. Every day or two the two young men
who had tortured him drove a landcar off in the morning with
a used girl and came back with a new one.

Of the two younger house bondswomen, the one called
Kamsa always carried her little baby around with her, and the
men ignored her. The other, Heo, was the scared one who had
waited on him. Tualenem used her every night. The other men
kept hands off.

When they or any of the bondspeople passed Esdan in the
house or outdoors they dropped their hands to their sides,
chin to the chest, looked down, and stood still: the formal
reverence expected of personal assets facing an owner.

"Good morning, Kamsa."

Her reply was the reverence.

It had been years now since he had been with the finished
product of generations of slavery, the kind of slave described as
"perfectly trained, obedient, selfless, loyal, the ideal personal
asset," when they were put up for sale. Most of the assets he had
known, his friends and colleagues, had been city rentspeople,
hired out by their owners to companies and corporations to
work in factories or shops or at skilled trades. He had also known
a good many fieldhands. Fieldhands seldom had any contact
with their owners; they worked under gareot bosses and their
compounds were run by cutfrees, eunuch assets. The ones he
knew had mostly been runaways protected by the Hame, the
underground railroad, on their way to independence in Yeowe.
None of them had been as utterly deprived of education, options, any imagination of freedom, as these bondspeople were.
He had forgotten what a good dusty was like. He had forgotten
the utter impenetrability of the person who has no private life,
the intactness of the wholly vulnerable.

Kamsa's face was smooth, serene, and showed no feeling,
though he heard her sometimes talking and singing very softly
to her baby, a joyful, merry little noise. It drew him. He saw

her one afternoon sitting at work on the coping of the great terrace, the baby in its sling on her back. He limped over and sat down nearby. He could not prevent her from setting her knife and board aside and standing head and hands and eyes down in reverence as he came near.

"Please sit down, please go on with your work," he said. She obeyed. "What's that you're cutting up?"

"Dueli, master," she whispered.

It was a vegetable he had often eaten and enjoyed. He watched her work. Each big, woody pod had to be split along a sealed seam, not an easy trick; it took a careful search for the opening-point and hard, repeated twists of the blade to open the pod. Then the fat edible seeds had to be removed one by one and scraped free of a stringy, clinging matrix.

"Does that part taste bad?" he asked.

"Yes, master."

It was a laborious process, requiring strength, skill, and patience. He was ashamed. "I never saw raw dueli before," he said.

"No, master."

"What a good baby," he said, a little at random. The tiny creature in its sling, its head lying on her shoulder, had opened large bluish-black eyes and was gazing vaguely at the world. He had never heard it cry. It seemed rather unearthly to him, but he had not had much to do with babies.

She smiled.

"A boy?"

"Yes, master."

He said, "Please, Kamsa, my name is Esdan. I'm not a master. I'm a prisoner. Your masters are my masters. Will you call me by my name?"

She did not answer.

"Our masters would disapprove."

She nodded. The Werelian nod was a tip back of the head, not a bob down. He was completely used to it after all these years. It was the way he nodded himself. He noticed himself noticing it now. His captivity, his treatment here, had displaced, disoriented him. These last few days he had thought more about Hain than he had for years, decades. He had been at home on Werel, and now was not. Inappropriate comparisons, irrelevant memories. Alienated.

"They put me in the cage," he said, speaking as low as she did and hesitating on the last word. He could not say the whole word, crouchcage.

Again the nod. This time, for the first time, she looked up at him, the flick of a glance. She said soundlessly, "I know," and went on with her work.

He found nothing more to say.

"I was a pup, then I did live there," she said, with a glance in the direction of the compound where the cage was. Her murmuring voice was profoundly controlled, as were all her gestures and movements. "Before that time the house burned. When the masters did live here. They did often hang up the cage. Once, a man for until he did die there. In that. I saw that."

Silence between them.

"We pups never did go under that. Never did run there."

"I saw the . . . the ground was different, underneath," Esdan said, speaking as softly and with a dry mouth, his breath coming short. "I saw, looking down. The grass. I thought maybe . . . where they . . ." His voice dried up entirely.

"One grandmother did take a stick, long, a cloth on the end of that, and wet it, and hold it up to him. The cutfrees did look away. But he did die. And rot some time."

"What had he done?"

"*Enna*," she said, the one-word denial he'd often heard assets use—I don't know, I didn't do it, I wasn't there, it's not my fault, who knows. . . .

He'd seen an owner's child who said "enna" be slapped, not for the cup she broke but for using a slave word.

"A useful lesson," he said. He knew she'd understand him. Underdogs know irony like they know air and water.

"They did put you in that, then I did fear," she said.

"The lesson was for me, not you, this time," he said.

She worked, carefully, ceaselessly. He watched her work. Her downcast face, clay-color with bluish shadows, was composed, peaceful. The baby was darker-skinned than she. She had not been bred to a bondsman, but used by an owner. They called rape "use." The baby's eyes closed slowly, translucent bluish lids like little shells. It was small and delicate, probably only a month or two old. Its head lay with infinite patience on her stooping shoulder.

No one else was out on the terraces. A slight wind stirred in the flowering trees behind them, streaked the distant river with silver.

"Your baby, Kamsa, you know, he will be free," Esdan said.

She looked up, not at him, but at the river and across it. She said, "Yes. He will be free." She went on working.

It heartened him, her saying that to him. It did him good to know she trusted him. He needed someone to trust him, for since the cage he could not trust himself. With Rayaye he was all right; he could still fence; that wasn't the trouble. It was when he was alone, thinking, sleeping. He was alone most of the time. Something in his mind, deep in him, was injured, broken, had not mended, could not be trusted to bear his weight.

He heard the flyer come down in the morning. That night Rayaye invited him down to dinner. Tualenem and the two veots ate with them and excused themselves, leaving him and Rayaye with a half-bottle of wine at the makeshift table set up in one of the least damaged downstairs rooms. It had been a hunting-lodge or trophy-room, here in this wing of the house that had been the azade, the men's side, where no women would ever have come; female assets, servants and usewomen, did not count as women. The head of a huge packdog snarled above the mantel, its fur singed and dusty and its glass eyes gone dull. Crossbows had been mounted on the facing wall. Their pale shadows were clear on the dark wood. The electric chandelier flickered and dimmed. The generator was uncertain. One of the old bondsmen was always tinkering at it.

"Going off to his usewoman," Rayaye said, nodding towards the door Tualenem had just closed with assiduous wishes for the Minister to have a good night. "Fucking a white. Like fucking turds. Makes my skin crawl. Sticking his cock into a slave cunt. When the war's over there'll be no more of that kind of thing. Halfbreeds are the root of this revolution. Keep the races separate. Keep the ruler blood clean. It's the only answer." He spoke as if expecting complete accord, but did not wait to receive any sign of it. He poured Esdan's glass full and went in his resonant politician's voice, kind host, lord of the manor, "Well, Mr. Old Music, I hope you've been having a pleasant stay at Yaramera, and that your health's improved."

A civil murmur.

"President Oyo was sorry to hear you'd been unwell and sends his wishes for your full recovery. He's glad to know you're safe from any further mistreatment by the insurgents. You can stay here in safety as long as you like. However, when the time is right, the President and his cabinet are looking forward to having you in Bellen."

Civil murmur.

Long habit prevented Esdan from asking questions that would reveal the extent of his ignorance. Rayaye like most politicians loved his own voice, and as he talked Esdan tried to piece together a rough sketch of the current situation. It appeared that the Legitimate Government had moved from the city to a town, Bellen, northeast of Yaramera, near the eastern coast. Some kind of command had been left in the city. Rayaye's references to it made Esdan wonder if the city was in fact semi-independent of the Oyo government, governed by a faction, perhaps a military faction.

When the Uprising began, Oyo had at once been given extraordinary powers; but the Legitimate Army of Voe Deo, after their stunning defeats in the west, had been restive under his command, wanting more autonomy in the field. The civilian government had demanded retaliation, attack, and victory. The army wanted to contain the insurrection. Rega-General Aydan had established the Divide in the city and tried to establish and hold a border between the new Free State and the Legitimate Provinces. Veots who had gone over to the Uprising with their asset troops had similarly urged a border truce to the Liberation Command. The army sought armistice, the warriors sought peace. But "So long as there is one slave I am not free," cried Nekam-Anna, Leader of the Free State, and President Oyo thundered, "The nation will not be divided! We will defend legitimate property with the last drop of blood in our veins!" The Rega-General had suddenly been replaced by a new Commander-in-Chief. Very soon after that the embassy was sealed, its access to information cut.

Esdan could only guess what had happened in the half year since. Rayaye talked of "our victories in the south" as if the Legitimate Army had been on the attack, pushing back into the Free State across the Devan River, south of the city. If so, if they had regained territory, why had the government pulled out of the city and dug in down at Bellen? Rayaye's talk of victories might be translated to mean that the Army of the Liberation had been trying to cross the river in the south and the Legitimates had been successful in holding them off. If they were willing to call that a victory, had they finally given up the dream of reversing the revolution, retaking the whole country, and decided to cut their losses?

"A divided nation is not an option," Rayaye said, squashing that hope. "You understand that, I think."

Civil assent.

Rayaye poured out the last of the wine. "But peace is our goal. Our very strong and urgent goal. Our unhappy country has suffered enough."

Definite assent.

"I know you to be a man of peace, Mr. Old Music. We know the Ekumen fosters harmony among and within its member states. Peace is what we all desire with all our hearts."

Assent, plus faint indication of inquiry.

"As you know, the Government of Voe Deo has always had the power to end the insurrection. The means to end it quickly and completely."

No response but alert attention.

"And I think you know that it is only our respect for the policies of the Ekumen, of which my nation is a member, that has prevented us from using that means."

Absolutely no response or acknowledgment.

"You do know that, Mr. Old Music."

"I assumed you had a natural wish to survive."

Rayaye shook his head as if bothered by an insect. "Since we joined the Ekumen—and long before we joined it, Mr. Old Music—we have loyally followed its policies and bowed to its theories. And so we lost Yeowe! And so we lost the West! Four million dead, Mr. Old Music. Four million in the first Uprising. Millions since. Millions. If we had contained it then, many, many fewer would have died. Assets as well as owners."

"Suicide," Esdan said in a soft mild voice, the way assets spoke.

"The pacifist sees all weapons as evil, disastrous, suicidal. For all the age-old wisdom of your people, Mr. Old Music, you have not the experiential perspective on matters of war we younger, cruder peoples are forced to have. Believe me, we are not suicidal. We want our people, our nation, to survive. We are determined that it shall. The bibo was fully tested, long before we joined the Ekumen. It is controllable, targetable, containable. It is an exact weapon, a precise tool of war. Rumor and fear have wildly exaggerated its capacities and nature. We know how to use it, how to limit its effects. Nothing but the response of the Stabiles through your Ambassador prevented us from selective deployment in the first summer of the insurrection."

"I had the impression the high command of the Army of Voe Deo was also opposed to deploying that weapon."

"Some generals were. Many veots are rigid in their thinking, as you know."

"That decision has been changed?"

"President Oyo has authorised deployment of the bibo against forces massing to invade this province from the west."

Such a cute word, bibo. Esdan closed his eyes for a moment.

"The destruction will be appalling," Rayaye said.

Assent.

"It is possible," Rayaye said, leaning forward, black eyes in black face, intense as a hunting cat, "that if the insurgents were warned, they might withdraw. Be willing to discuss terms. If they withdraw, we will not attack. If they will talk, we will talk. A holocaust can be prevented. They respect the Ekumen. They respect you personally, Mr. Old Music. They trust you. If you were to speak to them on the net, or if their leaders will agree to a meeting, they will listen to you, not as their enemy, their oppressor, but as the voice of a benevolent, peace-loving neutrality, the voice of wisdom, urging them to save themselves while there is yet time. This is the opportunity I offer you, and the Ekumen. To spare your friends among the rebels, to spare this world untold suffering. To open the way to lasting peace."

"I am not authorised to speak for the Ekumen. The Ambassador—"

"Will not. Cannot. Is not free to. You are. You are a free agent, Mr. Old Music. Your position on Werel is unique. Both sides respect you. Trust you. And your voice carries infinitely more weight among the whites than his. He came only a year before the insurrection. You are, I may say, one of us."

"I am not one of you. I neither own nor am owned. You must redefine yourselves to include me."

Rayaye, for a moment, had nothing to say. He was taken aback, and would be angry. Fool, Esdan said to himself, old fool, to take the moral high ground! But he did not know what ground to stand on.

It was true that his word would carry more weight than the Ambassador's. Nothing else Rayaye had said made sense. If President Oyo wanted the Ekumen's blessing on his use of this weapon and seriously thought Esdan would give it, why was he working through Rayaye, and keeping Esdan hidden at Yaramera? Was Rayaye working with Oyo, or was he working for a faction that favored using the bibo, while Oyo still refused?

Most likely the whole thing was a bluff. There was no weapon. Esdan's pleading was to lend credibility to it, while leaving Oyo out of the loop if the bluff failed.

The biobomb, the bibo, had been a curse on Voe Deo for decades, centuries. In panic fear of alien invasion after the Ekumen first contacted them almost four hundred years ago, the Werelians had put all their resources into developing space flight and weaponry. The scientists who invented this particular device repudiated it, informing their government that it could not be contained; it would destroy all human and animal life over an enormous area and cause profound and permanent genetic damage worldwide as it spread throughout the water and the atmosphere. The government never used the weapon but was never willing to destroy it, and its existence had kept Werel from membership in the Ekumen as long as the Embargo was in force. Voe Deo insisted it was their guarantee against extraterrestrial invasion and perhaps believed it would prevent revolution. Yet they had not used it when their slave-planet Yeowe rebelled. Then, after the Ekumen no longer observed the Embargo, they announced that they had destroyed the stockpiles. Werel joined the Ekumen. Voe Deo invited inspection of the weapon sites. The Ambassador politely declined, citing the Ekumenical policy of trust. Now the bibo existed again. In fact? In Rayaye's mind? Was he desperate? A hoax, an attempt to use the Ekumen to back a bogey threat to scare off an invasion: the likeliest scenario, yet it was not quite convincing.

"This war must end," Rayaye said.

"I agree."

"We will never surrender. You must understand that." Rayaye had dropped his blandishing, reasonable tone. "We will restore the holy order of the world," he said, and now he was fully credible. His eyes, the dark Werelian eyes that had no whites, were fathomless in the dim light. He drank down his wine. "You think we fight for our property. To keep what we own. But I tell you, we fight to defend our Lady. In that fight is no surrender. And no compromise."

"Your Lady is merciful."

"The Law is her mercy."

Esdan was silent.

"I must go again tomorrow to Bellen," Rayaye said after a while, resuming his masterful, easy tone. "Our plans for moving on the southern front must be fully coordinated. When I come back, I'll need to know if you will give us the help I've asked you for. Our response will depend largely on that. On your voice. It is known that you're here in the East Provinces—known to the insurgents, I mean, as well as our people—though your exact location is of course kept hidden for your own safety. It is known that you may be preparing a statement of a change in the Ekumen's attitude toward the conduct of the civil war. A change that could save millions of lives and bring a just peace to our land. I hope you'll employ your time here in doing so."

He is a factionalist, Esdan thought. He's not going to Bellen, or if he is, that's not where Oyo's government is. This is some scheme of his own. Crackbrained. It won't work. He doesn't have the bibo. But he has a gun. And he'll shoot me.

"Thank you for a pleasant dinner, Minister," he said.

Next morning he heard the flyer leave at dawn. He limped out into the morning sunshine after breakfast. One of his veot guards watched him from a window and then turned away. In a sheltered nook just under the balustrade of the south terrace, near a planting of great bushes with big, blowsy, sweet-smelling white flowers, he saw Kamsa with her baby and Heo. He made his way to them, dot-and-go-one. The distances at Yaramera, even inside the house, were daunting to a lamed man. When he finally got there he said, "I am lonely. May I sit with you?"

The women were afoot, of course, reverencing, though Kamsa's reverence had become pretty sketchy. He sat on a curved bench splotched all over with fallen flowers. They sat back down on the flagstone path with the baby. They had unwrapped the little body to the mild sunshine. It was a very thin baby, Esdan thought. The joints in the bluish-dark arms and legs were like the joints in flowerstems, translucent knobs. The baby was moving more than he had ever seen it move, stretching its arms and turning its head as if enjoying the feel of the air. The head was large for the neck, again like a flower, too large a flower on too thin a stalk. Kamsa dangled one of the real flowers over the baby. His dark eyes gazed up at it. His eyelids and eyebrows were exquisitely delicate. The sunlight shone through his fingers. He smiled. Esdan caught his breath. The baby's smile at the flower was the beauty of the flower, the beauty of the world.

"What is his name?"

"Rekam."

Grandson of Kamye. Kamye the Lord and slave, huntsman and husbandman, warrior and peacemaker.

"A beautiful name. How old is he?"

In the language they spoke that was, "How long has he lived?" Kamsa's answer was strange. "As long as his life," she said, or so he understood her whisper and her dialect. Maybe it was bad manners or bad luck to ask a child's age.

He sat back on the bench. "I feel very old," he said. "I haven't seen a baby for a hundred years."

Heo sat hunched over, her back to him; he felt that she wanted to cover her ears. She was terrified of him, the alien. Life had not left much to Heo but fear, he guessed. Was she twenty, twenty-five? She looked forty. Maybe she was seventeen. Usewomen, ill-used, aged fast. Kamsa he guessed to be not much over twenty. She was thin and plain, but there was bloom and juice in her as there was not in Heo.

"Master did have children?" Kamsa asked, lifting up her baby to her breast with a certain discreet pride, shyly flaunting.

"No."

"*A yera yera*," she murmured, another slave word he had often heard in the urban compounds: O pity, pity.

"How you get to the center of things, Kamsa," he said. She

glanced his way and smiled. Her teeth were bad but it was a good smile. He thought the baby was not sucking. It lay peacefully in the crook of her arm. Heo remained tense and jumped whenever he spoke, so he said no more. He looked away from them, past the bushes, out over the wonderful view that arranged itself, wherever you walked or sat, into a perfect balance: the levels of flagstone, of dun grass and blue water, the curves of the avenues, the masses and lines of shrubbery, the great old tree, the misty river and its green far bank. Presently the women began talking softly again. He did not listen to what they said. He was aware of their voices, aware of sunlight, aware of peace.

Old Gana came stumping across the upper terrace towards them, bobbed to him, said to Kamsa and Heo, "Choyo does want you. Leave me that baby." Kamsa set the baby down on the warm stone again. She and Heo sprang up and went off, thin, light women moving with easy haste. The old woman settled down piece by piece and with groans and grimaces onto the path beside Rekam. She immediately covered him up with a fold of his swaddling-cloth, frowning and muttering at the foolishness of his mother. Esdan watched her careful movements, her gentleness when she picked the child up, supporting that heavy head and tiny limbs, her tenderness cradling him, rocking her body to rock him.

She looked up at Esdan. She smiled, her face wrinkling up into a thousand wrinkles. "He is my great gift," she said.

He whispered, "Your grandson?"

The backward nod. She kept rocking gently. The baby's eyes were closed, his head lay softly on her thin, dry breast. "I think now he'll die not long now."

After a while Esdan said, "Die?"

The nod. She still smiled. Gently, gently rocking. "He is two years of age, master."

"I thought he was born this summer," Esdan said in a whisper.

The old woman said, "He did come to stay a little while with us."

"What is wrong?"

"The wasting."

Esdan had heard the term. He said, "Avo?" the name he

knew for it, a systemic viral infection common among Werelian children, frequently epidemic in the asset compounds of the cities.

She nodded.

"But it's curable!"

The old woman said nothing.

Avo was completely curable. Where there were doctors. Where there was medicine. Avo was curable in the city not the country. In the great house not the asset quarters. In peacetime not in wartime. Fool!

Maybe she knew it was curable, maybe she did not, maybe she did not know what the word meant. She rocked the baby, crooning in a whisper, paying no attention to the fool. But she had heard him, and answered him at last, not looking at him, watching the baby's sleeping face.

"I was born owned," she said, "and my daughters. But he was not. He is the gift. To us. Nobody can own him. The gift of the Lord Kamye of himself. Who could keep that gift?"

Esdan bowed his head down.

He had said to the mother, "He will be free." And she had said, "Yes."

He said at last, "May I hold him?"

The grandmother stopped rocking and held still a while. "Yes," she said. She raised herself up and very carefully transferred the sleeping baby into Esdan's arms, onto his lap.

"You do hold my joy," she said.

The child weighed nothing—six or seven pounds. It was like holding a warm flower, a tiny animal, a bird. The swaddling-cloth trailed down across the stones. Gana gathered it up and laid it softly around the baby, hiding his face. Tense and nervous, jealous, full of pride, she knelt there. Before long she took the baby back against her heart. "There," she said, and her face softened into happiness.

That night Esdan sleeping in the room that looked out over the terraces of Yaramera dreamed that he had lost a little round, flat stone that he always carried with him in a pouch. The stone was from the pueblo. When he held it in his palm and warmed it, it was able to speak, to talk with him. But he had not talked with it for a long time. Now he realised he did not have it. He had lost it, left it somewhere. He thought it was in the basement of the embassy. He tried to get into the basement, but the door was locked, and he could not find the other door.

He woke. Early morning. No need to get up. He should think about what to do, what to say, when Rayaye came back. He could not. He thought about the dream, the stone that talked. He wished he had heard what it said. He thought about the pueblo. His father's brother's family had lived in Arkanan Pueblo in the Far South Highlands. In his boyhood, every year in the heart of the northern winter, Esi had flown down there for forty days of summer. With his parents at first, later on alone. His uncle and aunt had grown up in Darranda and were not pueblo people. Their children were. They had grown up in Arkanan and belonged to it entirely. The eldest, Suhan, fourteen years older than Esdan, had been born with irreparable brain and neural defects, and it was for his sake that his parents had settled in a pueblo. There was a place for him there. He became a herdsman. He went up on the mountains with the yama, animals the South Hainish had brought over from O a millennium or so ago. He looked after the animals. He came back to live in the pueblo only in winter. Esi saw him seldom, and was glad of it, finding Suhan a fearful figure—big, shambling, foul-smelling, with a loud braying voice, mouthing incomprehensible words. Esi could not understand why Suhan's parents and sisters loved him. He thought they pretended to. No one could love him.

To adolescent Esdan it was still a problem. His cousin Noy, Suhan's sister, who had become the Water Chief of Arkanan, told him it was not a problem but a mystery. "You see how Suhan is our guide?" she said. "Look at it. He led my parents here to live. So my sister and I were born here. So you come to stay with us here. So you've learned to live in the pueblo. You'll never be just a city man. Because Suhan guided you here. Guided us all. Into the mountains."

"He didn't really guide us," the fourteen-year-old argued.

"Yes, he did. We followed his weakness. His incompleteness. Failure's open. Look at water, Esi. It finds the weak places in the rock, the openings, the hollows, the absences. Following water we come where we belong." Then she had gone off to arbitrate a dispute over the usage-rights to an irrigation system outside town, for the east side of the mountains was very dry country, and the people of Arkanan were contentious, though hospitable, and the Water Chief stayed busy.

But Suhan's condition had been irreparable, his weakness inaccessible even to the wondrous medical skills of Hain. This baby was dying of a disease that could be cured by a mere series of injections. It was wrong to accept his illness, his death. It was wrong to let him be cheated out of his life by circumstance, bad luck, an unjust society, a fatalistic religion. A religion that fostered and encouraged the terrible passivity of the slaves, that told these women to do nothing, to let the child waste away and die.

He should interfere, he should do something, what could be done?

"How long has he lived?"

"As long as his life."

There was nothing they could do. Nowhere to go. No one to turn to. A cure for avo existed, in some places, for some children. Not in this place, not for this child. Neither anger nor hope served any purpose. Nor grief. It was not the time for grief yet. Rekam was here with them, and they would delight in him as long as he was here. As long as his life. *He is my great gift. You do hold my joy.*

This was a strange place to come to learn the quality of joy. Water is my guide, he thought. His hands still felt what it had been like to hold the child, the light weight, the brief warmth.

He was out on the terrace late the next morning, waiting for Kamsa and the baby to come out as they usually did, but the older veot came instead. "Mr. Old Music, I must ask you to stay indoors for a time," he said.

"Zadyo, I'm not going to run away," Esdan said, sticking out his swathed lump of a foot.

"I'm sorry, sir."

He stumped crossly indoors after the veot and was locked into a downstairs room, a windowless storage space behind the kitchens. They had fixed it up with a cot, a table and chair, a pisspot, and a battery lamp for when the generator failed, as it did for a while most days. "Are you expecting an attack, then?" he said when he saw these preparations, but the veot replied only by locking the door. Esdan sat on the cot and meditated, as he had learned to do in Arkanan Pueblo. He cleared distress and anger from his mind by going through the long repetitions: health and good work, courage, patience, peace, for himself, health and good work, courage, patience, peace for the zadyo . . . for Kamsa, for baby Rekam, for Rayaye, for Heo, for Tualenem, for the oga, for Nemeo who had put him in the crouchcage, for Alatual who had put him in the crouchcage, for Gana who had bound his foot and blessed him, for people he knew in the embassy, in the city, health and good work, courage, patience, peace. . . . That went well, but the meditation itself was a failure. He could not stop thinking. So he thought. He thought about what he could do. He found nothing. He was weak as water, helpless as the baby. He imagined himself speaking on the holonet with a script saying that the Ekumen reluctantly approved the limited use of biological weapons in order to end the civil war. He imagined himself on the holonet dropping the script and saying that the Ekumen would never approve the use of biological weapons for any reason. Both imaginings were fantasies. Rayaye's schemes were fantasies. Seeing that his hostage was useless Rayaye would have him shot. How long has he lived? As long as sixty-two years. A much fairer share of time than Rekam was getting. His mind went on past thinking.

The zadyo opened the door and told him he could come out.

"How close is the Liberation Army, zadyo?" he asked. He expected no answer. He went out onto the terrace. It was late afternoon. Kamsa was there, sitting with the baby at her breast. Her nipple was in his mouth but he was not sucking. She covered her breast. Her face as she did so looked sad for the first time.

"Is he asleep? May I hold him?" Esdan said, sitting by her.

She shifted the little bundle over to his lap. Her face was still troubled. Esdan thought the child's breathing was more difficult, harder work. But he was awake, and looked up into Esdan's face with his big eyes. Esdan made faces, sticking out his lips and blinking. He won a soft little smile.

"The hands say, that army do come," Kamsa said in her very soft voice.

"The Liberation?"

"Enna. Some army."

"From across the river?"

"I think."

"They're assets—freedmen. They're your own people. They won't hurt you." Maybe.

She was frightened. Her control was perfect, but she was frightened. She had seen the Uprising, here. And the reprisals.

"Hide out, if you can, if there's bombing or fighting," he said. "Underground. There must be hiding places here."

She thought and said, "Yes."

It was peaceful in the gardens of Yaramera. No sound but the wind rustling leaves and the faint buzz of the generator. Even the burned, jagged ruins of the house looked mellowed, ageless. The worst has happened, said the ruins. To them. Maybe not to Kamsa and Heo, Gana and Esdan. But there was no hint of violence in the summer air. The baby smiled its vague smile again, nestling in Esdan's arms. He thought of the stone he had lost in his dream.

He was locked into the windowless room for the night. He had no way to know what time it was when he was roused by noise, brought stark awake by a series of shots and explosions, gunfire or handbombs. There was silence, then a second series of bangs and cracks, fainter. Silence again, stretching on and on. Then he heard a flyer right over the house as if circling, sounds inside the house: a shout, running. He lighted the lamp, struggled into his trousers, hard to pull on over the swathed foot. When he heard the flyer coming back and an explosion, he leapt in panic for the door, knowing nothing but that he had to get out of this deathtrap room. He had always feared fire, dying in fire. The door was solid wood, solidly bolted into its solid frame. He had no hope at all of breaking it down and knew it even in his panic. He shouted once, "Let me out of here!" then got control of himself, returned to the cot, and after a minute sat down on the floor between the cot and the wall, as sheltered a place as the room afforded, trying to imagine what was going on. A Liberation raid and Rayaye's men shooting back, trying to bring the flyer down, was what he imagined.

Dead silence. It went on and on.

His lamp flickered.

He got up and stood at the door.

"Let me out!"

No sound.

A single shot. Voices again, running feet again, shouting, calling. After another long silence, distant voices, the sound of men coming down the corridor outside the room. A man said, "Keep them out there for now," a flat, harsh voice. He hesitated and nerved himself and shouted out, "I'm a prisoner! In here!"

A pause.

"Who's in there?"

It was no voice he had heard. He was good at voices, faces, names, intentions.

"Esdardon Aya of the embassy of the Ekumen."

"Mighty Lord!" the voice said.

"Get me out of here, will you?"

There was no reply, but the door was rattled vainly on its massive hinges, was thumped; more voices outside, more thumping and banging. "Axe," somebody said. "Find the key," somebody else said; they went off. Esdan waited. He fought down a repeated impulse to laugh, afraid of hysteria, but it was funny, stupidly funny, all the shouting through the door and seeking keys and axes, a farce in the middle of a battle. What battle?

He had had it backwards. Liberation men had entered the house and killed Rayaye's men, taking most of them by surprise. They had been waiting for Rayaye's flyer when it came. They must have had contacts among the fieldhands, informers, guides. Sealed in his room, he had heard only the noisy end of the business. When he was let out, they were dragging out the dead. He saw the horribly maimed body of one of the young men, Alatual or Nemeo, come apart as they dragged it, ropy blood and entrails stretching out along the floor, the legs left behind. The man dragging the corpse was nonplussed and stood there holding the shoulders of the torso. "Well, shit," he said, and Esdan stood gasping, again trying not to laugh, not to vomit.

"Come on," said the men with him, and he came on.

Early morning light slanted through broken windows.

Esdan kept looking around, seeing none of the house people. The men took him into the room with the packdog head over the mantel. Six or seven men were gathered around the table there. They wore no uniforms, though some had the yellow knot or ribbon of the Liberation on their cap or sleeve. They were ragged, tough, hard. Some were dark, some had beige or clayey or bluish skin, all of them looked edgy and dangerous. One of those with him, a thin, tall man, said in the harsh voice that had said "Mighty Lord" outside the door: "This is him."

"I'm Esdardon Aya, Old Music, of the embassy of the Ekumen," he said again, as easily as he could. "I was being held here. Thank you for liberating me."

Several of them stared at him the way people who had never seen an alien stared, taking in his red-brown skin and deep-set, white-cornered eyes and the subtler differences of skull structure and features. One or two stared more aggressively, as if to test his assertion, show they'd believe he was what he said he was when he proved it. A big, broad-shouldered man, white-skinned and with brownish hair, pure dusty, pure blood of the ancient conquered race, looked at Esdan a long time. "We came to do that," he said.

He spoke softly, the asset voice. It might take them a generation or more to learn to raise their voices, to speak free.

"How did you know I was here? The fieldnet?"

It was what they had called the clandestine system of information passed from voice to ear, field to compound to city and back again, long before there was a holonet. The Hame had used the fieldnet and it had been the chief instrument of the Uprising.

A short, dark man smiled and nodded slightly, then froze his nod as he saw that the others weren't giving out any information.

"You know who brought me here, then—Rayaye. I don't know who he was acting for. What I can tell you, I will." Relief had made him stupid, he was talking too much, playing hands-around-the-flowerbed while they played tough guy. "I have friends here," he went on in a more neutral voice, looking at each of their faces in turn, direct but civil. "Bondswomen, house people. I hope they're all right."

"Depends," said a grey-haired, slight man who looked very tired.

"A woman with a baby, Kamsa. An old woman, Gana."

A couple of them shook their heads to signify ignorance or indifference. Most made no response at all. He looked around at them again, repressing anger and irritation at this pomposity, this tight-lipped stuff.

"We need to know what you were doing here," the brown-haired man said.

"A Liberation Army contact in the city was taking me from the embassy to Liberation Command, about fifteen days ago. We were intercepted in the Divide by Rayaye's men. They brought me here. I spent some time in a crouchcage," Esdan said in the same neutral voice. "My foot was hurt and I can't walk much. I talked twice with Rayaye. Before I say anything else I think you can understand that I need to know who I'm talking to."

The tall thin man who had released him from the locked room went around the table and conferred briefly with the grey-haired man. The brown-haired one listened, consented. The tall thin one spoke to Esdan in his uncharacteristically harsh, flat voice: "We are a special mission of the Advance Army of the World Liberation. I am Marshal Metoy." The others all said their names. The big brown-haired man was General Banarkamye, the tired older man was General Tueyo. They said their rank with their name, but didn't use it addressing one another, nor did they call him Mister. Before Liberation, rentspeople had seldom used any titles to one another but those of parentage: father, sister, aunty. Titles were something that went in front of an owner's name: Lord, Master, Mister, Boss. Evidently the Liberation had decided to do without them. It pleased him to find an army that didn't click its heels and shout Sir! But he wasn't certain what army he'd found.

"They kept you in that room?" Metoy asked him. He was a strange man, a flat, cold voice, a pale, cold face, but he wasn't as jumpy as the others. He seemed sure of himself, used to being in charge.

"They locked me in there last night. As if they'd had some kind of warning of trouble coming. Usually I had a room upstairs."

"You may go there now," Metoy said. "Stay indoors."

"I will. Thank you again," he said to them all. "Please, when you have word of Kamsa and Gana—?" He did not wait to be snubbed, but turned and went out.

One of the younger men went with him. He had named himself Zadyo Tema. The Army of the Liberation was using the old veot ranks, then. There were veots among them, Esdan knew, but Tema was not one. He was light-skinned and had the city-dusty accent, soft, dry, clipped. Esdan did not try to talk to him. Tema was extremely nervous, spooked by the night's work of killing at close quarters or by something else; there was an almost constant tremor in his shoulders, arms, and hands, and his pale face was set in a painful scowl. He was not in a mood for chitchat with an elderly civilian alien prisoner.

In war everybody is a prisoner, the historian Henennemores had written.

Esdan had thanked his new captors for liberating him, but he knew where, at the moment, he stood. It was still Yaramera.

Yet there was some relief in seeing his room again, sitting down in the one-armed chair by the window to look out at the early sunlight, the long shadows of trees across the lawns and terraces.

None of the housepeople came out as usual to go about their work or take a break from it. Nobody came to his room. The morning wore on. He did what exercises of the tanhai he could do with his foot as it was. He sat aware, dozed off, woke up, tried to sit aware, sat restless, anxious, working over words: *A special mission of the Advance Army of World Liberation.*

The Legitimate Government called the enemy army "insurgent forces" or "rebel hordes" on the holonews. It had started out calling itself the Army of the Liberation, nothing about World Liberation; but he had been cut off from any coherent contact with the freedom fighters ever since the Uprising, and cut off from all information of any kind since the embassy was sealed—except for information from other worlds light years away, of course, there'd been no end of that, the ansible was full of it, but of what was going on two streets away, nothing, not a word. In the embassy he'd been ignorant, useless, helpless, passive. Exactly as he was here. Since the war began he'd been, as Henennemores had said, a prisoner. Along with everybody else on Werel. A prisoner in the cause of liberty.

He feared that he would come to accept his helplessness, that it would persuade his soul. He must remember what this war was about. But let the Liberation come soon, he thought, come set me free!

In the middle of the afternoon the young zadyo brought him a plate of cold food, obviously scraps and leftovers they'd found in the kitchens, and a bottle of beer. He ate and drank gratefully. But it was clear that they had not released the housepeople. Or had killed them. He would not let his mind stay on that.

After sunset the zadyo came back and brought him downstairs to the packdog room. The generator was off, of course; nothing had kept it going but old Saka's eternal tinkering. Men carried electric torches, and in the packdog room a couple of big oil lamps burned on the table, putting a romantic, golden light on the faces round it, throwing deep shadows behind them.

"Sit down," said the brown-haired general, Banarkamye— Read-bible, his name could be translated. "We have some questions to ask you."

Silent but civil assent.

They asked how he had got out of the embassy, who his contacts with the Liberation had been, where he had been going, why he had tried to go, what happened during the kidnapping, who had brought him here, what they had asked him, what they had wanted from him. Having decided during the afternoon that candor would serve him best, he answered all the questions directly and briefly until the last one.

"I personally am on your side of this war," he said, "but the Ekumen is necessarily neutral. Since at the moment I'm the only alien on Werel free to speak, whatever I say may be taken, or mistaken, as coming from the embassy and the Stabiles. That was my value to Rayaye. It may be my value to you. But it's a false value. I can't speak for the Ekumen. I have no authority."

"They wanted you to say the Ekumen supports the Jits," the tired man, Tueyo, said.

Esdan nodded.

"Did they talk about using any special tactics, weapons?" That was Banarkamye, grim, trying not to weight the question.

"I'd rather answer that question when I'm behind your

lines, General, talking to people I know in Liberation Command."

"You're talking to the World Liberation Army Command. Refusal to answer can be taken as evidence of complicity with the enemy." That was Metoy, glib, hard, harsh-voiced.

"I know that, Marshal."

They exchanged a glance. Despite his open threat, Metoy was the one Esdan felt inclined to trust. He was solid. The others were nervy, unsteady. He was sure now that they were factionalists. How big their faction was, how much at odds with Liberation Command it was, he could learn only by what they might let slip.

"Listen, Mr. Old Music," Tueyo said. Old habits die hard. "We know you worked for the Hame. You helped send people to Yeowe. You backed us then." Esdan nodded. "You must back us now. We are speaking to you frankly. We have information that the Jits are planning a counterattack. What that means, now, it means that they're going to use the bibo. It can't mean anything else. That can't happen. They can't be let do that. They have to be stopped."

"You say the Ekumen is neutral," Banarkamye said. "That is a lie. A hundred years the Ekumen wouldn't let this world join them, because we had the bibo. Had it, didn't use it, just had it was enough. Now they say they're neutral. Now when it matters! Now when this world is part of them! They have got to act. To act against that weapon. They have got to stop the Jits from using it."

"If the Legitimates did have it, if they did plan to use it, and if I could get word to the Ekumen—what could they do?"

"You speak. You tell the Jit President: the Ekumen says stop there. The Ekumen will send ships, send troops. You back us! If you aren't with us, you are with them!"

"General, the nearest ship is light years away. The Legitimates know that."

"But you can call them, you have the transmitter."

"The ansible in the embassy?"

"The Jits have one of them too."

"The ansible in the foreign ministry was destroyed in the Uprising. In the first attack on the government buildings. They blew the whole block up."

"How do we know that?"

"Your own forces did it. General, do you think the Legitimates have an ansible link with the Ekumen that you don't have? They don't. They could have taken over the embassy and its ansible, but in so doing they'd have lost what credibility they have with the Ekumen. And what good would it have done them? The Ekumen has no troops to send," and he added, because he was suddenly not sure Banarkamye knew it, "as you know. If it did, it would take them years to get here. For that reason and many others, the Ekumen has no army and fights no wars."

He was deeply alarmed by their ignorance, their amateurishness, their fear. He kept alarm and impatience out of his voice, speaking quietly and looking at them unworriedly, as if expecting understanding and agreement. The mere appearance of such confidence sometimes fulfills itself. Unfortunately, from the looks of their faces, he was telling the two generals they'd been wrong and telling Metoy he'd been right. He was taking sides in a disagreement.

Banarkamye said, "Keep all that a while yet," and went back over the first interrogation, repeating questions, asking for more details, listening to them expressionlessly. Saving face. Showing he distrusted the hostage. He kept pressing for anything Rayaye had said concerning an invasion or a counterattack in the south. Esdan repeated several times that Rayaye had said President Oyo was expecting a Liberation invasion of this province, downriver from here. Each time he added, "I have no idea whether anything Rayaye told me was the truth." The fourth or fifth time round he said, "Excuse me, General. I must ask again for some word about the people here—"

"Did you know anybody at this place before you came here?" a younger man asked sharply.

"No. I'm asking about housepeople. They were kind to me. Kamsa's baby is sick, it needs care. I'd like to know they're being looked after."

The generals were conferring with each other, paying no attention to this diversion.

"Anybody stayed here, a place like this, after the Uprising, is a collaborator," said the zadyo, Tema.

"Where were they supposed to go?" Esdan asked, trying to

keep his tone easy. "This isn't liberated country. The bosses still work these fields with slaves. They still use the crouchcage here." His voice shook a little on the last words, and he cursed himself for it.

Banarkamye and Tueyo were still conferring, ignoring his question. Metoy stood up and said, "Enough for tonight. Come with me."

Esdan limped after him across the hall, up the stairs. The young zadyo followed, hurrying, evidently sent by Banarkamye. No private conversations allowed. Metoy, however, stopped at the door of Esdan's room and said, looking down at him, "The housepeople will be looked after."

"Thank you," Esdan said with warmth. He added, "Gana was caring for this injury. I need to see her." If they wanted him alive and undamaged, no harm using his ailments as leverage. If they didn't, no use in anything much.

He slept little and badly. He had always thrived on information and action. It was exhausting to be kept both ignorant and helpless, crippled mentally and physically. And he was hungry.

Soon after sunrise he tried his door and found it locked. He knocked and shouted a while before anybody came, a young fellow looking scared, probably a sentry, and then Tema, sleepy and scowling, with the door key.

"I want to see Gana," Esdan said, fairly peremptory. "She looks after this," gesturing to his swaddled foot. Tema shut the door without saying anything. After an hour or so, the key rattled in the lock again and Gana came in. Metoy followed her. Tema followed him.

Gana stood in the reverence to Esdan. He came forward quickly and put his hands on her arms and laid his cheek against hers. "Lord Kamye be praised I see you well!" he said, words that had often been said to him by people like her. "Kamsa, the baby, how are they?"

She was scared, shaky, her hair unkempt, her eyelids red, but she recovered herself pretty well from his utterly unexpected brotherly greeting. "They are in the kitchen now, sir," she said. "The army men, they said that foot do pain you."

"That's what I said to them. Maybe you'd re-bandage it for me."

He sat down on the bed and she got to work unwrapping the cloths.

"Are the other people all right? Heo? Choyo?"

She shook her head once.

"I'm sorry," he said. He could not ask her more.

She did not do as good a job bandaging his foot as before. She had little strength in her hands to pull the wrappings tight, and she hurried her work, unnerved by the strangers watching.

"I hope Choyo's back in the kitchen," he said, half to her half to them. "Somebody's got to do some cooking here."

"Yes, sir," she whispered.

Not sir, not master! he wanted to warn her, fearing for her. He looked up at Metoy, trying to judge his attitude, and could not.

Gana finished her job. Metoy sent her off with a word, and sent the zadyo after her. Gana went gladly, Tema resisted. "General Banarkamye—" he began. Metoy looked at him. The young man hesitated, scowled, obeyed.

"I will look after these people," Metoy said. "I always have. I was a compound boss." He gazed at Esdan with his cold black eyes. "I'm a cutfree. Not many like me left, these days."

Esdan said after a moment, "Thanks, Metoy. They need help. They don't understand."

Metoy nodded.

"I don't understand either," Esdan said. "Does the Liberation plan to invade? Or did Rayaye invent that as an excuse for talking about deploying the bibo? Does Oyo believe it? Do you believe it? Is the Liberation Army across the river there? Did you come from it? Who are you? I don't expect you to answer."

"I won't," the eunuch said.

If he was a double agent, Esdan thought after he left, he was working for Liberation Command. Or he hoped so. Metoy was a man he wanted on his side.

But I don't know what my side is, he thought, as he went back to his chair by the window. The Liberation, of course, yes, but what is the Liberation? Not an ideal, the freedom of the enslaved. Not now. Never again. Since the Uprising, the Liberation is an army, a political body, a great number of people and leaders and would-be leaders, ambitions and greed clogging hopes and strength, a clumsy amateur semi-government lurching from violence to compromise, ever more complicated, never again to know the beautiful simplicity of the ideal, the pure idea of liberty. And that's what I wanted, what I worked for, all these years. To muddle the nobly simple structure of the hierarchy of caste by infecting it with the idea of justice. And then to confuse the nobly simple structure of the ideal of human equality by trying to make it real. The monolithic lie frays out into a thousand incompatible truths, and that's what I wanted. But I am caught in the insanity, the stupidity, the meaningless brutality of the event.

They all want to use me, but I've outlived my usefulness, he thought; and the thought went through him like a shaft of clear light. He had kept thinking there was something he could do. There wasn't.

It was a kind of freedom.

No wonder he and Metoy had understood each other wordlessly and at once.

The zadyo Tema came to his door to conduct him downstairs. Back to the packdog room. All the leader-types were drawn to that room, its dour masculinity. Only five men were there this time, Metoy, the two generals, the two who used the rank of rega. Banarkamye dominated them all. He was through asking questions and was in the order-giving vein. "We leave here tomorrow," he said to Esdan. "You with us. We will have access to the Liberation holonet. You will speak for us. You will tell the Jit goverment that the Ekumen knows they are planning to deploy banned weapons and warns them that if they do, there will be instant and terrible retaliation."

Esdan was light-headed with hunger and sleeplessness. He stood still—he had not been invited to sit down—and looked down at the floor, his hands at his sides. He murmured barely audibly, "Yes, master."

Banarkamye's head snapped up, his eyes flashed. "What did you say?"

"Enna."

"Who do you think you are?"

"A prisoner of war."

"You can go."

Esdan left. Tema followed him but did not stop or direct

him. He made his way straight to the kitchen, where he heard the rattle of pans, and said, "Choyo, please, give me something to eat!" The old man, cowed and shaky, mumbled and apologised and fretted, but produced some fruit and stale bread. Esdan sat at the worktable and devoured it. He offered some to Tema, who refused stiffly. Esdan ate it all. When he was done he limped on out through the kitchen exitways to a side door leading to the great terrace. He hoped to see Kamsa there, but none of the housepeople were out. He sat on a bench in the balustrade that looked down on the long reflecting pool. Tema stood nearby, on duty.

"You said the bondspeople on a place like this, if they didn't join the Uprising, were collaborators," Esdan said.

Tema was motionless, but listening.

"You don't think any of them might just not have understood what was going on? And still don't understand? This is a benighted place, zadyo. Hard to even imagine freedom, here."

The young man resisted answering for a while, but Esdan talked on, trying to make some contact with him, get through to him. Suddenly something he said popped the lid.

"Usewomen," Tema said. "Get fucked by blacks, every night. All they are, fucks. Jits' whores. Bearing their black brats, yesmaster yesmaster. You said it, they don't know what freedom is. Never will. Can't liberate anybody lets a black fuck 'em. They're foul. Dirty, can't get clean. They got black jizz through and through 'em. Jit-jizz!" He spat on the terrace and wiped his mouth.

Esdan sat still, looking down over the still water of the pool to the lower terraces, the big tree, the misty river, the far green shore. May he be well and work well, have patience, compassion, peace. What use was I, ever? All I did. It never was any use. Patience, compassion, peace. They are your own people. . . . He looked down at the thick blob of spittle on the yellow sandstone of the terrace. Fool, to leave his own people a lifetime behind him and come to meddle with another world. Fool, to think you could give anybody freedom. That was what death was for. To get us out of the crouchcage.

He got up and limped towards the house in silence. The young man followed him.

The lights came back on just as it was getting dark. They

must have let old Saka go back to his tinkering. Preferring twilight, Esdan turned the room light off. He was lying on his bed when Kamsa knocked and came in, carrying a tray. "Kamsa!" he said, struggling up, and would have hugged her, but the tray prevented him. "Rekam is—?"

"With my mother," she murmured.

"He's all right?"

The backward nod. She set the tray down on the bed, as there was no table.

"You're all right? Be careful, Kamsa. I wish I— They're leaving tomorrow, they say. Stay out of their way if you can."

"I do. Do you be safe, sir," she said in her soft voice. He did not know if it was a question or a wish. He made a little rueful gesture, smiling. She turned to leave.

"Kamsa, is Heo—?"

"She was with that one. In his bed."

After a pause he said, "Is there anywhere you can hide out?" He was afraid that Banarkamye's men might execute these people when they left, as "collaborators" or to hide their own tracks.

"We got a hole to go to, like you said," she said.

"Good. Go there, if you can. Vanish! Stay out of sight."

She said, "I will hold fast, sir."

She was closing the door behind her when the sound of a flyer approaching buzzed the windows. They both stood still, she in the doorway, he near the window. Shouts downstairs, outside, men running. There was more than one flyer, approaching from the southeast. "Kill the lights!" somebody shouted. Men were running out to the flyers parked on the lawn and terrace. The window flared up with light, the air with a shattering explosion.

"Come with me," Kamsa said, and took his hand and pulled him after her, out the door, down the hall and through a service door he had never even seen. He hobbled with her as fast as he could down ladderlike stone stairs, through a back passage, out into the stable warren. They came outdoors just as a series of explosions rocked everything around them. They hurried across the courtyard through overwhelming noise and the leap of fire, Kamsa still pulling him along with complete sureness of where she was going, and ducked into one of the storerooms at the end of the stables. Gana was there and one of the old bondsmen, opening up a trap door in the floor. They went down, Kamsa with a leap, the others slow and awkward on the wooden ladder, Esdan most awkward, landing badly on his broken foot. The old man came last and pulled the trap shut over them. Gana had a battery lamp, but kept it on only briefly, showing a big, low, dirt-floored cellar, shelves, an archway to another room, a heap of wooden crates, five faces: the baby awake, gazing silent as ever from its sling on Gana's shoulder. Then darkness. And for some time silence.

They groped at the crates, set them down for seats at random in the darkness.

A new series of explosions, seeming far away, but the ground and the darkness shivered. They shivered in it. "O Kamye," one of them whispered.

Esdan sat on the shaky crate and let the jab and stab of pain in his foot sink into a burning throb.

Explosions: three, four.

Darkness was a substance, like thick water.

"Kamsa," he murmured.

She made some sound that located her near him.

"Thank you."

"You said hide, then we did talk of this place," she whispered.

The old man breathed wheezily and cleared his throat often. The baby's breathing was also audible, a small uneven sound, almost panting.

"Give me him." That was Gana. She must have transferred the baby to his mother.

Kamsa whispered, "Not now."

The old man spoke suddenly and loudly, startling them all: "No water in this!"

Kamsa shushed him and Gana hissed, "Don't shout, fool man!"

"Deaf," Kamsa murmured to Esdan, with a hint of laughter.

If they had no water, their hiding time was limited; the night, the next day; even that might be too long for a woman nursing a baby. Kamsa's mind was running on the same track as Esdan's. She said, "How do we know, should we come out?"

"Chance it, when we have to."

There was a long silence. It was hard to accept that one's eyes did not adjust to the darkness, that however long one waited one would see nothing. It was cave-cool. Esdan wished his shirt were warmer.

"You keep him warm," Gana said.

"I do," Kamsa murmured.

"Those men, they were bondsfolk?" That was Kamsa whispering to him. She was quite near him, to his left.

"Yes. Freed bondsfolk. From the north."

She said, "Lotsalot different men come here, since the old Owner did die. Army soldiers, some. But no bondsfolk before. They shot Heo. They shot Vey and old Seneo. He didn't die but he's shot."

"Somebody from the field compound must have led them, showed them where the guards were posted. But they couldn't tell the bondsfolk from the soldiers. Where were you when they came?"

"Sleeping, back of the kitchen. All us housefolk. Six. That man did stand there like a risen dead. He said, Lie down there! Don't stir a hair! So we did that. Heard them shooting and shouting all over the house. Oh, mighty Lord! I did fear! Then no more shooting, and that man did come back to us and hold his gun at us and take us out to the old house-compound. They did get that old gate shut on us. Like old days."

"For what did they do that if they are bondsfolk?" Gana's voice said from the darkness.

"Trying to get free," Esdan said dutifully.

"How free? Shooting and killing? Kill a girl in the bed?"

"They do all fight all the others, mama," Kamsa said.

"I thought all that was done, back three years," the old woman said. Her voice sounded strange. She was in tears. "I thought that was freedom then."

"They did kill the master in his bed!" the old man shouted out at the top of his voice, shrill, piercing. "What can come of that!"

There was a bit of a scuffle in the darkness. Gana was shaking the old fellow, hissing at him to shut up. He cried, "Let me go!" but quieted down, wheezing and muttering.

"Mighty Lord," Kamsa murmured, with that desperate laughter in her voice.

The crate was increasingly uncomfortable, and Esdan wanted to get his aching foot up or at least level. He lowered himself to the ground. It was cold, gritty, unpleasant to the hands. There was nothing to lean against. "If you made a light for a minute, Gana," he said, "we might find sacks, something to lie down on."

The world of the cellar flashed into being around them, amazing in its intricate precision. They found nothing to use but the loose board shelves. They set down several of these, making a kind of platform, and crept onto it as Gana switched them back into formless simple night. They were all cold. They huddled up against one another, side to side, back to back.

After a long time, an hour or more, in which the utter silence of the cellar was unbroken by any noise, Gana said in an impatient whisper, "Everybody up there did die, I think."

"That would simplify things for us," Esdan murmured.

"But we are the buried ones," said Kamsa.

Their voices roused the baby and he whimpered, the first complaint Esdan had ever heard him make. It was a tiny, weary grizzling or fretting, not a cry. It roughened his breathing and he gasped between his frettings. "Oh, baby, baby, hush now, hush," the mother murmured, and Esdan felt her rocking her body, cradling the baby close to keep him warm. She sang almost inaudibly, "*Suna meya, suna na . . . Sura rena, sura na . . .*" Monotonous, rhythmic, buzzy, purring, the sound made warmth, made comfort.

He must have dozed. He was lying curled up on the planks. He had no idea how long they had been in the cellar.

I have lived here forty years desiring freedom, his mind said to him. That desire brought me here. It will bring me out of here. I will hold fast.

He asked the others if they had heard anything since the bombing raid. They all whispered no.

He rubbed his head. "What do you think, Gana?" he said.

"I think the cold air does harm that baby," she said in almost her normal voice, which was always low.

"You do talk? What do you say?" the old man shouted. Kamsa, next to him, patted him and quieted him.

"I'll go look," Gana said.

"I'll go."

"You got one foot on you," the old woman said in a disgusted tone. She grunted and leaned hard on Esdan's shoulder as she stood up. "Now be still." She did not turn on the light, but felt her way over to the ladder and climbed it, with a little whuff of breath at each step up. She pushed, heaved at the trap door. An edge of light showed. They could dimly see the cellar and each other and the dark blob of Gana's head up in the light. She stood there a long time, then let the trap down. "Nobody," she whispered from the ladder. "No noise. Looks like first morning."

"Better wait," Esdan said.

She came back and lowered herself down among them again. After a time she said, "We go out, it's strangers in the house, some other army soldiers. Then where?"

"Can you get to the field compound?" Esdan suggested.

"It's a long road."

After a while he said, "Can't know what to do till we know who's up there. All right. But let me go out, Gana."

"For what?"

"Because I'll know who they are," he said, hoping he was right.

"And they too," Kamsa said, with that strange little edge of laughter. "No mistaking you, I guess."

"Right," he said. He struggled to his feet, found his way to the ladder, and climbed it laboriously. "I'm too old for this," he thought again. He pushed up the trap and looked out. He listened for a long time. At last he whispered to those below him in the dark, "I'll be back as soon as I can," and crawled out, scrambling awkwardly to his feet. He caught his breath: the air of the place was thick with burning. The light was strange, dim. He followed the wall till he could peer out of the storeroom doorway.

What had been left of the old house was down like the rest of it, blown open, smouldering and masked in stinking smoke. Black embers and broken glass covered the cobbled yard. Nothing moved except the smoke. Yellow smoke, grey smoke. Above it all was the even, clear blue of dawn.

He went around onto the terrace, limping and stumbling, for his foot shot blinding pains up his leg. Coming to the balustrade he saw the blackened wrecks of the two flyers. Half the upper terrace was a raw crater. Below it the gardens of Yara-mera stretched beautiful and serene as ever, level below level, to the old tree and the river. A man lay across the steps that went down to the lower terrace; he lay easily, restfully, his arms outflung. Nothing moved but the creeping smoke and the white-flowered bushes nodding in a breath of wind.

The sense of being watched from behind, from the blank windows of the fragments of the house that still stood, was intolerable. "Is anybody here?" Esdan suddenly called out.

Silence.

He shouted again, louder.

There was an answer, a distant call, from around in front of the house. He limped his way down onto the path, out in the open, not seeking to conceal himself; what was the use? Men came around from the front of the house, three men, then a fourth—a woman. They were assets, roughly clothed, field-hands they must be, come down from their compound. "I'm with some of the housepeople," he said, stopping when they stopped, ten meters apart. "We hid out in a cellar. Is anybody else around?"

"Who are you?" one of them said, coming closer, peering, seeing the wrong color skin, the wrong kind of eyes.

"I'll tell you who I am. But is it safe for us to come out? There's old people, a baby. Are the soldiers gone?"

"They are dead," the woman said, a tall, pale-skinned, bony-faced woman.

"One we found hurt," said one of the men. "All the house-people dead. Who did throw those bombs? What army?"

"I don't know what army," Esdan said. "Please, go tell my people they can come up. Back there, in the stables. Call out to them. Tell them who you are. I can't walk." The wrappings on his foot had worked loose, and the fractures had moved; the pain began to take away his breath. He sat down on the path, gasping. His head swam. The gardens of Yaramera grew very bright and very small and drew away and away from him, far-ther away than home.

He did not quite lose consciousness, but things were con-fused in his mind for a good while. There were a lot of people around, and they were outdoors, and everything stank of burnt meat, a smell that clung in the back of his mouth and made him retch. There was Kamsa, the tiny bluish shadowy sleeping face of the baby on her shoulder. There was Gana, saying to other people, "He did befriend us." A young man with big hands talked to him and did something to his foot, bound it up again, tighter, causing terrible pain and then the beginning of relief.

He was lying down on his back on grass. Beside him a man was lying down on his back on grass. It was Metoy, the eunuch. Metoy's scalp was bloody, the black hair burned short and brown. The dust-colored skin of his face was pale, bluish, like the baby's. He lay quietly, blinking sometimes.

The sun shone down. People were talking, a lot of people, somewhere nearby, but he and Metoy were lying on the grass and nobody bothered them.

"Were the flyers from Bellen, Metoy?" Esdan said.

"Came from the east." Metoy's harsh voice was weak and hoarse. "I guess they were." After a while he said, "They want to cross the river."

Esdan thought about this for a while. His mind still did not work well at all. "Who does?" he said finally.

"These people. The fieldhands. The assets of Yaramera. They want to go meet the Army."

"The Invasion?"

"The Liberation."

Esdan propped himself up on his elbows. Raising his head seemed to clear it, and he sat up. He looked over at Metoy. "Will they find them?" he asked.

"If the Lord so wills," said the eunuch.

Presently Metoy tried to prop himself up like Esdan, but failed. "I got blown up," he said, short of breath. "Something hit my head. I see two for one."

"Probably a concussion. Lie still. Stay awake. Were you with Banarkamye, or observing?"

"I'm in your line of work."

Esdan nodded, the backward nod.

"Factions will be the death of us," Metoy said faintly.

Kamsa came and squatted down beside Esdan. "They say we must go cross the river," she told him in her soft voice. "To where the people-army will keep us safe. I don't know."

"Nobody knows, Kamsa."

"I can't take Rekam cross a river," she whispered. Her face clenched up, her lips drawing back, her brows down. She wept, without tears and in silence. "The water is cold."

"They'll have boats, Kamsa. They'll look after you and Rekam. Don't worry. It'll be all right." He knew his words were meaningless.

"I can't go," she whispered.

"Stay here then," Metoy said.

"They said that other army will come here."

"It might. More likely ours will."

She looked at Metoy. "You are the cutfree," she said. "With those others." She looked back at Esdan. "Choyo got killed. All the kitchen is blown in pieces burning." She hid her face in her arms.

Esdan sat up and reached out to her, stroking her shoulder and arm. He touched the baby's fragile head with its thin, dry hair.

Gana came and stood over them. "All the fieldhands are going cross the river," she said. "To be safe."

"You'll be safer here. Where there's food and shelter." Metoy spoke in short bursts, his eyes closed. "Than walking to meet an invasion."

"I can't take him, mama," Kamsa whispered. "He has got to be warm. I can't, I can't take him."

Gana stooped and looked into the baby's face, touching it very softly with one finger. Her wrinkled face closed like a fist. She straightened up, but not erect as she used to stand. She stood bowed. "All right," she said. "We'll stay."

She sat down on the grass beside Kamsa. People were on the move around them. The woman Esdan had seen on the terrace stopped by Gana and said, "Come on, grandmother. Time to go. The boats are ready waiting."

"Staying," Gana said.

"Why? Can't leave that old house you worked in?" the woman said, jeering, humoring. "It's all burned up, grandmother! Come on now. Bring that girl and her baby." She looked at Esdan and Metoy, a flick-glance. They were not her concern. "Come on," she repeated. "Get up now."

"Staying," Gana said.

"You crazy housefolk," the woman said, turned away, turned back, gave it up with a shrug, and went on.

A few others stopped, but none for more than a question, a moment. They streamed on down the terraces, the sunlit paths beside the quiet pools, down towards the boathouses beyond the great tree. After a while they were all gone.

The sun had grown hot. It must be near noon. Metoy was whiter than ever, but he sat up, saying he could see single, most of the time.

"We should get into the shade, Gana," Esdan said. "Metoy, can you get up?"

He staggered and shambled, but walked without help, and they got to the shade of a garden wall. Gana went off to look for water. Kamsa was carrying Rekam in her arms, close against her breast, sheltered from the sun. She had not spoken for a long time. When they had settled down she said, half questioning, looking around dully, "We are all alone here."

"There'll be others stayed. In the compounds," Metoy said. "They'll turn up."

Gana came back; she had no vessel to carry water in, but had soaked her scarf, and laid the cold wet cloth on Metoy's head. He shuddered. "You can walk better, then we can go to the house-compound, cutfree," she said. "Places we can live in, there."

"House-compound is where I grew up, grandmother," he said.

And presently, when he said he could walk, they made their halt and lame way down a road which Esdan vaguely remembered, the road to the crouchcage. It seemed a long road. They came to the high compound wall and the gate standing open.

Esdan turned to look back at the ruins of the great house for a moment. Gana stopped beside him.

"Rekam died," she said under her breath.

He caught his breath. "When?"

She shook her head. "I don't know. She wants to hold him. She's done with holding him, then she will let him go." She looked in the open gateway at the rows of huts and longhouses, the dried-up garden patches, the dusty ground. "Lotsalot little babies are in there," she said. "In that ground. Two of my own. Her sisters." She went in, following Kamsa. Esdan stood a while longer in the gateway, and then he went in to do what there was for him to do: dig a grave for the child, and wait with the others for the Liberation.

Notes on Werel and Yeowe

I. PRONUNCIATION OF NAMES AND WORDS

In VOE DEAN (which is also the language of Yeowe) and
GATAYAN, vowels have the usual "European values":
    a as in father (ah)
    e as in hey (ay) or let (eh)
    i as in machine (ee) or it (ih)
    o as in go (o) or off (oh)
    u as in ruby (oo)

In Voe Dean the accent is normally on the next-to-last syllable.
Thus:
    Arkamye—ar-KAHM-yeh
    Bambur—BAHM-boor
    Boeba—bo-AY-bah
    Dosse—DOHS-she
    Erod—EH-rod
    gareot—gah-RAY-ot
    Gatay—gah-TAH-ee
    gede—GHEH-deh
    Geu—GAY-oo
    Hame—HAH-meh
    Hagayot—hah-GAH-yot
    Hayawa—hah-YAH-wah
    Kamye—KAHM-yeh
    Keo—KAY-o
    makil—MAH-kihl
    Nadami—nah-DAH-mee
    Noeha—no-AY-hah
    Ramayo—rah-MAH-yo
    rega—RAY-gah
    Rewe—REH-weh
    San Ubattat—sahn-oo-BAHT-taht
    Seugi—say-OO-ghee
    Shomeke—sho-MEH-keh
    Suhame—soo-HAH-meh

Tazeu—tah-ZAY-oo
Teyeo—teh-YAY-o
Tikuli—tee-KOO-lee
Toebawe—to-eh-BAH-weh
Tual—too-AHL or TWAHL
veot—VAY-ot
Voe Deo—vo-eh-DAY-o
Walsu—WAHL-soo
Werel—WEH-rehl
Yeowe—yay-O-way
Yeron—YEH-rohn
Yoke—YO-keh
Yotebber—yo-TEHB-ber
Yowa—YO-wah

Names formed with the name of the deities Kamye (Kam) and
Tual tend to keep a stress on that element, thus:
Abberkam—AHB-ber-KAHM
Batikam—BAH-tih-KAHM
Rakam—RAH-KAHM
Sezi-Tual—SAY-zih-TWAHL
Tualtak—TWAHL-tahk

HAINISH
(The extremely long lineage-names common among the
Hainish are cut down for daily use; thus Mattin-yehedarhed-
dyura-ga-muruskets becomes Yehedarhed.)

araha—ah-RAH-ha
Ekumen (*from an Ancient Terran word*)—EK-yoo-men
Esdardon Aya—ez-DAR-don-AH-ya
Havzhiva—HAHV-zhi-vah
Iyan Iyan—ee-YAHN-ee-YAHN
Kathhad—KAHTH-hahd
Mezhe—MEH-zheh
Stse—STSEH (*like the capitalized letters in English* "beST SEt")
Tiu—TYOO
Ve—VEH
Yehedarhed—yeh-heh-DAR-hed

2. THE PLANETS WEREL AND YEOWE

*From A Handbook of the Known Worlds, printed in Dar-
randa, Hain, Hainish Cycle 93, Local Year 5467.*

*Ekumenical Year 2102 is counted as Present when historical
dates are given as years Before Present (BP).*

The Werel-Yeowe solar system consists of 16 planets orbiting
a yellow-white star (RK-tamo-5544-34). Life developed on the
third, fourth, and fifth planets. The fifth, called Rakuli in Voe
Dean, has only invertebrate life-forms tolerant of arid cold,
and has not been exploited or colonised. The third and fourth
planets, Yeowe and Werel, are well within the Hainish Norm
of atmosphere, gravity, climate, etc. Werel was colonised by
Hain late in the Expansion, within the last million years. It
appears that there was no native fauna to displace, as all animal
life-forms found on Werel, as well as some flora, are of Hainish
derivation. Yeowe had no animal life until Werel colonised it
365 years BP.

WEREL

Natural History
    The fourth planet out from its sun, Werel has seven small
moons. Its current climate is cool temperate, severely cold at
the poles. Its flora is largely indigenous, its fauna entirely of
Hainish origin, modified deliberately to obtain cobiosis with
the native plants, and further modified through genetic drift and
adaptation. Human adaptations include a cyanotic skin color-
ation (from black to pale, with a bluish cast) and eyes without
visible whites, both evidently adjustments to elements in the
solar radiation spectrum.

Voe Deo: *Recent History*: 4000–3500 years BP, aggressive,
progressive black-skinned people from south of the equator on
the single great continent (the region that is now the nation of
Voe Deo) invaded and dominated the lighter-skinned peoples
of the north. These conquerors instituted a master-slave society based on skin color.

Voe Deo is the largest, most numerous, wealthiest nation on the planet; all other nations in both hemispheres are dependencies, client states, or economically dependent on Voe Deo. Voe Dean economics have been based on capitalism and slavery for at least 3000 years. Voe Dean hegemony permits the general description of Werel as if it were all one society. As the society is in rapid change, however, this account will be put in the past tense. *Social Classes under Slavery:*

Class: master (**owner** or **gareot**) and slave (**asset**). Your class was your mother's class, without exception.

Skin color ranges from blue-black through bluish or greyish beige to an almost depigmented white. (Only albinism affects hair and eyes, which are dark.) Ideally and in the abstract, class was skin color: owners black, assets white. Actually, many owners were black, most were dark; some assets were black, most beige, some white.

OWNERS were called men, women, children.

The unqualified word *owner* meant either the class as a whole or an individual/family owning two or more slaves.

The owner of one slave or no slaves was a staffless owner or *gareot*.

The *veot* was a member of an hereditary warrior caste of owners; the ranks were *rega, zadyo, oga*. Veot men almost invariably joined the Army; most veot families were landed proprietors; most were owners, some gareots.

Owner women formed a subclass or inferior caste. An owner woman was legally the property of a man (father, uncle, brother, husband, son, or guardian). Most observers hold that the gender division of Werelian society was as profound and essential as the master/slave division, but less visible, as it cut across it, owner women being considered socially superior to assets of both sexes. Since women were property, they could not own property, including human property. They could, however, manage property.

ASSETS were called bondsmen, bondswomen, pups or young. Pejorative terms: slaves, dusties, chalks, whites.

Luls were work-slaves, owned by a person or a family. All slaves on Werel were luls, except makils and asset-soldiers.

Makils were sold to and owned by the Entertainment Corporation.

Asset-soldiers were sold to and owned by the Army.

"*Cutfrees*" or eunuchs were male slaves castrated (more or less voluntarily, depending on age, etc.) to gain status and privilege. Werelian histories describe a number of cutfrees who rose to great power in various governments; many held posts of influence throughout the bureaucracy. The Bosses of the bondswomen's side of the compound were invariably cutfrees.

Manumission was extremely rare up until the last century, restricted to a few famous historical/legendary cases of slaves whose supernal loyalty and virtue induced their masters to give them freedom. About the time the War of Liberation began on Yeowe, the practice of manumission became more frequent on Werel, led by the owner group **The Community**, which advocated the abolition of slavery. A manumitted asset ranked legally, though seldom socially, as a gareot.

In Voe Deo at the time of the Liberation the proportion of assets to owners was 7:1. (About half these owners were gareots, owners of one or no assets.) In poorer countries the proportion dropped lower or reversed; in the Equatorial States the proportion of assets to owners was 1:5. In Werel as a whole, the proportion was estimated to be about three assets to one owner.

The House and the Compound

Historically and in the country, on the estates, farms, and plantations, the assets lived in a fenced or walled compound with a single gate. The compound was divided in halves by a ditch running parallel to the gate wall. The *gateside* was the men's quarters, the *inside* was the women's. Children lived on the inside, until boys reaching working age (8 to 10) were sent over to the longhouse. Women lived in huts, mothers and daughters, sisters or friends usually sharing a hut, two to four women with their children. The men and boys lived in gateside barracks called longhouses. Kitchen gardens were maintained by the old people and small children who did not go out to work; the old people generally cooked for the working people. The grandmothers ruled the compound.

Cutfrees (eunuchs) lived in separate houses built against the outside wall, with a surveillance station on the wall; they served as Compound Bosses, intermediaries between the grandmothers and the Work Bosses (members of the owner family, or hired gareots, in charge of the working assets). Work Bosses lived in houses outside the compound.

The owning family and their owner-class dependents occupied the House. The term House included any number of outbuildings, the Work Bosses' quarters, and animal barns, but specifically meant the family's large house. In conventional Houses the men's side (azade) and the women's side (beza) were strictly divided. The degree of restriction on the women reflected the wealth, power, and social pretension of the family. Gareot women might have considerable freedom of movement and occupation, but women of wealthy or distinguished family were kept indoors or in the walled gardens, never going out without a numerous male escort.

A number of female assets lived on the women's side as domestics and for use of the male owners. Some Houses kept male domestics, usually boys or old men; some kept cutfrees as servants.

In factories, mills, mines, etc., the compound system was maintained with some modifications. Where there was division of labor, all-male compounds were controlled entirely by hired gareots; in all-female compounds the grandmothers were allowed to keep order as in country compounds. Men rented to the all-male compounds had a life expectancy of about 28 years. During the shortage of assets caused by the slave trade to Yeowe in the early years of the Colony, some owners formed cooperative breeding compounds, where bondswomen were kept and bred annually, doing light work; some of these "breeders" bore a baby annually for twenty or more years.

Rentspeople: On Werel, all assets were individually owned. (The Corporations of Yeowe changed this practice; the Corporations owned the slaves, who had no private masters.)

In Werelian cities, assets traditionally lived in their owners' household as domestics. During the last millennium it became increasingly common for owners of superfluous assets to rent them to businesses and factories as skilled or unskilled labor. The owners or shareholders of a company bought and owned individual assets individually; the company rented the assets, controlled their use, and shared the profits. An owner could live on the rental of two skilled assets. Thus rentsmen and rentswomen became the largest group of assets in all cities and

many towns. Rentspeople lived in "union compounds"—
apartment houses supervised by hired gareot Bosses. They
were required to keep curfew and check in and out.

(Note the difference between Werelian *rentspeople*, rented
out by their owner, and the far more autonomous Yeowan
freedpeople, slaves who paid their owner a tithe or tax on freely
chosen work, called "freedom rental." One of the early objectives of the **Hame**, the Voe Dean underground asset liberation
group, was to institute "freedom rental" on Werel.)

Most union compounds and all city households were gender-
divided into azade and beza, but some private owners and
some companies allowed their assets or rentspeople to live as
couples, though not to marry. Their owners could separate
them for any reason at any time. The mother's owner owned
the children of any such asset couple.

In the conventional compound, heterosexual access was
controlled by the owners, the Bosses, and the grandmothers.
People who "jumped the ditch" did so at their peril. The
owner myth-ideal was of total separation of male and female
assets, with the Bosses managing selective breeding, chosen
stud asset males servicing the females at optimal intervals to
produce the desired number of young. Female assets were
mainly concerned, on exploitive farms, to avoid undesired
breeding and yearly pregnancy. In the hands of benevolent
owners, the grandmothers and cutfrees often could protect
girls and women from rape, and even allow some affectional
pairing. But bonding was discouraged both by the owners and
the grandmothers; and no form of slave marriage was admitted
by law or custom on Werel.

Religions

The worship of Tual, a Kwan Yin–like maternal deity of
peace and forgiveness, was the state religion of Voe Deo. *Phil-
osophically*, Tual is seen as the most important incarnation of
Ama the Increate or Creator Spirit. *Historically*, she is an
amalgam of many local and nature deities, and locally often
refragments into multiplicity. *Nationally*, enforcement of the
national religion tended to accompany Voe Dean hegemony in
other countries, although the religion is not inherently a proselytising or aggressive one. Tualite priests can and do hold

high office in the government. *Class*: Tualite images and worship were maintained by the owners in all slave compounds, both on Werel and Yeowe. Tualism was the owners' religion. The assets' practice of it was enforced, and while including aspects of Tualite myth and worship in their rituals, most assets were Kamyites. By considering Kamye as "the Bondsman" and a lesser aspect of Ama, the Tualite priesthood included and tolerated Kamyite practice (which had no official clergy) among slaves and soldiers (most veots were Kamyites).

The *Arkamye* or Life of Kamye the Swordsman (Kamye is also the Herdsman, a beastmaster deity, and the Bondsman, having been long in service to Lord Nightfall): a warrior epic, adopted about 3,000 years ago by the assets, pretty much worldwide, as the sourcebook of their own religion. It cultivates such warrior/slave virtues as obedience, courage, patience, and selflessness, as well as spiritual independence, a stoical indifference to the things of this world, and a passionate mysticism: reality is to be won only by letting the seeming-real go. Assets and veots include Tual in their worship as an incarnation of Kamye, himself an incarnation of Ama the Increate. The "stages of life" and "going into silence" are among the mystical ideas and practices shared by Kamyites and Tualites.

Relations with the Ekumen

The First Envoy (EY 1724) was met with extreme suspicion. After a closely guarded deputation was allowed to land from the ship *Hugum*, alliance was rejected. Aliens were forbidden to enter the solar system by the Government of Voe Deo and its allies. Werel, led by Voe Deo, then entered on a rapid, competitive development of space technology and intensification of all techno-industrial development. For many decades, Voe Dean government, industry, and military were driven by a paranoid expectation of the armed return of conquering Aliens. It was this development that led within only thirteen years to the colonisation of Yeowe.

During the next three centuries the Ekumen made contact at intervals with Werel. An exchange of information was initiated at the insistence of the University of Bambur, joined by a consortium of universities and research institutions. Finally, after over three hundred years, the Ekumen was permitted to send a few Observers. During the War of Liberation on Yeowe, the Ekumen was invited to send Ambassadors to Voe Deo and Bambur, and later Envoys to Gatay, the Forty States, and other nations. For some time nonobservance of the Arms Convention kept Werel from joining the Ekumen, despite pressure from Voe Deo on the other states, which insisted on retaining their weaponry. After the abrogation of the Arms Convention, Werel joined the Ekumen, 359 years after first contact and 14 years after the end of the War of Liberation.

As a property of the Corporations, having no government of its own, Yeowe Colony was considered by its Werelian owners to be ineligible for Ekumenical membership. The Ekumen continued to question the right of the Four Corporations to ownership of the planet and its people. During the last years of the War of Liberation, the Freedom Party invited Ekumenical observers to Yeowe, and the establishment of a regular Envoy there coincided with the end of the War. The Ekumen helped Yeowe negotiate an end to the economic control of the planet by the Corporations and the Government of Voe Deo. The World Party nearly succeeded in driving the Aliens as well as the Werelians off the planet, but when that movement collapsed, the Ekumen supported the Provisional Government until elections could be held. Yeowe joined the Ekumen in Year of Liberation 11, three years before Werel did.

YEOWE

Natural History

The third planet out from its sun, Yeowe has a warm-moderate climate with little seasonal variation.

Bacterial life is ancient and of normally vast complexity and adaptive variety. A number of microscopic marine Yeowan species are defined as animals; otherwise, the native biota of the planet were plants.

On land there was a great variety of complex species, photosynthetic or saprophytic. Most were sessile, with some "creepers," colonial or individual plants capable of slow movement. Trees were the principal large life-form. South Continent was almost entirely tropical jungle/temperate rain forest from the coastlines up to timberline in the Polar Range and to the taiga

of the Antarctic Circle. Great Continent, forested in the extreme north and south, was a steppe and savannah landscape at
the higher central altitudes, with immense areas of bog, marsh,
and sea marsh on the coastal plains. In the absence of pollinat-
ing animals, the plants had many devices to use wind and rain
to cross-fertilise and propagate: explosive seeds, winged seeds,
seednets that catch the wind and float for hundreds of miles,
waterproof spores, "burrowing" seeds, "swimming" seeds, and
plants with mobile vanes, cilia, etc.

The seas, which are warm and relatively shallow, and the vast
sea marshes nourish a huge variety of sessile and floating plants,
on the order of plankton, algaes, seaweeds, coral-type and
sponge-type plants forming permanent constructions (mostly
of silicon), and unique plants such as the "sailers" and the "mir-
rorweed." Vast connected "lily mats" were harvested by the
Corporations so efficiently as to render the species extinct
within thirty years.

Heedless introduction of Werelian plant and animal species
killed off or crowded out about 3/5 of the native species, aided
by industrial pollution and war. The owners brought in deer,
hunting dogs, hunting cats, and greathorses for their hunts. The
deer thrived and destroyed a great deal of native habitat. Most
introduced animal species failed in the long run. Werelian animal survivors other than humankind on Yeowe include:

  birds (domestic fowl brought in as game or as poultry; song-
    birds were released, and a few species adapted and survived)
  foxdogs and spotted cats (pets)
  cattle (domestic; many wild in abandoned districts)
  deer (wild, called fendeer, adapted to the marsh regions)
  hunting cats (feral, rare, in marshlands)

The introduction of some fish species in the rivers was disastrous to the native plant life, and what fish survived were destroyed by poison. All attempts to introduce ocean fish failed.

Horses were slaughtered during the War of Liberation, as
symbolic possessions of the owners; none remain.

The Colony: The Settlement

Early Werelian rockets reached Yeowe 365 years BP. Exploration, mapping, and prospecting were eagerly pursued. The
Yeowe Mines Corporation, owned principally by Voe Dean

investors, was given sole right to prospecting. Within twenty-five years, larger and more efficient ships made mining profitable, and the YMC began regular shipments of slaves to Yeowe and ores and minerals to Werel.

The next major company established was the Second Planet Forest Woods Corporation, cutting and shipping Yeowan timber to Werel, where industrial and population expansion had reduced forests drastically.

Exploitation of the oceans became a major industry by the end of the first century, the Yeowan Shippers Corporation harvesting the lily mats with immense profit. Having used up that resource, the YSC turned to the exploitation and processing of other sea species, especially the oil-rich bladderweed.

During the Colony's first century, the Agricultural Plantation Company of Yeowe began systematic culture of introduced grains and fruits and of native species such as the oe-reed and the pini fruit. The warm, equable climate of most of Yeowe and the absence of insect and animal pests (maintained by scrupulous quarantine regulations) permitted an enormous expansion of agriculture.

The individual enterprises of these four Corporations and the regions where they operated, whether in mining, forestry, mariculture, or agriculture, were called "Plantations."

The four great Corporations maintained absolute control over their respective products, though there were over the decades many battles (legal and physical) over conflicting rights to the exploitation of an area. No rival company was able to break the Corporations' monopoly, which had the full, active support—military, political, and scientific—of the Government of Voe Deo, a major beneficiary of Corporation profits. The principal investment of capital in the Corporations was always from the government and capitalists of Voe Deo. A powerful country at the time of the Settlement, after three centuries of the Colony Voe Deo was by far the richest country on Werel, dominating and controlling all the others. Its control over the Corporations on Yeowe, however, was nominal. It negotiated with them as with sovereign powers.

Population and Slavery

For the first century only male slaves were exported to Yeowe Colony by the Corporations, whose monopoly on slave shipment, via the Interplanet Cartel, was complete. In the first century, a high proportion of these slaves were from the poorer nations of Werel; later, as slave-breeding for the Yeowan market became profitable, more of them were sent from Bambur, the Forty States, and Voe Deo.

During this period, the population grew to about 40,000 of the owner class (80% male) and about 800,000 slaves (all male).

There were several experimental "Emigration Towns," settlements of gareots (owner-class people without slaves), mostly mills and service communities. These settlements were first tolerated, then abolished, by the Corporations, who induced the Werelian governments to limit emigration to Corporation personnel. The gareot settlers were shipped back to Werel and the services they had set up were staffed by slaves. The "middle class" of townsfolk and tradespeople on Yeowe thus came to be composed of semi-independent slaves (freedpeople) rather than gareots and rentspeople as on Werel.

Prices on bondsmen kept going up, as the Mining and Agricultural Corporations in particular squandered slave life (a mine slave during the first century was expected to have a "worklife" of five years). Individual owners increasingly often smuggled in female slaves as sexual and domestic servants. The Corporations, under these pressures, changed their rule and permitted the importation of bondswomen (238 BP).

At first bondswomen, considered as breeding stock, were restricted to the compounds on the plantations. As their usefulness for all kinds of work became evident, these restrictions were eased by the owners on most plantations. Slave women, however, had to fit into the century-old social system of slave men, which they entered as inferiors, slaves' slaves.

On Werel, all assets were personally owned, except the makils (bought from their owners by the Entertainment Corporation), and asset-soldiers (bought from their owners by the government). On Yeowe, all slaves were Corporation-owned, bought by the Corporation from their Werelian owners. No slave on Yeowe could be privately owned. No slave on Yeowe could be freed. Even those brought in as personal servants, such as maids of plantation owners' wives, had their ownership transferred to the Corporation that owned the plantation.

Though manumission was not allowed, as the slave population increased very rapidly, causing a surplus on many plantations, the status of *freedperson* became increasingly common. Freedpeople found work for hire or independently and "rented freedom," paying one or more Corporations monthly or annually whatever fee (usually about 50%) was levied on them as a tax on their independent work. Most freedpeople worked as sharecroppers, shopkeepers, or mill hands, and in service industries; during the Colony's third century a professional class of freedpeople became well established in the cities.

By the end of the third century, when the population growth had slowed somewhat, the total population of Yeowe was about 450 million; the proportion of owners to slaves was less than one to one hundred. About half the slave population were freedpeople. (The population 20 years after Liberation was again 450 million, all free.)

On the plantations, the original all-male social structure set the pattern of slave society. Work gangs early developed into social groups (called gangs), and gangs into tribes, each with a hierarchy of power: Tribesmen under a slave Headman or Chief, under the Boss, under the owner, under the Corporation. Bonding, competition, rivalry, homosexual privileges, and adoptive lineages became institutionalised and often elaborately codified. The only safety for a slave was membership in a tribe and strict adherence to its rules. Slaves sold away from their plantation had to serve as slaves' slaves, often for years, before they were accepted into membership of the local tribe.

As women slaves were brought in, most of them became tribal, as well as Corporate, property. The Corporations encouraged this. It was to their advantage to have slave women controlled by the tribes, as the tribes were controlled by the Corporations.

Opposition and insurrection, never able to organise widely, were always crushed with the instant and brutal finality of infinitely superior armaments. Headmen and chiefs colluded with the Bosses, who, working in the interest of owners and Corporations, exploited the rivalries between tribes and the power struggles within them, while maintaining an absolute embargo on "ideology," by which they meant education, information of any kind from outside the local plantation. (On most plantations, well into the second century, literacy was a crime. A slave caught reading was blinded by dropping acid in the eyes or scraping the eyes from the sockets. A slave caught using a radio or network outlet was deafened by white-hot picks thrust through the eardrums. The "Fit Punishment Lists" of the Corporations and plantations were long, detailed, and explicit.)

In the second century, as slave population shot up to the point of surplus on most plantations, a gradual trickle of both men and women towards the "shop-strips" run by freedpeople grew to a steady stream. Over the decades, the "shop-strips" grew into towns and the towns into cities entirely populated by freedpeople.

Although doomsayers among the owners began to point to the ever-increasing size and independence of the "Assetvilles" and "Whiteytowns" and "Dustyburgs" as a looming threat, the Corporations considered the cities safely under control. No large buildings were allowed, no defensive structures of any kind; possession of a firearm was punished by disembowelment; no slave was allowed to operate any flying vehicle; the Corporations kept tight guard on raw materials and industrial processes that could provide weaponry of any kind to the slaves or freedpeople.

"Ideology," education, did exist in the cities. Late in the second century of the Colony, the Corporations, while censoring, filtering, and altering information, formally gave permission for freedpeople's children and some tribal children to be schooled up to age 14. They allowed slave communities to set up schools, and sold them books and other materials. In the third century the Corporations instituted and maintained an information and entertainment network for the cities. Educated workers were becoming valuable. The limitations of the tribes had become increasingly evident. Rigidly conservative, most tribal chiefs and Bosses were unable or unwilling to change any practices in any way, at a time when the abuse of the planet's resources called for radical changes in methods and objectives. It was clear that profit on Yeowe would increasingly come not from strip-mining, clear-cutting, and monoculture, but from refined industry, modern plants staffed by skilled workers capable of learning new techniques and following unfamiliar orders.

On Werel, a capitalist slave society, work was done by people. Slave labor, whether simple brawnwork or highly skilled,
was hand labor, aided by an elegant but ancillary machine
technology: "The trained asset is the finest machine, and the
cheapest." Production, even of very high-technology items,
was essentially traditional craft of very high quality. Neither
speed nor great volume was particularly valued.

On Yeowe, late in the third century of the Colony, as raw
material exports failed, slave labor was used in a new way. The
assembly line was developed, with the conscious purpose not
only of speeding and cheapening production, but also of keeping the worker ignorant of the work process as a whole. The
Second Planet Corporation, dropping the words Forest Woods
from its name, led the new manufacture. The SPC quickly
surpassed the old giants, Mines and Agriculture, reaping huge
profits from the sale of mass-produced finished goods to the
poorer nations of Werel. By the time of the Uprising, more
than half the freedworkers of Yeowe were owned by or rented
to the Second Planet Corporation.

There was far more social unrest in the mills and mill towns
than on the tribal plantations. Corporation executives ascribed
it to the increase in the number of "uncontrolled" freedper-
sons, and many advocated closing the schools, destruction of
the cities, and reinstitution of sealed compounds for all slaves.
The Corporations' city militia (gareots hired and brought
from Werel, plus a police force of unarmed freedmen) increased to a considerable standing army, its gareot members
heavily armed. Much of the unrest in the cities and attempts at
protest centered on mills that used the assembly line. Workers
who, feeling themselves part of an intelligible process, would
tolerate very harsh conditions, found meaningless work intolerable, even though working conditions were in some ways
improved.

The Liberation began, however, not in the cities, but in the
compounds of the plantations.

The Uprising and the Liberation

The Uprising had its origin in organisations of tribal women
in plantations of Great Continent, joining together to prevent
ritual rape of girl-children and to demand tribal laws against

sexual enslavement of bondswomen by bondsmen, gang rape, and the beating and murder of women, for none of which was there any penalty.

They acted first by educating women and children of both sexes, then by demanding proportional voice in the all-male tribal councils. Their organisations, called Woman Clubs, spread across both continents throughout the third century of the Colony. The Clubs spirited so many girls and women off the plantations into the cities that the chiefs' and Bosses' complaints began to be heard by the Corporations. Local tribesmen and Bosses were encouraged to "go into the cities and get their women back."

These incursions, often led by plantation police and aided by the Corporation city militia, were often carried out with extreme brutality. City freedpeople, unused to the kind of violence normal on the plantations, reacted with outrage. City bondsmen were drawn to defend and fight with the women.

In 61 BP, in Eyu Province, in the town of Soyeso, the slaves' successful resistance to a police raid from Nadami Plantation (APC) escalated into an attack on the plantation itself. The police barracks were stormed and burned. Some of the chiefs of Nadami joined the uprising, opening their compounds to the rebels. Others joined in the defense of their owners in the Plantation House. A slave woman unlocked the doors of the plantation armory to the insurrection—the first time in the history of Yeowe Colony that any large group of slaves had access to powerful weapons. A massacre of owners followed, but it was partially restrained: most of the children of the Plantation House, and twenty women and men, were spared and put on a train to the capital. No adult slave who had fought against the uprising was spared.

From Nadami the Uprising spread, by way of guns and ammunition, to three neighboring plantations. All the tribes joined, defeating Corporation forces in the quick, fierce Battle of Nadami. Slaves and freedpeople from neighboring provinces poured into Eyu. The chiefs, the grandmothers of the compounds, and the leaders of the insurrection met at Nadami and declared Eyu Province a free state.

Within ten days, Corporation bombing raids and land troops had smashed the insurrection. Captured rebels were tortured

and executed. Particular revenge was taken on the town of Soyeso: all the people left there, mostly children and the old, were
herded into the town squares and trucks and tread-wheeled
ore-carriers ran over and over them. This was called "paving
with dust."

The Corporations' victory had been quick and easy, but it
was followed by a new insurrection at a different plantation,
the murder of an owner's family here, a strike of city freedworkers there, all over the world.

The unrest did not cease. Many attacks on plantation armor-
ies and militia barracks were successful; the insurrectionists
now had weapons, and learned how to make bombs and mines.
Hit-and-run warfare in the jungles and the great marshes gave
the guerrilla's advantage to the rebels. It became clear that the
Corporations needed more armaments and more manpower.
They imported mercenary soldiers from the poorer nations of
Werel. Not all of these were loyal or effective troops. The
Corporations soon persuaded the government of Voe Deo to
safeguard its national interest by investing troops in the defense of the Owners of Yeowe. At first the commitment was
reluctant, but 23 years after Nadami, Voe Deo decided to put
down the unrest once and for all, sending 45,000 troops, all
veots (members of the hereditary warrior caste) or owner-
volunteers.

Seven years later, at the end of the war, 300,000 soldiers
from Werel had been killed on Yeowe, most of them from Voe
Deo, and most of them veots.

The Corporations began to take their people off Yeowe several years before the end of the war, and during the final year
of fighting there were almost no civilian owners left on the
planet.

Throughout the thirty years of the War of Liberation, some
tribes and many individual slaves sided with the Corporations,
which promised them safety and rewards and furnished them
with weapons. Even during the Liberation there were battles
between rival tribes. After the Corporations and the army
pulled out, tribal wars smouldered and flared up all over Great
Continent. No central government was able to establish itself
until Abberkam's World Party, defeating the Freedom Party in
many local elections, seemed to be on the point of setting up

the first World Council elections. In Year 2 of Liberation the World Party collapsed abruptly under accusation of corruption. The Envoys of the Ekumen (invited to Yeowe by the Freedom Party during the final year of the war) supported the Freedom Party in activating their constitution and setting up elections. The First Election (Year 3 of the Liberation), managed by the Freedom Party, established the new Constitution on rather shaky ground; women were not allowed to vote, many tribal votes were cast by the chiefs alone, and some of the hierarchic tribal structures were retained and legalised. There were several more fierce tribal wars and years of unrest and protest while the society of free Yeowe constructed itself. Yeowe joined the Ekumen in Year 11 of the Liberation, 19 BP, and the First Ambassador was sent in that year. Major amendments to the Yeowan Constitution, assuring all people over 18 the vote by secret ballot and guaranteeing equal rights, were voted by free general election in Year 18 of the Liberation.

O Yeowe

O, O, Ye - o — we, No-bo-dy ne-ver come back.

THE TELLING

The day I was born I made my first mistake,

and by that path

have I sought wisdom ever since.

THE MAHABHARATA

Chapter One

WHEN SUTTY WENT back to Earth in the daytime, it was always to the village. At night, it was the Pale.

Yellow of brass, yellow of turmeric paste and of rice cooked with saffron, orange of marigolds, dull orange haze of sunset dust above the fields, henna red, passionflower red, dried-blood red, mud red: all the colors of sunlight in the day. A whiff of asafetida. The brook-babble of Aunty gossiping with Moti's mother on the verandah. Uncle Hurree's dark hand lying still on a white page. Ganesh's little piggy kindly eye. A match struck and the rich grey curl of incense smoke: pungent, vivid, gone. Scents, glimpses, echoes that drifted or glimmered through her mind when she was walking the streets, or eating, or taking a break from the sensory assault of the neareals she had to partiss in, in the daytime, under the other sun.

But night is the same on any world. Light's absence is only that. And in the darkness, it was the Pale she was in. Not in dream, never in dream. Awake, before she slept, or when she woke from dream, disturbed and tense, and could not get back to sleep. A scene would begin to happen, not in sweet, bright bits but in full recall of a place and a length of time; and once the memory began, she could not stop it. She had to go through it until it let her go. Maybe it was a kind of punishment, like the lovers' punishment in Dante's Hell, to remember being happy. But those lovers were lucky, they remembered it together.

The rain. The first winter in Vancouver rain. The sky like a roof of lead weighing down on the tops of buildings, flattening the huge black mountains up behind the city. Southward the rain-rough grey water of the Sound, under which lay Old Vancouver, drowned by the sea rise long ago. Black sleet on shining asphalt streets. Wind, the wind that made her whimper like a dog and cringe, shivering with a scared exhilaration, it was so fierce and crazy, that cold wind out of the Arctic, ice breath of the snow bear. It went right through her flimsy coat, but her boots were warm, huge ugly black plastic boots splashing in the gutters, and she'd soon be home. It made you feel safe, that awful cold. People hurried past not bothering each other, all their hates and passions frozen. She liked the North, the cold, the rain, the beautiful, dismal city.

Aunty looked so little, here, little and ephemeral, like a small butterfly. A red-and-orange cotton saree, thin brass bangles on insect wrists. Though there were plenty of Indians and Indo-Canadians here, plenty of neighbors, Aunty looked small even among them, displaced, misplaced. Her smile seemed foreign and apologetic. She had to wear shoes and stockings all the time. Only when she got ready for bed did her feet reappear, the small brown feet of great character which had always, in the village, been a visible part of her as much as her hands, her eyes. Here her feet were put away in leather cases, amputated by the cold. So she didn't walk much, didn't run about the house, bustle about the kitchen. She sat by the heater in the front room, wrapped up in a pale ragged knitted woollen blanket, a butterfly going back into its cocoon. Going away, farther away all the time, but not by walking.

Sutty found it easier now to know Mother and Father, whom she had scarcely known for the last fifteen years, than to know Aunty, whose lap and arms had been her haven. It was delightful to discover her parents, her mother's good-natured wit and intellect, her father's shy, unhandy efforts at showing affection. To converse with them as an adult while knowing herself unreasonably beloved as a child—it was easy, it was delightful. They talked about everything, they learned one another. While Aunty shrank, fluttered away very softly, deviously, seeming not to be going anywhere, back to the village, to Uncle Hurree's grave.

Spring came, fear came. Sunlight came back north here long and pale like an adolescent, a silvery shadowy radiance. Small pink plum trees blossomed all down the side streets of the neighborhood. The Fathers declared that the Treaty of Beijing contravened the Doctrine of Unique Destiny and must be abrogated. The Pales were to be opened, said the Fathers, their populations allowed to receive the Holy Light, their schools cleansed of unbelief, purified of alien error and deviance. Those who clung to sin would be re-educated.

Mother was down at the Link offices every day, coming home late and grim. This is their final push, she said; if they do this, we have nowhere to go but underground.

In late March, a squadron of planes from the Host of God flew from Colorado to the District of Washington and bombed the Library there, plane after plane, four hours of bombing that turned centuries of history and millions of books into dirt. Washington was not a Pale, but the beautiful old building, though often closed and kept locked, under guard, had never been attacked; it had endured through all the times of trouble and war, breakdown and revolution, until this one. The Time of Cleansing. The Commander-General of the Hosts of the Lord announced the bombing while it was in progress, as an educational action. Only one Word, only one Book. All other words, all other books were darkness, error. They were dirt. *Let the Lord shine out!* cried the pilots in their white uniforms and mirror-masks, back at the church at Colorado Base, facelessly facing the cameras and the singing, swaying crowds in ecstasy. *Wipe away the filth and let the Lord shine out!*

But the new Envoy who had arrived from Hain last year, Dalzul, was talking with the Fathers. They had admitted Dalzul to the Sanctum. There were neareals and holos and 2Ds of him in the net and *Godsword*. It seemed that the Commander-General of the Hosts had not received orders from the Fathers to destroy the Library of Washington. The error was not the Commander-General's, of course. Fathers made no errors. The pilots' zeal had been excessive, their action unauthorised. Word came from the Sanctum: the pilots were to be punished. They were led out in front of the ranks and the crowds and the cameras, publicly stripped of their weapons and white uniforms. Their hoods were taken off, their faces were bared. They were led away in shame to re-education.

All that was on the net, though Sutty could watch it without having to partiss in it, Father having disconnected the vr-proprios. *Godsword* was full of it, too. And full of the new Envoy, again. Dalzul was a Terran. Born right here on God's Earth, they said. A man who understood the men of Earth as no alien ever could, they said. A man from the stars who came to kneel at the feet of the Fathers and to discuss the implementation of the peaceful intentions of both the Holy Office and the Ekumen.

"Handsome fellow," Mother said, peering. "What is he? A white man?"

"Inordinately so," Father said.

"Wherever is he from?"

But no one knew. Iceland, Ireland, Siberia, everybody had a different story. Dalzul had left Terra to study on Hain, they all agreed on that. He had qualified very quickly as an Observer, then as a Mobile, and then had been sent back home: the first Terran Envoy to Terra.

"He left well over a century ago," Mother said. "Before the Unists took over East Asia and Europe. Before they even amounted to much in Western Asia. He must find his world quite changed."

Lucky man, Sutty was thinking. Oh lucky, lucky man! He got away, he went to Hain, he studied at the School on Ve, he's been where everything isn't God and hatred, where they've lived a million years of history, where they understand it all!

That same night she told Mother and Father that she wanted to study at the Training School, to try to qualify for the Ekumenical College. Told them very timidly, and found them undismayed, not even surprised. "This seems a rather good world to get off of, at present," Mother said.

They were so calm and favorable that she thought, Don't they realise, if I qualify and get sent to one of the other worlds, they'll never see me again? Fifty years, a hundred, hundreds, round trips in space were seldom less, often more. Didn't they care? It was only later that evening, when she was watching her father's profile at table, full lips, hook nose, hair beginning to go grey, a severe and fragile face, that it occurred to her that if she was sent to another world, she would never see them again either. They had thought about it before she did. Brief presence and long absence, that was all she and they had ever had. And made the best of it.

"Eat, Aunty," Mother said, but Aunty only patted her piece of naan with her little ant-antenna fingers and did not pick it up.

"Nobody could make good bread with such flour," she said, exonerating the baker.

"You were spoiled, living in the village," Mother teased her. "This is the best quality anybody can get in Canada. Best quality chopped straw and plaster dust."

"Yes, I was spoiled," Aunty said, smiling from a far country.

The older slogans were carved into facades of buildings: FOR-WARD TO THE FUTURE. PRODUCER-CONSUMERS OF AKA MARCH

TO THE STARS. Newer ones ran across the buildings in bands of dazzling electronic display: REACTIONARY THOUGHT IS THE DEFEATED ENEMY. When the displays malfunctioned, the messages became cryptic: OD   IS   ON. The newest ones hovered in holopro above the streets: PURE SCIENCE DESTROYS CORRUPTION. UPWARD ONWARD FORWARD. Music hovered with them, highly rhythmic, multivoiced, crowding the air. "Onward, onward to the stars!" an invisible choir shrilled to the stalled traffic at the intersection where Sutty's robocab sat. She turned up the cab sound to drown the tune out. "Superstition is a rotting corpse," the sound system said in a rich, attractive male voice. "Superstitious practices defile youthful minds. It is the responsibility of every citizen, whether adult or student, to report reactionary teachings and to bring teachers who permit sedition or introduce irrationality and superstition in their classroom to the attention of the authorities. In the light of Pure Science we know that the ardent cooperation of all the people is the first requisite of—" Sutty turned the sound down as far as it would go. The choir burst forth, "To the stars! To the stars!" and the robocab jerked forward about half its length. Two more jerks and it might get through the intersection at the next flowchange.

Sutty felt in her jacket pockets for an akagest, but she'd eaten them all. Her stomach hurt. Bad food, she'd eaten too much bad food for too long, processed stuff jacked up with proteins, condiments, stimulants, so you had to buy the stupid akagests. And the stupid unnecessary traffic jams because the stupid badly made cars broke down all the time, and the noise all the time, the slogans, the songs, the hype, a people hyping itself into making every mistake every other population in FF-tech mode had ever made. —Wrong.

Judgmentalism. Wrong to let frustration cloud her thinking and perceptions. Wrong to admit prejudice. Look, listen, notice: observe. That was her job. This wasn't her world.

But she was on it, in it, how could she observe it when there was no way to back off from it? Either the hyperstimulation of the neareals she had to study, or the clamor of the streets: nowhere to get away from the endless aggression of propaganda, except alone in her apartment, shutting out the world she'd come to observe.

The fact was, she was not suited to be an Observer here. In other words, she had failed on her first assignment. She knew that the Envoy had summoned her to tell her so.

She was already nearly late for the appointment. The robocab made another jerk forward, and its sound system came up loud for one of the Corporation announcements that overrode low settings. There was no off button. "An announcement from the Bureau of Astronautics!" said a woman's vibrant, energy-charged, self-confident voice, and Sutty put her hands over her ears and shouted, "Shut up!"

"Doors of vehicle are closed," the robocab said in the flat mechanical voice assigned to mechanisms responding to verbal orders. Sutty saw that this was funny, but she couldn't laugh. The announcement went on and on while the shrill voices in the air sang, "Ever higher, ever greater, marching to the stars!"

The Ekumenical Envoy, a doe-eyed Chiffewarian named Tong Ov, was even later than she for their appointment, having been delayed at the exit of his apartment house by a malfunction of the ZIL-screening system, which he laughed about. "And the system here has mislaid the microrec I wanted to give you," he said, going through files in his office. "I coded it, because of course they go through my files, and my code confused the system. But I know it's in here. . . . So, meanwhile, tell me how things have been going."

"Well," Sutty said, and paused. She had been speaking and thinking in Dovzan for months. She had to go through her own files for a moment: Hindi no, English no, Hainish yes. "You asked me to prepare a report on contemporary language and literature. But the social changes that took place here while I was in transit . . . Well, since it's against the law, now, to speak or study any language but Dovzan and Hainish, I can't work on the other languages. If they still exist. As for Dovzan, the First Observers did a pretty thorough linguistic survey. I can only add details and vocabulary."

"What about literature?" Tong asked.

"Everything that was written in the old scripts has been destroyed. Or if it exists, I don't know what it is, because the Ministry doesn't allow access to it. So all I was able to work on is modern aural literature. All written to Corporation specifications. It tends to be very—to be standardised."

She looked at Tong Ov to see if her whining bored him, but though still looking for the mislaid file, he seemed to be listening with lively interest. He said, "All aural, is it?"

"Except for the Corporation manuals hardly anything's printed, except printouts for the deaf, and primers to accompany sound texts for early learners. . . . The campaign against the old ideographic forms seems to have been very intense. Maybe it made people afraid to write—made them distrust writing in general. Anyway, all I've been able to get hold of by way of literature is sound tapes and neareals. Issued by the World Ministry of Information and the Central Ministry of Poetry and Art. Most of the works are actually information or educational material rather than, well, literature or poetry as I understand the terms. Though a lot of the neareals are dramatisations of practical or ethical problems and solutions. . . ." She was trying so hard to speak factually, unjudgmentally, without prejudice, that her voice was totally toneless.

"Sounds dull," said Tong, still flitting through files.

"Well, I'm, I think I'm insensitive to this aesthetic. It is so deeply and, and, and flatly political. Of course every art is political. But when it's *all* didactic, all in the service of a belief system, I resent, I mean, I resist it. But I try not to. Maybe, since they've essentially erased their history— Of course there was no way of knowing they were on the brink of a cultural revolution, at the time I was sent here— But anyhow, for this particular Observership, maybe a Terran was a bad choice. Given that we on Terra are living the future of a people who denied their past."

She stopped short, appalled at everything she had said.

Tong looked round at her, unappalled. He said, "I don't wonder that you feel that what you've been trying to do can't be done. But I needed your opinion. So it was worth it to me. But tiresome for you. A change is in order." There was a gleam in his dark eyes. "What do you say to going up the river?"

"The river?"

"It's how they say 'into the backwoods,' isn't it? But in fact I meant the Ereha."

When he said the name, she remembered that a big river ran through the capital, partly paved over and so hidden by buildings and embankments that she couldn't remember ever having seen it except on maps.

"You mean go outside Dovza City?"

"Yes," Tong said. "Outside the city! And not on a guided tour! For the first time in fifty years!" He beamed like a child revealing a hidden present, a beautiful surprise. "I've been here two years, and I've put in eighty-one requests for permission to send a staff member to live or stay somewhere outside Dovza City or Kang-negne or Ert. Politely evaded, eighty times, with offers of yet another guided tour of the space-program facilities or the beauty of spring in the Eastern Isles. I put in such requests by habit, by rote. And suddenly one is granted! Yes! 'A member of your staff is authorised to spend a month in Okzat-Ozkat.' Or is it Ozkat-Okzat? It's a small city, in the foothills, up the river. The Ereha rises in the High Headwaters Range, about fifteen hundred kilos inland. I asked for that area, Rangma, never expecting to get it, and I got it!" He beamed.

"Why there?"

"I heard about some people there who sound interesting."

"An ethnic fragment population?" she asked, hopeful. Early in her stay, when she first met Tong Ov and the other two Observers presently in Dovza City, they had all discussed the massive monoculturalism of modern Aka in its large cities, the only places the very few offworlders permitted on the planet were allowed to live. They were all convinced that Akan society must have diversities and regional variations and frustrated that they had no way to find out.

"Sectarians, I suspect, rather than ethnic. A cult. Possibly remnants in hiding of a banned religion."

"Ah," she said, trying to preserve her expression of interest.

Tong was still searching his files. "I'm looking for the little I've gathered on the subject. Sociocultural Bureau reports on surviving criminal antiscientific cult activities. And also a few rumors and tales. Secret rites, walking on the wind, miraculous cures, predictions of the future. The usual."

To fall heir to a history of three million years was to find little in human behavior or invention that could be called un-usual. Though the Hainish bore it lightly, it was a burden on their various descendants to know that they would have a hard time finding a new thing, even an imaginary new thing, under any sun.

Sutty said nothing.

"In the material the First Observers here sent to Terra," Tong pursued, "did anything concerning religions get through?"

"Well, since nothing but the language report came through undamaged, information about anything was pretty much only what we could infer from vocabulary."

"All that information from the only people ever allowed to study Aka freely—lost in a glitch," said Tong, sitting back and letting a search complete itself in his files. "What terrible luck! Or was it a glitch?"

Like all Chiffewarians, Tong was quite hairless—a chihuahua, in the slang of Valparaíso. To minimize his outlandishness here, where baldness was very uncommon, he wore a hat; but since the Akans seldom wore hats, he looked perhaps more alien with it than without it. He was a gentle-mannered man, informal, straightforward, putting Sutty as much at her ease as she was capable of being; yet he was so uninvasive as to be, finally, aloof. Himself uninvadable, he offered no intimacy. She was grateful that he accepted her distance. Up to now, he had kept his. But she felt his question as disingenuous. He knew, surely, that the loss of the transmission had been no accident. Why should she have to explain it? She had made it clear that she was traveling without luggage, just as Observers and Mobiles who'd been in space for centuries did. She was not answerable for the place she had left sixty light-years behind her. She was not responsible for Terra and its holy terrorism.

But the silence went on, and she said at last, "The Beijing ansible was sabotaged."

"Sabotaged?"

She nodded.

"By the Unists?"

"Toward the end of the regime there were attacks on most of the Ekumenical installations and the treaty areas. The Pales."

"Were many of them destroyed?"

He was trying to draw her out. To get her to talk about it. Anger flooded into her, rage. Her throat felt tight. She said nothing, because she was unable to say anything.

A considerable pause.

"Nothing but the language got through, then," Tong said.

"Almost nothing."

"Terrible luck!" he repeated energetically. "That the First

Observers were Terran, so they sent their report to Terra instead of Hain—not unnaturally, but still, bad luck. And even worse, maybe, that ansible transmissions sent *from* Terra all got through. All the technical information the Akans asked for and Terra sent, without any question or restriction. . . . Why, why would the First Observers have agreed to such a massive cultural intervention?"

"Maybe they didn't. Maybe the Unists sent it."

"Why would the Unists start Aka marching to the stars?"

She shrugged. "Proselytising."

"You mean, persuading others to believe what they believed? Was industrial technological progress incorporated as an element of the Unist religion?"

She kept herself from shrugging.

"So during that period when the Unists refused ansible contact with the Stabiles on Hain, they were . . . *converting* the Akans? Sutty, do you think they may have sent, what do you call them, missionaries, here?"

"I don't know."

He was not probing her, not trapping her. Eagerly pursuing his own thoughts, he was only trying to get her, a Terran, to explain to him what the Terrans had done and why. But she would not and could not explain or speak for the Unists.

Picking up her refusal to speculate, he said, "Yes, yes, I'm sorry. Of course you were scarcely in the confidence of the Unist leaders! But I've just had an idea, you see— If they did send missionaries, and if they transgressed Akan codes in some way, you see?—that might explain the Limit Law." He meant the abrupt announcement, made fifty years ago and enforced ever since, that only four offworlders would be allowed on Aka at a time, and only in the cities. "And it could explain the banning of religion a few years later!" He was carried away by his theory. He beamed, and then asked her almost pleadingly, "You never heard of a second group sent here from Terra?"

"No."

He sighed, sat back. After a minute he dismissed his speculations with a little flip of his hand. "We've been here seventy years," he said, "and all we know is the vocabulary."

She relaxed. They were off Terra, back on Aka. She was safe. She spoke carefully, but with the fluency of relief. "In my last year in training, some facsimile artifacts were reconstituted from the damaged records. Pictures, a few fragments of books. But not enough to extrapolate any major cultural elements from. And since the Corporation State was in place when I arrived, I don't know anything about what it replaced. I don't even know when religion was outlawed here. About forty years ago?" She heard her voice: placating, false, forced. Wrong.

Tong nodded. "Thirty years after the first contact with the Ekumen. The Corporation put out the first decree declaring 'religious practice and teaching' unlawful. Within a few years they were announcing appalling penalties. . . . But what's odd about it, what made me think the impetus might have come from offworld, is the word they use for religion."

"Derived from Hainish," Sutty said, nodding.

"Was there no native word? Do you know one?"

"No," she said, after conscientiously going through not only her Dovzan vocabulary but several other Akan languages she had studied at Valparaíso. "I don't."

A great deal of the recent vocabulary of Dovzan of course came from offworld, along with the industrial technologies; but that they should borrow a word for a native institution in order to outlaw it? Odd indeed. And she should have noticed it. She would have noticed it, if she had not tuned out the word, the thing, the subject, whenever it came up. Wrong. Wrong.

Tong had become a bit distracted; the item he had been searching for had turned up at last, and he set his noter to retrieve and decode. This took some time. "Akan microfiling leaves something to be desired," he said, poking a final key.

"'Everything breaks down on schedule,'" Sutty said. "That's the only Akan joke I know. The trouble with it is, it's true."

"But consider what they've accomplished in seventy years!" The Envoy sat back, warmly discursive, his hat slightly askew. "Rightly or wrongly, they were given the blueprint for a G86." G86 was Hainish historians' shorthand jargon for a society in fast-forward industrial technological mode. "And they devoured that information in one gulp. Remade their culture, established the Corporate worldstate, got a spaceship off to Hain—all in a single human lifetime! Amazing people, really. Amazing unity of discipline!"

Sutty nodded dutifully.

"But there must have been resistance along the way. This anti-religious obsession. . . . Even if we triggered it along with the technological expansion. . . ."

It was decent of him, Sutty thought, to keep saying "we," as if the Ekumen had been responsible for Terra's intervention in Aka. That was the underlying Hainish element in Ekumenical thinking: *Take responsibility.*

The Envoy was pursuing his thought. "The mechanisms of control are so pervasive and effective, they must have been set up in response to something powerful, don't you think? If resistance to the Corporate State centered in a religion—a well-established, widespread religion—that would explain the Corporation's suppression of religious practices. And the attempt to set up national theism as a replacement. God as Reason, the Hammer of Pure Science, all that. In the name of which to destroy the temples, ban the preachings. What do you think?"

"I think it understandable," Sutty said.

It was perhaps not the response he had expected. They were silent for a minute.

"The old writing, the ideograms," Tong said, "you can read them fluently?"

"It was all there was to learn when I was in training. It was the only writing on Aka, seventy years ago."

"Of course," he said, with the disarming Chiffewarian gesture that signified *Please forgive the idiot.* "Coming from only twelve years' distance, you see, I learned only the modern script."

"Sometimes I've wondered if I'm the only person on Aka who can read the ideograms. A foreigner, an offworlder. Surely not."

"Surely not. Although the Dovzans are a systematic people. So systematic that when they banned the old script, they also systematically destroyed whatever was written in it—poems, plays, history, philosophy. Everything, you think?"

She remembered the increasing bewilderment of her early weeks in Dovza City: her incredulity at the scant and vapid contents of what they called libraries, the blank wall that met all her attempts at research, when she had still believed there had to be some remnants, somewhere, of the literature of an entire world.

"If they find any books or texts, even now, they destroy them," she said. "One of the principal bureaus of the Ministry of Poetry is the Office of Book Location. They find books, confiscate them, and send them to be pulped for building material. Insulating material. The old books are referred to as pulpables. A woman there told me that she was going to be sent to another bureau because there were no more pulpables in Dovza. It was clean, she said. Cleansed."

She heard her voice getting edgy. She looked away, tried to ease the tension in her shoulders.

Tong Ov remained calm. "An entire history lost, wiped out, as if by a terrible disaster," he said. "Extraordinary!"

"Not that unusual," she said, very edgily— Wrong. She rearranged her shoulders again, breathed in once and out once, and spoke with conscious quietness. "The few Akan poems and drawings that were reconstructed at the Terran Ansible Center would be illegal here. I had copies with me in my noter. I erased them."

"Yes. Yes, quite right. We can't introduce anything that they don't want to have lying about."

"I hated to do it. I felt I was colluding."

"The margin between collusion and respect can be narrow," Tong said. "Unfortunately, we exist in that margin, here."

For a moment she felt a dark gravity in him. He was looking away, looking far away. Then he was back with her, genial and serene.

"But then," he said, "there are a good many scraps of the old calligraphy painted up here and there around the city, aren't there? No doubt it's considered harmless since no one now can read it. . . . And things tend to survive in out-of-the-way places. I was down in the river district one evening —it's quite disreputable, I shouldn't have been there, but now and then one can wander about in a city this size without one's hosts knowing it. At least I pretend they don't. At any rate, I heard some unusual music. Wooden instruments. Illegal intervals."

She looked her question.

"Composers are required by the Corporation State to use what I know as the Terran octave."

Sutty looked stupid.

Tong sang an octave.

Sutty tried to look intelligent.

"They call it the Scientific Scale of Intervals, here," Tong said. And still seeing no great sign of understanding, he asked, smiling, "Does Akan music sound rather more familiar to you than you had expected?"

"I hadn't thought about it—I don't know. I can't carry a tune. I don't know what keys are."

Tong's smile grew broad. "To my ear Akan music sounds as if none of them knew what a key is. Well, what I heard down in the river district wasn't like the music on the loudspeakers at all. Different intervals. Very subtle harmonies. 'Drug music,' the people there called it. I gathered that drug music is played by faith healers, witch doctors. So one way and another I managed eventually to arrange a chat with one of these doctors. He said, 'We know some of the old songs and medicines. We don't know the stories. We can't tell them. The people who told the stories are gone.' I pressed him a little, and he said, 'Maybe some of them are still up the river there. In the mountains.'" Tong Ov smiled again, but wistfully. "I longed for more, but of course my presence there put him at risk." He made rather a long pause. "One has this sense, sometimes, that . . ."

"That it's all our fault."

After a moment he said, "Yes. It is. But since we're here, we have to try to keep our presence light."

Chiffewarians took responsibility, but did not cultivate guilt the way Terrans did. She knew she had misinterpreted him. She knew he was surprised by what she had said. But she could not keep anything light. She said nothing.

"What do you think the witch doctor meant, about stories and the people who told them?"

She tried to get her mind around the question but couldn't. She could not follow him any further. She knew what the saying meant: to come to the end of your tether. Her tether choked her, tight around her throat.

She said, "I thought you sent for me to tell me you were transferring me."

"Off the planet? No! No, no," Tong said, with surprise and a quiet kindness.

"I shouldn't have been sent here."

"Why do you say that?"

"I trained as a linguist and in literature. Aka has one language left and no literature. I wanted to be a historian. How can I, on a world that's destroyed its history?"

"It's not easy," Tong said feelingly. He got up to check the file recorder. He said, "Please tell me, Sutty, is the institutionalised homophobia very difficult for you?"

"I grew up with it."

"Under the Unists."

"Not only the Unists."

"I see," Tong said. Still standing, he spoke carefully, looking at her; she looked down. "I know that you lived through a great religious upheaval. And I think of Terra as a world whose history has been shaped by religions. So I see you as the best fitted of us to investigate the vestiges, if they exist, of this world's religion. Ki Ala has no experience of religion, you see, and Garru has no detachment from it." He stopped again. She made no response. "Your experience," he said, "may have been of a kind that would make detachment difficult for you. To have lived all your life under theocratic repression, and the turmoil and violence of the last years of Unism. . . ."

She had to speak. She said coldly, "I believe my training will allow me to observe another culture without excessive prejudice."

"Your training and your own temperament: yes. I believe so too. But the pressures of an aggressive theocracy, the great weight of it all through your life, may well have left you a residue of distrust, of resistance. If I'm asking you—again!—to observe something you detest, please tell me that."

After a few seconds which seemed long to her she said, "I really am no good at all with music."

"I think the music is a small element of something very large," said Tong, doe-eyed, implacable.

"I see no problem, then," she said. She felt cold, false, defeated. Her throat ached.

Tong waited a little for her to say more, and then accepted her word. He picked up the microcrystal record and gave it to her. She took it automatically.

"Read this and listen to the music here in the library, please, and then erase it," he said. "Erasure is an art we must learn from the Akans. Seriously! I mean it. The Hainish want to hang on to everything. The Akans want to throw everything away. Maybe there's a middle way? At any rate, we have our first chance to get into an area where maybe history wasn't erased so thoroughly."

"I don't know if I'll know what I'm seeing when I see it. Ki Ala's been here ten years. You've had experience on four other worlds." She had told him there was no problem. She had said she could do what he asked. Now she heard herself still trying to whine her way out of it. Wrong. Shameful.

"I've never lived through a great social revolution," Tong said. "Nor has Ki Ala. We're children of peace, Sutty. I need a child of conflict. Anyhow, Ki Ala is illiterate. I am illiterate. You can read."

"Dead languages in a banned script."

Tong looked at her again for a minute in silence, with an intellectual, impersonal, real tenderness. "I believe you tend to undervalue your capacities, Sutty," he said. "The Stabiles chose you to be one of the four representatives of the Ekumen on Aka. I need you to accept the fact that your experience and your knowledge are essential to me, to our work here. Please consider that."

He waited until she said, "I will."

"Before you go up to the mountains, if you do, I also want you to consider the risks. Or rather to consider the fact that we don't know what the risks may be. The Akans seem not to be a violent people; but that's hard to judge from our insulated position. I don't know why they've suddenly given us this permission. Surely they have some reason or motive, but we can find what it is only by taking advantage of it." He paused, his eyes still on her. "There's no mention of your being accompanied, of having guides, watchdogs. You may be quite on your own. You may not. We don't know. None of us knows what life is like outside the cities. Every difference or sameness, everything you see, everything you read, everything you record, will be important. I know already that you're a sensitive and impartial observer. And if there's any history left on Aka, you're the member of my crew here best suited to find it. To go look for these 'stories,' or the people who know them. So, please, listen to these songs, and then go home and think about it, and tell me your decision tomorrow. *O.K.?*"

He said the old Terran phrase stiffly, with some pride in the accomplishment. Sutty tried to smile. "O.K.," she said.

Chapter Two

O N THE WAY home, in the monorail, she suddenly broke into tears. Nobody noticed. Crowded in the car, people tired from work and dulled by the long rocking ride all sat watching the holopro above the aisle: children doing gymnastics, hundreds of tiny children in red uniforms kicking and jumping in unison to shrill cheery music in the air.

On the long climb up the stairs to her apartment she wept again. There was no reason to cry. There had to be a reason. She must be sick. The misery she felt was fear, a wretched panic of fear. Dread. Terror. It was crazy to send her off on her own. Tong was crazy to think of it. She could never handle it. She sat down at her workdesk to send him a formal request for return to Terra. The Hainish words would not come. They were all wrong.

Her head ached. She got up to find something to eat. There was nothing in her foodstorage, nothing at all. When had she eaten last? Not at midday. Not in the morning. Not last night.

"What's wrong with me?" she said to the air. No wonder her stomach hurt. No wonder she had fits of weeping and panic. She had never in her life forgotten to eat. Even in that time, the time after, when she went back to Chile, even then she had cooked food and eaten it, forcing food salty with tears down her throat day after day after day.

"I won't do this," she said. She didn't know what she meant. She refused to go on crying.

She walked back down the stairs, flashed her ZIL at the exit, walked ten blocks to the nearest Corp-Star foodshop, flashed her ZIL at the entrance. All the foods were packaged, processed, frozen, convenient; nothing fresh, nothing to cook. The sight of the wrapped rows made her tears break out again. Furious and humiliated, she bought a hot stuffed roll at the Eat Quick counter. The man serving was too busy to look at her face.

She stood outside the shop on the street, turned away from people passing by, and crammed the food into her mouth, salty with tears, forced herself to swallow, just like back then, back there. Back then she had known she had to live. It was her job. To live life after joy. Leave love and death behind her. Go on. Go alone and work. And now she was going to ask to get sent back to Earth? Back to death?

She chewed and swallowed. Music and slogans blared in broken bursts from passing vehicles. The light at a crossing four blocks away had failed, and robocab horns outblared the music. People on foot, the producer-consumers of the Corporation State, in uniforms of rust, tan, blue, green, or in Corporation-made standard trousers, tunics, jackets, all wearing canvas StarMarch shoes, came crowding past, coming up from the underground garages, hurrying toward one apartment house or another.

Sutty chewed and swallowed the last tough, sweet-salt lump of food. She would not go back. She would go on. Go alone and work. She went back to her apartment house, flashed her ZIL at the entrance, and climbed the eight flights of stairs. She had been given a big, flashy, top-floor apartment because it was considered suitable for an honored guest of the Corporation State. The elevator had not been working for a month.

She nearly missed the boat. The robocab got lost trying to find the river. It took her to the Aquarium, then to the Bureau of Water Resources and Processing, then to the Aquarium again. She had to override it and reprogram it three times. As she scurried across the wharf, the crew of Ereha River Ferry Eight was just pulling in the gangway. She shouted, they shoved the gangway back down, she scrambled aboard. She tossed her bags into her tiny cabin and came out on deck to watch the city go by.

It showed a dingier, quieter side down here on the water, far under the canyon walls of the blocks and towers of business and government. Beneath huge concrete embankments were wooden docks and warehouses black with age, a water-beetle come-and-go of little boats on errands that were no doubt beneath the notice of the Ministry of Commerce, and house-boat communities wreathed in flowering vines, flapping laundry, and the stink of sewage.

A stream ran through a concrete ditch between high dark walls to join the great river. Above it a fisherman leaned on the rail of a humpback bridge: a silhouette, simple, immobile, timeless—the image of a drawing in one of the Akan books they had partially salvaged from the lost transmission.

How reverently she had handled those few pages of images, lines of poems, fragments of prose, how she had pored over them, back in Valparaíso, trying to feel from them what these people of another world were like, longing to know them. It had been hard to erase the copies from her noter, here, and no matter what Tong said, she still felt it as a wrong, a capitulation to the enemy. She had studied the copies in her noter one last time, lovingly, painfully, trying to hold on to them before she deleted them. *And there are no footprints in the dust behind us. . . .* She had shut her eyes as she deleted that poem. Doing so, she felt that she was erasing all her yearning hope that when she came to Aka she'd learn what it was about.

But she remembered the four lines of the poem, and the hope and yearning were still there.

The quiet engines of Ferry Eight drummed softly. Hour by hour the embankments grew lower, older, more often broken by stairs and landings. At last they sank away altogether into mud and reeds and shrubby banks, and the Ereha spread itself out wider and wider and amazingly wider across a flatness of green and yellow-green fields.

For five days the boat, moving steadily eastward on that steady breadth of water through mild sunshine and mild starry darkness, was the tallest thing in sight. Now and then it came to a riverside city where it would tie up at an old dock dwarfed under high new office and apartment towers and take on supplies and passengers.

Sutty found it amazingly easy to talk to people on the boat. In Dovza City everything had conspired to keep her reserved and silent. Though the four offworlders were given apartments and a certain freedom of movement, the Corporation scheduled their lives very closely with appointments, programming and supervising their work and amusements. Not that they were the only ones so controlled: Aka's abrupt and tremendous technological advance was sustained by rigid discipline universally enforced and self-enforced. It seemed that everybody in the city worked hard, worked long hours, slept short hours, ate in haste. Every hour was scheduled. Everybody she'd been in touch with in the Ministries of Poetry and of Information knew exactly what they wanted her to do and how she should do it, and as soon as she started doing as they directed, they hurried off about their business, leaving her to hers.

Though the technologies and achievements of the Ekumenical worlds were held as the shining model for everything on Aka, the four visitors from the Ekumen were kept, as Tong said, in a fish tank. From time to time they were put on display to the public and in the neareals, smiling figures sitting at a Corporation banquet or somewhere near the chief of a bureau giving a speech; but they were not asked to speak. Only to smile. Possibly the ministers did not trust them to say exactly what they ought to say. Possibly the ministers found them rather flat, dull examples of the superior civilisations Aka was striving so hard to emulate. Most civilisations, perhaps, look shinier in general terms and from several light-years away.

Though Sutty had met many Akans and disliked few of them, after a half year on the planet she had scarcely had anything deserving the name of a conversation with any one of them. She had seen nothing of Akan private life except the stiff dinner parties of upper-level bureaucrats and Corporation officials. No personal friendship had ever come even remotely into view. No doubt the people she met had been advised not to talk with her more than necessary, so that the Corporation could remain in full control of the information she received. But even with people she saw constantly, intimacy did not grow. She did not feel this distance as prejudice, xenophobia; the Akans were remarkably unconcerned about foreignness as such. It was that they were all so busy, and all bureaucrats. Conversation went by program. At the banquets people talked business, sports, and technology. Waiting in lines or at the laundry, they talked sports and the latest neareals. They avoided the personal and, in public, repeated the Corporation line on all matters of policy and opinion, to the point of contradicting her when her description of her world didn't tally with what they had been taught about wonderful, advanced, resourceful Terra.

But on the riverboat, people talked. They talked personally, intimately, and exhaustively. They leaned on the railing talking, sat around on the deck talking, stayed at the dinner table with a glass of wine talking.

A word or smile from her was enough to include her in their talk. And she realised, slowly, because it took her by surprise, that they didn't know she was an alien.

They all knew there were Observers from the Ekumen on Aka; they'd seen them on the neareals, four infinitely remote, meaningless figures among the ministers and executives, stuffed aliens among the stuffed shirts; but they had no expectation of meeting one among ordinary people.

She had expected not only to be recognised but to be set apart and kept at a remove wherever she traveled. But no guides had been offered and no supervisors were apparent. It seemed that the Corporation had decided to let her be genuinely on her own. She had been on her own in the city, but in the fish tank, a bubble of isolation. The bubble had popped. She was outside.

It was a little frightening when she thought about it, but she didn't think much about it, because it was such a pleasure. She was accepted—one of the travelers, one of the crowd. She didn't have to explain, didn't have to evade explanation, because they didn't ask. She spoke Dovzan with no more accent, indeed less, than many Akans from regions other than Dovza. People assumed from her physical type—short, slight, dark-skinned—that she came from the east of the continent. "You're from the east, aren't you?" they said. "My cousin Muniti married a man from Turu," and then they went on talking about themselves.

She heard about them, their cousins, their families, their jobs, their opinions, their houses, their hernias. People with pets traveled by riverboat, she discovered, petting a woman's furry and affable kittypup. People who disliked or feared flying took the boat, as a chatty old gentleman told her in vast detail. People not in a hurry went by boat and told each other their stories. Sutty got told even more stories than most, because she listened without interrupting, except to say, Really? What happened then? and How wonderful! or How terrible! She listened with greed, tireless. These dull and fragmentary relations of ordinary lives could not bore her. Everything she had missed in Dovza City, everything the official literature, the heroic propaganda left out, they told. If she had to choose between heroes and hernias, it was no contest.

As they got farther upstream, deeper inland, passengers of a different kind began to come aboard. Country people used the riverboat as the simplest and cheapest way to get from one town to another—walk onto the boat here and get off it there. The towns were smaller now, without tall buildings. By the seventh day, passengers were boarding not with pets and luggage but with fowls in baskets, goats on leashes.

They weren't exactly goats, or deer or cows or any other earthly thing; they were eberdin; but they blatted, and had silky hair, and in Sutty's mental ecology they occupied the goat niche. They were raised for milk, meat, and the silky hair. In the old days, according to a bright-colored page of a picture book that had survived the lost transmission, eberdin had pulled carts and even carried riders. She remembered the blue-and-red banners on the cart, and the inscription under the picture: SETTING OFF FOR THE GOLDEN MOUNTAIN. She wondered if it had been a fantasy for children, or a larger breed of eberdin. Nobody could ride these; they were only about knee-high. By the eighth day they were coming aboard in flocks. The aft deck was knee-deep in eberdin.

The city folk with pets and the aerophobes had all disembarked early that morning at Eltli, a big town that ran a railway line up into the South Headwaters Range resort country. Near Eltli the Ereha went through three locks, one very deep. Above them it was a different river—wilder, narrower, faster, its water not cloudy blue-brown but airy blue-green.

Long conversations also ended at Eltli. The country folk now on the boat were not unfriendly but were shy of strangers, talking mostly to their own acquaintances, in dialect. Sutty welcomed her recovered solitude, which left her eyes to see.

Off to the left as the stream bent north, mountain peaks spired up one after another, black rock, white glaciers. Ahead of the boat, upstream, no peaks were visible, nothing dramatic; the land just went slowly up, and up, and up. And Ferry Eight, now full of blatting and squawking and the quiet, intermittent voices of the country people, and smelling of manure, fried bread, fish, and sweet melons, moved slowly, her silent engines working hard against the drastic current, between wide rocky shores and treeless plains of thin, pale, plumy grass. Curtains of rain swept across the land, dropping from vast, quick clouds, and trailed off leaving sunlight, diamond air, the fragrance of the soil. Night was silent, cold, starlit. Sutty stayed up late and waked early. She came out on deck. The east was brightening. Over the shadowy western plains, dawn lit the far peaks one by one like matches.

The boat stopped where no town or village was, no sign of habitation. A woman in fleece tunic and felt hat crowded her flock onto the gangplank, and they ran ashore, she running with them, shouting curses at them and raucous goodbyes to friends aboard. From the aft rail Sutty watched the flock for miles, a shrinking pale blot on the grey-gold plain. All that ninth day passed in a trance of light. The boat moved slowly. The river, now clear as the wind, rushed by so silently that the boat seemed to float above it, between two airs. All around them were levels of rock and pale grass, pale distances. The mountains were lost, hidden by the vast swell of rising land. Land, and sky, and the river crossing from one to the other.

This is a longer journey, Sutty thought, standing again at the rail that evening, than my journey from Earth to Aka.

And she thought of Tong Ov, who might have made this journey himself and had given it to her to make, and wondered how to thank him. By seeing, by describing, by recording, yes. But she could not record her happiness. The word itself destroyed it.

She thought: Pao should be here. By me. She would have been here. We would have been happy.

The air darkened, the water held the light.

One other person was on deck. He was the only other passenger who had been on the boat all the way from the capital, a silent, fortyish man, a Corporation official in blue and tan. Uniforms were ubiquitous on Aka. Schoolchildren wore scarlet shorts and tunics: masses and lines and little hopping dots of brilliant red all over the streets of the cities, a startling, cheerful sight. College students wore green and rust. Blue and tan was the Sociocultural Bureau, which included the Central Ministry of Poetry and Art and the World Ministry of Information. Sutty was very familiar with blue and tan. Poets wore blue and tan—official poets, at any rate—and producers of tapes and neareals, and librarians, and bureaucrats in branches of the bureau with which Sutty was less familiar, such as Ethical Purity. The insignia on this man's jacket identified him as a Monitor, fairly high in the hierarchy. When she was first aboard, expecting some kind of official presence or supervision, some watchdog watching her excursion, Sutty had waited for him to show some attention to her or evidence of keeping an eye on her. She saw nothing of the kind. If he knew who she was, nothing in his demeanor showed it. He had been entirely silent and aloof, ate at the captain's table at meals, communicated only with his noter, and avoided the groups of talkers that she always joined.

Now he came to stand at the rail not far from her. She nodded and ignored him, which was what he had always appeared to want.

But he spoke, breaking the intense silence of the vast dusk landscape, where only the water murmured its resistance quietly and fiercely to the boat's prow and sides. "A dreary country," the Monitor said.

His voice roused a young eberdin tied to a stanchion nearby. It bleated softly, Ma-ma! and shook its head.

"Barren," the man said. "Backward. Are you interested in lovers' eyes?"

Ma-ma! said the little eberdin.

"Excuse me?" said Sutty.

"Lovers' eyes. Gems, jewels."

"Why are they called that?"

"Primitive fancy. Imagined resemblance." The man's glance crossed hers for a moment. In so far as she had thought anything about him at all, she had thought him stiff and dull, a little egocrat. The cold keenness of his look surprised her.

"They're found along stream banks, in the high country. Only there," he said, pointing upstream, "and only on this planet. I take it some other interest brought you here."

He did know who she was, then. And from his manner, he wished her to know that he disapproved of her being on the loose, on her own.

"In the short time I've been on Aka, I've seen only Dovza City. I received permission to do some sightseeing."

"To go upriver," the man said with a tight pseudo-smile. He

waited for more. She felt a pressure from him, an expectancy, as if he considered her accountable to him. She resisted.

He gazed at the purplish plains fading into night and then down at the water that seemed still to hold some transparency of light within it. He said, "Dovza is a land of beautiful scenery. Rich farmlands, prosperous industries, delightful resorts in the South Headwaters Range. Having seen nothing of that, why did you choose to visit this desert?"

"I come from a desert," Sutty said.

That shut him up for a bit.

"We know that Terra is a rich, progressive world." His voice was dark with disapproval.

"Some of my world is fertile. Much of it is still barren. We have misused it badly. . . . It's a whole world, Monitor. With room enough for a lot of variety. Just as here."

She heard the note of challenge in her voice.

"Yet you prefer barren places and backward methods of travel?"

This was not the exaggerated respect shown her by people in Dovza City, who had treated her as a fragile exotic that must be sheltered from reality. This was suspicion, distrust. He was telling her that aliens should not be allowed to wander about alone. The first xenophobia she'd met on Aka.

"I like boats," she said, with care, pleasantly. "And I find this country beautiful. Austere but beautiful. Don't you?"

"No," he said, an order. No disagreement allowed. The corporate, official voice.

"So what brings you up the river? Are you looking for lovers' eyes?" She spoke lightly, even a bit flirtily, allowing him to change tone and get out of the challenge-response mode if he wanted to.

He didn't. "Business," he said. *Vizdiat*, the ultimate Akan justification, the inarguable aim, the bottom line. "There are pockets of cultural fossilisation and recalcitrant reactionary activity in this area. I hope you have no intention of traveling out of town into the high country. Where education has not yet reached, the natives are brutal and dangerous. In so far as I have jurisdiction in this area, I must ask you to remain in touch with my office at all times, to report any evidence of illegal practices, and to inform us if you plan to travel."

"I appreciate your concern and shall endeavor to comply with your request," Sutty said, straight out of *Advanced Exercises in Dovzan Usage and Locutions for Barbarians.*

The Monitor nodded once, his eyes on the slowly passing, slowly darkening shore. When she looked again where he had stood he was gone.

Chapter Three

THE WONDERFUL VOYAGE of a ship climbing a river through a desert ended on the tenth day at Okzat-Ozkat. On the map the town had been a dot at the edge of an endless tangle of isobars, the High Headwaters Range. In the late evening it was a blur of whitish walls in the clear, cold darkness, dim horizontal windows set high, smells of dust and dung and rotten fruit and a dry sweetness of mountain air, a singsong of voices, the clatter of shod feet on stone. Scarcely any wheeled traffic. A gleam of rusty light shone on some kind of high, pale, distant wall, faintly visible above ornate roofs, against the last greenish clarity of the western sky.

Corporation announcements and music blared across the wharfs. That noise after ten days of quiet voices and river silence drove Sutty straight away.

No tour guide was waiting for her. Nobody followed her. Nobody asked her to show her ZIL.

Still in the passive trance of the journey, curious, nervous, alert, she wandered through the streets near the river till her shoulder bag began to drag her down and she felt the knife edge of the wind. In a dark, small street that ran uphill she stopped at a doorway. The house door was open, and a woman sat in a chair in the yellow light from within the house as if enjoying a balmy summer evening.

"Can you tell me where I might find an inn?"

"Here," the woman said. She was crippled, Sutty saw now, with legs like sticks. "Ki!" she called.

A boy of fifteen or so appeared. Wordlessly he invited Sutty into the house. He showed her to a high-ceilinged, big, dark room on the ground floor, furnished with a rug. It was a magnificent rug, crimson eberdin wool with severe, complex, concentric patterns in black and white. The only other thing in the room was the light fixture, a peculiar, squarish bulb, quite dim, fixed between two high-set, horizontal windows. Its cord came snaking in one of the windows.

"Is there a bed?"

The boy gestured shyly to a curtain in the shadows of the far corner.

"Bath?"

He ducked his head toward a door. Sutty went and opened it. Three tiled steps went down to a little tiled room in which were various strange but interpretable devices of wood, metal, and ceramic, shining in the warm glow of an electric heater.

"It looks very nice," she said. "How much is it?"

"Eleven haha," the boy murmured.

"The night?"

"For a week." The Akan week was ten days.

"Oh, that's very nice," Sutty said. "Thank you."

Wrong. She should not have thanked him. Thanks were "servile address." Honorifics and meaningless ritual phrases of greeting, leave-taking, permission-asking, and false gratitude, please, thank you, you're welcome, goodbye, fossil relics of primitive hypocrisy—all were stumbling blocks to truthfulness between producer-consumers. She had learned that lesson, in those terms, almost as soon as she arrived. She had trained herself quite out of any such bad habits acquired on Earth. What had made the uncouth thanks jump now from her mouth?

The boy only murmured something which she had to ask him to repeat: an offer of dinner. She accepted without thanks.

In half an hour he brought a low table into her room, set with a figured cloth and dishes of dark-red porcelain. She had found cushions and a fat bedroll behind the curtain; had hung up her clothes on the bar and pegs also behind the curtain; had set her books and notebooks on the polished floor under the single light; and now sat on the carpet doing nothing. She liked the extraordinary sense of room in this room—space, height, stillness.

The boy served her a dinner of roast poultry, roast vegetables, a white grain that tasted like corn, and lukewarm, aromatic tea. She sat on the silky rug and ate it all. The boy looked in silently a couple of times to see if she needed anything.

"Tell me the name of this cereal, please." No. Wrong. "But first, tell me your name."

"Akidan," he whispered. "That's tuzi."

"It's very good. I never ate it before. Does it grow here?"

Akidan nodded. He had a strong, sweet face, still childish, but the man visible. "It's good for the wood," he murmured.

Sutty nodded sagely. "And delicious."

"Thank you, yoz." Yoz: a term defined by the Corporation as servile address and banned for the last fifty years at least. It meant, more or less, fellow person. Sutty had never heard the word spoken except on the tapes from which she had learned Akan languages back on Earth. And 'good for the wood,' was that an evil fossil of some kind too? She might find out tomorrow. Tonight she'd have a bath, unroll her bed, and sleep in the dark, blessed silence of this high place.

A gentle knock, presumably by Akidan, guided her to breakfast waiting on the tray-table outside her door. There was a big piece of cut and seeded fruit, bits of something yellow and pungent in a saucer, a crumbly greyish cake, and a handleless mug of lukewarm tea, this time faintly bitter, with a taste she disliked at first but found increasingly satisfying. The fruit and bread were fresh and delicate. She left the yellow pickled bits. When the boy came to remove the tray, she asked the name of everything, for this food was entirely different from anything she had eaten in the capital, and it had been presented with significant care. The pickled thing was abid, Akidan said. "It's for the early morning," he said, "to help the sweet fruit."

"So I should eat it?"

He smiled, embarrassed. "It helps to balance."

"I see. I'll eat it, then." She ate it. Akidan seemed pleased. "I come from very far away, Akidan," she said.

"Dovza City."

"Farther. Another world. Terra of the Ekumen."

"Ah."

"So I'm ignorant about how to live here. I'd like to ask you lots of questions. Is that all right?"

He gave a little shrug-nod, very adolescent. Shy as he was, he was self-possessed. Whatever it meant to him, he accepted with aplomb the fact that an Observer of the Ekumen, an alien whom he could have expected to see only as an electronic image sent from the capital, was living in his house. Not a trace of the xenophobia she had diagnosed in the disagreeable man on the boat.

Akidan's aunt, the crippled woman, who looked as if she was in constant low-level pain, spoke little and did not smile, but had the same tranquil, acceptant manner. Sutty arranged with her to stay two weeks, possibly longer. She had wondered if she was the only guest at the inn; now, finding her way about the house, she saw there was only one guest room.

In the city, at every hotel and apartment house, restaurant, shop, store, office, or bureau, every entrance and exit ran an automatic check of your personal ID chip, the all-important ZIL, the warranty of your existence as a producer-consumer entered in the data banks of the Corporation. Her ZIL had been issued her during the lengthy formalities of entrance at the spaceport. Without it, she had been warned, she had no identity on Aka. She could not hire a room or a robocab, buy food at a market or in a restaurant, or enter any public building without setting off an alarm. Most Akans had their chip embedded in the left wrist. She had taken the option of wearing hers in a fitted bracelet. Speaking with Akidan's aunt in the little front office, she found herself looking around for the ZIL scanner, holding her left arm ready to make the universal gesture. But the woman pivoted her chair to a massive desk with dozens of small drawers in it. After quite a few tranquil mistakes and pauses to ponder, she found the drawer she wanted and extracted a dusty booklet of forms, one of which she tore off. She pivoted the chair back round and handed the form to Sutty to fill out by hand. It was so old that the paper was crumbly, but it did have a space for the ZIL code.

"Please, yoz, tell me how to address you," Sutty said, another sentence from the *Advanced Exercises.*

"My name is Iziezi. Please tell me how to address you, yoz and deyberienduin."

Welcome-my-roof-under. A nice word. "My name is Sutty, yoz and kind innkeeper." Invented for the occasion, but it seemed to serve the purpose. Iziezi's thin, drawn face warmed faintly. When Sutty gave her the form back, she drew her clasped hands against her breastbone with a slight but very formal inclination of the head. A banned gesture if ever there was one. Sutty returned it.

As she left, Iziezi was putting the form book and the form Sutty had filled out into a desk drawer, not the same one. It looked as if the Corporation State was not going to know, for a few hours anyhow, exactly where individual /EX/HH 440 T 386733849 H 4/4939 was staying.

I've escaped the net, Sutty thought, and walked out into the sunshine.

Inside the house it was rather dim, all the horizontal windows being set very high up in the wall so that they showed nothing but fierce blue sky. Coming outdoors, she was dazzled. White house walls, glittering roof tiles, steep streets of dark slate flashing back the light. Above the roofs westward, as she began to be able to see again, she saw the highest of the white walls—immensely high—a wrinkled curtain of light halfway up the sky. She stood blinking, staring. Was it a cloud? A volcanic eruption? The Northern Lights in daytime?

"Mother," said a small, toothless, dirt-colored man with a three-wheeled barrow, grinning at her from the street.

Sutty blinked at him.

"Ereha's mother," he said, and gestured at the wall of light. "Silong. Eh?"

Mount Silong. On the map, the highest point of the Headwaters Range and of the Great Continent of Aka. Yes. As they came up the river, the rise of the land had kept it hidden. Here you could see perhaps the upper half of it, a serrated radiance above which floated, still more remote, immense, ethereal, a horned peak half dissolved in golden light. From the summit streamed the thin snow-banners of eternal wind.

As she and the barrow man stood gazing, others stopped to help them gaze. That was the impression Sutty got. They all knew what Silong looked like and therefore could help her see it. They said its name and called it Mother, pointing to the glitter of the river down at the foot of the street. One of them said, "You might go to Silong, yoz?"

They were small, thin people, with the padded cheeks and narrow eyes of hill dwellers, bad teeth, patched clothes, thin, fine hands and feet coarsened by cold and injury. They were about the same color of brown she was.

"Go there?" She looked at them all smiling and could not help smiling. "Why?"

"On Silong you live forever," said a gnarly woman with a backpack full of what looked like pumice rock.

"Caves," said a man with a yellowish, scarred face. "Caves full of being."

"Good sex!" said the barrow man, and everybody laughed. "Sex for three hundred years!"

"It's too high," Sutty said, "how could anybody go there?"

They all grinned and said, "Fly!"

"Could a plane land on that?"

Cackles, headshakes. The gnarly woman said, "Nowhere," the yellow man said, "No planes," and the barrow man said, "After three-hundred-year sex, anybody can fly!" And then as they were all laughing they stopped, they wavered like shadows, they vanished, and nobody was there except the barrow man trundling his barrow halfway down the street, and Sutty staring at the Monitor.

On the ship she had not seen him as a big man, but here he loomed. His skin, his flesh, were different from that of the people here, smooth, tough, and even, like plastic. His blue-and-tan tunic and leggings were clean and smooth and like uniforms everywhere on every world, and he didn't belong in Okzat-Ozkat any more than she did. He was an alien.

"Begging is illegal," he said.

"I wasn't begging."

After a slight pause he said, "You misunderstand. Do not encourage beggars. They are parasites on the economy. Alms-giving is illegal."

"No one was begging."

He gave his short nod—all right then, consider yourself warned—and turned away.

"Thank you so much for your charm and courtesy!" Sutty said in her native language. Oh, wrong, wrong. She had no business being sarcastic in any language, even if the Monitor paid no attention. He was insufferable, but that did not excuse her. If she was to obtain any information here, she must stay in the good graces of local officialdom; if she was to learn anything here, she must not be judgmental. The old farfetchers' motto: *Opinion ends reception.* Maybe those people had in fact been beggars, working her. How did she know? She knew nothing, nothing about this place, these people.

She set off to learn her way around Okzat-Ozkat with the humble determination not to have any opinions about it at all.

The modern buildings—prison, district and civic prefectures, agricultural, cultural, and mining agencies, teachers' college, high school—looked like all such buildings in the other cities she'd seen: plain, massive blocks. Here they were only two or three stories high, but they loomed, the way the Monitor did. The rest of the city was small, subtle, dirty, fragile. Low house walls washed red or orange, horizontal windows set high under the eaves, roofs of red or olive-green tile with curlicues running up the angles and fantastic ceramic animals pulling up the corners in their toothy mouths; little shops, their outer and inner walls entirely covered with writing in the old ideographs, whitewashed over but showing through with a queer subliminal legibility. Steep slate-paved streets and steps leading up to locked doors painted red and blue and whitewashed over. Work yards where men made rope or cut stone. Narrow plots between houses where old women dug and hoed and weeded and changed the flow patterns of miniature irrigation systems. A few cars down by the docks and parked by the big white buildings, but the street traffic all on foot and by barrow and handcart. And, to Sutty's delight, a caravan coming in from the country: big eberdin pulling two-wheeled carts with green-fringed tent tops, and two even bigger eberdin, the size of ponies, with bells tied in the creamy wool of their necks, each ridden by a woman in a long red coat sitting impassive in the high, horned saddle.

The caravan passed the facade of the District Prefecture, a tiny, jaunty, jingling scrap of the past creeping by under the blank gaze of the future. Inspirational music interspersed with exhortations blared from the roof of the Prefecture. Sutty followed the caravan for several blocks and watched it stop at the foot of one of the long flights of steps. People in the street also stopped, with that same amiable air of helping her watch, though they said nothing to her. People came out the high red and blue doors and down the steps to welcome the riders and carry in the luggage. A hotel? The owners' townhouse?

She climbed back up to one of the shops she had passed in the higher part of town. If she had understood the signs around the door, the shop sold lotions, unguents, smells, and fertiliser. A purchase of hand cream might give her time to read some of the inscriptions that covered every wall from

floor to ceiling, all in the old, the illegal writing. On the facade
of the shop the inscriptions had been whitewashed out and
painted over with signs in the modern alphabet, but these had
faded enough that she could make out some of the underlying
words. That was where she had made out "smells and fertiliser." Probably perfumes and—what? Fertility? Fertility drugs,
maybe? She went in.

She was at once engulfed in the smells—powerful, sweet,
sharp, strange. A dim, pungent air. She had the curious sensation that the pictographs and ideograms that covered the walls
with bold black and dark-blue shapes were moving, not jump-
ily like half-seen print but evenly, regularly, expanding and
shrinking very gently, as if they were breathing.

The room was high, lighted by the usual high-set windows,
and lined with cabinets full of little drawers. As her eyes adjusted,
she saw that a thin old man stood behind a counter to her left.
Behind his head two characters stood out quite clearly on the
wall. She read them automatically, various of their various meanings arriving more or less at once: *eminent / peak / felt hat / look
down / start up*, and *two / duality / sides / loins / join / separate*.

"Yoz and deyberienduin, may I be of use to you?"

She asked if he had an unguent or lotion for dry skin. The
proprietor nodded pleasantly and began seeking among his
thousand little drawers with an air of peaceful certainty of
eventually finding what he wanted, like Iziezi at her desk.

This gave Sutty time to read the walls, but that distracting
illusion of movement continued, and she could not make
much sense of the writings. They seemed not to be advertise-
ments as she had assumed, but recipes, or charms, or quotations. A lot about branches and roots. A character she knew as
blood, but written with a different Elemental qualifier, which
might make it mean lymph, or sap. Formulas like "the five
from the three, the three from the five." Alchemy? Medicine,
prescriptions, charms? All she knew was that these were old
words, old meanings, that for the first time she was reading
Aka's past. And it made no sense.

To judge by his expression, the proprietor had found a
drawer he liked. He gazed into it for some while with a satisfied look before he took an unglazed clay jar out of it and put
it down on the counter. Then he went back to seeking gently

among the rows of unlabeled drawers until he found another one he approved of. He opened it and gazed into it and, after a while, took out a gold-paper box. With this he disappeared into an inner room. Presently he came back with the box, a small, brightly glazed pot, and a spoon. He set them all down on the counter in a row. He spooned out something from the unglazed pot into the glazed pot, wiped the spoon with a red cloth he took from under the counter, mixed two spoonfuls of a fine, talc-like powder from the gold box into the glazed pot, and began to stir the mixture with the same unhurried patience. "It will make the bark quite smooth," he said softly.

"The bark," Sutty repeated.

He smiled and, setting down the spoon, smoothed one hand over the back of the other.

"The body is like a tree?"

"Ah," he said, the way Akidan had said, "Ah." It was a sound of assent, but qualified. It was yes but not quite yes. Or yes but we don't use that word. Or yes but we don't need to talk about that. Yes with a loophole.

"In the dark cloud descending out of the sky . . . the forked . . . the twice-forked. . . ?" Sutty said, trying to read a faded but magnificently written inscription high on the wall.

The proprietor slapped one hand loudly on the counter and the other over his mouth.

Sutty jumped.

They stared at each other. The old man lowered his hand. He seemed undisturbed, despite his startling reaction. He was perhaps smiling. "Not aloud, yoz," he murmured.

Sutty went on staring for a moment, then shut her mouth.

"Just old decorations," the proprietor said. "Old-fashioned wallpaper. Senseless dots and lines. Old-fashioned people live around here. They leave these old decorations around instead of painting walls clean and white. White and silent. Silence is snowfall. Now, yoz and honored customer, this ointment permits the skin to breathe mildly. Will you try it?"

She dipped a finger in the pot and spread the dab of pale cream on her hands. "Oh, very nice. And what a pleasant smell. What is it called?"

"The scent is the herb immimi, and the ointment is my secret, and the price is nothing."

Sutty had picked up the pot and was admiring it; it was surely an old piece, enamel on heavy glass, with an elegantly fitted cap, a little jewel. "Oh, no, no, no," she said, but the old man raised his clasped hands as Iziezi had done and bowed his head with such dignity that further protest was impossible. She repeated his gesture. Then she smiled and said, "Why?"

". . . *the twice-forked lightning-tree grows up from earth*," he said almost inaudibly.

After a moment she looked back up at the inscription and saw that it ended with the words he had spoken. Their eyes met again. Then he melted into the dim back part of the room and she was out on the street, blinking in the glare, clutching the gift.

Walking back down the steep, complicated streets to her inn, she pondered. It seemed that first the Mobile, then the Monitor, and now the Fertiliser, or whatever he was, had promptly and painlessly co-opted her, involving her in their intentions without telling her what they were. Go find the people who know the stories and report back to me, Tong said. Avoid dissident reactionaries and report back to me, said the Monitor. As for the Fertiliser, had he bribed her to be silent or rewarded her for speaking? The latter, she thought. But all she was certain of was that she was far too ignorant to do what she was doing without danger to herself or others.

The government of this world, to gain technological power and intellectual freedom, had outlawed the past. She did not underestimate the enmity of the Akan Corporation State toward the "old decorations" and what they meant. To this government who had declared they would be free of tradition, custom, and history, all old habits, ways, modes, manners, ideas, pieties were sources of pestilence, rotten corpses to be burned or buried. The writing that had preserved them was to be erased.

If the educational tapes and historical neareal dramas she had studied in the capital were factual, as she thought they were at least in part, within the lifetime of people now living, men and women had been crushed under the walls of temples, burned alive with books they tried to save, imprisoned for life for teaching anachronistic sedition and reactionary ideology. The tapes and dramas glorified this war against the past, relating the bombings, burnings, bulldozings in sternly heroic terms. Brave young men and women broke free from stupid parents, conniving priests, teachers of superstition, fomentors of reaction, and unflinchingly burned the pestilential forests of error, planting healthy orchards in their place—denounced the wicked professor who had hidden a dictionary of ideograms under his bed—blew up the monstrous hives where the poison of ignorance was stored—drove tractors through the flimsy rituals of superstition—and then, hand in hand, led their fellow producer-consumers to join the March to the Stars.

Behind the glib and bloated rhetoric lay real suffering, real passion. On both sides. Sutty knew that. She was a child of violence, as Tong Ov had said. Still she found it hard to keep in mind, and bitterly ironical, that here it was all the reverse of what she had known, the negative: that here the believers weren't the persecutors but the persecuted.

But they were all true believers, both sides. Secular terrorists or holy terrorists, what difference?

The only thing she had found at all unusual in the endless propaganda from the Ministries of Information and Poetry was that the heroes of the exemplary tales usually came in pairs—a brother and sister, or a betrothed or married couple. If a sexual pair, heterosexual, always. The Akan government was obsessive in its detestation of "deviance." Tong had warned her about it as soon as she arrived: "We must conform. No discussion, no question is possible. Anything that can be seen and reported as a sexual advance to a person of the same sex is a capital offense. So tiresome, so sad. These poor people!" He sighed for the sufferings of bigots and puritans, the sufferings and cruelties.

She had scarcely needed his warning, since she had so little contact with people as individuals, but she had of course heeded it; and it had been an element of her early, severe disappointment, her discouragement. The old Akan usages and language she had learned on Earth had led her to think she was coming to a sexually easygoing society with little or no gender hierarchy. The society of her native corner of Earth had still been cramped by social and gender caste, further rigidified by Unist misogyny and intolerance. No place on Earth had been entirely out from under that shadow, not even the Pales. One of the reasons she had specialised in Aka, had learned the languages, was that she and Pao had read in the First Observers' reports that Akan society was not hierarchically gendered and that heterosexuality was not compulsory, not even privileged. But all that had changed, changed utterly, during the years of her flight from Earth to Aka. Arriving here, she had had to go back to circumspection, caution, self-suppression. And danger.

So, then, why did they all so promptly try to enlist her, to use her? She was scarcely a jewel in anybody's crown.

Tong's reasons were superficially plain: he'd jumped at the first chance to send somebody out unsupervised, and chose her because she knew the old writing and language and would know what she found when she found it. But if she found it, what was she supposed to do with it? It was contraband. Illicit goods. Anti-Corporation sedition. Tong had said she was right to delete the fragments of the old books from the ansible transmission. Yet now he wanted her to record such material?

As for the Monitor, he was playing power games. It must be a thrill for a middle-weight supervisor of cultural correctness to find a genuine alien, an authentic Observer of the Ekumen, to give orders to: Don't talk to social parasites—don't leave town without permission—report to the boss man, me.

What about the Fertiliser? She could not shake the impression that he knew who she was, and that his gift had some meaning beyond courtesy to a stranger. No telling what.

Given her ignorance, if she let any of them control her, she might do harm. But if she tried to do anything bold and decisive on her own, she would almost certainly do harm. She must go slow, wait, watch, learn.

Tong had given her a code word to use in a message in case of trouble: "devolve." But he hadn't really expected trouble. The Akans loved their alien guests, the cows from whom they milked the milk of high technology. They wouldn't let her get into danger. She mustn't paralyse herself with caution.

The Monitor's rumbling about brutal tribespeople was bogey talk. Okzat-Ozkat was a safe, a touchingly safe place to live. It was a small, poor, provincial city, dragged along in the rough wake of Akan progress, far enough behind that it still held tattered remnants of the old way of life—the old civilisation. Probably the Corporation had consented to let an offworlder come here because it was so very out of the way, a harmless, picturesque bywater. Tong had sent her here to follow up a hunch or hope of finding under the monolithic, univocal success story of modern Aka some traces of what the Ekumen treasured: the singular character of a people, their way of being, their history. The Akan Corporation State wanted to forget, hide, ban, bury all that, and if she learned anything here, it would not please them. But the days of burying and burning alive were over. Weren't they? The Monitor would bluster and bully, but what could he do?

Nothing much to her. A good deal, perhaps, to those who talked to her.

Hold still, she told herself. Listen. Listen to what they have to tell.

The air was dry at this altitude, cold in the shadow, hot in the sun. She stopped at a cafeteria near the Teachers' College to buy a bottle of fruit juice and sat with it at a table outdoors. Cheery music, exhortations, news about crops, production statistics, health programs blared across the square from the loudspeakers as always. Somehow she had to learn to listen through that noise to what it hid, the meaning under it.

Was its ceaselessness its meaning? Were the Akans afraid of silence?

Nobody about her seemed to be afraid of anything. They were students in green-and-rust Education uniforms. Many had the padded cheekbones and delicate bone structure of the old street people here, but they were plump and shiny with youth and confidence, chattering and shouting across her without seeing her. Any woman over thirty was an alien to them.

They were eating the kind of food she had eaten in the capital, high-protein, sweet-salt packaged stuff, and drinking akakafi, a native hot drink rebaptized with a semi-Terran name. The Corporation brand of akakafi was called Starbrew and was ubiquitous. Bittersweet, black, it contained a remarkable mixture of alkaloids, stimulants, and depressants. Sutty loathed the taste, and it made her tongue furry, but she had learned to swallow it, since sharing akakafi was one of the few rituals of social bonding the people of Dovza City allowed themselves, and therefore very important to them. "A cup of akakafi?" they cried as soon as you came into the house, the office, the meeting. To refuse was to offer a rebuff, even an insult. Much small talk centered around akakafi: where to go for the best powder (not Starbrew, of course), where it was grown and processed, how to brew it. People boasted about how many cups they drank a day, as if the mild addiction were somehow praiseworthy. These young Educators were drinking it by the liter.

She listened to them dutifully, hearing chatter about examinations, prize lists, vacation travel. Nobody talked about reading or course material except two students nearby arguing about teaching preschoolers to use the toilet. The boy insisted that shame was the best incentive. The girl said, "Wipe it up and smile," which annoyed the boy into giving quite a lecture on peer adjustment, ethical goal setting, and hygienic laxity.

Walking home, Sutty wondered if Aka was a guilt culture, a shame culture, or something all its own. How was it that everybody in the world was willing to move in the same direction, talk the same language, believe the same things? Fear of being evil, or fear of being different?

There she was, back with fear. Her problem, not theirs.

Her crippled hostess was sitting in the doorway when she got home. They greeted each other shyly with illegal civilities. Making conversation, Sutty said, "I like the teas you serve so much. Much better than akakafi."

Iziezi didn't slap one hand down and the other across her mouth, but her hands did move abruptly, and she said, "Ah," exactly as the Fertiliser had said it. Then, after a long pause, cautiously, shortening the invented word, she said, "But akafi comes from your country."

"Some people on Terra drink something like it. My people don't."

Iziezi looked tense. The subject was evidently fraught.

If every topic was a minefield, there was nothing to do but talk on through the blasts, Sutty thought. She said, "You don't like it either?"

Iziezi screwed up her face. After a nervous silence she said earnestly, "It's bad for people. It dries up the sap and disorders the flow. People who drink akafi, you can see their hands tremble and their heart jump. That's what they used to say, anyhow.

The old-time people. A long time ago. My grandmother. Now everybody drinks it. It was one of those old rules, you know. Not modern. Modern people like it."

Caution; confusion; conviction.

"I didn't like the breakfast tea at first, but then I did. What is it? What does it do?"

Iziezi's face smoothed out. "That's bezit. It starts the flow and reunites. It refreshes the liver a little, too."

"You're a . . . herb teacher," Sutty said, not knowing the word for herbalist.

"Ah!"

A small mine going off. A small warning.

"Herb teachers are respected and honored in my home-land," Sutty said. "Many of them are doctors."

Iziezi said nothing, but gradually her face smoothed out again.

As Sutty turned to enter the house, the crippled woman said, "I'm going to exercise class in a few minutes."

Exercises? Sutty thought, glancing at the immobile stick-shins that hung from Iziezi's knees.

"If you haven't found a class and would care to come. . . ."

The Corporation was very strong on gymnastics. Everybody in Dovza City belonged to a gymnogroup and went to fitness classes. Several times a day brisk music and shouts of One! Two! blared from the loudspeakers, and whole factories and office buildings poured their producer-consumers out into streets and courtyards to jump and punch and bend and swing in vigorous unison. As a foreigner, Sutty had mostly succeeded in evading these groups; but she looked at Iziezi's worn face and said, "I'd like to come."

She went in to find a place of honor in her bathroom for the Fertiliser's beautiful pot and to change from leggings into loose pants. When she came back out, Iziezi was transferring herself on crutches to a small powered wheelchair, Corporation issue, Starflight model. Sutty praised its design. Iziezi said dismissively, "It's all right in flat places," and took off, jolting and lurching up the steep, uneven street. Sutty walked alongside, lending a hand when the chair bucked and stuck, which it did about every two meters. They arrived at a low building with windows under the eaves and a high double door. One flap had been red and the other blue, with some kind of red-and-blue cloud motif painted above, now showing ghostly pink and grey through coats of whitewash. Iziezi headed her chair straight for the doors and barged them open. Sutty followed.

It seemed pitch-black inside. Sutty was getting used to these transitions from inside dark to outside dazzle and back, but her eyes weren't. Just inside the door, Iziezi paused for Sutty to take her shoes off and set them on a shelf at the end of a dim row of shoes, all black canvas StarMarch issue, of course. Then Iziezi steered her chair at a fearless clip down a long ramp, parked it behind a bench, and levered herself around onto the bench. It seemed to be at the edge of a large matted area, beyond which all was velvet gloom.

Sutty was able to make out shadowy figures sitting here and there cross-legged on the mat. Near Iziezi on the bench sat a man with one leg. Iziezi got herself arranged, set down her crutches, and looked up at Sutty. She made a little patting gesture at the mat near her. The door had opened briefly as someone came in, and in the brief grey visibility, Sutty saw Iziezi smile. It was a lovely and touching sight.

Sutty sat down on the mat cross-legged with her hands in her lap. For a long time nothing else happened. It was, she thought, certainly unlike any exercise class she had ever seen, and far more to her taste. People came in silently, one or two at a time. As her eyes adjusted fully, she saw the room was vast. It must be almost entirely dug into the ground. Its long, low windows, right up where the wall met the ceiling, were of a thick bluish glass that let in only diffuse light. Above them the ceiling went on up in a low dome or series of arches; she could just make out dark, branching beams. She restrained her curious eyes and tried to sit, breathe, and not fall asleep.

Unfortunately, in her experience, sitting meditation and sleep had always tended to converge. When the man sitting nearest her began to swell and shrink like the ideograms on the Fertiliser's shop wall, it roused only a dreamy interest in her. Then, sitting up a little straighter, she saw that he was raising his outstretched arms till the backs of his hands met above his head and then lowering them in a very slow, regular breath-rhythm. Iziezi and some others were doing the same, in more or less the same rhythm. The serene, soundless movements were like the pulsing of jellyfish in a dim aquarium. Sutty joined the pulsation.

Other motions were introduced here and there, one at a time, all arm movements, all in slow breath-rhythm. There would be periods of rest, and then the peaceful swelling and shrinking—stretch and relax, pulse out, draw in—would begin again, first one vague figure then another. A soft, soft sound accompanied the movements, a wordless rhythmic murmur, breath-music seemingly without source. Across the room one figure grew slowly up and up, whitish, undulant: a man or woman was afoot, making the arm gestures while bending forward or back or sideways from the waist. Two or three others rose in the same bonelessly supple way and stood reaching and swaying, never lifting a foot from the ground, more than ever like rooted sea creatures, anemones, a kelp forest, while the almost inaudible, ceaseless chanting pulsed like the sea swell, lifting and sinking . . .

Light, noise—a hard, loud, white blast as if the roof had been blown off. Bare square bulbs glared dangling from dusty vaultings. Sutty sat aghast as all around her people leapt to their feet and began to prance, kick, do jumping jacks, while a harsh voice shouted, "One! Two! One! Two! One! Two!" She stared round at Iziezi, who sat on her bench, jerking like a marionette, punching the air with her fists, one, two, one, two. The one-legged man next to her shouted out the beat, slamming his crutch against the bench in time.

Catching Sutty's eye, Iziezi gestured, Up!

Sutty stood up, obedient but disgusted. To achieve such a beautiful group meditation and then destroy it with this stupid muscle building—what kind of people were these?

Two women in blue and tan were striding down the ramp after a man in blue and tan. The Monitor. His eyes went straight to her.

She stood among the others, who were all motionless now, except for the quick rise and fall of breath.

Nobody said anything.

The ban on servile address, on greetings, goodbyes, any phrase acknowledging presence or departure, left holes in the texture of social process, gaps crossed only by a slight effort, a recurrent strain. City Akans had grown up with the artificiality and no doubt did not feel it, but Sutty still did, and it seemed these people did too. The stiff silence enforced by the three standing on the ramp put the others at a disadvantage. They had no way to defuse it. The one-legged man at last cleared his throat and said with some bravado, "We are performing hygienic aerobic exercises as prescribed in the *Health Manual for Producer-Consumers of the Corporation*."

The two women with the Monitor looked at each other, bored, sour, I-told-you-so. The Monitor spoke to Sutty across the air between them as if no one else were there: "You came here to practice aerobics?"

"We have very similar exercises in my homeland," she said, her dismay and indignation concentrating itself on him in a burst of eloquence. "I'm very glad to find a group here to practice them with. Exercise is often most profitable when performed with a sincerely interested group. Or so we believe in my homeland on Terra. And of course I hope to learn new exercises from my kind hosts here."

The Monitor, with no acknowledgment of any kind except a moment's pause, turned and followed the blue-and-tan women up the ramp. The women went out. He turned and stood just inside the doors, watching.

"Continue!" the one-legged man shouted. "One! Two! One! Two!" Everybody punched and kicked and bounced furiously for the next five or ten minutes. Sutty's fury was genuine at first; then it boiled off with the silly exercises, and she wanted to laugh, to laugh off the shock.

She pushed Iziezi's chair up the ramp, found her shoes among the row of shoes. The Monitor still stood there. She smiled at him. "You should join us," she said.

His gaze was impersonal, appraising, entirely without response. The Corporation was looking at her.

She felt her face change, felt her eyes flick over him with dismissive incredulity as if seeing something small, uncouth, a petty monster. Wrong! wrong! But it was done. She was past him, outside in the cold evening air.

She kept hold of the chair back to help Iziezi zigzag bumpily down the street and to distract herself from the crazy surge of hatred the Monitor had roused in her. "I see what you mean about level ground," she said.

"There's no—level—ground," Iziezi jerked out, holding on, but lifting one hand for a moment toward the vast verticalities of Silong, flaring white-gold over roofs and hills already drowned in dusk.

Back in the front hallway of the inn, Sutty said, "I hope I may join your exercise class again soon."

Iziezi made a gesture that might have been polite assent or hopeless apology.

"I preferred the quieter part," Sutty said. Getting no smile or response, she said, "I really would like to learn those movements. They're beautiful. They felt as if they had a meaning in them."

Iziezi still said nothing.

"Is there a book about them, maybe, that I could study?" The question seemed absurdly cautious yet foolishly rash.

Iziezi pointed into the common sitting room, where a vid/ neareal monitor sat blank in one corner. Stacks of Corporation-issue tapes were piled next to it. In addition to the manuals, which everybody got a new set of annually, new tapes were frequently delivered to one's door, informative, educational, admonitory, inspirational. Employees and students were frequently examined on them in regular and special sessions at work and in college. *Illness does not excuse ignorance!* blared the rich Corporational voice over vids of hospitalised workmen enthusiastically partissing in a neareal about plastic molding. *Wealth is work and work is wealth!* sang the chorus for the Capital-Labor instructional vid. Most of the literature Sutty had studied consisted of pieces of this kind in the poetic and inspirational style. She looked with malevolence at the piles of tapes.

"The health manual," Iziezi murmured vaguely.

"I was thinking of something I could read in my room at night. A book."

"Ah!" The mine went off very close this time. Then silence. "Yoz Sutty," the crippled woman whispered, "books . . ."

Silence, laden.

"I don't mean to put you at any risk."

Sutty found herself, ridiculously, whispering.

Iziezi shrugged. Her shrug said, Risk, so, everything's a risk.

"The Monitor seems to be following me."

Iziezi made a gesture that said, No, no. "They come often

to the class. We have a person to watch the street, turn the lights on. Then we . . ." Tiredly, she punched the air, One! Two!

"Tell me the penalties, yoz Iziezi."

"For doing the old exercises? Get fined. Maybe lose your license. Maybe you just have to go to the Prefecture or the High School and study the manuals."

"For a book? Owning it, reading it?"

"An . . . old book?"

Sutty made the gesture that said, Yes.

Iziezi was reluctant to answer. She looked down. She said finally, in a whisper, "Maybe a lot of trouble."

Iziezi sat in her wheelchair. Sutty stood. The light had died out of the street entirely. High over the roofs the barrier wall of Silong glowed dull rust-orange. Above it, far and radiant, the peak still burned gold.

"I can read the old writing. I want to learn the old ways. But I don't want you to lose your inn license, yoz Iziezi. Send me to somebody who isn't her nephew's sole support."

"Akidan?" Iziezi said with new energy. "Oh, he'd take you right up to the Taproot!" Then she slapped one hand on the wheelchair arm and put the other over her mouth. "So much is forbidden," she said from behind her hand, with a glance up at Sutty that was almost sly.

"And forgotten?"

"People remember. . . . People know, yoz. But I don't know anything. My sister knew. She was educated. I'm not. I know some people who are . . . educated. . . . But how far do you want to go?"

"As far as my guides lead me in kindness," Sutty said. It was a phrase not from the *Advanced Exercises in Grammar for Barbarians* but from the fragment of a book, the damaged page that had had on it the picture of a man fishing from a bridge and four lines of a poem:

> *Where my guides lead me in kindness*
> *I follow, follow lightly,*
> *and there are no footprints*
> *in the dust behind us.*

"Ah," Iziezi said, not a land mine, but a long sigh.

Chapter Four

IF THE MONITOR was keeping her under observation, she could go nowhere, learn nothing, without getting people into trouble. Possibly getting into trouble herself. And he was here to watch her; he had said so, if she'd only listened. It had taken all this time to dawn upon her that Corporation officials didn't travel by boat. They flew in Corporation planes and helis. Her conviction of her own insignificance had kept her from understanding his presence and heeding his warning.

She hadn't listened to what Tong Ov told her either: like it or not, admit it or not, she was important. She was the presence of the Ekumen on Aka. And the Monitor had told her, and she hadn't listened, that the Corporation had authorised him to prevent the Ekumen—her—from investigating and revealing the continued existence of reactionary practices, rotten-corpse ideologies.

A dog in a graveyard, that's how he saw her. *Keep far the Dog that's friend to men, or with his nails he'll dig it up again. . . .*

"Your heritage is Anglo-Hindic." Uncle Hurree, with his wild white eyebrows and his sad, fiery eyes. "You must know Shakespeare and the Upanishads, Sutty. You must know the Gita and the Lake Poets."

She did. She knew too many poets. She knew more poets, more poetry, she knew more grief, she knew more than anybody needed to know. So she had sought to be ignorant. To come to a place where she didn't know anything. She had succeeded beyond all expectation.

After long pondering in her peaceful room, long indecision and anxiety, some moments of despair, she sent her first report to Tong Ov—and incidentally to the Office of Peace and Surveillance, the Sociocultural Ministry, and whatever other bureaus of the Corporation intercepted everything that came to Tong's office. It took her two days to write two pages. She described her boat journey, the scenery, the city. She mentioned the excellent food and fine mountain air. She requested a prolongation of her holiday, which had proved both enjoyable and educational, though hampered by the well-intended but overprotective zeal of an official who thought it necessary to insulate her from conversations and interactions with the local people.

The corporative government of Aka, while driven to control everyone and everything, also wanted very much to please and impress their visitors from the Ekumen. To *measure up*, as Uncle Hurree would have said. The Envoy was expert at using that second motive to limit the first; but her message could cause him problems. They had let him send an Observer into a "primitive" area, but they had sent an observer of their own to observe the Observer.

She waited for Tong's reply, increasingly certain that he would be forced to call her back to the capital. The thought of Dovza City made her realise how much she did not want to leave the little city, the high country. For three days she went on hikes out into the farmlands and up along the bank of the glacier-blue, rowdy young river, sketched Silong above the curlicued roofs of Okzat-Ozkat, entered Iziezi's recipes for her exquisite food in her noter but did not return to "exercise class" with her, talked with Akidan about his schoolwork and sports but did not talk to any strangers or street people, was studiously touristic and innocuous.

Since she came to Okzat-Ozkat, she had slept well, without the long memory-excursions that had broken her nights in Dovza City; but during this time of waiting she woke every night in the depths of the darkness and was back in the Pale.

The first night, she was in the tiny living room of her parents' flat, watching Dalzul on the neareal. Father, a neurologist, abominated vr-proprios. "Lying to the body is worse than torturing it," he growled, looking like Uncle Hurree. He had long ago disconnected the vr modules from their set, so that it functioned merely as a holo TV. Having grown up in the village with no commtech but radios and an ancient 2D television in the town meeting hall, Sutty didn't miss vr-prop. She had been studying, but turned her chair round to see the Envoy of the Ekumen standing on the balcony of the Sanctum, flanked by the white-robed Fathers.

The Fathers' mirror masks reflected the immense throng, hundreds of thousands of people gathered in the Great Square, as a tiny dappling. Sunlight shone on Dalzul's bright, amazing hair. The Angel, they called him now, God's Herald, the Divine Messenger. Mother scoffed and grumbled at such terms, but she watched him as intently, listened to his words as devoutly as any Unist, as anybody, everybody in the world. How did Dalzul bring hope to the faithful and hope to the unbelievers at the same time, in the same words?

"I want to distrust him," Mother said. "But I can't. He is going to do it—to put the Meliorist Fathers into power. Incredible! He is going to set us free."

Sutty had no trouble believing it. She knew, from Uncle Hurree and from school and from her own apparently innate conviction, that the Rule of the Fathers under which she had lived all her life had been a fit of madness. Unism was a panic response to the great famines and epidemics, a spasm of global guilt and hysterical expiation, which had been working itself into its final orgy of violence when Dalzul the "Angel" came from "Heaven" and with his magic oratory turned all that zeal from destruction to loving-kindness, from mass murder to mild embrace. A matter of timing; a tip of the balance. Wise with the wisdom of Hainish teachers who had been through such episodes a thousand times in their endless history, canny as his white Terran ancestors who had convinced everybody else on Earth that their way was the only way, Dalzul had only to set his finger on the scales to turn blind, bigoted hatred into blind, universal love. And now peace and reason would return, and Terra would regain her place among the peaceful, reasonable worlds of the Ekumen. Sutty was twenty-three and had no trouble believing it at all.

Freedom Day, the day they opened the Pale: the restrictions on unbelievers lifted, all the restrictions on communications, books, women's clothing, travel, worship and nonworship, everything. The people of the Pale came pouring out of the shops and houses, the high schools and the training schools into the rainy streets of Vancouver.

They didn't know what to do, really, they had lived so long silent, demure, cautious, humble, while the Fathers preached and ruled and ranted and the Officers of the Faith confiscated, censored, threatened, punished. It had always been the faithful who gathered in huge crowds, shouted praises, sang songs, celebrated, marched here and marched there, while the unbelievers lay low and talked soft. But the rain let up, and people brought guitars and sitars and saxophones out into the streets and squares and began playing music and dancing. The sun came out, low and gold under big clouds, and they went on dancing the joyous dances of unbelief. In McKenzie Square there was a girl leading a round dance, black heavy glossy hair, ivory skin, Sino-Canadian, laughing, a noisy, laughing girl, too loud, brassy, self-confident, but Sutty joined her round dance because the people in it were having such a good time and the boy playing the concertina made such terrific music. She and the black-haired girl came face to face in some figure of the dance they had just invented. They took each other's hands. One laughed, and the other laughed. They never let go of each other's hands all night.

From that memory Sutty plunged soft and straight into sleep, the untroubled sleep she almost always had in this high, quiet room.

Next day she hiked a long way up the river, came back late and tired. She ate with Iziezi, read a while, unrolled her bed.

As soon as she turned the light off and lay down, she was back in Vancouver, the day after freedom.

They had gone for a walk up above the city in New Stanley Park, the two of them. There were still some big trees there, enormous trees from before the pollution. Firs, Pao said. Douglas firs, and spruce, they were called. Once the mountains had been black with them. "Black with them!" she said in her husky, unmodulated voice, and Sutty saw the great black forests, the heavy, glossy black hair.

"You grew up here?" she asked, for they had everything to learn about each other, and Pao said, "Yes I did, and now I want to get out!"

"Where to?"

"Hain, Ve, Chiffewar, Werel, Yeowe-Werel, Gethen, Urras-Anarres, O!"

"O, O, O!" Sutty crowed, laughing and half crying to hear her own litany, her secret mantra shouted out loud. "I do too! I will, I will, I'm going!"

"Are you in training?"

"Third year."

"I just started."

"Catch up!" Sutty said.

And Pao almost did so. She got through three years of work in two. Sutty graduated after the first of those years and stayed on the second as a graduate associate, teaching deep grammar and Hainish to beginning students. When she went to the Ekumenical School in Valparaíso, she and Pao would be apart only eight months; and she would fly back up to Vancouver for the December holiday, so they'd only actually be separated for four months and then four months again, and then together, together all the way through the Ekumenical School, and all the rest of their lives, all over the Known Worlds. "We'll be making love on a world nobody even knows the name of now, a thousand years from now!" Pao said, and laughed her lovely chortling laugh that started down inside her belly, in what she called her tan-tien-tummy, and ended up rocking her to and fro. She loved to laugh, she loved to tell jokes and be told them. Sometimes she laughed out loud in her sleep. Sutty would feel and hear the soft laughter in the darkness, and in the morning Pao would explain that her dreams had been so funny, and laugh again trying to tell the funny dreams.

They lived in the flat they'd found and moved into two weeks after freedom, the dear grubby basement flat on Souché Street, Sushi Street because there were three Japanese restaurants on it. They had two rooms: one with wall-to-wall futons, one with the stove, the sink, and the upright piano with four dead keys that came with the flat because it was too far gone to repair and too expensive to move. Pao played crashing waltzes with holes in them while Sutty cooked bhaigan tamatar. Sutty recited the poems of Esnanaridaratha of Darranda and filched almonds while Pao fried rice. A mouse gave birth to infant mice in the storage cabinet. Long discussions about what to do about the infant mice ensued. Ethnic slurs were exchanged: the ruthlessness of the Chinese, who treated animals as insentient, the wickedness of the Hindus, who fed sacred cows and let children starve. "I will not live with mice!" Pao shouted. "I will not live with a murderer!" Sutty shouted back. The infant mice became adolescents and began making forays. Sutty bought a secondhand box trap. They baited it with tofu. They caught the mice one by one and released them in New Stanley

Park. The mother mouse was the last to be caught, and when they released her they sang:

> *God will bless thee, loving mother*
> *Of thy faithful husband's child,*
> *Cling to him and know no other,*
> *Living pure and undefiled.*

Pao knew a lot of Unist hymns, and had one for most occasions.

Sutty got the flu. Flu was a frightening thing, so many strains of it were fatal. She remembered vividly her terror, standing in the crowded streetcar while the headache got worse and worse, and when she got home and couldn't focus her eyes on Pao's face. Pao cared for her night and day and when the fever went down made her drink Chinese medicinal teas that tasted like piss and mildew. She was weak for days and days, lying there on the futons staring at the dingy ceiling, weak and stupid, peaceful, coming back to life.

But in that epidemic little Aunty found her way back to the village. The first time Sutty was strong enough to visit home, it was strange to be there with Mother and Father and not with Aunty. She kept turning her head, thinking Aunty was standing in the doorway or sitting in her chair in the other room in her ragged blanket cocoon. Mother gave Sutty Aunty's bangles, the six everyday brass ones, the two gold ones for dressing up, tiny, frail circlets through which Sutty's hands would never pass. She gave them to Lakshmi for her baby girl to wear when she got bigger. "Don't hold on to things, they weigh you down. Keep in your head what's worth keeping," Uncle Hurree had said, preaching what he'd had to practice; but Sutty kept the red-and-orange saree of cotton gauze, which folded up into nothing and could not weigh her down. It was in the bottom of her suitcase here, in Okzat-Ozkat. Someday maybe she would show it to Iziezi. Tell her about Aunty. Show her how you wore a saree. Most women enjoyed that and liked to try it on themselves. Pao had tried on Sutty's old grey-and-silver saree once, to entertain Sutty while she was convalescing, but she said it felt too much like skirts, which of course she had been forced to wear in public all her life because of the

Unist clothing laws, and she couldn't get the trick of securing the top. "My tits are going to pop out!" she cried, and then, encouraging them to do so, had performed a remarkable version of what she called Indian classical dance all over the futons.

Sutty had been frightened again, very badly frightened, when she discovered that everything she'd learned in the months before she got the flu—the Ekumenical history, the poems she'd memorised, even simple words of Hainish she had known for years—seemed to have been wiped out. "What will I do, what will I do, if I can't keep things even in my head?" she whispered to Pao, when she finally broke down and confessed to the terror that had been tormenting her for a week. Pao hadn't comforted her much, just let her tell her fear and misery, and finally said, "I think that will wear off. I think you'll find it all coming back." And of course she was right. Talking about it changed it. The next day, as Sutty was riding the streetcar, the opening lines of *The Terraces of Darranda* suddenly flowered out in her mind like great fireworks, the marvelous impetuous orderly fiery words; and she knew that all the other words were there, not lost, waiting in the darkness, ready to come when she called them. She bought a huge bunch of daisies and took them home for Pao. They put them in the one vase they had, black plastic, and they looked like Pao, black and white and gold. With the vision of those flowers an intense and complete awareness of Pao's body and presence filled her now, here in the high quiet room on another world, as it had filled her constantly there, then, when she was with Pao, and when she wasn't with her, but there was no time that they weren't together, no time that they were truly apart, not even that long, long flight down all the coast of the Americas had separated them. Nothing had separated them. *Let me not to the marriage of true minds admit impediment* . . . "O my true mind," she whispered in the dark, and felt the warm arms holding her before she slept.

Tong Ov's brief reply came, a printout, received at a bureau of the District Prefecture and hand-delivered, after inspection of her ZIL bracelet, by a uniformed messenger. *Observer Sutty Dass: Consider your holiday the beginning of a field trip. Continue research and recording personal observations as you see fit.*

So much for the Monitor! Surprised and jubilant, Sutty went outdoors to look up at the bannered peak of Silong and think where to start.

She had gathered in her mind innumerable things to learn about: the meditation exercises; the double-cloud doors, which she had found all over the city, always whitewashed or painted over; the inscriptions in shops; the tree metaphors she kept hearing in talk about food or health or anything to do with the body; the possible existence of banned books; the certain existence of a web or net of information, subtler than the electronic one and uncontrolled by the Corporation, that kept people all over the city in touch and aware at all times of, for instance, Sutty: who she was, where she was, what she wanted. She saw this awareness in the eyes of street people, shopkeepers, schoolchildren, the old women who dug in the little gardens, the old men who sat in the sun on barrels on street corners. She felt it as uninvasive, as if she walked among faint lines of guidance, not bonds, not constraints, but reassurances. That she had not first entered either Iziezi's or the Fertiliser's door entirely by chance now seemed probable, though she could not explain it, and acceptable, though she did not know why.

Now that she was free, she wanted to go back to the Fertiliser's shop. She went up into the hills of the city, began to climb that narrow street. Halfway up it she came face to face with the Monitor.

Released from concern about either obeying or evading him, she looked at him as she had at first on the river journey, not as the object of bureaucratic control looks at the bureaucrat, but humanly. He had a straight back and good features, though ambition, anxiety, authority had made his face hard, tight. Nobody starts out that way, Sutty thought. There are no hard babies. Magnanimous, she greeted him, "Good morning, Monitor!"

Her cheery, foolish voice rang in her own ears. Wrong, wrong. To him such a greeting was mere provocation. He stood silent, facing her.

He cleared his throat and said, "I have been ordered to withdraw my request to you to inform my office of your contacts and travel plans. Since you did not comply with it, I attempted to keep some protective surveillance over you. I am informed that you complained of this. I apologise for any annoyance or inconvenience caused you by myself or my staff."

His tone was cold and dour but he had some dignity, and Sutty, ashamed, said, "No—I'm sorry, I—"

"I warn you," he said, paying no attention, his voice more intense, "that there are people here who intend to use you for their own ends. These people are not picturesque relics of a time gone by. They are not harmless. They are vicious. They are the dregs of a deadly poison—the drug that stupefied my people for ten thousand years. They seek to drag us back into that paralysis, that mindless barbarism. They may treat you kindly, but I tell you they are ruthless. You are a prize to them. They'll flatter you, teach you lies, promise you miracles. They are the enemies of truth, of science. Their so-called knowledge is rant, superstition, poetry. Their practices are illegal, their books and rites are banned, and you know that. Do not put my people into the painful position of finding a scientist of the Ekumen in possession of illegal materials—participating in obscene, unlawful rites. I ask this of you—as a scientist of the Ekumen—" He had begun to stammer, groping for words.

Sutty looked at him, finding his emotion unnerving, grotesque. She said drily, "I am not a scientist. I read poetry. And you need not tell me the evils religion can do. I know them."

"No," he said, "you do not." His hands clenched and unclenched. "You know nothing of what we were. How far we have come. We will never go back to barbarism."

"Do you know anything at all about my world?" she said with incredulous scorn. Then none of this talk seemed worthwhile to her, and she only wanted to get away from the zealot. "I assure you that no representative of the Ekumen will interfere in Akan concerns unless explicitly asked to do so," she said.

He looked straight at her and spoke with extraordinary passion. "Do not betray us!"

"I have no intention—"

He turned his head aside as if in denial or pain. Abruptly he walked on past her, down the street.

She felt a wave of hatred for him that frightened her.

She turned and went on, telling herself that she should be

sorry for him. He was sincere. Most bigots are sincere. The stupid, arrogant fool, trying to tell her that religion was dangerous! But he was merely parroting Dovzan propaganda. Trying to frighten her, angry because his superiors had put him in the wrong. That he couldn't control her was so intolerable to him that he'd lost control of himself. There was absolutely no need to think about him any more.

She walked on up the street to the little shop to ask the Fertiliser what the double-cloud doors were, as she had intended.

When she entered, the high dim room with its word-covered walls seemed part of a different reality altogether. She stood there for a minute, letting that reality become hers. She looked up at the inscription: *In the dark cloud's descent from sky the twice-forked lightning-tree grows up from earth.*

The elegant little pot the Fertiliser had given her bore a motif that she had taken to be a stylised shrub or tree before she saw that it might be a variation on the cloud-door shape. She had sketched the design from the pot. When the Fertiliser materialised from the dark backward and abysm of his shop, she put her sketch down on the counter and said, "Please, yoz, can you tell me what this design is?"

He studied the drawing. He observed in his thin, dry voice, "It's a very pretty drawing."

"It's from the gift you gave me. Has the design a meaning, a significance?"

"Why do you ask, yoz?"

"I'm interested in old things. Old words, old ways."

He watched her with age-faded eyes and said nothing.

"Your government"—she used the old word, *biedins*, "system of officials," rather than the modern *vizdestit*, "joint business" or "corporation"— "Your government, I know, prefers that its people learn new ways, not dwelling on their past." Again she used the old word for people, not *riyingdutey*, producer-consumers. "But the historians of the Ekumen are interested in everything that our member worlds have to teach, and we believe that a useful knowledge of the present is rooted in the past."

The Fertiliser listened, affably impassive.

She forged ahead. "I've been asked by the official senior to me in the capital to learn what I can about some of the old ways that no longer exist in the capital, the arts and beliefs and customs that flourished on Aka before my people came here. I've received assurance from a Sociocultural Monitor that his office won't interfere with my studies." She said the last sentence with a certain vengeful relish. She still felt shaken, sore, from her confrontation with the Monitor. But the peacefulness in this place, the dim air, the faint scents, the half-visible ancient writings, made all that seem far away.

A pause. The old man's thin forefinger hovered over the design she had drawn. "We do not see the roots," he said.

She listened.

"The trunk of the tree," he said, indicating the element of the design that, in a building, was the double-leafed door. "The branches and foliage of the tree, the crown of leaves." He indicated the five-lobed "cloud" that rose above the trunk. "Also this is the body, you see, yoz." He touched his own hips and sides, patted his head with a certain leafy motion of the fingers, and smiled a little. "The body is the body of the world. The world's body is my body. So, then, the one makes two." His finger showed where the trunk divided. "And the two bear each three branches, that rejoin, making five." His finger moved to the five lobes of foliage. "And the five bear the myriad, the leaves and flowers that die and return, return and die. The beings, creatures, stars. The being that can be told. But we don't see the roots. We cannot tell them."

"The roots are in the ground . . . ?"

"The mountain is the root." He made a beautiful formal gesture, the backs of his fingers touching at the tip to shape a peak, then moving in to touch his breast over his heart.

"The mountain is the root," she repeated. "These are mysteries."

He was silent.

"Can you tell me more? Tell me about the two, and the three, and the five, yoz."

"These are things that take a long time to tell, yoz."

"My time is all for listening. But I don't want to waste yours, or intrude on it. Or ask you to tell me anything you don't want to tell me, anything better kept secret."

"Everything's kept secret now," he said in that papery voice.

"And yet it's all in plain sight." He looked round at the cases of little drawers and the walls above them entirely covered with words, charms, poems, formulas. Today in Sutty's eyes the ideograms did not swell and shrink, did not breathe, but rested motionless on the high, dim walls. "But to so many they aren't words, only old scratches. So the police leave them alone. . . . In my mother's time, all children could read. They could begin to read the story. The telling never stopped. In the forests and the mountains, in the villages and the cities, they were telling the story, telling it aloud, reading it aloud. Yet it was all secret then too. The mystery of the beginning, of the roots of the world, the dark. The grave, yoz. Where it begins."

So her education began. Though later she thought it had truly begun when she sat at the little tray-table in her room in Iziezi's house, with the first taste of that food on her tongue.

One of the historians of Darranda said: *To learn a belief without belief is to sing a song without the tune.*

A yielding, an obedience, a willingness to accept these notes as the right notes, this pattern as the true pattern, is the essential gesture of performance, translation, and understanding. The gesture need not be permanent, a lasting posture of the mind or heart; yet it is not false. It is more than the suspension of disbelief needed to watch a play, yet less than a conversion. It is a position, a posture in the dance. So Sutty's teachers, gathered from many worlds to the city Valparaíso de Chile, had taught her, and she had had no cause to question their teaching.

She had come to Aka to learn how to sing this world's tune, to dance its dance; and at last, she thought, away from the city's endless noise, she was beginning to hear the music and to learn how to move to it.

Day after day she recorded her notes, observations that stumbled over each other, contradicted, amplified, back-tracked, speculated, a wild profusion of information on all sorts of subjects, a jumbled and jigsawed map that for all its complexity represented only a rough sketch of one corner of the vastness she had to explore: a way of thinking and living developed and elaborated over thousands of years by the vast majority of human beings on this world, an enormous interlocking system of symbols, metaphors, correspondences, theories, cosmology, cooking, calisthenics, physics, metaphysics, metallurgy, medicine, physiology, psychology, alchemy, chemistry, calligraphy, numerology, herbalism, diet, legend, parable, poetry, history, and story.

In this vast mental wilderness she looked for paths and signs, institutions that could be described, ideas that could be defined. Instinctively she avoided great cloudy concepts and sought tangibilities, such as architecture. The buildings in Okzat-Ozkat with the double doors that represented the Tree had been temples, *umyazu*, a word now banned, a nonword. Nonwords were useful markers of paths that might lead through the wilderness. Was "temple" the best translation? What had gone on in the umyazu?

Well, people said, people used to go there and listen.

To what?

Oh, well, the stories, you know.

Who told the stories?

Oh, the maz did. They lived there. Some of them.

Sutty gathered that the umyazu had been something like monasteries, something like churches, and very much like libraries: places where professionals gathered and kept books and people came to learn to read them, to read them, and to hear them read. In richer areas, there had been great, rich umyazu, to which people went on pilgrimage to see the treasures of the library and "hear the Telling." These had all been destroyed, pulled down or blown up, except the oldest and most famous of all, the Golden Mountain, far to the east.

From an official neareal she had partissed in while she was in Dovza City, she knew that the Golden Mountain had been made into a Corporate Site for the worship of the God of Reason: an artificial cult that had no existence except at this tourist center and in slogans and vague pronouncements of the Corporation. The Golden Mountain had been gutted, first, however. The neareal showed scenes of books being removed from a great underground archive by machinery, big scoops shoveling books up like dirt into dump trucks, backhoes ramming and scraping books into a landfill. The viewer of the neareal partissed in the operation of one of these machines, while lively, bouncy music played. Sutty had stopped the neareal in the midst of this scene and disconnected the vr-proprios from the set. After that she had watched and listened to Corporation neareals but never partissed in one again, though she reconnected the vr-p modules every day when she left her special research cubicle at the Central Ministry of Poetry and Art.

Memories such as that inclined her to some sympathy with this religion, or whatever it was she was studying, but caution and suspicion balanced her view. It was her job to avoid opinion and theory, stick to evidence and observation, listen and record what she was told.

Despite the fact that it was all banned, all illicit, people talked to her quite freely, trustfully answering her questions. She had no trouble finding out about the yearlong and lifelong cycles and patterns of feasts, fasts, indulgences, abstinences, passages, festivals. These observances, which seemed in a general way to resemble the practices of most of the religions she knew anything about, were now of course subterranean, hidden away, or so intricately and unobtrusively woven into the fabric of ordinary life that the Monitors of the Sociocultural Office couldn't put their finger on any act and say, "This is forbidden."

The menus of the little restaurants for working people in Okzat-Ozkat were a nice example of this kind of obscurely flourishing survival of illicit practices. The menu was written up in the modern alphabet on a board at the door. Along with akakafi, it featured the foods produced by the Corporation and advertised, distributed, and sold all over Aka by the Bureau of Public Health and Nutrition: produce from the great agrifactories, high-protein, vitamin-enriched, packaged, needing only heating. The restaurants kept some of these things in stock, freeze-dried, canned, or frozen, and a few people ordered them. Most people who came to these little places ordered nothing. They sat down, greeted the waiter, and waited to be served the fresh food and drink that was appropriate to the day, the time of day, the season, and the weather, according to an immemorial theory and practice of diet, the goal of which was to live long and well with a good digestion. Or with a peaceful heart. The two phrases were the same in Rangma, the local language.

In her noter in one of her long evening recording sessions, late in the autumn, sitting on the red rug in her quiet room, she defined the Akan system as a religion-philosophy of the type of Buddhism or Taoism, which she had learned about during her Terran education: what the Hainish, with their passion for lists and categories, called a religion of process. "There are no native Akan words for God, gods, the divine," she told her noter. "The Corporation bureaucrats made up a word for God and installed state theism when they learned that a concept of deity was important on the worlds they took as models. They saw that religion is a useful tool for those in power. But there was no native theism or deism here. On Aka, *god* is a word without referent. No capital letters. No creator, only creation. No eternal father to reward and punish, justify injustice, ordain cruelty, offer salvation. Eternity not an endpoint but a continuity. Primal division of being into material and spiritual only as two-as-one, or one in two aspects. No hierarchy of Nature and Supernatural. No binary Dark/Light, Evil/Good, or Body/Soul. No afterlife, no rebirth, no immortal disembodied or reincarnated soul. No heavens, no hells. The Akan system is a spiritual discipline with spiritual goals, but they're exactly the same goals it seeks for bodily and ethical well-being. Right action is its own end. Dharma without karma."

She had arrived at a definition of Akan religion. For a minute she was perfectly satisfied with it and with herself.

Then she found she was thinking about a group of myths that Ottiar Uming had been telling. The central figure, Ezid, a strange, romantic character who appeared sometimes as a beautiful, gentle young man and sometimes as a beautiful, fearless young woman, was called "the Immortal." She added a note: "What about 'Immortal Ezid'? Does this imply belief in an afterlife? Is Ezid one person, two, or many? *Immortal/ living-forever* seems to mean: intense, repeated many times, famous, perhaps also a special 'educated' meaning: in perfect bodily/spiritual health, living wisely. Check this."

Again and again in her notes, after every conclusion: *Check this.* Conclusions led to new beginnings. Terms changed, were corrected, recorrected. Before long she became unhappy with her definition of the system as a religion; it seemed not incorrect, but not wholly adequate. The term *philosophy* was even less adequate. She went back to calling it the system, the Great System. Later she called it the Forest, because she learned that in ancient times it had been called the way through the forest. She called it the Mountain when she found that some of her teachers called what they taught her the way to the mountain. She ended up calling it the Telling. But that was after she came to know Maz Elyed.

She had long debates with her noter about whether any word in Dovzan, or in the older and partly non-Dovzan vocabulary used by "educated" people, could be said to mean sacred or holy. There were words she translated as power, mystery, not-controlled-by-people, part-of-harmony. These terms were never reserved for a certain place or type of action. Rather it appeared that in the old Akan way of thinking any place, any act, if properly perceived, was actually mysterious and powerful, potentially sacred. And perception seemed to involve description—telling about the place, or the act, or the event, or the person. Talking about it, making it into a story.

But these stories weren't gospel. They weren't Truth. They were essays at the truth. Glances, glimpses of sacredness. One was not asked to believe, only to listen.

"Well, that's how I learned the story," they would say, having told a parable or recounted a historical episode or recited an ancient and familar legend. "Well, that's the way this telling goes."

The holy people in their stories achieved holiness, if that was what it was, by all kinds of different means, none of which seemed particularly holy to Sutty. There were no rules, such as poverty chastity obedience, or exchanging one's worldly goods for a wooden begging bowl, or reclusion on a mountaintop. Some of the heroes and famous maz in the stories were flamboyantly rich; their virtue had apparently consisted in generosity—building great beautiful umyazu to house their treasures, or going on processions with hundreds of companions all mounted on eberdin with silver harnesses. Some of the heroes were warriors, some were powerful leaders, some were shoemakers, some were shopkeepers. Some of the holy people in the stories were passionate lovers, and the story was about their passion. A lot of them were couples. There were no rules.

There was always an alternative. The story-tellers, when they commented on the legends and histories they told, might point out that that had been a good way or a right way of doing something, but they never talked about *the* right way. And good was an adjective, always: good food, good health, good sex, good weather. No capital letters. Good or Evil as entities, warring powers, never.

This system wasn't a religion at all, Sutty told her noter with increasing enthusiasm. Of course it had a spiritual dimension. In fact, it *was* the spiritual dimension of life for those who lived it. But religion as an institution demanding belief and claiming authority, religion as a community shaped by a knowledge of foreign deities or competing institutions, had never existed on Aka.

Until, perhaps, the present time.

Aka's habitable lands were a single huge continent with an immensely long archipelago off its eastern coast. Dovza was the farthest southwestern region of the great continent. Undivided by oceans, the Akans were physically all of one type with slight local variations. All the Observers had remarked on this, all had pointed out the ethnic homogeneity, the lack of societal and cultural diversity, but none of them had quite realised that among the Akans there *were no foreigners*. There had never been any foreigners, until the ships from the Ekumen landed.

It was a simple fact, but one remarkably difficult for the Terran mind to comprehend. No aliens. No others, in the deadly sense of otherness that existed on Terra, the implacable division between tribes, the arbitrary and impassable borders, the ethnic hatreds cherished over centuries and millennia. "The people" here meant not *my* people, but people—everybody, humanity. "Barbarian" didn't mean an incomprehensible outlander, but an uneducated person. On Aka, all competition was familial. All wars were civil wars.

One of the great epics Sutty was now recording in pieces and fragments concerned a long-running and bloody feud over a fertile valley, which began as a quarrel between a brother and sister over inheritance. Struggles between regions and city-states for economic dominance had gone on all through Akan history, flaring often into armed conflict. But these wars and feuds had been fought by professional soldiers, on battlefields. It was a very rare thing, and treated in the histories and annals as shamefully, punishably wrong, for soldiers to destroy cities or farmlands or to hurt civilians. Akans fought each other out of greed and ambition for power, not out of hatred and not in the name of a belief. They fought by the rules. They had the same rules. They were one people. Their system of thought and way of life had been universal. They had all sung one tune, though in many voices.

Much of this communality, Sutty thought, had depended on the writing. Before the Dovzan cultural revolution there had been several major languages and innumerable dialects, but they had all used the same ideograms, mutually intelligible to all. Clumsy and archaic as nonalphabetic scripts were in some respects, they could bond and preserve, as Chinese ideograms had done on Earth, a great diversity of languages and dialects; and they made texts written thousands of years ago readable without translation even though the sounds of the words had changed out of all recognition. Indeed, to the Dovzan reformers, that may have been the chief reason for getting rid of the old script: it was not only an impediment to progress but an actively conservative force. It kept the past alive.

In Dovza City she had met nobody who could, or who admitted they could, read the old writing. Her few early questions concerning it met with such disapproval and blank rejection that she promptly learned not to mention the fact that she could read it. And the officials dealing with her never asked. The old writing had not been used for decades; it probably never occurred to them that, through the accident of time lapse during space travel, it had been the writing she learned.

She had not been entirely foolish to wonder, there in Dovza City, if she might actually be the only person in the world who could now read it, and not entirely foolish to be frightened by the thought. If she carried the entire history of a people, not her own people, in her head, then if she forgot one word, one character, one diacritical mark, that much of all those lives, all those centuries of thought and feeling, would be lost forever. . . .

It had been a vast relief to her to find, here in Okzat-Ozkat, many people, old and young, even children, carrying and sharing that precious cargo. Most could read and write a few dozen characters, or a few hundred, and many went on to full literacy. In the Corporation schools, children learned the Hainish-derived alphabet and were educated as producer-consumers; at home or in illicit classes in little rooms behind a shop, a work-shop, a warehouse, they learned the ideograms. They practiced writing the characters on small blackboards that could be wiped clean with a stroke. Their teachers were working people, householders, shopkeepers, common people of the city.

These teachers of the old language and the old way, the "educated people," were called maz. Yoz was a term indicating respectful equality; maz as an address indicated increased re-spect. As a title or a noun, it meant, as Sutty began to under-stand it, a function or profession that wasn't definable as priest, teacher, doctor, or scholar, but contained aspects of them all.

All the maz Sutty met, and as the weeks went on she met most of the maz in Okzat-Ozkat, lived in more or less com-fortable poverty. Usually they had a trade or job to supplement what they were paid as maz for teaching, dispensing medicine and counsel on diet and health, performing certain ceremonies such as marriage and burial, and reading and talking in the evening meetings, the tellings. The maz were poor, not be-cause the old way was dying or was treasured only by the old, but because the people who paid them were poor. This was a hard-bitten little city, marginal, without wealth. But the people supported their maz, paid for their teaching "by the word," as they said. They came to the house of one maz or another in the evening to listen to the stories and the discussions, paying regular fees in copper money, small paper bills. There was no shame in the transaction on either side, no hypocrisy of "dona-tion": cash was paid for value received.

Many children were brought along in the evening to the tellings, to which they listened, more or less, or fell quietly asleep. No fee was charged for children until they were fifteen or so, when they began to pay the same fees as adults. Adoles-cents favored the sessions of certain maz who specialised in reciting or reading epics and romances, such as *The Valley War* and the tales of Ezid the Beautiful. Exercise classes of the more vigorous and martial kind were full of young men and women.

The maz, however, were mostly middle-aged or old, again

not because they were dying out as a group, but because, as they said, it took a lifetime to learn how to walk in the forest.

Sutty wanted to find out why the task of becoming educated was interminable; but the task of finding out seemed to be interminable itself. What was it these people believed? What was it they held sacred? She kept looking for the core of the matter, the words at the heart of the Telling, the holy books to study and memorise. She found them, but not it. No bible. No koran. Dozens of upanishads, a million sutras. Every maz gave her something else to read. Already she had read or heard countless texts, written, oral, both written and oral, many or most of them existing in more than one mode and more than one version. The subject matter of the tellings seemed to be endless, even now, when so much had been destroyed.

Early in the winter she thought she had found the central texts of the system in a series of poems and treatises called *The Arbor*. All the maz spoke of it with great respect, all of them quoted from it. She spent weeks studying it. As well as she could determine, it had mostly been written between fifteen hundred and a thousand years ago in the central region of the continent during a period of material prosperity and artistic and intellectual ferment. It was a vast compendium of sophisticated philosophical reasonings on being and becoming, form and chaos, mystical meditations on the Making and the Made, and beautiful, difficult, metaphysical poems concerning the One that is Two, the Two that are One, all interconnected, illuminated, and complicated by the commentaries and marginalia of all the centuries since. Uncle Hurree's niece, the scholar-pedant, rushed exulting into that jungle of significances, willing to be lost there for years. She was brought back to daylight only by her conscience, which trailed along carrying the heavy baggage of common sense, nagging: But this isn't the Telling, this is just a part of it, just a *small* part of it. . . .

Conscience finally got decisive help in its task from Maz Oryen Viya, who mentioned that the text of *The Arbor* that Sutty had been coming to study at his house every day for a month was only a portion of, and in many places entirely different from, a text he had seen many years ago in a great umyazu in Amareza.

There was no correct text. There was no standard version. Of anything. There was not one *Arbor* but many, many arbors. The jungle was endless, and it was not one jungle but endless jungles, all burning with bright tigers of meaning, endless tigers. . . .

Sutty finished scanning Oryen Viya's version of *The Arbor* into her noter, put the crystal away, knocked her inner pedant on the head, and started all over.

Whatever it was she was trying to learn, the education she was trying to get, was not a religion with a creed and a sacred book. It did not deal in belief. All its books were sacred. It could not be defined by symbols and ideas, no matter how beautiful, rich, and interesting its symbols and ideas. And it was not called the Forest, though sometimes it was, or the Mountain, though sometimes it was, but was mostly, as far as she could see, called the Telling. Why?

Well (said common sense, rudely), because what the educated people *do* all the time is tell stories.

Yes, of course (her intellect replied with some disdain) they tell parables, stories, that's how they *educate*. But what do they *do*?

She set out to observe the maz.

Back on Terra, when she first studied the languages of Aka, she had learned that all the major ones had a peculiar singular/dual pronoun, used for a pregnant woman or animal and for a married couple. She had met it again in *The Arbor* and many other texts, where it referred to the single/double trunk of the tree of being and also to the mythic-heroic figures of the stories and epics, who usually—like the producer-consumer heroes of Corporation propaganda—came in pairs. This pronoun had been banned by the Corporation. Use of it in speech or writing was punishable by fine. She had never heard it spoken in Dovza City. But here she heard it daily, though not publicly, spoken of and to the teacher-officiants, the maz. Why?

Because the maz were couples. They were always couples. A sexual partnership, heterosexual or homosexual, monogamous, lifelong. More than lifelong, for if widowed they never remarried. They took and kept each other's name. The Fertiliser's wife, Ang Sotyu, had been dead fifteen years, but he was still Sotyu Ang. They were two who were one, one who was two.

Why?

She got excited. She was on the track of the central principle of the system: it was the Two that are One. She must concentrate upon understanding it.

Obliging maz gave her many texts, all more or less relevant. She learned that from the interplay of the Two arise the triple Branches that join to make the Foliages, consisting of the Four Actions and the Five Elements, to which the cosmology and the medical and ethical systems constantly referred, and which were built into the architecture and were structural to the language, particularly in its ideogrammatic form. . . . She realised that she was getting into another jungle, a very ancient one, an appallingly exuberant one. She stood on the outskirts and peered in, yearning but cautious, with conscience whining behind her like a dog. Good dog, dharma dog. She did not go into that jungle.

She remembered that she had intended to find what it was that the maz actually did.

They performed, or enacted, or did, the Telling. They told.

Some people had only a little to tell. They owned a book or poem or map or treatise that they had inherited or been given, and that, at least once a year, generally in the winter, they displayed or read aloud or recited from memory to anybody who wanted to come. Such people were politely called educated people, and were respected for owning and sharing their treasure, but they were not maz.

The maz were professionals. They gave a major part of their life to acquiring and sharing what they told, and made their living by doing so.

Some of them, specialists in ceremonies, resembled the priests of conventional Terran religions, officiating at the rites of passage, marriages, funerals, welcoming the newborn into the community, celebrating the fifteenth birthday, which was considered an important and fortunate occasion (One plus Two plus Three plus Four plus Five). The tellings of such maz were mostly formulaic—chants and rituals and recitations of the most familiar hero tales.

Some maz were physicians, healers, herbalists, or botanists. Like the leaders of exercise and gymnastic arts, they told the body, and also listened to the body (the body that was the

Tree, that was the Mountain). Their tellings were factual, descriptive, medical teachings.

Some maz worked mostly with books: they taught children and adults to write and read the ideograms, they taught the texts and ways of understanding them.

But the essential work of the maz, what gave them honor among the people, was telling: reading aloud, reciting, telling stories, and talking about the stories. The more they told, the more they were honored, and the better they told it, the better they were paid. What they talked about depended on what they knew, what they possessed of the lore, what they invented on their own, and, evidently, what they felt like talking about at the moment.

The incoherence of it all was staggering. During the weeks that Sutty had laboriously learned about the Two and the One, the Tree and the Foliage, she had gone every evening to hear Maz Ottiar Uming tell a long mythico-historical saga about the explorations of the Rumay among the Eastern Isles six or seven thousand years ago, and also gone several mornings a week to hear Maz Imyen Katyan tell the origins and history of the cosmos, name the stars and constellations, and describe the movements of the other four planets in the Akan system, while displaying beautiful, accurate, ancient charts of the sky. How did it all hang together? Was there any relation at all among these disparate things?

Fed up with the abstractions of philosophy, for which she had little gift and less inclination, Sutty turned to what the maz called body-telling. The healer maz seemed to know a good deal about maintaining health. She asked Sotyu Ang to teach her about medicine. He patiently began to tell her the curative properties of each of the items in the immense herbary he had inherited from Ang Sotyu's parents, which filled most of the little drawers in his shop.

He was very pleased that she was recording all he told her in her noter. So far she had met no arcane wisdoms in the Telling, no holy secrets that could be told only to adepts, no knowledge withheld to fortify the authority of the learned, magnify their sanctity, or increase their fees. "Write down what I tell you!" all the maz kept saying. "Memorise it! Keep it to tell other people!" Sotyu Ang had spent his adult life learning the properties of the herbs, and having no disciple or apprentice, he was touchingly grateful to Sutty for preserving that knowledge. "It is all I have to give the Telling," he said. He was not a healer himself but an apothecary and herbalist. He wasn't strong on theory; his explanations of why this or that herb worked were often mere associative magic or went in pure verbal circles: this bark dispels fever because it is a febrifuge. . . . But the system of medicine that underlay this pharmaceutics was, as well as she could judge, pragmatic, preventive, and effective.

Pharmacy and medicine were one of the branches of the Great System. There were many, many branches. The endless story-telling of the maz was about many, many things. All things, all the leaves of the immense foliage of the Tree. She could not give up the conviction that there must be some guiding motive, some central concern. The trunk of the Tree. Was it ethics? the right conduct of life?

Having grown up under Unism, she was not so naive as to think there was any necessary relation between religion and morality, or that if there was a relation it was likely to be a benevolent one.

But she had begun to discern and learn a characteristic Akan ethic, expressed in all the parables and moral tales she heard in the tellings, and in the behavior and conversation of the people she knew in Okzat-Ozkat. Like the medicine, the ethic was pragmatic and preventive, and seemed to be pretty effective. It chiefly prescribed respect for your own and everybody else's body, and chiefly proscribed usury.

The frequency with which excess profit making was denounced in the stories and in public opinion showed that the root of all evil went deep on Aka. In Okzat-Ozkat, crime consisted mostly of theft, cheating, embezzlement. There was little personal violence. Assault and battery, perpetrated by thieves or by enraged victims of theft or extortion getting revenge, was so rare that every case of it was discussed for days or weeks. Crimes of passion were even rarer. They were not glamorised or condoned. In the tales and histories, heroism was not earned by murder or slaughter. Heroes were those who atoned for violent acts, or those who died bravely. The word for murderer was a cognate of the word for madman. Iziezi couldn't tell Sutty whether murderers were locked up in a jail or in a madhouse, because she didn't know of any murderers in Okzat-Ozkat. She had heard that in the old days rapists had been castrated, but wasn't sure how rape was punished now, because she didn't know of any cases of it either. Akans were gentle with their children, and Iziezi seemed to find the idea of mistreating children almost inconceivable; she knew some folktales of cruel parents, of children left orphaned who starved because nobody took them in, but she said, "Those stories are from long ago, before people were educated."

The Corporation, of course, had introduced a new ethic, with new virtues such as public spirit and patriotism, and a vast new area of crime: participation in banned activities. But Sutty had yet to meet anybody in Okzat-Ozkat, outside Corporation officials and perhaps some of the students at the Teachers' College, who thought of the maz or anything they did as criminal. Banned, illicit, illegal, deviant: these new categories redefined behavior, but they were without moral meaning except to their authors.

Had there been no crimes, then, in the old days, but rape, murder, and usury?

Maybe there had been no need for further sanctions. Maybe the system had been so universal that nobody could imagine living outside it, and only self-destructive insanity could subvert it. It had been the way of life. It had been the world.

That ubiquity of the system, its great antiquity, the tremendous force of habit it had acquired through its detailed patterning of daily life, food, drink, hours and aims of work and recreation—all this, Sutty told her noter, might explain modern Aka. At least it might explain how the Corporation of Dovza had achieved hegemony so easily, had been able to enforce uniform, minute control over how people lived, what they ate, drank, read, heard, thought, did. The system had been in place. Anciently, massively in place, all over the Continent and Isles of Aka. All Dovza had done was take the system over and change its goals. From a great consensual social pattern within which each individual sought physical and spiritual satisfaction, they had made it a great hierarchy in which each individual served the indefinite growth of the society's material wealth and complexity. From an active homeostatic balance they had turned it to an active forward-thrusting imbalance.

The difference, Sutty told her noter, was between somebody sitting thinking after a good meal and somebody running furiously to catch the bus.

She was pleased with that image.

She looked back on her first half year on Aka with incredulity and with pity both for herself and for the consumer-producers of Dovza City. "What sacrifices these people have made!" she told her noter. "They agreed to deny their entire culture and impoverish their lives for the 'March to the Stars' —an artificial, theoretical goal—an imitation of societies they assumed to be superior merely because they were capable of space flight. Why? There's a step missing. Something happened to cause or catalyse this enormous change. Was it nothing more than the arrival of the First Observers from the Ekumen? Of course that was an enormous event for a people who'd never known outsiders. . . ."

An enormous burden of responsibility on the outsiders, too, she thought.

"Do not betray us!" the Monitor had said. But her people, the starfarers of the Ekumen, the Observers who were so careful not to intervene, not to interfere, not to take control, had brought betrayal with them. A few Spaniards arrive, and the great empires of the Incas, the Aztecs, betray themselves, collapse, let their gods and their very language be denied. . . . So the Akans had been their own conquerors. Bewildered by foreign concepts, by the very concept of foreignness, they had let the ideologues of Dovza dominate and impoverish them. As the ideologues of Communocapitalism in the twentieth century, and the zealots of Unism in her own century, had dominated and impoverished the Earth.

If indeed this process had begun with first contact, perhaps it was by way of reparation that Tong Ov wanted to learn what could be learned of Aka before the First Observers came. Did he have some hope of eventually restoring to the Akans what they had thrown away? But the Corporation State would never allow it. "Look in the garbage for the gold piece," was a saying she had learned from Maz Ottiar Uming, but she didn't think the Monitor would agree with it. To him the gold piece was a rotten corpse.

She had mental conversations with the Monitor quite often during that long winter of learning and listening, reading and practicing, thinking and rethinking. She set him up as her boxing dummy. He didn't get to answer, only to listen to her. There were things she didn't want to record in her noter, things she thought in the privacy of her head, opinions that she couldn't cease to cherish but tried to keep separate from observation. Such as her opinion that if the Telling was a religion it was very different from Terran religions, since it entirely lacked dogmatic belief, emotional frenzy, deferral of reward to a future life, and sanctioned bigotry. All those elements, which the Akans had done so well without, she thought, had been introduced by Dovza. It was the Corporation State that was the religion. And so she liked to summon up the blue-and-tan uniform, the stiff back and cold face of the Monitor, and tell him what a zealot he was, and what a fool, along with all the other bureaucrat-ideologues, for grasping after other people's worthless goods while tossing his own treasure into the garbage.

The actual flesh-and-blood Monitor must have left Okzat-Ozkat; she had not met him in the streets for weeks. It was a relief. She much preferred him as a minatory figment.

She had stopped posing the question about what the maz did. Any four-year-old could have said what they did. They told. They retold, read, recited, discussed, explained, and invented. The infinite matter of their talk was not fixed and could not be defined. And it was still growing, even now; for not all the texts were learned from others, not all the stories were of ancient days, not all the thoughts and ideas had been handed down over the years.

The first time she met the maz Odiedin Manma was at a telling where he told the story of a young man, a villager up in the foothills of Silong, who dreamed that he could fly. The young man dreamed flying so often and so vividly that it seemed he began to take his dreams for waking life. He would describe the sensations of flight and the things he saw from the air. He drew maps of beautiful unknown lands on the other side of the world that he discovered in his flights. People came to hear him tell about flying and to see the marvelous maps.

But one day, climbing down a river gorge after a strayed eber-din, he missed his footing, fell, and was killed.

That was all the story. Odiedin Manma made no comment, and no one asked questions. The telling was at the house of the maz Ottiar and Uming. Sutty later asked Maz Ottiar Uming about the story, for it puzzled her.

The old woman said, "Odiedin's partner Manma was killed in a fall when he was twenty-seven. They had been maz only a year."

"And Manma used to tell his dreams of flying?"

Ottiar Uming shook her head. "No," she said. "That is the story, yoz. Odiedin Manma's story. He tells that one. The rest of his telling is in the body." She meant exercises, gymnastic practice, of which Odiedin was a highly respected teacher.

"I see," Sutty said, and went away and thought about it.

She knew one thing, she had learned one thing for sure, here in Okzat-Ozkat: she had learned how to listen. To listen, hear, keep listening to what she'd heard. To carry the words away and listen to them. If telling was the skill of the maz, listening was the skill of the yoz. As they all liked to remark, neither one was any use without the other.

Chapter Five

WINTER CAME WITHOUT much snow but bitterly cold, winds knifing down out of the immense wilderness of mountains to the west and north. Iziezi took Sutty to a secondhand clothing store to buy a worn but sturdy leather coat lined with its own silky fleece. The hood lining was the feathery fur of some mountain animal of which Iziezi said, "All gone now. Too many hunters." She said the leather was not eberdin, as Sutty had thought, but minule, from the high mountains. The coat came below her knees and was met by light, fleece-lined boots. These were new, made of artificial materials, for mountain sports and hiking. The people of the old way placidly accepted new technologies and products, so long as they worked better than the old ones and so long as using them did not require changing one's life in any important way. To Sutty this seemed a profound but reasonable conservatism. But to an economy predicated on endless growth, it was anathema.

Sutty tramped around the icy streets in her old coat and her new boots. In winter in Okzat-Ozkat everybody looked alike in their old leather coats and fleecy hoods, except for the uniformed bureaucrats, who all looked alike in their coats and hoods of artificial fabrics in bright uniform colors, purple, rust, and blue. The merciless cold gave a kind of fellowship of anonymity. When you got indoors the warmth was an unfailing source of relief, pleasure, companionly feeling. On a bitter blue evening, to struggle up the steep streets to some small, stuffy, dim-lit room and gather with the others at the hearth—an electric heater, for there was little wood here near timberline, and all warmth was generated by the ice-cold energy of the Ereha—and to take your mittens off and rub your hands, which seemed so naked and delicate, and look round at the other windburned faces and ice-dewed eyelashes, and hear the little drum go tabatt, tabatt, and the soft voice begin to speak, listing the names of the rivers of Hoying and how each flowed into the next, or telling the story of Ezid and Inamema on the Mountain of Gam, or describing how the Council of Mez raised an army against the western barbarians—that was a solid, enduring, reliable pleasure to Sutty, all winter long.

The western barbarians, she now knew, were the Dovzans. Almost everything the maz taught, all their legends and history and philosophy, came from the center and east of the great continent, and from past centuries, past millennia. Nothing came from Dovza but the language they spoke; and here that was full of words from the original language of this area, Rangma, and other tongues.

Words. A world made of words.

There was music. Some of the maz sang healing chants like those Tong Ov had recorded in the city; some played string instruments, plucked or bowed, to accompany narrative ballads and songs. Sutty recorded them when she could, though her musical stupidity kept her from appreciating them. There had been art, carvings and paintings and tapestries, using the symbols of the Tree and the Mountain and figures and events from the legends and histories. There had been dance, and there were still the various forms of exercise and moving meditation. But first and last there were the words.

When the maz put the mantle of their office—a flimsy length of red or blue cloth—over their shoulders, they were perceived as owning a sacred authority or power. What they said then was part of the Telling.

When they took the scarf off they returned to ordinary status, claiming no personal spiritual authority at all; what they said then weighed no more than what anybody said. Some people of course insisted on ascribing permanent authority to them. Like the people of Sutty's own tribe, many Akans longed to follow a leader, turn earned payment into tribute, load responsibility onto somebody else's shoulders. But if the maz had one quality in common, it was a stubborn modesty. They were not in the charisma business. Maz Imyen Katyan was as gentle a man as she had ever met, but when a woman called him by a reverent title, munan, used for famous maz in the stories and histories, he turned on her with real rage—"How dare you call me that?"—and then, having regained his calm, "When I've been dead a hundred years, yoz."

Sutty had assumed that since everything the maz did professionally was in defiance of the law, at real personal risk, some of this modest style, this very low profile, was a recent thing. But when she said so, Maz Ottiar Uming shook her head.

"Oh, no," the old woman said. "We have to hide, to keep everything secret, yes. But in my grandparents' time I think most of the maz lived the way we do. Nobody can wear the scarf all the time! Not even Maz Elyed Oni. . . . Of course it was different in the umyazu."

"Tell me about the umyazu, maz."

"They were places built so the power could gather in them. Places full of being. Full of people telling and listening. Full of books."

"Where were they?"

"Oh, everywhere. Here in Okzat-Ozkat there was one up where the High School is now, and one where the pumice works is now. And all the way to Silong, in the high valleys, on the trade roads, there were umyazu for the pilgrims. And down where the land's rich, there were huge, great umyazu, with hundreds of maz living in them, and visiting from one to another all their lives. They kept books, and wrote them, and made records, and kept on telling. They could give their whole life to it, you see. They could always be there where it was. People would go visit them to hear the telling and read the books in the libraries. People went in processions, with red and blue flags. They'd go and stay all winter, sometimes. Save up for years so they could pay the maz and pay for their lodging. My grandmother told me about going to the Red Umyazu of Tenban. She was eleven or twelve years old. It took them nearly the whole year to go and stay and come back. They were pretty wealthy, my grandmother's family, so they could ride all the way, the whole family, with eberdin pulling the wagon. They didn't have the cars and planes then, you know. Nobody did. Most people just walked. But everybody had flags and wore ribbons. Red and blue." Ottiar Uming laughed with pleasure at the thought of those processions. "My mother's mother wrote the story of that journey. I'll get it out and tell it sometime."

Her partner, Uming Ottiar, was unfolding a big, stiff square of paper on the table in the back room of their grocery shop. Ottiar Uming went to help him, setting a polished black stone on each curling corner to keep it flat. Then they invited their five listeners to come forward, salute the paper with the mountain-heart gesture, and study the chart and inscriptions on it. They displayed it thus every three weeks, and Sutty had come each time all winter. It had been her first formal intro-duction to the thought system of the Tree. The couple's most precious possession, given them fifty years ago by their teacher-maz, it was a marvelously painted map or mandala of the One that is Two giving rise to the Three, to the Five, to the Myriad, and the Myriad again to the Five, the Three, the Two, the One. . . . A Tree, a Body, a Mountain, inscribed within the circle that was everything and nothing. Delicate little figures, animals, people, plants, rocks, rivers, lively as flickering flames, made up each of the greater forms, which divided, rejoined, transformed each into the others and into the whole, the unity made up of infinite variety, the mystery plain as day.

Sutty loved to study it and try to make out the inscriptions and poems surrounding it. The painting was beautiful, the poetry was splendid and elusive, the whole chart was a work of high art, absorbing, enlightening. Maz Uming sat down and after a few knocks on his drum began intoning one of the in-terminable chants that accompanied the rituals and many of the tellings. Maz Ottiar read and discussed some of the in-scriptions, which were four or five hundred years old. Her voice was soft, full of silences. Softly and hesitantly, the stu-dents asked questions. She answered them the same way.

Then she drew back and sat down and took up the chant in a gnat voice, and old Uming, half blind, his speech thickened by a stroke, got up and talked about one of the poems.

"That's by Maz Niniu Raying, five, six, seven hundred years back, eh? It's in *The Arbor*. Somebody wrote it here, a good calligrapher, because it talks about how the leaves of the Tree perish but always return so long as we see them and say them. See, here it says: 'Word, the gold beyond the fall, returns the glory to the branch.' And underneath it here, see, somebody later on wrote, 'Mind's life is memory.'" He smiled round at them, a kind, lopsided smile. "Remember that, eh? 'Mind's life is memory.' Don't forget!" He laughed, they laughed. All the while, out front in the grocery shop, the maz' grandson kept the volume turned up high on the audio system, cheery music, exhortations, and news announcements blaring out to cover the illicit poetry, the forbidden laughter.

It was a pity, but no surprise, Sutty told her noter, that an ancient popular cosmology-philosophy-spiritual discipline should contain a large proportion of superstition and verge over into what she labeled in her noter HP, hocus-pocus. The great jungle of significance had its swamps and morasses, and she had at last stumbled into some of them. She met a few maz who claimed arcane knowledge and supernal powers. Boring as she found all such claims, she knew she could not be sure of what was valuable and what was drivel, and painstakingly recorded whatever information she could buy from these maz concerning alchemy, numerology, and literal readings of symbolic texts. They sold her bits of texts and snippets of methodology at a fairly stiff price, grudgingly, hedging the transactions with portentous warnings about the danger of this powerful knowledge.

She particularly detested the literal readings. By such literalism, fundamentalism, religions betrayed the best intentions of their founders. Reducing thought to formula, replacing choice by obedience, these preachers turned the living word into dead law. But she put it all into her noter—which she had now had to unload into crystal storage twice, for she could not transmit any of the treasure-and-trash she was amassing.

At this distance, with all means of communication monitored, there was no way to consult with Tong Ov as to what she should or he intended to do with all this material. She couldn't even tell him she'd found it. The problem remained, and grew.

Among the HP she came on a brand that was, as far as she knew, unique to Aka: a system of arcane significances attached to the various strokes that composed the ideogrammatic characters and the further strokes and dots that qualified them with verbal tense and mode and nominal case and with Action or Element (for everything, literally every thing, could be categorised under the Four Actions and the Five Elements). Every character of the old writing thus became a code to be interpreted by specialists, who functioned much as horoscope readers had in Sutty's homeland. She discovered that many people in Okzat-Ozkat, including officials of the Corporation, would undertake nothing of importance without calling in a "sign reader" to write out their name and other relevant words and, after poring over these and referring to impressively elaborate charts and diagrams, to advise and foretell. "This is the kind of thing that makes me sympathise with the Monitor," she told her noter. Then she said, "No. It's what the Monitor wants from his own kind of HP. Political HP. Everything locked in place, on course, under control. But he's handed over the controls just as much as they have."

Many of the practices she learned about had equivalents on Earth. The exercises, like yoga and tai chi, were physical-mental, a lifelong discipline, leading toward mindfulness, or toward a trance state, or toward martial vigor and readiness, depending on the style and the practitioner's desire. Trance seemed to be sought for its own sake as an experience of essential stillness and balance rather than as satori or revelation. Prayer . . . Well, what about prayer?

The Akans did not pray.

That seemed so strange, so unnatural, that as soon as she had the thought, she qualified it: it was very possible that she didn't properly understand what prayer was.

If it meant asking for something, they didn't do it. Not even to the extent that she did. She knew that when she was very startled she cried, "O Ram!" and when she was very frightened she whispered, "O please, please." The words were strictly meaningless, yet she knew they were a kind of prayer. She had never heard an Akan say anything of the kind. They could wish one another well—"May you have a good year, may your venture prosper"—just as they could curse one another—"May your sons eat stones," she had heard Diodi the barrow man murmur as a blue-and-tan stalked by. But those were wishes, not prayers. People didn't ask God to make them good or to destroy their enemy. They didn't ask the gods to win them the lottery or cure their sick child. They didn't ask the clouds to let the rain fall or the grain grow. They wished, they willed, they hoped, but they didn't pray.

If prayer was praise, then perhaps they did pray. She had come to understand their descriptions of natural phenomena, the Fertiliser's pharmacopoeia, the maps of the stars, the lists of ores and minerals, as litanies of praise. By naming the names they rejoiced in the complexity and specificity, the wealth and beauty of the world, they participated in the fullness of being. They described, they named, they told all about everything. But they did not pray for anything.

Nor did they sacrifice anything. Except money.

To get money, you had to give money: that was a firm and universal principle. Before any business undertaking, they buried silver and brass coins, or threw them into the river, or gave them to beggars. They pounded out gold coins into airy, translucent gold leaf with which they decorated niches, columns, even whole walls of buildings, or had them spun into thread and woven into gorgeous shawls and scarves to give away on New Year's Day. Silver and gold coins were hard to come by, as the Corporation, detesting this extravagant waste, had gone over mostly to paper; so people burned paper money like incense, made paper boats of it and sailed them off on the river, chopped it up fine and ate it with salad. The practice was pure HP, but Sutty found it irresistible. Slaughtering goats or one's firstborn to placate the supernatural seemed to her the worst kind of perversity, but she saw a gambler's gallantry in this money sacrifice. Easy come, easy go. At the New Year, when you met a friend or acquaintance, you each lighted a one-ha bill and waved it about like a little torch, wishing each other health and prosperity. She saw even employees of the Corporation doing this. She wondered if the Monitor had ever done it.

The more naive people that she came to know at the tellings and in the classes, and Diodi and other friendly acquaintances of the streets, all believed in sign reading and alchemical marvels and talked about diets that let you live forever, exercises that had given the ancient heroes the strength to withstand whole armies. Even Iziezi held firmly by sign reading. But most of the maz, the educated, the teachers, claimed no special powers or attainments at all. They lived firmly and wholly in the real world. Spiritual yearning and the sense of sacredness they knew, but they did not know anything holier than the world, they did not seek a power greater than nature. Sutty was certain of that. *No miracles!* she told her noter, jubilant.

She coded her notes, got into her coat and boots, and set off through the vicious early-spring wind for Maz Odiedin

Manma's exercise class. Silong was visible for the first time in weeks, not the barrier wall but only the peak above it, standing like a silver horn over dark storm clouds.

She went regularly to exercise with Iziezi now, often staying on to watch Akidan and other adolescents and young people do "two-one," an athletic form performed in pairs, with spectacular feints and falls. Odiedin Manma, the teller of the strange story about the man who dreamed he could fly, was much admired by these young people, and some of them had first taken Sutty to his class. He taught an austere, very beautiful form of exercise-meditation. He had invited her to join his group.

They met in an old warehouse down by the river, a less safe place than the umyazu-turned-gymnasium she went to with Iziezi, where legitimate health-manual gymnastics did take place and served as cover for the illegal ones. The warehouse was lighted only by dirty slit windows high up under the eaves. Nobody spoke above the barest whisper. There was no hocus-pocus about Odiedin, but Sutty found the class, the silent, slow movements in darkness, hauntingly strange, sometimes disturbing; it had entered into her dreams.

A man sitting near Sutty this morning stared at her as she took her place on the mat. While the group went through the first part of the form, he kept staring, winking, gesturing, grinning at her. Nobody behaved like that. She was annoyed and embarrassed until, during a long-held pose, she got a look at the man and realised that he was half-witted.

When the group began a set of movements she wasn't yet familiar with, she watched and followed along as best she could. Her mistakes and omissions upset her neighbor. He kept trying to show her when and how to move, pantomiming, exaggerating gestures. When they stood up, she stayed sitting, which was always permissible, but this distressed the poor fellow very much. He gestured, Up! up! He mouthed the word, and pointed upward. Finally, whispering, "Up—like this—see?," he took a step onto the air. He brought the other foot up on the invisible stair, and then climbed another step up the same way. He was standing barefoot half a meter above the floor, looking down at her, smiling anxiously and gesturing for her to join him. He was standing on the air.

Odiedin, a lithe, trim man of fifty with a scrap of blue cloth around his neck, came to him. All the others kept on steadily with the complex, swaying kelp-forest patterns. Odiedin murmured, "Come down, Uki." Reaching up, he took the man's hand and led him down two nonexistent steps to the floor, patted his shoulder gently, and moved on. Uki joined in the pattern, swaying and turning with flawless grace and power. He had evidently forgotten Sutty.

She could not bring herself to ask Odiedin any questions after the class. What would she ask? "Did you see what I saw? Did I?" That would be stupid. It couldn't have happened, and so he'd no doubt merely answer her question with a question.

Or perhaps the reason she didn't ask was that she was afraid he would simply answer, "Yes."

If a mime can make air into a box, if a fakir can climb a rope tied to air, maybe a poor fool can make air into a step. If spiritual strength can move mountains, maybe it can make stairs. Trance state. Hypnotic or hypnogogic suggestion.

She described the occurrence briefly in her daily notes, without comment. As she spoke into her noter, she became quite sure that there had in fact been some kind of step there that she hadn't seen in the dim light, a block, a box perhaps, painted black. Of course there had been something there. She paused, but did not say anything more. She could see the block or box, now. But she had not seen it.

But often in her mind's eye she saw those two callused, muscular, bare feet stepping up the absent mountain. She wondered what the air felt like on the soles of your feet when you walked on it. Cool? Resilient?

After that she made herself pay more attention to the old texts and tales that talked about walking on the wind, riding on clouds, traveling to the stars, destroying distant enemies with thunderbolts. Such feats were always ascribed to heroes and wise maz far away and long ago, even though a good many of them had been made commonplace fact by modern technologies. She still thought they were mythic, metaphoric, not meant to be taken literally. She arrived at no explanation.

But her attitude had been changed. She knew now that she'd still missed the point, a misunderstanding so gross and total that she couldn't see it.

A telling is not an explaining.

Can't see the forest for the trees, the pedants, the pundits, Uncle Hurree growled in her mind. *Poetry, girl, poetry. Read the Mahabharata. Everything's there.*

"Maz Elyed," she asked, "what is it you do?"

"I tell, yoz Sutty."

"Yes. But the stories, all the things you tell, what do they do?"

"They tell the world."

"Why, maz?"

"That's what people do, yoz. What we're here for."

Maz Elyed, like many of the maz, talked softly and rather hesitantly, pausing, starting up again about the time you thought she'd stopped. Silence was part of all she said.

She was small, lame, and very wrinkled. Her family owned a little hardware shop in the poorest district of the city, where many houses were not built of stone and wood but were tents or yurts of felt and canvas patched with plastic, set on platforms of beaten clay. Nephews and grandnieces abounded in the hardware shop. A very small great-grandnephew staggered about it, his goal in life to eat screws and washers. An old 2D photograph of Elyed with her partner Oni hung on the wall behind the counter: Oni Elyed tall and dreamy-eyed, Elyed Oni tiny, vivid, beautiful. Thirty years ago they had been arrested for sexual deviance and teaching rotten-corpse ideology. They were sent to a re-education camp on the west coast. Oni had died there. Elyed came back after ten years, lame, with no teeth: knocked out or lost to scurvy, she never said. She did not talk about herself or her wife or her age or her concerns. Her days were spent in an unbroken ritual continuity that included all bodily needs and functions, preparing and eating meals, sleeping, teaching, but above all reading and telling, a soft, endless repetition of the texts she had been learning her whole life long.

At first Elyed had appeared unearthly, inhuman to Sutty, as indifferent and inaccessible as a cloud, a domestic saint living entirely inside the ritual system, a sort of automaton of recitation without emotion or personality. Sutty had feared her. She was afraid that this woman who embodied the system fully, who lived it totally, would force her to admit that it was hysterical, obsessional, absolutist, everything she hated and feared and wanted it not to be. But as she listened to Elyed's tellings, she heard a disciplined, reasoning mind, though it spoke of what was unreasonable.

Elyed used that word often, unreasonable, in a literal sense: what cannot be understood by thinking. Once when Sutty was trying to find a coherent line of thought connecting several different tellings, Elyed said, "What we do is unreasonable, yoz."

"But there is a reason *for* it."

"Probably."

"What I don't understand is the pattern. The place, the importance of things in the pattern. Yesterday you were telling the story about Iaman and Deberren, but you didn't finish it, and today you read the descriptions of the leaves of the trees of the grove at the Golden Mountain. I don't understand what they have to do with each other. Or is it that on certain days a certain kind of material is proper? Or are my questions just stupid?"

"No," the maz said, and laughed her small laugh that had no teeth to show. "I get tired remembering. So I read. It doesn't matter. It's all the leaves of the tree."

"So . . . anything—anything that's in the books is equally important?"

Elyed considered. "No," she said. "Yes." She drew a shaky breath. She tired quickly when she could not rest in the stream of ritual act and language, but she never dismissed Sutty, never evaded her questions. "It's all we have. You see? It's the way we have the world. Without the telling, we don't have anything at all. The moment goes by like the water of the river. We'd tumble and spin and be helpless if we tried to live in the moment. We'd be like a baby. A baby can do it, but we'd drown. Our minds need to tell, need the telling. To hold. The past has passed, and there's nothing in the future to catch hold of. The future is nothing yet. How could anybody live there? So what we have is the words that tell what happened and what happens. What was and is."

"Memory?" Sutty said. "History?"

Elyed nodded, dubious, not satisfied by these terms. She sat thinking for some time and finally said, "We're not outside the world, yoz. You know? We are the world. We're its language. So we live and it lives. You see? If we don't say the words, what is there in our world?"

She was trembling, little spasms of the hands and mouth that she tried to conceal. Sutty thanked her with the mountain-heart gesture, apologised for wearing her out with talk. Elyed gave her small, black laugh. "Oh, yoz, I keep going with talk. Just the way the world does," she said.

Sutty went away and brooded. All this about language. It always came back to words. Like the Greeks with their Logos, the Hebrew Word that was God. But this was words. Not the Logos, the Word, but words. Not one but many, many. . . . Nobody made the world, ruled the world, told the world to be. It was. It did. And human beings made it be, made it be a human world, by saying it? By telling what was in it and what happened in it? Anything, everything—tales of heroes, maps of the stars, love songs, lists of the shapes of leaves. . . . For a moment she thought she understood.

She brought this half-formed understanding to Maz Ottiar Uming, who was easier to talk with than Elyed, wanting to try to put it into words. But Ottiar was busy with a chant, so Sutty talked to Uming, and somehow her words got contorted and pedantic. She couldn't speak her intuition.

As they struggled to understand each other, Uming Ottiar showed a bitterness, almost the first Sutty had met with among these soft-voiced teachers. Despite his impediment he was a fluent talker, and he got going, mildly enough at first: "Animals have no language. They have their nature. You see? They know the way, they know where to go and how to go, following their nature. But we're animals with no nature. Eh? Animals with no nature! That's strange! We're so strange! We have to talk about how to go and what to do, think about it, study it, learn it. Eh? We're born to be reasonable, so we're born ignorant. You see? If nobody teaches us the words, the thoughts, we stay ignorant. If nobody shows a little child, two, three years old, how to look for the way, the signs of the path, the landmarks, then it gets lost on the mountain, doesn't it? And dies in the night, in the cold. So. So." He rocked his body a little.

Maz Ottiar, across the little room, knocked on the drum, murmuring some long chronicle of ancient days to a single, sleepy, ten-year-old listener.

Maz Uming rocked and frowned. "So, without the telling,

the rocks and plants and animals go on all right. But the people don't. People wander around. They don't know a mountain from its reflection in a puddle. They don't know a path from a cliff. They hurt themselves. They get angry and hurt each other and the other things. They hurt animals because they're angry. They make quarrels and cheat each other. They want too much. They neglect things. Crops don't get planted. Too many crops get planted. Rivers get dirty with shit. Earth gets dirty with poison. People eat poison food. Everything is confused. Everybody's sick. Nobody looks after the sick people, the sick things. But that's very bad, very bad, eh? Because looking after things, that's our job, eh? Looking after things, looking after each other. Who else would do it? Trees? Rivers? Animals? They just do what they are. But we're here, and we have to learn how to be here, how to do things, how to keep things going the way they need to go. The rest of the world knows its business. Knows the One and the Myriad, the Tree and the Leaves. But all we know is how to learn. How to study, how to listen, how to talk, how to tell. If we don't tell the world, we don't know the world. We're lost in it, we die. But we have to tell it right, tell it truly. Eh? Take care and tell it truly. That's what went wrong. Down there, down there in Dovza, when they started telling lies. Those false maz, those big munan, those boss maz. Telling people that nobody knew the truth but them, nobody could speak but them, everybody had to tell the same lies they told. Traitors, usurers! Leading people astray for money! Getting rich off their lies, bossing people! No wonder the world stopped going around! No wonder the police took over!"

The old man was dark red in the face, shaking his good hand as if he held a stick in it. His wife got up, came over, and put the drum and drumstick into his hands, all the time going on with her droning recitation. Uming bit his lip, shook his head, fretted a bit, knocked the drum rather hard, and took up the recitation on the next line.

"I'm sorry," Sutty said to Ottiar as the old woman went with her to the door. "I didn't mean to upset Maz Uming."

"Oh, it's all right," Ottiar said. "All that was before I/we were born. Down in Dovza."

"You weren't part of Dovza, up here?"

"We're mostly Rangma here. My/our people all talked Rangma. The grandparents didn't know how to talk much Dovzan till after the Corporation police came and made everybody talk it. They hated it! They kept the worst accents they could!"

She had a merry smile, and Sutty smiled back; but she walked down the hill-street in a maze of thoughts. Uming's tirade against the "boss maz" had been about the period *before* the Dovzan Corporation ruled the world, before "the police came," possibly before the First Observers of the Ekumen came. As he spoke, it had occurred to her that of the hundreds of stories and histories she had heard in the tellings, none had to do with events in Dovza, or any events of the last five or six decades except very local ones. She had never heard a maz tell a tale about the coming of the offworlders, the rise of the Corporation State, or any public event of the last seventy years or more.

"Iziezi," she said that night, "who were the boss maz?"

She was helping Iziezi peel a kind of fungus that had just come into season up on the hills where the snow was melting at the edge of thawing drifts. It was called demyedi, first-of-spring, tasted like snow, and was good for balancing the peppery banam shoots and the richness of oilfish, thus keeping the sap thin and the heart easy. Whatever else she had missed and misunderstood in this world, she had learned when, and why, and how to cook its food.

"Oh, that was a long time ago," said Iziezi. "When they started bossing everybody around, down in Dovza."

"A hundred years ago?"

"Maybe that long ago."

"Who are 'the police'?"

"Oh, you know. The blue-and-tans."

"Just them?"

"Well, I guess we call all those people the police. From down there. Dovzans. . . . First they used to arrest the boss maz. Then they started to arrest all the maz. When they sent soldiers up here to arrest people in the umyazu, that's when people started calling them police. And people call skuyen the police, too. Or they say, 'They're working for the police.'"

"Skuyen?"

"People who tell the blue-and-tans about illegal things. Books, tellings, anything. . . . For money. Or for hatred." Iziezi's mild voice changed on the last words. Her face had closed into its tight look of pain.

Books, tellings, anything. What you cooked. Who you made love with. How you wrote the word for tree. Anything.

No wonder the system was incoherent, fragmented. No wonder Uming's world had stopped going around. The wonder was that anything remained of it at all.

As if her realisations had summoned him out of nothingness, the Monitor passed her on the street next morning. He did not look at her.

A few days later she went to visit Maz Sotyu Ang. His shop was closed. It had never been closed before. She asked a neighbor sweeping his front step if he would be back soon. "I think the producer-consumer is away," the man said vaguely.

Maz Elyed had lent her a beautiful old book—lent or given, she was not sure. "Keep it, it's safe with you," Elyed had said. It was an ancient anthology of poems from the Eastern Isles, an inexhaustible treasure. She was deep in studying and transferring it into her noter. Several days passed before she thought to visit her old friend the Fertiliser again. She walked up the steep street that shone blinding black in the sunshine. Spring came late but fast to these foothills of the great range. The air blazed with light. She walked past the shop without recognising it.

She was disoriented, turned back, found the shop. It was all white: whitewashed, a blank front. All the signs, the bold characters, the old words gone. Silenced. Snowfall. . . . The door stood ajar. She looked in. The counters and the walls of tiny drawers had been torn out. The room was empty, dirty, ransacked. The walls where she had seen the living words, the breathing words, had been smeared over with brown paint.

The twice-forked lightning tree. . . .

The neighbor had come out when she passed. He was sweeping his step again. She began to speak to him and then did not. Skuyen? How did you know?

She started back home and then, seeing the river glittering at the foot of the streets, turned and went along the hillside out of town to a path that led down to and followed the river.

She had hiked that path all one day, one of those days long, long ago in the early autumn when she was waiting for the Envoy to tell her to go back to the city.

She set off upriver beside thickets of newly leafed-out shrubs and the dwarfed trees that grew here not far from timberline. The Ereha ran milky blue with the first glacier melt. Ice crunched in the ruts of the road, but the sun was hot on her head and back. Her mouth was still dry with shock. Her throat ached.

Go back to the city. She should go back to the city. Now. With the three record crystals and the noter full of stuff, full of poetry. Get it all to Tong Ov before the Monitor got it.

There was no way to send it. She must take it. But travel must be authorised. O Ram! where was her ZIL? She hadn't worn it for months. Nobody here used ZILs, only if you worked for the Corporation or had to go to one of the bureaus. It was in her briefcase, in her room. She'd have to use her ZIL at the telephone on Dock Street, get through to Tong, ask him to get her an authorisation to come to the city. By plane. Take the riverboat down to Eltli and fly from there. Do it all out in the open, let them all know, so they couldn't stop her privately, trick her somehow. Confiscate her records. Silence her. Where was Maz Sotyu? What were they doing to him? Was it her fault?

She could not think about that now. What she had to do was save what she could of what Sotyu had given her. Sotyu and Ottiar and Uming and Odiedin and Elyed and Iziezi, dear Iziezi. She could not think about that now.

She turned round, walked hurriedly back along the river into town, found her ZIL bracelet in her briefcase in her room, went to Dock Street, and put in a call to Tong Ov at the Ekumenical Office in Dovza City.

His Dovzan secretary answered and said superciliously that he was in a meeting. "I must speak to him, now," Sutty said and was not surprised when the secretary said in a meek tone that she would call him.

When Sutty heard his voice she said, in Hainish, hearing the words as foreign and strange, "Envoy, I've been out of touch for so long, I feel as if we needed to talk."

"I see," Tong said, and a few other meaningless things, while she and probably he tried to figure out how to say anything meaningful. If only he knew any of her languages, if only she knew his! But their only common languages were Hainish and Dovzan.

"Nothing devolving in particular?" he inquired.

"No, no, not really. But I'd like to bring you the material I've been collecting," she said. "Just notes on daily life in Okzat-Ozkat."

"I was hoping to come see you there, but that seems to be contraindicated at present," Tong said. "With a window just wide enough for one, of course it's a pity to close the blinds. But I know how much you love Dovza City and must have been missing it. I'm equally sure that you've found nothing much interesting up there. So, if your work's all done, by all means come on back and enjoy yourself here."

Sutty groped and stammered, and finally said, "Well, as you know it's a very, the Corporation State is a very homogeneous culture, very powerful and definitely in control, very success-ful. So everything here is, yes, is very much the same here as there. But maybe I should stay on and finish the, finish the tapes before I bring them? They're not very interesting."

"Here, as you know," said Tong, "our hosts share all kinds of information with us. And we share ours with them. Every-body here is getting loads of fresh material, very educational and inspiring. So what you're doing there isn't really all that important. Don't worry about it. Of course I'm not at all un-easy about you. And have no need to be. Do I?"

"No, yes, of course not," she said. "Honestly."

She left the telephone office, showing her ZIL at the door, and hurried back to her inn, her home. She thought she had followed Tong's backward talk, but it destroyed itself in her memory. She thought he had been trying to tell her to stay there, not to try to bring what she had to him, because he would have to show it to officials there and it would be confis-cated, but she was not sure that was what he had meant. Maybe he truly meant it was not all that important. Maybe he meant he could not help her at all.

Helping Iziezi prepare dinner, she was sure that she had panicked, had been stupid to call Tong, thus bringing atten-tion to herself and her friends and informants here. Feeling that she must be careful, cautious, she said nothing about the desecrated shop.

Iziezi had known Maz Sotyu Ang for years, but she said nothing about him either. She showed no sign of anything being wrong. She showed Sutty how to slice the fresh numiem, thin and on the bias, to bring the flavor out.

It was one of Elyed's teaching nights. After she and Akidan and Iziezi had eaten, Sutty took her leave and went down River Street into the poor part of town, the yurt city, where the Corporation had not brought electric enlightenment and there were only the tiny gleams of oil lamps inside the shacks and tents. It was cold, but not the bone-dry, blade-keen cold of winter. A damp, spring-smelling cold, full of life. But Sutty's heart swelled with dread as she came near Elyed's shop: to find it all whited out, gutted, raped . . .

The great-grandnephew was screaming bloody murder as somebody separated him from a screwdriver, and nieces smiled at Sutty as she went through the shop to the back room. She was early for the teaching hour. Nobody was in the little room but the maz and an unobtrusive grandnephew setting up chairs.

"Maz Elyed Oni, do you know Maz Sotyu Ang—the herbalist —his shop—" She could not keep the words from bursting out.

"Yes," the old woman said. "He's staying with his daughter."

"The shop, the herbary—"

"That is gone."

"But—"

Her throat ached. She struggled with tears of rage and out-rage that wanted to be cried, here with this woman who could be her grandmother, who was her grandmother.

"It was my fault."

"No," Elyed said. "You did no wrong. Sotyu Ang did no wrong. There is no fault. Things are going badly. It's not pos-sible always to do right when things are difficult."

Sutty stood silent. She looked around the small, high-ceilinged room, its red rug almost hidden by chairs and cush-ions; everything poor, clean; a bunch of paper flowers stuck in an ugly vase on the low table; the grandnephew gently re-arranging floor cushions; the old, old woman lowering herself carefully, painfully onto a thin pillow near the table. On the table, a book. Old, worn, many times read.

"I think maybe, yoz Sutty, it was the other way round. Sotyu told us last summer that he thought a neighbor had informed the police about his herbary. Then you came, and nothing happened."

Sutty forced herself to understand what Elyed had said. "I was a safeguard?"

"I think so."

"Because they don't want me to see . . . what they do? But then why did they—now—?"

Elyed drew her thin shoulders together. "They don't study patience," she said.

"Then I should stay here," Sutty said slowly, trying to understand. "I thought it would be better for you if I left."

"I think you might go to Silong."

Her mind was clouded. "To Silong?"

"The last umyazu is there."

Sutty said nothing, and after a while Elyed added, scrupulous of fact, "The last I know of. Maybe some are left in the east, in the Isles. But here in the west they say the Lap of Silong is the last. Many, many books have been sent there. For many years now. It must be a great library. Not like the Golden Mountain, not like the Red Umyazu, not like Atangen. But what has been saved, most of it is there."

She looked at Sutty, her head a little on one side, a small old bird, keen-eyed. She had completed her cautious journey down onto the cushion, and now arranged her black wool vest, a bird getting its feathers straight. "You want to learn the Telling, I know that. You should go there," she said. "Here, nothing much is here. Bits and pieces. What I have, what a few maz have. Not much. Always less. Go to Silong, daughter Sutty. Maybe you can find a partner. Be a maz. Eh?" Her face creased up in a sudden, tremendous smile, toothless and radiant. She jiggled gently with laughter. "Go to Silong . . ."

Other people were coming in. Elyed put her hands in her lap and began to chant softly, "The two from one, the one from two. . . ."

Chapter Six

SHE WENT TO TALK to Odiedin Manma. Despite his enigmatic telling, despite the uncanny event (which she was now quite sure she had merely imagined) in his class, she had found him the most worldly and politically knowledgeable of the maz she knew, and she badly wanted some practical counsel. She waited till after his class and then begged him for advice.

"Does Maz Elyed want me to go to this place, this umyazu, because she thinks if I go there, my presence will help keep it safe? I think she might be wrong. I think the blue-and-tans are tracking me all the time. It's a secret place, a hidden place, isn't it? If I went, they could just follow me. They may have all kinds of tracking devices."

Odiedin held up his hand, mild but unsmiling. "I don't think they'll track you, yoz. They have orders from Dovza to let you be. Not to follow and observe you."

"You know that?"

He nodded.

She believed him. She remembered the invisible web she had sensed when she first lived here. Odiedin was one of the spiders.

"Anyhow, the way to Silong isn't an easy track to follow. And you could leave very quietly." He chewed his lip a little. A hint of warmth, a pleasurable look, had come into his dark, severe face. "If Maz Elyed suggested that you go there, and if you want to go there," he said, "I'd show you the way."

"You would?"

"I was at the Lap of Silong once. I was twelve. My parents were maz. It was a bad time then. When the books were burned. A lot of police. A lot of loss, destruction. Arrests. Fear. So we left Okzat, went up into the hills, to the hill towns. And then, in the summer, all the way round Zubuam, to the lap of the Mother. I'd like very much to go that way again before I die, yoz."

Sutty tried to leave no track, "no footprints in the dust." She sent no word to Tong except that she planned to do nothing much the next few months except a little hiking and climbing. She spoke to none of her friends, acquaintances, teachers, except Elyed and Odiedin. She fretted about her crystals—four, now, for she had cleared her noter again. She could not leave them at Iziezi's house, the first place the blue-and-tans would look for them. She was trying to decide where to bury them and how to do it without being seen, when Ottiar and Uming in the most casual way told her that since the police were so busy at the moment, they were storing their mandala away in a safe place for a while, and did she have anything she'd like to stash away with it? Their intuition seemed amazing, until Sutty remembered that they were part of the spiderweb—and had lived their adult lives in secrecy, hiding all that was most precious to them. She gave them the crystals. They told her where the hiding place was. "Just in case," Ottiar said mildly. She told them who Tong Ov was and what to tell him, just in case. They parted with loving embraces.

Finally she told Iziezi about the long hike she planned to take in the mountains.

"Akidan is going with you," Iziezi said with a cheerful smile.

Akidan was out with friends. The two women were eating dinner together at the table in the red-carpeted corner of Iziezi's immaculate kitchen. It was a "little-feast" night: several small dishes, delicately intense in flavor, surrounding a bland, creamy pile of tuzi. It reminded Sutty of the food of her far-off childhood. "You'd like basmati rice, Iziezi!" she said. Then she heard what her friend had said.

"Into the mountains? But it— We may be gone a long time."

"He's been up in the hills several times. He'll be seventeen this summer."

"But what will you do?" Akidan ran his aunt's errands, did her shopping, sweeping, fetching and carrying, helped her when a crutch slipped.

"My cousin's daughter will come stay with me."

"Mizi? But she's only six!"

"She's a help."

"Iziezi, I don't know if this is a good idea. I may go a long way. Even stay the winter in one of the villages up there."

"Dear Sutty, Ki isn't your responsibility. Maz Odiedin Manma told him to come. To go with a teacher to the Lap of

Silong is the dream of his life. He wants to be a maz. Of course he has to grow up and find a partner. Maybe finding a partner is what he's mostly thinking about, just now." She smiled a little, not so cheerfully. "His parents were maz," she said.

"Your sister?"

"She was Maz Ariezi Meneng." She used the forbidden pronoun, she/he/they. Her face had fallen into its set expression of pain. "They were young," she said. A long pause. "Ki's father, Meneng Ariezi, everybody loved him. He was like the old heroes, like Penan Teran, so handsome and brave. . . . He thought being a maz was like armor. He believed nothing could hurt her/him/them. There was a while, then, three or four years, when things were going along more like the old days. No arrests. No more troops of young people from down there breaking windows, painting everything white, shouting. . . . It quieted down. The police didn't come here much. We all thought it was over, it would go back to being like it used to be. Then all of a sudden there were a lot of them. That's how they are. All of a sudden. They said there were, you know, too many people here breaking the law, reading, telling. . . . They said they'd clean the city. They paid skuyen to inform on people. I knew people who took their money." Her face was tight, closed. "A lot of people got arrested. My sister and her husband. They took them to a place called Erriak. Somewhere way off, down there. An island, I think. An island in the sea. A rehabilitation center. Five years ago we heard that Ariezi was dead. A notice came. We never have heard anything about Meneng Ariezi. Maybe he's still alive."

"How long ago . . . ?"

"Twelve years."

"Ki was four?"

"Nearly five. He remembers them a little. I try to help him remember them. I tell him about them."

Sutty said nothing for a while. She cleared the table, came and sat down again. "Iziezi, you're my friend. He's your child. He *is* my responsibility. It could be dangerous. They could follow us."

"Nobody follows the people of the Mountain to the Mountain, dear Sutty."

They all had that serene, foolhardy confidence when they

talked about the mountains. No blame. Nothing to fear. Maybe they had to think that way in order to go on at all.

Sutty bought a nearly weightless, miraculously insulated sleeping bag for herself, and one for Akidan. Iziezi protested pro forma. Akidan was delighted and, like a child, slept in his sleeping bag from that night on, sweltering.

She got her boots and fleeces out again, packed her back-pack, and in the early morning of the appointed day walked with Akidan to the gathering place. It was spring on the edge of summer. The streets were dim blue in morning twilight, but up there to the northwest the great wall stood daylit, the peak was flying its radiant banners. We're going there, Sutty thought, we're going *there*! And she looked down to see if she was walking on the earth or on the air.

Vast slopes rose up all round to hanging glaciers and the glare of hidden ice fields. Their group of eight trudged along in line, so tiny in such hugeness that they seemed to be walking in place. Far up above them wheeled two geyma, the long-winged carrion birds that dwelt only among the high peaks, and flew always in pairs.

Six had set out: Sutty, Odiedin, Akidan, a young woman named Kieri, and a maz couple in their thirties, Tobadan and Siez. In a hill village four days out from Okzat-Ozkat two guides had joined them, shy, gentle-mannered men with weathered faces, whose age was hard to determine—somewhere between thirty and seventy. They were named Ieyu and Long.

The group had gone up and down in those hills for a week before they ever came to what these people called mountains. Then they had begun to climb. They had climbed steadily, daily, for eleven days now.

The luminous wall of Silong looked exactly the same, no nearer. A couple of insignificant 5,000-meter peaks to the north had shifted place and shrunk a bit. The guides and the three maz, with their trained memory for descriptive details and figures, knew the names and heights of all the peaks. They used a measure of altitude, pieng. As well as Sutty could recall, 15,000 pieng was about 5,000 meters; but since she wasn't certain her memory was correct, she mostly left the figures in pieng. She liked hearing these great heights, but she did not try to remember them, or the names of the mountains and passes. She had resolved before they set out never to ask where they were, where they were going, or how far they had yet to go. She had held to that resolve the more easily as it left her childishly free.

There was no trail as such except near villages, but there were charts that like river pilots' charts gave the course by landmarks and alignments: *When the north scarp of Mien falls behind the Ears of Taziu . . .* Odiedin and the other maz pored over these charts nightly with the two guides who had joined them in the foothills. Sutty listened to the poetry of the words. She did not ask the names of the tiny villages they passed through. If the Corporation, or even the Ekumen, ever demanded to know the way to the Lap of Silong, she could say in all truth that she did not know it.

She didn't know even the name of the place they were going to. She had heard it called the Mountain, Silong, the Lap of Silong, the Taproot, the High Umyazu. Possibly there was more than one place. She knew nothing about it. She resisted her desire to learn the name for everything, the word for everything. She was living among people to whom the highest spiritual attainment was to speak the world truly, and who had been silenced. Here, in this greater silence, where they could speak, she wanted to learn to listen to them. Not to question, only to listen. They had shared with her the sweetness of ordinary life lived mindfully. Now she shared with them the hard climb to the heights.

She had worried about her fitness for this trek. A month in the hill country of Ladakh and a few hiking holidays in the Chilean Andes were the sum of her mountaineering, and those had not been climbs, just steep walking. That was what they were doing now, but she wondered how high they would go. She had never walked above 4,000 meters. So far, though they must be that high by now, she had had no trouble except for running short of breath on stiff uphill stretches. Even Odiedin and the guides took it slow when the way got steep. Only Akidan and Kieri, a tough, rotund girl of twenty or so, raced up the endless slopes, and danced on outcroppings of granite over vast blue abysses, and were never out of breath. The eberdibi, the others called them—the kids, the calves.

They had walked a long day to get to a summer village: six or seven stone rings with yurts set up on them among steep, stony pastures tucked in the shelter of a huge curtain wall of granite. Sutty had been amazed to find how many people lived up here where it seemed there was nothing to live on but air and ice and rock. The vast, barren-seeming foothills far above Okzat-Ozkat had turned out to be full of villages, pasturages, small stone-walled fields. Even here among the high peaks there were habitations, the summer villages. Villagers came up from the hills through the late spring snow with their animals, the kind of eberdin called minule. Horned, half wild, with long legs and long pale wool, the minule pastured as high as grass grew and bore their young in the highest alpine meadows. Their fine, silky fleece was valuable even now in the days of artificial fibers. The villagers sold their wool, drank their milk, tanned their hides for shoes and clothing, burned their dung for fuel.

These people had lived this way forever. To them Okzat-Ozkat, a far provincial outpost of civilisation, was civilisation. They were all Rangma. They spoke some Dovzan in the foothills, and Sutty could converse well enough with Ieyu and Long; but up here, though her Rangma had improved greatly over the winter, she had to struggle to understand the mountain dialect.

The villagers all turned out to welcome the visitors, a jumble of dirty sunburnt smiling faces, racing children, shy babies laced into leather cocoons and hung up on stakes like little trophies, blatting minule with their white, silent, newborn young. Life, life abounding in the high, empty places.

Overhead, as always, were a couple of geyma spiraling lazily on slender dark wings in the dark dazzling blue.

Odiedin and the young maz couple, Siez and Tobadan, were already busy blessing huts and babies and livestock, salving sores and smoke-damaged eyes, and telling. The blessing, if that was the right word for it—the word they used meant something like including or bringing in—consisted of ritual chanting to the tabatt-batt-batt of the little drum, and handing out slips of red or blue paper on which the maz wrote the recipient's name and age and whatever autobiographical facts they asked to have written, such as—

"Married with Temazi this winter."

"Built my house in the village."

"Bore a son this winter past. He lived one day and night. His name was Enu."

"Twenty-two minulibi born this season to my flock."

"I am Ibien. I was six years old this spring."

As far as she could tell, the villagers could read only a few characters or none at all. They handled the written slips of paper with awe and deep satisfaction. They examined them for a long time from every direction, folded them carefully, slipped them into special pouches or finely decorated boxes in their house or tent. The maz had done a blessing or ingathering like this in every village they passed through that did not have a maz of its own. Some of the telling boxes in village houses, magnificently carved and decorated, had hundreds of these little red and blue record slips in them, tellings of lives present, lives past.

Odiedin was writing these for a family, Tobadan was dispensing herbs and salve to another family, and Siez, having finished the chant, had sat down with the rest of the population to tell. A narrow-eyed, taciturn young man, Siez in the villages became a fountain of words.

Tired and a little buzzy-headed—they must have come up another kilometer today—and liking the warmth of the afternoon sun, Sutty joined the half circle of intently gazing men and women and children, cross-legged on the stony dust, and listened with them.

"The telling!" Siez said, loudly, impressively, and paused.

His audience made a soft sound, *ah, ah,* and murmured to one another.

"The telling of a story!"

Ah, ah, murmur, murmur.

"The story is of Dear Takieki!"

Yes, yes. The dear Takieki, yes.

"Now the story begins! Now, the story begins when dear Takieki was still living with his old mother, being a grown man, but foolish. His mother died. She was poor. All she had to leave him was a sack of bean meal that she had been saving for them to eat in the winter. The landlord came and drove Takieki out of the house."

Ah, ah, the listeners murmured, nodding sadly.

"So there went Takieki walking down the road with the sack of bean meal slung over his shoulder. He walked and he walked, and on the next hill, walking toward him, he saw a ragged man. They met in the road. The man said, 'That's a heavy sack you carry, young man. Will you show me what is in it?' So Takieki did that. 'Bean meal!' says the ragged man.''

Bean meal, whispered a child.

"'And what fine bean meal it is! But it'll never last you through the winter. I'll make a bargain with you, young man. I'll give you a real brass button for that bean meal!'

"'Oh, ho,' says Takieki, 'you think you're going to cheat me, but I'm not so foolish as that!'"

Ah, ah.

"So Takieki hoisted his sack and went on. And he walked and he walked, and on the next hill, coming toward him, he saw a ragged girl. They met in the road, and the girl said, 'A heavy sack you're carrying, young man. How strong you must be! May I see what's in it?' So Takieki showed her the bean meal, and she said, 'Fine bean meal! If you'll share it with me, young man, I'll go along with you, and I'll make love with you whenever you like, as long as the bean meal lasts.'"

A woman nudged the woman sitting by her, grinning.

"'Oh, ho,' says Takieki, 'you think you're going to cheat me, but I'm not so foolish as that!'

"And he slung his sack over his shoulder and went on. And he walked and he walked, and on the next hill, coming toward him, he saw a man and woman."

Ah, ah, very softly.

"The man was dark as dusk and the woman bright as dawn, and they wore clothing all of bright colors and jewels of bright colors, red, blue. They met in the road, and he/she/they said, 'What a heavy sack you carry, young man. Will you show us what's in it?' So Takieki did that. Then the maz said, 'What fine bean meal! But it will never last you through the winter.' Takieki did not know what to say. The maz said, 'Dear Takieki, if you give us the sack of bean meal your mother gave you, you may have the farm that lies over that hill, with five barns full of grain, and five storehouses full of meal, and five stables full of eberdin. Five great rooms are in the farmhouse, and its roof is of coins of gold. And the mistress of the house is in the house, waiting to be your wife.'

"'Oh, ho,' said Takieki. 'You think you're going to cheat me, but I'm not so foolish as that!'

"And he walked on and he walked on, over the hill, past the farm with five barns and five storehouses and five stables and a roof of gold, and so he went walking on, the dear Takieki."

Ah, ah, ah! said all the listeners, with deep contentment. And they relaxed from their intensity of listening, and chatted a little, and brought Siez a cup and a pot of hot tea so that he could refresh himself, and waited respectfully for whatever he would tell next.

Why was Takieki "dear"? Sutty wondered. Because he was foolish? (Bare feet standing on air.) Because he was wise? But would a wise man have distrusted the maz? Surely he was foolish to turn down the farm and five barns and a wife. Did the story mean that to a holy man a farm and barns and a wife aren't worth a bag of bean meal? Or did it mean that a holy man, an ascetic, is a fool? The people she had lived with this year honored self-restraint but did not admire self-deprivation. They had no strenuous notions of fasting, and saw no virtue whatever in discomfort, hunger, poverty.

If it had been a Terran parable, most likely Takieki ought to have given the ragged man the bean meal for the brass button, or just given it for nothing, and then when he died he'd get his reward in heaven. But on Aka, reward, whether spiritual or fiscal, was immediate. By his performance of a maz's duties, Siez was not building up a bank account of virtue or sanctity; in return for his story-telling he would receive praise, shelter, dinner, supplies for their journey, and the knowledge that he had done his job. Exercises were performed not to attain an ideal of health or longevity but to achieve immediate well-being and for the pleasure of doing them. Meditation aimed toward a present and impermanent transcendance, not an ultimate nirvana. Aka was a cash, not a credit, economy.

Therefore their hatred of usury. A fair bargain and payment on the spot.

But then, what about the girl who offered to share what she had if he'd share what he had. Wasn't that a fair bargain?

Sutty puzzled over it all through the next tale, a famous bit of *The Valley War* that she had heard Siez tell several times in villages in the foothills—"I can tell that one when I'm sound asleep," he said. She decided that a good deal depended on how aware Takieki was of his own simplicity. Did he know the girl might trick him? Did he know he wasn't capable of managing a big farm? Maybe he did the right thing, hanging on to what his mother gave him. Maybe not.

As soon as the sun dropped behind the mountain wall to the west, the air in that vast shadow dropped below freezing. Everyone huddled into the hut-tents to eat, choking in the smoke and reek. The travelers would sleep in their own tents set up alongside the villagers' larger ones. The villagers would sleep naked, unwashed, promiscuous under heaps of silken pelts full of grease and fleas. In the tent she shared with Odiedin, Sutty thought about them before she slept. Brutal people, primitive people, the Monitor had said, leaning on the rail of the riverboat, looking up the long dark rise of the land that hid the Mountain. He was right. They were primitive, dirty, illiterate, ignorant, superstitious. They refused progress, hid from it, knew nothing of the March to the Stars. They hung on to their sack of bean meal.

Ten days or so after that, camped on névé in a long, shallow valley among pale cliffs and glaciers, Sutty heard an engine, an airplane or helicopter. The sound was distorted by wind and echoes. It might have been quite near or bounced from mountainside to mountainside from a long way off. There was ground fog blowing in tatters, a high overcast. Their tents, dun-colored, in the lee of an icefall, might be invisible in the vast landscape or might be plain to see from the air. They all held still as long as they could hear the stutter and rattle in the wind.

That was a weird place, the long valley. Icy air flowed down into it from the glaciers and pooled on its floor. Ghosts of mist snaked over the dead white snow.

Their food supplies were low. Sutty thought they must be close to their goal.

Instead of climbing up out of the long valley as she had expected, they descended from it on a long, wide slope of boulders. The wind blew without a pause and so hard that the gravel chattered ceaselessly against the larger stones. Every step was difficult, and every breath. Looking up now they saw Silong palpably nearer, the great barrier wall reaching across the sky. But the bannered crest still stood remote behind it. All Sutty's dreams that night were of a voice she could hear but could not understand, a jewel she had found but could not touch.

The next day they kept going down, down steeply, to the southwest. A chant formed itself in Sutty's dulled mind: *Go back to go forward, fail to succeed. Go down to go upward, fail to succeed.* It would not get out of her head but thumped itself over and over at every jolting step. Go *down* to go *up*ward, *fail* to suc*ceed.* . . .

They came to a path across the slope of stones, then to a road, to a wall of stones, to a building of stone. Was this their journey's end? Was this the Lap of the Mother? But it was only a stopping place, a shelter. Maybe it had been an umyazu once. It was silent now. It held no stories. They stayed two days and nights in the cheerless house, resting, sleeping in their sleeping bags. There was nothing to make a fire with, only their tiny cookers, and no food left but dried smoked fish, which they shared out in little portions, soaking it in boiled snow to make soup.

"They'll come," people said. She did not ask who. She was so tired, she thought she could lie forever in the stone house, like one of the inhabitants of the little white stone houses in the cities of the dead she had seen in South America, resting in peace. Her own people burned their dead. She had always dreaded fire. This was better, the cold silence.

On the third morning she heard bells, a long way off, a faint jangling of little bells. "Come see, Sutty," Kieri said, and coaxed her to get up and stand in the door of the stone house and look out.

People were coming up from the south, winding among the grey boulders that stood higher than they did, people leading minule laden with packs on high saddles. There were poles fixed to the saddles, and from them long red and blue ribbons snapped in the wind. Clusters of little bells were tied into the white neck wool of the young animals that ran beside their mothers.

The next day they started down with the people and the animals to their summer village. It took them three days, but the going was mostly easy. The villagers wanted Sutty to ride one of the minule, but nobody else was riding. She walked. At one place they had to round a cliff under a precipice that continued vertically down from the narrow ledge of the pathway. The path was level, but no wider than a foot's breadth in places, and the snow on it was softened and loosened by the summer thaw. There they let the minule loose and instead of leading them followed them. They showed Sutty that she should put her feet in the animals' tracks. She followed one minule meticulously, step by step. Its woolly buttocks swaying nonchalantly, it sauntered along, pausing now and then to look down the sheer drop into the hazy depths with a bored expression. Nobody said anything till they were all off the cliff path. Then there was some laughter and joking, and several villagers made the mountain-heart gesture to Silong.

Down in the village the horned peak could not be seen, only the big shoulder of a nearer mountain and a glimpse of the barrier wall closing off the northwestern sky. The village was in a green place, open to north and south, good summer pasturage, sheltered, idyllic. Trees grew by the river: Odiedin showed them to her. They were as tall as her little finger. Down in Okzat-Ozkat such trees were the shrubs beside the Ereha. In the parks of Dovza City she had walked in their deep shade.

There had been a death among the people, a young man who had neglected a cut on his foot and died of blood poisoning. They had kept the body frozen in snow till the maz could come and perform his funeral. How had they known Odiedin's group was coming? How had these arrangements been made? She didn't understand, but she didn't think about it much. Here in the mountains there was much she didn't understand. She went along in the moment, like a child. "Tumble and spin and be helpless, like a baby. . . ." Who had said that to her? She was content to walk, content to sit in the sun, content to follow in the footsteps of an animal. *Where my guides lead me in kindness, I follow, follow lightly* . . .

The two young maz told the funeral. That was how the people spoke of it. Like all the rites, it was a narrative. For two days Siez and Tobadan sat with the man's father and aunt, his sister, his friends, a woman who had been married to him for a while, hearing everybody who wanted to talk about him tell them who he had been, what he had done. Now the two young men retold all that, ceremonially and in the formal language, to the soft batt-tabatt of the drum, passing the word one to the other across the body wrapped in white, thin, still-frozen cloth: a praise-song, gathering a life up into words, making it part of the endless telling.

Then Siez recited in his beautiful voice the ending of the story of Penan Teran, a mythic hero couple dear to the Rangma people. Penan and Teran were men of Silong, young warriors who rode the north wind, saddling the wind from the mountains like an eberdin and riding it down to battle, banners flying, to fight the ancient enemy of the Rangma, the sea people, the barbarians of the western plains. But Teran was killed in battle. And Penan led his people out of danger and then saddled the south wind, the sea wind, and rode it up into the mountains, where he leapt from the wind and died.

The people listened and wept, and there were tears in Sutty's eyes.

Then Tobadan struck the drum as Sutty had never heard it struck, no soft heartbeat but a driving urgent rhythm, to which people lifted up the body and carried it away in procession, swiftly away from the village, always with the drum beating.

"Where will they bury him?" she asked Odiedin.

"In the bellies of the geyma," Odiedin said. He pointed to distant rock spires on one of the mighty slopes above the valley. "They'll leave him naked there."

That was better than lying in a stone house, Sutty thought. Better far than fire.

"So he'll ride the wind," she said.

Odiedin looked up at her and after a while quietly assented.

Odiedin never said much, and what he said was often dry; he was not a mild man; but she was by now altogether at ease with him and he with her. He was writing on the little slips of blue and red paper, of which he had a seemingly endless supply in his pack: writing the name and family names of the man who had died, she saw, for those who mourned him to take home and keep in their telling boxes.

"Maz," she said. "Before the Dovzans became so powerful

. . . before they began changing everything, using machinery, making things in factories instead of by hand, making new laws—all that—" Odiedin nodded. "It was after people from the Ekumen came here that they began that. Only about a lifetime ago. What were the Dovzans before that?"

"Barbarians."

He was a Rangma; he hadn't been able to resist saying it, saying it loud and clear. But she knew he was also a thoughtful, truthful man.

"Were they ignorant of the Telling?"

A pause. He set his pen down. "Long ago, yes. In the time of Penan Teran, yes. When *The Arbor* was written, yes. Then the people from the central plains, from Doy, began taming them. Trading with them, teaching them. So they learned to read and write and tell. But they were still barbarians, yoz Sutty. They'd rather make war than trade. When they traded, they made a war of it. They allowed usury, and sought great profits. They always had headmen to whom they paid tribute, men who were rich, and passed power down to their sons. Gobey—bosses. So when they began to have maz, they made the maz into bosses, with the power to rule and punish. Gave the maz the power to tax. They made them rich. They made the sons of maz all maz, by birth. They made the ordinary people into nothing. It was wrong. It was all wrong."

"Maz Uming Ottiar spoke of that time once. As if he remembered it."

Odiedin nodded. "I remember the end of it. It was a bad time. Not as bad as this," he added, with his brief, harsh laugh.

"But this time came from that time. Grew out of it. Didn't it?"

He looked dubious, thoughtful.

"Why don't you tell of it?"

No response.

"You don't tell it, maz. It's never part of all the histories and tales you tell about the whole world all through the ages. You tell about the far past. And you tell things from your own years, from ordinary people's lives—at funerals, and when children speak their tellings. But you don't tell about these great events. Nothing about how the world has changed in the last hundred years."

"None of that is part of the Telling," Odiedin said after a tense, pondering silence. "We tell what is right, what goes right, as it should go. Not what goes wrong."

"Penan Teran lost their battle, a battle with Dovza. It didn't go right, maz. But you tell it."

He looked up and studied her, not aggressively or with resentment, but from a very great distance. She had no idea what he was thinking or feeling, what he would say.

In the end he said only, "Ah."

The land mine going off? or the soft assent of the listener? She did not know.

He bent his head and wrote the name of the dead man, three bold, elegant characters across the slip of faded red paper. He had ground his ink from a block he carried, mixed it with river water in a tiny stoneware pot. The pen he was using for this writing was a geyma feather, ash-grey. He might have sat here cross-legged on the stony dust, writing a name, three hundred years ago. Three thousand years ago.

She had no business asking him what she had asked him. Wrong, wrong.

But the next day he said to her, "Maybe you've heard the Riddles of the Telling, yoz Sutty?"

"I don't think so."

"Children learn them. They're very old. What children tell is always the same. *What's the end of a story? When you begin telling it.* That's one of them."

"More a paradox than a riddle," Sutty said, thinking it over. "So the events must be over before the telling begins?"

Odiedin looked mildly surprised, as the maz generally did when she tried to interpret a saying or tale.

"That's not what it means," she said with resignation.

"It might mean that," he said. And after a while, "Penan leapt from the wind and died: that is Teran's story."

She had thought he was answering her question about why the maz did not tell about the Corporation State and the abuses that had preceded it. What did the ancient heroes have to do with that?

There was a gap between her mind and Odiedin's so wide light would need years to cross it.

"So the story went right, it's right to tell it; you see?" Odiedin said.

"I'm trying to see," she said.

They stayed six days in the summer village in the deep valley, resting. Then they set off again with new provisions and two new guides, north and up. And up, and up. Sutty kept no count of the days. Dawn came, they got up, the sun shone on them and on the endless slopes of rock and snow, and they walked. Dusk came, they camped, the sound of water ceased as the little thaw streams froze again, and they slept.

The air was thin, the way was steep. To the left, towering over them, rose the scarps and slopes of the mountain they were on. Behind them and to the right, peak after far peak rose out of mist and shadow into light, a motionless sea of icy broken waves to the remote horizon. The sun beat like a white drum in the dark blue sky. It was midsummer, avalanche season. They went very soft and silent among the unbalanced giants. Again and again in the daytime the silence quivered into a long, shuddering boom, multiplied and made sourceless by echoes.

Sutty heard people say the name of the mountain they were on, Zubuam. A Rangma word: Thunderer.

They had not seen Silong since they left the deep village. Zubuam's vast, deeply scored bulk closed off all the west. They inched along, north and up, north and up, in and out of the enormous wrinkles of the mountain's flank.

Breathing was slow work.

One night it began to snow. It snowed lightly but steadily all the next day.

Odiedin and the two guides who had joined them at the deep village squatted outside the tents that evening and conferred, sketching out lines, paths, zigzags on the snow with gloved fingers. Next morning the sun leapt brilliant over the icy sea of the eastern peaks. They inched on, sweating, north and up.

One morning as they walked, Sutty realised they were turning their backs to the sun. Two days they went northwest, crawling around the immense shoulder of Zubuam. On the third day at noon they turned a corner of rock and ice. Before them the immense barrier faced them across a vast abyss of air: Silong breaking like a white wave from the depths to the regions of light. The day was diamond-bright and still. The tip of the horned peak could be seen above the ramparts. From it the faintest gossamer wisp of silver trailed to the north.

The south wind was blowing, the wind Penan had leapt from to die.

"Not far now," Siez said as they trudged on, southwestward and down.

"I think I could walk here forever," Sutty said, and her mind said, *I will.* . . .

During their stay in the deep village, Kieri had moved into her tent. They had been the only women in the group before the new guides joined them. Until then Sutty had shared Odiedin's tent. A widowed maz, celibate, silent, orderly, he had been a self-effacing, reassuring presence. Sutty was reluctant to make the change, but Kieri pressed her to. Kieri had tented with Akidan till then and was sick of it. She told Sutty, "Ki's seventeen, he's in rut all the time. I don't like boys! I like men and women! I want to sleep with you. Do you want to? Maz Odiedin can share with Ki."

Her use of the words was specific: *share* meant share the tent, *sleep* meant join the sleeping bags.

When she realised that, Sutty was more hesitant than ever; but the passivity she had encouraged in herself during the whole of this journey was stronger than her hesitations, and she agreed. Nothing about sex had mattered much to her since Pao's death. Sometimes her body craved to be touched and roused. Sex was something people wanted and needed. She could respond physically, so long as that was all they asked.

Kieri was strong, soft, warm, and as clean as any of them could be in the circumstances. "Let's heat up!" she said every night as she got into their joined sleeping bags. She made love to Sutty briefly and energetically and then fell asleep pressed up close against her. They were like two logs in a glowing campfire, burning down, Sutty thought, sinking asleep in the deep warmth.

Akidan had been honored to share the tent with his master and teacher, but he was miffed or frustrated by Kieri's desertion. He moped around her for a day or two, and then became attentive to the woman who had joined them in the village. The new guides were a brother and sister, a long-legged, round-faced, tireless pair in their twenties, named Naba and Shui. After a day or so Ki moved in with Shui. Odiedin, patient, invited Naba to share his tent.

What had Diodi the barrow man said, years ago, light-years away, back down there in the streets where people lived? "Sex for three hundred years! After three-hundred-year sex anybody can fly!"

I can fly, Sutty thought, plodding on, southward and down. There's nothing really in the world but stone and light. All the other things, all the things, dissolve back into the two, the stone, the light, and the two back into the one, the flying. . . . And then it will all be born again, it is born again, always, in every moment it's being born, but all the time there's only the one, the flying. . . . She plodded on through glory.

They came to the Lap of the Earth.

Though she knew it was implausible, impossible, foolish, Sutty's imagination had insisted all along that the goal of their journey was a great temple, a mysterious city hidden at the top of the world, stone ramparts, flags flying, priests chanting, gold and gongs and processions. All the imagery of lost Lhasa, Dragon-Tiger Mountain, Machu Picchu. All the ruins of the Earth.

They came steeply down the western flanks of Zubuam for three days in cloudy weather, seldom able to see the barrier wall of Silong across the vast gulf of air where the wind chased coiling clouds and ghostly snow flurries that never came to earth. They followed the guides all one day through cloud and fog along an arête, a long spine of snow-covered rock with a steep drop to either side.

The weather cleared suddenly, clouds gone, sun blazing at the zenith. Sutty was disoriented, looking up for the barrier wall and not finding it. Odiedin came beside her. He said, smiling, "We're on Silong."

They had crossed over. The enormous mass of rock and ice behind them in the east was Zubuam. An avalanche went curling and smoking down a slanting face of the rock far up on the mountain. A long time later they heard the deep roar of it, the Thunderer telling them what it had to tell.

Zubuam and Silong, they were two and one, too. Old maz mountains. Old lovers.

She looked up at Silong. The heights of the barrier wall loomed directly over them, hiding the summit peak. Sky was a brilliant, jagged-edged slash from north to south.

Odiedin was pointing to the south. She looked and saw only rock, ice, the glitter of thaw water. No towers, no banners.

They set off, trudging along. They were on a path, level and quite clear, marked here and there with piles of flat stones. Often Sutty saw the dry, neat pellets of minule dung beside the way.

In mid-afternoon she made out a pair of rock spires that stuck up from a projecting corner of the mountain ahead like tusks from the lower jaw of a skull. The path narrowed as they got closer to this corner, becoming a ledge along a sheer cliff. When they got to the corner, the two reddish tusks of rock stood before them like a gateway, the path leading between them.

Here they stopped. Tobadan brought out his drum and patted it, and the three maz spoke and chanted. The words were all in Rangma and so old or so formalised that Sutty could not follow their meaning. The two guides from the village and their own guides delved into their packs and brought out little bundles of twigs tied with red and blue thread. They gave them to the maz, who received them with the mountain-heart gesture, facing toward Silong. They set them afire and fixed them among rocks by the pathway to burn down. The smoke smelled like sage, a dry incense. It curled small and blue and lazy among the rocks and along the path. The wind whistled by, a river of turbulent air rushing through the great gap between the mountains, but here in this gateway Silong sheltered them and there was no wind at all.

They picked up their packs and fell into line again, passing between the saber-tooth rocks. The path now bent back inward toward the slope of the mountain, and Sutty saw that it led across a cirque, a level-floored half-moon bay in the mountainside. In the nearly vertical, curving inner wall, still a half kilo or so distant, were black spots or holes. There was some snow on the floor of the cirque, trodden in an arabesque of paths leading to and from these black holes in the mountain.

Caves, scarred Adien, the ex-miner, who had died of the jaundice in the winter, whispered in her mind. *Caves full of being.*

The air seemed to thicken like syrup and to quiver, to shake. She was dizzy. Wind roared in her ears, deep and shrill, terrible. But they were out of the wind, here in the sunlit air of the cirque. She turned back in confusion, then in terror looked upward for the rockslide clattering down upon her. Black shadows crossed the air, the roar and rattle were deafening. She cowered, covering her head with her arms.

Silence.

She looked up, stood up. The others were all standing, like her, statues in the bright sunlight, pools of black shadow at their feet.

Behind them, between the tusks, the gateway rocks, something hung or lay crumpled. It gleamed blindingly and was shadow-black, like a lander seen from the ship in space. A lander—a flyer—a helicopter. She saw the rotor vane jammed up against the outer rock spire. "O Ram," she said.

"Mother Silong," Shui whispered, her clenched hand at her heart.

Then they started back toward the gate, toward the thing, Akidan in the lead, running.

"Wait, Akidan!" Odiedin shouted, but the boy was already there at the thing, the wreck. He shouted something back. Odiedin broke into a run.

Sutty could not breathe. She had to stand a while and still her heart. The older of their guides from the foothill country, Long, a kind, shy man, stood beside her, also trembling, also trying to breathe evenly, easily. They had come down, but they were still at 18,000 pieng, she had heard Siez say, 6,000 meters, a thin air, a terribly thin air. She said the numbers in her head.

"You all right, yoz Long?"

"Yes. You all right, yoz Sutty?"

They went forward together.

She heard Kieri talking: "I saw it, I looked around—I couldn't believe it—it was trying to fly between the pillars—"

"No, I saw it, it was out there, coming up alongside the pass, coming after us, and then it seemed like a flaw of wind hit it, and tipped it sideways, and just threw it down between the rocks!" That was Akidan.

"She took it in her hands," said Naba, the man from the deep village.

The three maz were at the wreck, in it.

Shui was kneeling near it, smashing something furiously, methodically, with a rock. The remains of a transmitter, Sutty saw. Stone Age revenge, her mind said coldly.

Her mind seemed to be very cold, detached from the rest of her, as if frostbitten.

She went closer and looked at the smashed helicopter. It had burst open in a strange way. The pilot was hanging in his seat straps, almost upside down. His face was mostly hidden by a blood-soaked woollen scarf. She saw his eyes, bits of jelly.

On the stony ground, between Odiedin and Siez, another man lay. His eyes were alive. He was staring up at her. After a while she recognised him.

Tobadan, the healer, was quickly, lightly running his hands over the man's body and limbs, though surely he couldn't tell much through the heavy clothing. He kept talking as if to keep the man awake. "Can you take off your helmet?" he asked. After a while the man tried to comply, fumbling with the fastening. Tobadan helped him. He continued gazing up at Sutty with a look of dull puzzlement. His face, always set and hard, was now slack.

"Is he hurt?"

"Yes," Tobadan said. "This knee. His back. Not broken, I think."

"You were lucky," Sutty's cold mind said, speaking aloud.

The man stared, looked away, made a weak gesture, tried to sit up. Odiedin pressed down gently on his shoulders, saying, "Be quiet. Wait. Sutty, don't let him get up. We need to get the other man out. People will be here soon."

Looking back into the cirque, toward the caves, she saw little figures hurrying to them across the snow.

She took Odiedin's place, standing over the Monitor. He lay flat on the dirt with his arms crossed on his chest. He shuddered violently every now and then. She herself was shivering. Her teeth chattered. She wrapped her arms around her body.

"Your pilot is dead," she said.

He said nothing. He trembled.

Suddenly there were people around them. They worked with efficiency, strapping the man onto a makeshift stretcher and lifting it and setting off for the caves, all within a minute or two. Others carried the dead man. Some gathered around Odiedin and the young maz. There was a soft buzz of voices that did nothing but buzz in Sutty's head, meaningless as the speech of flies.

She looked for Long, joined him, and walked with him across the cirque. It was farther than it had seemed to the mountain wall and the entrance to the caves. Overhead a pair of geyma soared in long, lazy spirals. The sun was already behind the top of the barrier wall. Silong's vast shadow rose blue against Zubuam.

The caves were like nothing she had ever seen. There were many of them, hundreds, some tiny, no more than bubbles in the rock, some big as the doors of hangars. They made a lacework of circles interlocking and overlapping in the wall of rock, patterns, traceries. The edges of the entrances were fretted with clusters of lesser circles, silvery stone shining against black shadow, like soapsuds, like foam, like the edges of Mandelbrot figures.

Against one entrance a little fence had been set up. Sutty looked in as they passed, and the white face of a young minule looked back at her with dark, quiet eyes. There was a whole stable of the animals built back into the caves. She could smell the pungent, warm, grassy odor of them. The entrances to the caves had been widened and brought down to ground level where necessary, but they kept their circularity. The people she and Long were following entered one of these great round doors into the mountain. Inside, she looked back for a moment at the entrance and saw daylight as a blazing, perfect circle set in dead black.

Chapter Seven

IT WAS NOT a city with banners and golden processions, a temple with drums and bells and the chanting of priests. It was very cold, very dark, very poor. It was silent.

Food, bedding, oil for lamps, stoves and heating devices, everything that made it possible for anyone to live at the Lap of Silong had to be brought up from the eastern hill country on the backs of minules or human beings, little by little, in tiny caravans that would attract no attention, during the few months when it was possible to reach the place at all. In the summer thirty or forty men and women stayed there, living in the caves. Some of them brought books, papers, texts of the Telling. They stayed to arrange and protect all the books already there, the thousands and thousands of volumes brought over the decades from all over the great continent. They stayed to read and study, to be with the books, to be in the caves full of being.

Sutty moved in her first days there through a dream of darkness, strangeness. The caves themselves were bewildering: endless bubble chambers interconnecting, interfacing, dark walls, floors, ceilings all curved into one another seamlessly, so disorienting that sometimes she felt she was floating weightless. Sounds echoed so they had no direction. There was never enough light.

Her group of pilgrims set up their tents in a great vaulted chamber and slept in them, huddled into them for warmth as they had done during their trek. In other caves were other little constellations of tents. One maz couple had taken a three-meter, almost perfectly spherical hollow and made a private nest of it. Cookstoves and tables were in a large, flat-floored cave that received daylight through a couple of high vents, and everybody met there at mealtimes. The cooks scrupulously shared out the food. Never quite enough, and the same few things over and over: thin tea, boiled bean meal, dry cheese, dried leaves of spinach-like yota, a taste of hot pickle. Winter food, though it was summer. Food for the roots, for endurance.

The maz and the students and guides staying there this

summer were all from the north and east, the vast hill countries and plains of the continent's center, Amareza, Doy, Kang-negne. These maz were city people, far more learned and so-phisticated than those of the little hill city Sutty knew. Trained in a profound and still unbroken intellectual and bodily and spiritual discipline, heirs to a tradition vaster, even in its ruin and enforced secrecy, than she had ever conceived, they had an impersonality about them as well as great personal authority. They did not play the pundit (Uncle Hurree's phrase), but even the mildest of them was surrounded by a kind of aura or field—Sutty hated such words yet had to use them—that kept one from informal approach. They were aloof, absorbed in the telling, the books, the treasures of the caves.

The morning after the newcomers' arrival, the maz named Igneba and Ikak took them to and through what they called the Library. Numbers daubed in luminous paint over the openings corresponded to a chart of the caves that the maz showed them. By going always to a lower number, if you lost your way in the labyrinth—and it was quite easy to do so—you would always return to the outer caves. The man, Igneba Ikak, carried an electric torch, but like so much Akan manufacture it was unreliable or defective and kept failing. Ikak Igneba carried an oil lantern. From it once or twice she lighted lamps hanging on the walls, to illuminate the caves of being, the round rooms full of words, where the Telling lay hidden, in silence. Under rock, under snow.

Books, thousands of books, in leather and cloth and wooden and paper bindings, unbound manuscripts in carved and painted boxes and jewelled caskets, fragments of ancient writing blaz-ing with gold leaf, scrolls in tubes and boxes or tied with tape, books on vellum, parchment, rag paper, pulp paper, handwrit-ten, printed, books on the floors, in boxes, in small crates, on rickety low shelves made of scrap wood from the crates. In one big cave the volumes stood ranked on two shelves, at waist height and eye level, dug into the walls right around the cir-cumference. Those shelves were the work of long ago, Ikak said, carved by maz living here when it was a small umyazu and that one room had been all its library. Those maz had had the time and means for such work. Now all they could do was lay plastic sheeting to keep the books from the dirt or bare rock, stack or arrange them as best they could, try to sort them to some degree, and keep them hidden, keep them safe. Protect them, guard them, and, when there was time, read them.

But nobody in one lifetime could read more than a fragment of what was here, this broken labyrinth of words, this shattered, interrupted, immense story of a people and a world through the centuries, the millennia.

Odiedin sat down on the floor in one of the silent, gleam-lit caves where the books stretched away from the entrance in rows, like rows of mown grass but dark, vanishing into darkness. He sat down between two rows on the stone floor, picked up a small book with a worn cloth cover, and held it in his lap. He bowed his head over it without opening it. Tears ran down his cheeks.

They were free to go into the book caves as they wanted. In the days that followed, Sutty went back and back, wandering with the small, keen beam of an oil lamp to guide her, settling down here and there to read. She had her noter with her and scanned into it what she read, often whole books she didn't have time to read. She read the texts of blessings, the protocols of ceremonies, recipes, prescriptions for curing cold sores and for living to a great age, stories, legends, annals, lives of famous maz, lives of obscure merchants, testimonies of people who lived thousands of years ago and a few years ago, tales of travel, meditations of mystics, treatises of philosophy and of mathematics, herbals, bestiaries, anatomies, geometries both real and metaphysical, maps of Aka, maps of imaginary worlds, histories of ancient lands, poems. All the poems in the world were here.

She knelt at a wooden crate filled with papers and worn, handmade books, the salvage of some small umyazu or town, saved from the bulldozer and the bonfire, carried here up the long hard ways of the Mountain to be safe, to be kept, to tell. By the light of her lamp on the rock floor she opened one of the books, a child's primer. The ideograms were written large and without any qualifiers of aspect, mood, number, and Element. On one page was a crude woodcut of a man fishing from a humpbacked bridge. THE MOUNTAIN IS THE MOTHER OF THE RIVER, said the ideograms beneath the picture.

She would stay in the caves reading till the words of the

dead, the utter silence, the cold, the globe of darkness surrounding her, grew too strange, and she made her way back to daylight and the sound of living voices.

She knew now that all she would ever know of the Telling was the least hint or fragment of what there was to know. But that was all right; that was how it was. So long as it was here.

One maz couple was making a catalogue of the books in their Akan version of Sutty's noter. They had been coming up to the caves for twenty years, working on the catalogue. They discussed it with her eagerly, and she promised to try to link her noter with theirs to duplicate and transfer the information.

Though the maz treated her with unfailing courtesy and respect, conversations were mostly formal and often difficult. They all had to speak in a language not their own, Dovzan. Though the Akans spoke it in public in their lives "down below," it was not the language in which they thought, and not the language of the Telling. It was the tongue of the enemy. It was a barrier. Sutty realized how much closer she had drawn to people in Okzat-Ozkat as she learned their Rangma speech. Several of the maz of the Library knew Hainish, which was taught in the Corporation universities as a mark of true education. It wasn't of much use here, except perhaps in one conversation Sutty had with the young maz Unroy Kigno.

They went out together to enjoy the daylight for an hour and to sweep footsteps away. Since the helicopter had come so close, the first aircraft that had ever done so, the people of the Library took more care to sweep away paths or tracks in the snow that might lead an eye in the sky to the entrances of the caves. Sutty and Unroy had finished the rather pleasant job of throwing the light, dry snow about with brooms, and were taking a breather, sitting on boulders near the minules' stable.

"What is history?" Unroy asked abruptly, using the Hainish word. "Who are historians? Are you one?"

"The Hainish say I am," Sutty said, and they launched into a long and intense linguistico-philosophical discussion about whether history and the Telling could be understood as the same thing, or similar things, or not alike at all; about what historians did, what maz did, and why.

"I think history and the Telling are the same thing," Unroy said at last. "They're ways of holding and keeping things sacred."

"What is sacredness?"

"What is true is sacred. What has been suffered. What is beautiful."

"So the Telling tries to find the truth in events . . . or the pain, or the beauty?"

"No need to try to find it," said Unroy. "The sacredness is there. In the truth, the pain, the beauty. So that the telling of it is sacred."

Her partner, Kigno, was in a prison camp in Doy. He had been arrested and sentenced for teaching atheist religion and reactionary antiscience dogma. Unroy knew where he was, a huge steel-mill complex manned by prisoners, but no communication was possible.

"There are hundreds of thousands of people in the rehabilitation centers," Unroy told Sutty. "The Corporation gets its labor cheap."

"What are you going to do with your prisoner here?"

Unroy shook her head. "I wish he'd been killed like the other one," she said. "He's a problem we have no solution to."

Sutty agreed in bitter silence.

The Monitor was being well looked after; several of the maz were professional healers. They had put him in a small tent by himself and kept him warm and fed. His tent was in a big cave among seven or eight tents belonging to guides and minule hostlers. There was always somebody there with an ear and an eye, as they put it. In any case there was no danger of his trying to escape until his wrenched back and badly damaged knee mended.

Odiedin visited him daily. Sutty had not yet brought herself to do so.

"His name is Yara," Odiedin told her.

"His name is Monitor," she said, contemptuous.

"Not any longer," Odiedin said drily. "His pursuit of us was unauthorised. If he goes back to Dovza, he'll be sent to a rehabilitation center."

"A forced labor camp? Why?"

"Officials must not exceed their orders or take unauthorised action."

"That wasn't a Corporation helicopter?"

Odiedin shook his head. "The pilot owned it. Used it to

bring supplies to mountain climbers in the South Range. Yara hired him. To look for us."

"How strange," Sutty said. "Was he after me, then?"

"As a guide."

"I was afraid of that."

"I was not." Odiedin sighed. "The Corporation is so big, its apparatus is so clumsy, we little people in these big hills are beneath their notice. We slip through the mesh. Or we've done so for many years. So I didn't worry. But he wasn't the Corporation police. He was one man. One fanatic."

"Fanatic?" She laughed. "He believes slogans? He loves the Corporation?"

"He hates us. The maz, the Telling. He fears you."

"As an alien?"

"He thinks you'll persuade the Ekumen to side with the maz against the Corporation."

"What makes him think that?"

"I don't know. He's a strange man. I think you should talk with him."

"What for?"

"To hear what he has to tell," Odiedin said.

She put it off, but conscience pushed her. Odiedin was no scholar, no sage like these maz from the lowlands, but he had a clear mind and a clear heart. On their long trek she had come to trust him entirely, and when she saw him crying over the books in the Library, she knew she loved him. She wanted to do what he asked her to do, even if it was to hear what the Monitor had to tell.

Maybe she could also tell the Monitor a little of what he ought to hear. In any case, sooner or later she'd have to face him. And the question of what to do about him. And the question of her responsibility for his being there.

Before the evening meal the next day, she went to the big cave where they had put him. A couple of minule handlers were gambling, tossing marked sticks, by lantern light. On the inner wall of the cave, a pure black concave curve ten meters high, the figure of the Tree had been incised by the dwellers here in centuries past: the single trunk, the two branches, the five lobes of foliage. Gold leaf still glittered in the lines of the drawing, and bits of crystal, jet, and moonstone winked among the carved leaves. Her eyes were well used to darkness now. The glow of a small electric light in a tent close under the back wall seemed as bright as sunlight.

"The Dovzan?" she asked the gamblers. One nodded with his chin toward the lighted tent.

The door flap was closed. She stood outside a while and finally said, "Monitor?"

The flap opened. She looked in cautiously. The small interior of the tent was warm and bright. They had fixed the injured man a bed pad with a slanted back support so he need not lie entirely flat. The cord of the door flap, a hand-crank-powered electric lamp, a tiny oil heater, a bottle of water, and a small noter lay within his reach.

He had been terribly bruised in the crash, and the bruising was still livid: blue-black-green all down the right side of his face, the right eye swollen half shut, both arms spotted with great brown-blue marks. Two fingers of his left hand were lightly splinted. But Sutty's eyes were on the little device, the noter.

She entered the tent on her knees, and kneeling in the narrow clear space, picked up the device and studied it.

"It doesn't transmit," the man said.

"So you say," Sutty said, beginning to play with it, to run it through its paces. After a while she said, ironically, "Apologies for going through your private files, Monitor. I'm not interested in them. But I have to test this thing's capacities."

He said nothing.

The device was a recorder notebook, rather flashily designed but with several serious design flaws, like so much Akan technology—undigested techshit, she thought. It had no sending or receiving functions. She set it back down where he could reach it.

That alarm relieved, she was aware of her embarrassment and intense discomfort at being shut in this small space with this man. She wanted nothing but distance from him. The only way to make it was with words.

"What were you trying to do?"

"Follow you."

"Your government had ordered you not to."

After a pause he said, "I could not accept that."

"So the cog is wiser than the wheel?"

He said nothing. He had not moved at all since opening the door flap. The rigidity of his body probably signified pain. She observed it with no feeling.

"If you hadn't crashed, what would you have done? Flown back to Dovza and reported—what? Some cave mouths?"

He said nothing.

"What do you know about this place?"

As she asked the question, she realised that he had seen nothing of it but this one cave, a few hostlers, a few maz. He need never learn what it was. They could blindfold him— probably no need even for that: just get him out, get him away as soon as he could be moved. He had seen nothing but a travelers' resting place. He had nothing to report.

"This is the Lap of Silong," he said. "The last Library."

"What makes you think that?" she said, made angry by disappointment.

"This is where you were coming. The Office of Ethical Purity has been looking for it for a long time. The place where they hide the books. This is it."

"Who are 'they,' Monitor?"

"The enemies of the state."

"O Ram!" she said. She sat back, as far from him as she could get, and hugged her knees. She spoke slowly, stopping after each sentence. "You people have learned everything we did wrong, and nothing we did right. I wish we'd never come to Aka. But since in our own stupid intellectual hubris we did so, we should either have refused you the information you demanded, or taught you Terran history. But of course you wouldn't have listened. You don't believe in history. You threw out your own history like garbage."

"It was garbage."

His brown skin was greyish where it wasn't black-and-blue. His voice was hoarse and dogged. The man is hurt and helpless, she thought with neither sympathy nor shame.

"I know who you are," she said. "You're my enemy. The true believer. The righteous man with the righteous mission. The one that jails people for reading and burns the books. That persecutes people who do exercises the wrong way. That dumps out the medicine and pisses on it. That pushes the button that sends the drones to drop the bombs. And hides behind a bunker and doesn't get hurt. Shielded by God. Or the state. Or whatever lie he uses to hide his envy and self-interest and cowardice and lust for power. It took me a while to see you, though. You saw me right away. You knew I was your enemy. Was unrighteous. How did you know it?"

"They sent you to the mountains," he said. He had been looking straight forward, but he turned his head stiffly now to meet her eyes. "To a place where you would meet the maz. I did not wish any harm to you, yoz."

After a moment she said, "Yoz!"

He had looked away again. She watched his swollen, unreadable face.

He reached out his good hand and began to pump the hand crank of his lamp up and down. The little square bulb inside it immediately brightened. For the hundredth time in a corner of her mind Sutty wondered why the Akans made their lightbulbs square. But the rest of her mind was full of shadows, anger, hate, contempt.

"Did your people let me go to Okzat-Ozkat as a decoy? A tool of your official ideologues? Were they hoping I'd lead them here?"

"I thought so," he said after a pause.

"But you told me to keep away from the maz!"

"I thought they were dangerous."

"To whom?"

"To . . . the Ekumen. And my government." He used the old word, and corrected it: "The Corporation."

"You don't make sense, Monitor."

He had stopped cranking the lamp. He looked straight ahead again.

"The pilot said, 'There they are,' and we came up alongside the path," he said. "And he shouted, and I saw your group on the path. And smoke, behind you, smoke coming out of the rocks. But we were being thrown sideways, into the mountain. Into the rocks. The helicopter was thrown. Pushed."

He held his injured left hand with his right hand, stiffly. He was controlling his shivering.

"Catabatic winds, yoz," Sutty said after a while, softly. "And very high altitude for a helicopter."

He nodded. He had told himself the same thing. Many times, no doubt.

"They hold this place sacred," she said.

Where did that word come from? Not a word she used. Why was she tormenting him? Wrong, wrong.

"Listen, Yara—that's your name?—don't let rotten-corpse superstition get hold of you. I don't think Mother Silong pays any attention to us at all."

He shook his head, mute. Maybe he had told himself that, too.

She did not know what else to say to him. After a long silence, he spoke.

"I deserve punishment," he said.

That shook her.

"Well, you got it," she said finally. "And you'll probably get more, one way or another. What are we going to do with you? That has to be decided. It's getting on into late summer. They're talking of leaving in a few weeks. So, until then you might as well take it easy. And get walking again. Because wherever you go from here, I don't think you'll be flying on the south wind."

He looked at her again. He was unmistakably frightened. By what she had said? By whatever guilt had made him say, "I deserve punishment"? Or merely because lying helpless among the enemy was a frightening job?

He gave his stiff, painful, single nod and said, "My knee will be healed soon."

As she went back through the caves, she thought that, grotesque as it seemed, there was something childlike about the man, something simple and pure. Then she said to herself, Simplistic, not simple, and what the hell does pure mean? Saintly, holy, all that stuff? (*Don't Mother-Teresa me, girl,* Uncle Hurree muttered in her mind.) He was simpleminded, with his "enemy of the state" jargon. And single-minded. A fanatic, as Odiedin had said. In fact, a terrorist. Pure and simple.

Talking with him had soured her. She wished she had not done it, had not seen him. Anxiety and frustration made her impatient with her friends.

Kieri, with whom she still shared the tent, though not lately the sleeping bag, was cheerful and affectionate, but her self-confidence was impervious. Kieri knew all she wanted to know. All she wanted of the Telling was stories and superstitions. She had no interest in learning from the maz here and never went into the caves of books. She had come for the mere adventure.

Akidan, on the other hand, was in a state of hero worship fatally mixed with lust. The guide Shui had gone back to her village soon after they came to the caves, leaving Akidan in his tent alone, and he had immediately fallen in love with Maz Unroy Kigno. He stuck to her like a minule kid to its mother, gazed at her with worshiping eyes, memorised her every word. Unfortunately, the only people under the old system whose sexual life was strictly regulated were the maz. Lifelong monogamy was their rule, whether they were or were not with their partner. The maz Sutty had known, as far as she could see, lived by this rule. And Akidan, a gentle-natured young man, had no real intention of questioning or testing it. He was simply smitten, head over heels, a pitiful victim of hormone-driven hagiolatry.

Unroy was sorry for him but did not let him know it. She discouraged him harshly, challenging his self-discipline, his learning, his capacity to become a maz. When he made his infatuation too clear, she turned on him and quoted a well-known tag from *The Arbor*, "The two that are one are not two, but the one that is two is one. . . ." It seemed a fairly subtle reproof, but Akidan turned pale with shame and slunk away. He had been miserable ever since. Kieri talked with him a good deal and seemed inclined to comfort him. Sutty rather wished she would. She didn't want the seethe and sway of adolescent emotions; she wanted adult counsel, mature certainty. She felt that she must go forward and was at a dead end; must decide and did not know what was to be decided.

The Lap of Silong was wholly cut off from the rest of the world. No radios or any kind of communicators were ever brought there, lest signals be traced. News could come only up the northeastern paths or along the long, difficult way Sutty's party had come from the southeast. This late in the summer, it was most unlikely that anyone else would arrive; indeed, as she had told the Monitor, the people here were already talking of leaving.

She listened to them discuss their plans. It was their custom to depart a few at a time and take different ways where the paths diverged. As soon as they could do so, they would join with the small caravans of summer-village people going down to the foothills. Thus the pilgrimage, the way to the caves, had been kept invisible for forty years.

It was already too late, Odiedin told her, to go back the way their group had come, on the southeast trail. The guides from the deep village had left for home promptly, and even so expected to meet storm and snow on Zubuam. The rest of them would have to go down into Amareza, the hill region northeast of Silong, and work their way around the end of the Headwaters Range and back up through the foothills to Okzat-Ozkat. On foot it would take a couple of months. Odiedin thought they could get lifts on trucks through the hill country, though they would have to split up into pairs to do so.

It all sounded frightening and improbable to Sutty. To follow her guides up into the mountains, to follow a hidden way through the clouds to a secret, sacred place, was one thing; to wander like a beggar, to hitchhike, anonymous and unprotected, in the vast countrysides of an alien world, was another thing altogether. She trusted Odiedin, yes, but she wanted very badly to get in touch with Tong Ov.

And what were they going to do with the Monitor? Let him loose to run and blab to the bureaus and the ministries about the last great cache of banned books? He might be in terminal disgrace, but before his bosses sent him off to the salt mines, they'd hear what he had to report.

And what would she say to Tong Ov when and if she ever did talk to him again? He had sent her to find Aka's history, its lost, outlawed past, its true being, and she had found it. But then what?

What the maz wanted of her was clear and urgent: they wanted her to save their treasure. It was the only thing clear to her in the obscure turmoil of her thoughts and feelings since she had talked to the Monitor.

What she herself wanted—would have wanted, if it had been possible—was to stay here. To live in the caves of being, to read, to hear the Telling, here where it was still complete or nearly complete, still one unbroken story. To live in the forest of words. To listen. That was what she was fitted for, what she longed to do, and could not.

As the maz longed to do and could not.

"We were stupid, yoz Sutty," said Goiri Engnake, a maz from the great city of Kangnegne in the center of the continent, a scholar of philosophy who had served fourteen years in an agricultural labor camp for disseminating reactionary ideology. She was a worn, tough, abrupt woman. "Carrying everything up here. We should have left it all over the place. Left the books with whoever had the books, and made copies. Spent our time copying, instead of bringing everything we have together where they can destroy it all at once. But you see we're old-fashioned. People thought about how long it takes to copy, how dangerous it is to try to print. They didn't look at the machines the Corporation started making, the ways to copy things in an instant, to put whole libraries into a computer. Now we've got our treasure where we can't use those technologies. We can't bring a computer up here, and if we could, how would we power it? And how long would it take to put all this into it?"

"With Akan technology, years," Sutty said. "With what's available to the Ekumen, a summer, maybe."

Looking at Goiri's face, she added, slowly, "If we were authorised to do so. By the Corporation of Aka. And by the Stabiles of the Ekumen."

"I understand."

They were in the "kitchen," the cave where they cooked and ate. It was sealed to the extent that it could be kept habitably warm, and was the gathering place, at all hours, for discussions and conversations. They had eaten breakfast and were each nursing along a cup of very weak bezit tea. *It starts the flow and reunites*, Iziezi murmured in her mind.

"Would you ask the Envoy to request such authorisation, yoz?"

"Yes, of course," Sutty said. After a pause, "That is, I would ask him if he considered it feasible, or wise. If such a request indicated to your government that this place exists, we'd have blown your cover, maz."

Goiri grinned at Sutty's choice of words. They were of course speaking in Dovzan. "But maybe the fact that you know about it, that the Ekumen is interested in it, would protect the Library," she said. "Prevent them from sending the police here to destroy it."

"Maybe."

"The Executives of the Corporation hold the Ekumen in very high respect."

"Yes. They also hold its Envoys completely out of touch with everybody on Aka except ministers and bureaucrats. The Corporation has been given a great deal of useful information. In return, the Ekumen has been given a great deal of useless propaganda."

Goiri pondered this, and asked at last, "If you know that, why do you allow it?"

"Well, Maz Goiri, the Ekumen takes a very long view. So long that it's often hard for a short-lived being to live with. The principle we work on is that withholding knowledge is always a mistake—in the long run. So if asked to tell what we know, we tell it. To that extent, we're like you, maz."

"No longer," Goiri said bitterly. "All we know, we hide."

"You have no choice. Your bureaucrats are dangerous people. They're believers." Sutty sipped her tea. Her throat was dry. "On my world, when I was growing up, there was a powerful group of believers. They believed that their beliefs should prevail absolutely, that no other way of thinking should exist. They sabotaged the information storage networks and destroyed libraries and schools all over the world. They didn't destroy everything, of course. It can be pieced back together. But . . . damage was done. That kind of damage is something like a stroke. One recovers, almost. But you know all that."

She stopped. She was talking too much. Her voice was shaking. She was getting too close to it. Far too close to it. Wrong.

Goiri looked shaken too. "All I know of your world, yoz . . ."

"Is that we fly around in space ships bringing enlightenment to lesser, backward worlds," Sutty said. Then she slapped one hand on the table and the other across her mouth.

Goiri stared.

"It's a way the Rangma have of reminding themselves to shut up," Sutty said. She smiled, but her hands were shaking now.

They were both silent for a while.

"I thought of you . . . of all the people of the Ekumen, as very wise, above error. How childish," Goiri said. "How unfair."

Another silence.

"I'll do what I can, maz," Sutty said. "If and when I get back to Dovza City. It might not be safe to try to get in touch with the Mobile by telephone from Amareza. I could say, for the wiretappers, that we got lost trying to hike up to Silong and found an eastern path out of the mountains. But if I turn up in Amareza, where I wasn't authorised to go, they'll ask questions. I can clam up, but I don't think I can lie. I mean, not well. . . . And there's the problem of the Monitor."

"Yes. I wish you would talk to him, yoz Sutty."

Et tu, Brute? said Uncle Hurree, his eyebrows sarcastic.

"Why, Maz Goiri?"

"Well, he is—as you call it—a believer. And as you say, that's dangerous. Tell him what you told me about your Earth. Tell him more than you told me. Tell him that belief is the wound that knowledge heals."

Sutty drank the last of her tea. The taste was bitter, delicate. "I can't remember where I heard that. Not in a book. I heard it told."

"Teran said it to Penan. After he was wounded fighting the barbarians."

Sutty remembered now: the circle of mourners in the green valley under the great slopes of stone and snow, the body of the young man covered with thin, ice-white cloth, the voice of the maz telling the story.

Goiri said, "Teran was dying. He said, 'My brother, my husband, my love, my self, you and I believed that we would defeat our enemy and bring peace to our land. But belief is the wound that knowledge heals, and death begins the Telling of our life.' Then he died in Penan's arms."

The grave, yoz. Where it begins.

"I can carry that message," Sutty said finally. "Though bigots have small ears."

Eight

HIS TENT WAS LIGHTED only by the faint glimmer of the heater. When she entered, he began pumping the little crank of the lantern. It took a long time to brighten, and the glow was small and feeble.

She sat down cross-legged in the empty half of the tent. As well as she could make out, his face was no longer swollen, though still discolored. The backboard was set so that he was sitting up almost straight.

"You lie here in the dark, night and day," she said. "It must be strange. Sensory deprivation. How do you pass the time?" She heard the cold sharpness of her voice.

"I sleep," he said. "I think."

"Therefore you are. . . . Do you recite slogans? Onward, upward, forward? Reactionary thought is the defeated enemy?"

He said nothing.

A book lay beside the bed pad. She picked it up. It was a schoolbook, a collection of poems, stories, exemplary lives, and so on, for children of ten or so. It took her some moments to realise that it was printed in ideograms, not in alphabet. She had practically forgotten that in the Monitor's world, in modern Aka, everything was in alphabet, that the ideograms were banned, illegal, unused, forgotten.

"Can you read this?" she demanded, startled and somehow unnerved.

"Odiedin Manma gave it to me."

"Can you read it?"

"Slowly."

"When did you learn to read rotten-corpse primitive anti-scientific writing, Monitor?"

"When I was a boy."

"Who taught you?"

"The people I lived with."

"Who were they?"

"My mother's parents."

His answers came always after a pause, and spoken low, almost mumbled, like the replies of a humiliated schoolboy to a goading questioner. Sutty was abruptly overcome with shame. She felt her cheeks burn, her head swim.

Wrong again. Worse than wrong.

After a prolonged silence she said, "I beg your pardon for the way I've been talking to you. I disliked your manner to me, on the boat and in Okzat-Ozkat. I came to hate you when I thought you responsible for destroying Maz Sotyu Ang's herbary, his lifework, his life. And for hounding my friends. And hounding me. I hate the bigotry you believe in. But I'll try not to hate you."

"Why?" he asked. His voice was cold, as she remembered it.

"Hate eats the hater," she quoted from a familiar text of the Telling.

He sat impassive, tense as always. She, however, began to relax. Her confession had relieved not only her shame but also the resentful oppression she had felt in his presence. She got her legs into a more comfortable semilotus, straightened her back. She was able to look at him instead of sneaking glances. She watched his rigid face for a while. He would not or could not say anything, but she could.

"They want me to talk to you," she said. "They want me to tell you what life is like on Terra. The sad and ugly truths you'll find at the end of the March to the Stars. So that maybe you'll begin to ask yourself that fatal question: Do I know what I'm doing? But you probably don't want to. . . . Also I'm curious about what life's like for someone like you. What makes a man a Monitor. Will you tell me? Why did you live with your grandparents? Why did you learn to read the old writing? You're about forty, I should think. It was already banned when you were a child, wasn't it?"

He nodded. She had put the book back down. He picked it up, seeming to study the flowing calligraphy of the title on the cover: JEWEL FRUITS FROM THE TREE OF LEARNING.

"Tell me," she said. "Where were you born?"

"Bolov Yeda. On the western coast."

"And they named you Yara—'Strong.'"

He shook his head. "They named me Azyaru," he said.

Azya Aru. She had been reading about them just a day or so ago in a *History of the Western Lands*, which Unroy showed her in one of their forays into the Library. A maz couple of two centuries ago, Azya and Aru had been the chief founders and apostles of the Telling in Dovza. The first boss maz. Dovzan culture heroes, until the secularisation. Under the Corporation, they had no doubt become culture villains, until they could be totally erased, whited out, deleted.

"Were your parents maz, then?"

"My grandparents." He held the book as if it were a talisman. "The first thing I remember is my grandfather showing me how to write the word 'tree.'" His finger on the cover of the book sketched the two-stroke ideogram. "We were sitting on the porch, in the shade, where we could see the sea. The fishing boats were coming in. Bolov Yeda is on hills above a bay. The biggest city on the coast. My grandparents had a beautiful house. There was a vine growing over the porch, up to the roof, with a thick trunk and yellow flowers. They held the Telling in the house every day. They went to the umyazu in the evenings."

He used the forbidden pronoun, he/she/they. He was not aware of it, Sutty thought. His voice had become soft, husky, easy.

"My parents were schoolteachers. They taught the new writing at the Corporation school. I learned it, but I liked the old writing better. I was interested in writing, in books. In the things my grandparents taught me. They thought I was born to be a maz. Grandmother would say, 'Oh, Kiem, let the child go play!' But Grandfather would want me to stay and learn one more set of characters, and I always wanted to please him. To do better. . . . Grandmother taught me the spoken things, the things children learned of the Telling. But I liked the writing better. I could make it look beautiful. I could keep it. The spoken words just went out like the wind, and you always had to say them all over again to keep them alive. But the writing stayed, and you could learn to make it better. More beautiful."

"So you went to live with your grandparents, to study with them?"

He answered with the same quietness and almost dreamy ease. "When I was a little child, we lived there all together. Then my father became a school administrator. And my mother entered the Ministry of Information. They were transferred to

Tambe, and then to Dovza City. My mother had to travel a great deal. They both rose very quickly in the Corporation. They were valuable officials. Very active. My grandparents said it would be better if I stayed home with them, while my parents were moving about and working so hard. So I did."

"And you wanted to stay with them?"

"Oh, yes," he said, with complete simplicity. "I was happy."

The word seemed to echo in his mind, to jar him out of the quietness from which he had been speaking. He turned his head away from Sutty, an abrupt movement that brought vividly to her mind the moment on the street in Okzat-Ozkat when he said to her with passionate anger and pleading, "Do not betray us!"

They sat a while without speaking. No one else was moving about or talking in the Tree Cave. Deep silence in the Lap of Silong.

"I grew up in a village," Sutty said. "With my uncle and aunt. Really my great-uncle and great-aunt. Uncle Hurree was thin and quite dark-skinned, with white bristly hair and eyebrows —terrible eyebrows. I thought he frowned lightning out of them, when I was little. Aunty was a tremendous cook and manager. She could organise anybody. I learned to cook before I learned how to read. But Uncle did teach me, finally. He'd been a professor at the University of Calcutta. A great city in my part of Terra. He taught literature. We had five rooms in the house in the village, and they were all full of books, except the kitchen. Aunty wouldn't allow books in the kitchen. But they were piled all over my room, all around the walls, under the bed and the table. When I first saw the Library caves here, I thought of my room at home."

"Did your uncle teach in the village?"

"No. He hid there. We hid. My parents were hiding in a different place. Lying low. There was a kind of revolution going on. Like yours here, but the other way round. People who . . . But I'd rather listen to you than talk about that. Tell me what happened. Did you have to leave your grandparents? How old were you?"

"Eleven," he said.

She listened. He spoke.

"My grandparents were very active too," he said. His tone

had become leaden, labored, though he did not hesitate for words. "But not as loyal producer-consumers. They were leaders of a band of underground reactionary activists. Fomenting cult activities and teaching antiscience. I didn't understand that. They took me to the meetings they organised. I didn't know they were illegal meetings. The umyazu was closed, but they didn't tell me that the police had closed it. They didn't send me to Corporation school. They kept me home and taught me only superstition and deviant morality. Finally my father realised what they were doing. He and my mother had separated. He hadn't been to see me for two years, but he sent for me. A man came. He came at night. I heard my grandmother talking very loudly, angrily. I'd never heard her talk that way. I got up and came into the front room. My grandfather was sitting in his chair, just sitting, he didn't look at me or say anything. Grandmother and a man were facing each other across the table. They looked at me, and then the man looked at her. She said, 'Go get dressed, Azyaru, your father wants you to come see him.' I went and got dressed. When I came out again, they were still just the way they had been, exactly the same: Grandfather sitting like an old, deaf, blind man staring at nothing, and Grandmother standing with her hands in fists on the table, and the man standing there. I began crying. I said, 'I don't want to go, I want to stay here.' Then Grandmother came and held my shoulders, but she pushed me. She pushed me at the man. He said, 'Come on.' And she said, 'Go, Azyaru!' And I . . . went with him."

"Where did you go?" Sutty asked in a whisper.

"To my father in Dovza City. I went to school there." A long silence. He said, "Tell me about . . . your village. Why you were hiding."

"Fair's fair," Sutty said. "But it's a long story."

"All stories are long," he murmured. The Fertiliser had said something like that once. *Short stories are only pieces of the long one*, he had said.

"What's hard to explain is about God, on my world," she said.

"I know God," Yara said.

That made her smile. It lightened her for a moment. "I'm sure you do," she said. "But what might be hard to understand, here, is what God is, there. Here, it's a word and not much else. In your state theism, it seems to mean what's good. What's right. Is that right?"

"God is Reason, yes," he said, rather uncertainly.

"Well, on Terra, the word has been an enormously important one for thousands of years, among many peoples. And usually it doesn't refer so much to what's reasonable as to what's mysterious. What can't be understood. So there are all kinds of ideas of God. One is that God is an entity that created everything else and is responsible for everything that exists and happens. Like a kind of universal, eternal Corporation."

He looked intent but puzzled.

"Where I grew up, in the village, we knew about that kind of God, but we had a lot of other kinds. Local ones. A great many of them. They all were each other, though, really. There were some great ones, but I didn't know much about them as a child. Only from my name. Aunty explained my name to me once. I asked, 'Why am I Sutty?' And she said, 'Sutty was God's wife.' And I asked, 'Am I Ganesh's wife?' Because Ganesh was the God I knew best, and I liked him. But she said, 'No, Shiva's.'

"All I knew about Shiva then was that he has a lovely white bull that's his friend. And he has long, dirty hair and he's the greatest dancer in the universe. He dances the worlds into being and out of being. He's very strange and ugly and he's always fasting. Aunty told me that Sutty loved him so much that she married him against her father's will. I knew that was hard for a girl to do in those days, and I thought she was very brave. But then Aunty told me that Sutty went back to see her father. And her father talked insultingly about Shiva and was extremely rude to him. And Sutty was so angry and ashamed that she died of it. She didn't *do* anything, she just *died*. And ever since then, faithful wives who die when their husbands die are called after her. Well, when Aunty told me that, I said, 'Why did you name me for a stupid silly woman like that!'

"And Uncle was listening, and he said, 'Because Sati is Shiva, and Shiva is Sati. You are the lover and the griever. You are the anger. You are the dance.'

"So I decided if I had to be Sutty, it was all right, so long as I could be Shiva too. . . .'"

She looked at Yara. He was absorbed and utterly bewildered.

"Well, never mind about that. It is terribly complicated. But all the same, when you have a lot of Gods, maybe it's easier than having one. We had a God rock among the roots of a big tree near the road. People in the village painted it red and fed it butter, to please it, to please themselves. Aunty put marigolds at Ganesh's feet every day. He was a little bronze God with an animal nose in the back room. He was Shiva's son, actually. Much kinder than Shiva. Aunty recited things and sang to him. Doing pooja. I used to help her do pooja. I could sing some of the songs. I liked the incense and the marigolds. . . . But these people I have to tell you about, the people we were hiding from, they didn't have any little Gods. They hated them. They only had one big one. A big boss God. Whatever they said God said to do was right. Whoever didn't do what they said God said to do was wrong. A lot of people believed this. They were called Unists. *One God, one Truth, one Earth.* And they . . . They made a lot of trouble."

The words came out foolish, babyish, primer words for the years of agony.

"You see, my people, I mean all of us on Earth, had done a lot of damage to our world, fought over it, used it up, wasted it. There'd been plagues, famines, misery for so long. People wanted comfort and help. They wanted to believe they were doing something right. I guess if they joined the Unists, they could believe everything they did was right."

He nodded. That he understood.

"The Unist Fathers said that what they called evil knowledge had brought all this misery. If there was no evil knowledge, people would be good. Unholy knowledge should be destroyed to make room for holy belief. They opposed science, all learning, everything except what was in their own books."

"Like the maz."

"No. No, I think that's a mistake, Yara. I can't see that the Telling excludes any knowledge, or calls any knowledge evil, or anything unholy. It doesn't include anything of what Aka has learned in the last century from contact with other civilisations —that's true. But I think that's only because the maz didn't have time to start working all that new information into the Telling before the Corporation State took over as your central social institution. It replaced the maz with bureaucrats, and then criminalised the Telling. Pushed it underground, where it couldn't develop and grow. Called it unholy knowledge, in fact. What I don't understand is why the Corporation thought such violence, such brutal use of power, was necessary."

"Because the maz had had all the wealth, all the power. They kept the people ignorant, drugged with rites and superstitions."

"But they *didn't* keep the people ignorant! What is the Telling but teaching whatever's known to whoever will listen?"

He hesitated, rubbed his hand over his mouth. "Maybe that was the old way," he said. "Maybe once. But it wasn't like that. In Dovza the maz were oppressors of the poor. All the land belonged to the umyazu. Their schools taught only fossilised, useless knowledge. They refused to let people have the new justice, the new learning—"

"Violently?"

Again he hesitated.

"Yes. In Belsi the reactionary mob killed two officials of the Corporation State. There was disobedience everywhere. Defiance of the law."

He rubbed his hand hard over his face, though it must have hurt the sore, discolored temple and cheek.

"This is how it was," he said. "Your people came here and they brought a new world with them. A promise of our own world made greater, made better. They wanted to give us that. But the people who wanted to accept that world were stopped, prevented, by the old ways. The old ways of doing everything. The maz mumbling forever about things that happened ten thousand years ago, claiming they knew everything about everything, refusing to learn anything new, keeping people poor, holding us back. They were wrong. They were selfish. Usurers of knowledge. They had to be pushed aside, to make way for the future. And if they kept standing in the way, they had to be punished. We had to show people that they were wrong. My grandparents were wrong. They were enemies of the state. They would not admit it. They refused to change."

He had begun talking evenly, but by the end he was breathing in gasps, staring ahead of him, his hand clenched on the little primer.

"What happened to them?"

"They were arrested soon after I came to live with my father. They were in prison for a year in Tambe." A long pause. "A great number of recalcitrant reactionary leaders were brought to Dovza City for a just public trial. Those who recanted were allowed to do rehabilitative work on the Corporate Farms." His voice was colorless. "Those who did not recant were executed by the producer-consumers of Aka."

"They were shot?"

"They were brought into the Great Square of Justice." He stopped short.

Sutty remembered the place, a plain of pavement surrounded by the four tall, ponderous buildings housing the Central Courts. It was usually jammed with stalled traffic and hurrying pedestrians.

Yara began to talk again, still looking straight ahead at what he was telling.

"They all stood in the middle of the square, inside a rope, with police guarding them. People had come from all over to see justice done. There were thousands of people in the square. All around the criminals. And in all the streets leading to the square. My father brought me to see. We stood in a high window in the Supreme Court building. He put me in front of him so that I could see. There were piles of stones, building stones from umyazu that had been pulled down, big piles at the corners of the square. I didn't know what they were for. Then the police gave an order, and everybody pushed in toward the middle of the square where the criminals were. They began to beat them with the stones. Their arms went up and down and . . . They were supposed to throw the rocks, to stone the criminals, but there were too many people. It was too crowded. Hundreds of police, and all the people. So they beat them to death. It went on for a long time."

"You had to watch?"

"My father wanted me to see that they had been wrong."

He spoke quite steadily, but his hand, his mouth gave him away. He had never left that window looking down into the square. He was twelve years old and stood there watching for the rest of his life.

So he saw his grandparents had been wrong. What else could he have seen?

Again a long silence. Shared.

To bury pain so deep, so deep you never need feel it. Bury it under anything, everything. Be a good son. A good girl. Walk over the graves and never look down. *Keep far the Dog that's friend to men.* . . . But there were no graves. Smashed faces, splintered skulls, blood-clotted grey hair in a heap in the middle of a square.

Fragments of bone, tooth fillings, a dust of exploded flesh, a whiff of gas. The smell of burning in the ruins of a building in the rain.

"So after that you lived in Dovza City. And entered the Corporation. The Sociocultural Bureau."

"My father hired tutors for me. To remedy my education. I qualified well in the examinations."

"Are you married, Yara?"

"I was. For two years."

"No child?"

He shook his head.

He continued to gaze straight ahead. He sat stiffly, not moving. His sleeping bag was tented up over one knee on a kind of frame Tobadan had made to immobilise the knee and relieve the pain. The little book lay by his hand, JEWEL FRUITS FROM THE TREE OF LEARNING.

Sutty bent forward to loosen her shoulder muscles, sat up straight again.

"Goiri asked me to tell you about my world. Maybe I can, because my life hasn't been so different from yours, in some ways. . . . I told you about the Unists. After they took over the government of our part of the country, they started having what they called cleansings in the villages. It got more and more unsafe for us. People told us we should hide our books, or throw them in the river. Uncle Hurree was dying then. His heart was tired, he said. He told Aunty she should get rid of his books, but she wouldn't. He died there with them around him.

"After that, my parents were able to get Aunty and me out of India. Clear across the world, to another continent, in the north, to a city where the government wasn't religious. There were some cities like that, mostly where the Ekumen had started schools that taught the Hainish learning. The Unists hated the Ekumen and wanted to keep all the extraterrestrials off Earth, but they were afraid to try to do it directly. So they encouraged terrorism against the Pales and the ansible installations and anything else the alien demons were responsible for."

She used the English word *demon*, there being no such word in Dovzan. She paused a while, took a deep, conscious breath. Yara sat in the intense silence of the listener.

"So I went to high school and college there, and started training to work for the Ekumen. About that time, the Ekumen sent a new Envoy to Terra, a man called Dalzul, who'd grown up on Terra. He came to have a great deal of influence among the Unist Fathers. Before very long they were giving him more and more control, taking orders from him. They said he was an angel—that's a messenger from God. Some of them began to say he was going to save all mankind and bring them to God, and so . . ." But there was no Akan word for worship. "They lay down on the ground in front of him and praised him and begged him to be kind to them. And they did whatever he told them to do, because that was their idea of how to do right—to obey orders from God. And they thought Dalzul spoke for God. Or was God. So within a year he got them to dismantle the theocratic regime. In the name of God.

"Most of the old regions or states were going back to democratic governments, choosing their leaders by election, and restoring the Terran Commonwealth, and welcoming people from the other worlds of the Ekumen. It was an exciting time. It was wonderful to watch Unism fall to pieces, crumble into fragments. More and more of the believers believed Dalzul was God, but also more and more of them decided that he was the . . . opposite of God, entirely wicked. There was one kind called the Repentants, who went around in processions throwing ashes on their heads and whipping each other to atone for having misunderstood what God wanted. And a lot of them broke off from all the others and set up some man, a Unist Father or a terrorist leader, as a Savior of their own, and took orders from him. They were all dangerous, they were all violent. The Dalzulites had to protect Dalzul from the anti-Dalzulites. They wanted to kill him. They were always planting bombs, trying suicide raids. All of them. They'd always used violence, because their belief justified it. It told them that God rewards those who destroy unbelief and the unbeliever. But mostly they were destroying each other, tearing each other to pieces. They called it the Holy Wars. It was a frightening time, but it seemed as if there was no real problem for the rest of us—Unism was just taking itself apart.

"Well, before it got as far as that, when the Liberation was just beginning, my city was set free. And we danced in the streets. And I saw a woman dancing. And I fell in love with her."

She stopped.

It had all been easy enough, to this point. This point beyond which she had never gone. The story that she had told only to herself, only in silence, before sleep, stopped here. Her throat began to tighten.

"I know you think that's wrong," she said.

After a hesitation, he said, "Because no children can be born of such union, the Committee on Moral Hygiene declared—"

"Yes, I know. The Unist Fathers declared the same thing. Because God created women to be vessels for men's semen. But after freedom we didn't have to hide for fear of being sent to revival camps. Like your maz couples who get sent to rehabilitation centers." She looked at him, challenging.

But he did not take the challenge. He accepted what she said and waited, listening.

She could not talk her away around it or away from it. She had to talk her way through it. She had to tell it.

"We lived together for two years," she said. Her voice came out so softly that he turned a little toward her to hear. "She was much prettier than me, and much more intelligent. And kinder. And she laughed. Sometimes she laughed in her sleep. Her name was Pao."

With the name came the tears, but she held them back.

"I was two years older and a year ahead of her in our training. I stayed back a year to be with her in Vancouver. Then I had to go and begin training in the Ekumenical Center, in Chile. A long way south. Pao was going to join me when she graduated from the university. We were going to study together and be a team, an Observer team. Go to new worlds together. We cried a lot when I had to leave for Chile, but it wasn't as bad as we thought it would be. It wasn't bad at all, really, because we could talk all the time on the phone and the

net and we knew we'd see each other in the winter, and then
after the spring she'd come down and we'd be together forever.
We *were* together. We were like maz. We were two that weren't
two, but one. It was a kind of pleasure or joy, missing her, because she was there, she was there to miss. And she told me the
same thing, she said that when I came back in the winter, she
was going to miss missing me. . . ."

She had begun crying, but the tears were easy, not hard.
Only she had to stop and sniff and wipe her eyes and nose.

"So I flew back to Vancouver for the holiday. It was summer
in Chile, but winter there. And we . . . we hugged and kissed
and cooked dinner. And we went to see my parents, and Pao's
parents, and walked in the park, where there were big trees,
old trees. It was raining. It rains a lot there. I love the rain."

Her tears had stopped.

"Pao went to the library, downtown, to look up something
for the examinations she'd be taking after the holiday. I was
going to go with her, but I had a cold, and she said, 'Stay here,
you'll just get soaked,' and I felt like lying around being lazy,
so I stayed in our apartment, and fell asleep.

"There was a Holy War raid. It was a group called the Puri-
fiers of Earth. They believed that Dalzul and the Ekumen were
servants of the anti-God and should be destroyed. A lot of
them had been in the Unist military forces. They had some of
the weapons the Unist Fathers had stockpiled. They used them
against the training schools."

She heard her voice, as flat as his had been.

"They used drones, unmanned bombers. From hundreds of
kilos away, in the Dakotas. They hid underground and pressed
a button and sent the drones. They blew up the college, the
library, blocks and blocks of the downtown. Thousands of
people were killed. Things like that happened all the time in
the Holy Wars. She was just one person. Nobody, nothing,
one person. I wasn't there. I heard the noise."

Her throat ached, but it always did. It always would.

She could not say anything more for a while.

Yara asked softly, "Were your parents killed?"

The question touched her. It moved her to a place where
she could respond. She said, "No. They were all right. I went
to stay with them. After that I went back to Chile."

They sat quietly. Inside the mountain, in the caves full of being. Sutty was weary, spent. She could see in Yara's face and hands that he was tired and still in pain. The silence they shared after their words was peaceful, a blessing earned.

After a long time she heard people talking, and roused herself from that silence.

She heard Odiedin's voice, and presently he spoke outside the tent: "Yara?"

"Come in," Yara said. Sutty pulled the flap aside.

"Ah," said Odiedin. In the weak light of the lantern his dark, high-cheekboned face peering in at them was an amiable goblin mask.

"We've been talking," Sutty said. She emerged from the tent, stood beside Odiedin, stretched.

"I came for your exercises," Odiedin said to Yara, kneeling at the entrance.

"Will he be on his feet soon?" she asked Odiedin.

"Using crutches is hard because of the way his back was hurt," he answered. "Some of the muscles haven't reattached. We keep working on it."

He went into the tent on his knees.

She turned away, then turned back and looked in. To leave without a word, after such a conversation as they had had, was wrong.

"I'll come again tomorrow, Yara," she said. He made some soft reply. She stood up, looking at the cave in the faint glow reflected from the sides of the other tents. She could not see the carving of the Tree on the high back wall, only one or two of the tiny, winking jewels in its foliage.

The Tree Cave had an exit to the outside, not far from Yara's tent. It led through a smaller cave to a short passage that ended in an arch so low that one had to crawl out into the light of day.

She emerged from that and stood up. She had pulled out her dark goggles, expecting to be dazzled, but the sun, hidden all afternoon by the great bulk of Silong, was setting or had set. The light was gentle, with a faint violet tinge. A little snow had fallen during the last few hours. The broad half circle of the cirque, like a stage seen from the backdrop, stretched away pale and untrodden to its outer edge. The air was quiet here under the wall of the mountain, but there at the edge, a hundred meters or so away, wind picked up and dropped the fine, dry snow in thin flurries and skeins, forever restless.

Sutty had been out to the edge only once. The cliff beneath it was sheer, slightly undercut, a mile-deep gulf. It had made her head swim, and as she stood there, the wind had tugged at her, gusting treacherously.

She gazed now over that small, ceaseless dance of the blown snow, across the emptiness of twilit air to Zubuam. The slopes of the Thunderer were vague, pale, remote in evening. She stood a long time watching the light die.

She went to talk with Yara most afternoons now, after she had explored another section of the Library and had worked with the maz who were cataloguing it. She and he never came back directly to what they had told each other of their lives, though it underlay everything they said, a dark foundation.

She asked him once if he knew why the Corporation had granted Tong's request, allowing an offworlder outside the information-restricted, controlled environment of Dovza City. "Was I a test case?" she asked. "Or a lure?"

It was not easy for him to overcome the habit of his official life, of all official lives: to protect and aggrandise his power by withholding information, and to let silence imply he had information even when he didn't. He had obeyed that rule all his adult life and probably could not have broken from it now, if he had not lived as a child within the Telling. As it was, he struggled visibly to answer. Sutty saw that struggle with compunction. Lying here, a prisoner of his injuries, dependent on his enemies, he had no power at all except in silence. To give it up, to let it go, to speak, took valor. It cost him all he had left.

"My department was not informed," he began, then stopped, and began again: "I believe that there have," and finally, doggedly, he started over, forcing himself through the jargon of his calling: "There have been high-level discussions concerning foreign policy for several years. Since an Akan ship is on its way to Hain, and being informed that an Ekumenical ship is scheduled to arrive next year, some elements within the Council have advocated a more relaxed policy. It was said that there might be profit if some doors were opened to an increase of mutual exchange of information. Others involved in decisions on these matters took the view that Corporation control of dissidence is still far too incomplete for any laxity to be advisable. A . . . a form of compromise was eventually attained among the factions of opinion on the matter."

When Yara had run out of passive constructions, Sutty made a rough mental translation and said, "So I was the compromise? A test case, then. And you were assigned to watch me and report."

"No," Yara said with sudden bluntness. "I asked to. Was allowed to. At first. They thought when you saw the poverty and backwardness of Rangma, you'd go back quickly to the city. When you settled in Okzat-Ozkat, the Central Executive didn't know how to exert control without giving offense. My department was overruled again. I advised that you be sent back to the capital. Even my superiors within the department ignored my reports. They ordered me back to the capital. They won't listen. They won't believe the strength of the maz in the towns and the countryside. They think the Telling is over!"

He spoke with intense and desolate anger, caught in the trap of his complex, insoluble pain. Sutty could think of nothing to say to him.

They sat there in a silence that gradually became more peaceful as they listened and surrendered to the pure silence of the caves.

"You were right," she said at last.

He shook his head, contemptuous, impatient. But when she left, saying she would look in again tomorrow, he muttered, "Thank you, yoz Sutty." Servile address, meaningless ritual phraseology. From the heart.

After that their conversations were easier. He wanted her to tell him about Earth, but it was hard for him to understand, and often, though she thought he did understand, he denied it. He protested: "All you tell me is about destruction, cruel actions, how things went badly. You hate your Earth."

"No," she said. She looked up at the tent wall. She saw the curve in the road just as you came to the village, and the roadside dust she and Moti played in. Red dust. Moti showed her how to make little villages out of mud and pebbles, planting flowers all around them. He was a whole year older than she was. The flowers wilted at once in the hot, hot sun of endless summer. They curled up and lay down and went back into the dark red mud that dried to silken dust.

"No, no," she said. "My world's beautiful beyond telling, and I love it, Yara. I'm telling you propaganda. I'm trying to tell you why, before your government started imitating what we do, they'd have done better to look at who we are. And at what we did to ourselves."

"But you came here. And you had so much knowledge we didn't have."

"I know. I know. The Hainish did the same thing to us. We've been trying to copy the Hainish, to catch up to the Hainish, ever since they found us. Maybe Unism was a protest against that as much as anything. An assertion of our God-given right to be self-righteous, irrational fools in our own particularly bloody way and not in anybody else's."

He pondered this. "But we need to learn. And you said that the Ekumen thinks it wrong to withhold any knowledge."

"I did. But the Historians study the way knowledge should be taught, so that what people learn is genuine knowledge, not a bit here and a bit there that don't fit together. There's a Hainish parable of the Mirror. If the glass is whole, it reflects the whole world, but broken, it shows only fragments, and cuts the hand that holds it. What Terra gave Aka is a splinter of the mirror."

"Maybe that's why the Executives sent the Legates back."

"The Legates?"

"The men on the second ship from Terra."

"Second ship?" Sutty said, startled and puzzled. "There was only one ship from Terra, before the one I came on."

But as she spoke, she remembered her last long conversation with Tong Ov. He had asked her if she thought the Unist Fathers, acting on their own without informing the Ekumen, might have sent missionaries to Aka.

"Tell me about it, Yara! I don't know anything about that ship."

She could see him physically draw back very slightly, struggling with his immediate reluctance to answer. This had been classified information, she thought, known only to the upper echelons, not part of official Corporation history. Though they no doubt assumed *we* knew it.

"A second ship came and was sent back to Terra?" she asked.

"It appears so."

She sent an exasperated silent message at his rigid profile: Oh, don't come the tight-lipped bureaucrat on me *now*! She said nothing. After a pause, he spoke again.

"There were records of the visit. I never saw them."

"What were you told about ships from Terra—can you tell me?"

He brooded a bit. "The first one came in the year Redan Thirty. Seventy-two years ago. It landed near Abazu, on the eastern coast. There were eighteen men and women aboard." He glanced at her to check this for accuracy, and she nodded. "The provincial governments that were still in power then in the east decided to let the aliens go wherever they liked. The aliens said they'd come to learn about us, and to invite us to join in the Ekumen. Whatever we asked them about Terra and the other worlds they'd tell us, but they came, they said, not as tellers but as listeners. As yoz, not maz. They stayed five years. A ship came for them, and on the ship's ansible they sent a telling of what they'd learned here back to Terra." Again he looked at her for confirmation.

"Most of that telling was lost," Sutty said.

"Did they get back to Terra?"

"I don't know. I left Terra sixty years ago, sixty-one years now. If they got back during the Unist rule, or during the Holy Wars, they might have been silenced, or jailed, or shot. . . . But there was a second ship?"

"Yes."

"The Ekumen sponsored that first ship. But it didn't sponsor another expedition from Terra, because the Unists had taken over. They cut communication with the Ekumen to a bare minimum. They kept closing ports and teaching centers, threatening aliens with expulsion, letting terrorists cripple the facilities, keeping them powerless. If a second ship came from Terra, the Unists sent it. I never heard anything about it, Yara. It certainly wasn't announced to the common people."

Accepting this, he said, "It came two years after the first ship left. There were fifty people on it, with a boss maz, a leader. His name was Fodderdon. It landed in Dovza, south of the capital. Its people got in touch with the Corporation Executives at once. They said Terra was going to give all its knowledge to Aka. They brought all kinds of information, technological information. They showed us how we'd have to stop doing things in the old, ignorant ways and change our thinking, to learn what they could teach us. They brought plans, and books, and engineers and theorists to teach us the techniques. They had an ansible on their ship, so that information could come from Terra as soon as we needed it."

"A great big box of toys," Sutty whispered.

"It changed everything. It strengthened the Corporation tremendously. It was the first step in the March to the Stars. Then . . . I don't know what happened. All we were told was that Fodderdon and the others gave us information freely at first, but then began to withhold it and to demand an unfair price for it."

"I can imagine what price," Sutty said.

He looked his question.

"Your immortal part," she said. There was no Akan word for soul. Yara waited for her to explain. "I imagine he said: You must believe. You must believe in the One God. You must believe that I alone, Father John, am God's voice on Aka. Only the story I tell is true. If you obey God and me, we'll tell you all the wonderful things we know. But the price of our Telling is high. More than any money."

Yara nodded dubiously, and pondered. "Fodderdon did say that the Executive Council would have to follow his orders. That's why I called him a boss maz."

"That's what he was."

"I don't know about the rest. We were told that there were policy disagreements, and the ship and the Legates were sent back to Terra. However. . . . I'm not certain that that's what happened." He looked uncomfortable, and deliberated for a long time over what he was going to say. "I knew an engineer in New Alyuna who worked on the *Aka One*." He meant the NAFAL ship now on its way from Aka to Hain, the pride of the Corporation. "He said they'd used the Terran ship as a model. He may have meant they had the plans for it. But he made it sound as if he'd actually been in the ship. He was drunk. I don't know."

The fifty Unist missionary-conquistadors had very likely

died in Corporation labor camps. But Sutty saw now how Dovza itself had been betrayed into betraying the rest of Aka.

It saddened her heart, this story. All the old mistakes, made over and over. She gave a deep sigh. "So, having no way to distinguish Unist Legates from Ekumenical Observers, you've handled us ever since with extreme distrust. . . . You know, Yara, I think your Executives were wise in refusing the bargain Father John offered. Though probably they saw it simply as a power struggle. What's harder to see is that even the gift of knowledge itself had a price attached. And still does."

"Yes, of course it does," Yara said. "Only we don't know what it is. Why do your people hide the price?"

She stared at him, nonplussed.

"I don't know," she said. "I didn't realise . . . I have to think about that."

Yara sat back, looking tired. He rubbed his eyes and closed them. He said softly, "The gift is lightning," evidently quoting some line of the Telling.

Sutty saw beautiful, arching ideograms, high on a shadowy white wall: *the twice-forked lightning-tree grows up from earth.* She saw Sotyu Ang's worn, dark hands meet in the shape of a mountain peak above his heart. *The price is nothing* . . .

They sat in the silence, following their thoughts.

After a long time, she asked, "Yara, do you know the story about Dear Takieki?"

He stared at her and then nodded. It was a memory from childhood, evidently, that required some retrieval. After a bit longer he said definitely, "Yes."

"Was Dear Takieki really a fool? I mean, it was his mother who gave him the bean meal. Maybe he was right not to give it away, no matter what they offered him."

Yara sat pondering. "My grandmother told me that story. I remember I thought I'd like to be able to walk anywhere, the way he did, without anybody looking after me. I was still little, my grandparents didn't let me go off by myself. So I said he must have wanted to go on walking. Not stay at a farm. And Grandmother asked, 'But what will he do when he runs out of food?' And I said, 'Maybe he can bargain. Maybe he can give the maz some of the bean meal and keep some, and take just a few of the gold coins. Then he could go on walking, and still buy food to eat when winter comes.'"

He smiled faintly, remembering, but his face remained troubled.

It was always a troubled face. She remembered it when it was hard, cold, closed. It had been beaten open.

He was worried for good reason. He was not progressing well with walking. His knee would still not bear weight for longer than a few minutes, and his back injury prevented him from using crutches without pain and risk of further damage. Odiedin and Tobadan worked with him daily, endlessly patient. Yara responded to them with his own dogged patience, but the look of trouble never left him.

Two groups had already left the Lap of Silong, slipping away in the dawn light, a few people, a couple of minule, heavy-laden. No bannered caravans.

Life in the caves was managed almost wholly by custom and consensus. Sutty had noted the conscious avoidance of hierarchy. People scrupulously did not pull rank. She mentioned this to Unroy, who said, "That was what went wrong in the century before the Ekumen came."

"Boss maz," Sutty said tentatively.

"Boss maz," Unroy confirmed, grinning. She was always tickled by Sutty's slang and her Rangma archaisms. "The Dovzan Reformation. Power hierarchies. Power struggles. Huge, rich umyazu taxing the villages. Fiscal and spiritual usury! Your people came at a bad time, yoz."

"The ships always come to the new world at a bad time," Sutty said. Unroy glanced at her with a little wonder.

In so far as any person or couple was in charge of things at the Lap of Silong, it was the maz Igneba and Ikak. After general consensus was established, specific decisions and responsibilities were made by them. The order and times at which people were to depart was one such decision. Ikak came to Sutty at dinnertime one night. "Yoz Sutty, if you have no objection, your group will leave four days from now."

"All of us from Okzat-Ozkat?"

"No. You, Maz Odiedin Manma, Long, and Ieyu, we thought. A small group, with one minule. You should be able to travel fast and get down into the hills before the autumn weather."

"Very well, maz," Sutty said. "I hate to leave the books unread."

"Maybe you can come back. Maybe you can save them for our children."

That burning, yearning hope they all shared, that hope in her and in the Ekumen: it frightened Sutty every time she saw its intensity.

"I will try to do that, maz," she said. Then— "But what about Yara?"

"He'll have to be carried. The healers say he won't be able to walk any long distance before the weather changes. Your two young ones will be in the group with him, and Tobadan Siez, and two of our guides, and three minule with a handler. A large party, but it has to be so. They'll go tomorrow morning, while this good weather holds. I wish we'd known the man would be unable to walk. We'd have sent them earlier. But they'll take the Reban Path, the easiest."

"What becomes of him when you reach Amareza?"

Ikak spread out her hands. "What can we do with him? Keep him prisoner! We have to! He could tell the police exactly where the caves are. They'd send people as soon as they could, plant explosives, destroy it. The way they destroyed the Great Library of Marang, and all the others. The Corporation hasn't changed their policy. Unless *you* can persuade them to change it, yoz Sutty. To let the books be, to let the Ekumen come and study them and save them. If that happened, we'd let him go, of course. But if we do, his own people will arrest and imprison him for unauthorised actions. Poor man, he hasn't a very bright future."

"It's possible that he won't tell the police."

Ikak, surprised, looked her question.

"I know he'd made it a personal mission to find the Library and destroy it. An obsession, in fact. But he . . . He was brought up by maz. And . . ."

She hesitated. She could not tell Ikak his grave-secret any more than she could tell her own.

"He had to become what he was," she said finally. "But I think all that really makes sense to him is the Telling. I think

he's come back to that. I know he feels no enmity toward
Odiedin or anybody here. Maybe he could stay with people in
Amareza without being kept prisoner. Just keep out of sight."

"Maybe," Ikak said, not unsympathetic but unconvinced.
"Except it's very hard to hide somebody like that, yoz Sutty. He
has an implanted ZIL. And he was a fairly high official, assigned
to watch an Observer of the Ekumen. They'll be looking for
him. Once they get him, I'm afraid, whatever he feels, they can
make him tell them anything he knows."

"He could stay hidden in a village through the winter,
maybe. Not go down into Amareza at all. I will need time,
Maz Ikak Igneba—the Envoy will need time—to talk to people
in Dovza. And if a ship comes next year, as it's due to, then we
can talk on the ansible with the Stabiles of the Ekumen about
these matters. But it will take time."

Ikak nodded. "I'll speak with the others about it. We'll do
what we can."

Sutty went immediately after dinner to Yara's tent.

Both Akidan and Odiedin were already there, Akidan with
the warm clothing Yara would need for the journey, Odiedin
to reassure him about making it. Akidan was excited about
leaving. Sutty was touched to see how kindly he spoke to Yara,
his handsome young face alight. "Don't worry, yoz," he said
earnestly, "it's an easy path and we've got a very strong group.
We'll be down in the hills in a week."

"Thank you," Yara said, expressionless. His face had closed.

"Tobadan Siez will be with you," Odiedin said.

Yara nodded. "Thank you," he said again.

Kieri arrived with a thermal poncho Akidan had forgotten,
and came crowding in with it, talking away. The tent was too
full. Sutty knelt in the entrance and put her hand on Yara's
hand. She had never touched him before.

"Thank you for telling me what you told me, Yara," she said,
feeling hurried and self-conscious. "And for letting me tell
you. I hope you—I hope things work out. Goodbye."

Looking up at her, he gave his brief nod, and turned his
head away.

She went back to her tent, anxious yet also relieved.

The tent was a mess: Kieri had thrown around everything
she owned in preparation for packing it. Sutty looked forward

to sharing a tent with Odiedin again, to order, silence, celibacy.

She had spent a long day working on the catalogue, tiring, tricky work with the balky and laborious Akan programs. She went to bed, intending to get up very early and see her friends off. She slept at once. Kieri's return and the fuss of her packing scarcely disturbed her. It seemed about five minutes before the lamp was on again and Kieri was up, dressed, leaving. Sutty struggled out of her sleeping bag and said, "I'll be at breakfast with you."

But when she got to the kitchen, the people of the departing group weren't there having the hot meal that would start them on their way. Nobody was there but Long, who was on cooking duty.

"Where is everybody, Long?" she asked, alarmed. "They haven't left already, have they?"

"No," Long said.

"Is something wrong?"

"I think so, yoz Sutty." His face was distressed. He nodded toward the outer caves. She went to the entrance that led to them. She met Odiedin coming in.

"What's wrong?"

"Oh Sutty," Odiedin said. He made an incomplete, hopeless gesture.

"What is it?"

"Yara."

"What?"

"Come with me."

She followed him into the Tree Cave. He walked past Yara's tent. There were a lot of people around it, but she did not see Yara. Odiedin strode on through the small cave with a rough floor, and from that to the short passage that led to the outside by the doorway arch they could get through only on hands and knees.

Odiedin stood up just outside it. Sutty emerged beside him. It was far from sunrise still, but the high pallor of the sky seemed wonderfully radiant and vast after the spaceless darkness of the caves.

"See where he went," Odiedin said.

She looked down from the light to where he pointed. Snow

lay ankle deep on the floor of the cirque. From the arch where they stood, boot tracks led straight out to the edge and back, tracks of three or four people, she thought.

"Not the tracks," Odiedin said. "Those are ours. He was on hands and knees. He couldn't walk. I don't know how he could crawl on that knee. It's a long way."

She saw, now, the marks in the snow, heavy, dragging furrows. All the boot tracks kept to the left of them.

"Nobody heard him. Sometime after midnight, he must have crept out."

Looking down, quite close to the arch, where the snow was thin on the black rock, she saw a blurred handprint.

"Out there at the edge," Odiedin said, "he stood up. So that he could leap."

Sutty made a little noise. She sank down squatting, rocking her body a little. No tears came, but her throat was tight, she could not breathe.

"Penan Teran," she said. Odiedin did not understand her. "Onto the wind," she said.

"He didn't have to do this." Odiedin's voice was fierce, desolate. "It was wrong."

"He thought it was right," Sutty said.

Chapter Nine

THE CORPORATION AIRPLANE that flew her from Soboy in Amareza to Dovza City gained altitude over the eastern Headwaters Range. Looking out the small window, due west, she saw a great, rough, rocky, bulky mountain: Zubuam. And then, soaring up behind it, the whiteness of the barrier wall, hiding somewhere in its luminous immensity the cirque and the caves of being. Above the serrate rim of the barrier, level with her eye, the horn of Silong soared white-gold against blue. She saw it whole, entire, this one time. The thin, eternal banner blew northward from the summit.

The trek south had been hard, two long weeks, on a good path but with bad weather along much of the way; and she had had no rest in Soboy. The Corporation had their police watching every road out of the Headwaters Range. Officials, very polite, very tense, had met her party just inside the city. "The Observer is to be flown at once to the capital."

She had demanded to speak to the Envoy by telephone, and they had put the call through for her at the airfield. "Come along, as soon as you can," Tong Ov said. "There's been much alarm. We all rejoice at your safe return. Akan and alien alike. Though especially this alien."

She said, "I have to make sure my friends are all right."

"Bring them with you," Tong said.

So Odiedin and the two guides from the village in the foothills west of Okzat-Ozkat were sitting together in the three seats behind hers. What Long and Ieyu made of it all she had no idea. Odiedin had explained or reassured them a little, and they had climbed aboard quite impassively. All four of them were tired, muzzy-headed, worn out.

The plane turned eastward. When she next looked down, she saw the yellow of snowless foothills, the silver thread of a river. The Ereha. Daughter of the Mountain. They followed the silver thread as it broadened and dulled to grey all the way down to Dovza City.

*

"The base culture, under the Dovzan overlay, is not vertical, not militant, not aggressive, and not progressive," Sutty said. "It's level, mercantile, discursive, and homeostatic. In crisis I think they fall back on it. I think we can bargain with them."

Napoleon Buonaparte called the English a nation of shopkeepers, Uncle Hurree said in her mind. *Maybe not altogether a bad thing?*

Too much was in her mind. Too much to tell Tong; too much to hear from him. They had had little over an hour to talk, and the Executives and Ministers were due to arrive any minute.

"Bargain?" asked the Envoy. They were speaking in Dovzan, since Odiedin was present.

"They owe us," Sutty said.

"Owe us?"

Chiffewar was neither a militant nor a mercantile culture. There were concepts that Chiffewarians, for all their breadth and subtlety of mind, had trouble understanding.

"You'll have to trust me," Sutty said.

"I do," said the Envoy. "But please explain, however cryptically, what this bargain is."

"Well, if you agree that we should try to preserve the Library at Silong. . . ."

"Yes, of course, in principle. But if it involves interference with Akan policy—"

"We've been interfering with Aka for seventy years."

"But how could we arbitrarily refuse them information—since we couldn't undo that first tremendous gift of technological specifics?"

"I think the point is that it wasn't a gift. There was a price on it: spiritual conversion."

"The missionaries," Tong said, nodding. Earlier in their hurried talk, he had shown the normal human pleasure at having his guess confirmed.

Odiedin listened, grave and intent.

"The Akans saw that as usury. They refused to pay it. Ever since then, we've actually given them more information than they asked for."

"Trying to show them that there are less exploitive modes —yes."

"The point is that we've always given it freely, offered it to them."

"Of course," Tong said.

"But Akans pay for value received. In cash, on the spot. As they see it, they didn't pay for all the blueprints for the March to the Stars, or anything since. They've been waiting for decades for us to tell them what they owe us. Till we do, they'll distrust us."

Tong removed his hat, rubbed his brown, satiny head, and replaced the hat a little lower over his eyes. "So we ask them for information in return?"

"Exactly. We've given them a treasure. They have a treasure we want. Tit for tat, as we say in English."

"But to them it's not a treasure. It's sedition and a pile of rotten-corpse superstition. No?"

"Well, yes and no. I think they know it's a treasure. If they didn't, would they bother blowing it up?"

"Then we don't have to persuade them that the Library of Silong is valuable?"

"Well, we do want them to be aware that it's worth fully as much as any information we gave them. And that its value depends on our having free access to it. Just as they have free access to all the information we give them."

"Tat for tit," Tong said, absorbing the concept if not quite the phrase.

"And another thing—very important— That it's not just the books in the Lap of Silong that we're talking about, but all the books, everywhere, and all the people who read the books. The whole system. The Telling. They'll have to decriminalise it."

"Sutty, they're not going to agree to that."

"Eventually they must. We have to try." She looked at Odiedin, who was sitting erect and alert beside her at the long table. "Am I right, maz?"

"Maybe not everything all at once, yoz Sutty," Odiedin said. "One thing at a time. So there's more to keep bargaining with. And for."

"A few gold coins, for some of the bean meal?"

It took Odiedin a while. "Something like that," he said at last, rather dubiously.

"Bean meal?" the Envoy inquired, looking from one to the other.

"It's a story we'll have to tell you," Sutty said.

But the first Executives were coming into the conference room. Two men and two women, all in blue and tan. There were, of course, no formalities of greeting, no servile addresses; but there had to be introductions. Sutty looked into each face as the names were named. Bureaucrat faces. Government faces. Self-assured, smooth, solid. Closed. Endlessly repeatable variations on the Monitor's face. But it was not the Monitor's, it was Yara's face that she held in her mind as the bargaining began.

His life, that was what underwrote her bargaining. His life, Pao's life. Those were the intangible, incalculable stakes. The money burned to ashes, the gold thrown away. Footsteps on the air.

APPENDIX

Introduction to
The Word for World Is Forest

THERE IS NOTHING in all Freud's writings that I like better than his assertion that artists' work is motivated by the desire "to achieve honour, power, riches, fame, and the love of women." It is such a comforting, such a complete statement; it explains everything about the artist. There have even been artists who agreed with it; Ernest Hemingway, for instance; at least, he said he wrote for money, and since he was an honored, powerful, rich, famous artist beloved by women, he ought to know.

There is another statement about the artist's desires that is, to me, less obscure; the first two stanzas of it read,

> Riches I hold in light esteem
> And Love I laugh to scorn
> And lust of Fame was but a dream
> That vanished with the morn—
>
> And if I pray, the only prayer
> That moves my lips for me
> Is—"Leave the heart that now I bear
> And give me liberty."

Emily Brontë wrote those lines when she was twenty-two. She was a young and inexperienced woman, not honored, not rich, not powerful, not famous, and you see that she was positively rude about love ("of women" or otherwise). I believe, however, that she was rather better qualified than Freud to talk about what motivates the artist. He had a theory. But she had authority.

It may well be useless, if not pernicious, to seek a single motive for a pursuit so complex, long-pursued, and various as art; I imagine that Brontë got as close to it as anyone needs to get, with her word "liberty."

The pursuit of art, then, by artist or audience, is the pursuit of liberty. If you accept that, you see at once why truly serious people reject and mistrust the arts, labeling them as "escapism." The captured soldier tunneling out of prison, the runaway slave, and Solzhenitsyn in exile are escapists. Aren't they? The definition also helps explain why all healthy children can sing, dance, paint, and play with words; why art is an increasingly important element in psychotherapy; why Winston Churchill painted, why mothers sing cradle-songs, and what is wrong with Plato's *Republic*. It really is a much more useful statement than Freud's, though nowhere near as funny.

I am not sure what Freud meant by "power," in this context. Perhaps significantly, Brontë does not mention power. Shelley does, indirectly: "Poets are the unacknowledged legislators of the world." This is perhaps not too far from what Freud had in mind, for I doubt he was thinking of the artist's immediate and joyous power over his material—the shaping hand, the dancer's leap, the novelist's power of life and death over his characters; it is more probable that he meant the power of the idea to influence other people.

The desire for power, in the sense of power over others, is what pulls most people off the path of the pursuit of liberty. The reason Brontë does not mention it is probably that it was never even a temptation to her, as it was to her sister Charlotte. Emily did not give a damn about other people's morals. But many artists, particularly artists of the word, whose ideas must actually be spoken in their work, succumb to the temptation. They begin to see that they can do good to other people. They forget about liberty, then, and instead of legislating in divine arrogance, like God or Shelley, they begin to preach.

In this tale, *The Word for World Is Forest*, which began as a pure pursuit of freedom and the dream, I succumbed, in part, to the lure of the pulpit. It is a very strong lure to a science fiction writer, who deals more directly than most novelists with ideas, whose metaphors are shaped by or embody ideas, and who therefore is always in danger of inextricably confusing ideas with opinions.

I wrote *The Little Green Men* (its first editor, Harlan Ellison, retitled it, with my rather morose permission) in the winter of 1968, during a year's stay in London. All through the sixties, in my home city in the States, I had been helping organize and participating in nonviolent demonstrations, first against atomic bomb testing, then against the pursuance of the war in Viet Nam. I don't know how many times I walked down Alder Street in the rain, feeling useless, foolish, and obstinate, along with ten or twenty or a hundred other foolish and obstinate souls. There was always somebody taking pictures of us—not the press—odd-looking people with cheap cameras: John Birchers? FBI? CIA? Crackpots? No telling. I used to grin at them, or stick out my tongue. One of my fiercer friends brought a camera once and took pictures of the picture-takers. Anyhow, there was a peace movement, and I was in it, and so had a channel of action and expression for my ethical and political opinions totally separate from my writing.

In England that year, a guest and a foreigner, I had no such outlet. And 1968 was a bitter year for those who opposed the war. The lies and hypocrisies redoubled; so did the killing. Moreover, it was becoming clear that the ethic which approved the defoliation of forests and grainlands and the murder of noncombatants in the name of "peace" was only a corollary of the ethic which permits the despoliation of natural resources for private profit or the GNP, and the murder of the creatures of the Earth in the name of "man." The victory of the ethic of exploitation, in all societies, seemed as inevitable as it was disastrous.

It was from such pressures, internalized, that this story resulted: forced out, in a sense, against my conscious resistance. I have said elsewhere that I never wrote a story more easily, fluently, surely—and with less pleasure.

I knew, because of the compulsive quality of the composition, that it was likely to become a preachment, and I struggled against this. Say not the struggle naught availeth. Neither Lyubov nor Selver is mere Virtue Triumphant; moral and psychological complexity was salvaged, at least, in those characters. But Davidson is, though not uncomplex, pure; he is purely evil— and I don't, consciously, believe purely evil people exist. But my unconscious has other opinions. It looked into itself and produced, from itself, Captain Davidson. I do not disclaim him.

American involvement in Viet Nam is now past; the immediately intolerable pressures have shifted to other areas; and so the moralizing aspects of the story are now plainly visible. These I regret, but I do not disclaim them either. The work must stand or fall on whatever elements it preserved of the yearning that underlies all specific outrage and protest, whatever tentative outreaching it made, amidst anger and despair, toward justice, or wit, or grace, or liberty.

SYNCHRONICITY CAN HAPPEN AT ALMOST ANY TIME

A few years ago, a few years after the first publication in America of *The Word for World Is Forest*, I had the great pleasure of meeting Dr. Charles Tart, a psychologist well known for his researches into and his book on *Altered States of Consciousness.* He asked me if I had modeled the Athsheans of the story upon the Senoi people of Malaysia. The who? said I, so he told me about them. The Senoi are, or were, a people whose culture includes and is indeed substantially based upon a deliberate training in and use of the dream. Dr. Tart's book includes a brief article on them by Kilton Stewart.[1]

> Breakfast in the Senoi house is like a dream clinic, with the father and older brothers listening to and analysing the dreams of all the children. . . .
> When the Senoi child reports a falling dream, the adult answers with enthusiasm, "That is a wonderful dream, one of the best dreams a man can have. Where did you fall to, and what did you discover?"

The Senoi dream is meaningful, active, and creative. Adults deliberately go into their dreams to solve problems of interpersonal and intercultural conflict. They come out of their dreams with a new song, tool, dance, idea. The waking and the dreaming states are equally valid, each acting upon the other in complementary fashion.

The article implies, by omission rather than by direct statement, that the men are the "great dreamers" among the Senoi; whether this means that the women are socially inferior, or that their role (as among the Athsheans) is equal and compensatory, is not clear. Nor is there any mention of the Senoi conception of divinity, the numinous, etc.; it is merely stated that they do not practice magic, though they are perfectly willing to let neighboring peoples think they do, as this discourages invasion.

They have built a system of inter-personal relations which, in the field of psychology, is perhaps on a level with our attainments in such areas as television and nuclear physics.

It appears that the Senoi have not had a war, or a murder, for several hundred years.

There they are, twelve thousand of them, farming, hunting, fishing, and dreaming, in the rain forests of the mountains of Malaysia. Or there they were, in 1935—perhaps. Kilton Stewart's report on them has had no professional sequels that I know of. Were they ever there, and if so, are they still there? In the waking time, I mean, in what we so fantastically call "the real world." In the dream time, of course, they are there, and here. I thought I was inventing my own lot of imaginary aliens, and I was only describing the Senoi. It is not only the Captain Davidsons who can be found in the unconscious, if one looks. The quiet people who do not kill each other are there, too. It seems that a great deal is there, the things we most fear (and therefore deny), the things we most need (and therefore deny). I wonder, couldn't we start listening to our dreams, and our children's dreams?

"Where did you fall to, and what did you discover?"

Note

1. "Dream Theory in Malaya," by Kilton Stewart, in *Altered States of Consciousness*, ed. Charles T. Tart, Wiley & Sons, 1969; Anchor-Doubleday, 1972. The quotations are on pp. 164 and 163 of the Anchor second edition.

On Not Reading Science Fiction

PEOPLE WHO DON'T read it, and even some of those who write it, like to assume or pretend that the ideas used in science fiction all rise from intimate familiarity with celestial mechanics and quantum theory, and are comprehensible only to readers who work for NASA and know how to program their VCR. This fantasy, while making the writers feel superior, gives the non-readers an excuse. I just don't understand it, they whimper, taking refuge in the deep, comfortable, anaerobic caves of technophobia. It is of no use to tell them that very few science fiction writers understand "it" either. We, too, generally find we have twenty minutes of *I Love Lucy* and half a wrestling match on our videocassettes when we meant to record *Masterpiece Theater*. Most of the scientific ideas in science fiction are totally accessible and indeed familiar to anybody who got through sixth grade, and in any case you aren't going to be tested on them at the end of the book. The stuff isn't disguised engineering lectures, after all. It isn't that invention of a mathematical Satan, "story problems." It's stories. It's fiction that plays with certain subjects for their inherent interest, beauty, relevance to the human condition. Even in its ungainly and inaccurate name, the "science" modifies, is in the service of, the "fiction."

For example, the main "idea" in my book *The Left Hand of Darkness* isn't scientific and has nothing to do with technology. It's a bit of physiological imagination—a body change. For the people of the invented world Gethen, individual gender doesn't exist. They're sexually neuter most of the time, coming into heat once a month, sometimes as a male, sometimes as a female. A Gethenian can both sire and bear children. Now, whether this invention strikes one as peculiar, or perverse, or fascinating, it certainly doesn't require a great scientific intellect to grasp it, or to follow its implications as they're played out in the novel.

Another element in the same book is the climate of the planet, which is deep in an ice age. A simple idea: It's cold; it's very cold; it's always cold. Ramifications, complexities, and resonance come with the detail of imagining.

The Left Hand of Darkness differs from a realistic novel only in asking the reader to accept, *pro tem*, certain limited and specific changes in narrative reality. Instead of being on Earth during an interglacial period among two-sexed people (as in, say, *Pride and Prejudice*, or any realistic novel you like), we're on Gethen during a period of glaciation among androgynes. It's useful to remember that both worlds are imaginary.

Science-fictional changes of parameter, though they may be both playful and decorative, are essential to the book's nature and structure; whether they are pursued and explored chiefly for their own interest, or serve predominantly as metaphor or symbol, they're worked out and embodied novelistically in terms of the society and the characters' psychology, in description, action, emotion, implication, and imagery. The description in science fiction is likely to be somewhat "thicker," to use Clifford Geertz's term, than in realistic fiction, which calls on an assumed common experience. But the difficulty of understanding it is no greater than the difficulty of following any complex fiction. The world of Gethen is less familiar, but actually infinitely simpler, than the English social world of two hundred years ago which Jane Austen explored and embodied so vividly. Both worlds take some getting to know, since neither is one we can experience except in words, by reading about them. All fiction offers us a world we can't otherwise reach, whether because it's in the past, or in far or imaginary places, or describes experiences we haven't had, or leads us into minds different from our own. To some people this change of worlds, this unfamiliarity, is an insurmountable barrier; to others, an adventure and a pleasure.

People who don't read science fiction, but who have at least given it a fair shot, often say they've found it inhuman, elitist, and escapist. Since its characters, they say, are both conventionalized and extraordinary, all geniuses, space heroes, superhackers, androgynous aliens, it evades what ordinary people really have to deal with in life, and so fails an essential function of fiction. However remote Jane Austen's England is, the people in it are immediately relevant and revelatory—reading about them we learn about ourselves. Has science fiction anything to offer but escape from ourselves?

The cardboard-character syndrome was largely true of early science fiction, but for decades writers have been using the form to explore character and human relationships. I'm one of them. An imagined setting may be the most appropriate in which to work out certain traits and destinies. But it's also true that a great deal of contemporary fiction isn't a fiction of character. This end of the century isn't an age of individuality as the Elizabethan and the Victorian ages were. Our stories, realistic or otherwise, with their unreliable narrators, dissolving points of view, multiple perceptions and perspectives, often don't have depth of character as their central value. Science fiction, with its tremendous freedom of metaphor, has sent many writers far ahead in this exploration beyond the confines of individuality—Sherpas on the slopes of the postmodern.

As for elitism, the problem may be scientism: technological edge mistaken for moral superiority. The imperialism of high technocracy equals the old racist imperialism in its arrogance; to the technophile, people who aren't in the know/in the net, who don't have the right artifacts, don't count. They're proles, masses, faceless nonentities. Whether it's fiction or history, the story isn't about them. The story's about the kids with the really neat, really expensive toys. So "people" comes to be operationally defined as those who have access to an extremely elaborate fast-growth industrial technology. And "technology" itself is restricted to that type. I have heard a man say perfectly seriously that the Native Americans before the Conquest had no technology. As we know, kiln-fired pottery is a naturally occurring substance, baskets ripen in the summer, and Machu Picchu just grew there.

Limiting humanity to the producer-consumers of a complex industrial growth technology is a really weird idea, on a par with defining humanity as Greeks, or Chinese, or the upper-middle-class British. It leaves out a little too much.

All fiction, however, has to leave out most people. A fiction interested in complex technology may legitimately leave out the (shall we say) differently technologized, as a fiction about suburban adulteries may ignore the city poor, and a fiction centered on the male psyche may omit women. Such omission

may, however, be read as a statement that advantage is superiority, or that the white middle class is the whole society, or that
only men are worth writing about. Moral and political state-
ments by omission are legitimated by the consciousness of
making them, insofar as the writer's culture permits that consciousness. It comes down to a matter of taking responsibility.
A denial of authorial responsibility, a willed unconsciousness, is
elitist, and it does impoverish much of our fiction in every
genre, including realism.

I don't accept the judgment that in using images and metaphors of other worlds, space travel, the future, imagined technologies, societies, or beings, science fiction escapes from
having human relevance to our lives. Those images and metaphors used by a serious writer are images and metaphors of our
lives, legitimately novelistic, symbolic ways of saying what
cannot otherwise be said about us, our being and choices, here
and now. What science fiction does is enlarge the here and
now.

What do you find interesting? To some people only other
people are interesting. Some people really don't care about
trees or fish or stars or how engines work or why the sky is
blue; they're exclusively human-centered, often with the encouragement of their religion; and they aren't going to like either science or science fiction. Like all the sciences except
anthropology, psychology, and medicine, science fiction is not
exclusively human-centered. It includes other beings, other
aspects of being. It may be about relationships between people
—the great subject of realist fiction—but it may be about the
relationship between a person and something else, another
kind of being, an idea, a machine, an experience, a society.

Finally, some people tell me that they avoid science fiction
because it's depressing. This is quite understandable if they
happened to hit a streak of post-holocaust cautionary tales or a
bunch of trendies trying to outwhine each other, or overdosed
on sleaze-metal-punk-virtual-noir Capitalist Realism. But the
accusation often, I think, reflects some timidity or gloom in
the reader's own mind: a distrust of change, a distrust of the
imagination. A lot of people really do get scared and depressed
if they have to think about anything they're not perfectly familiar with; they're afraid of losing control. If it isn't about

things they know all about already they won't read it, if it's a different color they hate it, if it isn't McDonald's they won't eat at it. They don't want to know that the world existed before they were, is bigger than they are, and will go on without them. They do not like history. They do not like science fiction. May they eat at McDonald's and be happy in Heaven.

Now, having talked about why people dislike science fiction, I'll say why I like it. I like most kinds of fiction, mostly for the same qualities, none of which is specific to a single genre. But what I like in and about science fiction includes these particular virtues: vitality, largeness, and exactness of imagination; playfulness, variety, and strength of metaphor; freedom from conventional literary expectations and mannerism; moral seriousness; wit; pizzazz; and beauty.

Let me ride a moment on that last word. The beauty of a story may be intellectual, like the beauty of a mathematical proof or a crystalline structure; it may be aesthetic, the beauty of a well-made work; it may be human, emotional, moral; it is likely to be all three. Yet science fiction critics and reviewers still often treat the story as if it were a mere exposition of ideas, as if the intellectual "message" were all. This reductionism does a serious disservice to the sophisticated and powerful techniques and experiments of much contemporary science fiction. The writers are using language as postmodernists; the critics are decades behind, not even discussing the language, deaf to the implications of sounds, rhythms, recurrences, patterns— as if text were a mere vehicle for ideas, a kind of gelatin coating for the medicine. This is naive. And it totally misses what I love best in the best science fiction, its beauty.

CHRONOLOGY

NOTE ON THE TEXTS

NOTES

Chronology

1929   Born in Berkeley, California, on St. Ursula's Day, October
        21, to Alfred Louis Kroeber and Theodora Covel Kracaw
        Brown Kroeber. (Father, born in 1876 in Hoboken, New
        Jersey, completed a doctorate in anthropology at Colum-
        bia College under Franz Boas in 1901 and moved to
        Berkeley to create a museum and department of anthro-
        pology at the University of California. In 1911, Ishi, a Yahi
        Indian and the last survivor of the Yana band, came to
        work with Kroeber and others at the Museum of Anthro-
        pology, where he remained until his death, from tubercu-
        losis, in 1916. Mother, born in 1897 in Denver, Colorado,
        completed a master's degree in clinical psychology at the
        University of California in 1920 and married Clifton Spen-
        cer Brown in July 1920; they had two children: Clifton Jr.,
        born September 7, 1921, and Theodore "Ted," born in
        May 1923. Brown died in October 1923, and mother began
        taking anthropology courses from Alfred Kroeber. They
        married in March 1926, and Kroeber adopted both sons.
        They bought a house designed by Berkeley architect Ber-
        nard Maybeck at 1325 Arch Street on the north side of the
        university campus. Le Guin will later cite (in an essay in
        the journal *Paradoxa*) the beauty and "integrity" of its
        design as an early influence. Parents took a field trip to
        Peru for eight months, shortly after marriage, living in a
        tent. Brother Karl Kroeber born in Berkeley on November
        26, 1926.)

1930   Parents buy a ranch in the Napa Valley, later named
        Kishamish from a myth invented by brother Karl. Family
        will spend summers there entertaining visiting scholars,
        including physicist J. Robert Oppenheimer and both na-
        tive and white storytellers.

1931   Juan Dolores, a Papago Indian friend and collaborator of
        A. L. Kroeber's, spends the first of many summers with the
        Kroeber family at Kishamish.

1932–1939 Is taught to write by her brother Ted and goes on doing it.
        Ursula and Karl, along with Berkeley neighbor Ernst

Landauer, invent a world of stuffed animals. Later discovers science fiction magazines, including *Amazing Stories*. Father tells her American Indian stories and myths; she also reads Norse myths. Mother later recalls, "The children wrote and acted plays; they had the 'Barn-top Players' in the loft of the old barn. They put out a weekly newspaper."

c. 1940   Submits first story to *Astounding Science Fiction* and collects her first rejection letter.

c. 1942   With her brothers in the armed services (Clifton joins in 1940, before the war starts for America, Ted in '43, and Karl in '44), Ursula is left without imaginative co-conspirators. In a later interview she recalls, "My older brothers had some beautiful little British figurines, a troop of nineteenth-century French cavalrymen and their horses. I inherited them, and played long stories with them in our big attic. They went on adventures, exploring, fighting off enemies, going on diplomatic missions, etc. The captain was particularly gallant and handsome, with his sabre drawn, and his white horse reared up nobly. Unfortunately, when you took one of them off his horse, he was extremely bow-legged, and had a little nail sticking downward from his bottom, which fit into the saddle. . . . So my brave adventurers lived entirely on horseback. Also unfortunately, there were no females at all for my stories; but when I wrote the stories down, I provided some."

1944–46   In fall, begins attending Berkeley High School. Socially marginal, a good student, reads voraciously outside school, Tolstoy and other nineteenth-century writers, including Austen, the Brontës, Turgenev, Dickens, and Hardy, as well as the Taoist writings of Chinese writer Lao Tzu. Her mother introduces her to Virginia Woolf's *A Room of One's Own* and *Three Guineas*, which she says she didn't really get until much later. In spring 1946, father retires from Berkeley. Parents travel to England, where father receives the Huxley Medal from the Royal Anthropological Institute.

1947   Graduates high school in class of 3,500, which includes Philip K. Dick. The two never meet, although they later correspond. Father accepts a one-year appointment at

Harvard University, and it is decided that, with parents nearby, Ursula will attend Radcliffe College instead of the University of California. Spends summer with parents and Karl in New York City, where father teaches at Columbia University until Harvard appointment begins. They rent an apartment from parents' friends near 116th and Broadway and spend the summer seeing many plays and Broadway shows. Takes recorder lessons with Blanche Knopf. Moves to Radcliffe in the fall. Lives last three college years in Radcliffe cooperative Everett House with close friends Jean Taylor and Marion Ives.

1948   Father returns to Columbia, where he will teach until 1952. Spends summer with parents in New York City, this time in another apartment rented from parents' friends, near 116th and Riverside Drive.

1950   A relationship in her senior year at Radcliffe results in an unplanned pregnancy; an illegal abortion is arranged with the help of friends and parents.

1951   Elected to Phi Beta Kappa. Graduates cum laude from Radcliffe in June, writing a senior thesis titled "The Metaphor of the Rose as an Illustration of the 'Carpe Diem' Theme in French and Italian Poetry of the Renaissance." College acquaintances include John Updike, who marries one of her housemates. Travels to Paris with Karl and begins writing novel *A Descendance*, about the imaginary Central European country of Orsinia, whose name reflects her own: both come from the Latin word for "bear." Starts graduate work at Columbia in the fall. Begins writing and attempting to publish poetry and stories. Father helps her submit poems for publication, mailing her submissions and also investigating subculture of little magazines.

1952   Completes an M.A. in Renaissance French and Italian language and literature at Columbia University, writing a thesis titled "Ideas of Death in Ronsard's Poetry" on the sixteenth-century French poet Pierre Ronsard. Begins work on a doctorate at Columbia on the early sixteenth-century poet Jean Lemaire de Belges. Submits *A Descendance* to Alfred Knopf, a friend of her father's, and receives an encouraging rejection letter. In a 2013 interview, Le

Guin will recall that "the first novel I ever wrote was very strange, very ambitious. It covered many generations in my invented Central European country, Orsinia. My father knew Alfred Knopf personally. . . . When I was about twenty-three, I asked my father if he felt that my submitting the novel to Knopf would presume on their friendship, and he said, No, go ahead and try him. So I did, and Knopf wrote a lovely letter back. He said, I can't take this damn thing. I would've done it ten years ago, but I can't afford to now. He said, This is a very strange book, but you're going somewhere! That was all I needed. I didn't need acceptance." Begins writing new Orsinian novel called, variously, *Malafrena* and *The Necessary Passion*.

1953   Receives a Fulbright Fellowship to study in France. Departs from New York on September 23 on the *Queen Mary*. On the ship she meets fellow Fulbrighter Charles Alfred Le Guin (born June 4, 1927, in Macon, Georgia), who is writing his thesis on the French Revolution. On December 22, marries Le Guin in Paris after numerous delays in procuring a marriage license—later says there was "always another tax stamp we needed across the city." (On the marriage license, a space between "Le" and "Guin" is restored, in a surname that had not had one in America.)

1954   Le Guins return to U.S. on the *Ile de France* ship in August. Ends graduate work and the Le Guins move to Macon, Georgia, where Charles teaches history and Ursula teaches freshman French at Mercer University. Meets Charles's large extended family. Sees, and is first puzzled and then appalled by, her first sign for a "Colored Drinking Fountain."

1955   Completes first version of novel *Malafrena*. Works as a physics department secretary at Emory University in Atlanta, where Charles is completing his Ph.D. Reads *The Lord of the Rings*.

1956   Charles receives his doctorate from Emory and they move to Moscow, Idaho, where they both begin teaching at the University of Idaho. Out of boredom in a rather insular community, together with friends they fabricate items about an imaginary poetry society (including poems by Le Guin's alter ego Mrs. R. R. Korsatoff) and succeed in placing them on the society page of the local newspaper.

1957   Oldest child Elisabeth Covel Le Guin is born, July 25.

1958   Moves to Portland, Oregon, where Charles takes up position as professor of French history at Portland State University (then College). They buy a Victorian house below Portland's Forest Park, where they will live for the next six decades.

1959   Spends summer at Berkeley with parents and Karl's family. The Orsinian poem "Folksong from the Montayna Province" appears in the fall issue of the journal *Prairie Poet*. It is her first published work. Second child Caroline DuPree Le Guin is born, November 4. Mother publishes *The Inland Whale*, a book of retold legends from California Indians, including the title story, which was learned from Yurok storyteller (and frequent guest at Kishamish) Robert Spott.

1960   Father dies in Paris on October 5 after conducting an anthropology conference in Austria the previous week. Later refers to this as the time when she "came of age, rather belatedly, at age 31."

1961   Mother publishes her most famous work, *Ishi in Two Worlds*, based on her husband's memories and on her own research. Le Guin's Orsinian story "An die Musik" is published in the summer issue of *Western Humanities Review*; she is paid five contributor's copies. The same week it is accepted, she also makes her first commercial sale: the time-travel story "April in Paris" is accepted by editor Cele Goldsmith Lalli for *Fantastic* magazine, for which Le Guin is paid $30. Rewrites *Malafrena*.

1962   Encouraged by a friend, begins reading science fiction writers Philip K. Dick, Harlan Ellison, Theodore Sturgeon, and Vonda McIntyre.

1964   Youngest child Theodore Alfred (Theo) Le Guin is born, June 4. (While the children are young she writes mostly after nine at night.) Moves for the academic year to Palo Alto, California, where Charles is a fellow at the Center for Advanced Study in the Behavioral Sciences. Writes her first science fiction novel, *Rocannon's World*. Her turn to science fiction is partly stimulated by reading the American author Cordwainer Smith and her resultant discovery that the genre has become a vehicle for inward as well as outward exploration. In a 1986 interview, she will explain,

"To me encountering his works was like a door opening. There is one story of his called 'Alpha Ralpha Boulevard' that was as important to me as reading Pasternak for the first time."

1966   Acting as her own agent, sells *Rocannon's World* to Donald A. Wollheim at Ace Books. It is published as half of a back-to-back edition, known as an Ace Double, with Avram Davidson's *The Kar-Chee Reign*. Wollheim speaks proudly of finding Le Guin's novel in the slush pile (of manuscripts sent without an agent). Soon afterward, Terry Carr creates the Ace Science Fiction Specials line to feature work by Le Guin, Joanna Russ, and R. A. Lafferty. The character Rocannon is a native of a world called Hain by its inhabitants and Davenant by others. In later books set in the same universe Hain is identified as the oldest human world, and the others (including Terra) as its colonies or (as in the case of Gethen) its experiments. *Planet of Exile* is published in October as half of an Ace Double with Thomas M. Disch's *Mankind Under the Leash*.

1967   *City of Illusions* is published by Ace Books.

1968   Writes to literary agent Virginia Kidd, herself a writer and editor of science fiction and poetry, asking her to try to sell hardcover rights to a new novel, *The Left Hand of Darkness*. Kidd replies that she will, but only if she can also represent the rest of Le Guin's work. The two work together (though they meet in person only four times) until Kidd's death in 2003. Publishes letter, along with eighty-one other science fiction writers (including Joanna Russ, Samuel R. Delany, and Gene Roddenberry), in *Galaxy* magazine in June protesting U.S. involvement in Vietnam. An opposing prowar letter is signed by seventy-two writers, including Robert A. Heinlein, John W. Campbell, and Marion Zimmer Bradley. In fall, moves to England as part of Charles's sabbatical. During that time she writes "The Word for World Is Forest," set in the Hainish universe but depicting some of the moral issues of the Vietnam War. Fantasy novel *A Wizard of Earthsea* is published in November by Parnassus Books.

1969   *A Wizard of Earthsea* wins the *Boston Globe–Horn Book* Award for children's literature. *The Left Hand of Darkness* is published by Ace Books as an Ace Science Fiction Special in March. The book's vision of androgyny is criticized by some feminists as overly cautious, a critique to which Le Guin responds defensively at first and then with a serious rethinking of her concept of gender in essays such as "Is Gender Necessary? Redux" (1976, revised 1987) and the story "Coming of Age in Karhide" (1995). The story "Nine Lives" appears in *Playboy* in November with the byline U. K. Le Guin. The initials are a deliberate ploy by Virginia Kidd, given the gender policies of the magazine. After the story is accepted, the magazine editors ask if they can keep the name in that form to veil the author's gender from readers. Le Guin agrees, in part because of the large payment the magazine offers, but when asked for an autobiographical statement offers the following, which *Playboy* prints: "The stories of U. K. Le Guin were not written by U. K. Le Guin but by another person of the same name." Children's writer and critic Eleanor Cameron writes in praise of *A Wizard of Earthsea* and begins a decades-long correspondence with Le Guin. The two writers are both, at the time, beginning to come to terms with feminism and are working at learning how to write *as* women and *about* female protagonists. This friendship with an older writer presages the many supportive relationships Le Guin is to form with younger women writers such as Vonda McIntyre, Karen Joy Fowler, and Molly Gloss. Mother remarries, to artist and art psychotherapist John Quinn, who is forty-three years her junior, on December 14.

1970   *The Left Hand of Darkness* wins both the Hugo and Nebula Awards for best novel, selected, respectively, by fans and fellow writers. The Science Fiction Foundation is created in England with Le Guin and Arthur C. Clarke as patrons. *The Tombs of Atuan*, second Earthsea novel, is serialized in December in *Worlds of Fantasy* and published by Atheneum in June the following year.

1971   *The Lathe of Heaven* is serialized in the March and May issues of *Amazing Science Fiction* and published in October by Charles Scribner's Sons. Le Guin's first science fiction novel set on Earth, it incorporates her thoughts on dreaming (pioneering dream researcher William Dement is a consultant), ecological catastrophe, and Taoist

ideas of inaction and integrity. At a Science Fiction Writ-
ers of America meeting in Berkeley meets Vonda N. Mc-
Intyre, who will become a close friend and collaborator.
McIntyre invites Le Guin to teach science fiction writing
at the first Clarion West workshop at the University of
Washington.

1972   *The Tombs of Atuan* is selected as a Newbery Honor
Book by the American Library Association. *The Lathe of
Heaven* wins the Locus Award for best novel. "The
Word for World Is Forest," written in 1968–69, appears
in Harlan Ellison's anthology *Again, Dangerous Visions*
in March. In part an allegory of the Vietnam War, the
novella (published as a separate volume in 1976) influences James Cameron's 2009 movie *Avatar.* Third
Earthsea novel, *The Farthest Shore*, is published in September by Atheneum.

1973   *The Farthest Shore* wins the National Book Award
for Children's Literature. Le Guin's acceptance speech,
"Why Are Americans Afraid of Dragons?," is a major defense of fantasy literature. "The Word for World Is Forest" wins the Hugo Award for best novella. "The Ones
Who Walk Away from Omelas," a story inspired by philosopher William James, is published in *New Dimensions
3* in October.

1974   "The Ones Who Walk Away from Omelas" wins the Hugo
Award for best short story. Douglas Barbour publishes an
academic investigation of Le Guin's work in *Science Fiction
Studies.* Completes novel *The Dispossessed*, its main character Shevek partly based on a childhood memory of physicist Robert Oppenheimer; revises ending at the urging of
her friend Darko Suvin, a Croatian literary critic. Senior
editor Buz Wyeth acquires the novel for Harper & Row,
which publishes it in May. Wyeth remains her editor for
several years.

Takes part in a virtual symposium on "Women in Science Fiction," organized by editor and fan Jeffrey D.
Smith. Participants such as Suzy McKee Charnas, Virginia
Kidd, Samuel R. Delany, Vonda McIntyre, Joanna Russ,
and James Tiptree Jr. write a round robin of letters and
responses on a variety of topics, starting in October 1974
and continuing until May 1975. Their discussions are
published in the fanzine *Khatru* in November 1975.

Tiptree, believed by the other participants to be a man (the writer's identity as Alice Sheldon is not revealed until 1977), expresses a number of challenging ideas about gender and power.

1975 Poetry collection *Wild Angels* is published in January. *The Dispossessed* wins the Hugo, Locus, and Nebula Awards. In August, attends the World Science Fiction Convention, or Worldcon, in Melbourne, Australia, where she is a guest of honor, and also spends a week conducting a science fiction writing workshop using the Clarion method. In May, dystopian novella "The New Atlantis" is published as part of a triptych with novellas by Gene Wolfe and James Tiptree Jr. The first collection of Le Guin's short stories is published under the title *The Wind's Twelve Quarters*. The Le Guins spend another sabbatical year in London starting in the fall; Ursula is a visiting fellow in creative writing at the University of Reading. In November *Science Fiction Studies* devotes a special issue to her work.

1976 During their stay in England, the Le Guins travel to Dorset to meet writer Sylvia Townsend Warner; Ursula says later, "I hold it one of the dearest honors of my life that I knew her for an hour." Young adult novel *Very Far Away from Anywhere Else* published in August by Atheneum. A second collection of stories, *Orsinian Tales,* published in October by Harper & Row.

1977 At the invitation of utopian scholar Robert Elliott, teaches a term at the University of California, San Diego. Among her students are aspiring writers Kim Stanley Robinson and Luis Alberto Urrea.

1978 Again rewrites early novel *Malafrena*, finishing in December. Science fiction novella "The Eye of the Heron" appears in the original anthology *Millennial Women*, edited by Virginia Kidd, in August. Mother falls ill.

1979 Wins the Gandalf Grand Master Award for life achievement in fantasy writing. Susan Wood edits the first volume of Le Guin's speeches and essays, *The Language of the Night*. Around this time she discovers the poetry of Rainer Maria Rilke, a favorite and acknowledged influence. Mother dies of cancer on July 4. Le Guin's first children's picture book, *Leese Webster*, is published with illustrations by James Brunsman in September by Atheneum. *Malafrena* is published in October by G. P. Putnam's Sons. Le Guin is invited to take part in a symposium on narrative at the University of Chicago, October 26–28, along with scholars and writers such as Seymour Chatman, Paul de Man, Jacques Derrida, Frank Kermode, Barbara Herrnstein Smith, Robert Scholes, Victor Turner, Paul Ricoeur, and Hayden White. Her contribution at the end of the symposium is "It Was a Dark and Stormy Night; or, Why Are We Huddling Around the Campfire?", a piece that is both a witty summary of the discussions and a metanarrative about the value of story. She wrote in a headnote to the published version that "I had bought my first and only pair of two-inch-heeled shoes, black French ones, to wear there, but I never dared put them on; there were so many Big Guns shooting at one another that it seemed unwise to try to increase my stature." Short story "Two Delays on the Northern Line" is published in *The New Yorker* in the November 12 issue.

1980   On January 9, television movie of *The Lathe of Heaven* airs, filmed by PBS station WNET with a script by Roger Swaybill and Diane English with extensive contributions by David Loxton and Le Guin. Charles and Ursula appear as extras, an experience she writes about in an essay called "Working on 'The Lathe.'" Le Guin likes the film and finds the whole experience quite positive, in contrast to later experiences with film adaptations of her work. Young adult novel *The Beginning Place* published in February by Harper & Row. It is reviewed in *The New Yorker* by John Updike in June. Collaborates with Virginia Kidd as editors of the anthologies *Edges* and *Interfaces*. From 1980 to 1993, teaches many times at The Flight of the Mind writing workshop for women in McKenzie Bridge, Oregon, in her opinion her most valuable teaching experience.

1981   Poetry collection *Hard Words* published by Harper.

1982   "Sur," a story that is not so much alternative history as crypto-history (the female explorers who are first to the South Pole keep their feat a secret), appears in *The New Yorker* in January. *The New Yorker* publishes two more of her stories this year, in July and October.

1984   Brian Booth founds the Oregon Institute of Literary Arts and invites Le Guin, along with Floyd Skloot and William Stafford, to become members of the advisory board.

1985   In January, *The New Yorker* publishes "She Unnames Them," a story of a type that Le Guin has called a "psychomyth." In October, publishes a major new science fiction novel, *Always Coming Home*, set in the future California. Novel involves collaboration with geologist George Hersh, artist Margaret Chodos, and composer Todd Barton, whose music of the imagined Kesh people is included on a cassette tape with the original boxed set (and creates problems with the Library of Congress, which objects to copyrighting the music of indigenous peoples). The book wins the Janet Heidinger Kafka Prize for fiction by an American woman and is a runner-up for the National Book Award. It also creates a stir among more conservative science fiction readers and writers for being what they consider antitechnology; Le Guin points out that the book is pervaded with technology, though the technology is predicated upon a sustainable use of resources. Publishes a screenplay, *King Dog*, based on a segment of Hindu epic the Mahabharata. Composer Elinor Armer composes song settings of poems from Le Guin's collection *Wild Angels*. The two meet and begin to collaborate on eight musical compositions for orchestra and voices called *Uses of Music in Uttermost Parts*.

1987   Novella "Buffalo Gals, Won't You Come Out Tonight" appears in *The Magazine of Fantasy and Science Fiction*. The story combines another critique of anthropocentrism with an homage to American Indian storytelling tradition.

1988   Publishes children's picture storybook *Catwings*, illustrated by S. D. Schindler. The saga of a family of flying cats continues with *Catwings Return* (1989), *Wonderful Alexander and the Catwings* (1994), and *Jane on Her Own* (1999). The origin of the whole set is a winged cat drawn as a doodle by Ursula, which prompts the writing of the first story. The Catwings are reminiscent of a much larger (and thus much less feasible) race of winged cats in *Rocannon's World*.

1989   Receives the Pilgrim Award from the Science Fiction Research Association for her critical contributions, following in the footsteps of scholars such as H. Bruce Franklin and Thomas Clareson as well as writer-critics like James Blish and Joanna Russ.

1990   A fourth Earthsea novel, *Tehanu*, is published by Athe-
        neum/Macmillan in March. It reexamines themes from
        earlier volumes such as the maleness and (implicit) celi-
        bacy of wizards and the relationship between dragons
        and humans. Despite controversy over what some see as a
        revisionist history of a beloved fantasy world, the novel
        receives much acclaim (in 1993 in "Earthsea Revisioned"
        Le Guin says she always knew there was more to tell
        about Earthsea, but the fourth volume had to wait until
        she was ready to tell a story about women's lives: "I
        couldn't continue my hero-tale until I had, as woman and
        artist, wrestled with the angels of the feminist conscious-
        ness").

1991   *Tehanu* wins Nebula Award and Locus Award. Publishes
        Searoad, a linked collection or story cycle about a fictional
        coastal town in Oregon. Wins Pushcart Prize for short
        story "Bill Weisler," which is collected in *Searoad*. In the
        fall, is writer-in-residence for a semester at Beloit College,
        in Wisconsin, holding the Lois and Willard Mackey Chair
        in Creative Writing.

1992   *Searoad* is shortlisted for the Pulitzer Prize in fiction. Wins
        the H. L. Davis Fiction Award from the Oregon Library
        Association.

1993   With Karen Joy Fowler and Brian Attebery, edits *The
        Norton Book of Science Fiction*, which, though initially
        criticized for being too inclusive or "politically correct," is
        widely used as a textbook not only in science fiction classes
        but also in courses in short fiction and fiction writing.

1995   Receives the World Fantasy Award for Lifetime Achieve-
        ment. Publishes *Four Ways to Forgiveness*, a collection of
        four linked novellas set in a world within the Hainish uni-
        verse. Charles retires from Portland State University.

1996   Publishes a volume of poetry, *The Twins, the Dream*
        (1996), in which she and Argentine poet Diana Bellessi
        translate each other's work. Receives a Retrospective Tip-
        tree Award from The James Tiptree, Jr. Literary Award
        Council for *The Left Hand of Darkness*.

1997   Short story collection *Unlocking the Air* is nominated for
        the Pulitzer Prize. Stories in the collection include the
        1982 *New Yorker* story "The Professor's Houses"; the title

story in which the postcommunist revolution comes to Orsinia; and "The Poacher," an exploration of what it means to be an interloper rather than the hero of a fairy tale. Publishes a version of the *Tao Te Ching*, which she describes as a rendering in English, rather than a direct translation. Though she doesn't know Chinese, she is a lifelong student of Lao Tzu's enigmatic text and of Taoist philosophy, introduced to both by her father. In producing her English version she consults many translations, loose and literal, and consults with scholar J. P. Seaton.

1998   Publishes *Steering the Craft*, a guide to writing based on her own practice and on the many workshops she has conducted. Her examples of excellence include Kipling, Twain, Woolf, and a Northern Paiute storyteller whose name is not recorded.

2000   The U.S. Library of Congress honors Le Guin as a Living Legend in the Writers and Artists category. Awarded the Robert Kirsch Lifetime Achievement Award by the *Los Angeles Times*. Publishes *The Telling* in September, the first new novel since 1974 to be set in the Hainish universe of her early science fiction. Many shorter works in the same universe have appeared over the years, including "Vaster Than Empires and More Slow" (1971), "The Shobies' Story" (1990), "Another Story or A Fisherman of the Inland Sea" (1994), and the four linked novellas of *Four Ways to Forgiveness* (1995).

2001   *The Telling* wins the Endeavor Award for best book by a writer from the Pacific Northwest and the Locus Award. Le Guin is inducted into the Science Fiction Hall of Fame. Publishes *Tales from Earthsea* and the final volume of the Earthsea story, *The Other Wind*.

2002   *Tales from Earthsea* wins the Endeavor Award and the Locus Award. *The Other Wind* wins the World Fantasy Award for Best Novel. Receives the PEN/Malamud Award for Short Fiction. Fellow winner Junot Díaz acknowledges her influence. Participates in artists' rallies against the Patriot Act, passed the previous year; she writes, "What do attacks on freedom of speech and writing mean to a writer? It means that somebody's there with a big plug they're trying to fit into your mouth."

2003   Translates science fiction novel *Kalpa Imperial* by Argentine writer Angélica Gorodischer. Publishes *Changing Planes*, a linked collection of partly satirical stories about people who slip between realities while waiting in airports. Named a Grand Master by the Science Fiction and Fantasy Writers of America.

2004   *Changing Planes* wins the Locus Award for best story collection. Publishes *Gifts*, the first of three volumes of the *Annals of the Western Shore*, a fantasy for young adults, in September. Receives the Margaret A. Edwards Award for contributions to children's literature from the American Library Association and delivers the May Hill Arbuthnot Lecture to the ALA's subdivision, the Association for Library Service to Children.

2005   *Gifts* wins the 2005 PEN Center Children's Literature Award.

2006   Publishes the middle volume of the *Annals of the Western Shore*, *Voices*, in September. The Washington Center for the Book awards Le Guin the Maxine Cushing Gray Fellowship for Writers for a distinguished body of work.

2007   Publishes the final volume of the *Annals of the Western Shore*, *Powers*, in September. Works through Virgil's *Aeneid* in Latin, ten lines a day, in preparation for writing the historical novel *Lavinia*, a retelling of the *Aeneid* from the point of view of the hero's Italic second wife, who is silent in the original version.

2008   *Lavinia* is published in April and wins the Locus Award. *Powers* wins the Nebula Award.

2009   Publishes *Cheek by Jowl*, a book of essays on fantasy and why it matters. Brother Karl dies on November 8 of cancer, age eighty-two, in Brooklyn, New York.

2010   *Cheek by Jowl* wins Locus Award for best nonfiction/art book. Is the subject of a festschrift, or celebratory volume, on the occasion of her eightieth birthday. *80! Memories & Reflections on Ursula K. Le Guin* is edited by Karen Joy Fowler and Debbie Notkin and includes essays and original works by many writers and scholars, including Kim Stanley Robinson, Andrea Hairston, Julie Phillips, Gwyneth Jones, Eleanor Arnason, and John Kessel. Publishes *Out Here, Poems and Images from Steens Mountain*

Country, with text, poems, and sketches by Le Guin, text and photographs by Roger Dorband.

2012   Publishes *Finding My Elegy: New and Selected Poems*, her sixth book of poems. Publishes two-volume edition of selected short stories under the title *The Unreal and the Real*. Receives the J. Lloyd Eaton Lifetime Achievement Award in Science Fiction at the University of California, Riverside.

2013   Interviewed in the *Paris Review* series "The Art of Fiction." Publishes a translation of *Squaring the Circle: A Pseudotreatise of Urbogony* (2013) by Romanian writer Gheorghe Sasarman, which is retranslated from the Spanish translation by Mariano Martín Rodríguez, with both translations being overseen by Sasarman.

2014   Awarded the National Book Foundation Medal for Distinguished Contribution to American Letters. In her widely quoted speech she calls for "writers who can see alternatives to how we live now, and can see through our fear-stricken society and its obsessive technologies, to other ways of being. We'll need writers who can remember freedom —poets, visionaries—realists of a larger reality."

2017   Elected to the American Academy of Arts and Letters.

Note on the Texts

This volume contains novels and stories set in Ursula K. Le Guin's Hainish universe, *The Word for World Is Forest* (1972), the story suite *Five Ways to Forgiveness* (1995, 2002), and *The Telling* (2000), along with seven short stories and two essays. A companion Library of America volume collects the remainder of Le Guin's Hainish novels and stories, *Rocannon's World* (1966), *Planet of Exile* (1966), *City of Illusions* (1967), *The Left Hand of Darkness* (1969), and *The Dispossessed* (1974), as well as four short stories and six essays.

THE WORD FOR WORLD IS FOREST

The Word for World Is Forest was originally published in *Again, Dangerous Visions*, edited by Harlan Ellison (Garden City: Doubleday, 1972), pp. 30–108. It was issued as a separate hardcover by Berkley-Putnam in 1976. A British edition was published by Gollancz in 1977 with a new introduction by the author but otherwise with no changes except to bring about conformity with British conventions of spelling and usage. *Again, Dangerous Visions*, which contains the author's preferred text, is the source of the text used here.

STORIES

"The Shobies' Story" was first published in *Universe 1*, edited by Robert Silverberg and Karen Haber (New York: Doubleday, 1990), pp. 35–66. It was then included in Le Guin's collection *A Fisherman of the Inland Sea* (New York: HarperPrism, 1994), which is the source of the text used here.

"Dancing to Ganam" was first published in *Amazing Stories*, Vol. 68, No. 6 (September 1993), pp. 9–21. It was then included in *A Fisherman of the Inland Sea*, the source of the text used here.

"Another Story or A Fisherman of the Inland Sea" was first published in *Tomorrow* (August 1994), pp. 20–35. It was then included in *A Fisherman of the Inland Sea*, the source of the text used here.

"Unchosen Love" was first published in *Amazing Stories*, Vol. 69, No. 2 (Fall 1994), pp. 11–26. It was then included in Le Guin's collection *The Birthday of the World and Other Stories* (New York: Harper-Collins, 2002), the source of the text used here.

"Mountain Ways" was first published in *Asimov's Science Fiction*, Vol. 20, No. 8 (August 1996), pp. 14–39. It was then included in *The Birthday of the World and Other Stories*, the source of the text used here.

"The Matter of Seggri" was first published in *Crank!* 3 (Spring 1994), pp. 3–36. It was then included in *The Birthday of the World and Other Stories*, the source of the text used here.

"Solitude" was first published in *The Magazine of Fantasy and Science Fiction*, Vol. 87, No. 6 (December 1994), pp. 132–58. It was then included in *The Birthday of the World and Other Stories*, the source of the text used here.

FIVE WAYS TO FORGIVENESS

Five Ways to Forgiveness contains five linked stories: the four stories previously collected as *Four Ways to Forgiveness* (New York: HarperPrism, 1995), as well as "Old Music and the Slave Women." They are published here as a complete story suite, as the author intended, for this first time.

Four Ways to Forgiveness contained four linked stories. The original publication of each of the stories is as follows:

"Betrayals," *Blue Motel*, Vol. 3, edited by Peter Crowther (London: Little, Brown, 1994), pp. 195–229.

"Forgiveness Day," *Asimov's Science Fiction*, Vol. 18, Nos. 12 & 13 (November 1994), pp. 264–303.

"A Man of the People," *Asimov's Science Fiction*, Vol. 19, Nos. 4 & 5 (April 1995), pp. 22–64.

"A Woman's Liberation," *Asimov's Science Fiction*, Vol. 19, No. 8 (July 1995), pp. 116–62.

The four stories were then collected as the story suite *Four Ways to Forgiveness* and published by HarperPrism in September 1995. A British edition was published by Gollancz in June 1996. The British edition is the same as the American edition except for changes to bring about conformity with British conventions of punctuation. The first American edition is the source of the text used here.

"Old Music and the Slave Women" was first published in *Far Horizons: All New Tales from the Greatest Worlds of Science Fiction*, edited by Robert Silverberg (New York: Avon Eos, 1999), pp. 5–52. It was then included in *The Birthday of the World and Other Stories*, the source of the text used here.

THE TELLING

The Telling was first published by Harcourt in September 2000. A British printing was published by Gollancz in October 2001 using the Harcourt plates. The first American edition is the source of the text used here.

APPENDIX

For the British publication of *The Word for World Is Forest* by Gollancz in 1977, Le Guin wrote a new introduction. It was then included in the collection *The Language of the Night: Essays on Fantasy and Science Fiction by Ursula K. Le Guin*, edited by Susan Wood (New York: Putnam's, 1979). *The Language of the Night* is the source of the text used here.

"On Not Reading Science Fiction" was composed as the introduction to the story collection *A Fisherman of the Inland Sea* (New York: HarperPrism, 1994), which is the source of the text used here.

This volume presents the texts of the original printings chosen for inclusion here, but it does not attempt to reproduce features of their typographic design. The texts are presented without change, except for the correction of typographical errors. Spelling, punctuation, and capitalization are often expressive features, and they are not altered, even when inconsistent or irregular. The following is a list of typographical errors corrected, cited by page and line number: 11.11, goloshes,; 20.19, yumen's; 27.36, and may; 82.22, forested; 91.2, creechies.; 210.29, meet a; 217.37, one other; 340.28, stole!"; 361.9, soon she; 362.31, somone; 428.17, doctors.); 480.20, owners'; 504.31, give; 546.5, inaccesible; 572.10, third and and; 585.10, tribesman; 758.20, Getheian; 759.6, people,.

Notes

In the notes below, the reference numbers denote page and line of this volume (the line count includes headings, but not rule lines). No note is made for material included in the eleventh edition of Merriam-Webster's Collegiate Dictionary, except for certain cases where common words and terms have specific historical meanings or inflections. Biblical quotations and allusions are keyed to the King James Version; references to Shakespeare to *The Riverside Shakespeare*, ed. G. Blackmore Evans (Boston: Houghton Mifflin, 1974). For further biographical background, references to other studies, and more detailed notes, see Elizabeth Cummins, *Understanding Ursula K. Le Guin*, revised edition (Columbia: University of South Carolina Press, 1993); Ursula K. Le Guin, "Introduction," in *The Norton Book of Science Fiction* (New York: W. W. Norton, 1993); John Wray, "Ursula K. Le Guin, The Art of Fiction No. 221," *The Paris Review*, No. 206 (Fall 2013); Richard D. Erlich, *Coyote's Song: The Teaching Stories of Ursula K. Le Guin* (Rockville, MD: Borgo, 2010); Donna R. White, *Dancing with Dragons: Ursula K. Le Guin and the Critics* (Columbia, SC: Camden House, 1999); Mike Cadden, Ursula K. Le Guin *Beyond Genre: Fiction for Children and Adults* (New York: Routledge, 2005); Sandra Lindow, *Dancing the Tao: Le Guin and Moral Development* (Newcastle upon Tyne, UK: Cambridge Scholars Publishing, 2012); and Susan M. Bernardo and Graham J. Murphy, *Ursula K. Le Guin: A Critical Companion* (Westport, CT: Greenwood, 2006).

THE WORD FOR WORLD IS FOREST

4.11–12 Colony Brides . . . Recreation Staff] Early science fiction (by men) could only imagine women in space as sex workers, rather than technicians or scientists; an example is Robert A. Heinlein's "—All You Zombies—" (1959) in which women's only option for work was the group known either as "W.E.N.C.H.E.S." (Women's Emergency National Corps, Hospitality & Entertainment Section" or "Women's Hospitality Order Refortifying & Encouraging Spacemen" (whose acronym Heinlein leaves to the reader to supply).

10.39 *Shackleton*] After Antarctic explorer Ernest Shackleton (1874–1922).

18.4 "Are you of the dream-time or of the world-time?"] *Dream-time* is a translation of the Aboriginal (Arandic) term *Alcheringa*. Anthropologist Adolphus Peter Elkin (1891–1979) helped popularize the translated term in his 1938 book *The Australian Aborigines: How to Understand Them*. The Dream-time is the period of original creation but is also always reachable through dreaming, ritual, and storytelling.

33.7 alpha waves] Rhythmic oscillations of neural activity, or brain waves, associated with meditation, deep relaxation, and REM (rapid eye movement) periods of sleep.

33.12–13 Time's winged chariot hurrying near] From Andrew Marvell's "To His Coy Mistress" (c. 1651–52), lines 21–22: "But at my back I always hear / Time's wingéd chariot hurrying near."

33.18–19 Over the hills and far away.] Traditional seventeenth-century Scottish song; also a line in the nursery rhyme "Tom, Tom, the Piper's Son."

33.19 Ashes, ashes, all fall down.] Line from an eighteenth-century nursery rhyme, "Ring Around the Rosie."

34.7 paradoxical sleep] REM sleep: paradoxical in that the brain is as active as in wakefulness.

48.30 firejelly] Napalm: one of many indirect references to events of the Vietnam War.

50.24 final solution] Possibly a reference to the Nazi "Final Solution to the Jewish Question," a plan to exterminate the Jewish people that culminated in the Holocaust.

59.36 Venus Genetrix] Latin: Venus the Parent/Mother; the Roman goddess Venus portrayed as the creative principle of the universe, as in Lucretius's *De rerum natura* (*On the Nature of Things*, first century B.C.E.), and as ancestor and patroness of the Romans.

66.16–17 And the truth shall make you free. . . .] Cf. John 8:32.

68.4–5 *machina ex machina*] Latin: machine from the machine. A reference to *deus ex machina*, the god from the machine: in Greek drama a divine figure brought in by stage machinery to intervene at the end of an otherwise insoluble plot.

93.11 Blacks and Rhodesians] Southern Rhodesia (now Zimbabwe) was a British colonial state in southern Africa. Named for English imperialist Cecil Rhodes, the country declared itself independent in 1965, with a minority white government and significant repression of the black population. Civil war ensued, and the minority government was overthrown in 1979.

STORIES

107.6 negative ions] Negative ions released into the atmosphere by waterfalls and crashing waves can have a soothing effect.

107.33 EYs] Earth years.

110.5   transilience] First mentioned as a theoretical possibility in *The Dispossessed*, chapter three.

110.28–29   "The heart has its reasons . . . know,"] Blaise Pascal, *Pensées*, 277.

114.6   nonduring] Since there is no duration to travel by churten, it can't be "during."

118.8–9   "thick" description] American cultural anthropologist Clifford Geertz (1926–2006) used the term "thick description" (which he borrowed from philosopher Gilbert Ryle) to describe a method of ethnological writing that starts with a single item such as a cockfight and then fills in social contexts and traces symbolic associations until one begins to glimpse an entire pattern of culture.

136.7   heroes were phenomena] In "The Carrier-Bag Theory of Fiction" (1986) Le Guin wrote: "The novel is a fundamentally unheroic kind of story. Of course the Hero has frequently taken it over, that being his imperial nature and uncontrollable impulse, to take everything over and run it while making stern decrees and laws to control his uncontrollable impulse to kill it."

144.3   elements of a rather familiar kind of fiction] One familiar example, mostly fictional, is Captain John Smith's account of his rescue by Pocahontas the Indian "princess," which only appears in his third account of his capture by Powhatan's band of Algonquians, written ten years after the "fact."

155.34–35   Faced with chaos, we seek . . . Babies do it] An echo of William James's *The Principles of Psychology* (1890), which describes the mental experience of an infant. It is directly quoted by Le Guin in the story "The Field of Vision" (1973): "A blooming buzzing confusion."

168.25–26   "The Fisherman of the Inland Sea,"] A Japanese folktale whose first written variant dates from the eighth century. It was retold by Lafcadio Hearn in *Out of the East* (1895) as "The Dream of a Summer Day"; Le Guin read it, under the title "Urashima," in Hearn's compilation of *Japanese Fairy Tales* (published in five volumes, 1898–1922, and as a single volume, 1926). It incorporates the common motif of a short stay in fairyland that turns out to be several lifetimes in the mortal world.

170.9   germanes] Obsolete: siblings or close kin; redefined in the complex marriage system of the planet O.

170.33   moiety] In many cultures, one of two halves of the population, usually with restrictions on marriage within or across moieties.

176.14   "thick planning"] Cf. note 118.8–9 for Clifford Geertz's "thick description."

186.38   s-tc point] A point in the space-time continuum.

233.10   pretending to be a man] Akal's masquerade echoes that of the many cross-dressers in literature, including several of Shakespeare's heroines.

251.16–17   There is a "battlefield" as they call it of this game] The idea of sport as practice warfare is summed up in the statement (mis)attributed to the Duke of Wellington that "the battle of Waterloo was won on the playing fields of Eton."

258.10   "'What goes to the brain takes from the testicles,'"] In the 1873 book *Sex in Education: Or, a Fair Chance for Girls*, American physician Edward H. Clarke claimed that educating girls diverted blood from the sexual organs to the brain, leading to shrinkage of the ovaries.

262.9   hornvaulting] Minoan frescoes in Crete show both women and men as bull-leapers.

290.20   brachiate] To swing from branch to branch like an orangutan.

312.22–23   this is a broken culture] Colonialism has left many broken cultures in its wake: those of most California Indian groups, Le Guin points out in correspondence, "were broken, some irreparably, between 1850 and 1920." As an example of a culture that might be more resilient than was apparent to outsiders, British-American anthropologist Colin Turnbull's 1972 ethnography of the Ik people of Uganda, *The Mountain People*, claimed that the extreme isolationism of their culture was a result of famines and other disasters. However, Turnbull's negative portrayal of Ik culture has been challenged as a product of imperfect understanding of their language and traditions.

FIVE WAYS TO FORGIVENESS

338.10   Cyanid skins] Cyan is a greenish blue color; "cyanid" is different from cyanosis, a bluish skin condition caused by lack of oxygen.

353.5   *aiji*] A given name in Japanese, meaning "beloved child," but here denoting a martial art.

417.26   There are two kinds of knowledge, local and universal.] "Local knowledge" usually refers to such minor items as weather patterns or road conditions, but Le Guin draws here on the work of anthropologist Clifford Geertz (see also note 118.8–9), who uses the phrase to show how complex cultural patterns such as religion are built upon, and defined by, those smaller sorts of understanding.

424.15   the Terran Altiplano] The high plateau (averaging over 12,000 feet in elevation) that sits amid the Andes Mountains in Bolivia and extends into parts of Peru, Argentina, and Chile.

433.29   I believe in it because it is impossible.] Adapted from a line by Carthaginian Christian philosopher Tertullian (c. 155–240 C.E.): *Certum est quia impossibile est*, "It [the resurrection of Christ] is certain because it is impossible."

459.36   "jump the ditch."] An echo of the custom of jumping the broom, originally a joking term in Britain for an unsanctioned elopement but later a marriage ceremony practiced by American slaves who were not allowed to marry legally.

518.23–25   But how do you get there? . . . the problem with Utopia] In "The Soul of Man Under Socialism" (1891), Oscar Wilde wrote, "A map of the world that does not include Utopia is not worth even glancing at, for it leaves out the one country at which Humanity is always landing."

572.25–26   cyanotic skin coloration] See note 338.10.

576.31   Kwan Yin–like] Kwan Yin or Guanyin, an East Asian Buddhist divinity commonly called the "Goddess of Mercy."

THE TELLING

590.1–4   The day I was born . . . THE MAHABHARATA] This quotation does not occur in the Sanskrit epic Mahabharata (c. 400 B.C.E.–400 C.E.), but in a retelling of the Mahabharata by American writer William Buck (1933–1970), published posthumously in 1973. In 1985, Le Guin published a screenplay, *King Dog*, based on an episode from the Mahabharata.

591.3   the Pale] The original Pale was the region of eastern Ireland, including Dublin, that was under English rule from the fourteenth through sixteenth centuries, and is the origin of the phrase, "beyond the pale." The word derives from Latin *palus*, "stake," or, by extension, "fence."

591.11   Ganesh] Ganesh or Ganesha is the elephant-headed Hindu deity of arts and sciences.

591.25   lovers' punishment in Dante's Hell] Cf. Dante's *Inferno*, Canto V.

593.31   vr-proprios] Virtual reality nerve connections; from *proprio*, Latin: "one's own," as in proprioception, the body's internal monitoring senses.

597.7   ideographic forms] Ideographs are written symbols that stand for concepts rather than sounds (as an alphabet does). Egyptian hieroglyphics and Chinese characters are hybrids (called logograms): partly conceptual and partly phonetic.

597.11–12   World Ministry of Information . . . Poetry and Art] Orwellian terms—modeled after the practice of the government in George Orwell's *1984* (1949) to give euphemistic titles to agencies whose purpose is the opposite of what the name denotes, such as the Ministry of Truth.

620.25   "It helps to balance."] Akan folk practice resembles Chinese traditional medicine in its emphasis on balancing contraries: sweet and sour or cool *yin* and fiery *yang*.

629.9   She was scarcely a jewel in anybody's crown.] India (from which Sutty's ancestors came) was called the jewel in the crown of the British empire.

629.30–31   a code word . . . 'devolve.'] *Devolve* can mean either to delegate authority or to degenerate from a more complex to a simpler state.

630.33   Starbrew] Satirical reference to a Terran chain of coffee shops.

631.15–16   a guilt culture, a shame culture, or something all its own.] *The Chrysanthemum and the Sword* (1946) by American anthropologist Ruth Benedict (1887–1948) distinguished between cultures of shame, such as Japan, and cultures of guilt, like the United States. Benedict defined shame as the result of failing to live up to expectations, while guilt follows the committing of misdeeds as defined by one's society.

638.17–18   *Keep far the Dog . . . dig it up again. . . .*] "Oh keep the Dog far hence, that's friend to men, / Or with his nails he'll dig it up again!" T. S. Eliot, *The Waste Land* (1922), lines 74–75, echoing a dirge from John Webster's play *The White Devil* (1612): "But keep the wolf far thence, that's foe to men, / For with his nails he'll dig them up again."

638.21–22   the Upanishads . . . the Gita and the Lake Poets.] English and Indian classics: the Lake poets included William Wordsworth (1770–1850), Robert Southey (1774–1843), and Samuel Taylor Coleridge (1772–1834). The Upanishads (eighth century B.C.E. through fifteenth century C.E.) are a collection of philosophical sayings outlining the principles of Hinduism; the Bhagavad Gita (composed sometime between the fifth and second centuries B.C.E.) is a long philosophical poem, part of the Mahabharata (see note 590.1–4), spoken to Prince Arjuna by charioteer (and god in disguise) Krishna.

642.15   tan-tien-tummy] Tan tien is an energy center and focal point (comparable to a yogic chakra) in Chinese traditional medicine; the lowest of three tan tiens is located in the lower abdomen.

642.28   bhaigan tamatar] A curry made with tomato and eggplant.

644.31–32   *Let me not to the marriage of true minds admit impediment . . .*] Shakespeare, Sonnet 116, lines 1–2.

657.9   sutras] A sutra (Sanskrit: "thread") is an aphorism or set of sayings found in Hindu scriptures.

658.3–4   endless jungles, all burning with bright tigers] Cf. William Blake's "The Tyger" (1794), lines 1–4: "Tyger, tyger, burning bright, / In the forests of the night: / What immortal hand or eye, / Could frame thy fearful symmetry?"

658.24–25   a peculiar singular/dual pronoun] Many languages, including Old English, have dual pronouns and verb forms, which are neither singular nor plural but indicate exactly two things or persons.

671.24   "O Ram!"] Rama, hero of the ancient Indian epic Ramayana and an incarnation of the god Vishnu.

702.22–23   Lhasa, Dragon-Tiger Mountain, Macchu Picchu] Religious centers located in mountains in Tibet, China, and Peru, respectively.

706.21–22   Mandelbrot figures] Fractals; named after French and American mathematician Benoit Mandelbrot (1924–2010).

716.32   *Don't Mother-Teresa me, girl*] Mother Teresa, born Anjezë Gonxhe Bojaxhiu (1910–1997) in Albania, moved in 1929 to India, where she founded the religious order Missionaries of Charity. She was canonized in 2016 by the Catholic Church.

721.14   *Et tu, Brute?*] Latin: "You also, Brutus?" Purportedly spoken by Julius Caesar to his friend Marcus Brutus at his assassination; the familiar line is from *Julius Caesar*, III.i.77.

722.13–14   "I think." ¶ "Therefore you are. . . ."] Echo of French philosopher René Descartes (1596–1650): "*Cogito ergo sum.*" Latin: "I think, therefore I am."

727.18–19   "Sutty was God's wife."] The consort of the god Shiva is Sati or Parvati (sometimes seen as different goddesses). "Sutty" and "suttee" (the act of self-immolation by widows) are Anglicizations of "Sati."

727.19–20   Ganesh] See note 591.11.

728.10   pooja] *Pūjā*, Sanskrit: an act of devotion to the gods.

731.4–5   *Keep far the Dog that's friend to men. . . .*] See note 638.17–18.

748.5   *Napoleon Buonaparte called the English a nation of shopkeepers*] Common slur on English character attributed to Napoleon Bonaparte (1769–1821) by his physician Barry Edward O'Meara (1786–1836).

APPENDIX

754.3   Solzhenitsyn in exile] Aleksandr Solzhenitsyn (1918–2008), a Russian dissident imprisoned by Stalin and then exiled to Kazakhstan. He wrote about his experiences in *The Gulag Archipelago* (1973) and used Soviet labor camps as a setting in *One Day in the Life of Ivan Denisovich* (1962). He was awarded the Nobel Prize in Literature in 1970.

754.12–13   "Poets are the unacknowledged legislators of the world."] Percy Bysshe Shelley, "A Defence of Poetry" (1821).

759.17–18   "thicker" . . . Clifford Geertz's term] See note 118.8–9.

SOME WORLDS OF
H

ALTERRA
also known as Werel
142 LY from Terra

AKA
60 LY from Terra

BELDENE
also known as the Garden Planet

CHIFFEWAR
12 LY from Aka

ENSBO

FARADAY

GAO

GDE

KAPTEYN

NEW SOUTH GEORGIA
8 LY from Rokanan

OLLUL
17 LY from Gethen

PRESTNO
also known as World 88
1.8 LY from Athshe

SEGGRI

SHEASHEL HAVEN

UTTERMOSTS

VE
Nearest planet to Hain
22 LY from Urras and Anarres